THE EDINBURGH EDITION OF WALTER SCOTT'S POETRY

GENERAL EDITOR
Professor Alison Lumsden

VOLUME SEVEN
THE SHORTER POEMS

THE EDINBURGH EDITION OF
WALTER SCOTT'S POETRY

to be complete in ten volumes

WALTER SCOTT

THE SHORTER POEMS

Edited by
P. D. Garside and Gillian Hughes

EDINBURGH
University
Press

Edinburgh University Press is one of the leading university presses in the UK. We publish academic books and journals in our selected subject areas across the humanities and social sciences, combining cutting-edge scholarship with high editorial and production values to produce academic works of lasting importance. For more information visit our website: edinburghuniversitypress.com

Edinburgh University Press Ltd
The Tun – Holyrood Road
12 (2f) Jackson's Entry
Edinburgh EH8 8PJ

Typeset in Linotype Ehrhardt by
Servis Filmsetting Ltd, Stockport, Cheshire,
and printed and bound in Great Britain

A CIP record for this book is available from the British Library

ISBN 978 1 4744 2443 1 (hardback)
ISBN 978 1 4744 2444 8 (webready PDF)
ISBN 978 1 4744 2445 5 (epub)

CONTENTS

ACKNOWLEDGEMENTS

Although the Edinburgh Edition of Walter Scott's Poetry (EEWSP) is mainly the work of scholars attached to universities, the project could not prosper without the help of the sponsors cited below. Their generosity has met the direct costs to initial research and of the preparation of the volumes. Those universities which employ the editors have also contributed greatly. Particular thanks are extended to the University of Aberdeen.

DR WALTER GRANT SCOTT
The editors and Advisory Board of the Edinburgh Edition of Walter Scott's Poetry wish to acknowledge with gratitude the financial support of Dr Walter Scott, senior partner of Scott Investments in Henley-on-Thames. It was inevitable that the editors would approach someone bearing this name; but it was not inevitable that he should provide assistance. His help has facilitated much of the editorial investigation, and paid for those activities which are essential to establishing the reliability of a scholarly edition such as the almost incessant processes of proof-reading and checking the text. He approaches investment with a view to fostering long-term growth, and that belief is further expressed in the very different field of literary scholarship and his trust in the editors of the EEWSP.

THE CARNEGIE TRUST FOR THE UNIVERSITIES OF SCOTLAND
The Carnegie Trust for the Universities of Scotland generously provided funding for a pilot project via its Larger Grants Fund. This funding was invaluable in developing a methodology for the edition and in employing a research assistant in its early stages.

THE BRITISH ACADEMY
The pilot project was also generously supported by a Small Research Grant from the British Academy. This funding facilitated travel to the National Library of Scotland and also supported the employment of a research assistant.

LIBRARIES
Without the generous assistance of the two great repositories of Scott manuscripts, the National Library of Scotland and the Morgan Library,

New York, it would not have been possible to undertake the editing of Scott's poetry and the Board and the editors cannot overstate the extent to which they are indebted to their Trustees and staffs. The generosity of the Manuscripts Department of the National Library of Scotland in allowing permission to quote from their holdings is warmly acknowledged. Particular thanks are also extended to the Special Collections Department of the Sir Duncan Rice Library at the University of Aberdeen, home to the Bernard C. Lloyd Collection of Scott Materials. The presence of the Lloyd Collection at Aberdeen offers an invaluable resource for editing Scott's poetry and the foresight of Bernard Lloyd in compiling this collection and finding a home for it at the University of Aberdeen is very much appreciated. The Faculty of Advocates Abbotsford Collection Trust is also thanked for its permission to grant access to Scott's books at Abbotsford, Scott's home in the Scottish Borders. In connection with the current volume the support of Andrea Longson, Sara Berry and Angela Schofield has been invaluable.

THE SHORTER POEMS
The editors would like to thank The Bibliographical Society for their award to Dr Gillian Hughes of the Fredson Bowers Award for 2014–15, which allowed research into manuscripts and other materials located in New York and New Haven for the current volume. Both editors have also benefited through their affiliation to the University of Edinburgh during the preparation of this volume, as Honorary Professorial Fellow and Honorary Research Fellow respectively.

   In a collection containing such a variety of materials it has naturally been necessary to call on a large number of institutions and individual owners for permission to examine and cite manuscripts and other rare materials in their care. In addition to those already mentioned, holding libraries include: Basel University Library; the Beinecke Rare Book and Manuscript Library, Yale University; the Berg Collection of English and American Literature, New York Public Library; the Bodleian Library; the Borders Council Libraries Service; Boston Public Library; the Howard Gottlieb Archival Research Center, University of Boston; the British Library; the Brotherton Library, University of Leeds; Cornell University Library; Libraries, Leisure and Culture, Dundee; University of Edinburgh Library; Fales Library, New York University; Fordham University Library, New York; University of Glasgow Library; the John Work Garrett Library, Sheridan Libraries, Johns Hopkins University; the Houghton Library, Harvard University; the Henry E. Huntington Library, San Marino, California; Lichfield Record Office; Senate House Library, University of London; the Mitchell Library, Glasgow; National Art Library, Victoria and Albert Museum; National Library of Wales, Aberystwyth; the National Trust (Belton House); National Records of Scotland; National

Register of Archives of Scotland; the New York Society Library; the Carl H. Pforzheimer Collection of Shelley and his Circle, New York Public Library; Manuscripts and Special Collections, University of Nottingham; Princeton University Library; Harry Ransom Center, Austin, Texas; the Signet Library, Edinburgh; Staffordshire Record Office, Stafford; Wisbech and Fenland Museum; and the Wordsworth Trust, Dove Cottage, Grasmere. The image from The Gem *on page 280 is reproduced with the kind permission of Aberdeen University Library. (More particular details concerning collections and departments will be found as appropriate in the Notes to particular entries.) Private owners who have kindly allowed access include: the Duke of Buccleuch and Queensberry KBE; the Earl of Home; Spencer Compton, the Marquess of Northampton; Lord Polwarth; and Bill Zachs. Individual librarians working for the above institutions and individuals often went above and beyond the call of duty to assist the editors and should not be forgotten. Among these are Paul Barnaby, Iain Gordon Brown, Mary Ellen Budney, Velvet Colton, Philip Compton, Jeff Cowton, Kim Downie, Steven Dearden, Sally Garden, Susan Glover, Anna Gurton-Wachter, James Hamilton, Patrice Kane, Amy Kimball, Cameron McAulay, AnnaLee Pauls, Julian Pooley of the Nichols Archive Project, Gayle Richardson, Laura Russo, Alison Rosie, Erin Schreiner, Mary-Jo Searle, and David Wright.*

Editing the present volume has required knowledge and expertise beyond the capacity of two people alone, and many people have helped the present editors. They would like to give particular thanks to David Hewitt and Alison Lumsden, amongst their closest colleagues, for vital work in helping research and shape the collection in its earlier stages, as well as in seeing it through to completion. They also wish to express their gratitude and acknowledgement to the wider community of Scott scholars, and in particular to J. H. Alexander, Barbara Bell, Ian Duncan, Lindsay Levy, Ainsley McIntosh, the late Jane Millgate, Sigrid Reiuwerts, and Michael Wood. It is important to recognise the significance of the pioneering work on the poetry of Walter Scott undertaken by the late Jill Rubenstein and by Nancy Moore Goslee. The editors are also indebted to the following for their input on specialist matters: Bruno Bower, Melvyn Cole, Heide Connell, Chris Henson, Donald Meek, Dorothy McMillan, Roy Pinkerton, and Rachel Sweet. While working as a research assistant at the University of Aberdeen Chriselle Mackinnon undertook editorial tasks and Erasmus interns visiting the Walter Scott Research Centre from the University of Mainz also undertook additional checks. Thanks are extended to Rosa Ciminello and Margun Schmitz and to Sigrid Rieuwerts for arranging their visits. In addition, the volume could not have been completed without the participation of the typesetting and editorial teams at Edinburgh University Press.

Finally, the editors would like to thank their family members for their support and patience throughout the lengthy gestation and preparation of the present volume, most especially and as ever Gillian Garside and David Sweet.

The General Editor for this volume was Professor Alison Lumsden.

GENERAL INTRODUCTION

Even although Scott's literary reputation has been transformed by a tide of critical studies by international scholars, and by the first critical edition of his novels which appeared between 1993 and 2012, little attention has been paid to the poetry. One of the reasons is that there has never been a scholarly edition, and no complete edition is in print. The Edinburgh Edition of Walter Scott's Poetry (EEWSP) will be the first to provide a reliable text, and it will be the first to make all his poetry available. No previous edition has been as comprehensive, and none claiming to be comprehensive has appeared for over one hundred years.

On historical grounds the neglect of Scott's poetry is curious. It was his poetry that defined the new sensibility which is now termed 'Romanticism'. His poetry was incomparably the most popular in the first decade of the nineteenth century: in 1810 the publication of *The Lady of the Lake* was the media event of the year and over 25,000 copies were sold in the first twelve months. His success was dazzling: readers could not get enough of his work. Further, to understand Scott it is necessary to understand his career as a poet, for it was his poetry, particularly *The Lay of the Last Minstrel*, *Marmion* and *The Lady of the Lake*, which first established his reputation.

Of course, Scott did not help himself. In the Introduction to *Rokeby*[1] he made a typically self-effacing suggestion that the emergence of Byron as a major (and arguably darker and sexier) poet caused him to abandon his poetic endeavours and turn to writing fiction; this almost certainly instigated in later generations a sense that his poetry was less significant than the novels that followed. In fact Scott's narrative distorts the actualities of his poetic career. What we now consider to be Scott's major poetic achievements, *The Lay of the Last Minstrel*, *Marmion* and *The Lady of the Lake*, were certainly all published before the appearance of *Childe Harold's Pilgrimage*, Cantos I and II, in 1812, but Scott wrote several more significant narrative poems after this date, including *Rokeby* (1813) and *The Lord of the Isles* (1815). The current volume of *The Shorter Poems*, moreover, demonstrates convincingly that Scott also wrote short and occasional verse throughout his life, and of course, as the Edinburgh Edition of the Waverley

Novels (EEWN) has shown, Scott wrote much original poetry for the novels as mottos and to represent the (sometimes deliberately inept) poetic aspirations of his characters. Writing poetry was an activity that spanned his whole career.

A new critical edition of Scott's poetry therefore seems timely but what it should include is less evident. While the body of Scott's fiction is fairly well defined the poetry is less so. Several models present themselves. The first lies in J. G. Lockhart's 1833–34 *Poetical Works* edition, but this is problematic. Volumes 1–5 comprise *Minstrelsy of the Scottish Border* and Scott's edition of the medieval romance *Sir Tristrem*. Early in its discussions the EEWSP team decided that edited works lie outside the scope of this edition. A second model is offered by J. Logie Robertson's Oxford edition of 1894, as republished in 1904, which does not include the *Minstrelsy* material but does include Scott's original contributions to it. It also expands upon Lockhart's body of miscellaneous and shorter poems, and incorporates the poetry and verse Scott wrote for the novels. After much discussion it was agreed that the EEWSP should include not just the narrative poems and all the shorter and lyric poems that appear in Lockhart's edition, but also the uncollected poetry then in process of being discovered by the editors of *The Shorter Poems*, which significantly expands the known body of Scott's work. Original works by Scott himself which appeared in the *Minstrelsy* are included, but not the poems and songs he collected. His verse drama appears in its own volume and its inclusion will facilitate scholarship and comparison with the plays of contemporaries like Wordsworth, Coleridge, and Byron. The incidental original poetry in the Waverley Novels also forms part of the edition, for Scott himself sanctioned its separate collection and publication by Archibald Constable in 1822. The Edinburgh Edition of Walter Scott's Poetry will also include Scott's own essays on poetry, published as the 1830 Introductions to *Poetical Works* and as essays in the 1833–34 edition. It is true to say that Scott never provides us with a formulated theory of fiction, although we can see one if we synthesise views articulated in the introductory chapters in the Waverley Novels, in reviews, and his 'Lives of the Novelists'. But nowhere does he provide so comprehensive a view of literature as he does in these essays on poetry.

The Edinburgh Edition of the Waverley Novels provided a wealth of information about publishing practices relating to Scott's fiction, and indeed nineteenth-century fiction more generally. But the EEWSP team recognised that the poetry was written and published in different conditions and so it examined the publishing history and the textual archaeology of a number of key texts; all textual witnesses published in Scott's lifetime were collated against a standard of collation and publishing papers were comprehensively examined. It was found that Scott's poetry, being published under his own name, was subjected to considerable social pressure, unlike the novels where the main problem was the copying which preserved Scott's anonymity, but generated many errors. It was concluded that the discoveries of the EEWN editors, and the methodologies developed from them, cannot be transferred and applied wholesale to editing the poetry. New approaches were required.

A new edition of Scott's longer poems could be based on the manuscripts, most of which are close to being intact: only that of the *Lay* is missing. However the manuscripts are not appropriate since Scott expected the conventions of print to be imposed upon his poetry before its publication. The 1833–34 *Poetical Works*, edited by Lockhart and appearing just after Scott's death, offers the model of a collection supposedly based on the latest texts approved by the author. However, it is clear that as a base-text for a new edition, at least for those poems examined to date, it would be wholly unsuitable. There is no evidence to suggest that Scott was artistically engaged in its production, and while Lockhart makes reference to the existence of an interleaved set of the poetry similar to that used in the preparation of the Magnum edition of the novels, no set has been found, and Lockhart makes almost no emendations on its supposed authority. In fact, Lockhart's edition reveals more about the commercial agenda that he and Robert Cadell were pursuing at the point of its publication than it does about Scott's 'final intentions' for his poetry. Unfortunately Lockhart's edition provided the textual basis for all other editions published in the nineteenth century, and for the collection most widely available in the twentieth century, that edited by J. Logie Robertson.

If Lockhart's edition is inappropriate what of the first editions of Scott's poems? While the EEWN never explicitly states that the first editions should form the base text, arguing instead that this should be the first fully articulated version of the work, in nearly every case it was the first edition that was chosen, since (with some notable exceptions such as *Waverley*) there is very little evidence that Scott intervened in the texts of his novels between the first editions and the late Magnum project. However, a very different picture emerges in relation to the long poems. The different versions of those works examined in detail reveal that the texts do not remain stable but evolve and change in subtle ways from one edition to the next. We can reflect on the reasons for this: when Scott was writing the early narrative poems he was a much younger and less influential figure and it is possible that he had less control over the publication of his work. However, Scott's open avowal of authorship and the freeness with which he communicated his plans to friends makes the production of the poetry significantly different to that of the novels of the 'Great Unknown'.

With no need for secrecy Scott's poetry reached print very publicly, with friends and correspondents contributing their thoughts and responses. After publication, this process continued, with correspondents advising Scott on how his poems could be improved and contributing additional material for notes; his friends too criticised what he had written, and made suggestions for revisions, and even rewrote lines of verse. Ainsley McIntosh, editor of *Marmion*, following Jerome McGann, has described this process as a highly 'socialised' form of development and production where dialogues and interactions between Scott and his audience had direct consequences for the development of the text in both its pre- and post-publication stages. This pattern is replicated in *The Lay of the Last Minstrel* (1805), *The Lady of the Lake* (1810) and, tellingly, even in *The Lord of the Isles* (1815), published after Scott had begun to publish fiction. In each Scott continues to be artistically engaged with the poem beyond its first appearance in print; the first edition is not the end point of its creative evolution. However there comes a point, usually about a year after a poem was first published, where the continuing process of adjustment and augmentation more or less ceases. The editors consider this point to be the culmination of the creative process. In other words, these early editions are part of what we might call an initial creative process which is in the main Scott's, but which takes in and responds to the public context. As a consequence the base-text for each of these long poems is the edition in which the poem settles into its fullest articulation.

Collation also revealed that while Scott may have been 'improving' his poems at this early stage, they were also simultaneously deteriorating: punctuation, layout, and even occasional words were inevitably corrupted as compositors 'translated' the manuscript into print, and repeatedly used the last published edition as the copy-text for the next. Scott's handwriting is much easier to read in his younger years than his later and the layout of a poem on the page mitigates against the kind of cramped script that is found in the manuscripts of the novels. However, this does not mean that there were no errors in reading them; as with his fiction, Scott's poetry reveals that he has a more extensive and technical vocabulary than those who were preparing his work for publication and it was not always understood. The manuscripts of his poems also reveal layers of revision which were sometimes brought into the printed text incorrectly. While the manuscripts are lightly punctuated, Scott is emphatic when punctuation is meaningful but his wishes were not always followed. At times he was also emphatic about the layout of his text: indentation is closely aligned with his complex rhyming pattern but it was not always followed and errors were made. As new editions appeared further deterioration inevitably ensued. Scott's texts, therefore, came under pressure both from what might be seen as authorial improvement and textual deterioration thus raising particularly interesting questions for legitimate emendation.

Our policy, therefore, is to emend copy-texts both where there are obvious misreadings of the manuscript and where there is clear deterioration which can be attributed to compositors' errors and blundered attempts at correction. By returning to manuscript readings the freshness of the original texts can be captured without detracting from the developed text, and by removing the accretions of printing errors Scott's intentions, as discerned in what *he* wrote, can be recovered. While emendation may not be as extensive as in the novels, it is nevertheless significant, and it is hoped that it results in a text that fully captures Scott's artistic vision.

Emendations to the poetic texts are not, however, the only changes. This edition is novel in its treatment of Scott's annotation. In the novels the majority of Scott's notes were introduced as part of the Magnum Opus edition of 1829–33, but the notes to his longer narrative poems, and indeed some of his shorter verse, were *always* intrinsic to the original texts. The notes constitute an important part of their paratextual dialogue, and they are frequently textually unstable. A cursory look reveals that they are not notes as we would now understand them: they give accounts of his sources; they provide supplementary material; at times they are narratives in their own right. Indeed, they are best understood as a kind of *surplusage*, indicative of a process which he describes late on in his career as an inability to resist the act of storytelling, stating in *Reliquiæ Trotcosienses* that he could never prevent himself from 'gliding into the true musing style of an antiquarian disposed in sailors' phrase to "spin a tough yarn"'.[2] Lockhart's approach to this annotation compounds the inadequacy of his edition. While Scott makes a clear distinction between end notes and what he calls 'glossarial' notes at the foot of the page Lockhart muddles this distinction and even adds his own observations about the poem and its reception amongst the annotatory material. Other editions omit the notes altogether. However, in the Edinburgh Edition of Walter Scott's Poetry his notes are presented, as they were in the early editions, as part of the text of his poems, thus restoring a relationship that was clear in Scott's mind but has been lost in later reprintings of his poems.

The notes introduce an additional textual complication: Scott often relied upon amanuenses to copy material from other works to include in his own notes, and examining the copies against their sources it is possible to see where mistakes were made. When Scott himself copied documents he often adjusted and modernised his source, and this is allowed to stand in this edition for it is what Scott intended. But when an amanuensis misread a manuscript, introduced errors, or provided an 'interpretation' of the source, the EEWSP emends.

This, then, is the textual policy and general procedure governing the treatment of the longer narrative poems. However, while these general principles are applied throughout the edition whenever possible, in some instances they require adjustment. In the case of the present volume, for example, the varied nature of the textual witnesses (including magazines, newspapers and even funerary inscriptions) had to be accommodated. The particular approach for *The Shorter Poems* is outlined in its Essay on the Texts, but at all times the overriding principle is that the text demonstrably closest to the author will be preferred. Of course the Edinburgh Edition of Walter Scott's Poetry also provides its own paratextual material to re-invigorate understanding of Scott's verse. The appropriate form of this material for *The Shorter Poems* is outlined in the Essay on the Texts but as elsewhere in the edition its aim is to support modern readers without imposing unnecessary interpretation upon the work they are encountering. In these respects the poetry volumes follow the pattern of the Edinburgh Edition of the Waverley Novels and provide a companion to it.

Walter Scott's poetry is truly innovative. In *Marmion* Scott suggests that the poet should 'scorn pedantic laws' (Canto 5, line 183) and while his extraordinary dexterity in handling verse forms was at times perplexing for critics, it also prompted a recognition that something new and radical was at work within his poetry. He was also experimenting with the supernatural as was Coleridge, and with the construction of memory in relation to time and locale long before Wordsworth's *Prelude* was published.

The aim of the Edinburgh Edition of Walter Scott's Poetry is to restore his poems to a form which best reflects his intentions during the initial creative process and which is freed as far as possible from the various errors and non-authorial interventions that arose in the course of their publication and successive reprintings. It also aims to enrich the reading experience of those who come fresh to Scott's poetry. It is the hope of all involved that by doing so his full significance as a poet will be realised, and that the complexities at work within his poetry, and the relevance of the issues with which it deals, will be revealed. The editorial team is not blind to the challenge; reading nineteenth-century narrative poetry of the kind that Scott writes, to say nothing of verse dramas, requires a re-discovery of a type of reading that has to some extent been forgotten. It is hoped that a critical edition, which

provides readers with clear and accurate texts along with the support
they need to understand them in a twenty-first century context, will
encourage a rediscovery of the pleasures of this kind of reading. The
rewards are, we are certain, invigorating.

Alison Lumsden

Notes

1 Walter Scott, Introduction to *Rokeby*, *The Poetical Works of Walter Scott,
Bart.*, [ed. J. G. Lockhart], 12 vols (Edinburgh 1833–34), 9.15–20.
2 Walter Scott, *Reliquiæ Trotcosienses or the Gabions of the Late Jonathan Oldbuck
Esq. of Monkbarns*, ed. Gerard Carruthers and Alison Lumsden (Edinburgh,
2004), 34.

1
His First Lines

In awful ruins Ætna thunders nigh,
And sends in pitchy whirlwinds to the sky
Black clouds of smoke, which, still as they aspire,
From their dark sides there bursts the glowing fire;
At other times huge balls of fire are toss'd,   5
That lick the stars, and in the smoke are lost:
Sometimes the mount, with vast convulsions torn,
Emits huge rocks, which instantly are borne
With loud explosions to the starry skies,
The stones made liquid as the huge mass flies,   10
Then back again with greater weight recoils,
While Ætna thundering from the bottom boils.

2
On a Thunder-storm

Loud o'er my head though awful thunders roll,
And vivid lightnings flash from pole to pole,
Yet 'tis thy voice, my God, that bids them fly,
Thy arm directs those lightnings through the sky.
Then let the good thy mighty name revere,   5
And hardened sinners thy just vengeance fear.

3

On the Setting Sun

Those evening clouds, that setting ray,
And beauteous tints, serve to display
   Their great Creator's praise;
Then let the short liv'd thing call'd man
Whose life's compris'd within a span,   5
   To Him his homage raise;

We often praise the evening clouds,
   And tints so gay, and bold,
But seldom think upon our God,
   Who ting'd these clouds with gold.   10

4

To Jessie

Lassie can ye love me weel?
   Ask your heart, and answer true,
Doth that gentle bosom feel
   Love for one who loveth you?
Say not out of mere compassion,   5
   Say not out of idle sport,
Ruth and folly lead a fashion
   Only for the foolish sort.

Lassie gin ye'll love me weel
   Weel I'll love ye in return,   10
Whilst the salmon fills the creel,
   Whilst the flow'r grows by the burn.
Teviot and Tweed ne'er change their places
   Nor Heav'n its stars on earth may rain,
But e'er I slight thy winning graces,   15
   Such must be and be again.

5

Lines Addressed to Miss J. —

How beautiful thou art I know
And ev'ry hour would tell thee so,
Yet what avails thy blooming charms
If they elude my eager arms?
What boots the beauty of that face   5
If love find there no dwelling place?
What matters if thine eyes are bright
Unless on me they turn their light?
Why should I heed thy magic smile
Whose charm seeks not my soul the while?   10
Or let those lips that soul betray
That from my own still keep away?
I ask, and would not ask in vain—
What love allows, let love obtain:
If in thy breast Love's burning fires   15
Have raised the flame that ne'er expires,
Let that delightful passion raise
Its genial presence in thy gaze,
Making thy smiles—like rosy morn—
Warming each place they should adorn,   20
And teaching that sweet mouth the way
Of those that own Affection's sway.

6

To the Flower of Kelso

How lags with me the weary hour
That owneth not thy witching power!
The day creeps on with tedious pace,
The night drags out a tortoise race,
At sunrise to the hills I roam   5
To change the weariness of home,
Yet—as the hare her speed applies
In hopes to 'scape her enemies—
O'er bank and brae my eager horse
Follows the grey-hounds' rapid course   10
Passes like lightning ford and crag—
Still the hot chase appears to drag.

By Teviot's far famed banks I stray
Seeking till eve the scaly prey:
But though the fisher's aim I court,   15
All the dull time I find no sport.

With dog and gun the wood I beat—
The feathered game fall to my feet:
Yet should success attend each fire,
It soon grows tame, and I soon tire.   20
To Roxburgh's crumbling walls I hie
Or to the ruined Abbey fly,
Seeking, mid relics of the past,
The pleasures they once round me cast,
But monuments of days of yore,   25
I find can int'rest me no more:
The more I seek, the more I see,
The more I long to be with thee.

7
Jessie

When first I met thine eyes of blue
I gazed upon their azure hue
   As if, had met my sight,
The cloudless skies in beauty clear
That fill the radiant atmosphere   5
   With beauty, joy, and light.

When first I heard thy voice's tone
Filled with a music all its own
   It so did charm my ears,
I thought 'twas harmony divine   10
Such as when seraph choirs combine
   In yon etherial spheres.

But when I first became so blest
To clasp thee fondly to my breast,
   And my deep love express;   15
I fancied in thy glowing charms
I held all Heaven within my arms,
   Its bliss in thy caress.

8
To the Pride of Teviotdale

When at the tryst we're fondly roaming,
   How gallant all things shine!
Thy loving looks make bright the gloaming,
   Thy voice, that answers mine—
   Whose ev'ry breath is thine—   5
Gives to the silent air a melody divine.

With thee each look a pleasure darted,
    In those delightful days
Our hearts and hands were never parted;
    Brightly each gaze met gaze,   10
    And ev'ry speech was praise,
Feeding our mutual love in a thousand diff'rent ways.

Away from thee, loud sounds surround me
    As screech-owl harsh and shrill;
But when with thee the hour hath found me   15
    By valley stream or hill,
    Or whereso'er Fate will,
Though thunder shake the ground all seemeth hushed
                          and still.

Teacher or preacher gains no hearing,
    The page remains unread,   20
For Ah! my heart for thee is speiring,
    My foot still longs to tread,
    With thee, by Tweed's fair bed,
Rifling the gems of dew that crown the daisy's head.

Corn rigs still shew their golden yellow,   25
    The poppy blushes yet:
Each heather bell sings to its fellow
    At sunrise or sunset—
    But not as when I met,
With theirs, the thrilling looks my soul can ne'er forget.   30

Still Teviot rolls her shining billow,
    But Oh no more I see
That form which made my breast its pillow;
    How can I then agree
    These things unchanged may be,   35
When they, Alas! appear so different to me?

9

𝔄 𝔖imple 𝔉act

Ah tell me no more with a face full of beauty
    That you ever can be in fault;
That the path of Affection's not fairer than Duty,
    Or that there we should now make a halt.

Your scruples are vain, and your arguments shallow,   5
    For believe me that this is owre true—
If discretion indeed be the best part of Valour,
    With Love it hath nothing to do.

10

𝔗he ℜesolve

My wayward fate I needs must plain,
    Though bootless be the theme;
I loved, and was beloved again,
    Yet all was but a dream:
For, as her love was quickly got,   5
    So it was quickly gone;
No more I'll bask in flame so hot,
    But coldly dwell alone.

Not maid more bright than maid was e'er
    My fancy shall beguile,   10
By flattering word, or feigned tear,
    By gesture, look, or smile:
No more I'll call the shaft fair shot,
    Till it has fairly flown,
Nor scorch me at a flame so hot;—   15
    I'll rather freeze alone.

Each ambush'd Cupid I'll defy,
   In cheek, or chin, or brow,
And deem the glance of woman's eye
   As weak as woman's vow: 20
I'll lightly hold the lady's heart,
   That is but lightly won;
I'll steel my breast to beauty's art,
   And learn to live alone.

The flaunting torch soon blazes out,   25
   The diamond's ray abides,
The flame its glory hurls about,
   The gem its lustre hides;
Such gem I fondly deem'd was mine,
   And glow'd for me alone;   30
But, since each eye may see it shine,
   I'll darkling dwell alone.

No waking dream shall tinge my thought
   With dyes so bright and vain,
No silken net, so slightly wrought,   35
   Shall tangle me again:
No more I'll pay so dear for wit,
   I'll live upon mine own;
Nor shall wild passion trouble it,
   I'll rather dwell alone.   40

And thus I'll hush my heart to rest,—
   "Thy loving labour's lost;
Thou shalt no more be wildly blest,
   To be so strangely crost:
The widow'd turtles mateless die,   45
   The phœnix is but one;
They seek no loves—no more will I—
   I'll rather dwell alone."

11

Lines to Miss J. —

Whilst those angelic orbs I see
    I feel such wondrous charm
As though some power of witcherie
    Dwelt in that lovely form.

But never yet was magic known   5
    So welcomed where it fell,
Nor object so inclined to own
    Th'enchantment of the spell.

Though far away from those fond eyes
    Reluctantly I rove,   10
Those charms before my vision rise
    And fill my thoughts with love.

Whilst wandering on with random feet
    By Fancy so beguiled,
I find thee in the busy street   15
    As in the pathless wild.

So far or near we're ne'er apart,
    And nought can us divide,
Whilst in my fond embrace thou art
    Wherever I abide.   20

Only dear Jessie this believe—
    Some once or twice at most
I rather would yourself receive,
    Than fifty times your ghost.

12

The Prisoner's Complaint

Come Jessie I impatient grow—
    Come hither quick I pray,
With meikle speed unlock the door,
    I can no longer stay.

The minutes into hours have grown   5
    Whilst I imprisoned wait,
E'en your old aunt would pity have
    On my unhappy state.

I came in hopes of welcome looks,
    And words more welcome still;   10
I'm shut up in a gloomy hole
    And can't do as I will.

Instead of loving words from you,
    No sort of sound I hear,
Save an old woman's sighs and groans   15
    That make my stomach queer.

Though tired of standing all this time
    I dare na stir a leg;
Though wishing sair to stretch my arms
    I canna move a peg.   20

The glasses tremble at my breath
    So close to me they stand,
Whilst jars are pressing 'gainst my feet,
    And jugs at either hand.

Haste to prevent the threatening harm   25
    Or your old aunt I fear
When glass and china fall and crash
    Will think the devil's here.

Here's haddocks dry and barley meal
    And marmalade and jam;   30
And high suspended by a hook
    Above me hangs a ham;

But mid such heap of fish and flesh
    I uncontented live;
I hunger after fresher food   35
    Which you alone can give.

Untouched the tempting honey pots
    Upon their shelves remain,
For that I taste upon your lips
    Makes me all else disdain.   40

Come hither! You my closet are,
    Where all my sweets are stored,
Oh save me from your aunt's good things
    And some of your's afford.

13

Law Versus Love

Away with parchments, warrants, bills—
    Come fairies, brownies, knights and giants;
Avaunt all stupid books of Law,
    Shakspeare and Spenser are my clients.

Heineccius to your shelf return   5
    With brother Erskine's dryer labours,
For I have—to supply your place—
    Romance and Love those pleasant neighbours.

Heav'n keep your slumbers undisturbed
    You weary dreary dull civilians!   10
Love's are the only Institutes—
    His Pandects are the laws of millions.

Glad as I 'scape from thy dull rule
    A fresher air seems breaking o'er me;
There tow'rs a castle strong and high   15
    Here blooms a fair pleasaunce before me.

A lady's bow'r mine eye invites
    My feet gang there in willing duty;
I enter, and amid its flow'rs
    I find a flow'r of matchless beauty.   20

There sits my peerless queen enthroned
    And whilst in haste my joy I'm proving,
I'm roused by Tom who sharply cries
    "Hey Wattie, man! Ye're unco loving!"

The dingy boards again transform   25
    To mother nature's verdant bosom;
The inkstands turn to goodly trees,
    And all the pens begin to blossom.

Our shabby cloth and corduroy
    Now change to richest silk and satin;   30
And nought but fairy music sounds
    Stead of broad Scotch or musty Latin.

But greater changes still ensue,
    (I fear I'm non compos mentis,)
I spy a horrid Saracen   35
    In ev'ry yawning gowk apprentice.

These paynims vile I fierce assault,
    Till stopped by cry of snoring dolour,
I find by Allan's bloody pate
    I've cracked his noddle with the ruler.   40

14

A Lover's Advice

Heed not what the world may say
   Should they spy our goings on;
Put off till the evil day
   What till then must be unknown.
They may blame ye—who would doubt it?   5
Dinna fash your thumb about it.

Ever since auld Adam's time
   This good fashion hath prevailed,
To be happy in our prime,
   Ere each proper sense hath failed.   10
If they preach 'gainst this, or flout it,
Dinna fash your thumb about it.

Youth hath been the age of joy
   And joy with love must ever hold;
Let us then our youth employ   15
   In the loving way of old.
If they say you're best without it,
Dinna fash your thumb about it.

For what were our young arms designed
   If not to twine in fond embrace?   20
And long as "like loves like" we find,
   Lips on lips have proper place.
Though Prudes such law condemn and knout it,
Dinna fash your thumb about it.

Happiness all folks allow   25
   The while a hope of it endures,
Take your honest pleasure now,
   Tomorrow it may not be yours.
If cant your bliss approach to rout it,
Dinna fash your thumb about it.   30

Then to my heart once more be pressed,
    And, as such natural bliss we prove,
Convince ourselves that we are bless'd
    As well and truly as we love.
Though some may whisper blame, or shout it,   35
Dinna fash your thumb about it.

15

𝕬n 𝕬nti-𝕮lassical 𝕺de

Written after beholding certain Specimens of Sculpture

Away with Venus, and the three
    Who her hand-maidens were, or would be,
I'm sure it's very plain to me
    They were no better than they should be.

The first sprang from the salt-sea foam,   5
    As heathen history hath stated;
But I suspect her earliest home
    Was in the *froth* her bard created.

Or else she never saw the floods
    In all their mighty spray and splashing: 10
But, stead of foam, rose from the *suds*—
    Having been used to take in washing.

Oft sat she by the shining nook
    Where haddock hung by pliant withy
And her good man—so says the book—   15
    Was known by all to keep a smithy.

And if the chronicles speak truth
    She could not keep from naughty courses;
But toyed with Mars—a handsome youth—
    The whilst her husband shoed his horses.   20

Yet not content with one *faux pas*—
   Which most dishonourable I own is;
She sinned 'gainst honest love and Law
   With a young neighbour laird, Adonis.

Doubtless she used to treat her subs   25
   "The Graces Three", to make them frisky,
When they had worked well at the tubs,
   With a wee drap of right good whisky.

Whether they chose to cheat or rob
   Has not been said by those who've seen 'em;   30
'Tis plain they were as poor as Job—
   I see they've scarce a rag between 'em!

My hand my much shocked vision shades,
   Nor can I gaze but in a passion:
They must have been bold forward jades   35
   Or they'd have dressed in decent fashion.

But as their unclad limbs I spy,
   I feel that I my time am losing:
For all may see with half an eye
   They've left me nothing for exposing.   40

16

To a Lady

For *thee* from Time's slow mouldering hold
Shall many an Antique lay be torn—
Recorded Deeds of Champions bold
Or plaints of Maids who wept forlorn.

The shade of each departed Bard   5
Who mourns his verse neglected long
Shall own o'erpaid by *thy* regard
The labours of his noblest song.

So the rich Diamond's blazing stone
Is drawn from darkness of the Mine   10
To grace some valued Monarch's throne
Or some loved Saint's heart-worshipped Shrine.

17

The Violet

The violet, in her green-wood bower,
    Where birchen boughs with hazles mingle,
May boast itself the fairest flower
    In glen, or copse, or forest dingle.

Though fair her gems of azure hue,   5
    Beneath the dew-drop's weight reclining;
I've seen an eye of lovelier blue,
    More sweet through wat'ry lustre shining.

The summer sun that dew shall dry,
    Ere yet the day be past its morrow;   10
Nor longer in my false love's eye,
    Remain'd the tear of parting sorrow.

18

To the Cruel Lady of the Mountains

Ah ! why wilt thou not be my love,
    Among these wild and pleasant mountains,
From whence the eye untired may rove,
    O'er mossy banks and sparkling fountains?

Thy fleeting form I oft have chaced,   5
    O'er craggy rocks thy steps pursuing;
By fancy lured through woods to haste,
    While hope beguiled me to my ruin.

Thou savage in an angel's form,
    No more will I such homage render;   10
For what avails each outward charm,
    Without a heart that's kind and tender!

I'll throw my idle crook aside,
    My pipe and sylvan haunts forsaking,
Beneath a friar's garb to hide   15
    The weakness of a heart that's breaking.

Then in my gown, of sober gray,
    Along that winding path I'll wander,
And wend my melancholy way,
    To the sad shrine that waits me yonder.   20

There, in the calm monastic shade,
    All injuries must be forgiven;
And there, for *thee*, obdurate Maid,
    My orisons shall rise to heaven.

No more I'll wear this cypress wreath,   25
    No more petition, or reprove thee;—
Silent I go to meet my death,
    Or learn the art no more to love thee.

19

Unpued on Yarrow's braes

Unpued on Yarrow's braes, the birk,
Untouched may Teviot's roses fa'
While thy pale flowers shall cheer my way—
Laid by the maid that's far awa'—

And while I wander lorn and drear   5
By many a time worn tottering ha'
Thy spriggs shall wake remembrance dear
Of pleasure past and far awa'.

Droop sune, ye birks in Yarrow's shade
While the keen north winds rudely blaw   10
Sune may thy roses Teviot fade
Born on his whirlwhins far awa'—

Come Winter with thy ruthless train
And cleed again our hills wi' snaw
For lovely in thy stormy van   15
Thou bringst the maid that's far awa'.

20

Poem on Caterthun

Cold the wild blast that chills thy brow
And bleak thy summit C—t—r T—n
Yet lonely on thy cliffs of snow
I lingering watch the setting sun.

Long have the bards been low in death   5
That bade thy rocky crown arise
And frowning o'er thy brow of heath
Crest its gray circle to the skies.

Perhaps stern freedom on thy head
Reared the rude Granite's flinty pile   10
What time her indignant votaries fled
The veteran Legion's lengthened file.

Perhaps in Denmark's conquering day
Here Odin's ruthless altar rose
And thro' the rough scarr'd Runic lay   15
Streamed the red gore of captive foes.

Or if we trust the Village tale
A wayward maid in witching hour
When stars were red and moon was pale
Rear'd thy dread mound by magic power.   20

Yet not to trace whose deeds of yore
Have marked thy summit C—t—r T—n
On thy rude rampart bleak and hoar
I lonely watch the setting sun.

Loth to resume my vagrant lot   25
While brightening in the distance far
Thy beams yet gild one sacred Spot
And fondly seem to linger there.

And linger still thou setting sun
And gild her walks and cheer her flowers   30
And chase each care, and chase each pain
That cloud my gentle Favourite's hours.

Mine be the blast on mountain brow
If evening sun beams round her play
And mine the storm and mine the snow   35
If hers the sheltered vale of May.

And ever thro' life's chequered years
Thus *ever* may our fortunes roll
Tho' *mine* be storms or *mine* be tears
Be *hers* the "sunshine of the soul"—   40

C—t—r T—n, 5 May 1796

21

𝔚illiam and ℌelen

From the German of Gottfried Augustus Bürger

From heavy dreams fair Helen rose
    And ey'd the dawning red:
"Alas, my love, thou tarriest long!
    O art thou false or dead?"

With gallant Fred'rick's princely power   5
    He sought the bold crusade;
But not a word from Judah's wars
    Told Helen how he sped.

With Paynim and with Saracen
    At length a truce was made,   10
And ev'ry knight return'd to dry
    The tears his love had shed.

Our gallant host was homeward bound
    With many a song of joy;
Green wav'd the laurel in each plume,   15
    The badge of victory.

And old and young, and sire and son,
    To meet them crowd the way,
With shouts, and mirth, and melody,
    The debt of love to pay.   20

Full many a maid her true love met,
    And sobb'd in his embrace,
And flutt'ring joy in tears and smiles
    Array'd full many a face.

Nor joy nor smile for Helen sad;   25
    She sought the host in vain;
For none could tell her William's fate,
    If faithless, or if slain.

The martial band is past and gone;
  She rends her raven hair, 30
And in distraction's bitter mood
  She weeps with wild despair.

"O rise, my child," her mother said,
  "Nor sorrow thus in vain;
A perjur'd lover's fleeting heart 35
  No tears recal again."

"O mother, what is gone, is gone,
  What's lost, for ever lorn:
Death, death alone can comfort me;
  O had I ne'er been born! 40

"O break, my heart, O break at once!
  Drink my life-blood despair!
No joy remains on earth for me,
  For me in heaven no share."

"O enter not in judgment, Lord!" 45
  The pious mother prays;
"Impute not guilt to thy frail child!
  She knows not what she says.

"O say thy pater noster, child!
  O turn to God and grace! 50
His will that turn'd thy bliss to bale
  Can change thy bale to bliss."

"O mother, mother! What is bliss?
  O mother, what is bale?
My William's love was heaven on earth, 55
  Without it earth is hell.

"Why should I pray to ruthless Heav'n
  Since my lov'd William's slain?
I only pray'd for William's sake,
  And all my pray'rs were vain." 60

"O take the sacrament, my child,
   And check these tears that flow;
By resignation's humble pray'r
   O hallow'd be thy woe!"

"No sacrament can quench this fire,   65
   Or slake this scorching pain:
No sacrament can bid the dead
   Arise and live again.

"O break, my heart, O break at once!
   Be thou my god, Despair!   70
Heav'n's heaviest blow has fall'n on me,
   And vain each fruitless pray'r."

"O enter not in judgment, Lord,
   With thy frail child of clay!
She knows not what her tongue has spoke;   75
   Impute it not, I pray!

"Forbear, my child, this desp'rate woe,
   And turn to God and grace;
Well can devotion's heav'nly glow
   Convert thy bale to bliss."   80

"O mother, mother, what is bliss?
   O mother, what is bale?
Without my William what were heav'n,
   Or with him what were hell?"

Wild she arraigns th' eternal doom,   85
   Upbraids each sacred pow'r,
Till spent, she sought her silent room
   All in the lonely tower.

She beat her breast, she wrung her hands,
   Till sun and day were o'er,   90
And through the glimm'ring lattice shone
   The twinkling of the star.

Then crash! the heavy draw-bridge fell,
   That o'er the moat was hung;
And clatter! clatter! on its boards   95
   The hoof of courser rung.

The clank of echoing steel was heard
   As off the rider bounded;
And slowly on the winding stair
   A heavy footstep sounded.   100

And hark! and hark! a knock—Tap! tap!
   A rustling stifled noise;—
Door latch and tinkling staples ring;—
   At length a whisp'ring voice.

"Awake, awake, arise my love!   105
   How, Helen, dost thou fare?
Wak'st thou, or sleep'st? laugh'st thou, or weep'st?
   Hast thought on me, my fair?"

"My love! my love!—so late by night!—
   I wak'd, I wept for thee;   110
Much have I borne since dawn of morn;—
   Where, William, could'st thou be?"

"We saddled late—From Hungary
   I rode since darkness fell;
And to its bourne we both return   115
   Before the matin bell."

"O rest this night within my arms,
   And warm thee in their fold!
Chill howls through hawthorn bush the wind;—
   My love is deadly cold."   120

"Let the wind howl through hawthorn bush!
   This night we must away;
The steed is wight, the spur is bright;
   I cannot stay till day.

"Busk, busk, and boune! Thou mount'st behind   125
    Upon my black barb steed:
O'er stock and stile, a hundred miles,
    We haste to bridal bed."

"To-night—to-night a hundred miles!—
    O dearest William, stay!   130
The bell strikes twelve—dark, dismal hour!
    O wait, my love, till day!"

"Look here, look here—the moon shines clear—
    Full fast I ween we ride;
Mount and away! for ere the day   135
    We reach our bridal bed.

"The black barb snorts, the bridle rings;
    Haste, busk, and boune, and seat thee!
The feast is made, the chamber spread,
    The bridal guests await thee."   140

Strong love prevail'd: She busks, she bounes,
    She mounts the barb behind,
And round her darling William's waist
    Her lily arms she twin'd.

And hurry! hurry! off they rode,   145
    As fast as fast might be;
Spurn'd from the courser's thundering heels
    The flashing pebbles flee.

And on the right, and on the left,
    Ere they could snatch a view,   150
Fast, fast each mountain, mead and plain,
    And cot and castle flew.

"Sit fast—dost fear?—The moon shines clear—
    Fleet rides my barb—keep hold!
Fear'st thou?" "O no!" she faintly said;   155
    "But why so stern and cold?

"What yonder rings? what yonder sings?
  Why shrieks the owlet gray?"
"'Tis death bells clang, 'tis funeral song,
  The body to the clay.   160

"With song and clang, at morrow's dawn,
  Ye may inter the dead:
To-night I ride, with my young bride,
  To deck our bridal bed.

"Come with thy choir, thou coffin'd guest,   165
  To swell our nuptial song!
Come priest, to bless our marriage feast!
  Come all, come all along!"

Ceas'd clang and song; down sunk the bier;
  The shrouded corpse arose: 170
And hurry, hurry! all the train
  The thund'ring steed pursues.

And forward! forward! on they go;
  High snorts the straining steed;
Thick pants the rider's labouring breath,   175
  As headlong on they speed.

"O William, why this savage haste?
  And where thy bridal bed?"
"'Tis distant far." "Still short and stern?"
  "'Tis narrow, trustless maid."   180

"No room for me?" "Enough for both;—
  Speed, speed, my Barb, thy course."
O'er thund'ring bridge, through boiling surge,
  He drove the furious horse.

Tramp! tramp! along the land they rode;   185
  Splash! splash! along the sea;
The steed is wight, the spur is bright,
  The flashing pebbles flee.

Fled past on right and left how fast
 Each forest, grove and bower;   190
On right and left fled past how fast
 Each city, town and tower.

"Dost fear? dost fear?—The moon shines clear;—
 Dost fear to ride with me?—
Hurrah! hurrah! The dead can ride!"   195
 "O William let them be!

"See there, see there! What yonder swings
 And creaks 'mid whistling rain?"
"Gibbet and steel, th' accursed wheel;
 A murd'rer in his chain.   200

"Hollo! thou felon, follow here:
 To bridal bed we ride;
And thou shalt prance a fetter dance
 Before me and my bride."

And hurry, hurry! clash, clash, clash!   205
 The wasted form descends;
And fleet as wind through hazel bush
 The wild career attends.

Tramp! tramp! along the land they rode,
 Splash! splash! along the sea;   210
The scourge is red, the spur drops blood,
 The flashing pebbles flee.

How fled what moonshine faintly show'd!
 How fled what darkness hid!
How fled the earth beneath their feet,   215
 The heav'n above their head!

"Dost fear? dost fear? The moon shines clear,
 And well the dead can ride;
Does faithful Helen fear for them?"
 "O leave in peace the dead!"   220

"Barb! Barb! methinks I hear the cock;
    The sand will soon be run:
Barb! Barb! I smell the morning air;
    The race is well nigh done."

Tramp! tramp! along the land they rode,   225
    Splash! splash! along the sea;
The scourge is red, the spur drops blood,
    The flashing pebbles flee.

"Hurrah! hurrah! well ride the dead;
    The bride, the bride is come!   230
And soon we reach the bridal bed,
    For, Helen, here's my home."

Reluctant on its rusty hinge
    Revolv'd an iron door,
And by the pale moon's setting beam   235
    Were seen a church and tow'r.

With many a shriek and cry whiz round
    The birds of midnight, scared;
And rustling like autumnal leaves
    Unhallow'd ghosts were heard.   240

O'er many a tomb and tomb-stone pale
    He spurr'd the fiery horse,
Till sudden at an open grave
    He check'd the wond'rous course.

The falling gauntlet quits the rein,   245
    Down drops the casque of steel,
The cuirass leaves his shrinking side,
    The spur his gory heel.

The eyes desert the naked skull,
    The mould'ring flesh the bone,   250
Till Helen's lily arms entwine
    A ghastly skeleton.

The furious Barb snorts fire and foam;
  And with a fearful bound
Dissolves at once in empty air,   255
  And leaves her on the ground.

Half seen by fits, by fits half heard,
  Pale spectres fleet along;
Wheel round the maid in dismal dance,
  And howl the fun'ral song: 260

"E'en when the heart's with anguish cleft,
  Revere the doom of Heav'n.
Her soul is from her body reft;
  Her spirit be forgiv'n!"

22

𝕿𝖍𝖊 𝕮𝖍𝖆𝖘𝖊

From the German of Gottfried Augustus Bürger

Earl Walter winds his bugle horn;
  To horse, to horse, halloo, halloo!
His fiery courser snuffs the morn,
  And thronging serfs their Lord pursue.

The eager pack, from couples freed,   5
  Dash through the bush, the brier, the brake;
While answering hound, and horn, and steed,
  The mountain echoes startling wake.

The beams of God's own hallow'd day
  Had painted yonder spire with gold,   10
And, calling sinful man to pray,
  Loud, long, and deep the bell had toll'd.

But still Earl Walter onward rides;
    Halloo, halloo, and hark again!
When, spurring from opposing sides,   15
    Two stranger horsemen join the train.

Who was each stranger, left and right,
    Well may I guess, but dare not tell:
The right-hand steed was silver white,
    The left, the swarthy hue of hell.   20

The right-hand horseman, young and fair,
    His smile was like the morn of May;
The left, from eye of tawny glare,
    Shot midnight lightning's lurid ray.

He wav'd his huntsman's cap on high,   25
    Cry'd, "Welcome, welcome, noble Lord!
What sport can earth, or sea, or sky,
    To match the princely chase, afford?"

"Cease thy loud bugle's clanging knell,"
    Cry'd the fair youth, with silver voice;   30
"And for Devotion's choral swell
    Exchange the rude discordant noise.

"To-day th' ill-omen'd chase forbear;
    Yon bell yet summons to the fane:
To-day the warning spirit hear,   35
    To-morrow thou may'st mourn in vain."

"Away, and sweep the glades along!"
    The sable hunter hoarse replies;
"To muttering Monks leave matin song,
    And bells, and books, and mysteries."   40

Earl Walter spurr'd his ardent steed,
    And, launching forward with a bound,
"Who for thy drowsy priestlike rede
    Would leave the jovial horn and hound?

"No! pious fool, I scorn thy lore;   45
    Let him who ne'er the chase durst prove
Go join with thee the droning choir,
    And leave me to the sport I love."

Fast, fast Earl Walter onward rides,
    O'er moss and moor, o'er holt and hill,   50
And onward fast on either side
    The stranger horsemen follow'd still.

Up springs, from yonder tangled thorn,
    A stag more white than mountain snow;
And louder rung Earl Walter's horn,   55
    "Hark forward, forward, holla, ho!"

A heedless wretch has cross'd the way,—
    He gasps the thundering hoofs below;
But, live who can, or die who may,
    Still forward, forward! On they go.   60

See where yon simple fences meet,
    A field with Autumn's blessings crown'd;
See prostrate at Earl Walter's feet
    A husbandman with toil embrown'd.

"O mercy! mercy! noble Lord;   65
    Spare the hard pittance of the poor,
Earn'd by the sweat these brows have pour'd
    In scorching July's sultry hour."

Earnest the right-hand stranger pleads,
    The left still cheering to the prey: 70
Th' impetuous Earl no warning heeds,
    But furious holds the onward way.

"Away, thou hound, so basely born,
    Or dread the scourge's echoing blow!"
Then loudly rung his bugle horn,   75
    "Hark forward, forward, holla, ho!"

So said, so done—a single bound
    Clears the poor labourer's humble pale:
Wild follows man, and horse, and hound,
    Like dark December's stormy gale.   80

And man, and horse, and hound, and horn,
    Destructive sweep the field along,
While joying o'er the wasted corn
    Fell Famine marks the madd'ning throng.

Again up rous'd the tim'rous prey   85
    Scours moss and moor, and holt and hill;
Hard run, he feels his strength decay,
    And trusts for life his simple skill.

Too dangerous solitude appear'd;
    He seeks the shelter of the crowd;   90
Amid the flock's domestic herd
    His harmless head he hopes to shroud.

O'er moss and moor, and holt and hill,
    His track the steady blood-hounds trace;
O'er moss and moor, and holt and hill,   95
    Th' unweary'd Earl pursues the chase.

The anxious herdsman lowly falls:
    "O spare, thou noble Baron, spare
These herds, a widow's little all,
    These flocks, an orphan's fleecy care."   100

Earnest the right-hand stranger pleads,
    The left still cheering to the prey;
Nor prayer nor pity Walter heeds,
    But furious keeps the onward way.

"Unmanner'd dog! To stop my sport   105
    Vain were thy cant and beggar whine,
Though human spirits of thy sort
    Were tenants of these carrion kine!"

Again he winds his bugle horn,
    "Hark forward, forward, holla, ho!"   110
And through the herd, in ruthless scorn,
    He cheers his furious hounds to go.

In heaps the throttled victims fall;
    Down sinks their mangled herdsman near;
The murd'rous cries the stag appal,   ·   115
    Again he starts, new-nerv'd by fear.

With blood besmear'd, and white with foam,
    While big the tears of anguish pour,
He seeks, amid the forest's gloom,
    The humble hermit's hut obscure.   120

But man and horse, and horn and hound,
    Fast rattling on his traces go;
The sacred chapel rung around
    With hark away, and holla, ho!

All mild, amid the route profane,   125
    The holy hermit pour'd his pray'r:
"Forbear with blood God's house to stain,
    Revere his altar, and forbear!

"The meanest brute has rights to plead,
    Which, wrong'd by cruelty or pride,   130
Draw vengeance on the ruthless head;—
    Be warn'd at length, and turn aside."

Still the fair horseman anxious pleads,
    The black wild whooping points the prey;
Alas! the Earl no warning heeds,   135
    But frantic keeps the forward way.

"Holy or not, or right or wrong,
    Thy altar and its rites I spurn;
Not sainted martyrs' sacred song,
    Not God himself shall make me turn."   140

He spurs his horse, he winds his horn,
  "Hark forward, forward, holla, ho!"
But off, on whirlwind's pinions borne,
  The stag, the hut, the hermit, go.

And horse and man, and horn and hound,   145
  And clamour of the chase was gone:
For hoofs and howls, and bugle sound,
  A deadly silence reign'd alone.

Wild gaz'd th' affrighted Earl around;—
  He strove in vain to wake his horn,   150
In vain to call; for not a sound
  Could from his anxious lips be borne.

He listens for his trusty hounds;
  No distant baying reach'd his ears;
His courser, rooted to the ground,   155
  The quick'ning spur unmindful bears.

Still dark and darker round it spreads,
  Dark as the darkness of the grave;
And not a sound the still invades,
  Save what a distant torrent gave.   160

High o'er the sinner's humbled head
  At length the solemn silence broke;
And from a cloud of swarthy red,
  The awful voice of thunder spoke.

"Oppressor of creation fair!   165
  Apostate spirits' harden'd tool!
Scorner of God! scourge of the poor!
  The measure of thy cup is full.

"Go, hunt for ever through the wood,
  For ever roam th' affrighted wild;   170
And let thy fate instruct the proud
  God's meanest creature is his child."

'Twas hush'd: one flash of sombre glare
 With yellow ting'd the forests brown;
Up rose Earl Walter's bristling hair,   175
 And horror chill'd each nerve and bone.

Cold pour'd the sweat in freezing rill;
 A rising wind began to sing;
And louder, louder, louder still,
 Brought storm and tempest on its wing. 180

The earth is rock'd, it quakes, it rends;
 From yawning rifts, with many a yell,
Mix'd with sulphureous flames, ascend
 The misbegotten dogs of hell.

What ghastly huntsman next arose,   185
 Well may I guess, but dare not tell:
His eye like midnight lightning glows,
 His steed the swarthy hue of hell.

Earl Walter flies o'er bush and thorn
 With many a shriek of helpless woe;   190
Behind him hound, and horse, and horn,
 And hark away, and holla, ho!

With wild despair's reverted eye,
 Close, close behind he marks the throng;
With bloody fangs, and eager cry,   195
 In frantic fear he scours along.

Still shall the dreadful chase endure
 Till time itself shall have an end;
By day earth's tortured womb they scour,
 At midnight's witching hour ascend.   200

This is the horn, and hound, and horse,
 That oft the lated peasant hears:
Appal'd he signs the frequent cross,
 When the wild din invades his ears.

The wakeful priest oft drops a tear   205
    For human pride, for human woe,
When at his midnight mass he hears
    Th' infernal cry of holla, ho!

23

The Lamentation of the Faithful Wife of Asan Aga

From the Morlachian Language

What yonder glimmers so white on the mountain
Glimmers so white where yon sycamores grow?
Is it wild swans around Vaga's fair fountain?
Or is it a wreath of the wintery snow?

Had it been snow glimmers white on the mountain   5
By this it had melted before the bright day
Or had it been swans around Vaga's fair fountain
They had stretched their broad pinions and sped them
                                    away.

It is not then swans round the fountain of Vaga
It is not a wreath of the wintery snow   10
But it is the gay tents of the fierce Asan Aga
Glimmering so white where yon sycamores grow.

Low lies the Chief on the couch of the wounded
There watch his sisters with tenderest care
There weeps his mother in sorrow unbounded   15
Every sad friend—but his lady—is there.—

She sorrowed more than the fondest of mothers
But from the thronged camp in which wounded he lay
Tho' there flocked sad friends, tender sisters and brothers
Timid shamefacedness compelled her to stay.

But at her absence high kindling his anger
Wrote the stern Chieftain this severing line
—"Away from my castle, its mistress no longer,
Away from my children and all that is mine."—

Anguish the heart of that lady deep rended   25
When the hard message was brought to her eye
Woe were the looks on her children she bended
Weeping around her tho' scarce knowing why.—

O'er the high drawbridge come horses loud prancing
—Wildly she started in desperate mood   30
She thought 'twas the signal of Asan advancing
And rushed to the turret to plunge in the flood.

"Stay thee, oh stay thee! my Mother! my Mother!
'Tis not the steeds of our father you hear
'Tis the fleet horse of Carazan thy brother"—   35
—Thus cried her children in sorrow and fear.—

Then the sad mourner turned back to her brother
Clinging around him with bitterest moan
—"Late of these five little darlings the mother
Now see me, Carazan, the mother of none."   40

Silent and sad stood her brother Carazan
Then drew from his bosom the severing bill
Speaking divorce to the lady of Asan
Leaving her free to espouse whom she will.

Then the sad dame to her girls gave her blessing   45
Kiss'd the red cheek of each fair featured boy
But from the suckling to her breast closely pressing
Woe's me! She could not unloosen the tie.

Torn was the tie by her harsh-tempered brother
He rais'd her behind him upon his fleet horse   50
And to the lofty abode of their mother
He bent with the sorrowful lady his course.

Scarce had a fortnight that widow past over
Only a fortnight, a fortnight and day
When to that lady came many a lover   55
All in her mourning as weeping she lay.

The greatest of all was Imoski's proud Cadi
Long had he loved her more dearly than life
Then to her brother spoke weeping that lady
—"Give me no more to another to wife.   60

—"Give me no more as a wife to another,"
Thus to her brother in sorrow she spoke
"Least when my poor orphans shall call on their mother
By anguish and longing my heart should be broke."—

Her brother cared not for the prayer of the lady   65
Firmly resolved to bestow her as spouse
To bestow her as spouse on Imoski's great Cadi
That the high marriage gifts might enrich his proud house.

"Yet bid the Cadi, my brother Carazan,
Bring a black veil this sad head to enfold,   70
Least when I pass by the dwelling of Asan
These widowed eyes should their orphans behold."

Scarce was the message received by the Cadi
Soon he assembled the gay bridal train
And bringing the veil as desired by the lady   75
Safely the towers of Carazan they gain.

Safely they gained the high towers of Carazan
But with the bride as returned the gay train
Lo! as they passed the proud dwelling of Asan
The children beheld their lost mother again.   80

Loudly they shouted "O art thou returned?
Comest thou our meals and our pastimes to share?
O for thy absence how long have we mourned
Pass on no further—thy children are here."—

At the fond voices a sudden pause made she　　　　85
"Rein in your steeds these loved turrets below"
Thus to the gallants in agony said she
"Till my last gifts on my babes I bestow."—

Beneath the proud turrets the bridal train rested
While her last gifts on her babes she bestowed　　　　90
While she the boys with rich girdles invested
And with gay sabres with jewels that glowed.

Decked she her daughters in silks richly rustling
And for those days when his strength might them wield
To the dear suckling in her bosom close nestling　　　　95
Gave she a girdle a sabre and shield.

All this from beside saw the stern Asan Aga
And loud to his children he haughtily cried
"Away from that woman more false than the Vaga
More light than its breeze and more cold than its
　　　　　　　　tide."—　　　　100

Away fled the children for fear loudly crying
All but the suckling she clasped to her breast
Down sunk the lady pale, shivering, and dying
Grasped it yet closer and sunk unto rest.

24

The Mermaid

From the German of Goethe

The western breezes fanned the brook
　　As pensive by its side
The Youthful Angler marked the hook
　　Float dancing down the tide.

And as he watched with heedful eye   5
　　The eddying ebbs and flows
From yon deep whirlpool swelling high
　　The wily Mermaid rose.

And blushing as her bosom fair
　　Came glistening to the sun;   10
She wrapped around her silken hair
　　With liquid pearls bedone.—

And sweet she spoke and sweet she sung,
　　"Oh wherefore should thy wile
To part their last in sultry sun   15
　　My guiltless tribes beguile?

"Oh couldst thou know how sweet the joy
　　Beneath the waves they share;
To grasp such bliss thou soon wouldst fly
　　And dive to meet it there.—   20

"Bathe not the moon and glorious sun
　　In waves of western light
And glittering from the fresh'ning main
　　Arise more lovely bright?

"Look down, behold yon azure sky   25
　　Array'd in brighter blue;
Look down, thine own fair cheek descry
　　Returned in rosier hue."

His throbbing bosom felt her lay
　　The witless youngling, he   30
Marked not the water's rising sway
　　Nor felt it bathe his knee.

Still sweet she sung, still sweet she spoke
　　Till he, mid billows green
A plunge half drawn half willing took   35
　　And never more was seen.

25

Trained by Adversity's Stern Hand

Trained by Adversity's stern hand
The Youth that courts renown in fight
Still foremost of the hardy band
In spite of toil, in climate's spite
All dreadful with the bloody spear   5
Urge, thundering on his broken rear
The quivered Parthian's headlong flight.

On him from Susa's hostile towers
The maid shall bend her timorous eye
While many a votive prayer she pours   10
And frequent heaves the anxious sigh
Least all unused to bloody strife
Her lover, prodigal of life,
Should yon grim lion's rage defy.

What nobler meed awaits the brave   15
Than to meet death's griesly form
While his country's cause to save
Firm he stems the battle's storm
Since not the recreant's rapid feet
Tho' as the hunted Roebuck's fleet   20
Shall save his caitiff corpse amid the dire alarm?

For virtue on herself relies
Nor heeds the voice of giddy fame
Whether the croud with rapturous cries
Applaud to heaven her favourite name   25
Or whether fired with idle rage
Against her war they madly wage
She scorns their giddy mood unaltered and the same.

And when her votaries guiltless die
In her blest cause at her command   30
She bids heaven's portals open fly
Close barred against the common band
On Honour's pinion upward born
The sordid earth they scornful spurn
And seek their native home amid the sky.   35

Nor yet shall private faith unstained
Neglected miss its due reward—
Nor shall the wretch, his word profaned
Unnoticed scape Jove's dire regard
Devoted Miscreant, ne'er shall he   40
Unmoor the feeble skiff with me
Least both o'erwhelmed should sink beneath the
                                        stern award.

For oft while all serene the skies
And calm the bosom of the deep
Altho' fresh crimes on crimes arise   45
The tempted thunders seem to sleep
Vengeance tho' slow yet deadly sure
Silent and stern awaits the fated hour
Then pours upon the wretch her whirlwind's
                                        deadly sweep—

26

𝔅𝔶 𝔞 𝔗𝔥𝔬𝔲𝔰𝔞𝔫𝔡 𝔍𝔬𝔫𝔡 𝔇𝔯𝔢𝔞𝔪𝔰

By a thousand fond dreams my weak Bosom betrayed
Believed thee for Love and for Constancy made
Believed that Indifference never could be
Where gentle Compassion had pleaded for me.

The phantom swift flies, the Delusion is plain   5
Delusion too lovely alas! and too vain
Too late now revealed with Anguish I see
No comfort from Love, no pity from thee.

Ah! fool to exult, as wild fancy has done—
While she dreamed such a conquest by thee could be
                                won—   10
Ah! fool to imagine such graces could be
By Nature formed only for Love and for thee!

For grandeur, for wealth, your poor friend you resign
If Bliss they can give, *O may it be thine*
Farewell to the raptures of lowly degree   15
You might have enjoyed with Love and with me.

Unfriended by fortune, untutored by Art
I gave You my all—when I gave You my heart
But many a gallant of higher degree
Has none, W——, for Love or for thee.   20

Too proud to solicit, too weak to contend
That heart can but break, for it never shall bend,
Nor bear the cold glance of *Acquaintance* to see
In the eye which once softened with *friendship* for me.

Ah! ne'er will that heart the last agony bear   25
When Envy must add to the pangs of Despair
When, forgot each fond tie that once bound thee to me
Thy charms the dear price of vain splendour may be—

O! then ere the turf o'er these limbs has grown green
Will my favourite forget that I ever have been?   30
No gentle Remembrance will whisper in thee
"He fell a sad victim to Love and to me"—

2 7

The Triumph of Constancy

From the German of G. A. Bürger

The brave Earl Marshal was gallant in fight
   The brave Earl Marshal was gentle in bower
On one lovely maid he had placed his delight
And hid her from Envy's and Jealousy's sight
   Retired in a wild woodland tower.   5

And all for her love Earl Marshal would ride
   By night thro' the tempest and rain
To spend but one hour by the lovely maid's side
And back thro' the forest at morning he hied
   To return to our King's court again.   10

And thro' the deep wood as he spurred on his steed
   While the dank mist disfigured the glade
"Haste, haste thee, my courser, O double thy speed
Let the sight of my Love be my Constancy's meed
   Ere the morning dispel the kind shade."   15

He spied the loved tower by the slow-dawning light
   Her window was gilt by its ray
"Now stay thee, thou sunbeam, ah gleam not so bright
Nor dart thro' yon window thy glare on her sight
   To chase my love's slumbers away."—   20

He came to the shadowy park of the tower
   His courser he bound to a tree
He glided so swift thro' the postern door
And thro' the dim twilight he reached his Love's bower
   Where fondly he dreamed her to be.   25

But empty the mansion of rapture and joy
   And cold was the couch where she lay.
O wild with surprise gleamed the Marshal's dark eye
And loudly the castle it rung with his cry
   "Some traitor has borne her away."—   30

Then fiercely Earl Marshal has traversed the tower
   From the battlements e'en to the ground
And raging he stormed thro' hall and thro' bower
Till deeply from under the lowermost floor
   Arose a sad answering sound.   35

It was the old Seneschal prison'd below
   To the Marshal so trusty and true
"O who, my old vassal, has wrought thee this woe?
Give me quick the audacious caitiff to know
   Who has dared such a treason to do."—   40

"Proud Falkenstein's Baron with main and with might
   Hath wrought thee dishonour and woe:
He hath broken thy bower in the dead of the night
And away hath he borne the damsel so bright
   And thy hounds that so fleetly can go."—   45

Thro' nerve and thro' vein he was thrilled by his tongue
   His faulchion like light'ning he drew
To his curses the turrets re-echoed and rung
In a whirlwind of rage to his courser he sprung
   And fast thro' the forest he flew.   50

The traces of hoofs on the dew-spangled mead
   Marked the course of the Baron and dame.
"Stretch forward, my courser, O double thy speed
Stretch forward this once in my uttermost need
   And save me from sorrow and shame.—   55

"Halloo! my brave courser, stretch forward, my steed,
    Let us but the fair maiden regain,
Hold out but this once in my uttermost need
And thy life thou in plenty and pleasure shalt lead
    Nor again feel the spur or the rein."—   60

The courser stretched forward and sped him enough
    The valleys and cliffs rung around
They redoubled the cries of the warrior so rough
The thundering clang of the galloping hoofs
    And the nostrils' shrill echoing sound.   65

And see, where the earth with the blue of the sky
    Appears to unite on yon brow
The glitter of armour far gleams from on high
And two dogs spring to meet him with welcoming cry
    And coursing around him they go.   70

"Abide thou, false felon, thou robber abide
    The knight thou hast injured, to face,
My faulchion so trusty shall dig from thy side
The treacherous heart that would reave me my bride
    And my greyhounds so fleet in the chase."—   75

The Baron was bold and the Baron was proud
    Strength sate on his arm of steel
He heard the wild gallop, the threatening so loud
He leaped from his steed and he faced to the wood
    The banquet so bloody to deal.   80

From the scabbard swift flew Baron Falkenstein's brand
    The Marshal sprung clanging from horse
Each hewed upon other with desperate hand
And stamping they spurned the flint and the sand
    So near were they matched in their force.   85

They struggled and tore like wild bears of the wood
    The faulchions like thunder bolts fell
The helmets and hauberks were streaming with blood
And neither the Marshal nor Falkenstein cou'd
    His stubborn antagonist quell.   90

The strength of each warrior began to decay
   So long in the battle they bode
When thus spoke the Baron "Lord Marshal, I pray
That you hearken a moment to what I shall say
   As we rest from the labour of blood."—   95

Earl Marshal he lowered his blade as he stood
   The words of the Baron to hear—
"Lord Marshal we spend here our labour and blood
Methinks it were better that 'twixt us we shou'd
   Make agreement so free and so fair.—   100

"We hew and we push, and we gain only blows
   And long may we strive in the gray
'Twere wise by heaven that the Lady should chuse
And when with her favourite lover she goes
   Let the other resign her for aye."—   105

The Marshal he listened with sparkling eye
   Secure of the faith of his love
"Since earliest friendship first fastened the tye
For her I have lived and for her I could die
   Ah surely she never can rove."   110

"Ah!" tenderly thought he "too deeply with me
   The goblet of Love has she tasted."—
Alas! simple knight, thou couldst not foresee
Tho' the flower of Affection at morn sprung for thee
   Ere noon might its fragrance be wasted.   115

The maid on her palfrey approached from afar
   And thus to the warriors said she
"Sir Knights, since 'tis mine to determine the jar
Sheath, sheath your keen blades and desist from the war
   I go forward Lord Baron with thee."—   120

No blush of contrition her features besprente
   As lightly she reined round her steed
No glance of compassion Earl Marshal she sent
Who blasted and breathless remained on the bent
   Like a corpse by blue light'ning struck dead.   125

Astounded the Marshal lay stretched on the grass
   When lo, came the two trusty hounds
They know their old master, they fawn and caress
And kindly they lick his cold hands and his face
   And cleanse the clogged gore from his wounds.   130

Their tenderness called the sad warrior to day
   It pressed in the heart's master key
His sullen despair melts in torrents away
And he pressed to his bosom as weeping he lay
   The friends that so faithful could be.   135

And strengthened at heart by sweet Gratitude's balm
   Earl Marshal arose from the ground
His steed he bestrode with demeanour so calm
And slowly he paced back the way that he came
   While frolicking followed each hound.   140

Again rung the wood with a shout all so hoarse
   And galloping fleet as the wind
Baron Falkenstein came on his foam-covered horse
And hollo'd, his voice almost choaked in the course
   "Our fight is not yet at an end.   145

"The Lady so freely who gave me her hand
   Resigned not to thee her two hounds
Descend from the saddle and out with the brand
And try we how fortune betwixt us shall stand
   As again we prove battle and wounds."   150

But calm on his steed sat the Marshal so bold
   The words of the Baron to hear
Then quickly he answered so careless and cold
"Methinks it were better that 'twixt us we should
   Make agreement so free and so fair.—   155

"We hew and we push and we gain nought but blows
   And long may we strive in the fray
'Twere wiser by heaven that each greyhound should chuse
And when with his favourite master he goes
   Let the other resign him for aye."—   160

The Baron of Falkenstein made the accord
   And soon on the dogs can he cry
He strove by each gesture and accent and word
To lure them away from their long beloved Lord
   And each bribe and each soothing can try.   165

But vain was each soothing and proffer he tried
   And vain was his whistle and call
The dogs they remained by their old master's side
Or turned but to snarl at the Baron who cried
   Their Constancy triumphed o'er all.   170

28

Which of Us Shall Join the Forces?

Which of us shall join the forces
When the Chiefs their levies gather?—
Best of Horsemen, best of Horses
Highest head and gayest feather.

When the Chiefs their levies gather   5
Which of us shall leave our mother?—
Fairest offspring of our father
Of our brothers youngest brother.

With the rash man forward ride not
Lag not with the coward, my brother,   10
For the rash the sword abide not
And dishonour stains the other.

Bide, my brother, by the Banner
Straggle not from the arraying
So shall safety so shall honour   15
Bless thy charging, grace thy staying.

Then our choicest steed preparing
Saddle him by dawn of morning
Him with thin maned crest uprearing
Fleet at speed and sharp at turning.   20

   (YOUNG HUSSAR SPEAKS)

Ah my courser fiercely bounding
Where—O where wilt thou remove me
From my cot and friends surrounding
All who know and all who love me?

Does a moment's stay thus pain ye   25
Does a moment's lingering tire ye
Wherefore snortst thou, wherefore strain ye
Wherefore glance thine eyes so fiery?

Heavier far will be your cumber
When our march is long and weary   30
Irksome nights devoid of slumber
Mountains wild and marshes dreary.

Then will War with Want beside her
Urge thee on to ceaseless labour
And the spur of thy keen rider   35
Dreadful with his naked sabre.

29
With Flowers from a Roman Wall

Take these flowers which, purple waving,
   On the ruined rampart grew,
Where, the sons of freedom braving,
   Rome's imperial standards flew.

Warriors from the breach of danger   5
   Pluck no longer laurels there:
They but yield the passing stranger
   Wild-flower wreaths for Beauty's hair.

30
The Erl-King
From the German of Goethe

It is necessary the Reader should be informed, that in the legends of German superstition, certain mischievous Spirits are supposed to preside over the different Elements, and to amuse themselves with inflicting calamities on Man. One of these is termed the WATER-KING, another the FIRE-KING, and a third the CLOUD-KING. The Hero of the present piece is the ERL or OAK-KING—a Fiend who is supposed to dwell in the recesses of the forest, and thence to issue forth upon the benighted traveller to lure him to his destruction.

O! who rides by night thro' the woodlands so wild?
It is the fond Father embracing his Child;
And close the Boy nestles within his lov'd arm,
From the blast of the tempest to keep himself warm.

"O Father! see yonder, see yonder!" he says.   5
"My Boy, upon what dost thou fearfully gaze?"
"O! 'tis the ERL-KING, with his staff and his shroud!"
"No, my Love! it is but a dark wreath of the cloud."

(THE PHANTOM SPEAKS)

"O! wilt thou go with me, thou loveliest Child!
By many gay sports shall thy hours be beguil'd;   10
My Mother keeps for thee full many a fair toy,
And many a fine flow'r shall she pluck for my Boy."

"O Father! my Father! and did you not hear,
The ERL-KING whisper so close in my ear?"
"Be still my lov'd Darling, my Child be at ease!   15
It was but the wild blast as it howl'd thro' the trees."

(THE PHANTOM)

"O wilt thou go with me, thou loveliest Boy!
My Daughter shall tend thee with care and with joy;
She shall bear thee so lightly thro' wet and thro' wild,
And hug thee, and kiss thee, and sing to my Child."   20

"O Father! my Father! and saw you not plain
The ERL-KING's pale daughter glide past thro' the rain?"
"O no, my heart's treasure! I knew it full soon,
It was the Grey Willow that danc'd to the Moon."

(THE PHANTOM)

"Come with me, come with me, no longer delay!   25
Or else, silly Child, I will drag thee away."
"O Father! O Father! now, now, keep your hold!
The ERL-KING has seiz'd me—his grasp is so cold."

Sore trembled the Father; he spurr'd thro' the wild,
Clasping close to his bosom his shuddering Child;   30
He reaches his dwelling in doubt and in dread;
But, clasp'd to his bosom, the Infant was dead!

31
Frederick and Alice

This Ballad is translated (but with such alterations and additions, that it may almost be called original) from the fragment of a Romance, sung in Goethe's Opera of "Claudina von Villa Bella."

Frederick leaves the land of France,
    Homewards hastes his steps to measure;
Careless casts the parting glance
    On the scene of former pleasure;

Joying in his prancing steed,   5
    Keen to prove his untried blade,
Hope's gay dreams the soldier lead
    Over mountain, moor, and glade.

Helpless, ruin'd, left forlorn,
    Lovely Alice wept alone;   10
Mourn'd o'er love's fond contract torn,
    Hope, and peace, and honour flown.

Mark her breast's convulsive throbs!
    See, the tear of anguish flows!
Mingling soon with bursting sobs,   15
    Loud the laugh of frenzy rose.

Wild she cursed, and wild she pray'd;
    Seven long days and nights are o'er;
Death in pity brought his aid,
    As the village bell struck four.   20

Far from her, and far from France,
    Faithless Frederick onward rides,
Marking blythe the morning's glance
    Mantling o'er the mountain's sides.

Heard ye not the boding sound,   25
    As the tongue of yonder tower,
Slowly, to the hills around,
    Told the fourth, the fated hour?

Starts the steed, and snuffs the air,
    Yet no cause of dread appears;   30
Bristles high the rider's hair,
    Struck with strange mysterious fears.

Desperate, as his terrors rise,
    In the steed the spur he hides;
From himself in vain he flies;   35
    Anxious, restless, on he rides.

Seven long days, and seven long nights,
    Wild he wander'd, woe the while!
Ceaseless care, and causeless fright,
    Urge his footsteps many a mile.   40

Dark the seventh sad night descends;
    Rivers swell, and rain-streams pour;
While the deafening thunder lends
    All the terrors of its roar.

Weary, wet, and spent with toil,   45
    Where his head shall Frederick hide?
Where, but in yon ruin'd aisle,
    By the lightning's flash descried.

To the portal dank and low,
    Fast his steed the wanderer bound;   50
Down a ruin'd staircase, slow
    Next his darkling way he wound.

Long drear vaults before him lie!
    Glimmering lights are seen to glide!
—"Blessed Mary hear my cry!   55
    Deign a sinner's steps to guide!"—

Often lost their quivering beam,
    Still the lights move slow before,
Till they rest their ghastly gleam,
    Right against an iron door.   60

Thundering voices from within,
    Mix'd with peals of laughter, rose;
As they fell, a solemn strain
    Lent its wild and wondrous close!

Midst the din, he seem'd to hear   65
    Voice of friends, by death removed;—
—Well he knew that solemn air,
    'Twas the lay that Alice loved.—

Hark! for now a solemn knell
    FOUR times on the still night broke;   70
FOUR times, at its deaden'd swell,
    Echoes from the ruins spoke.

As the lengthen'd clangours die,
    Slowly opes the iron door!
Straight a banquet met his eye,   75
    But a funeral's form it wore!

Coffins for the seats extend;
    All with black the board was spread,
Girt by parent, brother, friend,
    Long since number'd with the dead!   80

Alice, in her grave clothes bound,
    Ghastly smiling, points a seat;
All arose with thundering sound;
    All the expected stranger greet.

High their meagre arms they wave,   85
    Wild their notes of welcome swell;
—"Welcome, traitor, to the grave!
    Perjured, bid the light farewell!"—

32

The Rouze of The Royal Edinburgh Light Dragoons

To Horse! To Horse! the Standard flies!
   The Bugles sound the call,
The Gallic Navy stems the Seas,
The Voice of Battle's on the breeze,
   Arouze ye one and all.   5

From high Edina's Towers we come,
   A band of Brothers true,
Our Casques with loyal Tartan bound
With Scotland's hardy Thistle crown'd,
   We boast the red and blue.*   10

Tho tamely crouch to Gallia's frown,
   Dull Holland's tardy train,
Their ravish'd toys tho Romans mourn,
Tho gallant Switzers vainly spurn,
   And foaming gnaw the chain: 15

(O had they mark'd the avenging call
   Their Brethren's murder gave,†
Disunion ne'er their ranks had mown
Nor Patriot valour desperate grown,
   Sought freedom in the grave.)   20

Shall we too bend the stubborn head,
   In freedom's temple born,
Dress our pale cheek in timid smile
To hail a Master in our Isle,
   Or brook a Victor's scorn?   25

---

* The Royal Colours.
† Massacre of the Swiss Guards, 10 August 1792.

No!—Tho Destruction o'er the land
   Come pouring as a flood,
The Sun that sees our falling day,
Shall mark our Sabres' deadly sway,
   And set that night in blood.   30

For gold let Gallia's legions fight,
   Or plunder's bloody gain,
Unbribed, Unbought our Swords we draw,
To guard our King, to fence our Law,
   Nor shall their edge be vain.   35

If ever breath of British gale,
   Shall fan the Tricolor,
Or footstep of Invader rude,
With rapine foul, and red with blood,
   Pollute our happy shore: 40

Then farewell home, and farewell friends,
   Adieu each tender tie,
Resolved we mingle in the tide
Where charging squadrons furious ride,
   To conquer or to die.   45

To Horse! To Horse! the Sabres gleam;
   High sounds our Bugle call,
Combined by honour's sacred tie,
Our word is, Laws and Liberty;
   March forward one and all.   50

33
Glenfinlas, or Lord Ronald's Coronach[*]

"For them the viewless forms of air obey,
Their bidding heed, and at their beck repair:
    They know what spirit brews the stormful day,
And heartless oft, like moody madness, stare
To see the phantom train their secret work prepare."

Glenfinlas is a tract of forest ground lying in the Highlands of
Perthshire, not far from Callender, in Menteith. To the west of the
forest of Glenfinlas lies Loch Katrine, and its romantic avenue, called
the Troshachs. Benledi, Benmore, and Benvoirlich, are mountains in
the same district, and at no great distance from Glenfinlas. The river
Teith passes Callender and the castle of Doune, and joins the Forth
near Stirling. The Pass of Lenny is immediately above Callender, and
is the principal access to the Highlands, from that town. Glenartney is
a forest near Benvoirlich. The whole forms a sublime tract of Alpine
scenery.

O hone a rie! O hone a rie![†]
    The pride of Albin's line is o'er,
And fallen Glenartney's stateliest tree,—
    We ne'er shall see Lord Ronald more!

O, sprung from great Macgilliannore,   5
    The chief that never fear'd a foe,
How matchless was thy broad claymore,
    How deadly thine unerring bow.

Well can the *Saxon*[‡] widows tell
    How, on the Teith's resounding shore,   10
The boldest Lowland warriors fell,
    As down from Lenny's pass you bore.

---

[*] *Coronach* is the lamentation for a deceased warrior, sung by the aged of the clan.
[†] *O hone a rie* signifies—"Alas for the prince or chief."
[‡] The term Sassenach, or Saxon, is applied by the Highlanders to their
Low-country neighbours.

But o'er his hills, on festal day,
   How blazed Lord Ronald's *beltane** tree;
While youths and maids the light strathspey   15
   So nimbly danced with Highland glee.

Cheer'd by the strength of Ronald's shell,
   E'en age forgot his tresses hoar;—
But now the loud lament we swell,
   O ne'er to see Lord Ronald more!   20

From distant isles a chieftain came,
   The joys of Ronald's halls to find,
And chase with him the dark-brown game
   That bounds o'er Albin's hills of wind.

'Twas Moy; whom in Columba's isle   25
   The Seer's prophetic spirit† found,
As with a minstrel's fire the while
   He waked his harp's harmonious sound.

Full many a spell to him was known,
   Which wandering spirits shrink to hear,   30
And many a lay of potent tone
   Was never meant for mortal ear.

For there, 'tis said, in mystic mood
   High converse with the dead they hold,
And oft espy the fated shroud   35
   That shall the future corpse infold.

---

* *Beltane-tree*; the fires lighted by the Highlanders on the first of May, in compliance with a custom derived from the Pagan times, are so called. It is a festival celebrated with various superstitious rites, both in the north of Scotland and in Wales.
† *Seer's spirit*. I can only describe the second sight, by adopting Dr. Johnson's definition, who calls it "An impression either by the mind upon the eye, or by the eye upon the mind, by which things distant and future are perceived and seen as if they were present." To which I would only add, that the spectral appearances thus presented usually presage misfortune; that the faculty is painful to those who suppose they possess it; and that they usually acquire it while themselves under the pressure of melancholy.

O so it fell, that on a day,
    To rouse the red deer from their den,
The chiefs have ta'en their distant way,
    And scour'd the deep Glenfinlas glen.   40

No vassals wait their sports to aid,
    To watch their safety, deck their board,
Their simple dress, the Highland plaid;
    Their trusty guard, the Highland sword.

Three summer days, through brake and dell,   45
    Their whistling shafts successful flew,
And still, when dewy evening fell,
    The quarry to their hut they drew.

In grey Glenfinlas' deepest nook
    The solitary cabin stood,   50
Fast by Moneira's sullen brook,
    Which murmurs through that lonely wood.

Soft fell the night, the sky was calm,
    When three successive days had flown,
And summer mist, in dewy balm,   55
    Steep'd heathy bank and mossy stone.

The moon, half hid in silvery flakes,
    Afar her dubious radiance shed,
Quivering on Katrine's distant lakes,
    And resting on Benledi's head.   60

Now in their hut, in social guise,
    Their sylvan fare the chiefs enjoy,
And pleasure laughs in Ronald's eyes,
    As many a pledge he quaffs to Moy.

—"What lack we here to crown our bliss,   65
    While thus the pulse of joy beats high,
What but fair woman's yielding kiss,
    Her panting breath, and melting eye?

"To chase the deer of yonder shades,
    This morning left their father's pile   70
The fairest of our mountain maids,
    The daughters of the proud Glengyle.

"Long have I sought sweet Mary's heart,
    And dropp'd the tear, and heaved the sigh;
But vain the lover's wily art,   75
    Beneath a sister's watchful eye.

"But thou may'st teach that guardian fair
    While far with Mary I am flown,
Of other hearts to cease her care,
    And find it hard to guard her own.   80

"Touch but thy harp, thou soon shalt see
    The lovely Flora of Glengyle,
Unmindful of her charge, and me,
    Hang on thy notes 'twixt tear and smile.

"Or if she choose a melting tale,   85
    All underneath the greenwood bough,
Will good St. Oran's[*] rule prevail,
    Stern huntsman of the rigid brow?"—

—"Since Enrick's fight, since Morna's death,
    No more on me shall rapture rise,   90
Responsive to the panting breath,
    Or yielding kiss, or melting eyes.

"E'en then when o'er the heath of woe,
    Where sunk my hopes of love and fame,
I bade my harp's wild wailings flow,   95
    On me the Seer's sad spirit came.

"The last dread curse of angry heaven,
    With ghastly sights, and sounds of woe,
To dash each glimpse of joy was given,
    The gift, the future ill to know.   100

[*] St. Oran was a friend and follower of St. Columba, and was buried in Icolmkill.

"The bark thou saw'st yon summer morn
    So gaily part from Oban's bay,
My eye beheld her dash'd and torn
    Far on the rocky Colonsay.

"Thy Fergus too—thy sister's son,   105
    Thou saw'st with pride the gallant's power,
As, marching 'gainst the lord of Downe,
    He left the skirts of huge Benmore.

"Thou only saw'st his banners wave,
    As down Benvoirlich's side they wound,   110
Heard'st but the pibroch* answering brave
    To many a target clanking round.

"I heard the groans, I mark'd the tears,
    I saw the wound his bosom bore,
When on the serried Saxon spears   115
    He pour'd his clan's resistless roar.

"And thou who bidst me think of bliss,
    And bidst my heart awake to glee,
And court, like thee, the wanton kiss,
    That heart, O Ronald, bleeds for thee!   120

"I see the death damps chill thy brow,
    I hear the warning spirit cry;
The corpse-lights dance—they're gone, and now ....!
    No more is given to gifted eye!"—

—"Alone enjoy thy dreary dreams,   125
    Sad prophet of the evil hour;
Say, should we scorn joy's transient beams,
    Because to-morrow's storm may lour?

"Or sooth, or false thy words of woe,
    Clangillian's chieftain ne'er shall fear;   130
His blood shall bound at rapture's glow,
    Though doom'd to stain the Saxon spear.

* A piece of martial music adapted to the Highland bagpipes.

"E'en now, to meet me in yon dell,
    My Mary's buskins brush the dew;"—
He spoke, nor bade the chief farewell,   135
    But call'd his dogs, and gay withdrew.

Within an hour return'd each hound,
    In rush'd the rouzers of the deer;
They howl'd in melancholy sound,
    Then closely couch'd beside the Seer.   140

No Ronald yet—though midnight came,
    And sad were Moy's prophetic dreams,
As bending o'er the dying flame
    He fed the watch-fire's quivering gleams.

Sudden the hounds erect their ears,   145
    And sudden cease their moaning howl;
Close press'd to Moy, they mark their fears
    By shivering limbs, and stifled growl.

Untouch'd the harp began to ring,
    As softly, slowly, oped the door,   150
And shook responsive every string,
    As light a footstep press'd the floor.

And by the watch-fire's glimmering light,
    Close by the Minstrel's side was seen
An huntress maid, in beauty bright,   155
    All dropping wet her robes of green.

All dropping wet her garments seem,
    Chill'd was her cheek, her bosom bare,
As bending o'er the dying gleam,
    She wrung the moisture from her hair.   160

With maiden blush she softly said,
    —"O gentle huntsman, hast thou seen,
In deep Glenfinlas' moon-light glade,
    A lovely maid in vest of green:

"With her a chief in Highland pride,   165
  His shoulders bear the hunter's bow;
The mountain dirk adorns his side,
  Far on the wind his tartans flow?"—

—"And who art thou; and who are they?"
  All ghastly gazing, Moy replied;   170
"And why, beneath the moon's pale ray,
  Dare ye thus roam Glenfinlas' side?"—

—"Where wild Loch Katrine pours her tide
  Blue, dark, and deep, round many an isle,
Our father's towers o'erhang her side,   175
  The castle of the bold Glengyle.

"To chase the dun Glenfinlas deer,
  Our woodland course this morn we bore,
And haply met, while wandering here,
  The son of great Macgilliannore.   180

"O aid me then to seek the pair,
  Whom loitering in the woods I lost;
Alone I dare not venture there,
  Where walks, they say, the shrieking ghost."—

—"Yes, many a shrieking ghost walks there;   185
  Then first, my own sad vow to keep,
Here will I pour my midnight prayer,
  Which still must rise when mortals sleep."—

—"O first, for pity's gentle sake,
  Guide a lone wanderer on her way,   190
For I must cross the haunted brake,
  And reach my father's towers ere day."—

—"First three times tell each Ave-bead,
  And thrice a Pater-noster say,
Then kiss with me the holy reed,   195
  So shall we safely wind our way."—

—"O shame to knighthood strange and foul!
    Go doff the bonnet from thy brow,
And shroud thee in the monkish cowl,
    Which best befits thy sullen vow.   200

"Not so, by high Dunlathmon's fire,
    Thy heart was froze to faith and joy,
When gaily rung thy raptured lyre,
    To wanton Morna's melting eye."—

Wild stared the Minstrel's eyes of flame,   205
    And high his sable locks arose,
And quick his colour went and came,
    As fear and rage alternate rose.

—"And thou! when by the blazing oak
    I lay, to her and love resign'd,   210
Say, rode ye on the eddying smoke,
    Or sail'd ye on the midnight wind?

"Not thine a race of mortal blood,
    Nor old Glengyle's pretended line;
Thy dame, the Lady of the Flood,   215
    Thy sire, the Monarch of the Mine."—

He mutter'd thrice St. Oran's rhyme,
    And thrice St. Fillan's* powerful prayer,
Then turn'd him to the Eastern clime,
    And sternly shook his coal-black hair: 220

And bending o'er his harp, he flung
    His wildest witch-notes on the wind,
And loud, and high, and strange, they rung,
    As many a magic change they find.

---

* I know nothing of St. Fillan, but that he has given his name to many chapels, holy fountains, &c. in Scotland.

Tall wax'd the Spirit's altering form,   225
    Till to the roof her stature grew,
Then mingling with the rising storm,
    With one wild yell away she flew.

Rain beats, hail rattles, whirlwinds tear,
    The slender hut in fragments flew,   230
But not a lock of Moy's loose hair
    Was waved by wind, or wet by dew.

Wild mingling with the howling gale,
    Loud bursts of ghastly laughter rise,
High o'er the Minstrel's head they sail,   235
    And die amid the northern skies.

The voice of thunder shook the wood,
    As ceased the more than mortal yell,
And spattering foul a shower of blood,
    Upon the hissing firebrands fell.   240

Next dropp'd from high a mangled arm,
    The fingers strain'd an half-drawn blade:
And last, the life-blood streaming warm,
    Torn from the trunk, a gasping head.

Oft o'er that head, in battling field,   245
    Stream'd the proud crest of high Benmore;
That arm the broad claymore could wield,
    Which dyed the Teith with Saxon gore.

Woe to Moneira's sullen rills!
    Woe to Glenfinlas' dreary glen!   250
There never son of Albin's hills
    Shall draw the hunter's shaft agen!

E'en the tired pilgrim's burning feet
    At noon shall shun that sheltering den,
Lest, journeying in their rage, he meet   255
    The wayward Ladies of the Glen.

And we—behind the chieftain's shield
    No more shall we in safety dwell;
None leads the people to the field—
    And we the loud lament must swell.   260

O hone a rie! O hone a rie!
    The pride of Albin's line is o'er;
And fallen Glenartney's stateliest tree,
    We ne'er shall see Lord Ronald more!*

34

𝕿𝖍𝖊 𝕰𝖛𝖊 𝖔𝖋 𝕾𝖆𝖎𝖓𝖙 𝕵𝖔𝖍𝖓

Smaylho'me, or Smallholm Tower, the scene of the following Ballad,
is situated on the northern boundary of Roxburghshire, among a clus-
ter of wild rocks, called Sandiknow-Crags, the property of Hugh Scott,
Esq. of Harden. The tower is a high square building, surrounded by an
outer wall, now ruinous. The circuit of the outer court being defended,
on three sides, by a precipice and morass, is only accessible from the
west, by a steep and rocky path. The apartments, as usual, in a Border
Keep, or fortress, are placed one above another, and communicate by a
narrow stair; on the roof are two bartizans, or platforms, for defence or
pleasure. The inner door of the tower is wood, the outer an iron grate;
the distance between them being nine feet, the thickness, namely, of
the wall. From the elevated situation of Smaylho'me Tower, it is seen

---

* The simple tradition upon which the preceding stanzas are founded, runs as
follows. While two Highland hunters were passing the night in a solitary bathy
(a hut built for the purpose of hunting), and making merry over their venison
and whisky, one of them expressed a wish that they had pretty lasses to complete
their party. The words were scarcely uttered, when two beautiful young women,
habited in green, entered the hut, dancing and singing. One of the hunters was
seduced by the syren who attached herself particularly to him, to leave the hut:
the other remained, and, suspicious of the fair seducers, continued to play upon
a trump, or Jew's harp, some strain consecrated to the Virgin Mary. Day at
length came, and the temptress vanished. Searching in the forest, he found the
bones of his unfortunate friend, who had been torn to pieces and devoured by
the Fiend into whose toils he had fallen. The place was, from thence, called the
Glen of the Green Women.

many miles in every direction. Among the crags by which it is sur-
rounded, one more eminent is called the *Watchfold*, and is said to have
been the station of a beacon in the times of war with England. Without
the tower-court is a ruined Chapel.

The Baron of Smaylho'me rose with day,
    He spurr'd his courser on,
Without stop or stay, down the rocky way
    That leads to Brotherstone.

He went not with the bold Buccleuch,   5
    His banner broad to rear;
He went not 'gainst the English yew
    To lift the Scottish spear.

Yet his plate-jack* was braced, and his helmet was laced,
    And his vaunt-brace of proof he wore;   10
At his saddle-gerthe was a good steel sperthe,
    Full ten pound weight and more.

The Baron return'd in three days' space,
    And his looks were sad and sour,
And weary was his courser's pace   15
    As he reached his rocky tower.

He came not from where Ancram Moor†
    Ran red with English blood,
Where the Douglas true, and the bold Buccleuch,
    'Gainst keen Lord Ivers stood;   20

Yet was his helmet hack'd and hew'd,
    His acton pierced and tore,
His axe and his dagger with blood embrued,
    But it was not English gore.

*The plate-jack is coat armour; the vaunt-brace (avant-bras), armour for the
shoulders and arms; the sperthe, a battle-axe.
† A. D. 1555, was fought the battle of Ancram Moor, in which Archibald
Douglas Earl of Angus, and Sir Walter Scott of Buccleuch, routed a superior
English army, under Lord Ralph Ivers, and Sir Brian Latoun.

He lighted at the Chapellage,   25
   He held him close and still,
And he whistled twice for his little foot page,
   His name was *English Will.*

—"Come thou hither, my little foot page,
   Come hither to my knee,   30
Though thou art young, and tender of age,
   I think thou art true to me.

"Come, tell me all that thou hast seen,
   And look thou tell me true;
Since I from Smaylho'me Tower have been,   35
   What did thy Lady do?"—

—"My Lady each night, sought the lonely light,
   That burns on the wild *Watchfold;*
For from height to height, the beacons bright,
   Of the English foemen told.   40

"The bittern clamour'd from the moss,
   The wind blew loud and shrill,
Yet the craggy pathway she did cross
   To the eiry* beacon hill.

"I watch'd her steps, and silent came   45
   Where she sate her on a stone;
No watchman stood by the dreary flame,
   It burned all alone.

"The second night I kept her in sight,
   Till to the fire she came;   50
And by Mary's might, an armed knight
   Stood by the lonely flame.

---

* *Eiry* is a Scotch expression, signifying the feeling inspired by the dread of apparitions.

"And many a word that warlike lord
   Did speak to my Lady there,
But the rain fell fast, and loud blew the blast,   55
   And I heard not what they were.

"The third night there the sky was fair,
   And the mountain blast was still,
As again I watch'd the secret pair,
   On the lonesome beacon hill;   60

"And I heard her name the midnight hour,
   And name this holy eve;
And say, 'Come that night to thy Lady's bower;
   Ask no bold Baron's leave.

"'He lifts his spear with the bold Buccleuch,   65
   His Lady is alone;
The door she'll undo, to her knight so true,
   On the eve of good St. John.'—

—"'I cannot come, I must not come,
   I dare not come to thee;   70
On the eve of St. John I must wander alone,
   In thy bower I may not be.'—

—"'Now out on thee, faint-hearted knight!
   Thou should'st not say me nay,
For the eve is sweet, and when lovers meet,   75
   Is worth the whole summer's day.

"'And I'll chain the blood-hound, and the warder
                   shall not sound,
   And rushes shall be strew'd on the stair,
So by the rood-stone,* and by holy St. John,
   I conjure thee, my love, to be there.'—   80

---

* The Black-rood of Melrose was a crucifix of black marble, and of superior sanctity.

—"'Though the blood-hound be mute, and the rush
            beneath my foot,
  And the warder his bugle should not blow,
Yet there sleepeth a priest in the chamber to the east,
  And my footstep he would know.'—

—"'O fear not the priest who sleepeth to the east,   85
  For to Dryburgh[*] the way he has ta'en;
And there to say mass, till three days do pass,
  For the soul of a knight that is slayne.'—

"He turn'd him around, and grimly he frown'd,
  Then he laugh'd right scornfully—   90
—'He who says the mass rite, for the soul of that knight,
  May as well say mass for me.

"'At the lone midnight hour, when bad Spirits have power,
  In thy chamber will I be.'—
With that he was gone, and my Lady left alone,   95
  And no more did I see."—

Then changed I trow, was that bold Baron's brow,
  From dark to blood-red high.
—"Now tell me the mien of the knight thou hast seen,
  For by Mary he shall die!"—   100

—"His arms shone full bright, in the beacon's red light,
  His plume it was scarlet and blue;
On his shield was a hound in a silver leash bound,
  And his crest was a branch of the yew."—

—"Thou liest, thou liest, thou little foot page,   105
  Loud dost thou lie to me;
For that knight is cold, and low laid in the mould,
  All under the Eildon[†] tree."—

[*] Dryburgh Abbey is beautifully situated on the banks of the Tweed. After its dissolution it became the property of the Haliburtons of Newmains, and is now the seat of the Right Honourable the Earl of Buchan.
[†] *Eildon* is a high hill, terminating in three conical summits, immediately above the town of Melrose, where are the admired ruins of a magnificent monastery. *Eildon* tree was said to be the spot where Thomas the Rhymer uttered his prophecies.

—"Yet hear but my word, my noble lord,
   For I heard her name his name;   110
And that Lady bright she called the knight
   Sir Richard of Coldinghame."—

The bold Baron's brow then changed, I trow,
   From high blood-red to pale.
"The grave is deep and dark, and the corpse is stiff
                   and stark;   115
   So I may not trust thy tale.

"Where fair Tweed flows round holy Melrose,
   And Eildon slopes to the plain,
Full three nights ago, by some secret foe,
   That gallant knight was slain.   120

"The varying light deceiv'd thy sight,
   And the wild winds drown'd the name,
For the Dryburgh bells ring, and the white monks
                   they sing,
   For Sir Richard of Coldinghame."—

He pass'd the court-gate, and he oped the tower grate,   125
   And he mounted the narrow stair,
To the bartizan-seat, where, with maids that on her wait,
   He found his Lady fair.

That Lady sat in mournful mood,
   Look'd over hill and vale,   130
Over Tweed's fair flood, and Mertoun's wood,
   And all down Tiviotdale.

—"Now hail! now hail! thou Lady bright!"—
   —"Now hail! thou Baron true!
What news what news, from Ancram fight?   135
   What news from the bold Buccleuch?"—

—"The Ancram Moor is red with gore,
   For many a Southern fell;
And Buccleuch has charged us evermore,
   To watch our beacons well."—   140

The Lady blush'd red, but nothing she said,
   Nor added the Baron a word;
Then she stepp'd down the stair to her chamber fair,
   And so did her moody Lord.

In sleep the Lady mourn'd, and the Baron toss'd and
                turn'd,   145
   And oft to himself he said,
—"The worms around him creep, and his bloody
                grave is deep,
   It cannot give up the dead."—

It was near the ringing of matin bell,
   The night was well nigh done,   150
When a heavy sleep on that Baron fell,
   On the eve of good St. John.

The Lady look'd through the chamber fair,
   By the light of a dying flame,
And she was aware of a knight stood there,   155
   Sir Richard of Coldinghame.

—"Alas! away! away!"—she cried,
   "For the holy Virgin's sake."—
—"Lady, I know who sleeps by thy side;
   But, Lady, he will not awake.   160

"By Eildon-tree, for long nights three,
   In bloody grave have I lain;
The mass and the death-prayer are said for me,
   But, Lady, they're said in vain.

"By the Baron's brand, near Tweed's fair strand,   165
   Most foully slain I fell,
And my restless sprite on the beacon height
   For a space is doom'd to dwell.

"At our trysting-place,* for a certain space,
   I must wander to and fro; 170
But I had not had power to come to thy bower
   Had'st thou not conjured me so."—

Love master'd fear—her brow she cross'd;
   —"How, Richard, hast thou sped?
And art thou saved, or art thou lost?"— 175
   The vision shook his head!

—"Who spilleth life, shall forfeit life;
   So bid thy Lord believe:
And lawless love is guilt above;
   This awful sign receive."— 180

He laid his left hand on an oaken stand,
   His right hand on her arm:
The Lady shrunk, and fainting sunk,
   For the touch was fiery warm.

The sable score of fingers four 185
   Remain on that board impress'd,
And for evermore that Lady wore
   A covering on her wrist.

There is a nun in Melrose bower
   Ne'er looks upon the sun; 190
There is a monk in Dryburgh tower,
   He speaketh word to none.

That nun who ne'er beholds the day,
   That monk who speaks to none,
That nun was Smaylho'me's Lady gay, 195
   That monk the bold Baron.

* *Trysting*-place, Scottish for place of *rendezvous*.

35

𝕿𝖍𝖊 𝕲𝖗𝖆𝖞 𝕭𝖗𝖔𝖙𝖍𝖊𝖗

A Fragment

The imperfect state of this ballad, which was written several years ago, is not a circumstance affected for the purpose of giving it that peculiar interest, which is often found to arise from ungratified curiosity. On the contrary, it was the editor's intention to have completed the tale, if he had found himself able to succeed to his own satisfaction. Yielding to the opinion of persons, whose judgment, if not biassed by the partiality of friendship, is entitled to deference, the editor has preferred inserting these verses, as a fragment, to his intention of entirely suppressing them.

The tradition, upon which the tale is founded, regards a house, upon the barony of Gilmerton, near Lasswade, in Mid Lothian. This building, now called Gilmerton Grange, was originally named Burndale, from the following tragic adventure. The barony of Gilmerton belonged, of yore, to a gentleman, named Heron, who had one beautiful daughter. This young lady was seduced by the Abbot of Newbattle, a richly endowed abbey, upon the banks of the South Esk, now a seat of the Marquis of Lothian. Heron came to the knowledge of this circumstance, and learned, also, that the lovers carried on their guilty intercourse by the connivance of the lady's nurse, who lived at this house, of Gilmerton Grange, or Burndale. He formed a resolution of bloody vengeance, undeterred by the supposed sanctity of the clerical character, or by the stronger claims of natural affection. Chusing, therefore, a dark and windy night, when the objects of his vengeance were engaged in a stolen interview, he set fire to a stack of dried thorns, and other combustibles, which he had caused to be piled against the house, and reduced to a pile of glowing ashes the dwelling, with all its inmates.[*]

The scene, with which the ballad opens, was suggested by the following curious passage, extracted from the Life of Alexander Peden, one of the wandering and persecuted teachers of the sect of Cameronians, during the reign of Charles II. and his successor, James. This person was supposed by his followers, and, perhaps, really believed himself, to be possessed of supernatural gifts; for the wild scenes, which they frequented, and the constant dangers, which were incurred through

---

[*] This tradition was communicated to me by John Clerk, Esq. of Eldin, author of an *Essay upon Naval Tactics*, who will be remembered by posterity, as having taught the Genius of Britain to concentrate her thunders, and to launch them against her foes with an unerring aim.

their proscription, deepened upon their minds the gloom of superstition, so general in that age.

"About the same time he (Peden) came to Andrew Normand's house, in the parish of Alloway, in the shire of Ayr, being to preach at night in his barn. After he came in, he halted a little, leaning upon a chair-back, with his face covered; when he lifted up his head, he said, 'There are in this house that I have not one word of salvation unto;' he halted a little again, saying, 'This is strange, that the devil will not go out, that we may begin our work!' Then there was a woman went out, ill-looked upon almost all her life, and to her dying hour, for a witch, with many presumptions of the same. It escaped me, in the former passages, that John Muirhead (whom I have often mentioned) told me, that when he came from Ireland to Galloway, he was at family worship, and giving some notes upon the scripture, when a very ill-looking man came, and sate down within the door, at the back of the *hallan* (partition of the cottage): immediately he halted, and said, 'There is some unhappy body just now come into this house. I charge him to go out, and not stop my mouth!' The person went out, and he *insisted* (went on), yet he saw him neither come in nor go out."—*The Life and Prophecies of Mr Alexander Peden, late Minister of the Gospel at New Glenluce, in Galloway*, part 2. § 26.

THE GRAY BROTHER

The Pope he was saying the high, high mass,
    All on Saint Peter's day,
With the power to him given, by the saints in heaven,
    To wash men's sins away.

The Pope he was saying the blessed mass,   5
    And the people kneel'd around,
And from each man's soul his sins did pass,
    As he kiss'd the holy ground.

And all, among the crowded throng,
    Was still, both limb and tongue,   10
While thro' vaulted roof, and aisles aloof,
    The holy accents rung.

At the holiest word, he quiver'd for fear,
    And faulter'd in the sound—
And, when he would the chalice rear,   15
    He dropp'd it on the ground.

"The breath of one, of evil deed,
    Pollutes our sacred day;
He has no portion in our creed,
    No part in what I say.   20

"A being, whom no blessed word
    To ghostly peace can bring;
A wretch, at whose approach abhorr'd,
    Recoils each holy thing.

"Up! up! unhappy! haste, arise!   25
    My adjuration fear!
I charge thee not to stop my voice,
    Nor longer tarry here!"

Amid them all a pilgrim kneel'd,
    In gown of sackcloth gray;   30
Far journeying from his native field,
    He first saw Rome that day.

For forty days and nights, so drear,
    I ween, he had not spoke,
And, save with bread and water clear,   35
    His fast he ne'er had broke.

Amid the penitential flock,
    Seem'd none more bent to pray;
But, when the Holy Father spoke,
    He rose, and went his way.   40

Again unto his native land,
    His weary course he drew,
To Lothian's fair and fertile strand,
    And Pentland's mountains blue.

His unblest feet his native seat,   45
    Mid Eske's fair woods, regain;
Thro' woods more fair no stream more sweet
    Rolls to the eastern main.

And lords to meet the pilgrim came,
    And vassals bent the knee;   50
For all mid Scotland's chiefs of fame,
    Was none more famed than he.

And boldly for his country, still,
    In battle he had stood,
Aye, even when, on the banks of Till,   55
    Her noblest pour'd their blood.

Sweet are the paths, O passing sweet!
    By Eske's fair streams that run,
O'er airy steep, thro' copsewood deep,
    Impervious to the sun.   60

There the rapt poet's step may rove,
    And yield the muse the day;
There Beauty, led by timid Love,
    May shun the tell-tale ray.

From that fair dome, where suit is paid,   65
    By blast of bugle free,
To Auchendinny's hazel glade,
    And haunted Woodhouselee.

Who knows not Melville's beechy grove,
    And Roslin's rocky glen,   70
Dalkeith, which all the virtues love,
    And classic Hawthornden?

Yet never a path, from day to day,
    The pilgrim's footsteps range,
Save but the solitary way   75
    To Burndale's ruin'd Grange.

A woeful place was that, I ween,
  As sorrow could desire;
For, nodding to the fall was each crumbling wall,
  And the roof was scathed with fire.   80

It fell upon a summer's eve,
  While, on Carnethy's head,
The last faint gleams of the sun's low beams
  Had streak'd the gray with red;

And the convent bell did vespers tell,   85
  Newbattle's oaks among,
And mingled with the solemn knell
  Our Ladye's evening song:

The heavy knell, the choir's faint swell,
  Came slowly down the wind,   90
And on the pilgrim's ear they fell,
  As his wonted path he did find.

Deep sunk in thought, I ween, he was,
  Nor ever rais'd his eye,
Until he came to that dreary place,   95
  Which did all in ruins lie.

He gazed on the walls, so scathed with fire,
  With many a bitter groan—
And there was aware of a grey friar,
  Resting him on a stone.   100

"Now, Christ thee save!" said the Gray Brother;
  "Some pilgrim thou seemest to be."
But in sore amaze did Lord Albert gaze,
  Nor answer again made he.

"O come ye from east, or come ye from west,   105
  Or bring reliques from over the sea,
Or come ye from the shrine of St James the divine,
  Or St John of Beverly?"

"I come not from the shrine of St James the divine,
   Nor bring reliques from over the sea;   110
I bring but a curse from our father, the Pope,
   Which for ever will cling to me."

"Now, woeful pilgrim, say not so!
   But kneel thee down by me,
And shrive thee so clean of thy deadly sin,   115
   That absolved thou mayst be."

"And who art thou, thou Gray Brother,
   That I should shrive to thee,
When he, to whom are giv'n the keys of earth and
               heav'n,
   Has no power to pardon me?"   120

"O I am sent from a distant clime,
   Five thousand miles away,
And all to absolve a foul, foul crime,
   Done *here* 'twixt night and day."

The pilgrim kneel'd him on the sand,   125
   And thus began his saye—
When on his neck an ice-cold hand
   Did that Gray Brother laye.

      *   *   *   *   *   *

NOTES ON THE GRAY BROTHER

Note 1

From that fair dome, where suit is paid,
By blast of bugle free.—lines 65-66.

The barony of Pennycuik, the property of Sir George Clerk, Bart. is held by a singular tenure; the proprietor being bound to sit upon a large rocky fragment, called the Buckstane, and wind three blasts of a horn, when the king shall come to hunt on the Borough Muir, near Edinburgh. Hence, the family have adopted, as their crest, a demi-forester proper, winding a horn, with the motto, *Free for a Blast.* The beautiful mansion-house of Pennycuik is much admired, both on account of the architecture and surrounding scenery.

Note 2

To Auchendinny's hazel glade.—line 67.

Auchendinny, situated upon the Eske, below Pennycuik, the present residence of the ingenious H. Mackenzie, Esq., author of the *Man of Feeling*, &c.

Note 3

And haunted Woodhouselee.—line 68.

For the traditions connected with this ruinous mansion, see the Ballad of *Cadyow Castle*, p. 121.

Note 4

Who knows not Melville's beechy grove.—line 69.

Melville Castle, the seat of the Honourable Robert Dundas, member for the county of Mid-Lothian, is delightfully situated upon the Eske, near Lasswade. It gives the title of viscount to his father, Lord Melville.

Note 5

And Roslin's rocky glen.—line 70.

The ruins of Roslin Castle, the baronial residence of the ancient family of St Clair, the Gothic chapel, which is still in beautiful preservation, with the romantic and woody dell, in which they are situated, belong to Sir James St Clair Erskine, Bart., the representative of the former lords of Roslin.

Note 6

Dalkeith, which all the virtues love.—line 71.

The village and castle of Dalkeith belonged, of old, to the famous Earl of Morton, but is now the residence of the noble family of Buccleuch. The park extends along the Esk, which is there joined by its sister stream, of the same name.

Note 7

And classic Hawthornden.—line 72.

Hawthornden, the residence of the poet Drummond. A house, of more modern date, is inclosed, as it were, by the ruins of the ancient castle, and overhangs a tremendous precipice, upon the banks of the Eske, perforated by winding caves, which, in former times, formed a refuge to the oppressed patriots of Scotland. Here Drummond received Ben Jonson, who journeyed from London, on foot, in order to visit him. The beauty of this striking scene has been much injured, of late years, by the indiscriminate use of the axe. The traveller now looks in vain for the leafy bower,

"Where Jonson sate in Drummond's social shade."

Upon the whole, tracing the Eske from its source, till it joins the sea, at Musselburgh, no stream in Scotland can boast such a varied succession of the most interesting objects, as well as of the most romantic and beautiful scenery.

36

At Flodden

Go sit old Cheviot's crest below,
And pensive mark the lingering snow
   In all his scaurs abide,
And slow dissolving from the hill
In many a sightless soundless rill,   5
   Feed sparkling Bowmont's tide.

Fair shines the stream by bank and lea,
As wimpling to the eastern sea
   She seeks Till's sullen bed,
Indenting deep the fatal plain,   10
Where Scotland's noblest, brave in vain,
   Around their monarch bled.

And westward hills on hills you see,
Even as old Ocean's mightiest sea
   Heaves high her waves of foam,   15
Dark and snow-ridged from Cutsfeld's wold
To the proud foot of Cheviot roll'd,
   Earth's mountain billows come.

37

The Fire-King

"The blessings of the evil genii, which are curses, were upon him."
Eastern Tale.

Bold knights and fair dames, to my harp give an ear,
Of love, and of war, and of wonder to hear,
And you haply may sigh in the midst of your glee
At the tale of Count Albert and fair Rosalie.

O see you that castle, so strong and so high?   5
And see you that lady, the tear in her eye?
And see you that palmer, from Palestine's land,
The shell on his hat, and the staff in his hand?

—"Now palmer, grey palmer, O tell unto me
What news bring you home from the Holy Countrie;   10
And how goes the warfare by Gallilee's strand,
And how fare our nobles, the flower of the land?"—

—"O well goes the warfare by Gallilee's wave,
For Gilead, and Nablous, and Ramah we have,
And well fare our nobles by Mount Libanon,
For the Heathen have lost, and the Christians have won."—

A rich chain of gold mid her ringlets there hung;
That chain o'er the palmer's grey locks has she flung;
"—Oh! palmer, grey palmer, this chain be thy fee,
For the news thou hast brought from the East Countrie.   20

"And palmer, good palmer, by Gallilee's wave,
O saw ye Count Albert, the gentle and brave?
When the Crescent went back, and the Red-cross rush'd on,
O saw ye him foremost on Mount Libanon?"—

—"O lady, fair lady, the tree green it grows,   25
O lady, fair lady, the stream pure it flows,
Your castle stands strong, and your hopes soar on high,
But lady, fair lady, all blossoms to die.

"The green boughs they wither, the thunderbolt falls,
It leaves of your castle but levin-scorch'd walls,   30
The pure stream runs muddy, the gay hope is gone,
Count Albert is prisoner on Mount Libanon."—

O she's ta'en a horse should be fleet at her speed,
And she's ta'en a sword should be sharp at her need,
And she has ta'en shipping for Palestine's land,   35
To ransom Count Albert from Soldanrie's hand.

Small thought had Count Albert on fair Rosalie,
Small thought on his faith, or his knighthood had he;
A heathenish damsel his light heart had won,
The Soldan's fair daughter of Mount Libanon.   40

—"Oh! Christian, brave Christian, my love would'st
                    thou be?
Three things must thou do ere I hearken to thee—
Our laws and our worship on thee shalt thou take,
And this thou shalt first do for Zulema's sake.

"And next in the cavern, where burns evermore   45
The mystical flame which the Curdmans adore,
Alone and in silence three nights shalt thou wake,
And this thou shalt next do for Zulema's sake.

"And last, thou shalt aid us with council and hand,
To drive the Frank robbers from Palestine's land;   50
For my lord and my love then Count Albert I'll take,
When all this is accomplish'd for Zulema's sake."—

He has thrown by his helmet and cross-handled sword,
Renouncing his knighthood, denying his Lord;
He has ta'en the green caftan, and turban put on,   55
For the love of the maiden of fair Libanon.

And in the dread cavern, deep deep under ground,
Which fifty steel gates and steel portals surround,
He has watch'd until day-break, but sight saw he none,
Save the flame burning bright on its altar of stone.   60

Amazed was the princess, the Soldan amazed,
Sore murmur'd the priests as on Albert they gazed;
They search'd all his garments, and under his weeds,
They found, and took from him, his rosary beads.

Again in the cavern, deep deep under ground,   65
He watch'd the lone night, while the winds whistled
                          round;
Far off was their murmur, it came not more nigh,
The flame burn'd unmoved, and nought else did he spy.

Loud murmur'd the priests, and amazed was the king,
While many dark spells of their witchcraft they sing;   70
They search'd Albert's body, and lo! on his breast
Was the sign of the Cross, by his father impress'd.

The priests they eraze it with care and with pain,
And the recreant return'd to the cavern again;
But as he descended a whisper there fell!—   75
—It was his good angel, who bade him farewell!—

High bristled his hair, his heart flutter'd and beat,
And he turn'd him five steps, half resolved to retreat;
But his heart it was harden'd, his purpose was gone,
When he thought of the maiden of fair Libanon.   80

Scarce pass'd he the archway, the threshold scarce trod,
When the winds from the four points of heaven were
                          abroad;
They made each steel portal to rattle and ring,
And, borne on the blast, came the dread Fire-King.

Full sore rock'd the cavern whene'er he drew nigh,   85
The fire on the altar blazed bickering and high;
In volcanic explosions the mountains proclaim
The dreadful approach of the Monarch of Flame.

Unmeasured in height, undistinguish'd in form,
His breath it was lightning, his voice it was storm,   90
I ween the stout heart of Count Albert was tame,
When he saw in his terrors the Monarch of Flame.

In his hand a broad faulchion blue-glimmer'd through
                smoke,
And Mount Libanon shook as the monarch he spoke;—
—"With this brand shalt thou conquer, thus long, and
                no more,   95
Till thou bend to the Cross, and the Virgin adore."—

The cloud-shrouded arm gives the weapon—and see!
The recreant receives the charm'd gift on his knee.
The thunders growl distant, and faint gleam the fires
As, born on his whirlwind, the phantom retires.   100

Count Albert has arm'd him the Paynim among,
Though his heart it was false, yet his arm it was strong;
And the Red-cross wax'd faint, and the Crescent came on,
From the day he commanded on Mount Libanon.

From Libanon's forests to Gallilee's wave,   105
The sands of Samaar drank the blood of the brave,
Till the Knights of the Temple, and Knights of Saint John,
With Salem's King Baldwin, against him came on.

The war-cymbals clatter'd, the trumpets replied,
The lances were couch'd, and they closed on each side; 110
And horsemen and horses Count Albert o'erthrew,
Till he pierced the thick tumult King Baldwin unto.

Against the charm'd blade which Count Albert did wield,
The fence had been vain of the King's Red-cross shield;
But a page thrust him forward the monarch before,   115
And cleft the proud turban the renegade wore.

So fell was the dint, that Count Albert stoop'd low
Before the cross'd shield, to his steel saddle-bow;
And scarce had he bent to the Red-cross his head—
—"*Bonne grace, notre Dame*,"—he unwittingly said.   120

Sore sigh'd the charm'd sword, for its virtue was o'er,
It sprung from his grasp, and was never seen more;
But true men have said, that the lightning's red wing
Did waft back the brand to the dread Fire-King.

He clench'd his set teeth, and his gauntletted hand,   125
He stretch'd with one buffet that page on the strand;
As back from the stripling the broken casque roll'd,
You might see the blue eyes, and the ringlets of gold!

Short time had Count Albert in horror to stare
On those death-swimming eye-balls and blood-clotted
                              hair,   130
For down came the Templars, like Cedron in flood,
And dyed their long lances in Saracen blood.

The Saracens, Curdmans, and Ishmaelites yield
To the scallop, the saltier, and crosletted shield,
And the eagles were gorged with the infidel dead   135
From Bethsaida's fountains to Naphthali's head.

The battle is over on Bethsaida's plain—
Oh! who is yon Paynim lies stretch'd mid the slain?
And who is yon page lying cold at his knee?
Oh! who but Count Albert and fair Rosalie.   140

The lady was buried in Salem's bless'd bound,
The Count he was left to the vulture and hound;
Her soul to high mercy our Lady did bring,
His went on the blast to the dread Fire-King.

Yet many a minstrel in harping can tell   145
How the Red-cross it conquer'd, the Crescent it fell;
And lords and gay ladies have sigh'd, mid their glee,
At the Tale of Count Albert and fair Rosalie.

38

Bothwell's Sisters Three

When fruitful Clydesdale's apple bowers
    Are mellowing in the noon
When sighs round Pembroke's ruined towers
    The sultry breath of June

When Clyde despite his sheltering wood   5
    Must leave his channel dry
And vainly o'er the limpid flood
    The angler guides his fly

If chance by Bothwell's lovely braes
    A wanderer thou hast been   10
Or hid thee from the summer's blaze
    In Blantyre's bowers of green

Full where the copse woods open wild
    Thy pilgrim step hath staid
Where Bothwell's towers in ruin piled   15
    O'erlook the verdant glade

And many a tale of love and fear
    Hath mingled with the scene
Of Bothwell's banks that bloomed so dear
    And Bothwell's bonny Jean.   20

O if with rugged minstrel lays
    Unsated be thy ear
And thou of deeds of other days
    Another tale wilt hear

Then all beneath the spreading beech   25
    Flung careless on the lea
The Gothic muse the tale shall teach
    Of Bothwell's sisters three.

———————————

Wight Wallace stood on Dechmount head
  He blew his bugle round   30
Till the wild bull in Cadzow wood
  Has started at the sound.

St. George's cross o'er Bothwell hung
  Was waving far and wide
And from the lofty turrets flung   35
  Its crimson blaze on Clyde

And startling at the bugle blast
  That marked the advancing foe
Old England's yeomen mustered fast
  And bent the Norman bow.   40

Tall in the midst Sir Aymer rose
  Proud Pembroke's Earl was he
While

39

Verses to Lady Charlotte Campbell

Of old 'tis said, in Ilium's battling days
  Ere Friendship knew a price or Faith was sold
The Chief high-minded, famed in Homer's lays,
  For meanest brass exchanged his arms of gold.
                              (Iliad Book 6th)

Say, lovely Lady, know you not of one   5
  Who with the Lycian hero's generous fire
Gave lays might rival Græcia's sweetest tone
  For the rude numbers of a Northern lyre?—

Yet—tho' unequal all to match my debt—
    Yet take these lines to thy protecting hand,   10
Nor heedless hear a Gothick bard repeat
    The wizard harpings of thy native land.

For each (forgive the vaunt) a wreath may grow,
    At distance due as my rude verse from thine,
The Classic *Laurel* crowns thy lovely brow   15
    The Druid's "magic Mistletoe" be mine—

                    Castle Street, 1 November 1799

40

The Minstrel's Pipe

When Freedom's war-horn bade our land
    Her voluntary lances raise,
The Minstrel joined the patriot band,
    To view the deeds he loved to praise.

But ill exchanged his studious fire   5
    For winter chills and warlike labour;
And ill exchanged his ancient lyre
    For crested casque and glimmering sabre.

To banish from his threatened march
    The toils and terrors of the hour,   10
Thou gavest (considerably arch)
    A charmed pipe of magic power.

Not the frail pipe of simple oat
    That loves the shepherd's lore to tell,
Nor the war-pipe, whose marshal note   15
    Bids warmth in Highland bosoms swell;

But that within whose bosom burn
    The odours of the eastern clime,
Of power to bid past scenes return,
    And speed the wings of lingering time. 20

Content and quiet hope are nigh,
    When its bland vapours curl in air,
And reasonings deep and musings high;
    And many a kindly thought is there.

And dreams of many a happy day 25
    Shall charm the Minstrel's soul the while,
When the blithe hours dance light away
    At *Friendship's* laugh and *Beauty's* smile.

———————————

Enough—ay and more—for I feel at such time
Things not to be uttered in prose or in rhyme, 30
Yet to light your meer-*schaum* may these verses aspire,
Being pregnant with genuine poetical fire.
This conceited assertion, though bold, yet most true is,
If you will not believe me, pray ask Mr. Lewis.
On the tail of each line as his poetical eyes squint, 35
He will tell you at once if a false rhyme he spies in't.

In one point they defy his exertions so clever,
A false *rhyme* he may spy, a false *sentiment* never.
Halt, La—or you'll say, with a good-humoured damn,
That you *smoke* in my verses Damascus all sham; 40
Or tell your fair dame, while you show her such stuff,
You have lost a good *pipe*, and have got but a *puff*.
Then I'll stop in good time, lest my credit I blot,
While I live, I remain hers and yours—Walter Scott.

P. S. I cannot attend you this evening—that's flat,   45
For a thousand strong reasons which will not shew pat.
If instead you'll accept us to-morrow at dinner,
(I can't find a rhyme to't, unless it be sinner,)
At expense of your beef and your ale I will show it,
To bluff trooper's hunger and thirst of the poet,   50
And then in the evening together we'll scramble,
To storm the fair mansion of friend Mrs. ——.

41

𝔄 𝔖𝔬𝔫𝔤 𝔬𝔣 𝔙𝔦𝔠𝔱𝔬𝔯𝔶

Joy to the victors! the sons of old Aspen!
    Joy to the race of the battle and scar!
Glory's proud garland triumphantly grasping;
    Generous in peace, and victorious in war.
        Honour acquiring,   5
        Valour inspiring,
    Bursting, resistless, through foemen they go:
        War-axes wielding,
        Broken ranks yielding,
    Till from the battle proud Roderic retiring,   10
Yields in wild rout the fair palm to his foe.

Joy to each warrior, true follower of Aspen!
    Joy to the heroes that gain'd the bold day!
Health to our wounded, in agony gasping;
    Peace to our brethren that fell in the fray!   15
        Boldly this morning,
        Roderic's power scorning,
    Well for their chieftain their blades did they wield:
        Joy blest them dying,
        As Maltingen flying,   20
    Low laid his banners, our conquest adorning,
Their death-clouded eyeballs descried on the field!

Now to our home, the proud mansion of Aspen,
  Bend we, gay victors, triumphant away:
There each fond damsel, her gallant youth clasping,   25
  Shall wipe from his forehead the stains of the fray.
    Listening the prancing
    Of horses advancing;
  E'en now on the turrets our maidens appear.
    Love our hearts warming,   30
    Songs the night charming,
  Round goes the grape in the goblet gay dancing;
Love, wine, and song, our blithe evening shall cheer!

42

Rhein-Wein Lied

What makes the troopers' frozen courage muster?
  The grapes of juice divine.
Upon the Rhine, upon the Rhine they cluster:
  Oh, blessed be the Rhine!

Let fringe and furs, and many a rabbit skin, sirs,   5
  Bedeck your Saracen;
He'll freeze without what warms our hearts within, sirs,
  When the night-frost crusts the fen;

But on the Rhine, but on the Rhine they cluster,
  The grapes of juice divine,   10
That make our troopers' frozen courage muster:
  Oh, blessed be the Rhine!

43

The Shepherd's Tale

And ne'er but once, my son, he says
Was yon sad cavern trod
In persecution's iron days
When the land was left by God.

From Bewlie Bog with slaughter red   5
A wanderer hither drew
And often stopped and turned his head
As by fits the night wind blew.

For trampling round by Cheviot edge
Were heard the troopers keen   10
And frequent from the Whitelaw sedge
The death shot flashed between.

The moonbeams thro' the misty shower
On yon dark cavern that fell
Thro' the cloudy night the snow glimmered white   15
Which sunbeam ne'er could quell.

"Yon cavern dark is rough and rude
And cold its jaws of snow
But more rough and rude are the men of blood
That hunt my life below.   20

"Yon spell-formed den as the aged tell
Was hewn by Dæmon's hand
But I had lourd mell with the fiends of hell
Than with Clavers and his band."—

He heard the deep mouthed bloodhound bark   25
He heard the horses neigh
He plunged him in the cavern dark
And downward sped his way.

Now faintly down the winding path
Came the cry of the faulting hound   30
And the muttered oath of baulked wrath
Was lost in hollow sound.

He threw him on the flinted floor
And held his breath for fear
He rose and bitterly cursed his foes   35
As the sounds died on his ear—

"O bare thine arm, thou battling Lord
For Scotland's wandering band
Dash from fell Clavers' hand the sword
And sweep him from the land.   40

"Forget not thou thy people groans
From dark Dunottar's tower
Mixed with the sea fowls' shrilly moans
And ocean's bursting roar.

"O in the Oppressor's hour of pride   45
Een in his mightiest day
As bold he strides thro' conquest's tide
Extend him on the clay—

"His widow and his little ones
O may their tower of trust   50
Remove its strong foundation stones
And crush them to the dust"—

"Sweet prayers to me" a voice replied
"Thrice welcome guest of mine."
And glimmering on the cavern side   55
A light was seen to shine.

An aged man in amice brown
Stood by the wanderer's side
By powerful charm a dead man's arm
The torch's light supplied.   60

From each stiff finger stretched upright
Arose a ghastly flame
That waved not in the blast of night
Which thro' the cavern came.

O deadly blue was that taper's hue   65
That flamed the cavern o'er
But more deadly blue was the ghastly hue
Of his eyes who the taper bore.

He laid on his head a hand like lead
As heavy pale and cold   70
"Vengeance be thine, thou guest of mine
If thy heart be firm and bold.

"But if faint thy heart and caitiff fear
Thy recreant sinews know
The mountain erne thy heart shall tear   75
Thy nerves the hooded crow."

The Wanderer raised him undismayed
"My Soul by danger steeled
Is stubborn as my border blade
Which never knew to yield.   80

"And if thy power can speed the hour
Of vengeance on my foes
Theirs be the fate from bridge and gate
To feed the hooded crows"—

The Brownie looked him in the face   85
And his colour fled with speed
"I fear me" quoth he "uneath it will be
To match thy word and deed.

"In ancient days when English bands
Sore ravaged Scotland fair   90
The sword and shield of Border lands
Was valiant Halbert Kerr.

"A warlock loved the warrior well
Sir Michael Scott by name
And he sought for his sake a spell to make   95
Should the Southron foeman tame.

"'Look thou' he said 'from Cessford head
As the July sun sinks low
And when glimmering white on Cheviot's height
Thou shalt spy a wreath of snow.   100
The spell is compleat which shall bring to thy feet
The haughty Saxon foe.'

"For many a year wrought the wizard here
In Cheviot's bosom low
Till the spell was compleat and in July's heat   105
Appeared December's snow
But Cessford's Halbert never came
The wondrous cause to know.

"For years before in Bowden aisle
The warrior's bones had lain   110
And after short while by female guile
Sir Michael Scott was slain.

"But me and my brethren in this cell
His mighty charms retain
And he that can quell the powerful spell   115
Shall o'er broad Scotland reign."

He led him thro' an iron door
And up a winding stair
And in wild amaze did the wanderer gaze
At the sight which opened there.   120

Thro' the gloomy night flashed ruddy bright
A thousand torches' glow
The vault rose high like the vaulted sky
O'er stalls in double row.

In every stall of that endless hall   125
Stood a steed in barbing bright
At the foot of each steed all armed save the head
Lay stretched a stalwart knight.

In each mailed hand was a naked brand:
As they lay on the black bull's hide   130
Each visage stern did upwards turn
With eyeballs fixed and wide.

A lance gey strong full twelve ells long
By every warrior hung
At each pommel there for battle yare   135
A ponderous axe was slung.

The casque hung near each cavalier
The plumes waved mournfully
At every tread which the wanderer made
Thro' the hall of gramarye.   140

The ruddy beam of the torches' gleam
That glanced the warriors on
Reflected light from armour bright
In noontide splendour shone.

And onward seen in lustre sheen   145
Still lengthening on the sight
Thro' the boundless hall stood steeds in stall
And by each lay a sable knight.

Still as the dead lay each horseman dread
And moved not limb nor tongue   150
Each steed stood stiff as an earthfast cliff
Nor hoof nor bridle rung.

No sounds thro' all the spacious hall
The deadly still divide
Save when echoes aloof from the vaulted roof   155
To the wanderer's steps replied.

At length his wondering eyes
On an iron column borne
Of antique shape and giant size
Descried a sword and horn.   160

"Now chuse thou here," quoth his leader pale
"Thy venturous fortune try
Thy woe and weal, thy boot and bale
In yon brand and bugle lie."

To the fatal brand he minted his hand   165
But his soul did quiver and quail
The life blood did start to his shuddering heart
And left him wan and pale.

The brand he forsook and the horn he took
To 'say a gentle sound   170
But so wild a blast from the bugle brast
That the Cheviot rocked around.

From Forth to Tees, from sea to seas
The awful bugle rung
On Carlisle's wall and Berwick withal   175
To arms the warders sprung.

With clank and clang the cavern rang
The steeds did stamp and neigh
And loud was the yell as each warrior fell
Sterte up with hoop and cry.   180

"Woe, woe" they cried "thou caitiff coward
That ever thou wert born.
Why drew ye not the mighty sword
Before ye blew the horn?"—

The morning on the mountain shone   185
And on the bloody ground
Hurled from the cave with shivered bone
The mangled wretch was found.

And still beneath the cavern dread
Among the glidders gray   190
A shapeless stone with lichen spread
Marks where the wanderer lay—

44
Thomas the Rhymer

Few personages are so renowned in tradition as Thomas of Erceldoune, known by the appellation of *The Rhymer*. Uniting, or supposed to unite, in his person, the powers of poetical composition, and of vaticination, his memory, even after the lapse of five hundred years, is regarded with veneration by his countrymen. To give any thing like a certain history of this remarkable man, would be indeed difficult; but the curious may derive some satisfaction from the particulars brought together in the "Minstrelsy of the Scottish Border," and here abridged.

It is agreed, on all hands, that the residence, and probably the birth-place, of this ancient bard, was Erceldoune, a village situated upon the Leader, two miles above its junction with the Tweed. The ruins of an ancient tower are still pointed out as the Rhymer's castle. The uniform tradition bears, that his sirname was Lermont, or Learmont; and that the appellation of *The Rhymer* was conferred on him in consequence of his poetical compositions.

The Rhymer flourished in the reign of Alexander the Third of Scotland, whose death he is said to have predicted; and during the halcyon period of tranquillity which Scotland then enjoyed, he composed the Romance of "Sir Tristrem," a metrical tale, which obtained its author the highest celebrity. It was lately republished from an ancient manuscript by the author of these poems. In short, both as a prophet and poet, the memory of Thomas of Erceldoune was long held in veneration, and still lives in Border tradition.

Whatever doubts the learned might have, as to the source of the Rhymer's prophetic skill, the vulgar had no hesitation to ascribe the whole to the intercourse between the bard and the queen of Faëry. The popular tale bears, that Thomas was carried off, at an early age, to the Fairy Land, where he acquired all the knowledge, which made him afterwards so famous. After seven years residence, he was permitted to return to the earth, to enlighten and astonish his countrymen by his prophetic powers; still, however, remaining bound to return to his royal mistress, when she should intimate her pleasure. Accordingly, while Thomas was making merry with his friends, in the tower of Erceldoune, a person came running in, and told, with marks of fear and astonishment, that a hart and hind had left the neighbouring forest, and were, composedly and slowly, parading the street of the village. The prophet instantly arose, left his habitation, and followed the wonderful animals to the forest, whence he was never seen to return. According to the popular belief, he still "drees his weird" in Fairy Land, and is one day expected to revisit earth. In the meanwhile, his memory is held in the most profound respect. The Eildon Tree, from beneath the shade of which he delivered his prophecies, now no longer exists; but the spot is marked by a large stone, called Eildon Tree Stone. A neighbouring rivulet takes the name of the Bogle Burn (Goblin Brook) from the Rhymer's supernatural visitants. The veneration paid to his dwelling-place, even attached itself in some degree to a person, who, within the memory of man, chose to set up his residence in the ruins of Learmont's tower. The name of this man was Murray, a kind of herbalist; who, by dint of some knowledge in simples, the possession of a musical clock, an electrical machine, and a stuffed alligator, added to a supposed communication with Thomas the Rhymer, lived for many years in very good credit as a wizard.

It must not be omitted, that the prophet has, since his final retreat, been occasionally a visitant upon earth. He is said to have appeared to a shepherd slumbering on a Fairy ring, and to have conducted him into a subterranean recess, where he discovered an amazing range of stalls. In every stall stood a steed caparisoned for battle, and beside every steed lay a warrior in complete armour; but all were motionless. At the end of this immense stable hung a horn and sword, which the prophet offered to the choice of the visitant. The shepherd took the horn, and began to wind; but the sound excited such a stamping of steeds, and clattering of armour, that he dropped it from his hand in dismay. All the steeds and cavaliers were again motionless, and a voice repeated these lines:—

"Woe to the wretch, that ever he was born,
Who feared to draw the sword before he blew the horn."

He was then expelled from the cavern by a furious whirlwind. The story is told, with some variation, in the Discourse concerning Spirits, appended to Reginald Scott's "Discovery of Witchcraft," edit. 1665; and is thus beautifully alluded to in Dr Leyden's "Scenes of Infancy:"—

"By every thorn along the woodland damp,
The tiny glow-worm lights her emerald lamp;
Like the shot-star, whose yet unquenched light
Studs with faint gleam the raven-vest of night.
The Fairy ring-dance now, round Eildon-tree,
Moves to wild strains of elfin minstrelsy:
On glancing step appears the Fairy Queen;
The printed grass, beneath, springs soft and green;
While, hand in hand, she leads the frolic round,
The dinning tabor shakes the charmed ground;
Or, graceful mounted on her palfrey gray,
In robes, that glister like the sun in May,
With hawk and hound she leads the moonlight ranks,
Of knights and dames, to Huntly's ferny banks,
Where Rymour, long of yore, the nymph embraced,
The first of men unearthly lips to taste.
Rash was the vow, and fatal was the hour,
Which gave a mortal to a fairy's power!
A lingering leave he took of sun and moon;
—Dire to the minstrel was the fairy's boon!—
A sad farewell of grass and green-leaved tree,
The haunts of childhood doomed no more to see.
Through winding paths, that never saw the sun,
Where Eildon hides his roots in caverns dun,
They pass,—the hollow pavement, as they go,
Rocks to remurmuring waves, that boil below;
Silent they wade, where sounding torrents lave
The banks, and red the tinge of every wave;
For all the blood, that dyes the warrior's hand,
Runs through the thirsty springs of Fairy Land.
Level and green the downward region lies,
And low the ceiling of the Fairy skies;
Self-kindled gems a richer light display
Than gilds the earth, but not a purer day.
Resplendent crystal forms the palace-wall;
The diamond's trembling lustre lights the hall:
But where soft emeralds shed an umbered light,
Beside each coal-black courser sleeps a knight;
A raven plume waves o'er each helmed crest,
And black the mail, which binds each manly breast,
Girt with broad faulchion, and with bugle green—
Ah! could a mortal trust the Fairy Queen!
From mortal lips an earthly accent fell,

And Rymour's tongue confessed the numbing spell:
In iron sleep the minstrel lies forlorn,
Who breathed a sound before he blew the horn.
      *   *   *   *   *   *
Mysterious Rymour! doomed, by Fate's decree,
Still to revisit Eildon's lonely tree,
Where oft the swain, at dawn of Hallow-day,
Hears thy black barb with fierce impatience neigh!
Say, who is he, with summons strong and high,
That bids the charmed sleep of ages fly,
Rolls the long sound through Eildon's caverns vast,
While each dark warrior rouses at the blast,
His horn, his faulchion, grasps with mighty hand,
And peals proud Arthur's march from Fairy Land?"

In the "Minstrelsy of the Scottish Border," there are three ballads on the subject of the Rhymer: the First, narrating his first interview with the Fairy Queen, and his expedition to her subterranean kingdom, is taken down from tradition; the Second is a sort of *cento*, selected and arranged from the ancient metrical prophecies published under the Rhymer's name in 1615; the Third and Last Part, being entirely modern, is here reprinted, as a part of the author's original poetry.

THOMAS THE RHYMER

When seven years more had come and gone,
    Was war through Scotland spread,
And Ruberslaw shewed high Dunyon
    His beacon blazing red.

Then all by bonny Coldingknow,   5
    Pitched palliouns took their room,
And crested helms, and spears a rowe,
    Glanced gaily through the broom.

The Leader, rolling to the Tweed,
    Resounds the ensenzie;*   10
They roused the deer from Caddenhead,
    To distant Torwoodlee.

---

* *Ensenzie*—War-cry, or gathering word.

The feast was spread in Ercildoune,
    In Learmont's high and ancient hall;
And there were knights of great renown,   15
    And ladies, laced in pall.

Nor lacked they, while they sat at dine,
    The music, nor the tale,
Nor goblets of the blood-red wine,
    Nor mantling quaighs* of ale.   20

True Thomas rose, with harp in hand,
    When as the feast was done;
(In minstrel strife, in Fairy Land,
    The elfin harp he won.)

Hushed were the throng, both limb and tongue,   25
    And harpers for envy pale;
And armed lords leaned on their swords,
    And hearkened to the tale.

In numbers high, the witching tale
    The prophet poured along;   30
No after bard might e'er avail
    Those numbers to prolong.

Yet fragments of the lofty strain
    Float down the tide of years,
As, buoyant on the stormy main,   35
    A parted wreck appears.

He sung King Arthur's table round:
    The warrior of the lake;
How courteous Gawaine met the wound,
    And bled for ladie's sake.   40

But chief, in gentle Tristrem's praise,
    The notes melodious swell;
Was none excelled, in Arthur's days,
    The knight of Lionelle.

* _Quaighs_—Wooden cups, composed of staves hooped together.

For Marke, his cowardly uncle's right, 45
 A venomed wound he bore;
When fierce Morholde he slew in fight
 Upon the Irish shore.

No art the poison might withstand;
 No medicine could be found, 50
Till lovely Isolde's lily hand
 Had probed the rankling wound.

With gentle hand and soothing tongue,
 She bore the leech's part;
And, while she o'er his sick-bed hung, 55
 He paid her with his heart.

O fatal was the gift, I ween!
 For, doomed in evil tide,
The maid must be rude Cornwall's queen,
 His cowardly uncle's bride. 60

Their loves, their woes, the gifted bard
 In fairy tissue wove;
Where lords, and knights, and ladies bright,
 In gay confusion strove.

The Garde Joyeuse, amid the tale, 65
 High reared its glittering head;
And Avalon's enchanted vale
 In all its wonders spread.

Brengwain was there, and Segramore,
 And fiend-born Merlin's gramarye; 70
Of that famed wizard's mighty lore,
 O who could sing but he?

Through many a maze the winning song
 In changeful passion led,
Till bent at length the listening throng 75
 O'er Tristrem's dying bed.

His ancient wounds their scars expand;
　　With agony his heart is wrung:
O where is Isolde's lily hand,
　　And where her soothing tongue?　　　　　　80

She comes, she comes! like flash of flame
　　Can lovers' footsteps fly:
She comes, she comes!—she only came
　　To see her Tristrem die.

She saw him die: her latest sigh　　　　　　85
　　Joined in a kiss his parting breath:
The gentlest pair that Britain bare,
　　United are in death.

There paused the harp; its lingering sound
　　Died slowly on the ear;　　　　　　　　90
The silent guests still bent around,
　　For still they seemed to hear.

Then woe broke forth in murmurs weak,
　　Nor ladies heaved alone the sigh;
But, half-ashamed, the rugged cheek　　　　95
　　Did many a gauntlet dry.

On Leader's stream, and Learmont's tower,
　　The mists of evening close;
In camp, in castle, or in bower,
　　Each warrior sought repose.　　　　　　100

Lord Douglas, in his lofty tent,
　　Dreamed o'er the woeful tale;
When footsteps light, across the bent,
　　The warrior's ears assail.

He starts, he wakes:—"What, Richard, ho!　　105
　　Arise, my page, arise!
What venturous wight, at dead of night,
　　Dare step where Douglas lies!"—

Then forth they rushed: by Leader's tide
   A selcouth* sight they see—   110
A hart and hind pace side by side,
   As white as snow on Fairnalie.

Beneath the moon, with gesture proud,
   They stately move and slow;
Nor scare they at the gathering crowd,   115
   Who marvel as they go.

To Learmont's tower a message sped,
   As fast as page might run:
And Thomas started from his bed,
   And soon his clothes did on.   120

First he woxe pale, and then woxe red;
   Never a word he spake but three;—
"My sand is run; my thread is spun;
   This sign regardeth me."—

The elfin harp his neck around,   125
   In minstrel guise, he hung;
And on the wind, in doleful sound,
   Its dying accents rung.

Then forth he went; yet turned him oft
   To view his ancient hall;   130
On the grey tower, in lustre soft,
   The autumn moon-beams fall.

And Leader's waves, like silver sheen,
   Danced shimmering in the ray:
In deepening mass, at distance seen,   135
   Broad Soltra's mountains lay.

"Farewell, my father's ancient tower!
   A long farewell," said he:
"The scene of pleasure, pomp, or power,
   Thou never more shalt be.   140

* *Selcouth*—Wondrous.

"To Learmont's name no foot of earth
  Shall here again belong;
And on thy hospitable hearth
  The hare shall leave her young.

"Adieu! Adieu!" again he cried,   145
  All as he turned him roun'——
"Farewell to Leader's silver tide!
  Farewell to Ercildoune!"——

The hart and hind approached the place,
  As lingering yet he stood;   150
And there, before Lord Douglas' face,
  With them he crossed the flood.

Lord Douglas leaped on his berry-brown steed,
  And spurred him the Leader o'er;
But, though he rode with lightning speed,   155
  He never saw them more.

Some said to hill, and some to glen,
  Their wondrous course had been;
But ne'er in haunts of living men
  Again was Thomas seen.   160

NOTES ON THOMAS THE RHYMER

Note 1

And Ruberslaw shewed high Dunyon.—line 3.

Ruberslaw and Dunyon are two high hills above Jedburgh.

Note 2

Then all by bonny Coldingknow.—line 5.

An ancient tower near Erceldoune, belonging to a family of the name of Home. One of Thomas's prophecies is said to have run thus:—

> "Vengeance! vengeance!—when and where?
> On the house of Coldingknow, now and ever mair!"

The spot is rendered classical by its having given name to the beautiful melody, called the *Broom o' the Cowdenknows*.

Note 3

They roused the deer from Caddenhead,
To distant Torwoodlee.—lines 11-12.

Torwoodlee and Caddenhead are places in Selkirkshire.

Note 4

How courteous Gawaine met the wound.—line 39.

See, in the *Fabliaux* of Monsieur le Grand, elegantly translated by the late Gregory Way, Esq., the tale of the *Knight and the Sword*.

Note 5

As white as snow on Fairnalie.—line 112.

An ancient seat upon the Tweed, in Selkirkshire. In a popular edition of the First Part of Thomas the Rhymer, the Fairy Queen thus addresses him:—

> "Gin ye wad meet wi' me again,
> Gang to the bonny banks of Fairnalie."

45

Of old, when vassals to their head

Of old, when vassals to their head
Their little tribute freely paid
   Of faithful homage duteous proof—
Protector, o'er their little field
The Chieftain shook his feudal shield   5
   And bade Invasion stand aloof.

Now to apply—if in my lines
A single spark of merit shines
   A thousand errors to excuse—
The verse be yours—At your command   10
Shall Painting raise her glowing hand
   And stretch her buckler o'er the Muse.

And when in Antiquarian phrase
I tell the Raids of border days
   Of shivering spears and armour's rattle,   15
Hand o'er the tale to Harden's side—
Our sires together lived and died
   And *stole* the *Cows* and fought the *battle*.

But when, unhappy, on my toil
Nor Taste nor friendship's eye can smile   20
   When rhyme alike and reason faulter
Just to maintain your feudal claim
E'en to a Baby twist the theme
   And give it to my Chief Charles Walter.

46
Cadyow Castle

The ruins of Cadyow, or Cadzow castle, the ancient baronial residence of the family of Hamilton, are situated upon the precipitous banks of the river Evan, about two miles above its junction with the Clyde. It was dismantled, in the conclusion of the civil wars, during the reign of the unfortunate Mary, to whose cause the house of Hamilton devoted themselves with a generous zeal, which occasioned their temporary obscurity, and, very nearly, their total ruin. The situation of the ruins, embosomed in wood, darkened by ivy and creeping shrubs, and overhanging the brawling torrent, is romantic in the highest degree. In the immediate vicinity of Cadyow is a grove of immense oaks, the remains of the Caledonian Forest, which anciently extended through the south of Scotland, from the eastern to the Atlantic Ocean. Some of these trees measure twenty-five feet, and upwards, in circumference, and the state of decay, in which they now appear, shews, that they may have witnessed the rites of the Druids.—The whole scenery is included in the magnificent and extensive park of the Duke of Hamilton. There was long preserved in this forest the breed of the Scottish wild cattle, until their ferocity occasioned their being extirpated, about forty years ago. Their appearance was beautiful, being milk-white, with black muzzles, horns, and hoofs. The bulls are described by antient authors, as having white manes; but those of latter days had lost that peculiarity, perhaps by intermixture with the tame breed[*].

In detailing the death of the Regent Murray, which is made the subject of the following ballad, it would be injustice to my reader to use other words than those of Dr Robertson, whose account of that memorable event forms a beautiful piece of historical painting.

"Hamilton of Bothwellhaugh was the person who committed this barbarous action. He had been condemned to death soon after the battle of Langside, as we have already related, and owed his life to the regent's clemency. But part of his estate had been bestowed upon one of the regent's favourites[†], who seized his house, and turned out his wife, naked, in a cold night, into the open fields, where, before next morning, she became furiously mad. This injury made a deeper impression on him than the benefit he had received, and from that moment he vowed to be revenged of the regent. Party rage strengthened and inflamed his

---

[*] They were formerly kept in the park at Drumlanrig, and are still to be seen at Chillingham Castle in Northumberland. For their nature and ferocity see Notes.
[†] This was Sir James Ballenden, Lord Justice Clerk, whose shameful and inhuman rapacity occasioned the catastrophe in the text. *Spottiswoode*.

private resentment. His kinsmen, the Hamiltons, applauded the enter-
prize. The maxims of that age justified the most desperate course he
could take to obtain vengeance. He followed the regent for some time,
and watched for an opportunity to strike the blow. He resolved, at last,
to wait till his enemy should arrive at Linlithgow, through which he
was to pass, in his way from Stirling to Edinburgh. He took his stand
in a wooden gallery*, which had a window towards the street; spread
a feather-bed on the floor, to hinder the noise of his feet from being
heard; hung up a black cloth behind him, that his shadow might not be
observed from without; and, after all this preparation, calmly expected
the regent's approach, who had lodged, during the night, in a house
not far distant. Some indistinct information of the danger, which
threatened him, had been conveyed to the regent, and he paid so much
regard to it, that he resolved to return by the same gate through which
he had entered, and to fetch a compass round the town. But, as the
crowd about the gate was great, and he himself unacquainted with fear,
he proceeded directly along the street; and the throng of people oblig-
ing him to move very slowly, gave the assassin time to take so true an
aim, that he shot him, with a single bullet, through the lower part of his
belly, and killed the horse of a gentleman, who rode on his other side.
His followers instantly endeavoured to break into the house, whence
the blow had come; but they found the door strongly barricaded, and,
before it could be forced open, Hamilton had mounted a fleet horse†,
which stood ready for him at a back-passage, and was got far beyond
their reach. The regent died the same night of his wound."—*History
of Scotland*, book v.

   Bothwellhaugh rode straight to Hamilton, where he was received
in triumph; for the ashes of the houses in Clydesdale, which had been
burned by Murray's army, were yet smoking; and party prejudice,
the habits of the age, and the enormity of the provocation, seemed, to
his kinsmen, to justify his deed. After a short abode at Hamilton, this
fierce and determined man left Scotland, and served in France, under
the patronage of the family of Guise, to whom he was doubtless rec-
ommended by having avenged the cause of their niece, Queen Mary,
upon her ungrateful brother. De Thou has recorded, that an attempt
was made to engage him to assassinate Gaspar de Coligni, the famous
admiral of France, and the buckler of the Huguenot cause. But the

---

* This projecting gallery is still shewn. The house, to which it was attached,
was the property of the Archbishop of St Andrews, a natural brother of the
Duke of Chatelherault, and uncle to Bothwellhaugh. This, among many other
circumstances, seems to evince the aid, which Bothwellhaugh received from his
clan in effecting his purpose.
† The gift of Lord John Hamilton, commendator of Arbroath.

character of Bothwellhaugh was mistaken. He was no mercenary trader in blood, and rejected the offer with contempt and indignation. He had no authority, he said, from Scotland, to commit murders in France; he had avenged his own just quarrel, but he would neither, for price nor prayer, avenge that of another man.—*Thuanus*, cap. 46.

The Regent's death happened 23. January, 1569. It is applauded, or stigmatized, by contemporary historians, according to their religious or party prejudices. The triumph of Blackwood is unbounded. He not only extols the pious feat of Bothwellhaugh, "who," he observes, "satisfied, with a single ounce of lead, him, whose sacrilegious avarice had stripp'd the metropolitan church of St Andrew's of its covering;" but he ascribes it to immediate divine inspiration, and the escape of Hamilton to little less than the miraculous interference of the Deity.— *Jebb*, vol. II. p. 263. With equal injustice, it was, by others, made the ground of a general national reflection; for, when Mather urged Berney to assassinate Burleigh, and quoted the examples of Poltrot and Bothwellhaugh, the other conspirator answered, "that neyther Poltrot nor Hambleton did attempt their enterpryse, without some reason or consideration to lead them to it: as the one, by hyre, and promise of preferment or rewarde; the other, upon desperate mind of revenge, for a lytle wrong done unto him, as the report goethe, accordinge to the vyle trayterous dysposysyon of the hoole natyon of the Scottes."— *Murdin's State Papers*, vol. I. p. 197.

CADYOW CASTLE
ADDRESSED TO THE RIGHT HONOURABLE
LADY ANNE HAMILTON

When princely Hamilton's abode
    Ennobled Cadyow's Gothic towers,
The song went round, the goblet flow'd,
    And revel sped the laughing hours.

Then, thrilling to the harp's gay sound,   5
    So sweetly rung each vaulted wall,
And echoed light the dancer's bound,
    As mirth and music cheer'd the hall.

But Cadyow's towers, in ruins laid,
    And vaults, by ivy mantled o'er,   10
Thrill to the music of the shade,
    Or echo Evan's hoarser roar.

Yet still, of Cadyow's faded fame,
   You bid me tell a minstrel tale,
And tune my harp, of Border frame,   15
   On the wild banks of Evandale.

For thou, from scenes of courtly pride,
   From pleasure's lighter scenes, canst turn,
To draw oblivion's pall aside,
   And mark the long forgotten urn.   20

Then, noble maid! at thy command,
   Again the crumbled halls shall rise;
Lo! as on Evan's banks we stand,
   The past returns—the present flies.—

Where with the rock's wood-cover'd side   25
   Were blended late the ruins green,
Rise turrets in fantastic pride,
   And feudal banners flaunt between:

Where the rude torrent's brawling course
   Was shagg'd with thorn and tangling sloe,   30
The ashler buttress braves its force,
   And ramparts frown in battled row.

'Tis night—the shade of keep and spire
   Obscurely dance on Evan's stream,
And on the wave the warder's fire   35
   Is chequering the moon-light beam.

Fades slow their light; the east is grey;
   The weary warder leaves his tower;
Steeds snort; uncoupled stag-hounds bay,
   And merry hunters quit the bower.   40

The draw-bridge falls—they hurry out—
   Clatters each plank and swinging chain,
As, dashing o'er, the jovial route
   Urge the shy steed, and slack the rein.

First of his troop, the chief rode on; 45
    His shouting merry-men throng behind;
The steed of princely Hamilton
    Was fleeter than the mountain wind.

From the thick copse the roe-bucks bound,
    The startling red-deer scuds the plain, 50
For the hoarse bugle's warrior sound
    Has rouzed their mountain haunts again.

Through the huge oaks of Evandale,
    Whose limbs a thousand years have worn,
What sullen roar comes down the gale, 55
    And drowns the hunter's pealing horn?

Mightiest of all the beasts of chace,
    That roam in woody Caledon,
Crashing the forest in his race,
    The Mountain Bull comes thundering on. 60

Fierce, on the hunters' quiver'd band,
    He rolls his eyes of swarthy glow,
Spurns, with black hoof and horn, the sand,
    And tosses high his mane of snow.

Aim'd well, the chieftain's lance has flown; 65
    Struggling, in blood the savage lies;
His roar is sunk in hollow groan—
    Sound, merry huntsmen! sound the *pryse**!

'Tis noon—against the knotted oak
    The hunters rest the idle spear; 70
Curls through the trees the slender smoke,
    Where yeomen dight the woodland cheer.

Proudly the chieftain mark'd his clan,
    On greenwood lap all careless thrown,
Yet miss'd his eye the boldest man, 75
    That bore the name of Hamilton.

* *Pryse*—The note blown at the death of the game.

"Why fills not Bothwellhaugh his place,
   Still wont our weal and woe to share?
Why comes he not our sport to grace?
   Why shares he not our hunter's fare?"   80

Stern Claud replied, with darkening face,
   (Grey Pasley's haughty lord was he)
"At merry feast, or buxom chace,
   No more the warrior shalt thou see.

"Few suns have set, since Woodhouselee   85
   Saw Bothwellhaugh's bright goblets foam,
When to his hearths, in social glee,
   The war-worn soldier turn'd him home.

"There, wan from her maternal throes,
   His Margaret, beautiful and mild,   90
Sate in her bower, a pallid rose,
   And peaceful nursed her new-born child.

"O change accurs'd! past are those days;
   False Murray's ruthless spoilers came,
And, for the hearth's domestic blaze,   95
   Ascends destruction's volumed flame.

"What sheeted phantom wanders wild,
   Where mountain Eske through woodland flows,
Her arms enfold a shadowy child—
   Oh is it she, the pallid rose?   100

"The wildered traveller sees her glide,
   And hears her feeble voice with awe—
'Revenge,' she cries, 'on Murray's pride!
   And woe for injured Bothwellhaugh!'"

He ceased—and cries of rage and grief   105
   Burst mingling from the kindred band,
And half arose the kindling chief,
   And half unsheath'd his Arran brand.

But who, o'er bush, o'er stream and rock,
  Rides headlong, with resistless speed,   110
Whose bloody poniard's frantic stroke
  Drives to the leap his jaded steed;

Whose cheek is pale, whose eye-balls glare,
  As one, some visioned sight that saw,
Whose hands are bloody, loose his hair?—   115
  —'Tis he! 'tis he! 'tis Bothwellhaugh!

From gory selle*, and reeling steed,
  Sprung the fierce horseman with a bound,
And, reeking from the recent deed,
  He dashed his carbine on the ground.   120

Sternly he spoke—"'Tis sweet to hear
  In good green-wood the bugle blown,
But sweeter to Revenge's ear,
  To drink a tyrant's dying groan.

"Your slaughtered quarry proudly trod,   125
  At dawning morn, o'er dale and down,
But prouder base-born Murray rode
  Thro' old Linlithgow's crowded town.

"From the wild Border's humbled side,
  In haughty triumph, marched he,   130
While Knox relaxed his bigot pride,
  And smiled, the traitorous pomp to see.

"But, can stern Power, with all his vaunt,
  Or Pomp, with all her courtly glare,
The settled heart of Vengeance daunt,   135
  Or change the purpose of Despair?

* *Selle*—Saddle. A word used by Spenser, and other ancient authors.

"With hackbut bent*, my secret stand,
 Dark as the purposed deed, I chose,
And marked, where, mingling in his band,
 Troop'd Scottish pikes and English bows.   140

"Dark Morton, girt with many a spear,
 Murder's foul minion, led the van;
And clashed their broad-swords in the rear,
 The wild Macfarlanes' plaided clan.

"Glencairn and stout Parkhead were nigh,   145
 Obsequious at their regent's rein,
And haggard Lindesay's iron eye,
 That saw fair Mary weep in vain.

"Mid pennon'd spears, a steely grove,
 Proud Murray's plumage floated high;   150
Scarce could his trampling charger move,
 So close the minions crowded nigh.

"From the raised vizor's shade, his eye,
 Dark-rolling, glanced the ranks along,
And his steel truncheon, waved on high,   155
 Seem'd marshalling the iron throng.

"But yet his sadden'd brow confess'd
 A passing shade of doubt and awe;
Some fiend was whispering in his breast,
 'Beware of injured Bothwellhaugh!'   160

"The death-shot parts—the charger springs—
 Wild rises tumult's startling roar!—
And Murray's plumy helmet rings—
 —Rings on the ground, to rise no more.

"What joy the raptured youth can feel,   165
 To hear her love the loved one tell,
Or he, who broaches on his steel
 The wolf, by whom his infant fell!

* *Hackbut bent*—Gun cock'd.

"But dearer, to my injured eye,
  To see in dust proud Murray roll;   170
And mine was ten times trebled joy,
  To hear him groan his felon soul.

"My Margaret's spectre glided near;
  With pride her bleeding victim saw;
And shrieked in his death-deafen'd ear,   175
  'Remember injured Bothwellhaugh!'

"Then speed thee, noble Chatlerault!
  Spread to the wind thy bannered tree!
Each warrior bend his Clydesdale bow!—
  Murray is fallen, and Scotland free."   180

Vaults every warrior to his steed;
  Loud bugles join their wild acclaim—
"Murray is fallen, and Scotland freed!
  Couch, Arran! couch thy spear of flame!"

But, see! the minstrel vision fails—   185
  The glimmering spears are seen no more;
The shouts of war die on the gales,
  Or sink in Evan's lonely roar.

For the loud bugle, pealing high,
  The blackbird whistles down the vale,   190
And sunk in ivied ruins lie
  The banner'd towers of Evandale.

For chiefs, intent on bloody deed,
  And Vengeance, shouting o'er the slain,
Lo! highborn Beauty rules the steed,   195
  Or graceful guides the silken rein.

And long may Peace and Pleasure own
  The maids, who list the minstrel's tale;
Nor e'er a ruder guest be known
  On the fair banks of Evandale!   200

NOTES ON CADYOW CASTLE

Note 1

First of his troop, the chief rode on.—line 45.

The head of the family of Hamilton, at this period, was James, Earl of Arran, Duke of Chatelherault in France, and first peer of the Scottish realm. In 1569, he was appointed by Queen Mary her lieutenant-general in Scotland, under the singular title of her adopted father.

Note 2

The Mountain Bull comes thundering on.—line 60.

In Caledonia olim frequens erat sylvestris quidam bos, nunc vero rarior, qui colore candidissimo, jubam densam et demissam instar leonis gestat, truculentus ac ferus ab humano genere abhorrens, ut quæcunque homines vel manibus contrectarint, vel halitu perflaverint, ab iis multos post dies omnino abstinuerint. Ad hoc tanta audacia huic bovi indita erat, ut non solum irritatus equites furenter prosterneret, sed ne tantillum lacessitus omnes promiscue homines cornibus, ac ungulis peteret; ac canum, qui apud nos ferocissimi sunt impetus plane contemneret. Ejus carnes cartilaginosæ sed saporis suavissimi. Erat is olim per illam vastissimum Caledoniæ sylvam frequens, sed humana ingluvie jam assumptus tribus tantum locis est reliquus, Strivilingii Cumbernaldiæ et Kincarniæ.—Leslæus Scotiæ Descriptio, p. 18.

Note 3

Stern Claud replied, with darkening face,
(Grey Pasley's haughty lord was he).—lines 81–82.

Lord Claud Hamilton, second son of the Duke of Chatelherault, and commendator of the abbey of Pasley, acted a distinguished part during the troubles of Queen Mary's reign, and remained unalterably attached to the cause of that unfortunate princess. He led the van of her army at the fatal battle of Langside, and was one of the commanders at the Raid of Stirling, which had so nearly given complete success to the Queen's faction. He was ancestor of the present Marquis of Abercorn.

Note 4

Few suns have set, since Woodhouselee.—line 85.

This barony, stretching along the banks of the Esk, near Auchindinny, belonged to Bothwellhaugh, in right of his wife. The ruins of the mansion, from whence she was expelled in the brutal manner which occasioned her death, are still to be seen in a hollow glen beside the river. Popular report tenants them with the restless ghost of the lady Bothwellhaugh; whom, however, it confounds with Lady Anne Bothwell, whose *Lament* is so popular. This spectre is so tenacious of her rights, that, a part of the stones of the ancient edifice having been employed in building or repairing the present Woodhouselee, she has deemed it a part of her privilege to haunt that house also; and, even of very late years, has excited considerable disturbance and terror among the domestics. This is a more remarkable vindication of the *rights of ghosts*, as the present Woodhouselee, which gives his title to the Honourable Alexander Fraser Tytler, a senator of the College of Justice, is situated on the slope of the Pentland hills, distant at least four miles from her proper abode. She always appears in white, and with her child in her arms.

Note 5

Whose bloody poniard's frantic stroke
Drives to the leap his jaded steed.—lines 111–12.

Birrell informs us, that Bothwellhaugh, being closely pursued, "after that spur and wand had fail'd him, he drew forth his dagger, and strocke his horse behind, whilk caused the horse to leap a verey brode stanke (*i.e.* ditch), by whilk means he escaipit, and gat away from all the rest of the horses."—*Birrel's Diary*, p. 18.

Note 6

From the wild Border's humbled side,
In haughty triumph, marched he.—lines 129–30.

Murray's death took place shortly after an expedition to the Borders; which is thus commemorated by the author of his elegy.

> "So having stablischt all thing in this sort,
> To Liddisdaill agane he did resort,
> Throw Ewisdail, Eskdail, and all the daills rode he,
> And also lay three nights in Cannabie,

Whair na prince lay thir hundred yeiris before.
Nae thief durst stir, they did him feir so sair;
And, that thay suld na mair their thift allege,
Threescore and twelf he brocht of thame in pledge,
Syne wardit thame, whilk maid the rest keep ordour,
Than mycht the rasch-bus keep ky on the bordour."

Scotish Poems, 16th century, p. 232.

Note 7

With hackbut bent, my secret stand.—line 137.

The carbine, with which the Regent was shot, is preserved at Hamilton Palace. It is a brass piece, of a middling length, very small in the bore, and, what is rather extraordinary, appears to have been rifled or indented in the barrel. It had a matchlock, for which a modern fire-lock has been injudiciously substituted.

Note 8

Dark Morton, girt with many a spear.—line 141.

Of this noted person it is enough to say, that he was active in the murder of David Rizzio, and at least privy to that of Darnley.

Note 9

The wild Macfarlanes' plaided clan.—line 144.

This clan of Lennox Highlanders were attached to the Regent Murray. Holinshed, speaking of the battle of Langsyde, says, "in this batayle the valiancie of an hieland gentleman, named Macfarlane, stood the regent's part in great steede; for, in the hottest brunte of the fighte, he came up with two hundred of his friendes and countrymen, and so manfully gave in upon the flankes of the queen's people, that he was a great cause of the disordering of them. This Macfarlane had been lately before, as I have heard, condemned to die, for some outrage by him committed, and obtayning pardon through suyte of the countesse of Murray, he recompenced that clemencie by this peice of service now at this batayle." Calderwood's account is less favourable to the Macfarlanes. He states that "Macfarlane, with his highlandmen, fled from the wing where they were set. The lord Lindsay, who stood nearest to them in the regent's battle, said 'Let them go! I shall fill their place better:' and so, stepping forward, with a company of fresh men, charged the enemy, whose spears were now spent, with long weapons, so that they were driven back by force, being before almost overthrown by the avant-guard and harquebusiers, and so were turned to flight."— *Calderwood's MS. apud Keith*, p. 480. Melville mentions the flight of the vanguard, but states it to have been commanded by Morton, and composed chiefly of commoners of the barony of Renfrew.

Note 10

Glencairn and stout Parkhead were nigh,
Obsequious at their regent's rein.—lines 145–46.

The Earl of Glencairn was a steady adherent of the Regent. George Douglas of Parkhead was a natural brother of the Earl of Morton, whose horse was killed by the same ball, by which Murray fell.

Note 11

And haggard Lindesay's iron eye,
That saw fair Mary weep in vain.—lines 147–48.

Lord Lindsay, of the Byres, was the most ferocious and brutal of the Regent's faction, and, as such, was employed to extort Mary's signature to the deed of resignation, presented to her in Lochleven castle. He discharged his commission with the most savage rigour; and it is even said, that when the weeping captive, in the act of signing, averted her eyes from the fatal deed, he pinched her arm with the grasp of his iron glove.

Note 12

Scarce could his trampling charger move,
So close the minions crowded nigh.—lines 151–52.

Not only had the Regent notice of the intended attempt upon his life, but even of the very house from which it was threatened.—With that infatuation, at which men wonder, after such events have happened, he deemed it would be a sufficient precaution to ride briskly past the dangerous spot. But even this was prevented by the crowd: so that Bothwellhaugh had time to take a deliberate aim.—*Spottiswoode*, p. 233. *Buchanan.*

47
The Reiver's Wedding

O will ye hear a mirthful bourd
    Or will ye hear of courtesie
Or will ye hear how a gallant Lord
    Was wedded to a gay Ladie?

"Ca' out the kye" quo' the village herd   5
    As he stood on the know
"Ca' this ane's nine and that ane's ten
    And bauld Laird William's cow."

"Ah by my sooth," quo' William then
    "And stands it that way now   10
When knave and churl have nine and ten
    That the Laird has but his cow?

"I swear by the light of the Michaelmas moon
    That shews where the fauldfu's lye
And by the edge of my braidsword brown   15
    They shall soon say Laird William's kye.

"I swear by the rood of our dear Lord
    And the might of Mary high
And by the edge of my gude braid sword
    They shall soon say Harden's kye."   20

He took a bugle from his side
    With names carved o'er and o'er
For many a chief of meikle pride
    That Border bugle bore.

He blew a note baith sharp and hie   25
    Till rock and water rung around.
Three score of moss troopers and three
    Have mounted at that bugle sound.

The Michaelmas moon was waxing then
    But ere she wan the full
Ye might see by her light in Kirkhope glen
    A bow of kye and a bassened bull.   30

And loud and loud in Kirkhope tower
    The quaigh gaed round wi glee
For the English beef was brought in bower
    And the English ale flowed merrilie.   35

And many a guest from Teviot side
    And Yarrow's braes were there
Was never Lord in Scotlonde wide
    That made more dainty fare.   40

They ate and laughed, they sung and quaffed
    Till nought on board was seen
When knight and squire were bowne to dine
    But a spur of silver sheen.

Lord William has ta'en his berry brown steed   45
    A sore shente man was he
"Wait ye, my guests, a little stead
    And well feasted ye shall be.

"Thy gallant Lads in the English hills
    These three days past hae been   50
But never out o' Kirkhope's hall
    Must ye wander hungry men."

He rode him down by Falsehope Burn
    His cousin dear to see
With him to take a riding turn   55
    "*Wat Draw the Sword*" was he.

And when he came to Falsehope Glen
    Beneath the Trysting tree
On the smooth green was carved plain
    To Lochwood bound are we.   60

"O if they be gane to dark Lochwood
  To drive the Warden's gear
Betwixt our names I ween there's feud
  I'll go and have my share.

"For little reck I for Johnstone's feud   65
  The Warden tho' he be."
So Lord William is away to dark Lochwood
  With riders barely three.

In Lochwood sate three Ladies gay
  And two were fair to see   70
The third she was a gentle may
  But small beauty had she—

The Warden's daughters in Lochwood sate
  Were all both fair and gay
All save the Lady Margaret   75
  And she was sad and wae.

The sister Jean had a full fair skin
  And Grace was bauld and braw
But the heart that was Margaret's breast within
  I ween was weel worth them a'.   80

Her father pranked her sisters a'
  Wi' mickle joy and pride
But Margaret maun seek Dundrenan's wa'
  For she ne'er maun be a bride.

On spear and casque by gallants gent   85
  Her sisters' scarfs were borne
But ne'er at tilt or tournament
  Were Margaret's colours worn.

The sisters rode to Thirlestane bower
  And she was left at hame   90
To wander round the gloomy tower
  And sigh young Harden's name.

"Of all the knights the knight most fair,
    From Yarrow to the Tyne"
Soft sighed the maid "is Harden's heir   95
    But ne'er can he be mine.

"Of all the maids the foulest maid
    From Teviot to the Dee"
O sighing sad that lady said
    "Can ne'er young Harden's be."   100

She looked up the briery glen
    And up the mossy brae
And she saw a score of her father's men
    Yclad in the Johnstone gray—

O fast and fast they downwards sped   105
    The moss and briars among
And in the midst the troopers led
    A shackled knight along.

48

On the Death of Simon de Montfort

Literally versified from the Norman-French

In woeful wise my song shall rise,
  My heart impells the strain;
Tears fit the song, which tells the wrong
  Of gentle Barons slayn.

CHORUS
Now lowly lies the flower of pries,*   5
  That could so much of weir:†
Fayr peace to gaine they fought in vayn,
  Their house to ruin gave,
And limb and life to butcheryng knyfe,
  Our native land to save.   10
Erle Montfort's scathe, and heavy death,
  Shall cost the world a tear.

As I here say, upon Tuesdaye,
  The battle bold was done;
Each mounted knight there fell in fight,   15
  For ayd of foot was none:
There wounds were felt, and blows were dealt
  With brands that burnish'd be;
Sir Edward stoute, his numerous route
  Have won the maisterie.   20
      Now lowly lies, &c.

* Price.   † War.

But, though he died, on Montfort's side
   The victorye remain'd;
Like Becket's fayth, the Erle's in deathe
   The martyr's palm obtain'd;   25
That holy Saint would never graunt
   The Church should fall or slyde;
Like him, the Erle met deadly peril,
   And like him dauntless dyed.
      Now lowly lies, &c.   30

The bold Sir Hugh Despencer true,
   The kingdom's Justice he,
Was doom'd to dye, unrighteouslye,
   By passynge crueltie.
And Sir Henry, the son was he   35
   To Leister's nobile lord,
With many moe, as ye shall know,
   Fell by Erle Gloster's sword.
      Now lowly lies, &c.

He that dares dye, in standing by   40
   The country's peace and lawe,
To him the Saint the meed shall graunt
   Of conscience free from flawe.
Who suffers scathe, and faces death,
   To save the poor from wrong,   45
God speed his end, the poor man's friend,
   For suche we pray, and long!
      Now lowly lies, &c.

His bosom nere, a treasure dere,
   A sackclothe shirt they founde,—   50
The felons there full ruthless were
   Who stretch'd hym on the grounde.
More wrongs than be in butcherye,
   They did the knight who fell,
To wield his sword and keep his worde   55
   Who knew the way so well.
      Now lowly lies, &c.

Pray, as is meet, my brethren sweet,
   The maiden Mary's Son,
The infant fair, our noble heir,   60
   In grace to guide him on.
I will not name the habit's* claym,
   Of that I will not saye;
But for Jesus' love, that sits above,
   For churchmen ever pray.   65
      Now lowly lies, &c.

Seek not to see, of chivalrye
   Or count, or baron bold;
Each gallant knight, and squire of might,
   They all are bought and sold;   70
For loyaltie and veritie,
   They now are done awaye—
The losel vile may reign by guile,
   The fool by his foleye.
      Now lowly lies, &c.   75

Sir Simon wight, that gallant knight,
   And his companye eche one,
To heaven above, and joye and love,
   And endless life are gone.
May He on rood who bought our good,   80
   And God, their paine relieve,
Who captive ta'en, are kept in chaine,
   And depe in dungeon grieve!

   Now lowly lies the flower of pries,
      That could so much of weir: 85
   Erle Montfort's scathe, and heavy death,
      Shall cost the world a tear.†

* The clerical habit is obviously alluded to; and it seems to be cautiously and obscurely hinted, that the church was endangered by the defeat of De Montfort.
† It was the object of the Translator to imitate, as literally as possible, the style of the original, even in its rudeness, abrupt transitions, and obscurity; such being the particular request of Mr. Ritson, who supplied the old French model of this ballad minstrelsy.

49

The Recollections of Chastellain

He that will hear of marvels strange
    As story e'er enroll'd,
Of me shall learn such matchless change
    As ne'er in song was told.
Each wondrous hap since first my eyes   5
    The living light did view,
From memory's faithful treasuries
    I know to tell it true.

And some are piteous all to know,
    And draw the listeners' tears;   10
And some that augur future woe,
    Impress with boding fears;
Of some the dark mysterious maze
    Exceeds our human skill;
And some record the hero's praise,   15
    And some the felon's ill.

All in fair France, that lovely land,
    The flower of Christentie,
I saw lead on an armed band
    A maid of low degree;   20
I saw her sweep the siege away,
    Which girt fair Orleans round;
By her in Rheims' cathedral grey
    I saw her monarch crown'd.

I saw her as a saint adored,   25
    Who broke her country's chain;
Yet, changeful fortune of the sword!
    At length I saw her ta'en.
Mourn, Gallia, mourn! from Rouen's walls
    Her death-smoke blots the skies;   30
Yet, when again her country calls,
    The martyred maid shall rise.

And next I saw a petty friar
  Assume the sacred sway,
And dictate to our holy sire,   35
  And bid the church obey.
The saucy priest, his power down-borne,
  Incurr'd a traitor's doom;
His loathsome corpse in quarters shorn
  Defiled the streets of Rome.   40

I saw a feigned Carmelite
  Roam through the land to preach;
And there the frantic hypocrite
  Foul heresy did teach;
Unlicensed by the priestly name,   45
  The holy mass he sung;
For which upon a pile of flame
  Convicted he was flung.

Even in fair Scotland's kingly hall
  I saw her royal lord,   50
The gallant Stuart, butcher'd, fall,
  By halberd and by sword.
Vainly his lovely consort strove
  To ward their traitorous blows;
Yet well, though late, her injured love   55
  Wreaked vengeance on his foes.

I saw proud Savoy strive to seize,
  With ill-considered aim,
The Roman pontiff's holy keys
  And triple diadem.   60
Irregular ambition's wiles
  Dealt holy church a wound;
For which, long after, at Repailles,
  The duke his guerdon found.

At Rome I saw an ancient, grave,   65
    And pious cardinal
Murder'd by a domestic slave,
    Within his palace hall.
Him on his peaceful couch, at noon,
    The faithless ruffian slew;   70
For which in many a torment soon
    He paid the vengeance due.

'Midst hoots of shame I saw, in France,
    With boughs in triumph borne,
The root of all abuse advance,   75
    The nation's plague and scorn;
A female fiend, whose pride and lust
    Exceed all earthly measure;
From such a stem could spring, I trust,
    Small profit and small pleasure.   80

And next I saw, by secret means,
    A money-broker rise;
In trade and lucre's sordid scenes
    Was none so wondrous wise;
I saw him too in exile die,   85
    His fortune chang'd and gone,
Because full often fraudfully
    His craft had robb'd the throne.

A youth of twenty years, no more,
    A wondrous sight to see,   90
I saw attain each varied lore,
    And win each learn'd degree.
Whate'er his eye had once perused
    His tongue could say again;
But the young antichrist abused   95
    His gifts in science vain.

Then saw I well Duke Glo'ster reel,
   And hurled from on high,
Crush'd beneath fortune's restless wheel,
   By felon murder die.   100
Immersed within the luscious tun
   The villains choak'd his breath,
That wine quaff'd on till life was gone,
   Might drown the sense of death.

I saw the nephew of King Charles,   105
   Sir Giles of Britany,
Spite of his birth from ancient earls,
   A strangled captive die.
Such was his cruel brother's doom,
   Who cited from on high,   110
By ways as wondrous, to the tomb
   Was brought as suddenly.

Grand Master of Saint James's knights
   I saw triumphant reign
Alvarez, in his haughty might,   115
   High Constable of Spain;
Not all the baron's hoarded wealth,
   Not all his power and state,
Could shield him, when crept on by stealth
   His dark and doubtful fate.   120

I saw the wealth which Venice piles
   In piles, where long it lay,
By a shrewd Grecian's crafty wiles
   Bereft and borne away;
Doom'd I saw the thief, detected   125
   By his comrades' treachery,
On a gibbet high erected,
   Far too mild a death to die.

A distant province next I saw,
   Where stern accusers said   130
How that their prince, 'gainst nature's law,
   Defiled his sister's bed;
In vain a forged bull he pleads,
   To screen a crime so foul,
For honour spurns his vicious deeds,   135
   And conscience wrings his soul.

I saw a poor adventurer's prize
   Lie conquer'd Milan fair;
More honour gain'd his high emprize
   Than if the rightful heir.   140
To the bold knight is justly due
   Such tribute of renown;
His valour, known the nations through,
   Might grace a kingly crown.

I saw the English race expell'd   145
   From fruitful Aquitaine,
Which, for three hundred years, they held
   Their ancient rich domain;
And Bayonne fair and Bordeaux, now,
   The King of France has won: 150
Praise to the monarch's laurell'd brow
   By whom such deeds are done.

Eke have I seen fair Normandy
   To France's crown restored;
And Rouen's turrets blaze on high   155
   The banners of her lord;
Against the ancient enemy
   Defiance now they wave:
Such are the fruits of victory
   By France's conquering glaive.   160

I saw devised in Roman walls
   A plot of horror dread,
To murder holy cardinals,
   And seize the church's head;
But God, who made his church his care,   165
   Soon quell'd the enemy;
And daring Stephen de Procaire
   Did on the gallows die.

Old Ghent, invincible esteem'd,
   I saw it storm'd and won   170
By one, the most victorious deem'd
   Beneath the rolling sun.
The town was given to the flame,
   The people to the sword;
No deed of such deserved fame   175
   Shall ages ten afford.

I saw within a listed field
   A noble youth contend
'Gainst twenty-two, with spear and shield,
   To vanquish or defend.   180
So many noble knights were there,
   So many faiths they bore;
A field so strange, and fought so fair,
   Shall ne'er be heard of more.

I saw the seat of Constantine   185
   Storm'd by a heathen host;
Destroy'd, alas! her ancient line,
   Her ancient honours lost.
The aged Emperor of Greece
   The caitiff miscreants slew;   190
But let the tale of horror cease,
   Nor vain regrets renew.

And I have seen a fair Lucrece
  Unbounded homage claim;
Of Naples she, and not of Greece,   195
  And least of Roman fame.
Proud priests and prelates, many a one,
  Came bending to her knee;
Yet but a rampant courtezan,
  To speak the sooth, was she.   200

I saw the King of Hungary
  His marriage feast prepare,
And celebrate his nuptials high,
  With princely pomp and care.
The wedding cheer was richly dight,   205
  The bridal couch was spread;
But on that couch lay stretch'd at night
  The royal bridegroom dead.

And after him I saw arise
  A wandering soldier's son;   210
By feats of worth and bold emprise
  The kingdom he has won.
Thus fail'd the ancient royal root,
  Its branches shrunk and gone,
And thus a foreign lowly shoot   215
  Was grafted on the throne.

The first of France's royal line
  I saw his kindred flee,
And shelter seek beneath the vine
  Of ducal Burgundy;   220
A royal crown, back'd by his aid,
  Unhappily he won;
But God be judge how he repaid
  The mighty service done.

On Naples' fair and fertile coast,   225
   I saw the firm earth rend,
Towns, castles, cities, sunk and lost
   Through the dark gulph descend.
The column'd churches rock'd and reel'd,
   The air with flames was red,   230
A trembling people pray'd and kneel'd,
   For earthly hope was fled.

I saw even in the land of France
   Full many an English lord
'Gainst English bosoms couch the lance,   235
   And wield the civil sword;
For Calais and for Guines they fought:
   Such discord dire and strange
Within a hostile land, methought,
   Must bode some wondrous change.   240

I turn'd my eyes to England's soil,
   'Twas slaughter over all;
In mutual fight and wild turmoil
   I saw her mightiest fall.
To tell how wide the whirlwind reign'd   245
   Would chill your soul with fears;
No spot in all the land remain'd
   Undrench'd by blood and tears.

In high despiteous wilful mood,
   Another king they chose;   250
Their aged monarch, mild and good,
   Took refuge with his foes.
To Scotland's kind, though hostile, coast
   With his young heir he came;
Scotland that can for ages boast   255
   Her hospitable fame.

A royal fleur-de-lis of France
    I saw in dungeon thrown;
By fickle fate and fell mischance
    His honours past and gone. 260
His princely state and seignorie
    Were reft before the time;
Of France the royal fleur-de-lis
    Had perish'd ere the prime.

I saw the crown of Cyprus' isle 265
    To a proud soldan lent,
Of Babylon the tyrant vile,
    Her king to exile sent;
Of holy church a bastard bold,
    All reckless of the end, 270
I saw him the foul deed uphold,
    Nor care for foe nor friend.

The Queen of Cyprus next I saw
    Through ocean plow her way;
From France some succours meet to draw 275
    To fence the Christian fay.
But still her evil fates pursue,
    From watery Venice came,
Of loose corsairs a lawless crew,
    Who robb'd the royal dame. 280

Two monarchs whom two kingdoms own
    I saw high worth avow,
And swear before one power alone
    Their royalty should bow.
They own'd one master, and no more, 285
    For him to wield the sword,
Of him to hold their crowns they swore,
    Fair Virtue's sovereign lord.

Sicilia's monarch have I seen
  Assume the shepherd swain,   290
And tending, with his lovely queen,
  Their sheep upon the plain.
The shepherd's hat, the shepherd's hook,
  The shepherd's cloak they wear,
And rest at eve beside the brook   295
  Amid their fleecy care.

And stranger men of eastern lands,
  From climes remote, I saw,
From Georgian hills and Persian sands,
  And old Armenia;   300
Both Christian chiefs, and heathen too
  Who Mahound's maxims hold,
Against the tyrant Turk did sue
  For aid to Charles the Bold.

Of Burgundy the noble duke   305
  Received them wondrous well,
And honour'd them, as word and look,
  But best his actions, tell.
For them he did such actions high,
  And honour so profound,   310
The memory shall never die,
  Till the last trumpet sound.

And I have seen strange signs in heaven
  Of wondrous blazing stars,
Whose fiery trains have signal given   315
  Of bitter plagues and wars.
To seek what evils they portend
  In vain we may explore;
Enough for us to wait the end,
  And trembling to adore.   320

And have I seen a savage scene
   In Christendom display'd;
For holy churchmen have I seen
   Fall by the bloody blade.
In fair Mayence, to flames a prey,   325
   Such outrage foul was done
As never, till that direful day,
   Was witness'd by the sun.

High Duke, in whom we glory all,
   And thou, his son so bold,   330
Accept this brief memorial
   Of deeds which I have told.
Framed for your lesson and your praise,
   In heart devoid of flaw,
Heaven grant ye from my humble lays   335
   The wholesome moral draw.

And now chill age, I see, is nigh,
   To freeze my future time,
And check my hand and dim my eye,
   For record or for rhime;   340
Last, last of all, stern death I see
   To shut the scene draw near—
The sequel, MOLINET, from thee
   The listening world shall hear.

50

The Battle of Killiecrankie

Translated from the Latin

The glorious Graeme of deathless fame
    Brought down his mountain band
The southern race in rout they chace
    Claymore and targe in hand.
The Lowland prig and canting Whig   5
    In headlong flight were roll'd
In foul retreat the *Dutch be—t*
    Their breeches manifold.

O wondrous Graeme! Herculean frame
    And Faith unstained by fear!   10
Thou well couldst fire to deeds of ire
    The agile mountaineer:
Though twice thy force opposed thy course
    In deep and dark array
Yet swept thy sword the foreign Lord   15
    And stranger race away.

Of noble birth and nobler worth
    A peer of old renown
His blade so true Dunfermline drew
    And hewed the traitors down.   20
With heart of faith and hand of death
    Old Scotland's Hector gray
O'er helms of steel through ranks that reel
    Pitcur led on the way.

For James's right Glengarry's might   25
　　The field with slaughter strowed
Not he through fire, who bore his sire
　　Such zealous duty shewed.
The men of Skye of metal high
　　They shared their chieftain's toils   30
Both sire and son to fight rushed on
　　Macdonalds of the Isles.

Maclean the bold fought as of old
　　Amid his martial clan
From foemen such the tardy Dutch   35
　　With speed unwonted ran.
The stout Lochiel with dirk of steel
　　And many a Cameron there
The Southron fell dispatched to hell
　　And bore their spoils to Blair.   40

Barra, Glencoe, Keppoch also
　　And Balloch and his brother
They fenced the claims of good King James
　　And would not brook another.
And Appin too his faulchion drew   45
　　With Stuarts brought from far
And Cannon sage did guide their rage
　　And marshalled all the war.

There too was he from Hungary
　　Who for his prince did come   50
And turned his dirk from faithless Turk
　　Gainst false Whigs at home.
The tutor sage to battle's rage
　　Clanranald's broadswords brought
And with his clan in act a man   55
　　Their stripling Captain fought.

Glenmorison from wood and glen
   A huntsman warrior came
His carbine true to earth he threw
   And drew his sword of flame.   60
He left the doe and bounding roe
   He left the stag at bay
The Whiggish race like deer to chace
   And course the false Mackay.

While Tummell's wave by rock and cave   65
   From Blair to Tay shall run
Claymore and targe in Highland charge
   Shall rout the pike and gun.
And you, ye true, your blades that drew
   For Scotland's laws and king   70
In storied lays your deathless praise
   Immortal bards shall sing.

51

The Norman Horse-Shoe

Air—The War-song of the Men of Glamorgan

The Welch, inhabiting a mountainous country, and possessing only an
inferior breed of horses, were usually unable to encounter the shock
of the Anglo-Norman cavalry. Occasionally, however, they were suc-
cessful in repelling the invaders; and the following verses are supposed
to celebrate a defeat of CLARE, Earl of Striguil and Pembroke, and of
NEVILLE, Baron of Chepstow, Lords Marchers of Monmouthshire.
Rymny is a stream which divides the counties of Monmouth and
Glamorgan: Caerphili, the scene of the supposed battle, is a vale upon
its banks, dignified by the ruins of a very ancient castle.

Red glows the forge in Striguil's bounds,
And hammers din, and anvil sounds,
And armourers, with iron toil,
Barb many a steed for battle's broil.
Foul fall the hand which bends the steel   5
Around the courser's thundering heel,
That e'er shall dint a sable wound
On fair Glamorgan's velvet ground!

From Chepstow's towers, ere dawn of morn,
Was heard afar the bugle horn;   10
And forth, in banded pomp and pride,
Stout Clare and fiery Neville ride.
They swore, their banners broad should gleam,
In crimson light, on Rymny's stream;
They vowed Caerphili's sod should feel   15
The Norman charger's spurning heel.

And sooth they swore—the sun arose,
And Rymny's wave with crimson glows;
For Clare's red banner, floating wide,
Rolled down the stream to Severn's tide!   20
And sooth they vowed—the trampled green
Shewed where hot Neville's charge had been:
In every sable hoof-tramp stood
A Norman horseman's curdling blood!

Old Chepstow's brides may curse the toil,   25
That armed stout Clare for Cambrian broil;
Their orphans long the art may rue,
For Neville's war-horse forged the shoe.
No more the stamp of armed steed
Shall dint Glamorgan's velvet mead;   30
Nor trace be there, in early spring,
Save of the Fairies' emerald ring.

52
The Dying Bard

Air— *Dafydd y Garreg-Wen*

The Welch tradition bears, that a bard, on his death-bed, demanded
his harp, and played the air to which these verses are adapted; request-
ing that it might be performed at his funeral.

Dinas Emlinn, lament; for the moment is nigh,
When mute in the woodlands thine echoes shall die:
No more by sweet Teivi Cadwallon shall rave,
And mix his wild notes with the wild dashing wave.

In spring and in autumn thy glories of shade,   5
Unhonoured shall flourish, unhonoured shall fade;
For soon shall be lifeless the eye and the tongue,
That viewed them with rapture, with rapture that sung.

Thy sons, Dinas Emlinn, may march in their pride,
And chase the proud Saxon from Prestatyn's side;   10
But where is the harp shall give life to their name?
And where is the bard shall give heroes their fame?

And Oh, Dinas Emlinn! thy daughters so fair,
Who heave the white bosom, and wave the dark hair;
What tuneful enthusiast shall worship their eye,   15
When half of their charms with Cadwallon shall die?

Then adieu, silver Teivi! I quit thy loved scene,
To join the dim choir of the bards who have been;
With Lewarch, and Meilor, and Merlin the old,
And sage Taliessin, high harping to hold.   20

And adieu, Dinas Emlinn! still green be thy shades,
Unconquered thy warriors, and matchless thy maids!
And thou, whose faint warblings my weakness can tell,
Farewell, my loved Harp! my last treasure, farewell!

53

𝕿𝖍𝖊 𝕭𝖆𝖗𝖉'𝖘 𝕴𝖓𝖈𝖆𝖓𝖙𝖆𝖙𝖎𝖔𝖓*

The Forest of Glenmore is drear,
    It is all of black pine, and the dark oak-tree;
And the midnight wind, to the mountain deer,
    Is whistling the forest-lullaby:—
The moon looks through the drifting storm,   5
But the troubled lake reflects not her form,
For the waves roll whitening to the land,
And dash against the shelvy strand.

There is a voice among the trees
    That mingles with the groaning oak—   10
That mingles with the stormy breeze,
    And the lake-waves dashing against the rock;—
There is a voice within the wood,
The voice of the Bard in fitful mood,
His song was louder than the blast,   15
As the Bard of Glenmore through the forest past.

* Written under the threat of invasion, in the autumn of 1804.

"Wake ye from your sleep of death,
  Minstrels and Bards of other days!
For the midnight wind is on the heath,
  And the midnight meteors dimly blaze;   20
The spectre with his bloody hand,*
Is wandering through the wild woodland;
The owl and the raven are mute for dread,
And the time is meet to awake the dead!

"Souls of the mighty! wake and say,   25
  To what high strain your harps were strung,
When Lochlin ploughed her billowy way,
  And on your shores her Norsemen flung?
Her Norsemen, trained to spoil and blood,
Skilled to prepare the raven's food,   30
All by your harpings doom'd to die
On bloody Largs and Loncarty.†

"Mute are ye all? No murmurs strange
  Upon the midnight breeze sail by;
Nor through the pines with whistling change,   35
  Mimic the harp's wild harmony!
Mute are ye now?—Ye ne'er were mute,
When Murder with his bloody foot,
And Rapine with his iron hand,
Were hovering near your mountain strand.   40

"O yet awake the strain to tell,
  By every deed in song enroll'd,
By every chief who fought or fell,
  For Albion's weal in battle bold;—
From Coilgach,‡ first who roll'd his car   45
Through the deep ranks of Roman war,
To him, of veteran memory dear,
Who victor died on Aboukir.

* The forest of Glenmore is haunted by a spirit called Lhamdearg, or Red-hand.
† Where the Norwegian invader of Scotland received two bloody defeats.
‡ The Galgacus of Tacitus.

"By all their swords, by all their scars,
 By all their names, a mighty spell!   50
By all their wounds, by all their wars,
 Arise, the mighty strain to tell;
For fiercer than fierce Hengist's strain,
More impious than the heathen Dane,
More grasping than all-grasping Rome,   55
Gaul's ravening legions hither come!"—

The wind is hush'd, and still the lake—
 Strange murmurs fill my tingling ears,
Bristles my hair, my sinews quake,
 At the dread voice of other years—   60
"When targets clash'd, and bugles rung,
And blades round warriors' heads were flung,
The foremost of the band were we,
And hymn'd the joys of Liberty!"

54
The Maid of Toro

O, low shone the sun on the fair lake of Toro,
 And weak were the whispers that waved the dark wood,
All as a fair maiden, bewildered in sorrow,
 Sorely sighed to the breezes, and wept to the flood.
"O, saints! from the mansions of bliss lowly bending; 5
 Sweet Virgin! who hearest the suppliant's cry;
Now grant my petition, in anguish ascending,
 My Henry restore, or let Eleanor die!"

All distant and faint were the sounds of the battle,
　　With the breezes they rise, with the breezes they fail,
Till the shout, and the groan, and the conflict's dread rattle,
　　And the chace's wild clamour, came loading the gale.
Breathless she gazed on the woodlands so dreary:
　　Slowly approaching a warrior was seen;
Life's ebbing tide marked his footsteps so weary,   15
　　Cleft was his helmet, and woe was his mien.

"O, save thee, fair maid, for our armies are flying!
　　O, save thee, fair maid, for thy guardian is low!
Deadly cold on yon heath thy brave Henry is lying;
　　And fast through the woodland approaches the foe."—
Scarce could he faulter the tidings of sorrow,
　　And scarce could she hear them, benumbed with despair:
And when the sun sunk on the sweet lake of Toro,
　　Forever he set to the Brave, and the Fair.

55

Hellvellyn

In the spring of 1805, a young gentleman of talents, and of a most amiable disposition, perished by losing his way on the mountain Hellvellyn. His remains were not discovered till three months afterwards, when they were found guarded by a faithful terrier-bitch, his constant attendant during frequent solitary rambles through the wilds of Cumberland and Westmoreland.

I climbed the dark brow of the mighty Hellvellyn,
    Lakes and mountains beneath me gleamed misty and wide;
All was still, save by fits when the eagle was yelling,
    And starting around me the echoes replied.
On the right Striden-edge round the Red-tarn was bending,   5
And Catchedicam its left verge was defending,
One huge nameless rock in the front was ascending,
    When I marked the sad spot where the wanderer had died.

Dark green was that spot mid the brown mountain-heather,
    Where the Pilgrim of Nature lay stretched in decay;   10
Like the corpse of an outcast abandoned to weather,
    Till the mountain-winds wasted the tenantless clay.
Nor yet quite deserted, though lonely extended,
For, faithful in death, his mute favourite attended,
The much-loved remains of her master defended,   15
    And chased the hill-fox and the raven away.

How long didst thou think that his silence was slumber!
    When the wind waved his garment, how oft didst thou start!
How many long days and long weeks didst thou number,
    Ere he faded before thee, the friend of thy heart!   20
And, Oh! was it meet, that,—no requiem read o'er him,
No mother to weep, and no friend to deplore him,
And thou, little guardian, alone stretched before him,—
    Unhonoured the Pilgrim from life should depart?

When a Prince to the fate of the Peasant has yielded,   25
    The tapestry waves dark round the dim-lighted hall;
With scutcheons of silver the coffin is shielded,
    And pages stand mute by the canopied pall:
Through the courts, at deep midnight, the torches are
                    gleaming;
In the proudly-arched chapel the banners are beaming;   30
Far adown the long aisle sacred music is streaming,
    Lamenting a Chief of the People should fall.

But meeter for thee, gentle Lover of Nature,
    To lay down thy head like the meek mountain lamb;
When, wildered, he drops from some cliff huge in stature,   35
    And draws his last sob by the side of his dam.
And more stately thy couch by this desart lake lying,
Thy obsequies sung by the grey plover flying,
With one faithful friend but to witness thy dying,
    In the arms of Hellvellyn and Catchedicam.   40

56

𝔄 𝔥𝔢𝔞𝔩𝔱𝔥 𝔱𝔬 𝔏𝔬𝔯𝔡 𝔐𝔢𝔩𝔟𝔦𝔩𝔩𝔢

Being an Excellent New Song

Were they not forced with those that should be ours,
We might have met them dareful, beard to beard,
And beat them backwards home.

SHAKESPEARE

Air—*Carrickfergus*

Since here we are set in array round the table,
    Five hundred good fellows well met in a hall;
Come listen, brave boys, and I'll sing as I'm able,
    How Innocence triumph'd, and Pride got a fall.
        But push round the claret;   5
        Come, stewards, don't spare it,
With rapture you'll drink to the toasts that I give;
        Here, boys,
        Off with it merrily,
MELVILLE for ever, and long may he live.   10

What were the Whigs doing, what measures pursuing,
    When PITT quelled Rebellion, gave Treason a string?
Why, they swore on their honour for ARTHUR O'CONNOR,
    And fought hard for DESPARD, against country and King.
        Well then we knew, boys,   15
        PITT and MELVILLE were true boys,
And the tempest was raised by the friends of reform.
        Ah, woe!
        Weep for his memory,
Low lies the Pilot that weather'd the storm.   20

And pray don't you mind when the Blues first were raising,
  And we scarcely could think the house safe o'er our head,
When villains and coxcombs, French politics praising,
  Drove peace from our tables, and sleep from our bed;
      Our hearts they grew bolder,   25
      When, musket on shoulder,
Stepp'd forth our old Statesman example to give,
      Come, boys, never fear,
      Drink the Blue Grenadier,—
Here's to old Harry, and long may he live.   30

They would turn us adrift; though rely, Sir, upon it,
  Our own faithful chronicles warrant us that
The free mountaineer, and his bonny blue bonnet
  Have oft gone as far as the regular's hat.
      We laugh at their taunting,   35
      For all we are wanting,
Is license our life for our country to give.
      Off with it merrily;
      Horse, foot, and artillery,—
Each Loyal Volunteer, long may he live.   40

'Tis not us alone, boys—the Army and Navy,
  Have each got a slap 'mid their politic pranks;
CORNWALLIS cashier'd, that watch'd winters to save ye,
  And the Cape call'd a bauble, unworthy of thanks.
      But vain is their taunt,   45
      No Soldier shall want
The thanks that his Country to valour can give;
      Come, boys,
      Drink it off merrily,—
SIR DAVID and POPHAM, and long may they live.   50

And then our revenue, Lord knows how they view'd it!
   While each *petty* Statesman talk'd lofty and big;
But the Beer-tax was weak, as if W—— had brew'd it,
   And the Pig-iron duty, a shame to a pig:
      In vain is their vaunting,   55
      Too surely there's wanting,
What judgment, experience, and steadiness give;
      Come, boys,
      Drink about merrily,——
Health to sage MELVILLE, and long may he live.   60

Our King too,—our Princess,—I dare not say more, Sir,—
   May Providence watch them with mercy and might;
While there's one Scottish hand, that can wag a claymore, Sir,
   They shall ne'er want a friend to stand up for their right.
      Be damn'd he that dare not,   65
      For my part, I'll spare not,
To beauty afflicted, a tribute to give;
      Fill it up steadily,
      Drink it off readily,——
Here's to the Princess, and long may she live.   70

And since we must not set Auld Reekie in glory,
   And make her brown visage as light as her heart;
Till each man illumine his own upper story,
   Nor law-book, nor lawyer, shall force us to part;
      In G—LLE and SP—R,   75
      And some few good men, Sir,
High talents we honour, slight difference forgive;
      But the Brewer we'll hoax,
      Tallyho to the Fox,
And drink MELVILLE for ever as long as we live.   80

57

The Lawyer and the Archbishop of Canterbury

Come listen, brave boys, to a story so merry,
  'Tis of the Archbishop of fair Canterbury;
How the Mitre did keep the full bottom in awe,
  And the Gospel taught manners and justice to Law.
                      Derry down.   5

A great Lawyer rose up in a very great hall,
  Some call'd him Chief Justice, some Law did him call,
But neither like law nor like justice spoke he,
  But some foul-mouth'd attorney who rail'd for a fee.
                      Derry down.   10

Then up rose that Prelate so rev'rend and wise,
  And expressed to their Lordships regret and surprise;
You should ne'er, ere you try folks, hang, quarter, or draw,
  Said the head of the Church to the head of the Law.
                      Derry down.   15

Now Lauderdale gaz'd on Law's tablet of brass,
  And astonish'd beheld him sit mute like an ass;
Quoth his Lordship, "next day he'll reply and content us,"
  But from thenceforth the Lawyer was *Non est inventus.*
                      Derry down.   20

Whitbread's lost all his *hops* of conviction, we hear,
  But got plenty of wormwood to bitter his beer;
For when the plump question by Plumer was put,
  The brewer rung hollow, and proved a mere butt.
                      Derry down.   25

The party now find themselves in the wrong box,
  Though they thanked the Committee and voted with
                Fox,
They've found out the difference twixt merit and jaw,
  And the damnable odds betwixt Justice and Law.
                      Derry down.   30

Then here's to the health of that Prelate of fame,
  Tho' true Presbyterians, we'll drink to his name;
Long, long may he live, to teach prejudice awe,
  And since Melville's got justice, the devil take Law.

Derry down.   35

58

The Monks of Bangor's March

Air—Ymdaith Mwnge

ETHELFRID, or OLFRID, King of Northumberland, having besieged
Chester in 613, and BROCKMAEL, a British prince, advancing to relieve
it, the Religious of the neighbouring monastery of Bangor marched in
procession to pray for the success of their countrymen. But the British
being totally defeated, the heathen victor put the monks to the sword,
and destroyed their monastery. The tune to which these verses are
adapted, is called the Monks' March, and is supposed to have been
played at their ill-omened procession.

When the heathen trumpets clang
Round beleaguered Chester rang,
Veiled nun and friar grey
March'd from Bangor's fair abbaye:
High their holy anthem sounds,   5
Cestria's vale the hymn rebounds,
Floating down the sylvan Dee,
  O miserere Domine!

On, the long procession goes,
Glory round their crosses glows,   10
And the Virgin-mother mild
In their peaceful banner smiled;
Who could think such saintly band
Doom'd to feel unhallow'd hand?
Such was the divine decree,   15
  O miserere Domine!

Bands that masses only sung,
Hands that censers only swung,
Met the northern bow and bill,
Heard the war–cry, wild and shrill: 20
Woe to Brockmael's feeble hand,
Woe to Olfrid's bloody brand,
Woe to Saxon cruelty,
    O miserere Domine!

Weltering amid warriors slain,   25
Spurned by steeds with bloody mane,
Slaughter'd down by heathen blade,
Bangor's peaceful monks are laid:
Word of parting rest unspoke,
Mass unsung, and bread unbroke;   30
For their souls for charity
    Sing, *miserere Domine!*

Bangor! o'er the murder wail,
Long thy ruins told the tale,
Shatter'd tower and broken arch   35
Long recall'd the woeful march:[*]
On thy shrine no tapers burn,
Never shall thy priests return;
The pilgrim sighs and sings for thee,
    O miserere Domine!   40

---

[*] WILLIAM of MALMESBURY says, that in his time the extent of the ruins of the monastery bore ample witness to the desolation occasioned by the massacre;— "tot semiruti parietes ecclesiarum, tot anfractus porticuum, tanta turba ruderum quantum vix alibi cernas."

59

On Ettrick Forest's Mountains Dun

Air—*I Canna Come Ilka Day to Woo*

The following song was written after a week's shooting and fishing, in which the Poet had been engaged with some friends.

On Ettrick Forest's mountains dun,
'Tis blythe to bear the sportsman's gun,
And seek the heath-frequenting brood
Far through the noon day solitude;
By many a cairn and trenched mound,   5
Where chiefs of yore sleep lone and sound,
And springs, where grey-hair'd shepherds tell,
That still the Fairies love to dwell.

Along the silver streams of Tweed,
'Tis blythe the mimic fly to lead,   10
When to the hook the salmon springs,
And the line whistles through the rings;
The boiling eddy see him try,
Then dashing from the current high,
'Till watchful eye and cautious hand   15
Have led his wasted strength to land.

'Tis blythe along the midnight tide,
With stalwart arm the boat to guide;
On high the dazz'ling blaze to rear,
And heedful plunge the barbed spear;   20
Rock, wood, and scaur, emerging bright,
Fling on the stream their ruddy light,
And from the bank our band appears
Like Genii, armed with fiery spears.

'Tis blythe at eve to tell the tale   25
How we succeed, and how we fail,
Whether at ALWYN's* lordly meal,
Or lowlier board of Ashesteel;†
While the gay tapers cheerly shine,
Bickers the fire, and flows the wine,—   30
Days free from thought and nights from care,
My blessing on the Forest fair.

60
The Palmer

"O open the door, some pity to shew,
    Keen blows the northern wind;
The glen is white with the drifted snow,
    And the path is hard to find.

"No Outlaw seeks your castle gate,   5
    From chasing the king's deer,
Though even an Outlaw's wretched state
    Might claim compassion here.

"A weary Palmer, worn and weak,
    I wander for my sin;   10
O open for Our Lady's sake,
    A pilgrim's blessing win!

"I'll give you pardons from the pope,
    And reliques from o'er the sea,—
Or if for these you will not ope,   15
    Yet open for charity.

---

* *Alwyn*, the seat of Lord Somerville.
† *Ashesteel*, the Poet's residence at the time.

"The hare is crouching in her form,
   The hart beside the hind;
An aged man, amid the storm,
   No shelter can I find.   20

"You hear the Ettrick's sullen roar,
   Dark, deep, and strong is he,
And I must ford the Ettrick o'er,
   Unless you pity me.

"The iron gate is bolted hard,   25
   At which I knock in vain;
The owner's heart is closer barr'd,
   Who hears me thus complain.

"Farewell, farewell! and Mary grant,
   When old and frail you be,   30
You never may the shelter want,
   That's now denied to me."

The Ranger on his couch lay warm,
   And heard him plead in vain;
But oft amid December's storm,   35
   He'll hear that voice again:

For lo, when through the vapours dank,
   Morn shone on Ettrick fair,
A corpse amid the alders rank,
   The Palmer welter'd there.   40

61

Wandering Willie

All joy was bereft me the day that you left me,
  And climbed the tall vessel to sail yon wide sea;
O weary betide it! I wandered beside it,
  And banned it for parting my Willie and me.

Far o'er the wave hast thou followed thy fortune;   5
  Oft fought the squadrons of France and of Spain;
Ae kiss of welcome's worth twenty at parting,
  Now I hae gotten my Willie again.

When the sky it was mirk, and the winds they were wailing,
  I sate on the beach wi' the tear in my ee,
And thought o' the bark where my Willie was sailing,
  And wished that the tempest could a' blaw on me.

Now that thy gallant ship rides at her mooring,
  Now that my wanderer's in safety at hame,
Music to me were the wildest winds roaring,   15
  That ere o'er Inch Keith drove the dark ocean faem.

When the lights they did blaze, and the guns they did rattle,
  And blithe was each heart for the great victory,
In secret I wept for the dangers of battle,
  And thy glory itself was scarce comfort to me.   20

But now shalt thou tell, while I eagerly listen,
  Of each bold adventure, and every brave scar:
And, trust me, I'll smile, though my een they may glisten;
  For sweet after danger's the tale of the war.

And Oh how we doubt when there's distance 'tween lovers,
  When there's naething to speak to the heart thro' the e'e;
How often the kindest, and warmest, prove rovers,
  And the love of the faithfullest ebbs like the sea.

Till, at times, could I help it? I pined and I pondered
    If love could change notes like the bird on the tree—   30
Now I'll ne'er ask if thine eyes may hae wandered,
    Enough, thy leal heart has been constant to me.

Welcome, from sweeping o'er sea and through channel,
    Hardships and danger despising for fame,
Furnishing story for glory's bright annal,   35
    Welcome, my wanderer, to Jeanie and hame.

Enough now thy story in annals of glory
    Has humbled the pride of France, Holland, and Spain;
No more shalt thou grieve me, no more shalt thou leave me,
    I never will part with my Willie again.

62

The Maid of Neidpath

There is a tradition in Tweeddale, that, when Neidpath Castle, near
Peebles, was inhabited by the Earls of March, a mutual passion sub-
sisted between a daughter of that noble family, and a son of the laird of
Tushielaw, in Ettricke Forest. As the alliance was thought unsuitable
by her parents, the young man went abroad. During his absence, the
lady fell into a consumption; and at length, as the only means of saving
her life, her father consented, that her lover should be recalled. On
the day when he was expected to pass through Peebles, on the road to
Tushielaw, the young lady, though much exhausted, caused herself to
be carried to the balcony of a house in Peebles, belonging to the family,
that she might see him as he rode past. Her anxiety and eagerness
gave such force to her organs, that she is said to have distinguished his
horse's footsteps at an incredible distance. But Tushielaw, unprepared
for the change in her appearance, and not expecting to see her in that
place, rode on, without recognizing her, or even slackening his pace.
The lady was unable to support the shock, and, after a short struggle,
died in the arms of her attendants. There is an incident similar to this
traditional tale in Count Hamilton's "Fleur d'Épine".

O lovers' eyes are sharp to see,
 And lovers' ears in hearing;
And love, in life's extremity,
 Can lend an hour of cheering.
Disease had been in Mary's bower,   5
 And slow decay from mourning,
Though now she sits on Neidpath's tower,
 To watch her love's returning.

All sunk and dim her eyes so bright,
 Her form decayed by pining,   10
Till through her wasted hand, at night,
 You saw the taper shining;
By fits, a sultry hectic hue
 Across her cheek was flying;
By fits, so ashy pale she grew,   15
 Her maidens thought her dying.

Yet keenest powers, to see and hear,
 Seemed in her frame residing;
Before the watch-dog pricked his ear,
 She heard her lover's riding;   20
Ere scarce a distant form was ken'd,
 She knew, and waved, to greet him;
And o'er the battlement did bend,
 As on the wing to meet him.

He came—he passed—an heedless gaze, 25
 As o'er some stranger glancing,
Her welcome spoke, in faultering phrase,
 Lost in his courser's prancing—
The castle arch, whose hollow tone
 Returns each whisper spoken,   30
Could scarcely catch the feeble moan,
 Which told her heart was broken.

63

Address Written for Miss Smith

When the lone pilgrim views afar
The shrine that is his guiding star,
With awe his footsteps print the road
Which the loved saint of yore has trod.
As near he draws, and yet more near,   5
His dim eye sparkles with a tear;
The Gothic fane's unwonted show,
The choral hymn, the taper's glow,
Oppress his soul; while they delight,
And chasten rapture with affright.   10
No longer dare he think his toil
Can merit aught his patron's smile;
Too light appears the distant way,
The chilly eve, the sultry day—
All these endured no favour claim,   15
But, murmuring forth the sainted name,
He lays his little offering down,
And only deprecates a frown.

  We too who ply the Thespian art
Oft feel such bodings of the heart,   20
And, when our utmost powers are strained,
Dare hardly hope your favour gained.
She, who from sister climes has sought
The ancient land where Wallace fought—
Land long renowned for arms and arts,   25
And conquering eyes, and dauntless hearts—

She, as the flutterings *here* avow,
Feels all the pilgrim's terrors *now*;
Yet sure on Caledonian plain
The stranger never sued in vain.   30
'Tis yours the hospitable task
To give the applause she dare not ask;
And they who bid the pilgrim speed,
The pilgrim's blessing be their meed!

64
Hunting Song

Waken lords and ladies gay,
On the mountain dawns the day,
All the jolly chace is here,
With hawk and horse, and hunting spear;
Hounds are in their couples yelling,   5
Hawks are whistling, horns are knelling,
Merrily, merrily, mingle they,
"Waken lords and ladies gay."

Waken lords and ladies gay,
The mist has left the mountain gray,   10
Springlets in the dawn are streaming,
Diamonds on the brake are gleaming;
And foresters have busy been,
To track the buck in thicket green;
Now we come to chaunt our lay,   15
"Waken lords and ladies gay."

Waken lords and ladies gay,
To the green wood haste away;
We can shew you where he lies,
Fleet of foot, and tall of size,   20
We can shew the marks he made,
When 'gainst the oak his antlers frayed;
You shall see him brought to bay,
"Waken lords and ladies gay."

Louder, louder chaunt the lay,   25
Waken lords and ladies gay!
Tell them youth and mirth and glee,
Run a course as well as we;
Time, stern huntsman! who can baulk,
Staunch as hound, and fleet as hawk;   30
Think of this, and rise with day,
Gentle lords and ladies gay.

65

War-Song of Lachlan, High Chief of Maclean

From the Gaelic

This song appears to be imperfect, or at least, like many of the early Gaelic poems, makes a rapid transition from one subject to another; from the situation, namely, of one of the daughters of the clan, who opens the song by lamenting the absence of her lover, to a eulogium over the military glories of the Chieftain. The translator has endeavoured to imitate the abrupt style of the original.

A weary month has wander'd o'er
Since last we parted on the shore;
Heaven! that I saw thee, Love, once more,
    Safe on that shore again!—
'Twas valiant Lachlan gave the word;   5
Lachlan, of many a galley lord:
He call'd his kindred bands on board,
    And launch'd them on the main.

Clan-Gillian* is to ocean gone;
Clan-Gillian, fierce in foray known;   10
Rejoicing in the glory won
    In many a bloody broil:
For wide is heard the thundering fray,
The rout, the ruin, the dismay,
When from the twilight glens away   15
    Clan-Gillian drives the spoil.

Woe to the hills that shall rebound
Our banner'd bag-pipes' maddening sound;
Clan-Gillian's onset echoing round,
    Shall shake their inmost cell.   20
Woe to the bark whose crew shall gaze,
Where Lachlan's silken streamer plays;
The fools might face the lightning's blaze
    As wisely and as well!

* i.e. The clan of Maclean, literally the race of Gillian.

66

Prologue to *The Family Legend*

'Tis sweet to hear expiring summer's sigh,
Through forests tinged with russet, wail and die;
'Tis sweet and sad the latest notes to hear
Of distant music, dying on the ear;
But far more sadly sweet, on foreign strand,   5
We list the legends of our native land,
Linked as they come with every tender tie,
Memorials dear of youth and infancy.
   Chief, thy wild tales, romantic Caledon,
Wake keen remembrance in each hardy son;   10
Whether on India's burning coasts he toil,
Or till Acadia's* winter-fettered soil,
He hears with throbbing heart and moisten'd eyes,
And as he hears, what dear illusions rise!
It opens on his soul his native dell,   15
The woods wild-waving, and the water's swell,
Tradition's theme, the tower that threats the plain,
The mossy cairn that hides the hero slain;
The cot, beneath whose simple porch were told
By grey-hair'd patriarch, the tales of old,   20
The infant groupe that hush'd their sports the while,
And the dear maid who listen'd with a smile.
The wanderer, while the vision warms his brain,
Is denizen of Scotland once again.
   Are such keen feelings to the crowd confined,   25
And sleep they in the poet's gifted mind?
Oh no! For She, within whose mighty page
Each tyrant Passion shows his woe and rage,
Has felt the wizard influence they inspire,
And to your own traditions tuned her lyre.   30
Yourselves shall judge—whoe'er has raised the sail
By Mull's dark coast, has heard this evening's tale.

---

* Acadia, or Nova Scotia.

The plaided boatman, resting on his oar,
Points to the fatal rock amid the roar
Of whitening waves, and tells whate'er to-night   35
Our humble stage shall offer to your sight;
Proudly preferr'd, that first our efforts give
Scenes glowing from her pen to breathe and live;
More proudly yet, should Caledon approve
The filial token of a daughter's love.   40

67

Lines Addressed to Ranald Macdonald, Esq., of Staffa

Staffa! sprung from high Macdonald,
Worthy branch of old Clan-Ranald.
Staffa! king of all kind fellows,
Well befall thy hills and valleys,
Lakes and inlets, deeps and shallows,   5
Cliffs of darkness, caves of wonder,
Echoing the Atlantic's thunder;
Mountains which the grey mist covers,
Where the chieftain spirit hovers,
Pausing while his pinions quiver,   10
Stretch'd to quit our land for ever.
    Each kind influence reign above thee,
All thou lov'st, and all that love thee.
Warmer heart, 'twixt this and Jaffa,
Beats not than in the breast of Staffa.   15

68

The Battle of Sempach

SIR,

The verses inclosed are a literal translation of an ancient Swiss ballad upon the battle of Sempach, fought 9th July 1386, the victory by which the Swiss cantons established their independence. The author, Albert Tchudi, denominated the Souter, from his profession of a shoemaker. He was a citizen of Lucerne, esteemed highly among his countrymen, both for his powers as a *Meistersinger* or minstrel, and his courage as a soldier; so that he might share the praise conferred by Collins on Eschylus, that—

> Not alone he nursed the poet's flame,
> But reached from Virtue's hand the patriot steel.

The circumstance of their being written by a poet returning from the well-fought field he describes, and in which his country's fortune was secured, may confer on Tchudi's verses an interest which they are not entitled to claim from their poetical merit. But ballad poetry, the more literally it is translated, the more it loses its simplicity, without acquiring either grace or strength; and therefore some part of the faults of the verses must be imputed to the translator's feeling it a duty to keep as closely as possible to his original. The various puns, rude attempts at pleasantry, and disproportioned episodes, must be set down to Tchudi's account, or to the taste of his age.

The military antiquary will derive some amusement from the minute particulars which the martial poet has recorded. The mode in which the Austrian men-at-arms received the charge of the Swiss, was by forming a phalanx, which they defended with their long lances. The gallant Winkelried, who sacrificed his own life by rushing among the spears, clasping in his arms as many as he could grasp, and thus opening a gap in these iron battalions, is celebrated in Swiss history. When fairly mingled together, the unwieldy length of their weapons, and cumbrous weight of their defensive armour, rendered the Austrian gentry a very unequal match for the light-armed mountaineers. The victories obtained by the Swiss over the German men-at-arms, hitherto deemed as formidable on foot as on horseback, led to important changes in the art of war. The poet describes the Austrian knights and squires as cutting the peaks from their boots ere they could act upon foot, in allusion to an inconvenient piece of foppery, often mentioned in the middle ages. Leopold III. Arch-duke of Austria, called "The handsome man-at-arms," was slain in the battle of Sempach, with the flower of his chivalry.

'Twas when among our linden trees
The bees had housed in swarms;
And grey-hair'd peasants say that these
Betoken foreign arms.

Then look'd we down to Willisow,   5
The land was all in flame;
We knew the Archduke Leopold
With all his army came.

The Austrian nobles made their vow,
So hot their heart and bold,   10
"On Switzer carles we'll trample now,
And slay both young and old."

With clarion loud, and banner proud,
From Zurich on the lake,
In martial pomp and fair array,   15
Their onward march they make.

"Now list, ye lowland nobles all,
Ye seek the mountain strand,
Nor wot ye what shall be your lot
In such a dangerous land.   20

"I rede ye, shrive you of your sins,
Before you further go;
A skirmish in Helvetian hills
May send your souls to woe."

"But where now shall we find a priest   25
Our shrift that he may hear?"
"The Switzer priest* has ta'en the field,
He gives a penance drear.

"Right heavily upon your head
He'll lay his hand of steel;   30
And with his trusty partizan
Your absolution deal."

---

* All the Swiss clergy who were able to bear arms fought in this patriotic war.

'Twas on a Monday morning then,
The corn was steep'd in dew,
And merry maids had sickles ta'en,   35
When the host to Sempach drew.

The stalwart men of fair Lucerne
Together have they join'd;
The pith and core of manhood stern
Was none cast looks behind.   40

It was the Lord of Hare-castle,
And to the Duke he said,
"Yon little band of brethren true
Will meet us undismay'd."

"O Hare-castle,* thou heart of hare!"   45
Fierce Oxenstern replied,
"Shalt see then how the game will fare,"
The taunted knight replied.

There was lacing then of helmets bright,
And closing ranks amain;   50
The peaks they hew'd from their boot-points
Might well nigh load a wain.†

And thus, they to each other said,
"Yon handful down to hew
Will be no boastful tale to tell,   55
The peasants are so few."

* In the original, *Haasenstein*, or *Harestone*.
† This seems to allude to the preposterous fashion, during the middle ages, of
wearing boots with the points or peaks turned upwards, and so long, that in
some cases they were fastened to the knees of the wearer with small chains.
When they alighted to fight upon foot, it would seem that the Austrian
gentlemen found it necessary to cut off these peaks, that they might move with
the necessary activity.

The gallant Swiss Confederates there,
They pray'd to God aloud,
And he display'd his rainbow fair
Against a swarthy cloud.   60

Then heart and pulse throbb'd more and more
With courage firm and high,
And down the good Confed'rates bore
On the Austrian chivalry.

The Austrian Lion* 'gan to growl,   65
And toss his mane and tail;
And ball, and shaft, and cross-bow bolt,
Went whistling forth like hail.

Lance, pike, and halberd, mingled there,
The game was nothing sweet;   70
The boughs of many a stately tree
Lay shiver'd at their feet.

The Austrian men-at-arms stood fast,
So close their spears they laid;
It chafed the gallant Winkelried,   75
Who to his comrades said—

"I have a virtuous wife at home,
A wife and infant son;
I leave them to my country's care,—
This field shall soon be won.   80

"These nobles lay their spears right thick,
And keep full firm array,
Yet shall my charge their order break,
And make my brethren way."

* A pun on the Archduke's name, Leopold.

He rushed against the Austrian band,   85
In desperate career,
And with his body, breast, and hand,
Bore down each hostile spear.

Four lances splintered on his crest,
Six shivered in his side;   90
Still on the serried files he press'd—
He broke their ranks, and died.

This patriot's self-devoted deed,
First tamed the Lion's mood,
And the four forest cantons freed   95
From thraldom by his blood.

Right where his charge had made a lane,
His valiant comrades burst,
With sword, and axe, and partizan,
And hack, and stab, and thrust.   100

The daunted Lion 'gan to whine,
And granted ground amain,
The Mountain Bull,* he bent his brows,
And gored his sides again.

Then lost was banner, spear, and shield,   105
At Sempach in the flight,
The cloister vaults at König's field
Hold many an Austrian knight.

It was the Archduke Leopold,
So lordly would he ride,   110
But he came against the Switzer churls,
And they slew him in his pride.

The heifer said unto the bull,
"And shall I not complain;
There came a foreign nobleman   115
To milk me on the plain.

---

* A pun on the Urus, or wild bull, which gives name to the canton of Uri.

"One thrust of thine outrageous horn
Has gall'd the knight so sore,
That to the churchyard he is borne,
To rule our glens no more."   120

An Austrian noble left the stour,
And fast the flight 'gan take;
And he arrived in luckless hour
At Sempach on the lake.

He and his squire a fisher call'd,   125
(His name was Hans Von Rot)
"For love, or meed, or charity,
Receive us in thy boat."

Their anxious call the fisher heard,
And, glad the meed to win,   130
His shallop to the shore he steer'd,
And took the flyers in.

And while against the tide and wind
Hans stoutly row'd his way,
The noble to his follower sign'd   135
He should the boatman slay.

The fisher's back was to them turn'd,
The squire his dagger drew,
Hans saw his shadow in the lake,
The boat he overthrew.   140

He 'whelm'd the boat, and as they strove,
He stunn'd them with his oar,
"Now, drink ye deep my gentle sirs,
You'll ne'er stab boatman more.

"Two gilded fishes in the lake   145
This morning have I caught,
Their silver scales may much avail,
Their carrion flesh is naught."

It was a messenger of woe
Has sought the Austrian land;   150
"Ah! gracious lady, evil news!
My lord lies on the strand.

"At Sempach, on the battle field,
His bloody corpse lies there:"
"Ah gracious God!" the lady cried,   155
"What tidings of despair!"

Now would you know the minstrel wight,
Who sings of strife so stern,
Albert the Souter is he hight,
A burgher of Lucerne.   160

A merry man was he, I wot,
The night he made the lay,
Returning from the bloody spot,
Where God had judged the day.

69

The Poacher

Welcome, grave stranger, to our green retreats,
Where health with exercise and freedom meets!
Thrice welcome, sage, whose philosophic plan
By Nature's limits metes the rights of man;
Generous as he, who now for freedom bawls,   5
Now gives full value for true Indian shawls;
O'er court and custom-house, his shoe who flings,
Now bilks excisemen, and now bullies kings!
Like his, I ween, thy comprehensive mind
Holds laws as mouse-traps baited for mankind;   10
Thine eye, applausive, each sly vermin sees,
That baulks the snare, yet battens on the cheese;

Thine ear has heard, with scorn instead of awe,
Our buckskin'd justices expound the law,
Wire-draw the acts that fix for wires the pain,   15
And for the netted partridge noose the swain;
And thy vindictive arm would fain have broke
The last light fetter of the feudal yoke,
To give the denizens of wood and wild,
Nature's free race, to each her free-born child.
Hence hast thou marked, with grief, fair London's race
Mock'd with the boon of one poor Easter chace,
And long'd to send them forth as free as when
Pour'd o'er Chantilly the Parisian train,
When musquet, pistol, blunderbuss, combined,   25
And scarce the field-pieces were left behind!
A squadron's charge each leveret's heart dismayed,
On every covey fired a bold brigade—
La Douce Humanité approved the sport,
For great the alarm indeed, yet small the hurt.   30
Shouts patriotic solemnized the day,
And Seine re-echoed *vive la liberté!*
But mad *Citoyen*, meek *Monsieur* again,
With some few added links resumes his chain;
Then, since such scenes to France no more are known,
Come, view with me a hero of thine own!
One, whose free actions vindicate the cause
Of sylvan liberty o'er feudal laws.

    Seek we yon glades, where the proud oak o'ertops
Wide waving seas of birch and hazel copse,   40
Leaving between deserted isles of land,
Where stunted heath is patch'd with ruddy sand;
And lonely on the waste the yew is seen,
Or straggling hollies spread a brighter green.
Here, little-worn, and winding dark and steep,   45
Our scarce mark'd path descends yon dingle deep:
Follow—but heedful, cautious of a trip,
In earthly mire philosophy may slip.

Step slow and wary o'er that swampy stream,
Till, guided by the charcoal's smothering steam,   50
We reach the frail yet barricaded door
Of hovel formed for poorest of the poor;
No hearth the fire, no vent the smoke receives,
The walls are wattles, and the covering leaves;
For, if such hut, our forest statutes say,   55
Rise in the progress of one night and day;
Though placed where still the Conqueror's hests
        o'erawe,
And his son's stirrup shines the badge of law;
The builder claims the unenviable boon,
To tenant dwelling, framed as slight and soon   60
As wigwam wild, that shrouds the native frore
On the bleak coast of frost-barr'd Labrador.*

Approach, and through the unlatticed window peep—
Nay, shrink not back, the inmate is asleep;
Sunk mid yon sordid blankets, till the sun   65
Stoop to the west, the plunderer's toils are done.
Loaded and primed, and prompt for desperate hand,
Rifle and fowling-piece beside him stand,
While round the hut are in disorder laid
The tools and booty of his lawless trade;   70
For force or fraud, resistance or escape,
The crow, the saw, the bludgeon, and the crape.
His pilfered powder in yon nook he hoards,
And the filch'd lead the church's roof affords—
(Hence shall the rector's congregation fret,   75
That, while his sermon's dry, his walls are wet.)
The fish-spear barb'd, the sweeping net are there,
Doe-hides, and pheasant-plumes, and skins of hare,
Cordage for toils, and wiring for the snare;

* Such is the law in the New Forest, Hampshire, tending greatly to increase the various settlements of thieves, smugglers, and deer-stealers, who infest it. In the forest courts the presiding judge wears as a badge of office an antique stirrup, said to have been that of William Rufus. See Mr William Rose's spirited poem, entitled "The Red King."

Barter'd for game from chace or warren won,
Yon cask holds moonlight,* run when moon was none;
And late snatch'd spoils lie stow'd in hutch apart,
To wait the associate higgler's evening cart.

Look on his pallet foul, and mark his rest:
What scenes perturb'd are acting in his breast!   85
His sable brow is wet and wrung with pain,
And his dilated nostril toils in vain;
For short and scant the breath each effort draws,
And 'twixt each effort Nature claims a pause.
Beyond the loose and sable neck-cloth stretch'd,   90
His sinewy throat seems by convulsions twitch'd,
While the tongue faulters, as to utterance loth,
Sounds of dire import—watch-word, threat, and oath.
Though stupified by toil, and drugg'd with gin,
The body sleep, the restless guest within   95
Now plies on wood and wold his lawless trade,
Now in the fangs of justice wakes dismayed.—

"Was that wild start of terror and despair,
Those bursting eye-balls, and that wilder'd air,
Signs of compunction for a murdered hare?   100
Do the locks bristle and the eye-brows arch,
For grouse or partridge massacred in March?"—

No, scoffer, no! Attend, and mark with awe,
There is no wicket in the gate of law!
He, that would e'er so slightly set ajar   105
That awful portal, must undo each bar;
Tempting occasion, habit, passion, pride,
Will join to storm the breach, and force the barrier wide.

That ruffian, whom true men avoid and dread,
Whom bruisers, poachers, smugglers, call Black Ned,
Was Edward Mansell once;—the lightest heart,
That ever played on holiday his part!

---

* A cant name for smuggled spirits.

The leader he in every Christmas game,
The harvest feast grew blither when he came,
And liveliest on the chords the bow did glance,　　115
When Edward named the tune and led the dance.
Kind was his heart, his passions quick and strong,
Hearty his laugh, and jovial was his song;
And if he loved a gun, his father swore,
"'Twas but a trick of youth would soon be o'er,　　120
Himself had had the same, some thirty years before."

But he, whose humours spurn law's awful yoke,
Must herd with those by whom law's bonds are broke.
The common dread of justice soon allies
The clown, who robs the warren or excise,　　125
With sterner felons trained to act more dread,
Even with the wretch by whom his fellow bled.
Then,—as in plagues the foul contagions pass,
Leavening and festering the corrupted mass,—
Guilt leagues with guilt, while mutual motives draw, 130
Their hope impunity, their fear the law;
Their foes, their friends, their rendezvous the same,
Till the revenue baulked, or pilfered game,
Flesh the young culprit, and example leads
To darker villainy, and direr deeds.　　135

Wild howled the wind the forest glades along,
And oft the owl renewed her dismal song;
Around the spot where erst he felt the wound,
Red William's spectre walked his midnight round.
When o'er the swamp he cast his blighting look,　　140
From the green marshes of the stagnant brook
The bittern's sullen shout the sedges shook!
The wading moon, with storm-presaging gleam,
Now gave and now withheld her doubtful beam;
The old Oak stooped his arms, then flung them high,
Bellowing and groaning to the troubled sky—
'Twas then, that, couched amid the brushwood sere,
In Malwood-walk young Mansell watched the deer:

The fattest buck received his deadly shot—
The watchful keeper heard, and sought the spot.   150
Stout were their hearts, and stubborn was their strife,
O'erpowered at length the outlaw drew his knife!
Next morn a corpse was found upon the fell—
The rest his waking agony may tell!

70

Song

Oh say not, my love, with that mortified air,
    That your spring-time of pleasure is flown,
Nor bid me to maids that are younger repair,
    For those raptures that still are thine own!

Though April his temples may wreathe with the vine,   5
    Its tendrils in infancy curled,
'Tis the ardours of August mature us the wine
    Whose life-blood enlivens the world.

Though thy form, that was fashioned as light as a fay's,
    Has assumed a proportion more round,
And thy glance that was bright as a falcon's at gaze,
    Looks soberly now on the ground,—

Enough, after absence to meet me again,
    Thy steps still with ecstacy move;
Enough, that those dear sober glances retain   15
    For me the kind language of love!

71
The Vision of Triermain

Where is the maiden of mortal strain,
That may match with the Baron of Triermain?
She must be lovely and constant and kind,
Holy and pure and humble of mind,
Blithe of cheer and gentle of mood,   5
Courteous and generous and noble of blood—
Lovely as the sun's first ray
When it breaks the clouds of an April day;
Constant and true as the widow'd dove,
Kind as a minstrel that sings of love;   10
Pure as the fountain in rocky cave,
Where never sun-beam kiss'd the wave;
Humble as maiden that loves in vain,
Holy as hermit's vesper strain;
Gentle as breeze that but whispers and dies,   15
Yet blithe as the light leaves that dance in its sighs;
Courteous as monarch the morn he is crown'd,
Generous as spring-dews that bless the glad ground;
Noble her blood as the currents that met
In the veins of the noblest Plantagenet.   20
Such must her form be, her mood and her strain,
That shall match with Sir Roland of Triermain.

Sir Roland de Vaux he hath laid him to sleep,
His blood it was fevered, his breathing was deep.
He had been pricking against the Scot,   25
The foray was long and the skirmish hot;
His dinted helm and his buckler's plight
Bore token of a stubborn fight.
    All in the castle must hold them still,
Harpers must lull him to his rest,   30
With the slow soft tunes he loves the best,
Till sleep sink down upon his breast,
    Like the dew on a summer-hill.

It was the dawn of an autumn day;
The sun was struggling with frost-fog grey,   35
That like a silvery crape was spread
Round Glaramara's distant head,
And dimly gleam'd each painted pane
Of the lordly halls of Triermain,
   When that baron bold awoke.   40
Starting he woke, and loudly did call,
Rousing his menials in bower and hall,
   While hastily he spoke.

"Hearken, my minstrels! Which of you all
Touch'd his harp with that dying fall,   45
   So sweet, so soft, so faint,
It seem'd an angel's whisper'd call
   To an expiring saint?
And hearken, my merrymen! Whither or where
   Has she gone, that maid with her heav'nly brow,   50
With her look so sweet and her eyes so fair,
And her graceful step and her angel air,
And the eagle-plume on her dark-brown hair,
   That pass'd from my bower e'en now?"—

Answer'd him Richard de Brettville; he   55
Was chief of the baron's minstrelsy,—
"Silent, noble chieftain, we
   Have sate since midnight close,
When such lulling sounds as the brooklet sings,
Murmur'd from our melting strings,   60
   And hush'd you to repose.
Had a harp-note sounded here,
It had caught my watchful ear,
   Although it fell as faint and shy
   As bashful maiden's half-form'd sigh,   65
When she thinks her lover near."—
Answer'd Philip of Fasthwaite tall,
He kept guard in the outer-hall,—
"Since at eve our watch took post,

Not a foot has thy portal cross'd;   70
   Else had I heard the steps, though low
And light they fell as when earth receives,
In morn of frost, the wither'd leaves,
   That drop when no winds blow."—

"Then come thou hither, Henry, my page,   75
Whom I saved from the sack of Hermitage,
When that dark castle, tower, and spire,
Rose to the skies a pile of fire,
   And redden'd all the Nine-stane Hill,
And the shrieks of death, that wildly broke   80
Through devouring flame and smothering smoke,
   Made the warrior's heart-blood chill!
The trustiest thou of all my train,
My fleetest courser thou must rein,
   And ride to Lyulph's tow'r,   85
And from the baron of Triermain
   Greet well that sage of pow'r.
He is sprung from druid sires,
And British bards that tuned their lyres
To Arthur's and Pendragon's praise,   90
And his who sleeps at Dunmailraise.
Gifted like his gifted race,
He the characters can trace,
Graven deep in elder time
Upon Helvellyn's cliffs sublime;   95
Sign and sigil well doth he know,
And can bode of weal and woe,
Of kingdoms' fall, and fate of wars,
From mystic dreams and course of stars.
He shall tell me if nether earth   100
To that enchanting shape gave birth,
Or if 'twas but an airy thing,
Such as fantastic slumbers bring,
Fram'd from the rain-bow's varying dyes,
Or fading tints of western skies.   105

For, by the blessed rood I swear,
If that fair form breathes vital air,
No other maiden by my side
Shall ever rest De Vaux's bride!"—

The faithful page he mounts his steed,   110
And soon he cross'd green Irthing's mead,
Dash'd o'er Kirkoswald's verdant plain,
And Eden barr'd his course in vain.
He pass'd red Penrith's Table Round,
For feats of chivalry renown'd,   115
Left Mayburgh's mound and stones of pow'r,
By druids raised in magic hour,
And traced the Eamont's winding way,
Till Ulfo's lake beneath him lay.—

Onwards he rode, the path-way still   120
Winding betwixt the lake and hill;
Till on the fragment of a rock,
Struck from its base by lightning shock,
    He saw the druid sage:
The silver moss and lichen twined,   125
With the red deer-hair check'd and lined,
    A cushion fit for age;
And o'er him shook the aspin tree,
A restless rustling canopy.
    Then sprung young Henry from his selle,   130
        To greet the prophet grave,—
    But, ere his errand he could tell,
        The sage his answer gave.

        *   *   *   *   *   *

72

Epitaph,

Designed for a Monument in Lichfield Cathedral, at the Burial Place of the Family of Miss Seward

Amid these Aisles, where once his precepts show'd
The Heavenward path-way which in life he trod,
This simple tablet marks a Father's bier,
And those he loved in life, in death are near;
For him, for them, a Daughter bade it rise,   5
Memorial of domestic charities.
 Still would'st thou know why o'er the marble spread,
In female grace the willow droops her head;
Why on her branches, silent and unstrung,
The minstrel harp is emblematic hung;   10
What Poet's voice is smother'd here in dust
Till waked to join the chorus of the just,—
Lo! one brief line an answer sad supplies,
Honour'd, beloved, and mourned, here SEWARD lies!
Her worth, her warmth of heart, let friendship say,— 15
Go seek her genius in her living lay.

73

The British Light Dragoons; or,
The Plain of Badajos

Air—The Bold Dragoon

'Twas a Marechal of France, and he fain would honour gain,
And he long'd to take a passing glance at Portugal from Spain,
   With his flying guns this gallant gay,
   And boasted corps d'armée,
O he fear'd not our dragoons with their long swords
                     boldly riding.   5
   Whack fal de ral la la, lal, la la la la,
   And Whack fal de ral la la la la la la la.

To Campo Mayor come, he had quietly sat down,
Just a fricassee to pick, while his soldiers sack'd the town,
   When 'twas peste! morbleu! mon General,   10
   Hear th' English bugle call!
And behold the light dragoons with their long swords
                     boldly riding.
   Whack fal de ral, &c.

Right about went horse and foot, artillery and all,
And as the devil leaves a house they tumbled through the
                     wall;[*]   15
   They took no time to seek the door,
   But best foot set before,
O they ran from our dragoons with their long swords
                     boldly riding.
   Whack fal de ral, &c.

---

[*] In their hasty evacuation of Campo Mayor, the French pulled down a part of the rampart and marched out over the glacis.

Those valiant men of France they had scarcely fled a mile,   20
When on their flank there sous'd at once the British rank
                        and file,
   For Long, de Grey, and Otway then
   Ne'er minded one to ten,
But came on like light dragoons with their long swords
                        boldly riding.
   Whack fal de ral, &c.   25

Their squadrons form'd to front, their sabres then they drew,
And as if the ranks were spider-webs they broke the
                        Frenchmen through,
   Still as they strove to form again
   We rode them down amain!
For we fought like stout dragoons with their long swords
                        boldly riding.   30
   Whack fal de ral &c.

Three hundred British lads they made three thousand reel,
Their hearts were made of English Oak, their swords of
                        Sheffield steel,
   Their horses were in Yorkshire bred,
   And Beresford them led;   35
So huzza for brave dragoons with their long swords
                        boldly riding.
   Whack fal de ral, &c.

There here's a health to Wellington, to Beresford, to Long,
And a single word of Bonaparte before I close my song:
   The eagles that to fight he brings   40
   Should serve his men with wings,
When they meet the brave dragoons with their long
                        swords boldly riding.
   Whack fal de ral, &c.

74

On the Massacre of Glencoe

"O tell me, Harper, wherefore flow
Thy wayward notes of wail and woe
Far down the desert of Glencoe,
    Where none may list their melody?
Say, harp'st thou to the mists that fly,   5
Or to the dun deer glancing by,
Or to the eagle, that from high
    Screams chorus to thy minstrelsy."

"No, not to these, for they have rest,—
The mist-wreath has the mountain crest,   10
The stag his lair, the erne her nest,
    Abode of lone security.
But those for whom I pour the lay,
Not wild-wood deep, nor mountain grey,
Not this deep dell that shrouds from day,   15
    Could screen from treach'rous cruelty.

"Their flag was furl'd, and mute their drum,
The very household dogs were dumb,
Unwont to bay at guests that come
    In guise of hospitality.   20
His blythest notes the piper plied,
Her gayest snood the maiden tied,
The dame her distaff flung aside,
    To tend her kindly housewifery.

"The hand that mingled in the meal,   25
At midnight drew the felon steel,
And gave the host's kind breast to feel,
    Meed for his hospitality.
The friendly hearth which warm'd that hand,
At midnight arm'd it with the brand   30
That bade destruction's flames expand
    Their red and fearful blazonry.

"Then woman's shriek was heard in vain,
Nor infancy's unpitied plain
More than the warrior's groan, could gain   35
    Respite from ruthless butchery.
The winter wind that whistled shrill,
The snows that night that cloked the hill,
Though wild and pitiless, had still
    Far more than southron clemency.   40

"Long have my harp's best notes been gone,
Few are its strings, and faint their tone,
They can but sound in desert lone
    Their grey-hair'd master's misery.
Were each grey hair a minstrel string,   45
Each chord should imprecations fling,
'Till startled Scotland loud should ring,
    'Revenge for blood and treachery.'"

75

Lines Written in Susan Ferrier's Album

The mountain winds are up, and proud
O'er heath and hill careering loud;
The groaning forest to its power
Yields all that formed our summer bower.
The summons wakes the anxious swain,   5
Whose tardy shocks still load the plain,
And bids the sleepless merchant weep,
Whose richer hazard loads the deep.
For me the blast, or low or high,
Blows nought of wealth or poverty;   10
It can but whirl in whimsies vain
The windmill of a restless brain,
And bid me tell in slipshod verse
What honest prose might best rehearse;

How much we forest-dwellers grieve   15
Our valued friends our cot should leave,
Unseen each beauty that we boast,
The little wonders of our coast,
That still the pile of Melrose grey,
For you must rise in Minstrel's lay,   20
And Yarrow's birks immortal long
For you but bloom in rural song.
Yet Hope, who still in present sorrow,
Whispers the promise of to-morrow,
Tells us of future days to come,   25
When you shall glad our rustic home;
When this wild whirlwind shall be still
And summer sleep on glen and hill,
And Tweed, unvexed by storms, shall guide
In silvery maze his stately tide,   30
Doubling in mirror every rank
Of oak and alder on his bank;
And our kind guests such welcome prove
As most we wish to those we love.

Ashestiel, 13 October 1811

76

The Return to Ulster

Air—*Young Terence Macdonough*

Once again, but how chang'd, since my wand'rings began—
I have heard the deep voice of the Lagan and Bann,
And the pines of Clanbrassil resound to the roar
That wearies the echoes of fair Tullamore.
Alas! my poor bosom, and why shouldst thou burn!   5
With the scenes of my youth can its raptures return?
Can I live the dear life of delusion again,
That flow'd when these echoes first mix'd with my strain?

It was then that around me, though poor and unknown,
High spells of mysterious enchantment were thrown;   10
The streams were of silver, of diamond the dew,
The land was an Eden, for fancy was new.
I had heard of our bards, and my soul was on fire
At the rush of their verse, and the sweep of their lyre:
To me 'twas not legend, nor tale to the ear,   15
But a vision of noontide, distinguish'd and clear.

Ultonia's old heroes awoke at the call,
And renew'd the wild pomp of the chace and the hall;
And the standard of Fion flash'd fierce from on high,
Like a burst of the sun when the tempest is nigh.*   20
It seem'd that the harp of green Erin once more
Could renew all the glories she boasted of yore.—
Yet why at remembrance, fond heart, shouldst thou burn?
They were days of delusion, and cannot return.

---

* In ancient Irish poetry, the standard of Fion, or Fingal, is called the *Sun-burst*, an epithet feebly rendered by the *Sun-beam* of Macpherson.

But was she, too, a phantom, the maid who stood by,   25
And listed my lay, while she turn'd from mine eye?
Was she, too, a vision, just glancing to view,
Then dispers'd in the sun-beam, or melted to dew?
Oh! would it had been so,—O would that her eye
Had been but a star-glance that shot through the sky,   30
And her voice, that was moulded to melody's thrill,
Had been but a zephyr that sigh'd and was still.

Oh! would it had been so,—not then this poor heart
Had learn'd the sad lesson, to love and to part;
To bear, unassisted, its burthen of care,   35
While I toil'd for the wealth I had no one to share.
Not then had I said, when life's summer was done,
And the hours of her autumn were fast speeding on,
"Take the fame and the riches ye brought in your train,
And restore me the dream of my spring-tide again."   40

77

Prologue to Helga

Pondering the labours of his mimic reign
Our stage-director plann'd the year's campaign:
The Tragic Muse, the Comic, urged her claim—
Farce, Pastoral, Opera, Masque and Melo Drame
O'er his bewildered meditation past   5
With scenes unpainted yet, and parts uncast
Speeches ne'er spouted, dresses yet unmade
Songs never set and musick never played.
Then rushed the stage-auxiliaries along
Man, monster and machine, a moteley throng—   10
For now no more our mean processions pass
In Hamlet's phrase, each actor on his ass:
Car, camel, war-horse, water-dog appear
And Bluebeard's elephant o'erwhelms the rear.

Perplexed amid the dark and dubious choice 15
Our Chief Theatric caught young Ammon's voice
"Athenians of the North—alas!" he says
"How hard we labour to deserve our praise"—
   Twas then that wafted from a distant sky
In hour of need, our evening's theme was nigh 20
Brought from that isle where flames volcanic light
The half-year's darkness of the polar night
Where boiling streams from earth's vexed caverns driven
With sleet and snow-drift mix in middle heaven
Where meet in neighbourhood extreme and dire 25
The frozen glaciere and the gulph of fire.
Yet in a clime where elemental strife
Wrecks each fair trace of animated life
Midst Iceland's waste of ashes and of snows
Even there of old the Light of song arose: 30
From her dark bosom the historic lay
O'er realms more genial poured the mental day.
In monarchs' halls their harps her minstrels strung
And courts and camps were silent when they sung.
Not now we boast to wake their loftier strain 35
Or bid the Runic rhymes revive again:
Enough if simply, yet to nature true,
Our wandering bard his sketch dramatic drew,
List then and learn how northern Minstrels strove
Stung by the rivalry of fame and love. 40

78

For the Anniversary Meeting of the Pitt Club of Scotland, 1814

O Dread was the time, and more dreadful the omen,
   When the brave on Marengo lay slaughtered in vain,
And, beholding broad Europe bowed down by her foemen,
   PITT closed in his anguish the map of her reign!
Not the fate of broad Europe could bend his brave spirit   5
   To accept for his country the safety of shame;
O then in her triumph remember his merit,
   And hallow the goblet that flows to his name.

Round the husbandman's head, while he traces the furrow,
   The mists of the winter may mingle with rain,   10
He may plough it with labour, and sow it in sorrow,
   And sigh while he fears he has sowed it in vain;
He may die ere his children shall reap in their gladness,
   But the blithe harvest-home shall remember his claim;
And their jubilee-shout shall be softened with sadness,   15
   While they hallow the goblet that flows to his name.

Though anxious and timeless his life was expended,
   In toils for our country preserved by his care,
Though he died ere one ray o'er the nations ascended,
   To light the long darkness of doubt and despair;   20
The storms he endured in our Britain's December,
   The perils his wisdom foresaw and o'ercame,
In her glory's rich Harvest shall Britain remember,
   And hallow the goblet that flows to his name.

Nor forget HIS grey head, who, all dark in affliction,   25
   Is deaf to the tale of our victories won,
And to sounds the most dear to paternal affection,
   The shout of his People applauding his SON;
By his firmness unmoved in success or disaster,
   By his long reign of virtue, remember his claim!   30
With our tribute to PITT join the praise of his Master,
   Though a tear stain the goblet that flows to his name.

Yet again fill the wine-cup, and change the sad measure,
    The rites of our grief and our gratitude paid,
To our Prince, to our Heroes devote the bright treasure,   35
    The wisdom that planned, and the zeal that obeyed!
Fill WELLINGTON's cup till it beam like his glory,
    Forget not our own brave DALHOUSIE and GRÆME;
A thousand years hence hearts shall bound at their story,
    And hallow the goblet that flows to their fame.   40

79

For A' That an' A' That

Being a new Song to an old Tune

Though right be aft put down by strength,
    As mony a day we saw that,
The true and leilfu' cause at length
    Shall bear the grie for a' that.
For a' that, an' a' that,   5
    Guns, guillotines, and a' that;
The Fleur-de-lis, that lost her right,
    Is Queen again for a' that!

We'll twine her in a friendly knot
    With England's Rose and a' that,   10
The Shamrock shall not be forgot,
    For Wellington made bra' that.
The Thistle, though her leaf be rude,
    Yet faith we'll no misca' that;
She shelter'd in her solitude   15
    The Fleur-de-lis for a' that!

The Austrian Vine, the Prussian Pine,
   (For Blucher's sake hurra' that!)
The Spanish Olive too shall join,
   And bloom in Peace for a' that.   20
Stout Russia's Hemp, so surely twined,
   Around our wreath we'll draw that,
And he that would the cord unbind
   Shall have it for his gra-vat.

Or if to choke sae puir a sot,   25
   Your pity scorn to thraw that,
The Devil's Elbo' be his lot,
   Where he may sit and claw that.
In spite of sleight, in spite of might,
   In spite of brags and a' that,   30
The lads that battled for the right,
   Have won the day and a' that!

There's ae bit spot I had forgot,
   They ca'd America, that;
A coward plot her rats had got   35
   Their fathers' flag, to gnaw that;
Now see it fly top-gallant high,
   Atlantic winds shall blaw that,
And, Yankee loun! beware your croun,
   There's kames in hand to claw that.   40
     For on the land, or on the sea,
      Where'er the breezes blaw that,
    The British flag shall bear the grie,
     And win the day for a' that.

80

Pharos loquitur

Far in the bosom of the deep
O'er these wild shelves my watch I keep.
A ruddy gem of changeful light
Bound on the dusky brow of night,
The seaman bids my lustre hail   5
And scorns to strike his timorous sail.

81

Epistle to His Grace the Duke of Buccleuch

Light House Yacht in the Sound of Lerwick Zetland
8 August 1814

Health to the Chieftain from his clansman true
From her true minstrel Health to fair Buccleuch
Health from the isles where Dawn at morning weaves
Her chaplet with the tints that twilight leaves
Where late the Sun scarce vanished from the sight   5
And his bright path-way graced the short-lived night
Though darker now as autumn's shades extend
The north winds whistle and the mists ascend—
Health from the land where eddying whirl-winds toss
The storm-rocked *cradle** of the Cape of Noss   10
On out-stretched cords the giddy engine slides
His own strong arm the bold adventurer guides
And he that lists such desperate feat to try
May like the sea mew skim twixt surf and sky

---

* A machine so called which slides by two iron rings upon two cords from a very high rock in the isle of Noss to another rock which is divided from it by a narrow channel of the sea. The adventurer flies over a chasm of about 500 feet high warp'd along by his own hands. A most dizzy operation.

And feel the mid-air gales around him blow   15
And see the billows rage five hundred feet below—
Here by each stormy peak and desert shore
The hardy isles-man tugs the daring oar
Practised alike his venturous course to keep
Through the white breakers or the pathless deep   20
By ceaseless peril and by toil to gain
A wretched pittance from the niggard main.
And when the worn out drudge the ocean leaves
What comfort cheers him and what hut receives?
Lady, the worst thy presence ere has cheered   25
(When want and sorrow fled as you appeared)
Were to a Zetlander's as the high dome
Of proud Drumlanrig to my humble home.
Here rise no groves and here no gardens blow
Here even the hardy heath scarce deigns to grow   30
But rocks on rocks in mist and storm arrayed
Stretch far to sea their giant colonnade
With many a cavern seam'd, the dreary haunt
Of the dun seal and swarthy cormorant.
Wild round their rifled brows, with frequent cry   35
As of lament, the gulls and gannets fly
And from their sable base with sullen sound
In sheets of whitening foam the waves rebound.
    Yet even these coasts a touch of envy gain
From those whose land has known oppression's chain   40
For here the industrious Dutchman* comes once more
To moor his fishing craft by Brassa's shore
Greets every former mate and brother tar
Marvels how Lerwick 'scaped the rage of war
Tells many a tale of Gallic outrage done   45
And ends by blessing God and Wellington.

---

* We heard of some very affecting greetings between the Dutchmen and the natives of Lerwick, who had not seen a fishing schuyt for many years till this season. The poor Dutchmen seemed quite impoverished and expressed great wonder that the fishing town of Lerwick had thriven during the war.

Here too the Greenland tar—a fiercer guest—
Claims a brief hour of riot not of rest
Proves each wild frolic that in wine has birth
And wakes the land with brawls and barbarous mirth.   50
    A sadder sight on yon poor vessel's prow
The captive Norse-man sits in silent woe,
And eyes the flags of Britain as they flow:
Hard fate of war which bade her terrors sway
His destined course and seize so mean a prey—   55
A bark with planks so warped and seams so riven
She scarce might face the gentlest airs of heaven:
Pensive he sits and questions oft if none
Can list his speech and understand his moan
In vain—no islesman now can use the tongue   60
Of the bold Norse from whom their lineage sprung.
    Not thus of old the Norse men hither came
Won by the love of danger or of fame
On every storm-beat cape a shapeless tower
Tells of their wars their conquests and their power   65
For nor for Grecia's vales nor Latian land
Was fiercer strife than for this barren strand—
A race severe, the isle and ocean-lords
Loved for its own delights the strife of swords
With scornful laugh the mortal pang defied   70
And blessed their Gods that they in battle died.
    Such were the sires of Zetland's simple race
And still the eye may faint resemblance trace
In the blue eye, tall form, proportion fair,
The limbs athletic and the long light hair   75
(Such was the mien as Scald and minstrel sings
Of Fair-haired Harold first of Norway's Kings)
But their high deeds to scale those crags confined
Their only warfare is with waves and wind.
    Why should I tell of Mousa's castled coast   80
Why of the horrors of the Sumburgh-rost[*]

---

[*] A furious race of tide off Sumburgh-head.

May not these bald disjointed lines suffice
Penn'd while my comrades whirl the rattling dice
While down the cabin-skylight lessening shine
The rays, and eve is chaced with mirth and wine—   85
Imagined while down Mousa's desert bay
Our well trimm'd vessel waged her nimble way
While to the freshening breeze she leaned her side
And bade her bolt sprit kiss the foamy tide—
Such are the lays that Zetland's isles supply—   90
Drenched with the drizzly spray and dropping sky
Weary and wet a sea-sick Minstrel I.—

POSTSCRIPT

In respect that your Grace has commissioned a Kraken
You will please be informed that they seldom are taken
It is January two years, the Zetland folks say   95
Since they saw the last Kraken in Scalloway-bay:
He lay in the offing a fortnight or more
But the devil a Zetlander put from the shore
Though bold in the seas of the North to assail
The morse and the sea-horse the grampus and whale.   100
If your Grace thinks I'm writing the thing that is not
You may ask at a namesake of ours Mr Scott
(He's not from our land though his merits deserve it,
But springs I'm informed from the Scotts of Scotstarvit)
He questioned the folks who beheld it with eyes   105
But they differed confoundedly as to its size
For instance the modest and diffident swore
That it loom'd like the keel of a ship and no more
Those of eye-sight more clear or of fancy more high
Said it rose like an island twixt ocean and sky   110
But all of the hulk had a steady opinion
That 'twas sure a *live* subject of Neptune's dominion
And I think my Lord Duke your Grace would not wish
To cumber your house, such a kettle of fish.

Had your order related to night-caps or hose   115
Or mittens of worsted there's plenty of those.
Or would you be pleased but to fancy a whale,
And direct me to send it by sea or by mail,
The season I'm told is nigh over but still
I could get you one fit for the lake at Bowhill.   120
Indeed as to whales there's no need to be thrifty
Since one day last fortnight two hundred and fifty
Pursued by seven Orkney-men's boats and no more
Betwixt Triffness and Liffness were driven on the shore.
You'll ask if I saw this same wonder with sight   125
I own that I did not, but easily might—
For this mighty shoal of leviathans lay
On our lee-beam a mile in the loop of the bay
And the islesmen of Sanda were all at the spoil
And *flinching* (so term it) the blubber to boil   130
(Ye Spirits of lavender drown the reflection
That awakes at the thoughts of this odorous dissection)
To see this huge marvel full fain would we go
But Wilson* the winds and the current said no.

    We have now got to Kirkwall and needs I must stare   135
When I think that in verse I have once called it *fair*—
'Tis a base little burgh both dirty and mean
There's nothing to hear and there's nought to be seen
Save a Church where of old times a prelate harangued
And a palace that's built by an Earl that was hanged.   140
But farewell to Kirkwall—aboard we are going
The anchor's a peak and the breezes are blowing
Our Commodore calls all his band to their places
And 'tis time to relieve you—Good night to your Graces.

                        Kirkwall, Orkney, 13 August 1814

* Master of the cutter.

82

𝔉arewell to 𝔐ackenƷie, 𝕳igh 𝕮hief of 𝕂intail

From the Gaelic

The original verses are arranged to a beautiful Gaelic air, of which
the chorus is adapted to the double pull upon the oars of a galley, and
which is therefore distinct from the ordinary jorrams, or boat-songs.
They were composed by the Family Bard upon the departure of the
Earl of Seaforth, who was obliged to take refuge in Spain, after an
unsuccessful effort at insurrection in favour of the Stuart family, in
the year 1719.

Farewell to Mackenneth, great Earl of the North,
The Lord of Lochcarron, Glenshiel, and Seaforth;
To the Chieftain this morning his course who began,
Launching forth on the billows his bark like a swan.
For a far foreign land he has hoisted his sail,   5
Farewell to Mackenzie, High Chief of Kintail!

O swift be the galley, and hardy her crew,
May her captain be skilful, her mariners true,
In danger undaunted, unwearied by toil,
Though the whirlwind should rise, and the ocean
                                should boil: 10
On the brave vessel's gunnel I drank his bonnail,*
And farewell to Mackenzie, High Chief of Kintail.

Awake in thy chamber, thou sweet southland gale!
Like the sighs of his people, breathe soft on his sail;
Be prolong'd as regret that his vassals must know,   15
Be fair as their faith, and sincere as their woe:
Be so soft, and so fair, and so faithful, sweet gale,
Wafting onward Mackenzie, High Chief of Kintail!

---

* Bonail', or Bonallez, the old Scottish phrase for a feast at parting with a friend.

Be his pilot experienced, and trusty, and wise,
To measure the seas and to study the skies: 20
May he hoist all his canvass from streamer to deck,
But O! crowd it higher when wafting him back—
Till the cliffs of Skooroora, and Conan's glad vale,
Shall welcome Mackenzie, High Chief of Kintail!

83
Imitation of Farewell to Mackenzie

So sung the old Bard, in the grief of his heart,
When he saw his loved Lord from his people depart.
Now mute on thy mountains, O Albyn, are heard
Nor the voice of the song, nor the harp of the bard;
Or its strings are but waked by the stern winter gale,   5
As they mourn for Mackenzie, last Chief of Kintail.

From the far Southland border a Minstrel came forth,
And he waited the hour that some Bard of the north
His hand on the harp of the ancient should cast,
And bid its wild numbers mix high with the blast;   10
But no Bard was there left in the land of the Gael,
To lament for Mackenzie, last Chief of Kintail.

And shalt thou then sleep, did the Minstrel exclaim,
Like the son of the lowly, unnoticed by fame?
No, Son of Fitzgerald! in accents of woe,   15
The song thou hast loved o'er thy coffin shall flow,
And teach thy wild mountains to join in the wail,
That laments for Mackenzie, last Chief of Kintail.

In vain, the bright course of thy talents to wrong,
Fate deaden'd thine ear and imprison'd thy tongue;   20
For brighter o'er all her obstructions arose
The glow of the genius they could not oppose;
And who in the land of the Saxon or Gael,
Might match with Mackenzie, High Chief of Kintail?

Thy sons rose around thee in light and in love,   25
All a father could hope, all a friend could approve;
What vails it the tale of thy sorrows to tell,—
In the spring time of youth and of promise they fell!
Of the line of Fitzgerald remains not a male,
To bear the proud name of the Chief of Kintail.   30

And thou, gentle Dame, who must bear to thy grief,
For thy clan and thy country the cares of a Chief,
Whom brief rolling moons in six changes have left,
Of thy husband, and father, and brethren bereft,
To thine ear of affection how sad is the hail,   35
That salutes thee the Heir of the line of Kintail!

84

The Dance of Death

Night and morning were at meeting
　Over Waterloo;
Cocks had sung their earliest greeting,
　Faint and low they crew,
For no paly beam yet shone   5
On the heights of Mount Saint John;
Tempest-clouds prolong'd the sway
Of timeless darkness over day;
Whirlwind, thunder-clap, and shower,
Mark'd it a predestined hour.   10
Broad and frequent through the night
Flash'd the sheets of levin-light;
Musquets, glancing lightnings back,
Shew'd the dreary bivouack
　Where the soldier lay,   15
Chill and stiff, and drench'd with rain,
Wishing dawn of morn again
　Though death should come with day.

'Tis at such a tide and hour,
Wizard, witch, and fiend have power,   20
And ghastly forms through mist and shower
　Gleam on the gifted ken;
And then the affrighted prophet's ear
Drinks whispers strange of fate and fear,
Presaging death and ruin near   25
　Among the sons of men;—
Apart from Albyn's war-array,
'Twas then grey Allan sleepless lay;
Grey Allan, who, for many a day,
　Had follow'd stout and stern   30
Where, through battle's rout and reel,
Storm of shot and hedge of steel,

Led the grandson of Lochiel,
    Valiant Fassiefern.
Through steel and shot he leads no more,   35
Low-laid 'mid friends' and foemen's gore—
But long his native lake's wild shore,
And Sunart rough, and high Ardgower,
    And Morvern long shall tell,
And proud Bennevis hear with awe,   40
How, upon bloody Quatre-Bras,
Brave Cameron heard the wild hurra
    Of conquest as he fell.

'Lone on the outskirts of the host,
The weary sentinel held post,   45
And heard, through darkness far aloof,
The frequent clang of courser's hoof,
Where held the cloak'd patrole their course,
And spurr'd 'gainst storm the swerving horse;
But there are sounds in Allan's ear,   50
Patrole nor sentinel may hear,
And sights before his eye aghast
Invisible to them have pass'd,
    When down the destined plain
'Twixt Britain and the bands of France,   55
Wild as marsh-borne meteors glance,
Strange phantoms wheel'd a revel dance,
    And doom'd the future slain.—
Such forms were seen, such sounds were heard,
When Scotland's James his march prepared   60
    For Flodden's fatal plain;
Such, when he drew his ruthless sword,
As Chusers of the Slain, adored
    The yet unchristen'd Dane.
An indistinct and phantom band,   65
They wheel'd their ring-dance hand in hand,
    With gesture wild and dread;

The Seer, who watch'd them ride the storm,
Saw through their faint and shadowy form
   The lightning's flash more red;   70
And still their ghastly roundelay
Was of the coming battle-fray
   And of the destined dead.

Song

   Wheel the wild dance
   While lightnings glance,   75
      And thunders rattle loud,
   And call the brave
   To bloody grave,
      To sleep without a shroud.

   Our airy feet,   80
   So light and fleet,
      They do not bend the rye
   That sinks its head when whirlwinds rave,
   And swells again in eddying wave,
   As each wild gust blows by;   85
   But still the corn,
   At dawn of morn,
      Our fatal steps that bore,
   At eve lies waste
   A trampled paste   90
      Of blackening mud and gore.

   Wheel the wild dance
   While lightnings glance,
      And thunders rattle loud,
   And call the brave   95
   To bloody grave,
      To sleep without a shroud.

Wheel the wild dance!
Brave sons of France,
   For you our ring makes room;   100
Makes space full wide
For martial pride,
   For banner, spear, and plume.
Approach, draw near,
Proud cuirassier!   105
   Room for the men of steel!
Through crest and plate
The broad-sword's weight
   Both head and heart shall feel.

Wheel the wild dance   110
While lightnings glance,
   And thunders rattle loud,
And call the brave
To bloody grave,
   To sleep without a shroud.   115

Sons of the spear!
You feel us near
   In many a ghastly dream;
With fancy's eye
Our forms you spy,   120
   And hear our fatal scream.
With clearer sight
Ere falls the night,
   Just when to weal or woe
Your disembodied souls take flight   125
On trembling wing—each startled sprite
   Our choir of death shall know.

Wheel the wild dance
While lightnings glance,
   And thunders rattle loud,   130
And call the brave
To bloody grave,
   To sleep without a shroud.

Burst, ye clouds, in tempest showers,
Redder rain shall soon be ours—   135
   See the east grows wan—
Yield we place to sterner game,
Ere deadlier bolts and drearer flame
Shall the welkin's thunders shame;
Elemental rage is tame   140
   To the wrath of man.

At morn, grey Allan's mates with awe
Heard of the vision'd sights he saw,
   The legend heard him say;
But the seer's gifted eye was dim,   145
Deafen'd his ear, and stark his limb,
   Ere closed that bloody day—
He sleeps far from his Highland heath,—
But often of the Dance of Death
   His comrades tell the tale   150
On picquet-post, when ebbs the night,
And waning watch-fires glow less bright,
   And dawn is glimmering pale.

Abbotsford, 1 October 1815

85

Saint Cloud

Soft spread the southern Summer night
   Her veil of darksome blue;
Ten thousand stars combined to light
   The terrace of Saint Cloud.

The evening breezes gently sigh'd,   5
   Like breath of lover true,
Bewailing the deserted pride
   And wreck of sweet Saint Cloud.

The drum's deep roll was heard afar,
   The bugle wildly blew   10
Good night to Hulan and Hussar,
   That garrison Saint Cloud.

The startled Naiads from the shade
   With broken urns withdrew,
And silenced was that proud cascade,   15
   The glory of Saint Cloud.

We sate upon its steps of stone,
   Nor could its silence rue,
When waked, to music of our own,
   The echoes of Saint Cloud.   20

Slow Seine might hear each lovely note
   Fall light as summer-dew,
While through the moonless air they float,
   Prolong'd from fair Saint Cloud.

And sure a melody more sweet   25
   His waters never knew,
Though Music's self was wont to meet
   With princes at Saint Cloud.

Nor then, with more delighted ear,
   The circle round her drew,   30
Than ours, when gather'd round to hear
   Our songstress at Saint Cloud.

Few happy hours poor mortals pass,—
   Then give those hours their due,
And rank among the foremost class   35
   Our evenings at Saint Cloud.

          Paris, 5 September 1815

86

Romance of Dunois

From the French

The original of this little Romance makes part of a manuscript collection of French songs, probably compiled by some young officer, which was found on the Field of Waterloo, so much stained with clay and with blood, as sufficiently to indicate what had been the fate of its late owner. The song is popular in France, and is rather a good specimen of the style of composition to which it belongs.—The translation is strictly literal.

It was Dunois, the young and brave, was bound for Palestine,
But first he made his orisons before Saint Mary's shrine:
"And grant, immortal Queen of Heaven," was still the
                              soldier's prayer,
"That I may prove the bravest knight, and love the
                              fairest fair."

His oath of honour on the shrine he graved it with his sword, 5
And follow'd to the Holy Land the banner of his Lord;
Where, faithful to his noble vow, his war-cry fill'd the air,
"Be honour'd aye the bravest knight, beloved the fairest fair."

They owed the conquest to his arm, and then his liege-lord
                              said,
"The heart that has for honour beat by bliss must be
                              repaid,—   10
My daughter Isabel and thou shall be a wedded pair,
For thou art bravest of the brave, she fairest of the fair."

And then they bound the holy knot before Saint Mary's shrine,
That makes a paradise on earth if hearts and hands combine;
And every lord and lady bright that were in chapel there, 15
Cried, "Honour'd be the bravest knight, beloved the
                              fairest fair."

87

The Troubadour

Glowing with love, on fire for fame,
    A Troubadour that hated sorrow,
Beneath his Lady's window came,
    And thus he sung his last good-morrow:
"My arm it is my country's right,   5
    My heart is in my true love's bower;
Gaily for love and fame to fight
    Befits the gallant Troubadour."

And while he march'd with helm on head
    And harp in hand, the descant rung,   10
As faithful to his favourite maid,
    The minstrel-burthen still he sung:
"My arm it is my country's right,
    My heart is in my lady's bower;
Resolved for love and fame to fight,   15
    I come, a gallant Troubadour."

Even when the battle-roar was deep,
    With dauntless heart he hewed his way,
Mid splintering lance and falchion-sweep,
    And still was heard his warrior-lay;   20
"My life it is my country's right,
    My heart is in my lady's bower;
For love to die, for fame to fight,
    Becomes the valiant Troubadour."

Alas! upon the bloody field   25
    He fell beneath the foeman's glaive,
But still, reclining on his shield,
    Expiring sung the exulting stave:
"My life it is my country's right,
    My heart is in my lady's bower;   30
For love and fame to fall in fight
    Becomes the valiant Troubadour."

88
Song of Folly

It chanced that Cupid on a season,
    By Fancy urged, resolved to wed,
But could not settle whether Reason
    Or Folly should partake his bed.

What does he then?—Upon my life,   5
    'Twas bad example for a deity—
He takes me Reason for his wife,
    And Folly for his hours of gaiety.

Though thus he dealt in petty treason,
    He loved them both in equal measure;   10
Fidelity was born of Reason,
    And Folly brought to bed of Pleasure.

89
The Lifting of the Banner

From the brown crest of Newark its summons extending,
    Our signal is waving in smoke and in flame;
And each forester blithe from his mountain descending,
    Bounds light o'er the heather to join in the game.

CHORUS

Then up with the Banner, let forest winds fan her,   5
She has blazed over Ettricke eight ages and more;
In sport we'll attend her, in battle defend her,
With heart and with hand, like our fathers before.

When the Southern invader spread waste and disorder,
   At the glance of her crescents he paused and withdrew;   10
For around them were marshall'd the pride of the Border,
   The Flowers of the Forest, the Bands of BUCCLEUCH.
       Then up with the Banner, &c.

A stripling's weak hand to our revel has borne her,
   No mail-glove has grasp'd her, no spearmen surround;   15
But ere a bold foeman should scathe or should scorn her,
   A thousand true hearts would be cold on the ground.
       Then up with the Banner, &c.

We forget each contention of civil dissension,
   And hail, like our brethren, HOME, DOUGLAS, and CAR;   20
And ELLIOT and PRINGLE in pastime shall mingle,
   As welcome in peace as their fathers in war.
       Then up with the Banner, &c.

Then strip, lads, and to it, though sharp be the weather,
   And if, by mischance, you should happen to fall,   25
There are worse things in life than a tumble on heather,
   And life is itself but a game of football.
       Then up with the Banner, &c.

And when it is over, we'll drink a blithe measure
   To each laird and each lady that witness'd our fun,   30
And to every blithe heart that took part in our pleasure,
   To the lads that have lost and the lads that have won.
       Then up with the Banner, &c.

May the Forest still flourish, both Borough and Landward,
   From the hall of the Peer to the herd's ingle-nook;   35
And huzza! my brave hearts, for BUCCLEUCH and his standard,
   For the King and the Country, the Clan and the Duke.

Then up with the Banner, let forest winds fan her,
She has blazed over Ettricke eight ages and more;
In sport we'll attend her, in battle defend her, 40
With heart and with hand, like our fathers before.

Quoth the Sheriff of the Forest

Abbotsford, 1 December 1815

90
Lullaby of an Infant Chief

*Air—Cadil gu lo**

O hush thee, my babie, thy sire was a knight;
Thy mother a lady, both lovely and bright;
The woods and the glens, from the towers which we see,
They all are belonging, dear baby, to thee.
   O ho ro, i ri ri, cadil gu lo,   5
   O ho ro, i ri ri, &c.

O fear not the bugle, though loudly it blows,
It calls but the warders that guard thy repose;
Their bows would be bended, their blades would be red,
Ere the step of a foeman draws near to thy bed.   10
   O ho ro, i ri ri, &c.

O hush thee, my baby, the time soon will come,
When thy sleep shall be broken by trumpet and drum;
Then hush thee, my darling, take rest while you may,
For strife comes with manhood, and waking with day.   15
   O ho ro, i ri ri, &c.

* "Sleep on till day." These words, adapted to a melody somewhat different from the original, are sung in my friend Mr Terry's drama of Guy Mannering.

91

𝕵𝖔𝖈𝖐 𝖔𝖋 𝕳𝖆𝖟𝖊𝖑𝖉𝖊𝖆𝖓

Air—*A Border Melody*

"Why weep ye by the tide, ladie?
   Why weep ye by the tide?
I'll wed you to my youngest son,
   And ye sall be his bride:
And ye sall be his bride, ladie,   5
   Sae comely to be seen—"
But aye she loot the tears down fa',
   For Jock of Hazeldean.

"Now let this wilful grief be done,
   And dry that cheek so pale;   10
Young Frank is chief of Errington,
   And lord of Langley-dale;
His step is first in peaceful ha',
   His sword in battle keen—"
But aye she loot the tears down fa',   15
   For Jock of Hazeldean.

"O' chain o' gold ye sall not lack,
   Nor braid to bind your hair;
Nor mettled hound, nor managed hawk,
   Nor palfrey fresh and fair;   20
And you, the foremost of them a',
   Shall ride our forest queen—"
But aye she loot the tears down fa',
   For Jock of Hazeldean.

The kirk was deck'd at morning-tide,   25
   The tapers glimmer'd fair;
The priest and bridegroom wait the bride,
   And dame and knight are there.
They sought her both by bower and ha',
   The ladie was not seen!   30
She's o'er the border, and awa
   Wi' Jock of Hazeldean.

92

Pibroch of Donald Dhu

Air—*Piobair of Dhonuil Duibh*[*]

This is a very ancient Pibroch belonging to the Clan MacDonald, and
supposed to refer to the expedition of Donald Balloch, who, in 1431,
launched from the Isles with a considerable force, invaded Lochaber,
and at Inverlochy defeated and put to flight the Earls of Mar and
Caithness, though at the head of an army superior to his own. The
words of the set, theme, or melody, to which the pipe variations are
applied, run thus in Gaelic:

> Piobaireachd Dhonuil, piobaireachd Dhonuil;
> Piobaireachd Dhonuil Duidh, piobaireachd Dhonuil;
> Piobaireachd Dhonuil Dhuidh, piobaireachd Donuil;
> Piob agus bratach air faiche Inverlochi.

> The pipe-summons of Donald the Black,
> The pipe-summons of Donald the Black,
> The war-pipe and the pennon are on the gathering place
>   at Inverlochy.

Pibroch of Donuil Dhu,
    Pibroch of Donuil,
Wake thy wild voice anew,
    Summon Clan-Conuil.
Come away, come away,   5
    Hark to the summons!
Come in your war array,
    Gentles and commons.

Come from deep glen, and
    From mountain so rocky,   10
The war-pipe and pennon
    Are at Inverlocky:
Come every hill-plaid, and
    True heart that wears one,
Come every steel blade, and   15
    Strong hand that bears one.

[*] The pibroch of Donald the Black.

Leave untended the herd,
 The flock without shelter;
Leave the corpse uninterr'd,
 The bride at the altar;   20
Leave the deer, leave the steer,
 Leave nets and barges;
Come with your fighting gear,
 Broad swords and targes.

Come as the winds come, when   25
 Forests are rended;
Come as the waves come, when
 Navies are stranded:
Faster come, faster come,
 Faster and faster,   30
Chief, vassal, page, and groom,
 Tenant and master.

Fast they come, fast they come;
 See how they gather!
Wide waves the eagle plume,   35
 Blended with heather.
Cast your plaids, draw your blades,
 Forward each man set!
Pibroch of Donuil Dhu,
 Knell for the onset!   40

93

Nora's Vow

Air—*Cha teid mis a chaoidh**

In the original Gaelic, the lady makes protestations that she will not
go with the Red Earl's son until the swan should build in the cliff, and
the eagle in the lake—until one mountain should change places with
another, and so forth. It is but fair to add that there is no authority for
supposing that she altered her mind—except the vehemence of her
protestation.

Hear what Highland Nora said,
"The Earlie's son I will not wed,
Should all the race of nature die,
And none be left but he and I.
For all the gold, for all the gear,   5
And all the lands both far and near,
That ever valour lost or won,
I would not wed the Earlie's son."

"A maiden's vows," old Callum spoke,
"Are lightly made, and lightly broke;   10
The heather on the mountain's height
Begins to bloom in purple light;
The frost-wind soon shall sweep away
That lustre deep from glen and brae;
Yet, Nora, ere its bloom be gone,   15
May blythely wed the Earlie's son."

"The swan," she said, "the lake's clear breast
May barter for the eagle's nest;
The Awe's fierce stream may backward turn,
Ben-Cruaichan fall, and crush Kilchurn,   20
Our kilted clans, when blood is high,
Before their foes may turn and fly;
But I, were all these marvels done,
Would never wed the Earlie's son."

* "I will never go with him."

Still in the water-lily's shade   25
Her wonted nest the wild swan made,
Ben-Cruaichan stands as fast as ever,
Still downward foams the Awe's fierce river;
To shun the clash of foeman's steel,
No Highland brogue has turn'd the heel;   30
But Nora's heart is lost and won,
—She's wedded to the Earlie's son!

94
MacGregor's Gathering

Air—Thain a' Grigalach*

These verses are adapted to a very wild, yet lively gathering-tune, used
by the MacGregors. The severe treatment of this clan, their outlawry,
and the prescription of their very name, are alluded to in the ballad.

The moon's on the lake, and the mist's on the brae,
And the Clan has a name that is nameless by day!
    Then gather, gather, gather, Gregalach!
    Gather, gather, gather, &c.

Our signal for fight, that from monarchs we drew,   5
Must be heard but by night in our vengeful haloo!
    Then haloo, Gregalach! haloo, Gregalach!
    Haloo, haloo, haloo, Gregalach, &c.

Glen Orchy's proud mountains, Coalchuirn and her towers,
Glenstrae and Glenlyon no longer are ours:
    We're landless, landless, landless, Gregalach!
    Landless, landless, landless, &c.

* "The MacGregor is come."

But doom'd and devoted by vassal and lord,
MacGregor has still both his heart and his sword!
   Then courage, courage, courage, Gregalach,   15
   Courage, courage, courage, &c.

If they rob us of name and pursue us with beagles,
Give their roofs to the flames, and their flesh to the eagles!
   Then vengeance, vengeance, vengeance, Gregalach!
   Vengeance, vengeance, vengeance, &c.   20

While there's leaves in the forest, and foam on the river,
MacGregor, despite them, shall flourish forever!
   Come then, Gregalach, come then, Gregalach,
   Come then, come then, come then, &c.

Through the depths of Loch Katrine the steed shall career,
O'er the peak of Ben-Lomond the galley shall steer,
And the rocks of Craig Royston like icicles melt,
Ere our wrongs be forgot, or our vengeance unfelt!
   Then gather, gather, gather, Gregalach!
   Gather, gather, gather, &c.   30

95
Verses, Composed for the Occasion

God protect brave ALEXANDER!
   Heaven defend the noble Czar!
Mighty Russia's high Commander,
   First in Europe's banded war.
For the realms he did deliver   5
   From the Tyrant overthrown,
Thou, of every good the Giver,
   Grant him long to bless his own.

Bless him! mid his land's disaster,
    For her rights who battled brave;   10
Of the land of foemen master,
    Bless him, who their wrongs forgave.
O'er his just resentment victor,
    Victor over Europe's foes,
Late and long, Supreme Director,   15
    Grant in peace his reign may close.

Hail! then, hail! ILLUSTRIOUS STRANGER!
    Welcome to our mountain strand;
Mutual interests, hopes, and danger,
    Link us with thy native land.   20
Foemen's force, or false beguiling,
    Shall that union ne'er divide:
Hand in hand, while Peace is smiling;
    And, in battle, side by side.

96

The Search After Happiness; or, The Quest of Sultaun Solimaun

O, for a glance of that gay Muse's eye,
    That lighten'd on Bandello's laughing tale,
And twinkled with a lustre shrewd and sly
    When Giam Battista bade her vision hail!*
Yet fear not, ladies, the *naïve* detail   5
    Given by the natives of that land canorous;
Italian license loves to leap the pale,
    We Britons have the fear of shame before us,
And, if not wise in mirth, at least must be decorous.

*The hint of the following tale is taken from *La Camiscia Magica*, a novel of Giam Battista Casti.

In the far eastern clime, no great while since,   10
Lived Sultaun Solimaun, a mighty prince,
Whose eyes, as oft as they perform'd their round,
Beheld all others fix'd upon the ground;
Whose ears received the same unvaried phrase,
"Sultaun! thy vassal hears, and he obeys!"—   15
All have their tastes—this may the fancy strike
Of such grave folks as pomp and grandeur like;
For me, I love the honest heart and warm
Of Monarch who can amble round his farm,
Or, when the toil of state no more annoys,   20
In chimney corner seek domestic joys—
I love a Prince will bid the bottle pass,
Exchanging with his subjects glance and glass;
In fitting time, can, gayest of the gay,
Keep up the jest and mingle in the lay—   25
Such Monarchs best our free-born humours suit,
But Despots must be stately, stern, and mute.

This Solimaun, Serendib had in sway—
And where's Serendib? may some critic say.—
Good lack, mine honest friend, consult the chart,   30
Scare not my Pegasus before I start!
If Rennell has it not, you'll find, mayhap,
The isle laid down in Captain Sindbad's map,—
Famed mariner! whose merciless narrations
Drove every friend and kinsman out of patience,   35
Till, fain to find a guest who thought them shorter,
He deign'd to tell them over to a porter—
The last edition see by Long: and Co.,
Rees, Hurst, and Orme, our fathers in the Row.

Serendib found, deem not my tale a fiction—   40
This Sultaun, whether lacking contradiction—
(A sort of stimulant which hath its uses,
To raise the spirits and reform the juices,
Sovereign specific for all sorts of cures
In my wife's practice, and perhaps in yours,)   45

The Sultaun lacking this same wholesome bitter,
Or cordial smooth for prince's palate fitter—
Or if some Mollah had hag-rid his dreams
With Degial, Ginnistan, and such wild themes
Belonging to the Mollah's subtle craft,   50
I wot not—but the Sultaun never laugh'd,
Scarce ate or drank, and took a melancholy
That scorn'd all remedy profane or holy;
In his long list of melancholies, mad,
Or mazed, or dumb, hath Burton none so bad.   55

Physicians soon arrived, sage, ware, and tried,
     As e'er scrawl'd jargon in a darken'd room;
With heedful glance the Sultaun's tongue they eyed,
Peep'd in his bath, and God knows where beside,
     And then in solemn accents spoke their doom,   60
"His Majesty is very far from well."
Then each to work with his specific fell:
The Hakim Ibrahim *instanter* brought
His unguent Mahazzim al Zerdukkaut,*
While Roompot, a practitioner more wily,   65
Relied on his Munaskif al fillfily.*
More and yet more in deep array appear,
And some the front assail and some the rear;
Their remedies to reinforce and vary,
Came surgeon eke, and eke apothecary;   70
Till the tired Monarch, though of words grown chary,
Yet dropt, to recompense their fruitless labour,
Some hint about a bowstring or a sabre.
There lack'd, I promise you, no longer speeches,
To rid the palace of those learned leeches.   75

Then was the council call'd—by their advice,
(They deem'd the matter ticklish all, and nice,
     And sought to shift it off from their own shoulders)

---

* For these hard words see D'Herbelot, or the learned editor of the Receipts of Avicenna.

Tatārs and couriers in all speed were sent,
To call a sort of Eastern parliament   80
   Of feudatory chieftains and freeholders—
Such have the Persians at this very day,
My learned Malcolm calls them *couroultai*;
I'm not prepared to show in this slight song
That to Serendib the same forms belong,—
E'en let the learn'd go search, and tell me if I'm wrong.

The Omrahs,* each with hand on scymitar,
Gave, like Sempronius, still their voice for war—
"The sabre of the Sultaun in its sheath
Too long has slept, nor own'd the work of death;   90
Let the Tambourgi bid his signal rattle,
Bang the loud gong and raise the shout of battle!
This dreary cloud that dims our sovereign's day,
Shall from his kindled bosom flit away,
When the bold Lootie wheels his courser round,   95
And the arm'd elephant shall shake the ground.
Each Noble pants to own the glorious summons—
And for the charges—Lo! your faithful Commons!"—
The Riots who attended in their places
   (Serendib-language calls a farmer Riot)   100
Look'd ruefully in one another's faces,
   From this oration auguring much disquiet,
Double assessment, forage, and free quarters;
And fearing these as China-men the Tartars,
Or as the whisker'd vermin fear the mousers,   105
Each fumbled in the pocket of his trowsers.

And next came forth the reverend Convocation,
   Bald heads, white beards, and many a turban green;
Imaum and Mollah there of every station,
   Santon, Fakir, and Calendar were seen.   110
Their votes were various—some advised a Mosque
   With fitting revenues should be erected,

* Nobility.

With seemly gardens and with gay Kiosque,
   To recreate a band of priests selected;
Others opined that through the realm a dole   115
   Be made to holy men, whose prayers might profit
The Sultaun's weal in body and in soul;
   But their long-headed chief, the Sheik Ul-Sofit,
More closely touch'd the point;—"Thy studious mood,"
Quoth he, "O Prince! hath thicken'd all thy blood,
And dull'd thy brain with labour beyond measure;
Wherefore relax a space and take thy pleasure,
And toy with beauty or tell o'er thy treasure;
From all the cares of state, my liege, enlarge thee,
And leave the burthen to thy faithful clergy."   125

These councils sage availed not a whit,
   And so the patient (as is not uncommon
Where grave physicians lose their time and wit)
   Resolved to take advice of an old woman;
His mother she, a dame who once was beauteous,   130
And still was call'd so by each subject duteous.
Now, whether Fatima was witch in earnest,
   Or only made believe, I cannot say—
But she profess'd to cure disease the sternest,
   By dint of magic amulet or lay;   135
And, when all other skill in vain was shown,
She deem'd it fitting time to use her own.

"*Sympathia magica* hath wonders done,"
(Thus did old Fatima bespeak her son,)
"It works upon the fibres and the pores,   140
And thus, insensibly, our health restores,
And it must help us here.—Thou must endure
The ill, my son, or travel for the cure.
Search land and sea, and get, where'er you can,
The inmost vesture of a happy man,   145
I mean his SHIRT, my son, which, if worn warm
And fresh from off his back, shall chase your harm,

Bid every current of your veins rejoice,
And your dull heart leap light as shepherd boy's."—
Such was the counsel from his mother came.   150
I know not if she had some under-game,
As Doctors have, who bid their patients roam
And live abroad, when sure to die at home;
Or if she thought, that somehow or another,
Queen Regent sounded better than Queen Mother;   155
But, says the Chronicle, (who will go look it,)
That such was her advice—the Sultaun took it.

All are on board—the Sultaun and his train,
In gilded galley prompt to plough the main:
   The old Rais* was the first who question'd,
              "Whither?"   160
They paused—"Arabia," thought the pensive Prince,
"Was call'd The Happy many ages since—
   For Mokha, Rais."—And they came safely thither.
But not in Araby with all her balm,
Not where Judæa weeps beneath her palm,   165
Not in rich Egypt, not in Nubian waste,
Could there the step of Happiness be traced.
One Copt alone profess'd to have seen her smile,
When Bruce his goblet fill'd at infant Nile;
She bless'd the dauntless traveller as he quaff'd,   170
But vanish'd from him with the ended draught.

"Enough of turbans," said the weary King,
"These dolimans of ours are not the thing;
Try we the Giaours, these men of coat and cap, I
Incline to think some of them must be happy;   175
At least they have as fair a cause as any can,
They drink good wine and keep no Ramazan.
Then northward, ho!" The vessel cuts the sea,
And fair Italia lies upon her lee.—
But fair Italia, she who once unfurl'd   180

* Master of the vessel.

Her eagle-banners o'er a conquer'd world,
Long from her throne of domination tumbled,
Lay, by her quondam vassals, sorely humbled;
The Pope himself looked pensive, pale, and lean,
And was not half the man he once had been.   185
"While these the priest and those the noble fleeces,
Our poor old boot,"* they said, "is torn to pieces.
Its top† the vengeful claws of Austria feel,
And the Great Devil is rending toe and heel.‡
If happiness you seek, to tell you truly,   190
We think she dwells with one Giovanni Bulli;
A tramontane, a heretic, the buck,
Poffaredio! still has all the luck;
By land or ocean never strikes his flag—
And then—a perfect walking money-bag."   195
Off set our Prince to seek John Bull's abode,
But first took France—it lay upon the road.

Monsieur Baboon, after much late commotion,
Was agitated like a settling ocean,
Quite out of sorts, and could not tell what ail'd him,   200
Only the glory of his house had fail'd him;
Besides, some tumours on his noddle biding,
Gave indication of a recent hiding.§
Our Prince, though Sultauns of such things are heedless,
Thought it a thing indelicate and needless
To ask, if at that moment he was happy.
And Monsieur, seeing that he was *comme il faut*, a
Loud voice mustered up, for "*Vive le Roi!*"
Then whisper'd, "Ave you any news of Nappy?"
The Sultaun answer'd him with a cross question,—   210
"Pray, can you tell me aught of one John Bull,
That dwells somewhere beyond your herring-pool?"

* The well-known resemblance of Italy in the map.
† Florence, Venice, &c.
‡ The Calabrias infested by bands of assassins. One of the leaders was called Fra Diavolo, *i.e.* Brother Devil.
§ Or drubbing, so called in the Slang Dictionary.

The query seem'd of difficult digestion,
The party shrugg'd, and grinn'd, and took his snuff,
And found his whole good breeding scarce enough.   215

Twitching his visage into as many puckers
As damsels wont to put into their tuckers,
Ere liberal Fashion damn'd both lace and lawn,
And bade the veil of modesty be drawn;
Replied the Frenchman, after a brief pause,   220
"Jean Bool!—I vas not know him—yes, I vas—
I vas remember dat von year or two,
I saw him at von place called Vaterloo—
Ma foi! il s'est tres joliment battu,
Dat is for Englishman,—m' entendez vous?   225
But den he had wit him one damn son-gun,
Rogue I no like—dey call him Vellington."—
Monsieur's politeness could not hide his fret,
So Solimaun took leave and cross'd the streight.

John Bull was in his very worst of moods,   230
Raving of sterile farms and unsold goods;
His sugar-loaves and bales about he threw,
And on his counter beat the Devil's tattoo.
His wars were ended, and the victory won,
But then, 'twas reckoning-day with honest John,   235
And authors vouch 'twas still this Worthy's way,
"Never to grumble till he came to pay;
And then he always thinks, his temper's such,
The work too little, and the pay too much."*
Yet, grumbler as he is, so kind and hearty,   240
    That when his mortal foe was on the floor,
    And past the power to harm his quiet more,
Poor John had well nigh wept for Bonaparte!
Such was the wight whom Solimaun salam'd,—
"And who are you," John answer'd, "and be d—d?" 245

* See the True-Born Englishman, by Daniel De Foe.

"A stranger come, to see the happiest man,—
So, Seignior, all avouch,—in Frangistan."*—
"Happy? my tenants breaking on my hand,
Unstock'd my pastures, and untill'd my land;
Sugar and rum a drug, and mice and moths   250
The sole consumers of my good broad-cloths—
Happy?—why, cursed war and racking tax
Have left us scarcely raiment to our backs."
"In that case, Seignior, I may take my leave;
I came to ask a favour—but I grieve"—   255
"Favour?" said John, and eyed the Sultaun hard,
"It's my belief you came to break the yard—
But, stay, you look like some poor foreign sinner,—
Take that, to buy yourself a shirt and dinner."—
With that he chuck'd a guinea at his head;   260
But, with due dignity, the Sultaun said,—
"Permit me, sir, your bounty to decline;
A *shirt* indeed I seek, but none of thine.
Seignior, I kiss your hands, so fare you well."
And John said,—"Kiss my breech, and go to hell!"   265

Next door to John there dwelt his sister Peg,
Once a wild lass as ever shook a leg
When the blithe bagpipe blew—but soberer now,
She *doucely* span her flax and milked her cow.
And whereas erst she was a needy slattern,   270
Nor now of wealth or cleanliness a pattern,
Yet once a-month her house was partly swept,
And once a-week a plenteous board she kept.
And whereas eke the vixen used her claws,
    And teeth, of yore, on slender provocation,   275
She now was grown amenable to laws,
    A quiet soul as any in the nation;
The sole remembrance of her warlike joys
Was in old songs she sang to please her boys.

* Europe.

John Bull, whom, in their years of early strife,   280
She wont to lead a cat-and-doggish life,
Now found the woman, as he said, a neighbour,
Who look'd to the main chance, declined no labour,
Loved a long grace and spoke a northern jargon,
And was d—d close in making of a bargain.   285

The Sultaun enter'd, and he made his leg,
And with decorum curtsied sister Peg;
(She loved a book, and knew a thing or two,
And guess'd at once with whom she had to do)
She bade him "sit into the fire," and took   290
Her dram, her cake, her kebbock, from the nook;
Asked him "about the news from eastern parts;
And of her absent bairns, puir Highland hearts!
If peace brought down the price of tea and pepper,
And if the *nitmugs* were grown *ony* cheaper;—   295
Were there nae *speerings* of our Mungo Park—
Ye'll be the gentleman that wants the sark?
If ye wad buy a web o' auld wife's spinning,
I'll warrant ye it's a weel-wearing linen."

Then up got Peg, and round the house 'gan scuttle,   300
     In search of goods her customer to nail,
Until the Sultaun strain'd his princely throttle,
     And hollowed,—"Ma'am, that is not what I ail.
Pray, are you happy, ma'am, in this snug glen?"
"Happy?" said Peg, "What for d'ye want to ken?—   305
Besides, just think upon this by-gane year,
     Grain wadna pay the yoking of the pleugh."
"What say you to the present?"—"Meal's sae dear,
     To mak their *brose* my bairns have scarce aneugh."
"The devil take the shirt," said Solimaun,   310
"I think my quest will end as it began.
Farewell, ma'am; nay, no ceremony, I beg"—
"Ye'll no be for the linen then?" said Peg.

Now, for the land of verdant Erin,
The Sultaun's royal bark is steering,   315
The emerald isle where honest Paddy dwells,
The cousin of John Bull, as story tells.
For a long space had John, with words of thunder,
Hard looks, and harder knocks, kept Paddy under,
Till the poor lad, like boy that's flogg'd unduly,   320
Had gotten somewhat restive and unruly.
Hard was his lot and lodging you'll allow,
A wigwam that would hardly serve a sow;
His landlord, and of middlemen two brace,
Had screw'd his rent up to the starving place;   325
His garment was a top-coat, and an old one,
His meal was a potatoe, and a cold one;
But still for fun or frolic, and all that,
In the round world was not the match of Pat.

The Sultaun saw him on a holiday,   330
Which is with Paddy still a jolly day:
When mass is ended, and his load of sins
Confess'd, and Mother Church hath from her binns
Dealt forth a bonus of imputed merit,
Then is Pat's time for fancy, whim, and spirit!   335
To jest, to sing, to caper fair and free,
And dance as light as leaf upon the tree.
"By Mahomet," said Sultaun Solimaun,
"That ragged fellow is our very man!
Rush in and seize him—do not do him hurt,   340
But, will he nill he, let me have his *shirt*."

Shilela their plan was well nigh after baulking,
(Much less provocation will set it a-walking,)
But the odds that foil'd Hercules foil'd Paddy Whack;
They seized, and they floor'd, and they stripp'd
                       him—Alack!   345
Ub-bubboo! Paddy had not—a shirt to his back!!!
And the King disappointed, with sorrow and shame,
Went back to Serendib as sad as he came.

97

Mr Kemble's Farewell Address,

On Taking Leave of the Edinburgh Stage

As the worn war-horse, at the trumpet's sound,
Erects his mane, and neighs, and paws the ground—
Disdains the ease his generous lord assigns,
And longs to rush on the embattled lines,
So I, your plaudits ringing on mine ear,   5
Can scarce sustain to think our parting near;
To think my scenic hour for ever past,
And that those valued plaudits are my last.
Why should we part, while still some powers remain,
That in your service strive not yet in vain?   10
Cannot high zeal the strength of youth supply,
And sense of duty fire the fading eye;
And all the wrongs of age remain subdued
Beneath the burning glow of gratitude?
Ah no! the taper, wearing to its close,   15
Oft for a space in fitful lustre glows;
But all too soon the transient gleam is past,
It cannot be renew'd, and will not last;
Even duty, zeal, and gratitude, can wage
But short-lived conflict with the frosts of age.   20
Yes! It were poor, remembering what I was,
To live a pensioner on your applause,
To drain the dregs of your endurance dry,
And take, as alms, the praise I once could buy,
Till every sneering youth around enquires,   25
"Is this the man who once could please our sires?"
And scorn assumes compassion's doubtful mien,
To warn me off from the encumber'd scene.
This must not be; —and higher duties crave
Some space between the theatre and the grave;   30
That, like the Roman in the Capitol,
I may adjust my mantle ere I fall:
My life's brief act in public service flown,
The last, the closing scene, must be my own.

Here, then, adieu! while yet some well-graced parts
May fix an ancient favourite in your hearts,
Not quite to be forgotten, even when
You look on better actors, younger men:
And if your bosoms own this kindly debt
Of old remembrance, how shall mine forget—   40
O, how forget!—how oft I hither came
In anxious hope, how oft return'd with fame!
How oft around your circle this weak hand
Has waved immortal Shakespeare's magic wand,
Till the full burst of inspiration came,   45
And I have felt, and you have fann'd, the flame!
By mem'ry treasured, while her reign endures,
Those hours must live—and all their charms are your's.

O favour'd Land! renown'd for arts and arms,
For manly talent and for female charms,   50
Could this full bosom prompt the sinking line,
What fervent benedictions now were thine!
But my last part is play'd, my knell is rung,
When e'en your praise falls faultering from my tongue;
And all that you can hear, or I can tell,   55
Is—Friends and Patrons, hail, and FARE YOU WELL!

98

The Foray

The last of the steers on our board has been spread,
And the last flask of wine in our goblets is red;
Up! up! my brave kinsmen! belt swords and be gone!
There are dangers to dare, and there's spoil to be won.

The eyes, that so lately mix'd glances with our's,   5
For a space must be dim, as they gaze from the towers,
And strive to distinguish, through tempest and gloom,
The prance of the steed, and the toss of the plume.

The rain is descending; the wind rises loud;
And the moon her red beacon has veil'd with a cloud;   10
'Tis the better, my mates; for the Warder's dull eye
Shall in confidence slumber, nor dream we are nigh.

Our steeds are impatient! I hear my blythe Grey!
There is life in his hoof-clang, and hope in his neigh;
Like the flash of a meteor, the glance of his mane
Shall marshal your march through the darkness and rain.

The drawbridge has dropp'd, and the bugle has blown;
One pledge is to quaff yet—then mount and be gone!—
To their honour and peace, that shall rest with the slain;
To their health and their glee, that see Teviot again!

99

Epistle to His Grace the Duke of Buccleuch, at Drumlanrig Castle

From Ross where the clouds on Ben-Lomond are sleeping
From Greenock where Clyde to the Ocean is sweeping
From Largs where the Scotch gave the Northmen a drilling
From Ardrossan whose harbour cost many a shilling
From Old Cumnock where beds are as hard as a plank Sir   5
From a chop and green pease and a chicken at Sanquhar
This eve please the fates at Drumlanrigg we anchor.

100
Mackrimmon's Lament

Air—*Cha till mi tuille**

Mackrimmon, hereditary piper to the Laird of Macleod, is said to have composed this lament when the Clan was about to depart upon a distant and dangerous expedition. The Minstrel was impressed with a belief, which the event verified, that he was to be slain in the approaching feud; and hence the Gaelic words, "*Cha till mi tuille; ged thillis Macleod, cha till Macrimmon*," "I shall never return; although Macleod returns, yet Mackrimmon shall never return!" The piece is but too well known, from its being the strain with which the emigrants from the West Highlands and Isles usually take leave of their native shore.

Macleod's wizard flag from the gray castle sallies,
The rowers are seated, unmoor'd are the gallies;
Gleam war-axe and broad-sword, clang target and quiver,
As Mackrimmon sings, "Farewell to Dunvegan for ever!
Farewell to each cliff, on which breakers are foaming; 5
Farewell each dark glen, in which red deer are roaming;
Farewell lonely SKYE, to lake, mountain, and river,
Macleod may return, but Mackrimmon shall never!

"Farewell the bright clouds that on Quillan are sleeping;
Farewell the bright eyes in the Dun that are weeping; 10
To each minstrel delusion, farewell!—and for ever—
Mackrimmon departs, to return to you never!
The *Banshee*'s wild voice sings the death-dirge before me,
The pall of the dead for a mantle hangs o'er me;
But my heart shall not flag, and my nerves shall not shiver,
Though devoted I go—to return again never!

---

* "We return no more."

"Too oft shall the notes of Mackrimmon's bewailing
Be heard when the GAEL on their exile are sailing;
Dear land! to the shores, whence unwilling we sever,
Return—return—return—shall we never!   20
Cha till, cha till, cha till sin tuille!
Cha till, cha till, cha till sin tuille,
Cha till, cha till, cha till sin tuille,
Ged thillis Macleod, cha till Macrimmon!"

101

Donald Caird's Come Again!

Air—*Malcolm Caird's come again**

CHORUS
Donald Caird's come again!
Donald Caird's come again!
Tell the news in burgh and glen
Donald Caird's come again!

Donald Caird can lilt and sing,   5
Blithely dance the Hieland fling,
Drink till the gudeman be blind,
Fleech till the gudewife be kind;
Hoop a leglen, clout a pan,
Or crack a pow wi' ony man;   10
Tell the news in burgh and glen
Donald Caird's come again!
    Donald Caird's come again!
    Donald Caird's come again!
    Tell the news in burgh and glen   15
    Donald Caird's come again!

* Caird, or Ceard, (Gaelic,) *Tinker.*

Donald Caird can wire a maukin,
Kens the wiles o' dun deer staukin'
Leisters kipper, makes a shift
To shoot a moor-fowl in the drift,   20
Water-bailiffs, rangers, keepers,
He can wauk when you are sleepers;
Not for bountith or reward,
Dare ye mell wi' Donald Caird!
    Donald Caird's come again!   25
    Donald Caird's come again!
    Gar the bag-pipes hum amain
    Donald Caird's come again!

Donald Caird can drink a gill
Fast as hostler-wife can fill;   30
Ilka ane that sells gude liquor
Kens how Donald bends a bicker;
When he's fou he's stout and saucy,
Keeps the cantle of the cawsey;
Highland chief and Lawland laird   35
Maun gie room to Donald Caird!
    Donald Caird's come again!
    Donald Caird's come again!
    Tell the news in burgh and glen,
    Donald Caird's come again!   40

Steek the amrie, lock the kist,
Else some gear may weel be mist;
Donald Caird finds orra things
Where Allan Gregor fund the tings;
Dunts of kebbuck, taits of woo',   45
Whiles a hen, and whiles a sow,
Webs or duds frae hedge or yard—
'Ware the widdie Donald Caird!
    Donald Caird's come again!
    Donald Caird's come again!   50
    Dinna let the Shirra ken
    Donald Caird's come again!

On Donald Caird the doom was stern,
Craig to tether, legs to airn;
But Donald Caird, wi' mickle study,   55
Caught the gift to cheat the woodie;
Rings of airn, and bolts of steel,
Fell like ice frae hand and heel!—
Watch the sheep, in fauld and glen,
Donald Caird's loose again!—   60
    Donald Caird's come again!
    Donald Caird's come again!
    Dinna let the Justice ken,
    Donald Caird's come again!

102
The Sun upon the Weirdlaw Hill

Air—*Rimhin aluin 'stu mo rùn*

The sun upon the Weirdlaw hill,
  In Ettrick's vale, is sinking sweet;
The westland wind is hush and still,
  The lake lies sleeping at my feet.
Yet not the landscape to mine eye   5
  Bears those bright hues that once it bore;
Though Evening, with her richest dye,
  Flames o'er the hills on Ettrick's shore.

With listless look along the plain,
  I see Tweed's silver current glide,   10
And coldly mark the holy fane
  Of Melrose rise in ruin'd pride.
The quiet lake, the balmy air,
  The hill, the stream, the tower, the tree,—
Are they still such as once they were,   15
  Or is the dreary change in me?

Alas, the warp'd and broken board,
   How can it bear the painter's dye!
The harp of strain'd and tuneless chord,
   How to the minstrel's skill reply!   20
To aching eyes each landscape lowers,
   To feverish pulse each gale blows chill;
And Araby's or Eden's bowers,
   Were barren as this moorland hill.

103

ꟻarewell to the Muse

Enchantress, farewell, who so oft has decoy'd me,
At the close of the evening, through woodlands to roam,
Where the forester, lated, with wonder espied me
Seek out the wild scenes he was quitting, for home.
Farewell, and take with thee thy numbers wild speaking, 5
The language alternate of rapture and woe;
Oh! none but some lover whose heart-strings are breaking,
The pang that I feel at our parting can know.

Each joy thou could'st double, and when there came
                sorrow,
Or pale disappointment, to darken my way,   10
What voice was like thine that could sing of to-morrow,
'Till forgot in the strain was the grief of to-day!
But when friends drop around us in life's weary waneing,
The grief, Queen of numbers, thou can'st not assuage;
Nor the gradual estrangement of those yet remaining, 15
The languor of pain, and the chillness of age.

'Twas thou that once taught me in accents bewailing,
To sing how a warrior lay stretch'd on the plain,
And a maiden hung o'er him with aid unavailing,
And held to his lips the cold goblet in vain.   20

As vain those enchantments, O Queen of wild numbers,
To a bard when the reign of his fancy is o'er,
And the quick pulse of feeling in apathy slumbers—
Farewell then, Enchantress!—I meet thee no more.

104
Epilogue to *The Appeal*

A cat of yore (or else old Æsop lied)
Was chang'd into a fair and blooming bride,
But spied a mouse upon her marriage day,
Forgot her spouse and seiz'd upon her prey;
Even thus my bridegroom lawyer, as you saw,   5
Threw off poor me and pounc'd upon papa,
His neck from Hymen's mystic knot made loose,
He twisted round my sire's the literal noose.
Such are the fruits of our dramatic labour
Since the New Jail became our next door neighbour.*   10

Yes, times *are* changed, for in your fathers' age
The lawyers were the patrons of the stage;
However high advanced by future fate,
There stands the bench *(points to the Pit)* that first
                                        receiv'd their weight.

The future legal sage, 'twas ours to see,   15
Doom though unwigg'd, and plead without a fee;
But now astounding each poor mimic elf,
Instead of lawyers comes the law herself;
Alarming neighbours, on our right she dwells,
Builds high her towers and excavates her cells;   20

---

* It is necessary to mention, that the allusions in this piece are all local, and addressed only to the Edinburgh audience. The new prisons of the city, on the Calton Hill, are not far from the Theatre.

While on the left, she agitates the town
With the tremendous question, Up or down?*
'Twixt Scylla and Charybdis thus stand we,
Law's final end and law's uncertainty.
But soft, who lives at Rome the Pope must flatter,   25
And jails and lawsuits are no jesting matter;
Then just farewell, we wait with serious awe
'Till your applause or censure gives the law,
Trusting our humble efforts may assure ye
We hold you Court and Counsel, Judge and Jury.   30

105

The Maid of Isla

Imitated from the Gaelic

Air—The Maid of Isla

O Maid of Isla, from yon cliff,
That looks on troubled wave and sky,
Dost thou not see yon little skiff,
Contend with ocean gallantly?
Now beating 'gainst the breeze and surge,   5
And steep'd her leeward deck in foam,
Why does she war unequal urge?—
O Isla's Maid, she seeks her home.

O Isla's Maid, yon sea-bird mark,
Her white wing gleams through mist and spray,   10
Against the storm-cloud, lowering dark,
As to the rock she wheels her way.

---

* The new buildings on the North Bridge, which have given rise to so many picturesque conversations about the scenery of the town, and so many debates as to whether they should be allowed to stand as a protection from the high winds of the west, or removed as a deformity in view of the inhabitants of Prince's Street towards the east.

ف

Where clouds are dark and billows rave,
Why to the shelter should she come
Of cliff exposed to wind and wave?—   15
O Maid of Isla, 'tis her home.

As breeze and tide to yonder skiff,
Thou'rt adverse to the suit I bring,
And cold as is yon wintery cliff,
Where sea-birds close their wearied wing.   20
Yet cold as rock, unkind as wave,
Still, Isla's Maid, to thee I come;
For in thy love, or in his grave,
Must Allan Vourich find his home.

106
I, Walter Scott of Abbotsford

I, Walter Scott of Abbotsford, a poor scholar, no
                              soldier but a soldier's lover
In the stile of my namesake and kinsman do hereby discover
That I have written the twenty-four letters twenty-
                              four million times over.—
And to every true-born Scott I do wish as many
                              golden pieces
As ever were hairs on Jason's and Medea's golden fleeces. 5

107
My Mither is of Sturdy Airn

My Mither is of sturdy airn,
A copper Dwarf am I, her Bairn;
Of Silver ore, a tray I hold,
And am clad o'er with beaten gold.

The airn speaks stalworth heart and hand,   5
The copper wealth and wide command,
The Silver rank and noble name,
The gold true worth and spotless fame.

Long have they flourish'd, long may they
Still flourish in the House of GRAY.   10

108
𝕷ines on the 𝕮aledonian 𝕮anal

Far in the desert Scottish bounds I saw
Art's proudest triumph over Nature's law;
Where, distant shores and oceans to combine,
Her daring hand has traced a liquid line,
Uniting lakes, around whose verges rise   5
Mountains which hide their heads in misty skies;
Each, bound within such adamantine chain,
For ages lash'd its lonely shores in vain,
Till, through their barriers, skill and labour led
The willing waves along a level bed.   10
Thus, e'en within her wildest fastness, man
Subdued his step-dame Nature's churlish plan.
The barren wilds, divested of their shade,
No trees could yield the giant-work to aid.
To mould the gates the skilful artist hied,   15
And iron frames the want of oak supplied.
Form'd of such stern material, portals nine,
In basins eight, the sever'd waves confine;
Locking each portion in its separate cell,
Whose gloomy grots might seem the gates of hell.   20
But better-augur'd name the passage bears,
Call'd by the hardy pilot NEPTUNE'S STAIRS.

There might the Sea-God and his vassals meet,
And gratulate the fair descending fleet,
When down those wat'ry stairs were seen to glide   25
Eight gallant sail that sought th'Atlantic tide.
Commerce and Art the floating wonder hail'd,
And triumph'd where the Roman arms had fail'd.

109

The Noble Moringer

An Ancient Ballad, Translated from the German

The original of these verses occurs in a collection of German popular songs, entitled *Sammlung Deutscher Volkslieder*, Berlin, 1807, published by Messrs Busching and Von der Hagen, both, and more especially the last, distinguished for their acquaintance with the ancient popular poetry and legendary history of Germany.

In the German Editor's notice of the ballad, it is stated to have been extracted from a manuscript Chronicle of Nicolaus Thomann, chaplain to Saint Leonard in Weisenhorn, which bears the date 1533; and the song is stated by the author to have been generally sung in the neighbourhood at that early period. Thomann, as quoted by the German Editor, seems faithfully to have believed the event he narrates. He quotes tomb-stones and obituaries to prove the existence of the personages of the ballad, and discovers that there actually died on the 11th May 1349, a Lady Von Neuffen, Countess of Marstetten, who was by birth of the house of Moringer. This Lady he supposes to have been Moringer's daughter mentioned in the ballad. He quotes the same authority for the death of Berckhold Von Neuffen in the same year. The editors, on the whole, seem to embrace the opinion of Professor Smith of Ulm, who, from the language of the ballad, ascribes its date to the fifteenth century.

The legend itself turns on an incident not peculiar to Germany, and which perhaps was not unlikely to happen in more instances than one, when crusaders abode long in the Holy Land, and their disconsolate dames received no tidings of their fate. A story very similar in circumstances, but without the miraculous machinery of Saint Thomas, is told of one of the ancient Lords of Haigh-hall in Lancashire, the patrimonial inheritance of the late Countess of Balcarras; and the particulars are represented on stained glass upon a window in that ancient manor house.

O, will you hear a knightly tale of old Bohemian day,
It was the noble Moringer in wedlock bed he lay,
He halsed and kiss'd his dearest dame, that was as sweet
                         as May,
And said, "Now, Lady of my heart, attend the words I say.

"'Tis I have vow'd a pilgrimage unto a distant shrine,   5
And I must seek Saint Thomas-land, and leave the land
                         that's mine;
Here shalt thou dwell the while in state, so thou wilt
                         pledge thy fay,
That thou for my return wilt wait seven twelvemonths
                         and a day."

Then out and spoke that Lady bright, sore troubled in
                         her cheer,
"Now tell me true, thou noble knight, what order takest
                         thou here;   10
And who shall lead thy vassal band, and hold thy lordly sway,
And be thy Lady's guardian true when thou art far away?"

Out spoke the noble Moringer, "Of that have thou no care,
There's many a valiant gentleman of me holds living fair;
The trustiest shall rule my land, my vassals and my state,
And be a guardian tried and true to thee, my lovely mate.

"As Christian-man, I needs must keep the vow which I
                         have plight,
When I am far in foreign land, remember thy true knight;
And cease, my dearest dame, to grieve, for vain were
                         sorrow now,
But grant thy Moringer his leave, since God hath heard
                         his vow."   20

It was the noble Moringer from bed he made him bowne,
And met him there his Chamberlain, with ewer and with
                         gown;
He flung the mantle on his back, 'twas furr'd with miniver,
He dipp'd his hand in water cold, and bathed his forehead fair.

"Now hear," he said, "Sir Chamberlain, true vassal art
                thou mine,
And such the trust that I repose in that proved worth of thine;
For seven years shalt thou rule my towers, and lead my
                vassal train,
And pledge thee for my Lady's faith till I return again."

The Chamberlain was blunt and true, and sturdily said he,
"Abide, my Lord, and rule your own, and take this rede
                from me;   30
That woman's faith's a brittle trust—Seven
                twelvemonths did'st thou say
I'll pledge me for no Lady's truth beyond the seventh fair
                day."

The noble Baron turn'd him round, his heart was full of care,
His gallant Esquire stood him nigh, he was Marstetten's heir,
To whom he spoke right anxiously, "Thou trusty squire
                to me,   35
Wilt thou receive this weighty trust when I am o'er the sea?

"To watch and ward my castle strong, and to protect my land,
And to the hunting or the host to lead my vassal band;
And pledge thee for my Lady's faith, till seven long years
                are gone,
And guard her as Our Lady dear was guarded by Saint
                John."   40

Marstetten's heir was kind and true, but fiery, hot and young,
And readily he answer made with too presumptuous tongue;
"My noble Lord, cast care away, and on your journey wend,
And trust this charge to me until your pilgrimage have end.

"Rely upon my plighted faith, which shall be truly tried,   45
To guard your lands, and ward your towers, and with
                your vassals ride;
And for your lovely Lady's faith, so virtuous and so dear,
I'll gage my head it knows no change, be absent thirty year."

The noble Moringer took cheer when thus he heard him speak,
And doubt forsook his troubled brow, and sorrow left his
                              cheek;   50
A long adieu he bids to all—hoists top-sails, and away,
And wanders in Saint Thomas-land seven twelvemonths
                              and a day.

It was the noble Moringer within an orchard slept,
When on the Baron's slumbering sense a boding vision crept,
And whisper'd in his ear a voice, "'Tis time, Sir Knight,
                              to wake,   55
Thy Lady and thine heritage another master take.

"Thy tower another banner knows, thy steeds another rein,
And stoop them to another's will thy gallant vassal train;
And she, the Lady of thy love, so faithful once and fair,
This night within thy father's hall she weds Marstetten's
                              heir."   60

It is the noble Moringer starts up and tears his beard,
"Oh would that I had ne'er been born! what tidings have
                              I heard?
To lose my lordship and my lands the less would be my care,
But God, that ere a squire untrue should wed my Lady fair!

"O good Saint Thomas hear," he pray'd, "my patron
                              Saint art thou,   65
A traitor robs me of my land even while I pay my vow!
My wife he brings to infamy, that was so pure of name,
And I am far in foreign land, and must endure the shame!"

It was the good Saint Thomas, then, who heard his
                              pilgrim's prayer
And sent a sleep so deep and dead that it o'erpower'd his care;
He waked in fair Bohemian land outstretch'd beside a rill,
High on the right a castle stood, low on the left a mill.

The Moringer he started up as one from spell unbound,
And dizzy with surprise and joy gazed wildly all around;
"I know my father's ancient towers, the mill, the stream I
　　　　　know,　　　　　　　　　　　　　　75
Now blessed be my patron Saint who cheer'd his
　　　　　pilgrim's woe."

He leant upon his pilgrim staff, and to the mill he drew,
So alter'd was his goodly form that none their master knew;
The Baron to the miller said, "Good friend, for charity,
Tell a poor palmer in your land what tidings may there be?" 80

The miller answer'd him again, "He knew of little news,
Save that the Lady of the land did a new bridegroom chuse;
Her husband died in distant land, such is the constant word,—
His death sits heavy on our souls, he was a worthy Lord.

"Of him I held this little mill, which wins me living free,　85
God rest the Baron in his grave, he still was kind to me;
And when Saint Martin's tide comes round, and millers
　　　　　take their toll,
The priest that prays for Moringer shall have both cope
　　　　　and stole."

It was the noble Moringer to climb the hill began,
And stood before the bolted gate a woe and weary man;
"Now help me, every saint in heaven that can compassion take,
To gain the entrance of my hall this woful match to break!"

His very knock it sounded sad, his call was sad and slow,
For heart and head, and voice and hand, were heavy all
　　　　　with woe;
And to the warder thus he spoke: "Friend, to thy Lady say, 95
A pilgrim from Saint Thomas-land craves harbour for a day.

"I've wander'd many a weary step, my strength is well
　　　　　nigh done,
And if she turn me from her gate I'll see no morrow's sun;

I pray, for sweet Saint Thomas' sake, a pilgrim's bed and dole,
And for the sake of Moringer's, her once loved husband's
        soul." 100

It was the stalwart warder then he came his dame before,
"A pilgrim worn and travel-toil'd stands at the castle door;
And prays for sweet Saint Thomas' sake for harbour and
        for dole,
And for the sake of Moringer thy noble husband's soul."

The Lady's gentle heart was moved, "Do up the gate,"
        she said, 105
"And bid the wanderer welcome be to banquet and to bed;
And since he names my husband's name, so that he lists
        to stay,
These towers shall be his harbourage a twelvemonth and
        a day."

It was the stalwart warder then undid the portal broad,
It was the noble Moringer that o'er the threshold strode;
"And have thou thanks, kind heaven," he said, "though
        from a man of sin,
That the true Lord stands here once more his castle gate
        within."

Then up the hall paced Moringer, his step was sad and slow,
It sat full heavy on his heart, none seem'd their Lord to know;
He sat him on a lowly bench, oppress'd with woe and
        wrong,—
Short space he sat, but ne'er to him seem'd little space so long.

Now spent was day and feasting o'er, and come was
        evening hour,
The time was nigh when new-made brides retire to
        nuptial bower;
"Our castle's wont," a brides-man said, "hath been both
        firm and long,
No guest to harbour in our halls till he shall chaunt a
        song." 120

Then spoke the youthful bridegroom there as he sat by
      the bride,
"My merry minstrel folks," quoth he, "lay shalm and
      harp aside;
Our pilgrim guest must sing a lay, the castle's rule to hold,
And well his guerdon will I pay with garment and with gold."

"Chill flows the lay of frozen age," 'twas thus the pilgrim
      sung,
"Nor golden meed, nor garment gay unlocks her heavy tongue;
Once did I sit, thou bridegroom gay, at board as rich as thine,
And by my side as fair a bride with all her charms was mine.

"But time traced furrows on my face, and I grew silver-haired,
For locks of brown, and cheeks of youth, she left this
      brow and beard;   130
Once rich, but now a palmer poor, I tread life's latest stage,
And mingle with your bridal mirth the lay of frozen age."

It was the noble Lady there this woeful lay that hears,
And for the aged pilgrim's grief her eye was dimm'd with
      tears;
She bade her gallant cup-bearer a golden beaker take, 135
And bear it to the palmer poor to quaff it for her sake.

It was the noble Moringer that dropp'd amid the wine
A bridal ring of burnish'd gold so costly and so fine:
Now listen, gentles, to my song, it tells you but the sooth,
'Twas with that very ring of gold he pledged his bridal
      truth.   140

Then to the cup-bearer he said, "Do me one kindly deed,
And should my better days return, full rich shall be thy meed;
Bear back the golden cup again to yonder bride so gay,
And crave her of her courtesy to pledge the palmer gray."

The cup-bearer was courtly bred, nor was the boon denied,
The golden cup he took again, and bore it to the bride;

"Lady," he said, "your reverend guest sends this, and
                bids me pray,
That, in thy noble courtesy, thou pledge the palmer gray."

The ring hath caught the Lady's eye, she views it close
                and near,
Then might you hear her shriek aloud, "The Moringer is
                here!"   150
Then might you see her start from seat, while tears in
                torrents fell,—
But whether 'twas for joy or woe the ladies best can tell.

But loud she utter'd thanks to heaven, and every saintly power,
That had return'd the Moringer before the midnight hour;
And loud she utter'd vow on vow, that never was there
                bride
That had like her preserved her troth, or been so sorely tried.

"Yes, here I claim the praise," she said, "to constant
                matrons due,
Who keep the troth that they have plight so stedfastly and true;
For count the term howe'er you will, so that you count aright,
Seven twelvemonths and a day are out when bells toll
                twelve to-night."   160

It was Marstetten then rose up, his falchion there he drew,
He kneel'd before the Moringer, and down his weapon threw;
"My oath and knightly faith are broke," these were the
                words he said,
"Then take, my liege, thy vassal's sword, and take thy
                vassal's head."

The noble Moringer he smiled, and then aloud did say,   165
"He gathers wisdom that hath roam'd seven
                twelvemonths and a day;
My daughter now hath fifteen years, fame speaks her
                sweet and fair,
I give her for the bride you lose, and name her for my heir."

The young bridegroom hath youthful bride, the old
                    bridegroom the old,
Whose faith was kept till term and tide so punctually
                    were told;   170
"But blessings on the warder kind that oped my castle gate,
For had I come at morrow tide, I came a day too late!"

110
Epitaph on Mrs Erskine

Plain, as her native dignity of mind,
Arise the tomb of her we have resign'd:
Unflaw'd and stainless be the marble scroll,
Emblem of lovely form, and candid soul.
But, Oh! what symbol may avail, to tell   5
The kindness, wit, and sense, we lov'd so well!
What sculpture shew the broken ties of life,
Here buried, with the Parent, Friend, and Wife!
Or, on the tablet, stamp each title dear,
By which thine urn, EUPHEMIA, claims the tear!   10
Yet, taught, by thy meek sufferance, to assume
Patience in anguish, hope beyond the tomb,
Resign'd, though sad, this votive verse shall flow,
And brief, alas! as thy brief span below.

111

For Mrs Siddons's Farewell to Dublin

The sinking curtain and the prompter's bell
Give the last signal—I must say Farewell—
Farewell—Brief mournful word—when that is spoken
What dreams of human happiness are broken!
Mirth hushes at the sound his joyous bands   5
Reluctant Friendship hears and severs hands
Parental smiles are changed to anxious sighs
And in a tear the lover's rapture dies.
A counter-charm to each delightful spell
That sweetens life lies in the word Farewell.   10
It wakes each sorrow, chills each genial fire
Till in Farewell even life itself expire.

   Beyond my proudest hope indulged, approved,
Think not that I can speak such word unmoved—
Unmoved when from the genial land I part   15
Where the hand owns the impulse of the heart
Waits not to weigh in critic scales our fame
But generous gives the applause we cannot claim?
Fair Isle to Genius, Wit and Honour dear
Land of the ready smile and ready tear   20
Ere from your shore the favoured wanderer stray
O hear her own the debt she cannot pay
While words unequal to her feelings tell
She faulters blessings as she says Farewell.

112

The Death of Don Pedro

Henry and King Pedro clasping,
  Hold in straining arms each other;
Tugging hard, and closely grasping,
  Brother proves his strength with brother.

Harmless pastime, sport fraternal,   5
  Blends not thus their limbs in strife;
Either aims, with rage infernal,
  Naked dagger, sharpen'd knife.

Close Don Henry grapples Pedro,
  Pedro holds Don Henry strait,   10
Breathing, this, triumphant fury,
  That, despair and mortal hate.

Sole spectator of the struggle,
  Stands Don Henry's page afar,
In the chase who bore his bugle,   15
  And who bore his sword in war.

Down they go in deadly wrestle,
  Down upon the earth they go,
Fierce King Pedro has the vantage,
  Stout Don Henry falls below.   20

Marking then the fatal crisis,
  Up the page of Henry ran,
By the waist he caught Don Pedro,
  Aiding thus the fallen man.

"King to place, or to depose him,   25
  Dwelleth not in my desire,
But the duty which he owes him,
  To his master pays the squire."—

Now Don Henry has the upmost,
  Now King Pedro lies beneath,   30
In his heart his brother's poniard
  Instant finds its bloody sheath.

Thus with mortal gasp and quiver,
  While the blood in bubbles well'd,
Fled the fiercest soul that ever   35
  In a Christian bosom dwell'd.

113

Carle, now the King's Come!

Being New Words to an Auld Spring

PART FIRST

The news has flown frae mouth to mouth,
The North for anes has bang'd the South;
The de'il a Scotsman's die of drouth,
        Carle, now the King's come!

> CHORUS
> *Carle, now the King's come!*   5
> *Carle, now the King's come!*
> *Thou shalt dance, and I will sing,*
>   *Carle, now the King's come!*

Auld England held him lang and fast;
And Ireland had a joyfu' cast;   10
But Scotland's turn is come at last—
        Carle, now the King's come!

Auld Reekie, in her rokela gray,
Thought never to have seen the day;
He's been a weary time away—   15
        But, Carle, now the King's come!

She's skirling frae the Castle Hill;
The Carline's voice is grown sae shrill,
Ye'll hear her at the Canon Mill,
   Carle, now the King's come!   20

"Up, bairns!" she cries, "baith grit and sma',
And busk ye for the weapon-shaw!—
Stand by me, and we'll bang them a'!
   Carle, now the King's come!

"Come from Newbattle's ancient spires,   25
Bauld Lothian, with your knights and squires,
And match the mettle of your sires,
   Carle, now the King's come!

"You're welcome hame, my Montagu!
Bring in your hand the young Buccleuch;— 30
I'm missing some that I may rue,
   Carle, now the King's come!

"Come, Haddington, the kind and gay,
You've graced my causeway mony a day;
I'll weep the cause if you should stay,   35
   Carle, now the King's come!

"Come, premier Duke, and carry doun,
Frae yonder craig, his ancient croun;
It's had a lang sleep and a soun'—
   But, Carle, now the King's come! 40

"Come, Athole, from the hill and wood,
Bring down your clansmen like a cloud;—
Come, Morton, shew the Douglas' blood,—
   Carle, now the King's come!

"Come, Tweeddale, true as sword to sheath; 45
Come, Hopetoun, fear'd on fields of death;
Come, Clerk, and give yon bugle breath;
   Carle, now the King's come!

"Come, Wemyss, who modest merit aids;
Come, Rosebery, from Dalmeny shades;   50
Breadalbane, bring your belted plaids;
          Carle, now the King's come!

"Come, stately Niddrie, auld and true,
Girt with the sword that Minden knew;
We have ower few such lairds as you—   55
          Carle, now the King's come!

"King Arthur's grown a common crier,
He's heard in Fife and far Cantire,—
'Fie, lads, behold my crest of fire!'
          Carle, now the King's come!   60

"Saint Abb roars out, 'I see him pass
Between Tantallon and the Bass!'—
Calton, get out your keeking-glass,
          Carle, now the King's come!"—

The Carline stopp'd; and, sure I am,   65
For very glee had ta'en a dwam,
But Oman help'd her to a dram.—
          Cogie, now the King's come!

          Cogie, now the King's come!
          Cogie, now the King's come!   70
          I'se be fou, and ye's be toom,
                    Cogie, now the King's come!

PART SECOND

A Hawick gill of mountain dew,
Heised up Auld Reekie's heart, I trow,
It minded her of Waterloo—   75
          Carle, now the King's come!

CHORUS

Carle, now the King's come!
Carle, now the King's come!
Thou shalt dance, and I will sing,
    Carle, now the King's come!   80

Again I heard her summons swell
Wi' sic a dirdum and a yell,
It drown'd Saint Giles's jowing bell—
    Carle, now the King's come!

"My trusty Provost, tried and tight,   85
Stand forward for the Good Town's right,—
There's waur than you been made a Knight—
    Carle, now the King's come!

"My reverend Clergy, look ye say
The best of thanksgivings ye ha'e,   90
And warstle for a sunny day—
    Carle, now the King's come!

"My Doctors, look that you agree,
Cure a' the town without a fee;—
My lawyers, dinna pike a plea—   95
    Carle, now the King's come!

"Come forth, each sturdy burgher's bairn,
That dunts on wood or clanks on airn,
That fires the oon, or winds the pirn—
    Carle, now the King's come!   100

"Come forth beneath the Blanket Blue,
Your sires were loyal men and true,
As Scotland's foemen oft might rue—
    Carle, now the King's come!

"Scots downa loup, and rin and rave,—   105
We're steady folks, and something grave,
We'll keep the causeway firm and brave—
    Carle, now the King's come!

"Sir Thomas, thunder from your rock
Till Pentland dinnles wi' the shock,   110
And lace with fire my snood o' smoke—
          Carle, now the King's come!

"Melville, lead out your bands of blue,
A' Louden lads, baith stout and true,
With Elcho, Hope, and Cockburn too—   115
          Carle, now the King's come!

"And you, who on yon bluidy braes
Compell'd the falling Despot's praise,
Rank out—rank out—my gallant Greys—
          Carle, now the King's come!   120

"Cock of the North, my Huntly bra',
Where are ye with the Forty-twa,
Ah! waes my heart that ye're awa'—
          Carle, now the King's come!

"But yonder come my canty Celts,   125
With durk and pistols at their belts,
Thank God, we've still some plaids and kilts—
          Carle, now the King's come!

"Lord, how the pibrochs groan and yell!
MacDonnell's ta'en the field himsel,   130
MacLeod comes branking ower the fell—
          Carle, now the King's come!

"Bend up your bow, each Archer spark,
For you're to guard him light and dark;
Faith, lads, for ance ye've hit the mark—   135
          Carle, now the King's come!

"Young Errol, take the sword of state,
The sceptre Panie-Morarchate,
Knight Mareschal, see ye clear the gate—
          Carle, now the King's come!   140

"Kind cummer Leith, ye've been mis-set,
But dinna be upon the fret—
Ye'se hae the handsel of him yet—
    Carle, now the King's come!

"My daughters, come with e'en sae blue,   145
Your garlands weave, your blossoms strew,
He ne'er saw fairer flowers than you—
    Carle, now the King's come!

"What shall we do for the propine—
We used to offer something fine,   150
But ne'er a groat's in pouch of mine—
    Carle, now the King's come!

"De'il care—for that I'se never start,
We'll welcome him with Highland heart,
Whate'er we have he's hae his part—   155
    Carle, now the King's come!

"I'll shew him mason-work the day—
Nane of your bricks of Babel clay,
But towers shall stand till Time's away—
    Carle, now the King's come!   160

"I'll shew him wit, I'll shew him lair,
And gallant lads and lasses fair,
And what wad kind heart wish for mair?—
    Carle, now the King's come!

"Step out, Sir John, of projects rife,   165
Come win the thanks of an auld wife,
And bring HIM HEALTH AND LENGTH OF LIFE—
    Carle, now the King's come!"

114

Lines added to the King's Anthem

Bright beams are soon o'ercast,
Soon our brief hour is past,
    Losing our King:
Honoured, beloved, and dear,
Still shall his parting ear,   5
Our latest accents hear,
    GOD SAVE THE KING!

115

Epilogue

Written for a Tragedy entitled 'Mary Stuart'

The sages—for authority pray look,
Seneca's Morals, or the copy-book—
The sages, to disparage woman's power,
Say Beauty is a fair but fading flower.
I cannot tell—I've small philosophy—   5
Yet if it fades, it does not surely die;
But like the violet, when decayed in bloom,
Survives through many a year in rich perfume.
Witness our theme to-night—two ages gone,
A third wanes fast since Mary filled the throne.   10
Brief was her bloom, with scarce one sunny day
'Twixt Pinkie's field—and fatal Fotheringay;
But when, while Scottish hearts and blood you boast,
Shall sympathy with Mary's woes be lost?
O'er Mary's memory the learned quarrel;   15
By Mary's grave the poet plants his laurel;

Time's echo, old Tradition, makes her name
The constant burthen of his faultering theme;
In each old hall his gray-haired heralds tell
Of Mary's picture, and of Mary's cell,—   20
And show—my fingers tingle at the thought—
The loads of tapestry that poor Queen wrought.
In vain did fate bestow a double dower
Of every ill that waits on rank and power,
Of every ill on beauty that attends,—   25
False ministers, false lovers, and false friends.
Spite of three wedlocks, so completely curst,
They rose in ill, from bad to worse and worst;—
In spite of errors—I dare not say more,
For Duncan Targe lays hand on his claymore:—   30
In spite of all, however humours vary,
There is a talisman in that word Mary
That unto Scottish bosoms all and some
Is found the genuine *open sesamum!*
In history, ballad, poetry, or novel,   35
It charms alike the castle and the hovel.
Even you—forgive me—who, demure and shy,
Gorge not each bait, nor stir at every fly,
Must rise to this; else, in her ancient reign,
The Rose of Scotland has survived in vain.   40

116

A Bannatyne Garland

Assist me, ye friends of old books and old wine,
To sing in the praises of sage Bannatyne,
Who left such a treasure of old Scottish lore,
As enables each age to print one volume more.
    One volume more, my friends, one volume more,   5
    We'll ransack old Banny for one volume more.

And first Allan Ramsay was eager to glean
From Bannatyne's hortus his bright Evergreen,
Two tight little volumes (intended for four,)
Still leave us the task to print one volume more.   10
    One volume more, &c.

His ways were not ours, for he cared not a pin,
How much he left out, or how much he put in;
The truth of the reading he thought was a bore,
So this accurate age calls for one volume more.   15
    One volume more, &c.

Correct and sagacious then came my Lord Hailes,
And weigh'd every letter in critical scales,
But left out some brief words, which the prudish abhor,
And castrated Banny in one volume more.   20
    One volume more, my friends, one volume more,
    We'll restore Banny's manhood in one volume more.

John Pinkerton's next, and I'm truly concern'd,
I cannot quite call him so candid as learn'd;
He rail'd at the plaid, and blasphemed the claymore,   25
And set Scots by the ears in his one volume more.
    One volume more, my friends, one volume more
    Celt and Goth shall be pleased with one volume more.

As bitter as gall, and as sharp as a razor,
And feeding on herbs like a Nebuchadnezzar;   30
His diet too acid, his temper too sore,
Little Ritson came out with his two volumes more.
    But one volume more, my friends, one volume more,
    We will dine on roast beef, and print one volume more.

The stout Gothic Yeditour's next on the roll,   35
With his beard like a brush, and as black as a coal;
And honest Gray-steel, that was true to the core,
Lent their hearts and their hands each to one volume more.
    One volume more, &c.

Since by these single champions such wonders were
                    done,   40
What may not be achieved by our Thirty and One;
Law, Gospel, and Commerce, we count in our corps,
And the Trade and the Press join for one volume more.
    One volume more, &c.

Ancient libels and contraband books, I assure ye,   45
We'll print as secure of Exchequer or Jury.
Then hear your Committee, and let them count o'er
The deeds they intend in their three volumes more.
    Three volumes more, &c.

They'll produce you King Jamie the Sapient and Sext,   50
And the Bob of Dumblaine and the Bishops come next;
One tome miscellaneous they'll add to your store,
Resolving next year to print four volumes more.
    Four volumes more, my friends, four volumes more,
    Pay down your subscriptions for four volumes more.   55

𝔉𝔦𝔫𝔦𝔰, 𝔮𝔲𝔬𝔱𝔥 𝔱𝔥𝔢 𝔎𝔫𝔦𝔤𝔥𝔱 𝔬𝔣 𝔄𝔟𝔟𝔬𝔱𝔰𝔣𝔬𝔯𝔡

117
To Mons. Alexandre

Of yore, in old England, it was not thought good
To carry two visages under one hood:
What should folks say to *you*? who have faces such plenty,
That from under one hood you last night show'd us twenty!
Stand forth, Arch-deceiver! and tell us in truth,   5
Are you handsome or ugly, in age or in youth?
Man, woman, or child? or a dog, or a mouse?
Or are you, at once, each live thing in the house?
Each live thing, did I ask? each dead implement too!
A work-shop in your person—saw, chisel, and screw.   10

Above all, are you *one* individual? I know
You must be, at the least, Alexandre *and Co.·*
But I think you're a troop—an assemblage—a mob—
And that I, as the Sheriff, must take up the job;
And, instead of rehearsing your wonders in verse,   15
Must read you the Riot Act, and bid you disperse!

Abbotsford, 23 April 1824

118

Epilogue to Saint Ronan's Well

Enter Meg Dods, one or two boys following and teazing her—The
Stage-keeper interposes and drives them off.

That's right, friend—drive the gaitlings back
And lend yon muckle ane a whack—
Your Embrugh bairns are grown a pack
        Sae bauld and saucy
They scarce will let an auld wife walk   5
        Upon your causey.

I've seen the day they wad been scared
Wi' the Tolbooth or wi' the Guard
Or maybe wad had some regard
        For Jamie Laing.   10
The water-hole was right weel wared
        On sic a gang.

But where's the gude Tolbooth ee'noo?
Where's the Auld Claught in red and blue?
Where's Jamie Laing and where's John Doo?   15
        And where's the Weigh House?
Deil ha'et I see but what is new
        Except the playhouse.

Yoursels are changed frae heed to heel
There's some that gar the causeway reel   20
Wi' clashing hufe and rattling wheel
      And horses cantering
Whose fathers daundered hame as weel
      Wi' lass and lanthorn.

Mysell being in the public line   25
I looked for howffs I kend lang syne
Where gentles used to drink good wine
      And eat cheap dinners
But deil a soul gangs there to dine
      Of saints or sinners.   30

Fortune's and Hunter's gane, alas!
And Bayle's is lost in empty space
And now if folk would splice a brace
      Or crack a bottle
They gang to a new-fangled place   35
      They caa'd a hottle.

The Devil hoddle them for Meg!
They are sae greedy and sae glegg
That if ye're served but wi' an egg
      And that's puir picking   40
In comes a chield and makes a leg
      And charges chicken.

"And wha may ye be" gin ye speir
"That brings your auld warld clavers here?"
Troth, if there's ony body near   45
      That kens the roads
I'll haud ye Burgundy to beer
      He kens Meg Dods.

I come a piece frae west of Currie
And since I see ye're in a hurry   50
Your patience I'll nae langer worry
      But be sae crouse
As speak a word for ane Will Murray
      That keeps the house.

Plays are auld–fashioned things in truth   55
And you've seen wonders mair uncouth
Yet actors should na suffer drowth
      Or want of dramock
Although they speak but with their mouth
      Not with their stomach.   60

But yese take care of a' folks pantry
And surely to have stooden sentry
Ower this big house that's far frae rent-free
      For a lone sister
Is claim as good as to be a ventri- —   65
      How'st caa'd?— -loquister.

Weel, Sirs, Gude'en and have a care
The bairns mak fun of Meg nae mair
For gin they do she tells you fair
      And without failyie   70
As sure as ever you sit there
      She'll tell the *Bailyie*.

119
Beam forth fair opening Dawn

Beam forth fair opening Dawn of ours
    Though tears obscured thy earlier ray
Our Shepherds tell that morning showers
    Give token of the brightest day.

        Bowhill, 13 November 1824

120

Epistle to John Gibson Lockhart, on the Composition of Maida's Epitaph

Dear John,—I some time ago wrote to inform his
Fat worship of *jaces*, misprinted for *dormis*;
But that several Southrons assured me the *januam*,
Was a twitch to both ears of Ass Priscian's cranium.
You, perhaps, may observe that one Lionel Berguer,   5
In defence of our blunder appears a stout arguer:
But at length I have settled, I hope, all these clatters,
By a *rowt* in the papers—fine place for such matters.
I have, therefore, to make it for once my command, sir,
That my gudeson shall leave the whole thing in my
                              hand, sir,   10
And by no means accomplish what James says you threaten,
Some banter in Blackwood to claim your dog-Latin.
I have various reasons of weight, on my word, sir,
For pronouncing a step of this sort were absurd, sir.
Firstly, erudite sir, 'twas against your advising   15
I adopted the lines this monstrosity lies in;
For you modestly hinted my English translation
Would become better far such a dignified station.
Second—how, in God's name, would my bacon be saved,
By not having writ what I clearly engraved?   20
On the contrary, I, on the whole, think it better
To be whipped as the thief, than his lousy resetter.
Thirdly—don't you perceive that I don't care a boddle
Although fifty false metres were flung at my noddle,
For my back is as broad and as hard as Benlomon's,   25
And I treat as I please both the Greeks and the Romans;
Whereas the said heathens might look rather serious
At a kick on their drum from the scribe of Valerius.
And, fourthly and lastly—it is my good pleasure
To remain the sole source of that murderous measure.   30
So *stet pro ratione voluntas*—be tractile,
Invade not, I say, my own dear little dactyl;

If you do, you'll occasion a breach in our intercourse:
To-morrow will see me in town for the winter-course,
But not at your door, at the usual hour, sir,   35
My own pye-house daughter's good prog to devour, sir.
Ergo—peace, on your duty, your squeamishness throttle,
And we'll soothe Priscian's spleen with a canny third bottle.
A fig for all dactyls, a fig for all spondees,
A fig for all dunces and Dominie Grundys;   40
A fig for dry thrapples, south, north, east, and west, sir,
Speates and raxes ere five for a famishing guest, sir;
And as Fatsman and I have some topics for haver, he'll
Be invited, I hope, to meet me and Dame Peveril,
Upon whom, to say nothing of Oury and Anne, you a   45
Dog shall be deemed if you fasten your *Janua*.

121

Come ower the Tweed Adam

Being an excellent New song to the Old Tune of Come ower the sea Charlie &c.

Come ower the Tweed Adam
Dear Adam Sir Adam
Come ower the Tweed Adam
   And dine with us all.
We'll welcome you truly   5
We'll stuff you most duly
With broth, greens and boullie
   In Abbotsford hall.
        Come ower the Tweed Adam
          Da capo

Bring here your dear lady   10
In friendship so steady
The welcomest tread aye
    That visits our hall.
Bring your guests too and spare not
For numbers we care not   15
In especiall Miss Arnot
    So comely and tall.
              Come ower the Tweed

With wine we'll regale ye
We'll dram, punch and ale ye   20
And song, tune and tale ye
    Shall have at your call.
T'will be worth a gold guinea
To hear Mrs. Jeanie
Lilting blithe as a queenie   25
    In Abbotsford hall.

    Then come ower the Tweed Adam
    Dear Adam Sir Adam
    Come ower the Tweed Adam
        And gladden us all.   30

122

The Bonnets of Bonnie Dundee

To the Lords of Convention, 'twas Clavers who spoke,
Ere the king's crown go down there are crowns to be broke;
So each Cavalier who loves honour and me—
Let him follow the bonnet of bonnie Dundee.

Come fill up my cup, come fill up my can,   5
Come saddle my horses, and call up my men;
Come open the West-port, and let me gae free,
And it's room for the bonnets of bonnie Dundee.

Dundee he is mounted—he rides up the street,
The bells are rung backwards, the drums they are beat;   10
But the Provost, douce man, said, "Just e'en let him be,
The Town is weel quit of that deil of Dundee."
    Come fill up, &c.

As he rode down the sanctified bends of the Bow,
Each carline was flyting and shaking her pow;   15
But some young plants of grace—they look'd couthy
                    and slee,
Thinking "luck to thy bonnet, thou bonnie Dundee."
    Come fill up, &c.

With sour-featured saints the Grass-market was pang'd,
As if half the West had set tryste to be hang'd;   20
There was spite in each face, there was fear in each ee,
As they watch'd for the bonnet of bonnie Dundee.
    Come fill up, &c.

These cowls of Kilmarnock had spits and had spears,
And lang-hafted gullies to kill Cavaliers;
But they shrunk to close-heads, and the causeway left free,
At a toss of the bonnet of bonnie Dundee.
    Come fill up, &c.

He spurr'd to the foot of the high Castle Rock,
And to the gay Gordon he gallantly spoke—   30
"Let Mons Meg and her marrows three vollies let flee,
For the love of the bonnets of bonnie Dundee."
    Come fill up, &c.

The Gordon has ask'd of him whither he goes,
"Wherever shall guide me the spirit of Montrose,   35
Your Grace in short space shall have tidings of me,
Or that low lies the bonnet of bonnie Dundee."
    Come fill up, &c.

There are hills beyond Pentland, and streams beyond
           Forth,
If there's Lords in the Southland, there's Chiefs in the
           North;
There are wild dunnie-wassels, three thousand times three,
Will cry *Hoigh!* for the bonnets of bonnie Dundee.
    Come fill up, &c.

"Away to the hills, to the woods, to the rocks,
Ere I own a usurper I'll couch with the fox;   45
And tremble, false Whigs, tho' triumphant ye be,
You have not seen the last of my bonnet and me."
    Come fill up, &c.

He wav'd his proud arm, and the trumpets were blown,
The kettle-drums clash'd, and the horsemen rode on,   50
Till on Ravelston Craigs and on Clermiston lee,
Died away the wild war-note of bonnie Dundee.
    Come fill up my cup, come fill up my can,
    Come saddle my horses, and call up my men;
    Fling all your gates open, and let me gae free,   55
    For 'tis up with the bonnets of bonnie Dundee.

123

When Noble Duke

When Noble Duke in joy we met
The shout of thousands owned a debt
A debt so weighty and so large
As never Britain can discharge
To one whose triumphs did not cease   5
Till she had triumph, Europe peace.
While some folks thought the thriftiest way
Was rather to disown than pay,
But not so Sunderland's stout tars
Welcomed the ender of our wars.   10
The Patriarch Prince of Durham grey

124

Translation from Grillparzer

Of the Nine the loveliest three
Are Painting, Music, Poetry
But thou art freest of the free
Matchless Muse of Harmony.

Gags can stop the Poet's tongue   5
Chains on Painter's arms are flung
Fetter-bolts and dungeon tower
O'er speech and pencil have the power.

But Music speaks a loftier tone
To tyrant and to spy unknown   10
And free as angels watch with men
Can pass unscathed the jailor's ken.

Then hail thou freest of the free
Mid times of wrong and tyranny
Music, the proudest lot is thine   15
And those who bend at Music's shrine.

125

Song from the German

Der Dichter liebt den guten Wein &c.

The poet loves the generous wine
    And if his verse be good
For him shall bloom the purple vine
And all her flexile tendrils twine
    To cheer him with her blood.   5

The gentle poet loves the fair
  Nor knows a traitor's art
The Mother hears the poet's prayer
The fairest maiden lends her ear
  And yields the bard her heart.   10

Then if a wish such prize could gain
  The poet's lot were mine:
For gaudy stars and ribbands vain
And wealth and titles I'd disdain
  For Beauty and for Wine.   15

126

Verses to Sir Cuthbert Sharp

Written by one of the Guests at the Wellington Dinner, to the Vice, who reminded him of a Promise to revisit Sunderland, which he appeared to have forgotten.

Forget you? No; my knightly fere;—
Forget blythe mirth and gallant cheer—
Death, sooner stretch me on my bier:
    Forget thee? No!

Forget the universal shout,   5
When canny Sunderland spoke out;
A truth which knaves affect to doubt.
    Forget thee? No!

Forget you? No! though now a-day,
I've heard your knowing people say—   10
"Disown the debt you cannot pay,
You'll find it far the thriftiest way."
    But I—Oh No!

Forget your kindness found for all room,
In which, though large, seem'd then a small room;   15
Forget my Surtees in a ball room.
      Forget you? No!

Forget your sprightly twiddle diddles,
And beauty tripping to the fiddles—
Forget my lively friends, the Liddles.   20
      Forget you? No!

127

The Death of Keeldar

Percy or Percival Rede, of Trochend, in Redesdale, Northumberland,
is celebrated in tradition as a huntsman and a soldier. He was, upon
two occasions, singularly unfortunate: once when an arrow, which he
had discharged at a deer, killed his celebrated dog Keeldar; and again
when, being on a hunting party, he was betrayed into the hands of a
clan called Crossar, by whom he was murdered. Mr. Cooper's Painting
of the first of these incidents suggested the following stanzas.

Up rose the sun o'er moor and mead;
Up with the sun rose Percy Rede;
Brave Keeldar, from his couples freed,
    Career'd along the lea;
The palfrey sprung with sprightly bound,   5
As if to match the gamesome hound;
His horn the gallant Huntsman wound:
    They were a jovial three!

Painted by A. Cooper R.A.   Engraved by A.W. Warren.

Man, hound, or horse, of higher fame,
To wake the wild deer never came,   10
Since Alnwick's Earl pursued the game
    On Cheviot's rueful day;
Keeldar was matchless in his speed,
Than Tarras ne'er was stauncher steed,
A peerless archer Percy Rede: 15
    And right dear friends were they.

The chase engross'd their joys and woes,
Together at the dawn they rose,
Together shared the noon's repose,
    By fountain or by stream;   20
And oft, when evening skies were red,
The heather was their common bed,
Where each, as wildering fancy led,
    Still hunted in his dream.

Now is the thrilling moment near   25
Of sylvan hope and sylvan fear,
Yon thicket holds the harbour'd deer,
    The signs the hunters know;—
With eyes of flame, and quivering ears,
The brake sagacious Keeldar nears;   30
The restless palfrey paws and rears;
    The archer strings his bow.

The game's afoot!—Halloo! Halloo!
Hunter, and horse, and hound pursue;—
But woe the shaft that erring flew—   35
    That e'er it left the string!
And ill betide the faithless yew!
The stag bounds scatheless o'er the dew,
And gallant Keeldar's life-blood true
    Has drench'd the grey-goose wing.   40

The noble hound—he dies, he dies,
Death, death has glazed his fixed eyes,
Stiff on the bloody heath he lies,
    Without a moan or quiver.
Now day may break and bugle sound,   45
And whoop and hollow ring around,
And o'er his couch the stag may bound,
    But Keeldar sleeps for ever.

Dilated nostrils, staring eyes,
Mark the poor palfrey's mute surprise,   50
He knows not that his comrade dies,
    Nor what is death—but still
His aspect hath expression drear
Of grief, and wonder, mix'd with fear,
Like startled children when they hear   55
    Some mystic tale of ill.

But he that bent the fatal bow,
Can well the sum of evil know,
And o'er his favourite bending low,
    In speechless grief recline;   60
Can think he hears the senseless clay
In unreproachful accents say,
"The hand that took my life away,
    Dear Master, was it thine?

"And if it be, the shaft be bless'd,   65
Which sure some erring aim address'd,
Since in your service, priz'd, caress'd,
    I in your service die;
And you may have a fleeter hound,
To match the dun deer's merry bound,   70
But by your couch will ne'er be found
    So true a guard as I."

And to his last stout Percy rued
The fatal chance, for when he stood,
'Gainst fearful odds in deadly feud,   75
   And fell amid the fray,
E'en with his dying voice he cried,
"Had Keeldar but been at my side,
Your treacherous ambush had been spied—
   I had not died to-day!"   80

Remembrance of the erring bow
Long since had join'd the tides which flow,
Conveying human bliss and woe,
   Down dark Oblivion's river;
But Art can Time's stern doom arrest,   85
And snatch his spoils from Lethe's breast,
And, in her Cooper's colours drest,
   The scene shall live for ever.

128

To General David Stewart of Garth

Brave Stuart, name without a blot
Yours to command is Walter Scott.

What ere in Waverley is wrote
I bear the blame, quoth Walter Scott.

A grey auld man sore failed I wot   5
There's life in't yet, said Walter Scott.

Trees did he plant and lands he bought
A Darnick Laird was Walter Scott.

He loved a man that bravely fought
And Garth was friend to Walter Scott.   10

With Highland Chiefs he had a vote
For well the plaids loved Walter Scott.

The greyhounds good were fleet as thought
Till age lamed them and Walter Scott.

Call this vile stuff—I reck it not   15
So there's an end of Walter Scott.

129

Farewell Address for Mrs Siddons

The curtain drops—the mimic scene is past
One word remains, the saddest and the last
A word which oft in careless mood we say
When parting friends have passed a social day
As oft pronounced in agony of heart   5
When friends must sever or when lovers part
Or o'er the dying couch in whisper spoken
When the frail thread of life is all but broken
When all that ear can list or tongue can tell
Are the last faultering accents "Fare you well."   10
   Such is the spell the actress must divide
From duties long her pleasure and her pride
So brief the syllables must bid adieu
To public life, to Scotland and to you
To hopes, to doubts, to efforts and to fears   15
And all the business of my scenic years.
    Would this were all. The poor Performer's lot
Is but to bloom, to fade and be forgot
But deeper thoughts of recollection rise
Throb at my heart and glisten in my eyes.   20
Can you remember?—Ah the good forget
Nor register a kindness as a debt.
But in what phrase shall I the Kindness own
In Misery's hours of deprivation shewn
When Sympathy Hope's dying lamp renewed   25
And Anguish softened into gratitude?
Ah generous soothers of a widow's cares
Despise not now her blessings and her prayers
Tis all she has—but warrant high is given
Such prayers and blessings find the path to heaven.   30
   Not with the sad remembrance of my woes
This space of final audience would I close:
One suit remains—you will not scorn to hear
The last my lips shall faulter on your ear?

When I am far, my patrons, O be kind   35
To the dear relative I leave behind!
He is your own and like yourselves may claim
A Scottish origin, a Scottish name.
His opening talents—Let the truth be told
A sister in a brother's cause is bold—   40
Shall cater for your eve of leisure still
With equal ardour and improving skill.

130

Ettricke's Forest and Fountains

I have seen Ettricke's forest and fountains
    When their flowrets were weeded away
But the Day Spring has risen on her mountains
    With all the gay promise of May.

While I gaze do not think it surprizing   5
    If my eyes should grow misty and wet
While I look on the beams that are rising
    I think upon those that have set.

But my sad recollections suppressing
    In verse, gentle Lady, I've tried   10
To frame for my Hostess a blessing
    Which Providence has not supplied.

Thou hast youth, rank and riches and beauty
    And more valued possessions than these
The art to find pleasure in duty   15
    The desire to be pleased and to please.

A hand stretched to comfort affliction
    A heart that is true to the North
And the right of exchanging affection
    With an object of spirit and worth.   20

What then can I wish the fair Duchess
  Nor do her prosperity wrong—
But that Heaven whose benevolence such is
  May preserve that prosperity long.

             Bowhill, 24 March 1830

131

Inscription for the Monument of the Rev. George Scott

To youth, to age, alike, this tablet pale
Tells the brief moral of its tragic tale.
Art thou a parent? Reverence this bier,
The parents' fondest hopes lie buried here.
Art thou a youth, prepared on life to start,   5
With opening talents and a generous heart,
Fair hopes and flattering prospects all thine own?
Lo! here their end—a monumental stone.
But let submission tame each murmuring thought,
Heaven crown'd its champion ere the fight was fought.   10

132
ℑantastic ℳaid

Fantastic Maid whose step from dewy morn
Till Evening's sober shade I oft have traced
And every shadowy change obscurely seen
Grow fresher, *wilder* by thy slipper traced.
And can it be and must I say farewell   5
Because advancing time hath marked with gray
The hair which once was tinged with youthful brown
While pale December fogs the bloom of May?

It will not aid, the fairy tinge is gone
That painted o'er each scene with fancies new   10
Far oe'r my aged head the glance is flown
Which bade Reality assume Romance's tone.
Oft have I thought amid thy wandering train
Of things that owed their beings to our selves
Entangled in the mesh we wove ourselves   15
That thou and I were like the netted bird.

133
ℒines 𝔚ritten in 𝔇ora 𝔚ordsworth's 𝔄lbum

Tis well the gifted eye which saw
    The first light sparks of fancy burn
Should mark its latest flash with awe
    Low glimmering from its funeral urn.

And thou mayst mark the hint, fair maid   5
    How vain is worldly esteem
Good fortune turns, Affections fade
    And fancy is an idle dream.

Yet not on this poor form alone
　　My palsied hand and deafened ear   10
But on my country's fate
　　The bolts of fate seem doomed to speed.

The storm might whistle round my head
　　I would not deprecate the ill
So I might say when it was sped   15
　　My Country be thou Glorious still.

　　　　　Abbotsford, 22 September 1831

134
Verses Written at the Request of the Countess Wolkonsky, A Russian Lady

Lady, they say thy Native land
　　Unlike this clime of fruit and flowers
Loves like the Minstrel's northern strand
　　The sterner shore of nature's powers
Even Beauty's powers of Empery   5
　　Grow feeble mid decaying bowers
Until even you mayst set a task
　　Too heavy for the poet's powers.

Mortals in vain—so says the Text—
　　Seek grapes from briars, from thistles corn   10
Say can fair Wolkonsky expect
　　Fruit from a withered Scottish thorn?
Time once there was alas but now
　　That time returns not new again
The shades upon the Dial cast   15
　　Proceed but pass not back again.

Yet in this land of lengthened day
  Where April wears the autumn's hue
Awakened by the genial ray
  Thoughts of past visions strive to blow   20
The blood grows warm the nerves expand
  The stiffened fingers take the pen
And

ESSAY ON THE TEXTS

1. CONTENTS OF THE VOLUME

The present volume, as the title implies, consists of the shorter poems of Walter Scott. Brief and impromptu forays into verse within his letters and in his Journal more closely resembling those within the novels, in being embedded in his other writing and thus not fully comprehensible out of context, are excluded: they will appear in the volume of the Edinburgh Edition of Walter Scott's Poetry mainly devoted to the Poetry from the Waverley Novels. The present volume also excludes the traditional ballads from *Minstrelsy of the Scottish Border* and those by Scott's literary friends published there as ballad imitations. It does, however, include those poems in that collection of which Scott himself is the author.

2. THE SEQUENCE OF POEMS IN THE VOLUME

As a poet Scott is best known for his series of long poetic narratives commencing with *The Lay of the Last Minstrel* (1805), but he also wrote a variety of shorter poems composed in a surprising variety of different genres and for different purposes. Scott was a translator and interpreter of poems written originally in German, French, Spanish, and in Latin: he also brought poems from other European cultures such as Scottish-Gaelic and Serbo-Croat to the attention of the English-language reading public. In response to requests from publishers and from friends, as an afficionado of the theatre and as a good citizen of Edinburgh, he wrote epitaphs, addresses to be delivered orally in the theatre, and songs for public dinners and civic occasions. He responded to the appeals of music-collectors and publishers for song lyrics, and wrote inscriptions in books. He contributed verses to the albums of admirers, and communicated various *jeux d'esprit* to his friends.

Ordering these poems thematically would have been both possible and interesting, but a chronological sequence has been preferred since this allows the reader to discern the shape of Scott's career as a poet, a career which by no means ceased with the publication of

Waverley in July 1814, the outset of his career as an historical novelist: Scott remained a poet to the end. The poems in the present volume were written by Scott over the long period of half a century, and range from the earliest efforts at versification of a clever schoolboy at Edinburgh's High School in the early 1780s to the final attempts of a seriously unwell, though internationally celebrated, author in the period preceding his death in September 1832. Wherever possible a poem appears in the order of its date of composition, since accidents could, and sometimes did, delay publication for several years. In a number of cases, however, insufficient evidence exists to determine a precise, or even an approximate, date of composition. In such cases the editors have sometimes placed an individual poem by its consonance with others written at a particular stage of Scott's career, but they have had occasionally to fall back upon the date of first publication. In every instance the editorial matter summarises the evidence for the date of composition or reasoning behind the placement of a poem within the sequence of the volume, as well as providing a publication history for it within Scott's lifetime and, where pertinent, beyond it.

Each poem has been given a sequential number for ease of reference in addition to its title. Where multiple titles have been used for the same poem the title at the head of the poem is generally that provided by the copy-text and alternative titles may be found in the Index of Titles at the end of the volume (648–51). Where a poem is untitled, or the title provided by the copy-text is in some way inapposite, it has either been suitably modified or supplied editorially from the first lines of the poem or given a descriptive title from its original context, and the fact recorded in the editorial matter.

In keeping with the overall policy of the EEWSP, the present volume provides the reader with a clean reading text of Scott's poems, and, where relevant, the apparatus he supplied to accompany them, without the intrusion of editorial material. Editorial notes are provided in a separate and following section of the volume, arranged in the same order as the sequence of the texts themselves, and under headings referring to each poem by number and title. The editorial material for each poem is divided in each case into three sections: Textual Note; Historical Note; and Explanatory Notes. Within these references to the text of a poem are given by page and line number. An account of the kind of information provided by each of these sections is given at the head of the Combined Editorial Notes (298–300), together with a list of abbreviations for works frequently cited in the present volume. Since the Explanatory Notes include the glossing of unfamiliar, outmoded, foreign language, and Scots words there is no separate Glossary.

3. EXCLUSIONS FROM THE SEQUENCE OF POEMS

With the possible exception of Byron, Scott was the most famous and widely-read British poet of his day, and his popularity continued throughout the nineteenth century and beyond. A bewildering variety of volume editions of his poems was published, and additions to the accepted body of his work were eagerly made by the various compilers of these as well as by literary scholars, general readers and contributors to periodical publications, sometimes on reliable grounds and sometimes rather less reliably. Besides adding a number of items to the generally accepted body of Scott's work, the present editors have excluded several poems previously attributed to or otherwise associated with him from the present volume, because research has enabled them to demonstrate that they are the work of another author or were published before Scott's time. A further group of poems previously attributed to Scott has been excluded because research has not provided the editors with sufficient evidence to decide in favour of Scott's authorship and thus attribution to him remains doubtful. Poems in both categories are listed, separately, in the Appendix of Suppositious and Doubtful Works (639–47).

4. SELECTION OF THE INDIVIDUAL COPY TEXT

In keeping with the general editorial policy of the EEWSP, the copy-text for each poem is normally that which best reflects Scott's intentions during the initial creative process, representing the earliest fully articulated and coherent form of the poem. Scott expected his work to be subjected to a process of socialisation that involved its completion through work at the printing-house and revisions made by him in response to the comments and suggestions of friends and correspondents. In general, then, the editors have seen this state of completion as represented by an early printed form of the poem in question rather than in Scott's fair-copy manuscript (where this has survived), and have merely sought to free this as far as possible from the various errors and non-authorial interventions that arose in the course of publication and successive reprintings. Each case is, however, slightly different in a volume made up of so many disparate poems. A contribution to an album or a personal *jeu d'esprit* might well not be intended for publication at all, and for these and for some incomplete and unpublished poems, Scott's manuscript is the copy-text. For some of his work intended for oral delivery at the theatre and considerably altered by the actors and theatre management in performance and as hastily printed by contemporary newspapers, the editors have preferred Scott's poem as he wrote it, represented by his fair-copy manuscript or by a printing more under his control.

Scott's lyrics for songs are also a special case. Although modern practice favours providing the accompanying music notation where songs are included in critical editions of a poet's work, such a practice is not entirely appropriate in the case of Walter Scott. Although he had a patriotic and sentimental attachment to traditional Scots song, Scott was not adept at reading printed music and was by some accounts virtually tone deaf. Though willing to provide verses in response to requests from song-collectors and musicians he concerned himself remarkably little over the music they were meant to suit, working mostly by a given rhythm. Evidently he sometimes heard the tune for a song only after he had composed his lyrics and there is no evidence that he felt particularly concerned when a different tune was substituted for the one to which his verses had been nominally written. Song-collectors were naturally eager to attach Scott's name to their productions as that of one of the most prestigious and best-selling poets of the age, but his possession of musical sensitivity and knowledge was not their primary consideration. When Scott's song-lyrics were reprinted in the various lifetime collected editions of his poetical works, publications particularly subject to his authorial control, the music was not generally included: sometimes the tune was named or the reader was referred to the music-book in which it had previously been published, but by no means was this invariably so. Nor is there any overall demarcation of songs from other kinds of shorter poems in these lifetime collected editions. The present editors have therefore decided that to provide music notation for these songs would distort the flow between them and the other short poems that exists overall, creating a false dichotomy between texts Scott himself seems to have regarded more as equivalents. The present volume represents Scott's intentions and practice more accurately by providing musical information and background relating to each of Scott's song-lyrics in the editorial matter for that item.

Where in a song book the first verse (or sometimes the whole) of Scott's lyrics is printed twice, both as independent letterpress and spaced underneath the relevant notes of the musical setting, unless otherwise stated the editors have chosen the letterpress version as their copy-text of the song.

5. OVERALL PRESENTATIONAL CONVENTIONS FOR THE POEMS

In a volume like the present the sources for the component poems inevitably vary widely, from manuscripts prepared for publication to entries in albums, from printed broadsides and song-books to volume collections of Scott's own work. While respecting the nature of these sources, the editors have also tried not to give undue prominence to their merely accidental or arbitrary features.

Stanza-numbering occurs for some poems and not others (as well as in some states but not others of the same poem), and appears to have little or no intrinsic significance. The editors have therefore decided to remove stanza-numbering from the texts of the poems in all cases.

Individual features of many copy-texts appear to have been governed primarily by the local preferences of the printer or periodical in question. The occurrence of small capitals for individual words within a poem was frequently determined by the nature of the medium in which it appeared. In general these capitals have been normalised unless they serve a clear purpose. Likewise, some publications commonly italicised the name of every person mentioned in an article and continued the practice when printing poetry. Such italics have been removed except for instances where there seems to be some more specific and particular significance in their use. The use of black letter type has also been retained only where it appears to have a particular application for the poem. There is considerable variation in the presentation of directions given within a poem concerning matters such as the name of a speaker or where a discrete section comprises a refrain or chorus. These have been standardised in the present edition to small capitals, as when centring the word 'CHORUS' above the section to which the direction refers. Initial address lines to verse epistles and end-datings have been placed on the right. End punctuation has been removed from headings and sub-headings. Where the air or tune has been named in a song the form 'Air—*The Maid of Isla*' has been used.

Printers varied their practice in the representation of speech marks within a poem, and the present volume has standardised these according to the following conventions. Double speech marks are employed at the start and at the conclusion of a speech, and where a speech continues from one stanza to the next the opening speech marks are repeated at the start of each succeeding stanza of the speech but not at the start of each line of it. Where a speech occurs within a speech single opening and closing speech marks have been applied.

For some of his poems Scott himself has provided apparatus such as a contextualising headnote, brief glossing footnotes keyed to the text, or longer explanatory and expository endnotes. In keeping with the overall procedures and policies of the EEWSP these appear as an integral part of Scott's poem and are firmly distinguished from the paratextual material provided by the editors of the present volume, which is placed after the main sequence of poems. The presentation of Scott's own accompanying apparatus has, however, been standardised in order to avoid giving a misleading significance to accidental features of the copy-text and to facilitate the reader's access to them: Scott's headnotes are invariably presented in the present volume in roman type; his footnotes appear as footnotes still, but keyed to the text by arbitrary symbols; his endnotes appear immediately after the poem itself and are given under the sub-heading 'NOTES ON X' and numbered sequentially, with verse-tags cross-referenced to the poem by line numbers. Any initial indents in the body of these notes have been removed. In some cases Scott has continued to add to his to a poem in subsequent reprintings, and although these additions are not part of the copy-text they are obviously of considerable interest to the reader. Wherever possible they have been summarised or quoted within the editors' Explanatory Notes, but where their length renders this impractical they have been given in an Appendix to the editorial material for the poem in question.

Some poems have been signed or initialled or end-dated by Scott, sometimes for a reason related to the poem itself and sometimes reflexively. The editors have tried to distinguish between the two, retaining only those signatures or end-datings which seem to bear a significant relation to the poem itself. The presentation of those end-datings retained as an integral part of a poem has been standardised over the volume as a whole in the form '13 October 1811', but the original form is either mentioned in the Textual Note or included in the Emendation List to the poem.

There is an immediately observable disparity between the punctuation of poems from a printed source and poems taken from Scott's manuscripts, which are lightly and sometimes inadequately punctuated in their holograph form. No attempt has been made in editing poems taken from a manuscript copy-text to eliminate this disparity by imposing the full, dense punctuation typical of an early nineteenth-century printed text. The manuscript punctuation has, however, been corrected and supplemented where appropriate to aid legibility, rather perhaps as a compositor with a lightly interventionist hand might have provided it, and the editorial matter to such poems gives an account of how this has been achieved. In some instances an overall statement is given that specific routine changes have been implemented silently. Such changes, varying according to the individual poem, include the application of routine apostrophes, speech marks, and stops at the ends of sentences or stanzas, and the expansion of ampersands to 'and', and of verb forms ending with 'd' to end in 'ed'. All other emendations, including the lowering of Scott's idiosyncratic initial upper-case letters at the start of words, are noted individually in an emendation list within the Textual Note to each poem, as in the case of poems with a printed copy-text. Such a procedure presents the detailed editorial process concisely as well as accurately. In supplementing the punctuation of poems with a manuscript copy-text a distinction has also been made between personal and essentially private poems and those of a kind which were probably drafted with eventual public dissemination or publication in mind even if they were never actually completed or published, the former category seeming to invite less editorial intervention.

Overall, the editors have attempted to balance the need to re-examine and present the main corpus of Scott's shorter poems with proper editorial consistency against a wish to demonstrate due sensitivity to the very different circumstances in which the individual poems were written. The present volume brings together hitherto unpublished poems as well as poems that have previously only been accessible through a variety of disparate publications. The result implicitly challenges many existing preconceptions about Scott's career as a poet.

COMBINED EDITORIAL NOTES

Notes are provided for each of the 134 poems in this volume, organised consecutively and headed by item number with main title. The entry for each poem is divided into three sections: Textual Note; Historical Note; and Explanatory Notes. Within these, references to the text of a poem are given by page and line number. References to another poem in the present volume are given by item number and title thus: see no. 16, 'To a Lady'. Reference to the editorial matter to another poem is indicated thus: see Notes to no. 16, 'To a Lady'. Reference to a specific section of the editorial matter to another poem, where appropriate, is signalled thus: see Historical Note to no. 16, 'To a Lady'.

The Textual Note typically comprises an account of the genesis of the poem, its composition and the process by which it came to publication, its evolution through various subsequent publications in Scott's lifetime, and concludes with the reasons for the choice of copy-text, followed by a list of emendations. Specific references are provided where the discussion involves the landmark collected editions of the 1820 *Poetical Works* and the Lockhart 1833–34 posthumous edition. In transcriptions from manuscript material additions have been marked between pairs of vertical arrows ↑thus↓ and deletions between pointed brackets <thus>.

The Historical Note summarises contextual and historical information relating to the poem, with general reference to Scott's influences and use of sources. Where relevant it also includes information on the immediate reception of a poem, as well as the history of that version of the tune for which Scott's lyrics were requested. In the individual Explanatory Notes a more detailed effort has been made to identify Scott's sources, quotations, references, historical events, and historical personages; to explain proverbs, and to translate difficult or obscure language, including single Scots words and those which have changed meaning since Scott's day (there is no separate Glossary). The notes are usually brief and offer information rather than critical comment or exposition. In cases where the text of the poem includes Scott's own notes these too are annotated, but not the material quoted by Scott within his notes.

References are to standard editions, or to editions Scott himself used. Books in the Abbotsford Library are identified as in '*ALC*' (*Abbotsford Library Catalogue*: see also abbreviations below). 'See *ALC*' indicates that Scott possessed an edition of the relevant work, but not the one cited in the note. When quotations reproduce their sources accurately, the reference is given without comment. Verbal differences in the source are indicated by a prefatory 'see', while a general rather than a verbal indebtedness is indicated by 'compare'. When a quotation has not been recognised this is stated: any new information from readers will be welcomed. Biblical references are to the Authorised (King James) Version, and when relevant to the metrical psalms authorised for use by the Church of Scotland. Plays by Shakespeare are cited without authorial ascription, and references are to *The Oxford Shakespeare: the Complete Works*, 2nd edn, ed. John Jowett, William Montgomery, Gary Taylor, and Stanley Wells (Oxford, 2005). The following works are distinguished by abbreviations:

By Scott

Ballads *Ballads and Lyrical Pieces* (Edinburgh, 1806).
Journal *The Journal of Sir Walter Scott*, ed. W. E. K. Anderson (Oxford, 1972).
Lay Ed8 *The Lay of the Last Minstrel ... With Ballads and Lyrical Pieces*, 8th edn (London, 1808).
Letters *The Letters of Sir Walter Scott*, ed. H. J. C. Grierson and others, 12 vols (London, 1932–37).
Minstrelsy *Minstrelsy of the Scottish Border*, 2nd edn, 3 vols (Edinburgh, 1803).
MiscPoems *Miscellaneous Poems* (Edinburgh, 1820).
1820*PW* *Poetical Works*, 12 vols (Edinburgh, 1820).
1821*PW* *Poetical Works*, 10 vols (Edinburgh, 1821).
1822*PW* *Poetical Works*, 8 vols (Edinburgh, 1822).
1823*PW* *Poetical Works*, 10 vols (Edinburgh, 1823).
1825*PW* *Poetical Works*, 10 vols (Edinburgh, 1825).
8vo1830*PW* *Poetical Works*, 11 vols, 8vo (Edinburgh, 1830).
18mo1830*PW* *Poetical Works*, 11 vols, 18mo (Edinburgh, 1830).
1833–34*PW* *Poetical Works*, 12 vols (Edinburgh, 1833–34).

Other Frequently Referenced Sources

ALC Abbotsford Library Catalogue, which is part of the online catalogue of the Advocates Library.
Berg Berg Collection, New York Public Library.
BL British Library.
Child Francis James Child, *The English and Scottish Popular Ballads*, 5 vols (Boston and New York, 1882–98): ballads are identified by item number, such as 'Child, 7B'.
EAR *Edinburgh Annual Register*.
EEWN *The Edinburgh Edition of the Waverley Novels*, 30 vols (Edinburgh, 1993–2012).
EEWSP *The Edinburgh Edition of Walter Scott's Poetry* (Edinburgh, 2018–).
EUL Edinburgh University Library.
Johnson Edgar Johnson, *Sir Walter Scott: The Great Unknown*, 2 vols (London, 1970).
Kinsley *The Poems and Songs of Robert Burns*, ed. James Kinsley, 3 vols (Oxford, 1968): poems are identified by item number.
Life J. G. Lockhart, *Memoirs of the Life of Sir Walter Scott, Bart.*, 7 vols (Edinburgh, 1837–38).
Morgan Morgan Library, New York.
N&I James C. Corson, *Notes and Index to Sir Herbert Grierson's Edition of the Letters of Sir Walter Scott* (Oxford, 1979).
NAL National Art Library, Victoria & Albert Museum.
NLS National Library of Scotland.
NRAS National Register of Archives for Scotland.
NRS National Records of Scotland.
ODEP *The Oxford Dictionary of English Proverbs*, 3rd edn, rev. F. P. Wilson (Oxford, 1970).
Ramsay Allan Ramsay, *A Collection of Scots Proverbs* (1737), in *The Works*

of Allan Ramsay, 6 vols, Vol. 5, ed. Alexander M. Kinghorn and Alexander
    Law (Edinburgh and London, 1972), 59–133.
Ray   J[ohn] Ray, *A Compleat Collection of English Proverbs*, 3rd edn (London,
    1737): *ALC*.
Ruff   William Ruff, *Bibliography of the Poetical Works of Sir Walter Scott*,
    Transactions of the Edinburgh Bibliographical Society, 1 (1937): entries are
    referred to by item number.
T&B   William B. Todd and Ann Bowden, *Sir Walter Scott: A Bibliographical
    History 1796–1832* (New Castle, Delaware, 1998): entries are referred to by
    item number.

1. His First Lines

Textual Note
These lines were first published in 1837 in J. G. Lockhart's *Life* of Scott, 1.95,
introduced there in the following terms:

> The autobiography tells us that his translations in verse from Horace and Virgil were
> often approved by Dr Adam. One of these little pieces, written in a weak boyish
> scrawl, within pencilled marks still visible, had been carefully preserved by his
> mother; it was found folded up in a cover inscribed by the old lady—"*My Walter's
> first lines*, 1782." (94–95)

Scott's fragmentary Ashestiel 'Memoirs' does indeed recall his Latin lessons at
the Edinburgh High School, first from 1779 under Luke Fraser, 'a good latin
scholar', then with the Rector, Dr Alexander Adam (1741-1809), whose class he
entered in October 1781:

> It was the fashion to remain two years at his class where we read Cæsar and Livy and
> Sallust in prose, Virgil, Horace and Terence in verse. I had by this time mastered in
> some degree the difficulties of the language and began to be sensible of its beauties. ...
> I distinguished myself by some attempts at poetical versions from Horace and Virgil.
> (*Scott on Himself* (Edinburgh, 1981), ed. David Hewitt, 20, 22–23)

What Lockhart provides is evidently one of these exercises, offering a fairly
literal translation of Bk 3, lines 571–77 of the epic *Aeneid* by the Roman poet
Virgil (70–19 BC): see also Historical Note. How Lockhart came to possess the
manuscript is unclear, Scott's mother having died in 1819. No evidence of its
having survived has been discovered.
    The present text follows that in Lockhart's *Life*, 1.95, without emendation.
The title, as found in J. Logie Robertson's edition of *The Poetical Works of Sir
Walter Scott* (London, 1904), 694, has been supplied editorially.

Historical Note
The translated passage from Virgil (see above) occurs after Aeneas with his
Trojan companions have sailed along the southern coast of Italy, escaping the
twin perils of Scylla and Charybdis, and then landed on the coast of Sicily, where
they spend a fearful night near Mount Etna. The relevant eight lines of Latin
pentameter in the original ('sed horrificis iuxta tonat Aetna ruinis ... glomerat
fundoque exaestuat imo') are rendered with some efficiency in the twelve lines
of decasyllabic couplets of Scott's version. In its use of heroic couplets, Scott's
approach parallels that of John Dryden in his classic English Augustan version
(1697) of the *Aeneid*, though Dryden's translation is somewhat freer than his
own: see *Works of Dryden*, ed. Scott, 18 vols (London, 1808), 14.317.

2.   On a Thunder-storm

Textual Note
This is the first of two short juvenile poems published in 1837 in the third
chapter of J. G. Lockhart's *Life* of Scott, 1.96. According to Lockhart the
pieces were found wrapped in a cover inscribed by Scott's schoolmaster at
the Edinburgh High School, Dr Alexander Adam (1741–1809), 'Walter Scott,
July, 1783'. A footnote acknowledges receipt of these materials from the Rev.
William Steven (1796–1857), author of *The History of the Scottish Church,
Rotterdam* (1833), who was then researching materials for his *History of the
High School of Edinburgh* (1849). Apparently unknown to Lockhart these par-
ticular lines had previously featured in an article headed 'Anecdotes of Sir
Walter Scott' in the *Imperial Magazine*, 2nd series, 3 (July 1833), 315. Here
they are given as part of a letter 'received from a northern correspondent some
years ago', the framing narrative of which recalls how they were originally writ-
ten by Scott to impress his mother. Comparison between this version and the
text in Lockhart shows a number of verbal differences, especially at the start
of individual lines. The second line thus begins 'What vivid' rather than 'And
vivid', the third reads 'It is' instead of 'Yet 'tis', while the first word in the final
line is 'Let' rather than 'And'. Line 4 also has (repetitively) 'Thy voice' rather
than 'Thy arm'. As a whole, there is a suggestion of slippage in the magazine
version, as if the original was being repeated in mediated form. Lockhart on
the other hand gives a strong impression of working directly from an autograph
manuscript: one which, according to evidence relating to its companion piece
(see Textual Note to no. 3, 'On the Setting Sun'), he would appear to have
transcribed accurately.
      This item did not appear in any of the collected sets of Scott's poetry up to
and including the posthumous edition of 1833–34, but became a fairly regular
feature in compilations following Lockhart's *Life* of Scott. The present text fol-
lows that in Lockhart's *Life*, 1.96, without emendation.

Historical Note
Scott gave his own account of the composition of these lines while surveying
his early career as a poet in his 'Essay on Imitations of the Ancient Ballad'
(1830):

> At one period of my schoolboy days I was so far left to my own desires as to become
> guilty of Verses on a Thunder-storm, which were much approved of, until a
> malevolent critic sprung up, in the shape of an apothecary's blue-buskined wife, who
> affirmed that my most sweet poetry was stolen from an old magazine. (8vo1830*PW*,
> 3.lvi)

Unlike the letter accompanying the verses in the *Imperial Magazine* (see
Textual Note), which ends with Scott's mother tearfully repeating to the
correspondent 'the first effusion of her son's genius' (315), the above account
tends to frame events more in terms of Scott's early education, with this effort
at originality following on from the 'metrical translations which were occa-
sionally recommended to us at the High School' (3.lvi). As Scott concedes,
if not exactly plagiaristic the lines were certainly derivative. In fact, most
of the set phrases there ('awful thunders', 'vivid lightnings', 'mighty name',
'hardened sinners') can be traced in metrical versions of the Psalms and Hymn
books common in the later eighteenth century, though no one specific text
containing all has been discovered. There appears to be a particular affinity
to the second verse of the hymn 'Divine Power', attributed to Thomas Jervis
(1748–1833), itself loosely based on Psalm 29: 'Thine awful thunder fills the

air, / Resounding through the sky; / While vivid lightning midst the gloom, / Proclaim Jehovah nigh.' However, it has not been possible to locate an instance of this in print prior to 1810.

3. On the Setting Sun

Textual Note
This is the second of two juvenile pieces reproduced in J. G. Lockhart's *Life* of Scott (1.96), from manuscript materials relating to the Edinburgh High School inscribed 'Walter Scott, July, 1783' by Scott's old teacher, Dr Alexander Adam (see also Textual Note to no. 2, 'On a Thunder-storm'). In the present instance, however, an engraved facsimile of Scott's original manuscript is to be found (facing page 131) in *The History of the High School of Edinburgh* (Edinburgh, 1849), by William Steven, Lockhart's original informant. In a large open hand, and (unusually in light of Scott's later practice) fully punctuated, this is headed by Scott 'To Dʳ. Adam. / On the Setting Sun'. According to Stevens's accompanying commentary:

> Among the papers of the late Dr Adam, we were much gratified in discovering several prosaic translations from the classics, and two metrical school exercises of Sir Walter Scott. Though the verses have already been printed in the Life of the Poet, a *facsimile* of one of the pieces has now, for the first time, been executed as an appropriate ornament to this volume. The lines in question, written by the Author of 'Waverley' in July 1783, when in his twelfth year, will doubtless be regarded as a valuable and curious memorial to that distinguished individual. (131)

Comparison between the facsimile and Lockhart's printed version shows no verbal differences, and only minor changes in punctuation. The layout of the verses in the facsimile however differs slightly in the indentation there of the third and sixth lines, reflecting that of the alternate lines in the final quatrain.

Like its fellow, this item did not appear in any of the collected sets of Scott's poetry up to and including the posthumous Lockhart edition of 1833–34, but became a fairly regular feature in compilations following Lockhart's *Life*. The present text is based on that in the facsimile manuscript in *The History of the High School of Edinburgh* (see above), with the following emendations from the printed version in Lockhart's *Life*:

2.3   Creator's (*Life*) / Creators
2.5   life's (*Life*) / lifes
2.6   Him (*Life*) / him

Explanatory Notes
2.3   **great Creator's praise**   compare John Dryden, 'A Song on St Cecilia's Day' (1697), line 57 (*Works*, ed. Scott, 18 vols (1808), 11.170) ['And sung the great Creator's praise']. The phrase is also found fairly commonly in 18th-century Hymn and Psalm books, as often given to children. See, e.g, Isaac Watts, *The Psalms of David* (London, 1719: see *ALC*), Psalm 104, line 1: 'My Soul, thy great Creator praise' (269).

4. To Jessie

Textual Note

This item is the first in a sequence of apparently original poems written for an unidentified girl named Jessie from Kelso in the Scottish Borders, where Scott lodged as a young man at Rosebank, the home of his uncle and patron Captain Robert Scott (1739–1804). They have survived along with several of Scott's letters to Jessie, both in the form of transcripts, in an unpublished two-volume manuscript biography of Scott now held in the National Art Library [NAL], Victoria and Albert Museum, as part of the Forster Collection (MS 470: Forster 48.F.53). Titled 'Sir Walter Scott and his Contemporaries', the work's authorship is as yet unknown, but references within to a number of other recently published accounts of Scott, including Lockhart's *Life* of 1837–38, would seem to place its composition somewhere around 1838–40. The letters contained all feature in H. J. C. Grierson's edition of the *Letters* (1.1–8), positioned so as to represent the first known correspondence of Scott. The record is supplemented by Davidson Cook's *New Love-Poems by Sir Walter Scott Discovered in the Narrative of an Unknown Love Episode with Jessie —— of Kelso* (Oxford, 1932), which effectively reproduces in full the unknown biographer's narrative of the affair, including transcripts of the Scott poems found among papers presumably originating from Jessie herself.

These particular verses are referred to in what would appear to be Scott's first amorous approach in letter form, undated and addressed 'To Miss J. ——, Kelso': 'I have scribbled the enclosed lines, which, though I am well aware they are quite unworthy of their subject I hope will not be unfavourably recieved [*sic*]' (*Letters*, 1.1–2). They are positioned immediately after the letter in the manuscript account and Cook's transcript (*New Love-Poems*, 3–4).

The present text follows the transcript in the original manuscript copy of 'Sir Walter Scott and his Contemporaries', Forster Collection (NAL, MS 470, Vol. 1, f. 53), where the poem appears in two octets rather than as in Cook in four quatrains. Apart from the omission of the 'W.S.' end-signature there, it is reproduced without emendation.

Historical Note

According to the unknown author of 'Sir Walter Scott and his Contemporaries' (see above): 'The poems are numerous but the letters do not amount to any great number. They were written at distant intervals during three or four years at least. ... none however are dated' (see *New Love-Poems*, ed. Cook, 2).The timespan indicated here clashes with the head dating of '1787' supplied for the run of 'Jessie' correspondence in the Grierson *Letters*, 1.1–8, as well as more generally with a tendency in some later accounts to place the heart of the affair in 1787–88 when Scott as an adolescent was recuperating from illness at Rosebank. Internal evidence points to a more prolonged involvement, leading up to and perhaps even beyond Scott's qualification as an Advocate in 1792. One pointer is the fourth of the letters in Grierson to Jessie (*Letters*, 1.7-8: compare *N&I*, 3, note to 1.7(b)), in which Scott quotes in modernised form two old English poems while attaching in full another, all of which must have come from Joseph Ritson's *Ancient Songs, from the Time of King Henry the Third, to the Revolution* (London, 1790; but evidently published 1792: *ALC*). Later poems in the sequence also appear to relate to another phase in the affair, supposedly reignited by a chance meeting when Jessie was in Edinburgh tending to an infirm aunt, and with Scott in a fairly late stage of his legal studies. From both its positioning and contents, however, the present item would seem to belong to the beginning of the affair, with Scott residing with his uncle Robert at Rosebank, on the banks of the Tweed at Kelso, aged about seventeen.

Explanatory Notes
2.1   Lassie can ye love me   compare the traditional ballad 'The Beggar Laddie', stanza 3, line 4: 'Bonnie lassie, can ye loo me?' (Child, 280B). Also more broadly echoing songs by Robert Burns, such as 'The birks of Aberfeldey', whose chorus begins 'Bony lassie will ye go' (Kinsley, no. 170).
2.9   gin ye'll love me   *gin* in the conditional sense of 'if only', 'granted that'. Used here in a formulation common in Scots verse, as in 'Gin ye meet a Bonnie Lassie', found in both Allan Ramsay and James Hogg.
2.11   fills the creel   i.e. fills the fisherman's basket, a *creel* referring either to a holding basket worn on the back or over the shoulder, or a wickerwork trap for catching fish. The idea of plenitude as suggested by a full catch is a familiar feature of 18th-century pastoral poetry.
2.13   Teviot and Tweed   the river Teviot which flows through Hawick joins the Tweed at Kelso, a main feature of the neighbourhood noted by Scott in his Ashestiel 'Memoirs': 'The meeting of two superb rivers, the Tweed and the Teviot, both renowned in song' (*Scott on Himself,* ed. David Hewitt (Edinburgh, 1981), 28).

5.   Lines Addressed to Miss J. ——

Textual Note
This features as the second poem in the unpublished two-volume manuscript 'Sir Walter Scott and his Contemporaries', and occurs there unaccompanied by any correspondence from Scott, though the unknown biographer comments how it might contain clues as to the result of Scott's original amatory letter to Jessie in Kelso: see *New Love-Poems by Sir Walter Scott Discovered in the Narrative of an Unknown Love Episode with Jessie —— of Kelso,* ed. Davidson Cook (Oxford, 1932), 4–5. (For more general information on the Jessie poems and their source, see Notes to no. 4, 'To Jessie'.)
     The present text follows the transcript in the original manuscript copy of 'Sir Walter Scott and his Contemporaries', Forster Collection (NAL, MS 470, Vol. 1, f. 54), omitting the 'W.S.' end-signature, but without any other emendation.

Historical Note
In a footnote to this item, Davidson Cook suggests that Scott 'seems to have had in mind a song by George Wither [1588–1667], no doubt well known to him in his youth' (*New-Love Poems,* 4n), quoting then the first octet beginning 'Shall I wasting in despair, / Die because a woman's fair?'. Though there are no clear direct verbal parallels, and while Wither's import differs in protesting an element of unconcern if rejected, there are nevertheless a number of affinities between the two poems in terms of rhetoric and tone. The same song had appeared in three stanzas anonymously under the title of 'The Shepherd's Resolution' in Thomas Percy's *Reliques of Ancient English Poetry,* 3 vols (London, 1765: see *ALC*), 3.120–21, a collection which Scott famously records as having first read as a boy while staying with his aunt at Kelso (see *Life,* 1.38, 116). At the same time, Scott might have come across Wither's poetry (or verse in the same vein) through a variety of sources, including other popular compilations such as Allan Ramsay's *Tea-Table Miscellany* (Edinburgh, 1724–37: see *ALC*). Set phrases

of the order of 'blooming charms' and 'burning fires' are also commonplace in eighteenth-century periodical literature.

6.   To the Flower of Kelso

Textual Note
This is the third in the sequence of poems to Jessie in the unpublished two-volume manuscript 'Sir Walter Scott and his Contemporaries'. (For more general information on these and their source, see Notes to no. 4, 'To Jessie'.) It occurs unaccompanied by any correspondence from Scott, with the unknown biographer merely commenting how 'The maid was coy but her young lover was of too ardent a nature to raise the siege on that account' (see *New Love-Poems by Sir Walter Scott Discovered in the Narrative of an Unknown Love Episode with Jessie —— of Kelso*, ed. Davidson Cook (Oxford, 1932), 5–6). The transcription in the original manuscript, which carries over between folios (ff. 55–56), leaves a certain amount of uncertainty regarding stanza structure, which Cook arguably interprets rather liberally in creating four breaks. Cook also apparently makes an egregious error in misreading 'night' as 'light' in line 4.
     The present text follows the transcript in the original manuscript copy of 'Sir Walter Scott and his Contemporaries', Forster Collection (NAL, MS 470, Vol. 1, ff. 55–56), omitting the 'W.S.' end-signature, and with the following emendation:

4.10   grey-hounds' (Editorial) / grey-hounds

Historical Note
Notwithstanding the continuing theme of unfulfilled love, this item differs from the preceding Jessie poems in its particular focus on the landscape around Kelso as well as historical antiquities there. In these respects, it matches Scott's recollection of 'the awaking of that delightful feeling for the beauties of natural objects' during his youthful visits to the region in the Ashestiel 'Memoirs':

> The neighbourhood of Kelso, the most beautiful if not the most romantic village in Scotland, is eminently calculated to awaken these ideas. ... The meeting of two superb rivers, the Tweed and the Teviot, both renowned in song, the ruins of an ancient abbey, the more distant vestiges of Roxburgh Castle, the modern mansion of Fleurs ... are so mixed, united and melted among a thousand other beauties of a less prominent description that they harmonize into one general picture and please rather by unison than by concord. (*Scott on Himself*, ed. David Hewitt (Edinburgh 1981), 28–29)

Though presented in a less picturesque light, similar landmarks are observed in this poem. The lines also bear witness (albeit again indirectly) to Scott's growing enthusiasm for country sports, as expressed to his friend William Clerk in a letter of 26 August 1791 describing an excursion from Kelso into Northumberland: 'all the day we shoot, fish, walk and ride' (*Letters*, 1.20). In other respects, the poem is somewhat heavily laden with the kind of poetic diction common in eighteenth-century pastoral poetry, as noticeable in set periphrases such as 'scaly prey' and 'feathered game'.

Explanatory Notes
4.title   **Flower of Kelso**   echoing 'The Flower of Yarrow', the name given to Mary Scott, the bride of Scott's namesake and ancestor Walter Scott, 3rd

Laird of Harden (*c.* 1550–1629?), known as 'Auld Wat', whose peel tower was by a stream which eventually flowed into the river Teviot (see *Life*, 1.66–67).

4.13   Teviot's far famed banks   Scott refers to fishing on Teviot Water with his uncle, Captain Robert Scott, in a letter to his friend William Clerk on 6 August 1790 (*Letters*, 1.12). Upper Teviotdale was the ancestral home of the Scotts of Buccleuch, and the 'Legendary Lore' (*Letters*, 1.237) associated with the valley of the Teviot was to play a major part in Scott's work on the Border ballads.

4.21   Roxburgh's crumbling walls   Roxburgh Castle, once a major fortification central to the royal burgh of Roxburgh; it was much disputed, and eventually destroyed by the Scots after its capture in 1460. Over the river Tweed from Kelso, close to its junction with the Teviot, it is now mainly a large mound with little stonework apparent.

4.22   ruined Abbey   Kelso Abbey, founded in the 12th century, overlooking the confluence of the Tweed and Teviot.

7. Jessie

Textual Note
Fourth in the sequence of poems in the unpublished two-volume manuscript 'Sir Walter Scott and his Contemporaries', this item occurs unattached to any correspondence from Scott, with the unknown biographer noting only its 'intimation that the young poet was not unsuccessful in his suit': see *New Love-Poems by Sir Walter Scott Discovered in the Narrative of an Unknown Love Episode with Jessie —— of Kelso*, ed. Davidson Cook (Oxford, 1932), 6–7. (For more general information on the Jessie poems and their source, see Notes to no. 4, 'To Jessie'.)

The present text follows the transcript in the original manuscript copy of 'Sir Walter Scott and his Contemporaries', Forster Collection (NAL, MS 470, Vol. 1, ff. 56–57), omitting the 'W.S' end-signature there, but otherwise without emendation.

Historical Note
This item follows in the tradition of English amatory poetry from the sixteenth century onwards. In particular, there are echoes of the love-songs anthologised in Joseph Ritson's *A Select Collection of English Songs*, 3 vols (London, 1783: *ALC*), a long-time favourite of Scott's (see *Letters*, 3.93), though there is no direct evidence of his having access to a copy at this early period. More generally, songs in this manner are found in periodical literature throughout the eighteenth century.

Explanatory Notes
5.1   When first I met   a fairly standard opening in old songs, as found on at least three occasions in the first volume of Joseph Ritson's *Select Collection of English Songs* (see above): 'When first I fair Celinda knew' (26); 'When fair Serena first I knew' (27); 'When gentle Celia first I knew' (137).

5.11   seraph choirs   seraphs are the highest order of angels in Christian and Jewish mythology, associated with light and harmony. Compare Samuel Wesley (1662–1735): 'The Seraph-Choir in every Note agree, / And all is Peace, and all is Harmonie' ('An Hymn on Peace', lines 19–20).

5.12   **etherial spheres**   alluding to the music of the spheres, an ethereal (light, airy and unworldly) sound supposed to be produced by the movement of the heavenly bodies. The spelling *etherial* is common in the period.
5.16   **glowing charms**   compare 'glowing with resistless charms': Ritson, *Select Collection*, 1.137 (Song 32, line 12).

8.   To the Pride of Teviotdale

Textual Note
Fifth in the sequence of poems to Jessie in the unpublished two-volume manuscript 'Sir Walter Scott and his Contemporaries' (see below), this item appears in the wake of a letter of Scott's showing him reluctantly about to leave Kelso for Edinburgh, and with the relationship with Jessie still being of a covert nature (*Letters*, 1.2–3). The unknown biographer's narrative then resumes with Scott returning after a short break, and composing the present poem 'at his uncle's upon finding on his arrival that his fair mistress was absent on a visit to a relative', it being then 'presented to her on her return a few days after': *New Love-Poems by Sir Walter Scott Discovered in the Narrative of an Unknown Love Episode with Jessie —— of Kelso*, ed. Davidson Cook (Oxford, 1932), 9. No source is given for this additional information, which was probably extrapolated, at least in part, from the preceding letter and the poem itself. (For more general information on the Jessie poems and their source, see Notes to no. 4, 'To Jessie'.) In addition to Cook's *New Love-Poems* (9–10), this poem is reprinted in *Sir Walter Scott: Selected Poems*, ed. James Reed (Manchester, 1992), 21–22. The dating given there of 1788–89, however, is almost certainly too early, with Scott probably by this time having entered the second phase of his university studies in Edinburgh (see also no. 13, 'Law Versus Love').
   The present text follows the transcript in the original manuscript copy of 'Sir Walter Scott and his Contemporaries', Forster Collection (NAL, MS 470, Vol. 1, ff. 60–61), with the following emendation:

6.24   head. (Editorial) / head

Historical Note
In this poem Scott again focuses on the landscape surrounding Kelso, after the fashion of 'To the Flower of Kelso' (no. 6). The twin rivers of Tweed and Teviot once more feature prominently, in stanzas 4 and 6 respectively, while the details of nature in stanza 5 suggest a late-summer season. The versification is also noticeably more ambitious than in earlier efforts.

Explanatory Notes
5.title   **Pride of Teviotdale**   *Pride* in the sense of the foremost, best, distinguished, in this case of all in Teviotdale, the valley of the River Teviot.
5.1   **tryst**   lovers' rendezvous or assignation.
5.3   **gloaming**   evening twilight, dusk.
6.21   **heart for thee is speiring**   *speiring* in the sense of asking, enquiring; here evidently with an added element of yearning, with something of the overall sense of 'my heart is enquiring for where you are'.
6.23   **Tweed's fair bed**   the river Tweed flows by Kelso and directly past Rosebank, where Scott stayed (see *Letters*, 1.10–11).
6.25   **Corn rigs**   ridges of land planted with grain. Compare Robert Burns's 'Corn rigs are bonie' (Kinsley, no. 8).

6.27   heather bell   *erica cinera*, a species of heather, with bell-shaped purple flowers.
6.31   Teviot   rises on the border of Dumfriesshire, running in a NE direction through Hawick and Ancrum before joining the River Tweed at Kelso.

9. A Simple Fact

Textual Note
This is the sixth original poem in the unpublished two-volume manuscript 'Sir Walter Scott and his Contemporaries', and occurs there after further correspondence from Scott to Jessie in Kelso, in which he refers to his increasing poetic output and experimentation (see *New Love-Poems by Sir Walter Scott Discovered in the Narrative of an Unknown Love Episode with Jessie —— of Kelso*, ed. Davidson Cook (Oxford, 1932), 10–12; *Letters*, 1.3–7). Scott also reveals a developing interest in balladry, enclosing in full one ballad titled 'The False Knight and the King's Daughter', while quoting liberally from another identifiable as a version of 'Lammikin'. Scott's stated source for these is an Irish nurse when he was staying at Bath as a child, though both can also be found in modified form in David Herd's *Ancient and Modern Scottish Songs*, 2nd edn, 2 vols (Edinburgh, 1776: *ALC*), 1.93–95 (as 'May Colvin') and 1.145–48 ('Lammikin'), as well as in other printed sources. 'A Simple Fact' appears independently after the above correspondence in the manuscript biography, and is seen as reflecting efforts made by Jessie to check the 'too rapid growth' of the relationship (*New Love-Poems*, 21). (For more general information on the Jessie poems and their source, see Notes to no. 4, 'To Jessie'.)
    The present text follows the transcript in the original manuscript copy of 'Sir Walter Scott and his Contemporaries', Forster Collection (NAL, MS 470, Vol. 1, f. 70), without emendation.

Explanatory Notes
7.6   owre true   over true, in the sense of 'only too true'. Compare 'AN OWER TRUE TALE' near the end of *The Bride of Lammermoor*, ed. J. H. Alexander, EEWN 7a (Edinburgh, 1995), 262.21–22 (and note).
7.7   discretion ... Valour   proverbial (*ODEP*, 189).

10. The Resolve

Textual Note
This is the seventh original poem to Jessie mentioned in the unpublished two-volume manuscript 'Sir Walter Scott and his Contemporaries', but is not transcribed there on the grounds that Scott himself, having retained a copy, later published it as 'The Resolve'. (For more general information on the Jessie poems and their source, see Notes to no. 4, 'To Jessie'.) Davidson Cook supplies the resulting gap by printing the text from the *Edinburgh Annual Register* for 1808, while adding 'It is inserted where mentioned by the unknown author but chronologically it is probably out of place as it seems to belong to the close of the episode' (*New Love-Poems by Sir Walter Scott Discovered in the Narrative of an Unknown Love Episode with Jessie —— of Kelso*, ed. Davidson Cook (Oxford, 1932), 25–27n). Interestingly, however, it is positioned in the manuscript biography immediately after the letter to Jessie in Kelso in which Scott quotes in

modernised form two old English poems while attaching in full another, 'Song on an Inconstant Mistress', all of which must have come from Joseph Ritson's *Ancient Songs, from the Time of King Henry the Third, to the Revolution* (London, 1790; but evidently published 1792: *ALC*). In the same undated letter, Scott states how 'lately I have managed to get hold of more than one collection of old songs native of the other side of the Border' (*New Love-Poems*, 23; *Letters*, 1.7). Granting that the positioning of the MS biography is correct, reflecting perhaps the order of the original papers received, then this item could represent the first clear product of the 'second phase' of the Jessie poems, after Scott's resolution to train and practise as an Advocate. In any event there is a danger of placing these poems entirely in terms of their supposed biographical content, especially in view of what by this stage had become a more sophisticated form of literary communication.

The first known printing of this poem is in Scott's *English Minstrelsy*, 2 vols (Edinburgh, 1810), 1.212–14, first published in Edinburgh in February 1810, in which it is given as 'Anonymous'. It then appeared under Scott's name later in the same year in the *Edinburgh Annual Register, for 1808*, 1: 2 (Edinburgh, 1810), xxxvi–xxxvii, described there in a sub-title as 'In Imitation of an Old English Poem. 1809'. How far these texts matched the poem originally sent to Jessie is uncertain, though one would expect the unknown author of 'Sir Walter Scott and his Contemporaries' to have remarked on the fact had it been substantially different from the printed versions. Signs of a possible continuing authorial involvement can be found in line 30, where the *English Minstrelsy*'s 'glow'd for me alone' is changed in the *Edinburgh Annual Register* to 'glow'd a diamond stone'. On the other hand, the later reading (which might just as well have derived from an intermediary, such as James Ballantyne) diffuses the clarity of the original version, avoiding the doubled rhyming of 'alone' but also creating a fresh and potentially confusing repetition with 'diamond's ray' at line 26. Nevertheless it was the *Edinburgh Annual Register*'s wording (along with the sub-title) that was followed in *The Vision of Don Roderick, and Other Poems* (Edinburgh, 1811), 159–62, then again in the lifetime collected editions where the poem regularly featured, beginning with the 1820 *Poetical Works* (12.131–34). Only minor changes in punctuation of the kind attributable to the printer occur up to and including the Lockhart 1833–34 posthumous edition (8.374–76), in which the link with the magazine is reinforced by a footnote stating 'Published in the Edinburgh Annual Register of 1808' (374n). The text also featured in the same form in George Thomson's *Select Melodies of Scotland*, 5 vols (Edinburgh, 1822–23), 3.item 22, accompanied by the tune 'O'er Boggie' as set by Joseph Haydn.

The present text follows that in *English Minstrelsy* (1810), 1.212–14, probably the closest to the original manuscript presented to Jessie in the early 1790s, and most likely representing the culmination of the original creative impulse. There are no emendations.

Historical Note
An immediate context for the earliest printings of this poem is suggested in a letter from Scott to his brother Tom of 30 December 1810:

> As to the Resolve it is mine & it is not—or to be less enigmatical it is an old fragment which I cooperd up into its present state with the purpose of quizzing certain judges of poetry who were extremely delighted & declared no living poet could write in the same exquisite taste. It is as you justly observe in the stile of the earlier part of the 17th Century. How it got into the papers I know not. (*Letters*, 7.454).

Tom had written earlier that month claiming to have seen the poem with an ascription to Scott in newspapers on the Isle of Man, where he was stationed: 'I cannot think it is your production. It is an imitation of the manner of the Marquis of Montrose' (NLS, MS 3879, f. 281v). This association of the piece with the Cavalier verse of James Graham, 1st Marquess of Montrose (1612–50), correctly responds to the 'antique' feel of the poem as it was first publicly presented, and is supported more particularly by at least one strong echo there (see note to 8.45 below). More broadly, however, the imagery and rhetoric are likely to reflect 'the collection[s] of old songs' (see Textual Note) which Scott told Jessie he was accumulating around 1792, among which almost certainly was Ritson's *Ancient Songs*. In this respect, the poem emerges as less of a pastiche, and more as an example of Scott's continuing development of his poetical repertoire.

Explanatory Notes

8.17   ambush'd Cupid   possibly echoing Matthew Prior's poem 'Cupid in Ambush', *Miscellaneous Works*, 2 vols (London, 1740), 68–69. The image is of Love lying in hiding to catch the unwary male in the girl's features.

8.42   loving labour's lost   see Shakespeare's *Love's Labour's Lost*.

8.45   widow'd turtles   compare 'I'll ne'er love thee more', by James Graham, 1st Marquess of Montrose: 'As doth the turtle chaste and true / Her fellow's death regrete, / And daily mourns for his adieu, / And ne'er renews her mate' (lines 121–24): see David Herd, *Ancient and Modern Scottish Songs*, 2nd edn, 2 vols (Edinburgh, 1776: *ALC*), 1.240. The turtle dove is by reputation monogamous.

8.46   phœnix is but one   in Greek mythology the Phoenix is solitary in life and death, singing its own lamentations, and being reborn from the ashes of its dead self. There may be an echo here of Shakespeare's poem 'The Phoenix and the Turtle' (1601), concerning the death of an ideal love, the two birds having created a perfect unity transcending the material world.

11.   Lines to Miss J. ——

Textual Note

This is the eighth original poem to Jessie to be mentioned in the unpublished two-volume manuscript 'Sir Walter Scott and his Contemporaries', and the seventh for which a transcript is provided. (For more general information on the Jessie poems and their source, see Notes to no. 4, 'To Jessie'.) According to the unknown biographer it was offered to Jessie after a long separation had taken place—presumably with Scott in Edinburgh—and was the 'first offering' made on the resumption of the affair: *New Love-Poems by Sir Walter Scott Discovered in the Narrative of an Unknown Love Episode with Jessie —— of Kelso*, ed. Davidson Cook (Oxford, 1932), 27. Whether this information has a separate source or is extrapolated from the poem itself remains unclear.

   The present text follows the transcript in the original manuscript copy of 'Sir Walter Scott and his Contemporaries', Forster Collection (NAL, MS 470, Vol. 1, ff. 76–77), and is reproduced without emendation.

12.   The Prisoner's Complaint

Textual Note
This is the ninth original poem to Jessie to be mentioned in the unpublished two-volume manuscript 'Sir Walter Scott and his Contemporaries', and the eighth for which a transcript is provided. (For more general information on the Jessie poems and their source, see Notes to no. 4, 'To Jessie'.) It is positioned in the biography after the start of a new chapter pointing to a fresh phase in the lovers' relationship, with Jessie coming to Edinburgh to tend to 'an invalid aunt', and Scott eventually crossing paths with her again when visiting a friend who by chance happened to live in the flat below where the aunt resided. The situation described in the poem is interpreted literally by the unknown biographer, who imagines Scott as secreted in the aunt's pantry and even being given 'writing materials' to occupy himself while there: *New Love-Poems by Sir Walter Scott Discovered in the Narrative of an Unknown Love Episode with Jessie —— of Kelso*, ed. Davidson Cook (Oxford, 1932), 29–30. Cook's transcript of this poem contains one verbal error, with 'impatient' instead of 'imprisoned' in the sixth line: a misreading carried over into its reprinting in *Sir Walter Scott: Selected Poems*, ed. James Reed (Manchester, 1992), 22–23. The dating given in the latter of 1788–89 is almost certainly too early, given that the relationship appears to have entered a new phase with both participants as adults in Edinburgh.

The present text follows the transcript in the original manuscript copy of 'Sir Walter Scott and his Contemporaries', Forster Collection (NAL, MS 470, Vol. 1, ff. 82–84), with the omission of the 'W.S.' end-signature, and the following emendation:

10.23   'gainst (Editorial) / gainst

Historical Note
Notwithstanding the supposed biographical connection (see above), the trope of the secreted lover overhearing or peeping at occurrences taking place externally is common in story-telling and literature, not least in the comic mode. More particularly this reflects a popular folk tradition in Scotland, whose contemporary practitioners included James Hogg in his 'Love Adventures of Mr George Cochrane' (1810/1820): see *Winter Evening Tales*, ed. Ian Duncan (Edinburgh, 2002), 166–228. The connection with this folk tradition is also accentuated by Scott's own use of Scots at significant points.

Explanatory Notes
10.3   **meikle speed**   great haste.
10.18   **dare na stir a leg**   daren't so much as move a leg.
10.20   **canna move a peg**   cannot make a move.
11.29   **haddocks dry**   haddock fish salted and hung up in a dry place.
11.29   **barley meal**   wholemeal barley flour, lighter than wheat but darker in colour, used in porridge and gruel in Scotland.

13.   Law Versus Love

Textual Note
This is the tenth original poem to Jessie in the unpublished two-volume manuscript 'Sir Walter Scott and his Contemporaries', and the ninth for which a transcript is provided. (For more general information on the Jessie poems and

their source, see Notes to no. 4, 'To Jessie'.) It is placed there almost imme-
diately after its predecessor, 'The Prisoner's Complaint' (no. 12), as further
illustrating signs of humour in Scott: see *New Love-Poems by Sir Walter Scott
Discovered in the Narrative of an Unknown Love Episode with Jessie —— of Kelso*,
ed. Davidson Cook (Oxford, 1932), 32–34. The text of the poem is also given
in Arthur Melville Clark, *Sir Walter Scott: The Formative Years* (Edinburgh,
1969), 188–89, where it is seen in the context of Scott's study of Civil and Scots
Law during the period 1790–92.

The present text follows the transcript in the original manuscript copy of 'Sir
Walter Scott and his Contemporaries', Forster Collection (NAL, MS 470, Vol. I,
ff. 84–85A), omitting the 'W.S.' end-signature, but otherwise without emenda-
tion. It does not include the word 'that' in line 34 which has been added in pencil
by another hand in the MS transcript to read 'I fear that I'm non compos mentis'.

Historical Note
This poem draws on two facets of Scott's life while studying law in Edinburgh,
both of which were later recalled in his Ashestiel 'Memoirs'. The first involved
the acquisition of a 'fund of romantic lore', extending from native writers like
Edmund Spenser to take in also French romances and early Italian poets such
as Tasso, Ariosto, Dante, and Boiardo: see *Scott on Himself*, ed. David Hewitt
(Edinburgh, 1981), 26, 33. The other involved a more arduous application,
along with his friend William Clerk, to key legal text-books in order to meet the
qualifications for an Advocate: 'we went by way of question and answer through
the whole of Heineccius's analysis of the Institutes and Pandects, as well as
through the smaller copy of Erskine's Institutes of the Law of Scotland' (*Scott
on Himself*, 43). The differing values represented by these two kinds of text vie
with each other in the poem, as the following explanatory notes illustrate.

Explanatory Notes
11.title **Law … Love** a fairly common juxtaposition. Compare George
Granville, Baron Lansdowne (1666–1735), 'Beauty and Love: A Poetical
Pleading'.
11.2 **brownies** goblins of shaggy appearance, often represented as
benevolent spirits connected to a dwelling, and only appearing at night.
11.3 **Avaunt** be gone!
11.4 **Shakspeare and Spenser** for the early influence on Scott of William
Shakespeare's plays, and of the Elizabethan poet Edmund Spenser (1552?–99),
see *Scott on Himself*, ed. Hewitt, 16, 26.
11.5 **Heineccius** Johann Gottlieb Heineccius (1681–1741), German jurist.
Scott acquired two titles of his among three Civil Law textbooks in 1789:
Elementa Juris Civilis and *Recitationes in Elementa Juris Civilis* (see Clark, *Sir
Walter Scott*, 194 n.31; editions of 1728 and 1773, along with another work by
him, are in *ALC*). See also *Scott on Himself* (quoted in Historical Note above),
and Scott's letter from Rosebank in Kelso to William Clerk of 6 August 1790:
'Heineccius and his fellow worthies have ample time to gather a venerable coat
of dust, which they merit by their dulness' (*Letters*, 1.11).
11.6 **Erskine's dryer labours** referring to John Erskine of Carnock
(1695–1768), Professor of Scots Law at Edinburgh University from 1737 to
1765. He was the author of *Principles of the Law of Scotland* (1754: see *ALC*), a
standard text-book which went through many editions, and *An Institute of the
Law of Scotland* (1773: see *ALC*), published posthumously.
11.8 **Romance** here in the sense of Romance literature, such as tales of
chivalry (see also Historical Note).

11.11–12   **Institutes … Pandects**   terms derived from Roman Emperor Justinian's commissioning of two legal works, known as the *Institutes* and the *Digest*. The *Institutes* was a manual intended as a text-book for students. The *Digest*, also known as the *Pandects* (the full title being *Digesta seu Pandectae*), was a codification of the works of the classical jurists.

12.16   **pleasaunce**   pleasure garden, often with the sole purpose of appealing to the senses but not offering material sustenance. The ensuing vision follows the convention of the enticing, but sometimes treacherous, enchanted garden in medieval romance, as well as in early modern texts such as Edmund Spenser's *Faerie Queene* (1590–96), Matteo Maria Boiardo's *Orlando Innamorato* (1487), and Ludovico Ariosto's *Orlando Furioso* (1532).

12.23   **roused by Tom**   evidently referring to Scott's younger brother, Thomas Scott (1774–1823), who was taken on as an apprentice in their father's legal practice when Scott decided to qualify as an Advocate (see *Scott on Himself*, ed. Hewitt, 41).

12.24   **unco loving**   extraordinarily amorous, besotted.

12.34   **non compos mentis**   *Latin* not of sound mind.

12.35   **Saracen**   Arab, Muslim.

12.36   **gowk**   foolish, loutish: from *gowk*, a cuckoo.

12.37   **paynims**   pagans, especially Muslims.

12.39   **Allan's bloody pate**   the Allan whose head is bloodied is presumably an apprentice or clerk (as yet unidentified) of Scott senior. Compare *King Henry VI, Part 1*, 3.1: 'Enter in skirmish, the Retainers of Gloucester and Winchester, with bloody pates.'

12.40   **cracked his noddle**   broken open the back of his head.

14.   A Lover's Advice

Textual Note
This is the eleventh original poem to Jessie to be mentioned in the unpublished two-volume manuscript 'Sir Walter Scott and his Contemporaries', and the tenth for which a transcript is provided. (For more general information on the Jessie poems and their source, see Notes to no. 4, 'To Jessie'.) It is prefaced there by comments on the drollery sometimes shown by Scott during the covert affair, and is introduced more particularly as exhibiting 'one of the arguments employed to combat her [Jessie's] scruples': see *New Love-Poems by Sir Walter Scott Discovered in the Narrative of an Unknown Love Episode with Jessie —— of Kelso*, ed. Davidson Cook (Oxford, 1932), 34–36.

   The present text is based on the transcript in the original manuscript copy of 'Sir Walter Scott and his Contemporaries', Forster Collection (NAL, MS 470, Vol. 1, ff. 86–88), omitting the 'W.S.' end-signature. It does not however implement the pencilled transposition there in another hand of 'your bliss' and 'approach' in line 29. The following emendations have also been made:

13.10   Ere (Editorial) / 'Ere
13.21   loves (Editorial) / love's

Explanatory Notes
13.6   **Dinna fash your thumb**   proverbial 'don't worry, don't bother': see *ODEP*, 246. Compare Allan Ramsay, *The Gentle Shepherd* (1725), 1.1.140: 'Do ye sae too, an' never fash your thumb.'

13.7   auld Adam's time 'old Adam' is a proverbial expression, used to signify man's fallen nature inherited from Adam: see *ODEP*, 3.

13.21   like loves like proverbial expression, signifying the attraction of similar qualities. Compare Robert Baron (b. 1630): 'If like loves like, why shouldst thou love the night / And deeds of darknesse, since thou art so light?' ('XXVI To Kate common', in *Pocula Castalia* (1650)).

13.23   knout it flog or scourge it.

13.29   If cant your bliss approach to rout it presumably in the approximate sense of 'if bigotry threatens to assail your happiness'. The word *cant* was used in particular for language used unthinkingly and sometimes hypocritically by a religious sect.

15. An Anti-Classical Ode

Textual Note
This is the twelfth and last original poem to Jessie to be mentioned in the unpublished two-volume manuscript 'Sir Walter Scott and his Contemporaries', and the eleventh for which a transcript is provided. (For more general information on the Jessie poems and their source, see Notes to no. 4, 'To Jessie'.) The unknown biographer introduces it as the 'next poem in the order of date', though as with other items no specific chronological evidence is supplied: see *New Love-Poems by Sir Walter Scott Discovered in the Narrative of an Unknown Love Episode with Jessie —— of Kelso*, ed. Davidson Cook (Oxford, 1932), 36–38. Cook's printed text misrepresents the original transcript twice in the fifth stanza, reading 'But if the characters' rather than 'And if the chronicles' at its beginning, and 'beauteous' instead of 'handsome' in the third line.

The present text follows the transcript in the original manuscript copy of 'Sir Walter Scott and his Contemporaries', Forster Collection (NAL, MS 470, Vol. 1, ff. 88–89), omitting the 'W.S' end-signature there, and with the following emendation:

14.3   it's (Editorial) / its

Historical Note
No evidence has so far been discovered about any sculptures Scott might have seen, or exhibitions where he could have viewed them. The most famous depiction of the Three Graces (see note to 14.1 below) in his day was undoubtedly the nude group in marble by Antonio Canova (1757–1822), sculpted first for the Empress Josephine in 1810, and then for John Russell, 6th Duke of Bedford in 1814–17. Though Scott was clearly familiar with Canova's work in later life (see *Saint Ronan's Well*, ed. Mark Weinstein, EEWN 16 (Edinburgh, 1995), 299.8 and note), the apparent origin of this poem in the early 1790s would seem to preclude any direct connection in this case. Representations of Venus and the Three Graces however are common to both Classical and Renaissance art, from the ancient Greek Venus de Milo to Botticelli's 'The Birth of Venus' and 'The Three Graces presenting Gifts to a Young Woman'. Scott's own approach here matches an eighteenth-century penchant for treating serious or 'high' subject-matter anti-bathetically in 'low' or scurrilous fashion as humour. Compare, for example, Robert Burns's anti-Classical manner in 'Ode to Spring' (Kinsley, no. 481).

Explanatory Notes

14.1 Venus Roman goddess, principally associated with love, beauty, and fertility.

14.1 the three the Three Graces, daughters of Jupiter (Zeus in Greek mythology): comprising Thalia (youth and beauty), Euphrosyne (mirth), and Aglaia (elegance). Often depicted dancing in a circle, they presided over banquets entertaining the guests of the gods.

14.5 salt-sea foam Venus is supposed to have arisen from foam on the sea-shore.

14.13–14 shining nook … pliant withy the image is of haddock fish hung to smoke on a rope made of thin, flexible twigs (*widdie*) by the ingle nook or fire hearth.

14.16 keep a smithy Venus was the wife of Vulcan, the Roman god of fire and metalwork, an unsightly spouse with whom she was permanently dissatisfied.

14.19 toyed with Mars the Roman god of war, Mars was Venus's preferred lover. On discovering the affair, Vulcan devised a net to capture the lovers in bed, and then exhibited them together to the other gods.

15.21 *faux pas* *French* mistake, indiscretion.

15.24 Adonis Venus's first mortal lover, with whom she went hunting, eventually killed by a boar (as recounted in Ovid *Metamorphoses*, Bk 2). This was also the subject of Shakespeare's poem *Venus and Adonis*, published in 1593.

15.26 Graces Three see note to 14.1 above.

15.31 poor as Job proverbial (*ODEP*, 638). See Job 1–2.

16. To a Lady

Textual Note

This poem is the second item belonging to a commonplace book of Scott's in the Abbotsford Library, notable in its earlier stages for containing a number of poems relating to his ultimately unsuccessful pursuit of Williamina Belsches (1776–1810), the only child of Sir John Belsches of Fettercairn and his wife Lady Jane Stuart, eldest daughter of the 6th Earl of Leven and 5th Earl of Melville. A small calf leather-bound volume, this was originally marked in hand on the spine 'MS ADVERSARIA / 1792 / MSS SCOTT' (the markings are now partly lost), while the recto of the third blank leaf bears the inscription 'Common places—14 May 1792'. In some respects the collection resembles a scrapbook, with many items pasted in or inserted, while only about half of the book is used.

'To a Lady' is found on a single leaf, measuring approx. 18.8 x 11.8 cm, pasted onto the third page of the Abbotsford commonplace book ('Adversaria'), in Scott's formal hand, and with the last two stanzas numbered 2 and 3. The text is largely without alteration, the one substantive change being the replacement of 'spirit' with 'shade' in the fifth line. This poem was first printed with additional punctuation as item 3 (taken from a negative photostat in NLS, MS 2232, f. 3) in W. M. Parker's 'Sir Walter Scott: Thirteen New Poems?', *Poetry Review*, 40: 4 (August–September 1949), 263–75 (p. 265).

The present text follows the original manuscript in the 'Adversaria' commonplace book (p. 3), with stops supplied editorially at the end of each fourth line. The following emendations have also been made:

15.1   Time's (Editorial) / Times
16.9   Diamond's (Editorial) / Di'monds
16.12   heart-worshipped (Editorial) / heart-worshipd

Historical Note
Various accounts have been given of the start of Scott's relationship with
Williamina Belsches (see above), one of the most durable being that the two first
met after a service at Greyfriars Kirk in Edinburgh, most probably in 1790, with
Walter shielding the young girl then in her fifteenth year from the rain. This is
by no means implausible, the homes of both parents (who were known to each
other) being in the same vicinity, though if any amorous interest developed at
this point it would have overlapped with Scott's continuing affair with Jessie of
Kelso (see Notes to no. 4, 'To Jessie'). Far more likely is that the relationship
approached something closer to courtship during the spring and winter seasons
of 1792–95, when Williamina resided in Edinburgh with her parents, attend-
ing functions such as those in the Assembly Rooms at the same time that Scott
reportedly was gaining new social graces. The initial dating of the 'Adversaria'
commonplace book (see above) in this case would place it close to the onset of
any fuller liaison.
    Compared with the apparently largely one-sided literary involvement with
Jessie, in this case there are signs of a fuller interchange, with Williamina herself
a collector and (to some extent) composer of poetry. A large sheaf of poems in
her writing, connected with these years and most probably handed to Scott
by her mother, Lady Jane, during a painful rapprochement in 1827, survives
amongst the Abbotsford Collection at the National Library of Scotland (MS 894,
ff. 60–80). A commonplace book of Williamina's own, now in private hands,
similarly contains a group of poems belonging to the years 1792–95, as well as
others from after 1800, and like the Abbotsford papers shows a special penchant
for the poems of Mrs Anne Hunter (1742/3–1821), whose sombre and some-
what mournful lyrical verse was in circulation well before the publication of her
retrospective collection of *Poems* in 1802. One item in the Abbotsford papers,
'The Farewell', seems to relate particularly to the relationship with Scott, with
a coded reference to both names in one stanza : 'O say my S— canst thou go /
Far from thy friend & Britains shore / And leave W—a sad alone / Thy loss
forever to deplore' (f. 63). (While there was evidently no question of Scott
going overseas, the adoption and sometimes reversal of a literary established
trope—here the convention of the departing sailor leaving his Highland lassie—
seems to have been a common feature of the pair's exchanges.) Several of the
apparently Williamina-related items of the 'Adversaria' reflect a similar kind of
literary courtship, which Williamina for her part might have viewed more in
terms of affectionate flirtation rather than as a prelude to marital union. Scott
himself clearly viewed matters differently, and in the summer of 1795 ventured
to disclose his intentions by letter, receiving a reply which, while advising cau-
tion, apparently did not shut off his hopes (see *Letters*, 1.40–42). In the following
April, after attending the Aberdeen Circuit Court, he took the matter further
by venturing into the proximity of Fettercairn and securing an invitation to
stay at the family house, where he spent some time with Williamina after her
recovery from a supposed illness. By then, however, Williamina had almost
certainly received approaches from (Sir) William Forbes (1773–1828), the son
of a wealthy banker, more acceptable socially and financially to the family and
whom she might well have personally preferred. A succession of events later
in the year, commencing with rumours early in September that Forbes and his
father had visited Fettercairn (*Letters*, 1.54), followed by news of the official

engagement of the couple on 12 October (they were married in January), meant the collapse of any remaining hopes, leaving Scott in a potentially dangerous state of mind. At least four original pieces in the 'Adversaria', along with several kindred poems from other sources, bear the marks of this emotional journey over several years.

The positioning of 'To a Lady' close to the beginning of 'Adversaria' indicates a relatively early provenance, though it should also be borne in mind that its immediate predecessor is dated 1796 (see no. 20, 'Poem on Caterthun') and that chronology might not have been Scott's first priority when reassembling these materials. The proximity of the poem in subject-matter to one of Williamina's favourites nevertheless would seem to place it nearer the beginning than end of the affair. In his *Life* of Scott, Lockhart gives the text of a poem entitled 'To Time—by A Lady', as written out by Scott in later life and bearing initials on the back identifying its true origin in the 'object of his first passion' (1.243–44). This same poem can also be found as 'To Time', in nine rather than eight stanzas, in Williamina's commonplace book, without authorial ascription. In later editions of *Life* a footnote served to identify the author as Anne Hunter, though in fact Hunter's published poem with that title is another piece. In this light there must be some possibility that the lines are Williamina's own composition; though alternatively the poem might be one of the myriad of pieces circulating privately at the time whose authorship is now untraceable. In any event, Scott in 'To a Lady' appears to be offering a direct and uplifting response to a favourite poem of Williamina's, replacing the sombre plea there for time and its 'torpid calm' to negate the pains of youth with the promise of imaginative riches to be found in the past. As Lindsay Levy has argued, Scott probably also presented to Williamina about this time his volume of *Legendary Fragments*, now in the Abbotsford Library and dated near its beginning 1792, containing fair transcripts of poems by others on mythological, historical, and traditional themes, this then most likely being handed back by Lady Jane Stuart during their exchanges in 1827: see 'Scott's Early Love Poems to Williamina Belsches', *Scottish Literary Review*, 3: 2 (2011), 45–53 (pp. 49–50). Indeed, it is not impossible that the present item, with its stress on the riches to be found in bardic lore, was somehow connected with this gift of the *Legendary Fragments* volume, though the opening epigraph found there is from Alexander Pope's 'The Temple of Fame'.

Explanatory Notes

15.1 For *thee* the emphasis given to 'thee' here (as to 'thy' in line 7) matches a similar treatment of such pronouns in verse collected by Williamina Belsches, as in 'Reply to Dr Percy's Beautiful Ballad "O Nancy wilt thou go"', where each of the three stanzas concludes with an underlined 'thee' (NLS, MS 894, f. 60).

15.5 shade of each departed Bard *shade* in the sense of the impalpable form of a dead person, especially in allusion to the Hades of classical mythology, and common (as in 'departed shade') in 18th-century verse. Reference to the *Bard* also evokes the tradition of Celtic poetry, as celebrated in Thomas Gray's 1757 Ode of that name and the Ossian poems of James Macpherson (1736–96).

17.   The Violet

Textual Note
This poem was first published, under Scott's name, in *English Minstrelsy*, ed. Scott, 2 vols (Edinburgh, 1810), 2.197–98, and then reprinted in the *Edinburgh Annual Register, for 1808*, 1: 2 (1810), xxiii. A manuscript version, probably used as a copy-text, survives in the Beinecke Rare Book and Manuscript Library, Yale University (GEN MSS 266, Box 1, Folder 40). Consisting of a small single leaf, measuring approx. 12.1 x 10.1 cm, this is pasted onto a larger piece of paper, so it is not possible to see any watermark, if such exists. At the head Scott has written 'For the Minstrelsy—if you like it—' (subsequently deleted); and in another hand 'Tenth' has been added, possibly as a marker in the printing-house—though the actual number given to the piece in the printed collection is 'XLV'. There are no verbal differences between this manuscript and the version in *English Minstrelsy*, apart from the interpretation of Scott's mistaken 'ay' as 'eye' (line 11), the few other variants found in the latter (addition of two hyphens, and reduction of 'watery' to 'wat'ry') being of the kind attributable to the printer.

On the other hand, some dissimilarities can be found in two instances where Scott included versions of his poem in letters to friends while soliciting contributions for his anthology. Writing to J. B. S. Morritt on 17 August 1809, he presented it as a 'trifle' of his own, a 'pitiful sonnet wrote in former days to my mistresses eye-brow or rather eyelid after it had wept itself dry' (*Letters*, 2.225). In the text that follows 'green-wood' (line 1) reads 'summer [bower]' and 'fair her' (line 5) appears as 'sweet its' (see also NLS, MS 144, item 4, f. 8r). Equivalent differences are found in the version given in a letter of 16 September to William Robert Spencer, which introduces the poem as 'a sort of *nothing* written before I had laid aside violets and lilies for nightshade and miseltoe [*sic*]... found ... among some old scraps, and now destined to the Miscellany' (*Letters*, 2.243–44). In this instance 'bracken' is found instead of 'birchen' (line 2), 'herself' rather than 'itself' (line 3), and 'sweet' rather than 'fair' (line 5). Owing to the uncertain date of the Beinecke manuscript, it is not possible to chart anything like a full sequence of composition. All the available evidence, however, points to an earlier initial conception, as is again indicated by Scott's description of the poem in a letter of 17 August to Margaret Clephane as 'some lack-a-daysical lines on a violet which I divind for the nonce in the non-age of my Muse' (*Letters*, 2.227).

There are hardly any variants, none of them substantive, in the various printed texts that followed in Scott's lifetime. The only differences in the *Edinburgh Annual Register* compared with the *English Minstrelsy* are found in the former's omission of the comma after 'violet' in the first line and rendition of 'wat'ry' as 'watry' (line 8). The next printing, in *The Vision of Don Roderick, and Other Poems* (Edinburgh, 1811), 151–52, likewise omits the comma, but restores 'wat'ry'; it also, for the first time, removes a comma after 'eye' at the end of line 11. The poem entered the lifetime collected editions with the 1820 *Poetical Works* (12.124), where the comma after 'eye' is restored. Only minute changes in punctuation of the kind attributable to the printer subsequently occur up to and including the Lockhart posthumous 1833–34 edition (8.372), in which a new footnote correctly identifies the piece as having first appeared in the *English Minstrelsy*.

The present text follows *English Minstrelsy* (1810), 2.197–98, as a first printing authorised by Scott, and one which in its wording conscientiously follows the MS copy-text provided by him for this purpose.

Historical Note
Strong secondary evidence connects this item with the body of poetry relating to Scott's relationship with Williamina Belsches (for further details see Historical Note to no. 16, 'To a Lady'). According to William Erskine (later Lord Kinedder), as reported in Lockhart, it is one of the few survivors from that phase in his life:

> 'O yes, he made many little stanzas about the lady, and he sometimes showed them to [George] Cranstoun, [William] Clerk, and myself—but we really thought them in general very poor. Two things of the kind, however, have been preserved—and one of them was done just after the conclusion of the business.' He then took down a volume of the English Minstrelsy, and pointed out to me some lines *on a violet*, which had not at that time been included in Scott's collected works. Lord Kinedder read them over in his usual impressive, though not quite unaffected, manner, and said, 'I remember well that, when I first saw these, I told him they were his best; but he had touched them up afterwards.' (*Life*, 1.243).

Some later editions of Scott's poetry, including J. Logie Robertson's *The Poetical Works of Sir Walter Scott* (London, 1904), 695, affix the date 1797, presumably following the half-suggestion in the above account that the poem came in the wake of the affair with Williamina, the apparent bitterness in the final two lines thus expressing Scott's own anguish. However, it is possible that the conception came earlier in the relationship, forming part of a poetical interchange which included a fair element of role-playing. Amongst the sheaf of poems in Williamina's hand, preserved in the Abbotsford Collection, is a poem titled 'The Wither'd Violet', subscribed '*W B* Melville House / Decr 1792'. Melville House was Williamina's mother's family house in Edinburgh, and the dating places it at a period when she and her parents would have been in town, at a point when Scott was just beginning his courtship in earnest. In the poem itself, a male protagonist associates himself with the 'sweet flower' and its now closed 'blue eye', likening its drooping state with his own cold treatment by Julia, in spite of his (as the final stanza makes clear) continuing to adore her: '"Tis but like me who doom'd to sigh / Condemn'd by Julia's frowns to smart / Yet still must bless that scornful eye / Yet still must love that cruel heart' (NLS, MS 894, f. 62v).

This same poem can also be found anonymously in several early nineteenth-century miscellanies, as well as (more surprisingly) in George Moore's Gothic novel *Theodosius de Zulvin*, 4 vols (London, 1802), 3.57, asterisked there 'Author Unknown'. In the Preface, Moore describes how on acquiring these lines he had written to his fellow-novelist Henry Mackenzie about rumours that he was the author, only to be met with a carefully-worded denial: 'The Withered Violet he [i.e. Mackenzie] rather supposed to be the work of some other person; for although he had formerly written some lines on a similar subject, they did not bear that title' (1.xii). While much (or all) of this of this could be part of the larger fiction, a connection with Henry Mackenzie is not unlikely, in view of both his sentimentalism and interest in German literature. Johann Wolfgang von Goethe's 'Das Veilchen' (The Violet) (1774) would almost certainly have been known by Mackenzie and, like 'The Wither'd Violet', features an imperilled flower, in this case crushed (rather than, as wished, caressed) by an insensitive young shepherdess. Scott's own poem, which in its original may have differed somewhat from the printed version, was almost certainly conceived in such a literary context. By the time of its retrieval (and possible revision) in the summer of 1809 Scott would no doubt also have been aware of William Wordsworth's 'Lucy' poem 'She dwelt among the untrodden ways', notably the lines 'A Violet by a mossy stone / Half-hidden from the Eye' (*Lyrical Ballads*, 2 vols (London, 1800), 2.52: see *ALC*).

18.   To the Cruel Lady of the Mountains

Textual Note
This poem was printed in *English Minstrelsy*, ed. Scott, 2 vols (Edinburgh, 1810), 1.224–26, where it is given as Anonymous both in the title and contents list, lacking the asterisk used to denote original pieces. No earlier printing has been discovered, and the poem has apparently never been published in any collected edition of Scott's work. The manuscript record however indicates a much closer association, and there is compelling evidence to suggest that this is his own composition. An early autograph version exists in NLS, MS 3220, ff. 35–36, in the form of a two-page booklet, with pages measuring approx. 19 x 11.5 cm, incorporating a crown and horn watermark with the initials 'G R'. Written in Scott's fair hand, the stanzas are numbered from 2–7, the whole piece being end-dated '14 Feby. 1793'. The same bound volume in the library also contains versions of 'The Sang of the Outlaw Murray' (ff. 37–45, on similar paper to the 'Cruel Lady'), and of Matthew Gregory Lewis's 'Alonzo the Brave and Fair Imogine' (ff. 53–60), both of which items were evidently presented by Scott to his aunt Miss Christian Rutherford. The dating of the present piece on St Valentine's Day 1793, close to the beginning of Scott's relationship with Williamina Belsches (for further details see Historical Note to no. 16, 'To a Lady'), encourages the view that the booklet was originally prepared as a presentation piece, addressed either to his aunt (who was party to the secret of his courtship) or to Williamina herself.

Another autograph version is found in a larger presentation booklet consisting of eight leaves (4 sheets folded) prepared for Lady Charlotte Campbell [later Bury] (1775–1861), now held in Aberdeen University Library (WS C2), the outside leaves of which bear the watermark 'T STAINS / 1799', and which is apparently dated in its inscription 16 January 1805, although it is possible that the year is in fact 1801. Here the poem (f. 7) is accompanied by several other items, including versions of 'The Maid of Toro' (see no. 54), originally written for 'The House of Aspen' around 1799, and the song 'O tell me how to woo thee', which appeared in print in the first edition of *Minstrelsy of the Scottish Border* (1802), 2.304–05. Granted that Scott was unlikely to offer up already-published poems, the earlier of the two dates mentioned above for the inscription seems more likely, this relating to a time when Lady Charlotte held sway in Edinburgh as a leader of society (see *Letters*, 1.130, 130n). There are a number of verbal variants in the Aberdeen MS compared with that in MS 3220, consistent with Scott recalling the poem at least partly from memory. In the sixth line 'rocks' and 'steps' become respectively 'steeps' and 'course', while line 18 reads 'No more these woodland scenes I ll wander' as opposed to 'Along yon winding path I'll wander'. Additionally, the protagonist proposes to throw away his 'pipe' rather than 'crook' (line 13), and trusts his prayers will 'rise' rather than 'mount' heavenward (line 24). A transcript of this poem also exists in Lady Charlotte's own commonplace book, in the Huntington Library, San Marino, California, HM 33691, written in her hand, amongst materials largely belonging to the late 1790s, a fair proportion communicated through personal acquaintance. Perhaps significantly the 'Cruel Lady' is positioned midway between versions of Scott's 'The Erl-King' and 'Glenfinlas' (see nos 30 and 33), both with origins around 1797–98. The text here too is much closer to the one in MS 3220, the only verbal variant matching those in the Aberdeen booklet being the use of 'rise' rather than 'mount' in line 24. It could be then that Lady Charlotte was already in possession of the poem before being more formally presented it by Scott.

No direct information has been found concerning the decision to include this item in the *English Minstrelsy*. Verbally the printed text is closer to the original version in MS 3220 than the presentation booklet to Lady Charlotte Campbell. At the same time, there are some telling variants, for instance the replacement of a rhyming 'aside' in line 13 with 'away' (the latter having previously been deleted in favour of the former in MS 3220). One possibility is that Scott's printer James Ballantyne had a hand in making the language more conventionally acceptable; another is that Scott himself was working from memory and in the process toning down still potentially hurtful expressions.

The association of Scott with this poem is further broadened by the reappearance of the penultimate two stanzas as an uncredited motto to Ch. 22 of *The Monastery* (1820): see *The Monastery*, ed. Penny Fielding, EEWN 9 (Edinburgh, 2000), 292, where line 18 reads 'Along the mountain path I'll wander' and the following line 'wind my solitary way'. This motto subsequently appeared in *The Poetry contained in the Novels, Tales, and Romances of the Author of Waverley* (Edinburgh, 1822), 30–31, tacitly acknowledging Scott's authorship of the full poem.

The present text is based on the printed version in *English Minstrelsy* (1810), 1.224–26, which has the advantage of being fully punctuated, and may in some respects represent Scott's final intentions. The following two emendations however have been made, the first maintaining the rhyme scheme and reflecting a change in that direction previously made by Scott, the second restoring a form of personal emphasis used elsewhere by Scott in poetry relating to Williamina Belsches:

17.13   aside (NLS, MS 3320) / away
17.23   *thee* (NLS, MS 3320) / thee

Historical Note
Written in a consciously pastoral style, this item matches other appropriations of established modes by Scott during the 1790s. In the present case there appears to be an especially strong affinity with Christopher Marlowe's 'The Passionate Shepherd to his Love' (1599), in which the shepherd-lover implores his loved one in lavish terms to enter into a pastoral idyll with him ('The shepherd swains shall dance and sing / For thy delight each May morning'), following a tradition dating back to the Greek poet Theocritus. Almost as well-known was Sir Walter Raleigh's more cynical 'The Nymph's Reply to the Shepherd' (1600), in which the nymph declines the invitation, pointing to the transitory nature of the supposed golden world on offer. Both poems were anthologised, either together or in close proximity, in works familiar to Scott, such as Joseph Ritson's *Select Collection of English Songs*, 3 vols (London, 1783: *ALC*), 1.228–31, and George Ellis's *Specimens of the Early English Poets* (London, 1790: see *ALC*), 75, 85–86. Viewed in this light, the present item adds a third ingredient to the exchange, the shepherd responding in turn to the nymph's rejection. In personal terms it contains a number of elements inviting comparison with the relationship between Scott and Williamina Belsches (see above), with Scott here featuring as a distraught lover and Williamina the ice-maiden in her mountain fortress at Fettercairn. The sense of absolute rejection, propelling the male protagonist in an obverse direction as a hermit, might seem to fit especially the circumstances of the autumn of 1796, when Scott realised that Williamina was to marry another, but this is countered by the 14 February 1793 dating of the first manuscript version. Granted that this poem is indeed one of those passing between Williamina and Scott earlier in their relationship, it serves to confirm

the sense that their poetical exchanges were marked by a considerable amount of role-playing, though with the parts adopted in this case subsequently gaining a darker hue.

Explanatory Notes

17.title   Cruel Lady   possibly alluding in obverse terms to 'The Nymph of the Mountain Stream' by Mrs Anne Hunter, a favourite poetess of Williamina Belsches, and in which Hunter recalls her youth in Scotland (opening lines: 'Nymph of the mountain-stream, thy foaming urn / Wastes its pure waters on the rock below'). This was reprinted in the *Edinburgh Annual Register, for 1808*, 1: 2 (1810), xxiv; then again in *English Minstrelsy* (1810), 2.219–20.

17.1   wilt thou not be my love   compare the opening line of Marlowe's 'The Passionate Shepherd' (see Historical Note): 'Come live with me, and be my love'.

17.23   for *thee*   the emphasis in 'thee' matches that found in other poems involving Williamina Belsches: see no. 16, 'To a Lady', note to 15.1.

17.23   obdurate Maid   a fairly common expression in pastoral poetry and drama during the 18th century, following on from the pattern set by Marlowe (see Historical Note). Compare Daniel Bellamy, 'Love and Despair: or, the Disconsolate Shepherd' (1722): 'Obdurate Maid! whose Comprehensive Name / Shews that the Sweets of Love are dash'd with Gall' (lines 1–2).

17.24   orisons   prayers.

17.25   cypress wreath   used to deck funerals, but also symbolically worn by tragic poets. Compare William Collins, 'Ode to Fear' (1746) [of Shakespeare]: 'His cypress wreath my Meed decree, / And I, oh Fear! will dwell with thee' (lines 70–71). 'The Cypress Wreath' is also the title of the song in *Rokeby* (1813), Canto 5, stanza 13.

19.   Unpued on Yarrow's braes

Textual Note

This constitutes the ninth item in Scott's commonplace book ('Adversaria') in the Abbotsford library, and has strong claims to be part of the body of verse there apparently relating to Williamina Belsches (for more general information on the book, and Scott's relationship with Williamina, see Notes to no. 16, 'To a Lady'). Consisting of four unnumbered stanzas, it is written in Scott's hand in ink on a single leaf, measuring approx. 13.3 x 12 cm, pasted onto p. 17 of the commonplace book. The MS text contains a number of corrections and interpolations, evidently made by Scott in the course of composition, these including the substitution of the Scots 'Unpued' for 'Untouchd' at the beginning, and the insertion of 'Thy spriggs shall wake' to replace 'To cherish sad' at line 7. A printed version (taken from the photostat in NLS, MS 2232, f. 8), with added punctuation, appears as item 4 in W. M. Parker's 'Sir Walter Scott: Thirteen New Poems?', *Poetry Review*, 40: 4 (August–September 1949), 263–75 (p. 266). The verses are also quoted in full as expressive of Scott's emotional longing in Johnson, 1.111.

The present text follows the original manuscript in the 'Adversaria' commonplace book, p. 17, though with the expansion of two ampersands, provision of five routine apostrophes (lines 1, 2, 4, 9, and 16), and normalisation of the original spelling of 'Untouchd' in the second line. A title is also provided editorially from the opening line. The following emendations have also been made:

18.9   shade (Editorial) / shad
18.12   awa'. (Editorial) / awa
18.16   awa'. (Editorial) / awa

Historical Note
This poem follows the pattern found in Scott's relationship with Williamina
Belsches of adapting established tropes and conventions for the purposes of
literary courtship. In this instance there is a clear indebtedness to a tradi-
tion of Scots pastoral songs centred on the Yarrow and Ettrick valleys in the
southern uplands of Scotland, and in particular to 'The Braes of Yarrow',
written by William Hamilton of Bangour (1704–54) after the manner of
the old traditional ballad. Somewhat longer than Scott's own poem, this
had featured in both Allan Ramsay's *Tea-Table Miscellany* (1724–37) and
Thomas Percy's *Reliques of Ancient English Poetry* (1765), the latter identify-
ing Hamilton as the author. More specifically, there is a strong similarity
between Scott's opening line and 'Puing the birks on the braes [Plucking the
birch on the high banks] of Yarrow', the refrain-like final line of quatrains
2–4 in 'The Braes of Yarrow'. While one should be cautious in drawing
biographical parallels, Scott in his correspondence is more than once found
yearning for the winter that will bring Williamina and her family back to
reside in Edinburgh (*Letters*, 1.25, 42), and much of his own summer vaca-
tions were spent in Roxburghshire, with Lockhart noting that the greater part
of his long vacation was spent there in 1794 (*Life*, 1.218).

Explanatory Notes
18.1   Unpued on Yarrow's braes, the birk   for an explanation, and
possible literary source, see Historical Note above. Yarrow Water, in the old
county of Selkirkshire, flows for about 23 km (14 miles) in a NE direction from
St Mary's Loch before joining Ettrick Water 3 km (2 miles) SW of Selkirk, the
two then falling into the Tweed.
18.2   Teviot's roses   the River Teviot flows in a NE direction through
Teviotdale, passing Hawick and Roxburgh, before joining the Tweed SW of
Kelso, where Scott himself resided when on vacation.
18.6   tottering ha'   *ha'* in the sense of a farm-house or main dwelling.
18.14   cleed … wi' snaw   cover or clothe with snow.

20.   Poem on Caterthun

Textual Note
This is the first item in Scott's commonplace book titled 'Adversaria' in the
Abbotsford Library, notable for its inclusion of a number of poems apparently
relating to Williamina Belsches (for more general information on this book,
and Scott's relationship with Williamina, see Notes to no. 16, 'To a Lady').
Untitled, it is written in pencil in Scott's hand on two pasted-on leaves, covering
pp. 1–2, the first measuring approx. 17.4 x 11 cm, and the second (with a tear
to the top right) approx. 13.8 x 11 cm. Numbering is provided for stanzas 2–10,
and the whole poem is subscribed '5ᵗʰ May 1796 / C—t—r T—n'. Changes
made apparently in the course of writing include the substitution of 'Granites'
for 'ramparts' and 'lonely' for 'lingering' (lines 10 and 24). A printed version,
with a number of verbal errors, is provided in Herbert Grierson's *Sir Walter
Scott, Bart.* (London, 1938), 36–38, while extracts have subsequently been given
in Johnson (1.117), and by Lindsay Levy in her article 'Scott's Early Love

Poems to Williamina Belsches', *Scottish Literary Review*, 3: 2 (2011), 45–53 (p. 48).

The present text follows the original manuscript in the 'Adversaria' commonplace book, pp. 1–2, with stops provided at the end of each quatrain. Ampersands have been expanded, apostrophes supplied where unambiguously required, and shorthand spellings such as 'lengthend' (see line 12) normalised. The title has also been supplied editorially. In addition the following emendations have been made.

18.4   sun (Editorial) / Sun
18.8   its (Editorial) / it's
19.12   Legion's (Editorial) / Legions
19.29   setting sun (Editorial) / Setting Sun
19.37   chequered (Editorial) / checquerd

Historical Note
The end-dating of this poem at 5 May 1796 helps place it precisely at the time Scott started to head southwards after a stay at Fettercairn House, the family home of Williamina Belsches, situated in the old county of Kincardineshire, some 18 km (11 miles) NW of Montrose. The two Iron Age hill-forts at Caterthun, known respectively as Brown and White Caterthun, are about 12 and 14 km (7.5 and 9 miles) respectively SW of Fettercairn, and Scott had evidently made a detour there and to nearby Edzell Castle on his way homeward. In a letter of 6 May to the Rev. James Walker, Minister of Dunnottar, he recalled how he had been 'detaind at Fettercairn house by the hospitality of Sir John and Lady Jane two or three days longer than I expected, from which you will easily guess Miss Belsches was recoverd and able to see company'. Subsequently he had 'visited a beautiful ruin called Eagle Castle and was delighted—I have seen Cater Thun, and was astonishd' (*Letters*, 1.48–49, 51). From the details in the poem, it would seem that Scott has chiefly in mind White Caterthun, which is capped by the ruins of a stone fort, now mostly consisting of masses of small boulders. Brown Caterthun by contrast has several earthen ramparts but no stone walls. An extensive area of low-lying countryside is visible to the NE from both Caterthuns.

Explanatory Notes
19.12   veteran Legion's   concerning the Roman military invasion of Scotland, which commenced around AD 71. More specifically perhaps alluding to the veteran Ninth Legion, which according to legend disappeared mysteriously after entering the Highlands. 'Legions' appears without any guiding apostrophe in the MS.
19.13   Denmark's conquering day   referring to the dominance of the Norsemen or Vikings in large areas of northern Scotland before and during the early medieval period.
19.14   Odin's ruthless altar   in Norse mythology Odin was the supreme god and creator, only appeased by human blood and the sacrifice of prisoners.
19.15   Runic lay   a recitation or legendary tale written or carved in runes (the earliest Teutonic alphabet) or more generally one belonging to ancient Scandinavia. Compare the chant of 'The billows know my Runic lay' by Norna of the Fitful-head in *The Pirate*, ed. Mark Weinstein and Alison Lumsden, EEWN 12 (Edinburgh, 2001), 177.7, 9.
19.17   Village tale   according to local tradition, a witch carried the stones to the summit at Caterthun, and would have brought more had not her

apron string broken, depositing one of the largest stones on the side of the mountain.

19.27   one sacred Spot   i.e. Fettercairn House, 0.75 km (0.5 miles) NE of Fettercairn village, the original three-storey building of which bears the date 1666 (see also Historical Note).

19.37   life's chequered years   compare *Marmion* (1808), Introduction to Canto Third, line 4 ('Life's chequered scene of joy and sorrow'): ed. Ainsley McIntosh, EEWSP 2 (Edinburgh, 2018), 69 and note to 3.4 (398–99).

19.40   sunshine of the soul   echoing a sonnet by Anne Hunter (a favourite poet of Williamina's), 'To the Memory of a Lovely Infant, written several years after his death', lines 11–12: 'Must woes on woes accumulated roll, / And cloud with care the sunshine of the soul?' (*Poems*, 1802, 55).

21.   William and Helen

Textual Note
In the 1820 *Poetical Works* (11.187) Scott stated that his translation of Bürger's 'Lenore' had been written in 1795. His working manuscript in the Houghton Library, Harvard University (MS Eng 253), which bears a 1795 watermark, consists of sixteen leaves with text in Scott's hand written on the rectos and numerous corrections and insertions on the facing versos. However, as the two outside leaves form a cover and title-page it also bears some signs of a finished copy. Two further manuscripts in Scott's hand are presentation copies, for Lady Charlotte Home (NRAS, 859/Box 201/Bundle 8) and a Miss Haldane (NLS, MS 5278), and are dated respectively 26 and 24 August 1796. These ladies suffered a carriage accident while travelling in Perthshire and Scott assisted them in their difficulties, and afterwards presented each with a copy of his poem. Although apparently written so close together these presentation copies are not identical: the first has a motto from Walpole and the second from Ossian, and there are also variations in the text itself. For instance, in line 10 Miss Haldane's copy reads 'a peace' whereas Lady Charlotte's copy like the Houghton Library manuscript has 'a truce', and in line 35 'faithless' where the other manuscript versions read 'fleeting'. Both presentation copies, however, contain the final stanza of moral reflection, lacking in the Houghton Library manuscript. Until the details of his translation were fixed by print, it seems likely that Scott was still trying out potential variations in his mind.

The date when Scott submitted copy for his publication of *The Chase, and William and Helen: Two Ballads from the German of Gottfried Augustus Bürger* to the Edinburgh publisher Manners and Miller is not exactly known, although in writing to William Erskine on 26 September 1796 he mentions having received that day 'a letter from Miller on the important subject of the Ballads' (*Letters*, 1.54) which clearly discussed the title-page and date of publication. The book was published in Edinburgh on 1 November that year. 'William and Helen' was subsequently republished in Scott's *An Apology for Tales of Terror* (Kelso, 1799), 41–57, with only changes of the kind normally associated with the printer.

During the intervening time Scott had, flatteringly, been chosen by the fashionable Matthew Gregory Lewis (1775–1818) as a contributor to the collection that was then intended to be called *Tales of Terror* and eventually published in 1801 as *Tales of Wonder*. William Erskine had met Lewis in London during the spring of 1798, drawing his attention to Scott's poems and eliciting a request from Lewis to include them in his collection. A letter from Scott to Lewis of 29 May 1798 (Morgan, MA 12) enclosed a copy of his first publication. Lewis would supervise the publication of Scott's translation of Goethe's play *Götz von Berlichingen* in London in 1799, and Scott subsequently recollected receiving 'instruction' from Lewis for his verses, relating to 'the rhymes in which he was justly *superior* and to the structure of versification' (*Letters*, 8.409). Lewis suggested a number of detailed corrections to Scott for this poem in a letter of 1799 (8vo1830*PW*, 3.ciii–civ), and it may have been excluded from *Tales of Wonder* only because of its previous appearance in *An Apology for Tales of Terror*.

In later life Scott was somewhat ashamed of his earliest German-influenced ballads. When he published 'William and Helen' in his *Poetical Works* of 1820 (11.187–211) he added a prefatory note stating that he had decided to omit it and that it was included only because the publishers had 'pleaded for its admission' (11.187). He also made some revisions: in line 154 the barb now 'goes' rather than 'rides' fleetly; in line 179 Helen's response of "Still short and stern?" is eliminated and instead William continues his speech with the words 'low, damp, and chill'; and in line 187 it is now the 'scourge' rather than the 'steed' that is wight. The poem afterwards passed into the successive lifetime collected editions of Scott's poetry and into the Lockhart posthumous edition of 1833–34 (6.291–306), with only changes of the kind normally associated with the printer.

The present text is taken from the poem's first publication in Scott's *The Chase, and William and Helen: Two Ballads from the German of Gottfried Augustus Bürger* (Edinburgh, 1796), 19–41, as representing the culmination of Scott's initial process of composition. The following emendations have been made to correct minor errors of punctuation, and in addition the sub-title 'From the German of Gottfried Augustus Bürger' has been added, reflecting the description on the title-page that applies both to 'William and Helen' and to 'The Chase'.

21.33   "O rise, my (1820*PW*) / "O, rise my
21.36   again." (1820*PW*) / again.
21.49   noster, (1820*PW*) / noster
22.68   again. (1820*PW*) / again."
23.108   me, (1820*PW*) / me

Historical Note
The 'Lenore' of Gottfried Augustus Bürger (1747–94) was first published in German in the *Göttinger Musenalmanach* in 1774, part of the German response to the examples given by the Ossian poems of James Macpherson (1736–96) and Thomas Percy's *Reliques of Ancient English Poetry* (1765) of seeking inspiration for a native tradition of poetry through folk verse and legend. It was not translated into English until 1796 when a number of translations appeared more or less simultaneously, the first and best known of them being by William Taylor of Norwich, published in the *Monthly Magazine*, 1 (March 1796), 135–37. Scott knew of Taylor's version previous to publication, for Mrs Barbauld had recited it at an evening party at the house of Professor Dugald Stewart during a visit to Edinburgh. Scott himself was not present, but heard of the translation from Stewart's brother-in-law George Cranstoun, who repeated to him the lines 'Tramp, tramp, across the land they speed; / Splash, splash, across the sea'. Scott himself, reminiscing towards the end of his life in his 1830 'Essay on Imitations of the Ancient Ballad', dates this incident rather vaguely to '[a]bout the summer of 1793 or 1794' (8vo1830*PW*, 3.lix). A copy of the original was obtained for him from Hamburg by Harriet, the wife of Scott of Harden, presumably after her marriage on 29 September 1795. By his own account he not only enthused to a friend within a few hours of obtaining the book, but 'rashly

added a promise to furnish a copy in English ballad verse', beginning to work after supper and finishing his translation 'about daybreak the next morning' (8vo1830*PW*, 3.lxii). The two-volume copy of Bürger's *Sämmtliche Schriften* in the Abbotsford Library was published at Göttingen in 1796, but Scott may have once owned an earlier printing containing 'Lenore'.

Scott's version of Bürger's ballad bears an obvious debt to Taylor's translation published towards the end of March 1796, not only in its inclusion of the couplet Scott heard from Cranstoun (which is not in Bürger), but also in its changing the location and historical setting of the original. Bürger's poem is set in Germany during the aftermath of the battle of Prague on 6 May 1757, when the forces of Frederick the Great of Prussia had caused the Austrian army to retreat from before the city. Frederick's army afterwards began a siege of Prague, but when it failed retreated from Bohemia altogether. Taylor's version in explaining that Lenore's lover 'went abroade with Richard's host, / The Paynim foes to quell' makes him an Englishman fighting in the Third Crusade (1189–92) in the army of Richard I of England (1157–99). Scott makes William a follower of the Holy Roman Emperor Frederick I (1122–92) and thus still a German, but follows Taylor in dating the story to the Third Crusade and renders it more precise in locating William's grave as in Hungary, which the crusaders had passed through en route to Constantinople. In other respects Scott's poem differs both from Bürger's original and Taylor's version, notably in substituting the animated corpse of a criminal executed in chains for the spirits who follow William's horse. Scott's description of his poem's relationship to Bürger's varied: his 1796 title-page describes both ballads as 'from the German' of Bürger, while from 1820 onwards in successive editions of his *Poetical Works* it is rather described as 'Imitated from' Bürger's poem.

Explanatory Notes

20.5 Fred'rick's princely power Frederick I, Holy Roman Emperor (1122–90) was a key figure in the Third Crusade to the Holy Land of 1189–92.

20.7 Judah's wars the ancient Jewish kingdom of Judah had Jerusalem as its capital. Between the 11th and 13th centuries a series of religious wars, known as the Crusades, were sanctioned by the church with the object of capturing Jerusalem and other sites in the Holy Land from Muslim rule.

20.9 Paynim and with Saracen a *paynim* is a pagan, especially a Muslim, while a *saracen* is an Arab.

21.49 pater noster from the first two words in Latin of the Lord's Prayer ('Our father'): a special bead in a rosary indicating that this prayer is to be said, or by extension to the rosary as a whole.

21.51 bale torment, misery or grief.

22.61 sacrament the Eucharist, or Holy Communion.

22.74 child of clay alluding to God's creation of Adam, the first man, from earth in Genesis 2.7.

22.75 knows not what her tongue has spoke an appeal for forgiveness since the sin is based on ignorance, and based on Jesus's words on the cross in Luke 23.34, 'Father, forgive them; for they know not what they do'.

23.113 From Hungary William supposedly died on his way to the Holy Land, the crusaders having passed through Hungary on their way to Constantinople.

23.116 matin bell an ecclesiastical service often performed at day-break, to which a bell would summon worshippers.

23.123 wight strong and vigorous.

24.125 busk, and boune dress, and get ready.

24.126   barb steed   a horse from Barbary, of a kind noted for its speed and endurance.
24.127   stock   the lower part of a tree-trunk left standing.
26.199   accursed wheel   a contrivance resembling a large wheel used as an instrument of torture.
27.221   hear the cock   apparitions must vanish at cock–crow: compare *Hamlet*, 1.1.130–36.
27.222   sand will soon be run   time is running short, an allusion to an hour-glass where the passage of time is marked by sand trickling from an upper to a lower glass chamber.
27.246   casque   helmet, armour to cover and protect the head.
27.247   cuirass   armour for the body, a breast-plate and back-plate hinged or buckled together and reaching down as far as the waist.

22.   The Chase

Textual Note
Scott almost certainly composed his verse translation of 'Der wilde Jäger' by Gottfried Augustus Bürger (1747–94) soon after his translation of the same poet's 'Lenore' as 'William and Helen', which he later stated to have been written in 1795 (1820*PW*, 11.187). There is no surviving manuscript in Scott's hand, but the poem was first published in Scott's *The Chase, and William and Helen: Two Ballads, from the German of Gottfried Augustus Bürger* (Edinburgh, 1796), 1–18. (For further details of this publication see Textual Note to no. 21, 'William and Helen'.) 'The Chase' was republished in *An Apology for Tales of Terror* (Kelso, 1799), 27–40, with only changes of the kind normally associated with the printer: for instance, the stanzas, which were numbered in the first printing, are unnumbered in *An Apology*.
More substantial revisions are evident in the poem's next incarnation under the title of 'The Wild Huntsmen' in Matthew Gregory Lewis's *Tales of Wonder*, 2 vols (1801), 1.153–63. (For details of Scott's connection with Lewis's collection see Textual Note to no. 21, 'William and Helen'.) Many of these revisions can be seen marked in pencil in Scott's hand in an imperfect copy of the printed text of 1796 in the Abbotsford Library, presumably as part of his preparation for adapting his poem for Lewis's work. Some of the changes in *Tales of Wonder* seem to reflect the author's desire to move his translation nearer to the German original: the title of 'The Wild Huntsmen' is closer to Bürger's 'Der wilde Jäger' (The Wild Huntsman), and the earlier Scottish (and Scott-like) 'Earl Walter' is changed to 'The Wildgrave' with a footnote to explain that this German title corresponds to the English Earl Warden of a royal forest. Most of the revisions, however, can be attributed to Lewis's mending Scott's supposedly imperfect rhymes. In the 12th stanza, for instance, Scott had rhymed 'lore' with 'choir' and 'prove' with 'love' in 1796, and the stanza was reshaped to have 'offend/ friend' and 'pray/away' instead:

> "Hence, if our manly sport offend:
>   "With pious fools go chaunt and pray;
> "Well hast thou spoke, my dark-brow'd friend,—
>   "Halloo! halloo! and hark away!"—

Scott's original wording is similarly rephrased to eliminate his uncertain rhymes in stanzas 13, 17, 25, 30, 46, and 50.

Scott apparently deferred to Lewis's judgement, for when he came to include the poem in his own *Ballads and Lyrical Pieces* of 1806 (148–61) he retained these alterations, as he did when the poem was reprinted in the eighth edition of *The Lay of the Last Minstrel* (1808), 224–41. 'The Wild Huntsmen' then passed into the various lifetime collected editions of his *Poetical Works* beginning with that of 1820 (2.213–30) with only the usual changes of the kind normally associated with the printer, except that for 1825*PW* (5.368–84) Scott has corrected his title to read 'The Wild Huntsman' in the singular, as in Bürger's original. Scott also revised the headnote to his poem in his 1806 *Ballads* to suit a collected edition of his own poetical works, providing the reader with a prose version of the story of his poem and adding comparative instances in the legends of France and of Scotland.

The present text follows that of *The Chase, and William and Helen: Two Ballads, from the German of Gottfried Augustus Bürger* (Edinburgh, 1796), 1–18, as representing the culmination of Scott's own initial creative processes for the poem. The sub-title 'From the German of Gottfried Augustus Bürger' has been added, reflecting the description on the title-page that applies both to 'William and Helen' and to 'The Chase', but no further emendations have been made. Scott's subsequent headnote in his 1806 *Ballads* (148–50) is printed after the Explanatory Notes below.

Historical Note
The example given by the Ossian poems of James Macpherson (1736–96) and by Percy's *Reliques of Ancient English Poetry* (1765) of seeking inspiration for a native tradition of poetry through folk verse and legend had been eagerly followed up in Germany. When Gottfried Augustus Bürger (1747–94) published his poems in two volumes in 1778 he included German versions of five of Percy's poems as well as 'Der wilde Jäger'. Scott presumably first encountered the poem, along with others by the same author, in a volume containing Bürger's poems obtained for him from Hamburg by Harriet, the wife of his kinsman Scott of Harden, her marriage having taken place on 29 September 1795. However, the two-volume copy of Bürger's *Sämmtliche Schriften* in the Abbotsford Library (*ALC*) was published at Göttingen in 1796. In his 'Essay on Imitations of the Ancient Ballad' of 1830, Scott relates that he 'accomplished a translation of "Der Wilde Jäger"—a romantic superstition universally current in Germany, and known also in Scotland and France. In this I took rather more license than in versifying "Lenore;" and I balladized one or two other poems of Bürger with more or less success' (8vo1830*PW*, 3.lxiii). Scott's reference to his own 'license' is partly perhaps an allusion to his omission of specific details, such as the seventeen-pronged antlers of the stag. Scott is also sometimes more ambiguous than Bürger about the otherworldly nature of his supernatural riders, who are a 'fair youth' and a 'sable hunter', where in the original poem they are 'den guten Engel' (the good angel) and the 'Bösen' (wicked one). He also removes indications that the hunter is a representative rather than an aberrant aristocrat. The thunderous voice of judgement in Bürger makes it clear that when the Wildgrave is hunted by the hounds of hell he will become a terror to other lords who are similarly heedless of the poor in pursuing their pleasures: the evil-doer hears the noise of the hunt at night and hunters bear witness to the truth of the legend. In Scott's poem, however, it is rather the belated peasant that is frightened by the noise of the infernal hunt and the wakeful priest who bewails human misery.

Explanatory Notes
28.4   serfs   bondsmen, labourers attached to the lands of their overlord.
28.5   couples   braces or leashes, joining two hounds together.
29.34   fane   a temple.
29.39   matin song   one of the canonical services of the church, often chanted at daybreak.
29.43   rede   advice or counsel.
31.78   pale   a fence, or enclosure marked by pales or planks of wood.
31.84   Fell Famine   a personification perhaps recalling the plagues attending the fall of Babylon in Revelation 18.8: 'in one day, death, and mourning, and famine'.
31.108   kine   cows.
32.120   hermit's hut   a hermit is a person living in solitude, the religious inhabitant of a remote cell.
33.166   Apostate   a turncoat, or renegade, particularly Satan and his devils who have rebelled against God.
33.168   measure of thy cup   used figuratively as in the Bible, a cup is one's allotted portion or destiny. See, for example, Matthew 26.39.

Appendix: 1806 Headnote

This is a translation, or rather an imitation, of the *Wilde Jäger* of the German poet Bürger. The tradition upon which it is founded bears, that formerly a Wildgrave, or keeper of a royal forest, named Falkenburg, was so much addicted to the pleasures of the chace, and otherwise so extremely profligate and cruel, that he not only followed this unhallowed amusement on the Sabbath, and other days consecrated to religious duty, but accompanied it with the most unheard-of oppression upon the poor peasants, who were under his vassalage. When this second Nimrod died, the people adopted a superstition, founded probably on the many various uncouth sounds heard in the depth of a German forest, during the silence of the night. They conceived they still heard the cry of the Wildgrave's hounds; and the well-known cheer of the deceased hunter, the sounds of his horses' feet, and the rustling of the branches before the game, the pack, and the sportsmen, are also distinctly discriminated; but the phantoms are rarely, if ever, visible. Once, as a benighted *Chasseur* heard this infernal chace pass by him, at the sound of the halloo, with which the Spectre Huntsman cheered his hounds, he could not refrain from crying, "*Gluck zu, Falkenburg!*" (Good sport to ye, Falkenburg!) "Dost thou wish me good sport?" answered a hoarse voice, "thou shalt share the game;" and there was thrown at him what seemed to be a huge piece of foul carrion. The daring *Chasseur* lost two of his best horses soon after, and never perfectly recovered the personal effects of this ghostly greeting. This tale, though told with some variations, is universally believed all over Germany.

The French had a similar tradition concerning an aërial hunter, who infested the forest of Fontainebleau. He was sometimes visible; when he appeared as a huntsman, surrounded with dogs, a tall grisly figure. Some account of him may be found in "Sully's Memoirs," who says he was called, *Le Grand Veneur.* At one time he chose to hunt so near the palace, that the attendants, and, if I mistake not, Sully himself, came out into the court, supposing it was the sound of the king returning from the chace. This phantom is elsewhere called Saint Hubert.

The superstition seems to have been very general, as appears from the following fine poetical description of this phantom chace, as it was heard in the wilds of Ross-shire.

> "Ere since, of old, the haughty thanes of Ross,—
> So to the simple swain tradition tells,—
> Were wont with clans, and ready vassals thronged,
> To wake the bounding stag, or guilty wolf,
> There oft is heard, at midnight, or at noon,
> Beginning faint, but rising still more loud,
> And nearer, voice of hunters, and of hounds,
> And horns, hoarse-winded, blowing far and keen:—
> Forthwith the hubbub multiplies; the gale
> Labours with wilder shrieks, and rifer din
> Of hot pursuit; the broken cry of deer
> Mangled by throttling dogs; the shouts of men,
> And hoofs, thick beating on the hollow hill.
> Sudden the grazing heifer in the vale
> Starts at the noise, and both the herdsman's ears
> Tingle with inward dread. Aghast, he eyes
> The mountain's height, and all the ridges round,
> Yet not one trace of living wight discerns;
> Nor knows, o'erawed, and trembling as he stands,
> To what, or whom, he owes his idle fear,
> To ghost, to witch, to fairy, or to fiend;
> But wonders, and no end of wondering finds."
> *Scottish Descriptive Poems*, pp. 167, 168.

A posthumous miracle of Father Lesly, a Scottish capuchin, related to his being buried on a hill haunted by these unearthly cries of hounds and huntsmen. After his sainted reliques had been deposited there, the noise was never heard more. The reader will find this, and other miracles, recorded in the life of Father Bonaventura, which is written in the choicest Italian.

23. The Lamentation of the Faithful Wife of Asan Aga

Textual Note
'The Lamentation of the Faithful Wife of Asan Aga' clearly dates from the late 1790s when Scott was enthusiastically engaged in translating poems from German originals. Lockhart mentions that a 'Morlachian fragment' was among the poems shown by Scott to James Ballantyne at Rosebank in October 1799 (*Life*, 1.315–16). Despite Ballantyne's admiration, however, it was not included in his publication for Scott of *An Apology for Tales of Terror* (Kelso, 1799) nor in Lewis's *Tales of Wonder* (London, 1801), probably because the story lacks a supernatural element. In fact it was never published in Scott's lifetime.

An autograph manuscript for this poem has been inserted near the front of a bound volume in Edinburgh University Library, La.III.827. According to a covering letter of 1 April 1871 bound in with it, the manuscript was sent to David Laing by the publisher Adam Black. It consists of six leaves, probably three conjugate pairs, of which the outer acts as a cover and title-page, with the text of the poem on the rectos and versos of the inside leaves. Each leaf measures approx. 22.7 x 18.0 cm, with a watermark '1794 / J WHATMAN'. The name 'Miss Tytler' is written on the verso of the first leaf containing the title, presumably a member of the family of Alexander Tytler, Lord Woodhouselee (1747–1813), to whom Scott presented his manuscript, which resembles other presentation copies of his early work. It contains few revisions but is not fully or consistently punctuated, and the stanza numbering is defective in that there is no stanza VIII. A version based on this manuscript was given by D. H. Low in 'The First Link between English and Serbo-Croat Literature', *Slavonic Review*, 3: 8 (December 1924), 362–69. Another manuscript in NLS, MS 5841, ff. 24–25, does not appear to be in Scott's hand, the writing in that matching that of copies of Scott poems in NLS, MS 2536, so that it is possible that this copy was also made by the novelist Henry Mackenzie (1745–1831). It is written on two conjugate leaves, each measuring approx. 22.5 x 18.6 cm and bearing a 1796 watermark, and the stanzas are unnumbered. There are a number of verbal variations between the EUL manuscript and this one, most notably in the fifth and beginning of the sixth stanzas, which here read:

> She sorrowed more than the fondest of mothers
> Weeping for Asan—as wounded he lay
> She sorrow'd more than friends, sisters, or Brothers,
> But matronly modesty prompted her stay—
>
> Thus spoke the Chief in his high flaming anger
> "Bear to the false one this severing line—

Scott seems to have had problems with this passage concerning the heroine's failure to appear publicly to wait upon her sick husband.

Mackenzie also seems to have copied just the first three stanzas of Scott's poem into a small leather-bound notebook (NLS, MS 2536, f. 3), which bears the inscription 'Poems by Wᵣ Scott Esqᵣ' on the recto of an early leaf and on the verso 'H Mackenzie / Heriot Row Edinᵣ', and the leaves of which are approx. 19.8 x 12 cm, with a 1798 watermark. Possibly when Scott gave his completed poem to Miss Tytler he retained a working version of the opening stanzas among his own papers. There is also an autograph copy of these three opening stanzas on a single leaf of paper, measuring roughly 22.1 x 18.4 cm with no visible watermark, signed and dated from London in April 1807 in NLS, MS 997, f. 5, perhaps written out by Scott in response for a request for an album contribution or an autograph. And again, when attempting to respond to the request of the musical collector and editor George Thomson (1757–1851) for the words of a song to suit a tune called 'The Sheriff's Fancy', Scott sent with a letter of July 1806 just the first twelve lines of his poem. The accompanying description sounds as though he then had it in mind to use them as a starting point for a rousing song of war rather than the tragedy of a forsaken wife:

> I enclose you the beginning of a war song imitated from the Morlachian—it is a fragment but could easily be completed if you think it will suit the character of the tune called "The Sheriff's fancy". The verses are uncommonly dashing. (*Letters*, 1.310)

Thomson responded with a regretful refusal:

> The beginning of the war song is very fine & promises great things—I regret therefore that it will not suit the measure of the sherrifs conceit; I have written & divided the notes in different ways, to make them echo the sense but in vain ...
> If you do work up the fragment into a War Song, I hope you will favour me with a sight of it, perhaps I may light upon an air suited to its character & measure— (BL, Add. MS 35,266, f. 98)

Scott never apparently fulfilled his intention of using the opening lines of his Morlachian ballad as the starting point for such a song, however.

The present text is based upon Scott's autograph manuscript in EUL, La.III.827, with some necessary emendations. The manuscript, for instance, contains an unusual number of nouns with initial upper-case letters, probably unconsciously retained from the German original. In addition to the following listed emendations ampersands have been routinely expanded to 'and', verb forms ending with 'd' to 'ed', routine apostrophes have been introduced as required, as have full stops at the ends of sentences and verse paragraphs.

35.2	sycamores (Editorial) / Sycamores
35.3	swans (Editorial) / Swans
35.4	Or is it (Editorial) / Or Is it
35.4	snow? (Editorial) / snow
35.7	had it been (Editorial) / had been
35.7	swans (Editorial) / Swans
35.9	swans (Editorial) / Swans
35.12	sycamores (Editorial) / Sycamores
35.14	sisters (Editorial) / Sisters
35.16	friend (Editorial) / freind
35.16	lady (Editorial) / Lady
35.19	friends, (Editorial) / freinds
35.20	shamefacedness (Editorial) / Shamefacedness
36.23	castle (Editorial) / Castle
36.23	mistress (Editorial) / Mistress
36.24	children (Editorial) / Children
36.25	lady (Editorial) / Lady
36.26	message (Editorial) / Message
36.27	children (Editorial) / Children
36.28	tho' (Editorial) / tho
36.29	drawbridge (Editorial) / Drawbridge
36.32	turret (Editorial) / Turret
36.33	thee, (Editorial) / thee
36.40	me, Carazan, (Editorial) / me Carazan
36.40	none." (Editorial) / none.
36.41	brother (Editorial) / Brother
36.42	bill (Editorial) / Bill
36.43	lady (Editorial) / Lady
36.45	dame (Editorial) / Dame
36.46	boy (Editorial) / Boy
36.47	suckling (Editorial) / Suckling
36.49	harsh-tempered brother (Editorial) / harsh temperd Brother
37.57	Cadi (Editorial) / Cady
37.59	lady (Editorial) / Lady
37.61	another," (Editorial) / another"
37.62	brother (Editorial) / Brother
37.65	brother (Editorial) / Brother
37.65	lady (Editorial) / Lady
37.67	Cadi (Editorial) / Cady
37.69	Carazan, (Editorial) / Carazan
37.70	enfold, (Editorial) / enfold
37.72	orphans behold." (Editorial) / Orphans behold
37.74	train (Editorial) / Train

37.75   lady (Editorial) / Lady
37.76   towers (Editorial) / Towers
37.78   bride (Editorial) / Bride
37.80   children (Editorial) / Children
37.81   returned? (Editorial) / returned
37.82   Comest (Editorial) / "Comest
37.82   share? (Editorial) / share
37.84   children (Editorial) / Children
38.87   gallants (Editorial) / Gallants
38.89   turrets (Editorial) / Turrets
38.90   babes (Editorial) / Babes
38.91   boys (Editorial) / Boys
38.92   sabres (Editorial) / Sabres
38.95   suckling (Editorial) / Suckling
38.96   sabre (Editorial) / Sabre
38.98   children (Editorial) / Children
38.102   suckling (Editorial) / Suckling
38.103   lady (Editorial) / Lady

Historical Note
'Klaggesang von der edlen Frauen des Asan Aga' (Song of Lamentation of the noble Wife of Asan Aga), translated by Johann Wolfgang von Goethe (1749–1832) in 1775 'from the Morlachian', was subsequently published (and probably first seen by Scott) in Johann Gottfried von Herder's *Volkslieder*, 2 vols (Leipzig, 1778–79), 1.309–14: *ALC*. The traditional ballad *Hasanaginica* is a Bosnian folk ballad, probably originating in the mid-seventeenth century in the region of Imotski (in present-day Croatia), then part of the Ottoman empire. It was first published by an Italian named Alberto Fortis in his book *Viaggio in Dalmazia* (Travels in Dalmatia) of 1774 as a 'Morlachian' ballad, the word being used to describe peoples from coastal Dalmatia as opposed to the people found inland. The version Goethe saw derives from Fortis's book, and Scott translated it from Goethe: see D. H. Low, 'The First Link between English and Serbo-Croat Literature' (as cited in the Textual Note).
    Scott's translation follows the main events of Goethe's poem but with certain adaptations in the details. Goethe's first six lines are elaborated by Scott into twelve, and Scott also lays more emphasis on the lady's sorrows for her husband's injuries than Goethe, who simply says that she was restrained by modesty from coming to him. Scott renders the brother a less sympathetic character, who is impetuous rather than harsh-tempered in Goethe. In Goethe's poem the wife has not been in her mother's house a week, rather than Scott's fortnight, before the suitors appear. Scott also adapts some of Goethe's details to suit English habits and expectations of a ballad. The children no longer invite their mother to share the evening meal of the household but to join them in their meals and pastimes, and in Goethe her gifts to her boys are gold-embroidered boots and to her baby a little coat rather than weaponry. The legal situation of a divorced wife is also closer to that of contemporary British law than to that of Sharia law.

Explanatory Notes
35.title   Asan Aga   Aga is an arabic title meaning chief or lord, while Hassan is a fairly common male given name, particularly associated with Mohammed's grandson.
35.3   Vaga's fair fountain   the River Vaga is not in Croatia but in the far northern Archangelsk region of Russia. Goethe's poem does not mention

the Vaga, a detail apparently added by Scott. Fountain suggests the source or head-spring of the river.

36.22 severing line according to Sharia law a husband may divorce his wife either verbally (preferably before two witnesses) or in writing, but he must then restore her dowry to her and a cooling-off period is specified, often of thirty days, when the wife lives in the marital home but without sexual contact with the husband. At the end of this time he either confirms or rescinds his decision.

36.40 mother of none this reflects British law in the early 19th century, which regarded the children of a marriage as belonging exclusively to the husband. Sharia law gives custody of the children of a divorcing couple to the mother provided that they are below the age of discernment (though she loses this right if she remarries), and their father is obliged to support them financially.

37.57 Imoski's proud Cadi a *Cadi* is a civil judge among the Turks or Arabs, often the judge of a town. Imoski is probably modern-day Imotski, a small town on the border with Bosnia-Herzegovina, known for its medieval fortress on the rocks of the Blue Lake.

24. The Mermaid

Textual Note
The only copy of Scott's 'The Mermaid' appears in a small leather-bound note-book (NLS, MS 2536, ff. 4–5), which contains transcriptions of Scott's early poems by the Scottish novelist Henry Mackenzie (1745–1831). (For further details see Textual Note to no. 23, 'The Lamentation of the Faithful Wife of Asan Aga'). It is undated, but most probably dates from the late 1790s when Scott was enthu-siastically translating the *Sturm und Drang* poems of Gottfried Augustus Bürger (1747–94) and Johann Wolfgang von Goethe (1749–1832). Another English ver-sion of this Goethe poem was published by Matthew Gregory Lewis in *Tales of Wonder*, 2 vols (London, 1801), 1.79–80, which is perhaps why Scott did not apparently offer his own translation as a contribution to this collection. Scott's version was never published in his lifetime, and was not printed until included as item 1 in W. M. Parker's 'Sir Walter Scott: Thirteen New Poems?', *Poetry Review*, 40: 4 (August–September 1949), 263–75 (pp. 263–64).

The present text is, inevitably, that of the Mackenzie notebook in NLS, MS 2536, ff. 4–5, with the following emendations:

39.23 fresh'ning (Editorial) / freshning
39.24 bright? (Editorial) / bright.
39.25 down, (Editorial) / down
39.27 down, (Editorial) / down
39.28 hue." (Editorial) / hue.
39.31 water's (Editorial) / waters
39.32 knee. (Editorial) / knee
39.33 sung, (Editorial) / sung
39.34 he, mid (Editorial) / he mid

Historical Note
Scott's poem is a translation of Goethe's 'Der Fischer' (1779), which tells of the appearance of a mermaid to a fisherman and her persuading him into the water where he presumably drowns. Scott changes the original title, and also

loses the rhythmic intensity of the original poem which, for instance, opens dramatically with 'Das Wasser rauscht, das Wasser schwoll' (The water rushed, the water swelled). In contrast Scott's setting is conventional and peaceful with no drama of surging waters but rather a peaceful brook and a contemplative angler, and lacks some of the ballad-like repetitions and near-repetitions of phrases in Goethe's original.

25. Trained by Adversity's Stern Hand

Textual Note
This poem appears consecutively as the seventeenth item in Scott's commonplace book ('Adversaria') in the Abbotsford Library (for more general information on this book, see Textual Note to no. 16, 'To a Lady'). Untitled, it is written on three pages, the first two of which are inserted so that both sides can be seen. Chain lines and part of a watermark are visible on the first leaf, but no countermark date is apparent. The seven verses are unnumbered, and there are multiple alterations within the text, with single words, phrases, and sometimes complete lines being deleted and replaced, in a way characteristic of an early draft. Amongst substantive changes, for example, in line 8 'Susa's' is substituted for 'Tauris'' and 'hostile towers' for 'Barbarous walls'; while the first line of the last stanza originally read 'For oft tho' 'mid the silent skies'. A printed version of the poem can be found as item 5 (taken from a negative photostat in NLS, MS 2232, ff. 14–16), in W. M. Parker's 'Sir Walter Scott: Thirteen New Poems?', *Poetry Review*, 40: 4 (August–September 1949), 263–75 (pp. 267–68).

The present text follows the original manuscript in the 'Adversaria' commonplace book, pp. 37–39, though routinely representing verbs ending with 'd' as 'ed', expanding ampersands, and adding apostrophes as appropriate. Punctuation has been supplied at the end of the first six stanzas, and a title taken from the poem's first line. The following emendations have also been made:

40.4   toil, (Editorial) / toil
40.5   dreadful (Editorial) / dreadfull
40.13   life, (Editorial) / life
40.14   Should (Editorial) / Shoud
41.32   against (Editorial) / ag^t·
41.34   scornful (Editorial) / scornfull
41.49   whirlwind's (Editorial) / whirlwinds

Historical Note
Little has been discovered about the circumstances or possible sources underlying this poem. The setting seems to place it at the time of the Parthian Empire, which ran from about 227 BC to AD 224, stretching at its height from the northern reaches of the Euphrates, in present-day Turkey, to eastern Iran. More particularly, it might refer to the conflict with the Roman Republic, leading to the defeat of Marcus Licinius Crassus at the battle of Carrhae in 53 BC, followed by successful counter-attacks under Mark Antony in following years. In terms of Scott's own career, the bellicose nature of the piece and its stress on defiant opposition might place it near the time of his volunteering for the Royal Edinburgh Volunteers early in 1797. An affinity to some of Scott's German-related compositions at this period, such as 'The Lamentation of the Faithful Wife of Asan Aga' (see no. 23), might indicate a similar source, though none as yet has been located.

Explanatory Notes

40.7   quivered Parthian's headlong flight   the Parthians were a semi-nomadic people, renowned for their horsemanship. The 'Parthian shot', exercised by archers on horseback shooting arrows at the enemy while retreating at full gallop, required immense skill. It could also be a tactic in feigning retreat, and was used to great effect against the Romans at the Battle of Carrhae (see Historical Note).

40.8   Susa's hostile towers   Susa, one of the oldest urban settlements in the world, was the principal city of both the Persian and Parthian empires. The present city of Shush, in Iran, occupies the ancient site.

40.20   hunted Roebuck's   the *roebuck* is the male roe deer.

41.39   Jove's dire regard   in Roman mythology Jove or Jupiter is the king of the gods, often associated with using thunder and lightning as a weapon. Compare Alexander Pope's translation (1715–20) of Homer's *Iliad*: 'as when angry Jove / Hurls down the forky lightning from above' (Bk 2, lines 950–51).

41.48   fated hour   the time when a prophecy or prediction is fulfilled. Compare *The Lay of the Last Minstrel* (1805): 'the fated hour is come' (Canto 2, stanza 4).

26.   By a Thousand Fond Dreams

Textual Note

This poem represents the eighteenth item in Scott's commonplace book ('Adversaria') in the Abbotsford Library, notable for its inclusion of a number of poems apparently relating to Williamina Belsches (for more general information on this book, and Scott's relationship with Williamina, see Notes to no. 16, 'To a Lady'). Untitled, it is written on several slips of paper mounted sideways, of varying size though uniformly approx. 19 cm in width. The text contains multiple deletions and alterations, indicative of an intense first composition. In line 4, for example, Scott had originally written 'With a bosom so gentle & spirit so free', before deleting this in favour of the present reading. And at the head of the second stanza, false starts are indicated by the deletion of 'Ah friend! To exult as wild fancy has done' and 'To dream such a conquest'. A full printed version is given in Sir Herbert Grierson's *Sir Walter Scott, Bart.* (London, 1938), 40–41, though with a number of substantive verbal errors (including 'When' for 'Where', 'flew' for flies', and 'plain' for 'vain' (lines 4, 5, 6).

The present text follows the original manuscript in the 'Adversaria' commonplace book, pp. 40–42, with a title supplied editorially from the first line. Spellings such as 'reveald' have been normalised and ampersands expanded. Stops have been provided at the end of stanzas 1–2 and 4–6, and the following punctuation within stanzas added to aid reading:

42.5   flies, (Editorial) / flies
42.8   Love, (Editorial) / Love
42.13   grandeur, (Editorial) / grandeur
43.30   been? (Editorial) / been

Historical Note

Following on from publication in Grierson's 1938 biography (cited above), these verses are now generally viewed as reflecting Scott's anger and despair at the realisation that Williamina Belsches was to marry a richer and socially more advantaged rival in the person of William Forbes. An early sign of that realisation is found in his statement to his friend William Erskine of 9 September 1796—alluding to Forbes senior's position as a wealthy banker—that "'*Dot & carry one*" is certainly gone to F[ettercair]n': news which he acknowledges as having the potential to cast him in the 'slough of Despond' (*Letters*, 1.54). Lockhart quotes a letter from one of Scott's friends to another, on 12 October (the day the engagement was announced), which gives the impression that Scott's mental stability was under threat: 'I always dreaded there was some self-deception on the part of our romantic friend, and I now shudder at the violence of his most irritable and ungovernable mind' (*Life*, 1.242). Scott's own letters of this period convey more of a determination, through hectic physical and social activity, 'to banish the Blue Devils and white black Devils and grey which insist upon being the companions of my Solitude' (*Letters*, 1.57). It is quite feasible that in a moment of heightened despair Scott gave vent to feelings of betrayal on Williamina's part in an uncharacteristically personal poem. On the other hand, some allowance perhaps ought to be made for the element of role-playing that had always been a feature of Scott's poetical exchanges with Williamina, an aspect which might arguably come to his aid when truly left as a solitary lover.

Explanatory Notes
42.1   a thousand fond dreams   compare 'The Frantic Lover', by the Shakespeare editor George Steevens (1736–1800), lines 45–46: 'A thousand soft thoughts in thy fancy combine! / A thousand wild horrors assemble in mine!': *The New Foundling Hospital for Wit*, 6 vols (London, 1786), 5.37.
42.22   break … bend   echoing Aesop's fable of 'The Oak and the Reed', itself the source of several proverbs such as 'Better bend than break' (*ODEP*, 52).

27.   The Triumph of Constancy

Textual Note
Scott's manuscript of 'The Triumph of Constancy' is in his commonplace book in the Abbotsford Library, known as 'Adversaria', for further details of which see Textual Note to no. 16, 'To a Lady'. It is item 84, located between pages 83 and 85, and consists of six leaves, each measuring approx. 19 x 12 cm, some of which have a partial watermark with a shield device. The first leaf resembles a title-page, bearing the title, the date of 1796, and a presentation inscription to Mrs Scott of Harden. Possibly this and the final blank leaf are conjugate, since they clearly form a cover for the rest. From its incorporation into Scott's own commonplace book, however, it would seem that the booklet was never given to the intended recipient, perhaps due to the presence of several deletions and replacements in the text. It may be that Scott then prepared a clean presentation copy for Mrs Scott, since she mentions in a letter to Lockhart from Mertoun of 6 October 1832 (NLS, MS 1554, ff. 59–60) that she had helped Scott to revise the poem and that at the time of writing she had 'that and several other of his early Poems in M.S.'.

In 1798 Matthew Gregory Lewis (1775–1818) invited Scott to contribute to his projected collection of poems of diablerie, published in 1801 as *Tales of Wonder* (for further details see Textual Note to no. 21, 'William and Helen'). Scott mentions this poem as among his possible contributions in his letter to Lewis of 29 May 1798: 'Erskine & Cranstoun, have been teasing me to send you other two translations from the German which have never seen the Light—One is from the "Lied von Treue" of Bürger' (Morgan, MA 1432). In his undated reply, however, Lewis rejected it, on the grounds that 'as a Ghost or a Witch is a sine-qua-non ingredient in all the dishes, of which I mean to compose my hobgoblin repast, I am afraid, the "Lied von Treue" does not come within my plan' (NLS, MS 3874, ff. 47–48). Scott's poem was never published in his lifetime. It was first printed by Coleman O. Parsons in his 'Scott's Translation of Bürger's "Das Lied von Treue"', *Journal of English and Germanic Philology*, 33: 2 (April 1934), 240–49. Parsons points out that there must have been another manuscript, since the Lichfield poet Anna Seward (1742–1809) in her letter to Colin Mackenzie of 3 February 1799 acknowledges his gift of a copy of some of Scott's early poems and comments specifically on this one: see *Letters of Anna Seward*, 6 vols (Edinburgh, 1811), 5.197–200. This manuscript, however, has not apparently survived.

The present text follows that of item 84 of the 'Adversaria' commonplace book, with some necessary emendations. The manuscript, for instance, contains an unusual number of nouns with initial upper-case letters, probably unconsciously retained from the German original. In addition to the following listed emendations ampersands have been routinely expanded to 'and', and verb forms ending with 'd' to 'ed'; routine apostrophes have been introduced as required, as have full stops at the ends of stanzas where these are lacking.

43.8	maid's (Editorial) / Maids
43.11	thro' (Editorial) / thro
43.15	morning (Editorial) / Morning
43.15	shade." (Editorial) / shade
43.16	light (Editorial) / Light
44.21	tower (Editorial) / Tower
44.26	mansion (Editorial) / Mansion
44.27	lay. (Editorial) / lay
44.29	castle (Editorial) / Castle
44.32	e'en (Editorial) / een
44.33	thro' hall (Editorial) / thro hall
44.38	who, my old vassal, (Editorial) / who my old vassal
44.42	dishonour (Editorial) / Dishonour
44.42	woe: (Editorial) / woe
44.44	borne (Editorial) / born
44.44	damsel (Editorial) / Damsel
44.46	thro' (Editorial) / thro
44.49	whirlwind (Editorial) / whirlwhind
44.50	thro' (Editorial) / thro
44.52	dame. (Editorial) / dame
44.53	forward, (Editorial) / forward
45.57	Let us but the fair maiden (Editorial) / Let us, but, the fair maiden,
45.66	earth (Editorial) / Earth
45.69	welcoming (Editorial) / wellcoming
46.93	Marshal, (Editorial) / Marshal
46.96	Earl (Editorial) / "Earl
46.99	'twixt (Editorial) / twixt
46.112	tasted."— (Editorial) / tasted"—
46.116	maid (Editorial) / Maid
46.118	Knights, (Editorial) / Knights
46.125	corpse (Editorial) / Corpse
47.135	friends (Editorial) / freinds
47.142	galloping (Editorial) / galopping

47.150   wounds." (Editorial) / wounds
47.155   fair.— (Editorial) / fair"—
47.159   master (Editorial) / Master
48.168   master's (Editorial) / Masters

Historical Note
It seems probable that Scott first encountered 'Das Lied von Treue' by Gottfried Augustus Bürger (1747–94), along with others by the same author, in a volume of Bürger's poems obtained for him from Hamburg by Harriet, the wife of his kinsman Scott of Harden, presumably only a few months after her marriage in September 1795. His manuscript translation dated 1796 seems originally to have been intended as a gift to her. This volume was probably not the two-volume edition of Bürger's *Sämmtliche Schriften* in the Abbotsford Library (*ALC*), which was published at Göttingen only in 1796. Scott may, however, once have owned an earlier printing of some of Bürger's poems.
    Scott's translation sticks quite closely to Bürger's tale about the abduction of the lady of the Marshal von Holm by the Baron of Stein, except that in the original the lady is not the Marshal's bride nor is there any mention of an early friendship between the two. In Bürger's tale the Marshal's false security as to her loyalty is based simply on the sexual gratification he supposes she has received during their love-affair. Anna Seward objected to the evident misogyny of the poem, writing to Colin Mackenzie on 3 February 1799 that 'there is something ludicrous in the canine consolation for the perfidy of a charming woman. It piques the pride of the ladies not a little' (*Letters of Anna Seward*, 5.200). Perhaps this may partly account for the fact that Scott never published it.

Explanatory Notes
43.1   **Earl Marshal**   one of the chief functionaries of a royal household or court.
43.13   **courser**   a charger.
44.23   **postern**   a door or gate distinct from the main entrance.
44.36   **Seneschal**   steward.
44.39   **caitiff**   a villain, a base wretch.
44.47   **faulchion**   a broad sword, originally a curved one with the edge on the convex side.
44.51   **mead**   meadow.
45.74   **reave**   to rob, or forcibly deprive a person of something.
45.88   **hauberks**   originally defensive armour for the neck and shoulders, but usually long military tunics made of ring or chain mail.
46.116   **palfrey**   a small saddle-horse for a lady.
46.121   **besprente**   sprinkled or strewed with.
46.124   **bent**   a place covered with rough grass, a heath.
47.148   **brand**   the blade of a sword.

28.   Which of Us Shall Join the Forces?

Textual Note
There are two drafts of this item in Scott's commonplace book ('Adversaria') in the Abbotsford Library (for more general information on this book, see Textual Note to no. 16, 'To a Lady'). The first, consisting of a single leaf pasted sideways on page 57, contains only a few opening lines, indicative of Scott having started and then left off writing. The second version, comprising nine

partly-numbered 4-line verses and written on two inserted leaves (approx. 16.3 x 14.5 cm and 17 x 14.5 cm), is found appreciably later in the book at pp. 93–95. A Britannia watermark is visible, but no date. The positioning of this later draft places it at some distance from other Scott compositions in the common-place book, especially those apparently relating to his courtship of Williamina Belsches, and it is perhaps significant that the immediately following item is a newspaper cutting dated 24 September 1800. While the text in this version is clearer than that in the earlier draft, there are still signs of Scott being actively engaged in the process of composition. For lines 3 and 4 of the fourth stanza, for instance, he originally wrote 'So with safety & with honour / Homeward shalt thou bend thy way'. A printed version of this poem can be found as item 6 (taken from a negative photostat in NLS, MS 2232, ff. 38–40) in W. M. Parker's 'Sir Walter Scott: Thirteen New Poems?', *Poetry Review*, 40: 4 (August–September 1949), 263–75 (pp. 269–70).

The present text follows that in the 'Adversaria' commonplace book, pp. 93–95, with an expansion of ampersands, addition of routine apostrophes as required, and punctuation provided at the end of each stanza. A title has also been supplied editorially guided by the opening line. The following emendations have also been made:

48.3   Horsemen, (Editorial) / Horsemen
48.6   mother?— (Editorial) / mother
48.10   coward, my brother, (Editorial) / coward my brother
48.13   Bide, my brother, (Editorial) / Bide my brother
48.16   charging, (Editorial) / charging
49.23   From (Editorial) / from
49.27   Wherefore (Editorial) / Where
49.27   thou, (Editorial) / thou

Historical Note
Although previously not identified as such, this piece probably started as an attempted loose translation of the Estonian folk song 'Lied vom Kriege' as translated into German in Johann Gottfried von Herder's collection *Volkslieder*, 2 vols (Leipzig, 1778–79), 2.237–39: *ALC*. There are strong affinities and some distinct verbal parallels especially in the first five stanzas, where in the German version the young soldier apprehensively prepares for battle. However, in the later section, where Scott's hussar is the sole speaker, the protagonist in the original is presented as returning home unrecognised and in a traumatised state. According to Lockhart, Scott was familiar with Herder's collection when first writing to Matthew Gregory Lewis in May 1798: 'He immediately wrote to Lewis, placing whatever pieces he had translated and imitated from the German "*Volkslieder*" at his disposal' (*Life*, 1.291). Scott's knowledge of the *Volkslieder* is also apparent in the case of his 'The Lamentation of the Faithful Wife of Asan Aga' (no. 23), itself a translation of a Bosnian folk ballad by Johann Wolfgang von Goethe that had first appeared in Herder's collection in 1778.

In a number of other respects this item shows a similarity to Scott's 'War-Song of the Royal Edinburgh Light Dragoons', first published in *Minstrelsy of the Scottish Border* in 1803, but originally issued as a song sheet several years earlier (see no. 32, 'The Rouze of The Royal Edinburgh Light Dragoons'). Scott was appointed Quartermaster, and in spite of lameness energetically joined in the drilling that took place, on Leith Sands and other nearby locations. As he wrote in a letter of 8 March 1797: 'Our number is 80 at present, and we mean to compleat two troops of 50 Gentlemen each mounted on horses worth from 30 to 60 guineas a piece, armed equipped &c at our own expence. ... We can perform most of the common manœuvres at the hard trot & Gallop' (*Letters*, 1.64). While the present item makes no specific reference to this embodiment, its concern for drills relating to light cavalry tallies with Scott's enthusiastic participation at this time.

Explanatory Notes

48.2   Chiefs their levies   *levy* in the sense of a body of enrolled men, though here with a suggestion of the raising of troops in feudal times. Scott regarded the Duke of Buccleuch as his 'Chief'.

48.16   charging ... staying   two main actions in cavalry drill, with troops in the *staying* position being lined shoulder to shoulder, swords drawn from the scabbard, with horses inclined to the left or right.

49.speech indicator   YOUNG HUSSAR   *hussar* is a term used for a number of types of light cavalry, originating from the Hungarian army in the 15th century. Hussar regiments existed in both the British and French armies in Scott's time. Scott's elder son, Walter, joined the 18th Regiment of Hussars in 1819, later transferring to the 15th Hussars, in whose uniform he appears in the portrait by Sir William Allan (1782–1850) which hangs prominently at Abbotsford. Scott refers to his son as 'my young Hussar' in a letter to Lord Montagu in 1820 (*Letters*, 6.174).

49.21   courser   powerful horse, as ridden in battle or tournaments.

29.   With Flowers from a Roman Wall

Textual Note

This poem was first published in *English Minstrelsy*, ed. Scott, 2 vols (Edinburgh, 1810), 2.191, under Scott's name and among several other items evidently retrieved from an earlier period of his career. No manuscript has been discovered. The verses were subsequently published, as 'To a Lady, with Flowers from a Roman Wall', once more as by Scott, in the *Edinburgh Annual Register, for 1808*, 1: 2 (1810), xxiii; then again in *The Vision of Don Roderick, and Other Poems* (Edinburgh, 1811), 153. The only internal variant between these versions is a somewhat fussy grammatical comma before 'which' in the first line added by the *Edinburgh Annual Register*. The poem then entered the collected sets with the *Poetical Works* of 1820 (12.125), and appeared, without any further significant alterations, through its successors up to the posthumous Lockhart edition of 1833–34 (8.373), maintaining in the process the slightly enlarged title introduced by the *Register*.

The present text follows that in *English Minstrelsy* (1810), 2.191, without emendation.

Historical Note

According to Lockhart, this poem was written during Scott's first visit to the Cumbrian spa resort at Gilsland, in September 1797, when he met his future wife Charlotte Carpenter, though the lines were not in fact addressed to her:

> Scott was, on his first arrival in Gilsland, not a little engaged with the beauty of one of the young ladies lodged under the same roof with him; and it was on occasion of a visit in her company to some part of the Roman Wall that he indited his lines. (*Life*, 1.266)

Acknowledging that he had previously assumed Charlotte to be the addressee, Lockhart in a footnote gives his source as 'Mr Claud Russel[l], accountant in

Edinburgh, who was one of the party' (1.266n). The presence of Russell (1769–1846) in the party is confirmed in Scott's correspondence, which seems to point to a rather officious companion, not unwilling—as Scott himself confided to Charlotte—to tell all about others' romantic engagements: 'Claud Russell being the only person who can put the *Natives* upon the right Scent has not faild to make use of his superior information by assuring every person that it is *certainly* Miss C—— & that she is a most agreeable & accomplishd young Lady' (*Letters*, 12.65; compare 1.80). Corson nevertheless points to a letter from Russell of 4 April 1833 to Robert Cadell, stating that at Gilsland he had rallied Scott about Charlotte 'when he was at pains to persuade me he thought more of another young lady, a very pretty girl, to whom he one day on returning from his ride presented a bunch of heath gathered on the Roman Wall in that neighbourhood accompanied by a copy of verses' (*N&I*, 318, note to 12.65(c)). Whether or not two ladies attracted Scott's attention, many readers of the poem apart from Lockhart must have assumed that this concerns Charlotte, an interpretation that may possibly have gathered in Scott's own mind as time passed.

Explanatory Notes
50.title Roman Wall Hadrian's Wall, begun in AD 122 in the reign of the Roman Emperor Hadrian, running for about 117 km (72 miles) from Wallsend on the River Tyne to Bowness-on-Solway to the west, built to protect Roman settlers from the Celtic tribes in Scotland. Gilsland, some 25 km (16 miles) NE of Carlisle, is one of the earliest points from the west where the wall is still visible.
50.1 flowers … purple waving possibly *Valerian*, a hardy perennial herb with dark pink flowers and the capacity to root in walls, whose name has been variously given a Latin derivation, including its originating from the 3rd-century Roman Emperor Valerius. (The colour purple is also associated with imperial Rome.) Alternatively, an *erica* (or heather) in bloom.
50.3 sons of freedom presumably the Scottish tribes, traditionally figured as standing for liberty in the face of Roman oppression.
50.6 laurels branches and leaves from the bay laurel, used in ancient Rome to create circular laurel wreaths as worn by commanding soldiers at their triumphs.

30. The Erl-King

Textual Note
According to William Ruff, Scott's translation of Goethe's 'Der Erlkönig' was first published in the *Kelso Mail* on 1 March 1798, signed 'Alonzo', although a copy of the newspaper of this date has not been located by the present editors: see 'Walter Scott and *The Erl-King*', *Englische Studien*, 69: 1 (1934), 106–08. It was subsequently published in *An Apology for Tales of Terror* (Kelso, 1799), 1–3. Ruff provides a transcription of the text from the *Kelso Mail*, which indicates that the stanzas of the poem were numbered there, but otherwise reveals only one difference from the later printing apart from those of the kind normally associated with the printer, in that where Ruff has 'many a gay sport' in line 10 *An Apology* has 'many gay sports'.
　　Two manuscript versions survive, both also dating from about this time. The first is in a letter from Scott of November 1797 to his aunt Christian Rutherford (NLS, MS 3220, ff. 13–14: *Letters*, 1.76–77), and perhaps represents the earliest surviving version of Scott's translation since it contains some readings not

found in subsequent versions: for instance, line 4 begins 'To hold himself fast', lines 9 and 25 begin 'O come & go with me', and line 20 has 'press thee & kiss thee'. The second manuscript text forms part of a presentation booklet in Scott's hand of his 'Ghost ballads' to Montagu, the wife of George Abercromby of Tullibody, Clackmannanshire (1770–1843) and daughter of Lord Melville (NRS, GD45/26/107): since it is addressed to her in her married name, the booklet must post-date her marriage in January 1799. Several readings of this manuscript agree with those of the Ruff transcription of the newspaper printing in the *Kelso Mail* and the subsequent printing in *An Apology for Tales of Terror*, as, for instance, the beginnings of lines 4, 9 and 25 and the reading 'hug thee & kiss thee' in line 20. (Both manuscripts, incidentally, have the 'Erl-King' rather than 'the Phantom' at the head of his speeches.) At this point Scott was probably still experimenting with the details of his translation. In the version for Mrs Abercromby he moved the final stanza partly into the present tense ('Sore trembles the father, he spurs thro the wild ... / He reaches'), which is also a feature of its subsequent anonymous appearance in the *Scots Magazine*, 64 (January 1802), 72, as the work of 'a Scotish [*sic*] literary gentleman, whom we do not hesitate to place at the head of those who have cultivated this species of poetry in this country'.

Scott provided various headnotes to the poem to suit the different readership he envisaged. To his aunt, for instance, he jocularly issued the instruction that the poem is 'to be read by a candle particularly long in the snuff', while for Mrs Abercromby he provided the brief and formal explanation, 'The *Erl-King* is a malignant phantom supposed by the Germans to haunt the Black Forest'. No headnote was supplied to the readership of the *Scots Magazine*, the editor supplying a footnote which focuses chiefly on the previous translation history of Goethe's original. Apart from the headnote and attempt to shift the final stanza into the present tense, however, the variations between the versions in *An Apology for Tales of Terror* and the *Scots Magazine* simply represent changes of the kind normally associated with the work of the printer. Neither has stanza numbering, although this is a feature both of the transcription from the *Kelso Mail* and the two manuscript versions.

'The Erl-King' was not included in the first edition of Scott's *Ballads and Lyrical Pieces* of 1806, but it was added to the second edition published the same year (162–64). This version varies from the earlier one in *An Apology for Tales of Terror* only in the kind of changes normally associated with the work of the printer, and in adjusting 'German superstition' to 'Danish superstition' in the headnote to the poem. It might be supposed that the poem had been omitted inadvertently from the first edition of *Ballads* and that Scott was now conscientiously rectifying an error, but perhaps he may rather have been wavering as to its worthiness to be included in this collected edition of his poems to date. 'The Erl-King' appeared in similar fashion in subsequent editions of *Ballads* and in the section of additional poems in the eighth edition of *The Lay of the Last Minstrel* of 1808 (242–44). However, it was neither reprinted in *Miscellaneous Poems* of 1820 nor in any of the subsequent lifetime editions of Scott's *Poetical Works*, nor in the Lockhart 1833–34 posthumous edition. Its appeal to Scott's contemporaries, however, is shown by its inclusion in Lady Charlotte Bury's commonplace book (Huntington Library, San Marino, California, HM 33691) and in a notebook of transcriptions of Scott's poems by the novelist Henry Mackenzie (NLS, MS 2536, ff. 1–2).

The present text follows that of *An Apology for Tales of Terror* (Kelso, 1799), 1–3, viewed as the culmination of Scott's initial creative process, with the addition of closing speech marks at the end of line 24.

Historical Note
Scott's poem is a translation of 'Der Erlkönig' (1782) by Johann Wolfgang von Goethe (1749–1832), now probably best known in its musical setting by Schubert. It had been previously translated into English by Matthew Gregory Lewis (1775–1818) and published in the *Monthly Mirror*, 2 (October 1796), 372–73, and afterwards in the fourth edition of his novel *Ambrosio, or The Monk*, 3 vols (London, 1798), 3.21–23, in the context of Theodore telling a group of nuns about four fiends called the Water-King, the Erl-King, the Fire-King, and the Cloud-King. Scott was aware of Lewis's translation as early as November 1797, since in giving the earliest version of his own translation in his letter to his aunt Christian Rutherford he remarks that 'there is no small impudence in attempting a version of that Ballad as it has been translated by Lewis' (*Letters*, 1.77). It was not until the spring of the following year that William Erskine met Lewis in London and showed him Scott's versions of Bürger's 'Lenore' and 'Der wilde Jäger' and Lewis invited Scott to contribute to his projected collection of poems of diablerie, eventually published in two volumes in January 1801 as *Tales of Wonder* (*Life*, 1.290–92). With a pre-existing English version of 'The Erl-King' by Lewis himself, Scott could not have expected that his own translation would appear in *Tales of Wonder*: rather it shows him testing himself as a poet influenced by German *Sturm und Drang* against the celebrated English poet and his participation in Lewis's scheme for having within the volume a group of poems each concerning one of the four fiends mentioned in the passage from his novel referred to above. (Scott's 'The Fire-King', no. 37, also fits neatly into this scheme.) Its subsequent inclusion in Scott's own *An Apology for Tales of Terror* shows that this publication was in part an attempt to compete with Lewis on his own ground and not just to hasten the appearance of poems to appear in Lewis's long-delayed collection. By the time Lewis's publication did appear, the vogue for German-inspired poetic horrors was rapidly passing and Lewis himself not such a prominent literary figure as he had been.

   Scott's diction in his translation from Goethe is less consciously poetic than Lewis's and therefore closer to the mood of the German original. Scott renders the final line 'But, clasp'd to his bosom, the Infant was dead!', which is closer to Goethe's 'In seinen Armen das Kind war tot' (In his arms the child was dead) than Lewis's more elaborate 'Life throbb'd in the sweet baby's bosom no more': see *Tales of Wonder*, 2 vols (London, 1801), 1.52. In general Scott's translation follows the sense and imagery of the original fairly closely, though he has the boy rather than the father initiate their exchanges about the apparition during their night-ride and sets the scene by a reference to 'the woodlands so wild' where Goethe simply has 'durch Nacht und Wind' (through night and wind). Like Lewis before him, Scott misinterprets the reference to 'Erlkönigs Töchter' as the 'Erl-King's daughter' rather than the plural 'Erl-King's daughters', and for the Erl-King's regal 'Kron und Schweif' (crown and train) he substitutes the more ghostly 'staff and … shroud'.

Explanatory Notes
50.headnote   German superstition   although written in German, 'Der Erlkönig' was ultimately based on a Danish ballad called Elveskud, translated into German by Herder as 'Erlkönigs Tochter' (Earl King's Daughter), and from this Goethe derived his poem about the Erl-King himself.
50. headnote   WATER-KING   included, as a translation from Danish, by Lewis in *Tales of Wonder*, 2 vols (London, 1801), 1.56–61.
50.headnote   FIRE-KING   the subject of a ballad by Scott, intended for and

subsequently published in Lewis's *Tales of Wonder*, 2 vols (London, 1801), 1.62–69 (see no. 37, 'The Fire-King').

50.headnote CLOUD-KING   the subject of a ballad by Lewis included in his *Tales of Wonder*, 2 vols (London, 1801), 1.70–78.

50.7   staff and his shroud   possibly a reference to the figure being shrouded in mist, and carrying a staff like a traveller. In Christian iconography the staff signifies pilgrimage and the shroud death.

51.22   pale daughter   pallor is associated with ill-health, death and with the spirit world.

51.24   Grey Willow that danc'd to the Moon   the grey willow, *salix cinerea*, is sometimes thought to have a magical association with the moon. An infusion made from its bark is a traditional remedy for fever.

31.   Frederick and Alice

Textual Note
An early version of 'Frederick and Alice' exists in Scott's commonplace book in the Abbotsford Library, known as 'Adversaria' (for further details of which see Textual Note to no. 16, 'To a Lady'). Clearly Scott was filling in this notebook during the 1790s, although no specific date is given for 'Frederick and Alice', which is the sixteenth item, on pages 31–35. The poem is written on three leaves pasted into cut-out windows of the notebook so that both sides are visible, but there is no watermark. Scott was translating Goethe's plays during the late 1790s, when it seems most likely that Goethe's *Singspiel* (see Historical Note) would have caught his attention. Certainly Scott had composed the ballad by 29 May 1798 when he tentatively offered a version to Matthew Gregory Lewis (1775–1818) for inclusion in Lewis's projected *Tales of Wonder*:

> Erskine & Cranstoun, have been teasing me to send you other two translations from the German which have never seen the Light—One is from the "Lied von Treue" of Bürger, the other an imitation of a Ghostly Ballad in the "Claudina von Billa Bella [*sic*] of Goethe—" I cannot think however of using such a freedom unless the nature of your proposed Collection be more extensive than I at present suppose. (Morgan, MA 1432)

A letter from Lewis to Scott of November 1798 shows that a version of Scott's poem was then in his possession, for it contains criticisms of specific passages for Scott's further consideration:

> Stanza 1st, '*hies*' and '*joys*' are not rhymes; the 1st stanza ends with '*joys*;' the 2d begins with '*joying*'. In the 4th, there is too sudden a change of tenses, '*flows*' and '*rose*'. 6th, 7th, and 8th, I like much. 9th, Does not '*ring his ears*' sound ludicrous in yours? The first idea that presents itself is, that his ears were pulled; but even *the ringing of the ears* does not please. 12th, '*Shower*' and '*roar*', not rhymes. '*Soil*' and '*aisle*,' in the 13th, are not much better; but '*head*' and '*descried*' are execrable. In the 14th, '*bar*' and '*stair*' are ditto; and '*groping*' is a nasty word. *Vide* Johnson, '*He gropes his breeches with a monarch's air*'. In the 15th, you change your metre, which has always an unpleasant effect; and '*safe*' and '*receive*' rhyme just about as well as Scott and Lewis would. 16th, '*within*' and '*strain*' are not rhymes. 17th, '*hear*' & '*air*,' not rhymes. 18th, two metres are mixed; the same objection to the third line of the 19th. Observe, that, in the Ballad, I do not always object to a variation of metre; but then it ought to increase the melody, whereas, in my opinion, in these instances, it is diminished. (8vo1830*PW*, 3.cii–ciii)

From the details given in Lewis's letter, it is clear that the manuscript Scott sent to Lewis was closer to the version of 'Frederick and Alice' in the 'Adversaria' commonplace book than that published in *Tales of Wonder*, 2 vols (London, 1801), 1.148–52. For instance, the first stanza in 'Adversaria' reads:

> Frederick leaves the land of France
> Gay and gallant on he hies
> Careless casts the parting glance
> On the scene of former joys—

This contains the hies/joys rhyme that Lewis objected to, the second word of which he also felt was repeated at the start of the following stanza. The published text takes account of this criticism, so that Lewis makes a valid contribution to the socialisation of the text. In other places, however, Scott ignored Lewis's criticisms: for instance, the rhyme of 'flows/rose' in the fourth stanza occurs in the published text as well as in the 'Adversaria' commonplace book version. Of the fourteen criticisms made by Lewis, roughly two thirds of them seem to have generated revisions in the published text with the remaining third being rejected. While in his letter to Scott of 15 December 1798 (NLS, MS 3874, ff. 30–31) Lewis says, 'I will alter your "Frederick and Alice" for you with pleasure', it seems unlikely that Scott left the task wholly in Lewis's hands even though he respected Lewis's judgement. In his subsequent 'Essay on Imitations of the Ancient Ballad' Scott described Lewis as 'a martinet ... in the accuracy of rhymes and of numbers' but one who 'had a right to be so, for few persons have exhibited more mastery of rhyme, or greater command over the melody of poetry' (8vo1830*PW*, 3.lxxvii).

When Scott came to include 'Frederick and Alice' in subsequent collections of his own poetry he retained almost all of the revisions he had made rather than reverting to the earlier readings indicated by the 'Adversaria' commonplace book version. The single exception lies in lines 43–44, where he undid the personification of ' Thunder ... his roar' and reverted to 'thunder ... its roar' when the poem was included in his 1806 *Ballads and Lyrical Pieces* (143–47) and in the eighth edition of *The Lay of the Last Minstrel* of 1808. Significantly, Scott also then supplied a longer headnote, which gratefully acknowledged Lewis's work on the poem:

> This tale is imitated, rather than translated, from a fragment introduced in Goethe's *'Claudina von Villa Bella'*, where it is sung by a member of a gang of banditti, to engage the attention of the family, while his companions break into the castle. It owes any little merit it may possess to my friend Mr LEWIS, to whom it was sent in an extremely rude state; and who, after some material improvements, published it in his *'Tales of Wonder'*. (*Ballads*, 143)

Variations are otherwise confined to changes of the kind normally associated with the printer. 'Frederick and Alice' was subsequently included in Scott's 1820 *Poetical Works* (2.207–12), in the subsequent lifetime editions, and in the Lockhart 1833–34 posthumous edition (6.327–31), with no indication of further authorial involvement.

The present text follows that of *Tales of Wonder*, 2 vols (London, 1801), 1.148–52, as representing the socialised text at the culmination of Scott's initial creative process, with the following emendations:

53.43   thunder ('Adversaria' MS) / Thunder
53.44   its roar ('Adversaria' MS it's roar) / his roar

Historical Note
Goethe's poem 'Der untreue Knabe' (The Faithless Boy) was included in his *Claudine von Villa Bella* (1776), a *Singspiel* or simplified form of opera in which songs are linked by spoken dialogue instead of accompanied recitative. In the

course of Goethe's light-hearted *Singspiel* a girl is carried off to a brigands' lair, this ballad being sung by the brigand chief, Rugantino, who whispers to her between the verses. As a result of interruption his song is incomplete in Goethe's original, being broken off at the point where the protagonist arrives at the spectral feast and sees the bride. The *Sturm und Drang* tone of the song, therefore, seems more tongue-in-cheek than that of Bürger's 'Lenore' which also concerns a ghostly bridal and was translated by Scott. Scott's version follows the events of Goethe's original with some variation of detail so that instead of coming from France (i.e. being a Frenchman) his hero leaves France. The chief difference is one of tone, in that Scott seems to take the story more seriously, losing the roughness of Rugantino's Gothic shocker, which verges on the comic.

Explanatory Notes
52.18   Seven long days   literally meaning here that a week has passed, but seven is also widely acknowledged as a magical number. There are seven days in creation, seven virtues, seven ages in the life of man, and the number is associated with a variety of occurrences in the Bible.
54.70–71   FOUR times ... FOUR times   this number is not in capital letters in the 'Adversaria' MS, but they may have been adopted for publication as a reminder to the reader that Alice's death had occurred a week previously at the same hour.

32.   The Rouze of The Royal Edinburgh Light Dragoons

Textual Note
This item first officially entered the Scott canon through its inclusion as 'War-Song of the Royal Edinburgh Light Dragoons' at the end of the second edition of *Minstrelsy of the Scottish Border* (1803), 3.415–20. In his introductory note there, however, Scott states that it had originally been written 'during the apprehension of an invasion', the author then having 'little thought that the circumstances of the nation would so speedily justify its republication' (416). Internal references as well as other circumstances have been adduced to claim an original composition, probably in 1798, though without any direct evidence regarding an earlier printed version. This situation can now be clarified through an anonymous song sheet, 'The Rouze of The Royal Edinburgh Light Dragoons', in the Inglis collection of printed music in the National Library of Scotland (Ing.291(4a)). Consisting of a once-folded sheet, with pages measuring approx. 33.5 x 24 cm, and watermarked 'WS / 1796', Scott's text is found on the middle two pages, with the first stanza written in under the lines of the musical notation. The imprint, placed at the head of the notation, is that of 'J[ohn] Watlen, at his Music Warehouse No. 34 North Bridge', an Edinburgh music publisher who issued many hundred song sheets from that address, before removing to London in 1800. The first printed page is also stamped at the foot 'Sold by N. Stewart & Co Edinr.', referring to the firm of Neil Stewart, another prolific music seller, who between 1792 and 1802 operated from 37 South Bridge Street. The musical notation is described 'As a March', and the 'Bugle Horn' given as an opening instrument. Scott's stanzas following the notation are numbered 2–10, matching in length the text in *Minstrelsy*. Two short footnotes are also supplied. Though no originating manuscript has been discovered, a typewritten transcript titled 'The Rouse of the Royal Edinr. Light Dragoons' can be found at NLS, MS 1753, ff. 97–99, as part of a volume con-

sisting mainly of materials rejected in the preparation of the Grierson edition of Scott *Letters*. The source given here is 'Cholmondeley', referring to R. H. Cholmondeley, sometime owner of a number of letters from Scott to George Ellis (1753–1815) and Richard Heber (1774–1833) near the turn of the century, the originals of which are now mostly not recoverable. It is not unlikely that Scott would have transmitted a written copy of his song as an enclosure to such politically sympathetic correspondents as these. Apart from the absence of the second stanza, the wording in the MS 1753 transcript is similar to that found in the printed music sheet. The end signature used by Scott in the transcript, 'Quod Le Seneschal / De La Tour Smaylhome', is also indicative of a relatively early point in his poetical career (see, for instance, Textual Note to no. 34, 'The Eve of Saint John').

As Scott himself indicates, the republication of the text of the song in the third volume of *Minstrelsy*, issued in May 1803, was at least partly triggered by a new wave of anti-invasion fears early that year. In the process, the wording of the second stanza was changed substantively, with 'Edina's Towers' becoming 'Dunedin's towers' in the first line, and 'our Casques with loyal Tartan bound' being replaced by 'Our casques the leopard's spoils surround' for the third. *Minstrelsy* also increases punctuation, with an influx of new exclamation marks, while generally lowering initial capital letters (for example 'Navy' and 'Seas' in line 3), as well as providing apostrophes where the song sheet is deficient. At the same time, the song acquires an encompassing editorial framework, more in keeping with *Minstrelsy*'s organisation, and involving a long epigraph from John Fletcher's play *Bonduca* (*c.* 1613), 1.1.168–90, an introductory note (already cited) outlining the formation and history of the Edinburgh Volunteer Cavalry, and an end 'Note on the War Song' about the Swiss guards, expanding at some length the concise second footnote of the song sheet. The 'War Song' subsequently featured under Scott's name in the *Scots Magazine* for October 1803 (65.725–26), minus the apparatus, but with a new headnote applauding 'the admirable effusion of the warlike and animated muse of this ingenious author'. Apart from a handful of small changes mainly to punctuation, the text generally matches that in *Minstrelsy*; though with a tendency to reintroduce initial capitals for certain words (for example 'Brethren's' and 'Patriot' in the fourth stanza); while the printer is clearly at fault in the placing of the apostrophe in 'sabre's' at line 29. The song first entered collections of Scott's verse with *Ballads and Lyrical Pieces* (1806), 165–70, in the section headed 'Songs'; and where the paratextual materials found in *Minstrelsy* are all preserved, with minor adjustments in the wording to allow for changes in the national situation. The same apparatus also carried through into the various sets of *Poetical Works*, starting with that of 1820 (2.233–39). No significant variations in the text either in these lifetime collections or in the posthumous Lockhart edition of 1833–34 (4.230–34), apart from routine changes that can be associated with the printer, have been discovered. The Lockhart edition, however, does add a few footnotes of its own, one of which wrongly states that 'The song originally appeared in the Scots Magazine for 1802' (231n).

The present text is based on the original music sheet located at NLS, Ing.291(4a), as representing the earliest known printing, and one with marks of having been based fairly directly on MS copy provided by Scott. In the first stanza, however, it omits the music sheet's repetition of the final line, apparently offered there as a prompt for the singer: a repetition that is not present in the remaining stanzas. The same is true of the sheet's long-hyphenation of 'A–rouze' in the same lines. Routine apostrophes have also been added in lines 12, 25, 29, 32 and 48. The following emendations have also been made:

55.17   Brethren's (Editorial) / Brethern's
55.footnote 2   10 August 1792 (Editorial) / 10th. Augt. 1794
          Year corrected to actual date of event: see note to 55.17 below.

Historical Note
Plans to form a force of Volunteer Cavalry in Edinburgh were first broached
at a meeting on 14 February 1797, after which another meeting was held on 15
March at which five names were nominated for commissions and Scott himself
formally proposed as Quartermaster and Secretary. These details, leading to
the authorisation on 4 April of 'two troops of Cavalry, wearing the Royal col-
ours' (6), are carefully set out in a small booklet, almost certainly written by
Scott, titled *Rules and Regulations of The Royal Edinburgh Light Dragoons* (1798).
Granted his overall enthusiasm, it is not improbable that Scott offered a rallying
song for the corps at much the same time as drafting its regulations. As the indi-
vidual notes below illustrate more fully, political references in the song match
particularly well the situation in the first half of 1798, when Napoleon was under
instruction from the French Directory to plan an invasion of Britain. According
to J. G. Lockhart, composition occurred in the summer of 1798 when Scott was
quartered at Musselburgh, and visited for a short while by Matthew Gregory
Lewis (1775–1818), the immediate trigger coming from Scott's Germanist
friend James Skene (1775–1864), himself serving as a cornet in the troop:

> While walking about before dinner on one of these days, Mr Skene's recitation of
> the German *Kriegslied*, 'Der Abschied's Tag ist da' (the day of departure is come),
> delighted both Lewis and Scott; and the latter produced next morning that spirited
> little piece in the same measure, which ... was forthwith adopted as the troop-song of
> the Edinburgh Light Horse. (*Life*, 1.294)

Skene's own record in his *Memories of Sir Walter Scott* tends to corroborate
such an origin: 'He composed a troop song ... It was set to the music of the
German Kriegslied, *Der Abschiedstag ist da*, and, when sung at mess ... every
trooper stood up and unsheathed his sabre' (ed. Basil Thomson (London, 1909),
14). This timeframe also accords well with a letter of 20 July 1798 from Scott's
friend, Jane Cranstoun, Countess Pürgstall (d. 1835), who had recently settled
in Germany, thanking him for 'your little translation & eke yr. March' (NLS,
MS 3874, f. 24v).
     These accounts are further supported by the music provided on the song sheet
'Rouze' in the Inglis collection, which in its basic melody matches that accom-
panying the *Abschiedslied* (Farewell Song) by the German poet and composer
Christian Friedrich Daniel Schubart (1739–91). The first of *Zwei Kaplieder*
(Two Cape Songs), this had been written and set to music by Schubart a few
weeks before the departure of a battalion of German mercenaries to Cape Town
in February 1787 in the service of the Dutch East India Company. Consisting
of twelve verses, with a similar rhyme scheme of abccb, its first two lines echo
especially Scott's rousing opening: 'Auf, auf! ihr Brüder und seid stark / der
Abschiedstag ist da!' (On on! Brethren, be strong, / The departure day is here).
Schubart's *Kriegslied* (War Song) enjoyed considerable popularity as a military
march, and was evidently familiar to Scott and/or his associates by the late
1790s, though presumably another person was engaged to provide the some-
what different harmonisation for the song sheet. The line 'Der Abschiedstag
ist da!' remained long in Scott's memory, being quoted by him twice in more
poignant circumstances in Journal entries of 11 May 1826 and 13 January 1829
(*Journal*, 142, 503).

Explanatory Notes

55.title Rouze in military terms *rouse* is a signal call (typically on the bugle and traditionally after reveille) to indicate that it is time to get out. See Charles James, *A New and Enlarged Military Dictionary* (London, 1802): '*Rouse*, One of the bugle-call soundings for duty.' In German *rouse* signifies 'to awaken, get up, put in motion'.

55.3 Gallic Navy stems the Seas in 1797/98 French naval activity had increased sharply off the coast of Scotland, though the threat to communications was partly averted by the defeat of the Dutch navy (allied with the French) at the Battle of Camperdown in October 1797; *stems* here is used in the sense of making headway.

55.6 high Edina's Towers referring to Edinburgh, and more specifically the Castle Rock, Castle and its fortifications, and possibly other high-rise buildings clustered around it. One interpretation of Edina is that it derives from the Celtic *eidyn*, meaning a hill or rock face. In its Latinate form (as here) it can be found as a name for the city in the poetry of Robert Fergusson, Burns, and Thomas Campbell. The term *Dunedin*, as introduced by Scott in the *Border Minstrelsy* version of the song (see Textual Note), derives from the Scots Gaelic 'Dun Eideann', and was employed by him again in both *The Lay of the Last Minstrel* (1805) and *Marmion* (1808).

55.8–9 Our Casques with loyal Tartan bound … hardy Thistle crown'd no information concerning the *casques* (helmets) of the corps being so adorned has been discovered. The *Rules and Regulations of the Royal Edinburgh Light Drag*oons (1798) only mentions, for full dress, a 'white feather tipped with red in the helmet' (13). The changed wording in the *Border Minstrelsy* version to 'Our casques the leopard's spoils surround' might signify a shift in design.

55.10 red and blue as Scott's 1st footnote partly indicates, the royal livery of England/Britain was traditionally crimson or scarlet with blue trimmings, a colouring presumably reflected in the uniforms of the present troop. According to *Rules and Regulations*, in particular, 'Serjeants wear blue and red sashes' (13).

55.11 Gallia's frown alluding to the domineering spirit of Revolutionary France in setting up client states throughout continental Europe in the wake of military conquest.

55.12 Dull Holland's after occupation of the Netherlands by French Revolutionary forces, the Batavian Republic was proclaimed in 1795, this lasting until 1806 when Napoleon's brother, Louis, was crowned as King of Holland.

55.13 ravish'd toys … Romans mourn alluding to the French seizure of art treasures in Italy for the Louvre in Paris, from which the Papal States suffered especially badly. By the terms of the Armistice of Bologna in June 1796, later reinforced by the Treaty of Tolentino of February 1797, numerous art works and manuscripts were appropriated, for which the Pope was even obliged to pay shipping costs to Paris. In *Paul's Letters to his Kinsfolk* (1816), Scott described the plundered treasures in the Louvre as illustrating 'perhaps the worst point' in Napoleon's character: 'Each picture, indeed, has its own separate history of murder, rapine, and sacrilege' (322). After Napoleon's successful campaigns in Italy 1796–97, French troops eventually deposed Pope Pius VI, establishing a Republic of Rome in February 1798.

55.14 gallant Switzers early in 1798 Switzerland was completely overrun by French forces, with a Helvetic Republic being proclaimed on 12 April. This however was unpopular, and several uprisings took place in April/May 1798, only to be crushed by the French.

55.17   Brethren's murder   referring, as Scott's 2nd footnote indicates, to
the massacre of the Swiss Guards at the storming by insurrectionists of the
French Royal Palace of the Tuileries. In *Minstrelsy of the Scottish Border*, 2nd
edn (1803), this was expanded as follows: 'The allusion is to the massacre of
the Swiss guards, on the fatal 10th August, 1792. It is painful, but not useless,
to remark, that the passive temper with which the Swiss regarded the death of
their bravest countrymen, mercilessly slaughtered in discharge of their duty,
encouraged and authorized the progressive injustice, by which the Alps, once
the seat of the most virtuous and free people upon the continent, have, at
length, been converted into the citadel of a foreign and military despot. A state
degraded is half enslaved.' (3.420)

56.31–32   Gallia's legions ... plunder's bloody gain   the French
revolutionary army was organised in legions, after the ancient Roman model,
and *La Légion Noire* (Black Legion) was specially prepared for the invasion
of Britain, participating in a landing at Fishguard, Wales, in 1797. British
propaganda regularly featured a ragged citizen army, often including convicts,
motivated alone by the prospect of booty.

56.37   Tricolor   the French revolutionary flag, featuring three vertical
bands coloured blue, white, and red; first adopted in 1790.

56.41   farewell home   according to a resolution of 17 March 1798, 'in
consequence of the threatened invasion in Spring 1798', the corps of the Royal
Edinburgh Light Dragoons declared 'themselves ready and willing, in case of
actual invasion, or the imminent danger thereof, to march to any part of Great
Britain' (*Rules and Regulations*, 7).

56.49   Laws and Liberty   contrasting with the French Revolutionary
'Liberty, Equality, and Fraternity'. Compare the conservative writer Edmund
Burke on the English Revolution Settlement of 1688: 'The Revolution was
made to preserve our *antient* indisputable laws and liberties, and that *antient*
constitution of government which is our only security for law and liberty'
(*Reflections on the Revolution in France*, 2nd edn (London, 1790), 44).

33.   Glenfinlas, or Lord Ronald's Coronach

Textual Note
In his 'Essay on Imitations of the Ancient Ballad' Scott described 'Glenfinlas'
as 'I think, the first original poem which I ventured to compose' (8vo1830*PW*,
3.lxviii). This was presumably before the end of 1798 since Matthew Gregory
Lewis (1775–1818), to whom Scott submitted it as a potential contribution to
his *Tales of Wonder*, refers to it in his letter to Scott of 6 January 1799 (3.cv).
Scott's working manuscript does not appear to have survived, although there is
a copy in his hand in a presentation booklet of his 'Ghost ballads', written out
for Montagu, the wife of George Abercromby of Tullibody, Clackmannanshire
(1770–1843) and daughter of Lord Melville (NRS, GD45/26/107): since it is
addressed to her in her married name, the booklet must post-date her marriage
in January 1799. In this there are one or two repetitious or infelicitous words
and phrases, suggesting that Scott has not yet perhaps worked out his poem
fully. Moy tells Lord Ronald in lines 121–22, for instance, 'Even now the death
damps chill thy brow / I hear—I hear the funeral cry!', while in line 224 his
harp finds 'many a magic pause'. Other early copies are not in Scott's hand but
those of his acquaintances, reflecting the manuscript circulation of Scott's early
works in Edinburgh. A somewhat carelessly transcribed version, for example,
is included in Lady Charlotte Bury's commonplace book (Huntington Library,

San Marino, California, HM 33691) under the title 'The Glen of the Green Women', and the poem is one of those in a small leather-bound notebook of copies of Scott's early poems (NLS, MS 2536, ff. 6–20) by the novelist Henry Mackenzie (1745–1831).

Lewis must have asked Scott to revise his poem substantially previous to publication, since a letter to Scott of 1799 acknowledges receipt of 'your revised "Glenfinlas"' and comments 'I do not despair of convincing you in time, that a *bad* rhyme is, in fact, no rhyme at all' (8vo1830*PW*, 3.cii). In his letter of 6 January 1799 Lewis mentions showing the poem to fellow guests while on a visit to Lord Melbourne's house, warning Scott 'that nobody understood the *Lady* Flora of Glengyle to be a disguised demon till the catastrophe arrived' and advising him to introduce 'some previous stanzas ... of the nature and office of *the wayward Ladies of the Wood*' (8vo1830*PW*, 3.cv). He also mentioned the opinion of a fellow-guest that the penultimate stanza should be omitted, although it is not clear whether this is the same as the penultimate stanza as published. The extent of Scott's revisions is unknown, but all the evidence shows that he respected Lewis's judgement (see Textual Note to no. 31, 'Frederick and Alice'). It seems likely that some at least of Lewis's corrections were willingly adopted by Scott prior to the first publication of 'Glenfinlas' in January 1801 in *Tales of Wonder*, 2 vols (London, 1801), 1.122–36.

'Glenfinlas' was subsequently included in Scott's own *Minstrelsy of the Scottish Border*, 2 vols (Kelso, 1802), 2.373–92, with a note of its previous publication in Lewis's collection. Here Scott took the opportunity to correct a few errors in the first printing and make some minor adjustments to his verses. Lewis's unfamiliarity with Scottish place-names and culture may have led to 'Lulan's bay' in line 102 (altered to 'Oban's bay'), to the spelling of 'Colensay' (line 104), as well as to the reference to 'St Columbus' in the footnote concerning St Oran. Scott changes 'The Fergus' to 'Thy Fergus' in line 105 and 'the Laird of Downe' to 'the lord of Downe' in line 107. He moves Lord Ronald's beltane-fire outside by mentioning it as 'o'er his hills' rather than 'in his halls' (line 13), while in line 129 'Or sooth, or false' becomes 'Or false, or sooth'. Moy's 'sullen brow' in line 200 becomes his 'sullen vow', perhaps because the original reading was the accidental result of eyeslip from the rhyme word two lines above. Other changes are of the kind normally associated with the printer.

Scott substantially reorganised his annotation for 'Glenfinlas' in *Minstrelsy*. His former endnote outlining the tradition on which the poem is based was added to his previous headnote explaining the localities mentioned, and the connection of these localities with the Macgregors emphasised. In this new context of an antiquarian project footnotes became endnotes, and some were made very much more substantial. Much fresh information was provided on St Oran, for instance. Scott's earlier declaration of knowing nothing of St Fillan is rescinded, and a detailed account of his miraculous arm is supplied. Scott also adds a new endnote giving a substantial extract from 'a descriptive poem, entituled *Albania*, published at Aberdeen, in the year 1757' (*Minstrelsy*, 2.392). In the second edition of *Minstrelsy* Scott adds even more information to his note on St Fillan's wonder-working arm (2.426) though removing the information about *Albania*.

'Glenfinlas' was subsequently included in Scott's 1806 *Ballads and Lyrical Pieces* (1–20) and in the section of additional poems in the eighth edition of *The Lay of the Last Minstrel* of 1808, 261–80, cxliii–cxlvi. It afterwards appeared in his 1820 *Poetical Works* (2.109–32), and in successive lifetime editions of his poetry, as well as the Lockhart 1833–34 posthumous edition (4.167–82), where (for the first time) a basic musical setting 'To an Ancient Highland Air' with pianoforte accompaniment was provided, almost certainly inserted by Lockhart himself, between pages 168 and 169. Changes to Scott's 'Glenfinlas' in these later reprintings of the text in *Minstrelsy* were almost exclusively of the kind normally associated with the work of the printers, although some editions omit 'simple' from the opening words of the headnote there, 'The simple tradition' (2.373). 1821*PW* adds to the final endnote the detail that the Quegrich was 'apparently the head of a pastoral staff' (3.326).

The present text follows that in *Tales of Wonder*, 2 vols (London, 1801), 1.122–36, as best representing the culmination of Scott's initial creation, an imitation of the German Romantic ballads he then admired. It adopts some of the obvious corrections made by him for *Minstrelsy of the Scottish Border*, but without reflecting the poem's changed inflection as a contribution to a primarily antiquarian project. In addition to the following emendations, the first two of Scott's footnotes, presented mistakenly as one in the copy-text, have been separated.

58.13	o'er his hills (*Minstrelsy*) / in his halls
58.footnote 1	*Beltane-tree* (*Tales of Wonder* Ed2) / Beltane-tree
60.footnote	St. Columba (Editorial) / St. Columbus
61.102	Oban's (*Minstrelsy*) / Lulan's
61.104	Colonsay (*Minstrelsy*) / Colensay
61.105	"Thy (*Minstrelsy*) / "The
61.107	lord (*Minstrelsy*) / Laird
64.200	vow (*Minstrelsy*) / brow

Historical Note

By Scott's own account in his 'Essay on Imitations of the Ancient Ballad', 'Glenfinlas', besides being an attempt to imitate the German poems he so much admired in the late 1790s, was also a 'versification of an Ossianic fragment' (8vo1830*PW*, 3.lxix). Scott felt that, despite the controversy about the authenticity of the supposed Ossian poems of James Macpherson (1736–96), the most competent judges of Gaelic language and culture agreed that 'in their spirit and diction they exactly resemble fragments of existing poetry of that language, to which no doubt can attach', and concluded that the 'Celtic people of Erin and Albyn had, in short, a style of poetry properly called national' (lxix–lxx). The setting of 'Glenfinlas' in the spectacular scenery around Loch Katrine reflects Scott's jaunts there in the early 1790s, while the demonic women and the grisly dismembering of Lord Ronald are symptomatic of his absorption in the wild poems of Gottfried Augustus Bürger (1747–94) at the start of his career as a poet. It is this last element that made the poem such an appropriate contribution to Lewis's *Tales of Wonder*, when Scott was invited to become a contributor in 1798 (see Textual Note to no. 21, 'William and Helen'). As outlined in the present Textual Note, Scott offered Lewis this ballad of his own composition alongside some of his translations from the German and was sufficiently proud of his achievement to circulate copies among his friends.

Explanatory Notes

57.title   Glenfinlas, or Glenfinglas (the Gaelic *gleann-fionn-glas* means 'grey white valley') is a rocky glen in Callander parish in SW Perthshire. It is traversed by the Turk rivulet and was once an ancient deer-forest.

57.motto   William Collins, 'An Ode on the Popular Superstitions of the Highlands of Scotland, Considered as the Subject of Poetry', lines 65–69: see *Thomas Gray and William Collins: Poetical Works*, ed. Roger Lonsdale (Oxford, 1977), 169.

57.2 Albin's line   the Clan Gregor is supposed to be descended from Griogar, the third son of Alpin, an 8th-century Celtic King of Scotland.
57.3 Glenartney's   Glenartney is a wooded glen in Comrie parish in Upper Strathearn in Perthshire, traversed by Ruchell Water. It is an ancient deer forest.
57.5 great Macgilliannore   not identified as a title for the chief of the Macgregors, although apparently based on 'Mac Cailein Mor' as a way of referring to the Campbell chief.
57.7 claymore   a two-edged Highland broadsword.
58.14 *beltane* tree   Beltane in Scotland is an ancient Celtic festival of 1 May when fires were kindled on hill-tops and cattle driven between the flames for magical purposes of protection. Traditionally embers were taken from the fires to relight hearths.
58.15 strathspey   a lively Scottish reel or dance for two dancers.
58.17 Ronald's shell   a drinking-vessel, made of shell or perhaps horn.
58.25 Moy   a place 16 km (10 miles) S of Inverness, the home of the chief of the Mackintosh clan. Scottish landowners are often addressed or referred to by the name of their estate.
58.25 Columba's isle   Iona, or Icolmkill, near Mull in the Inner Hebrides, where St Columba landed in AD 563 and founded a monastery.
58.footnote 2 Dr. Johnson's definition   see Samuel Johnson, *A Journey to the Western Islands of Scotland* (London, 1775), 248–49.
59.41 No vassals wait   numerous clan members were normally present when Highland chiefs were hunting. Scott commented in his 'Essay on Imitations of the Ancient Ballad' that in this respect his poem was unhistorical: 'The ancient Highland chieftains, when they had a mind to "hunt the dun deer down," did not retreat into solitary bothies, or trust the success of the chase to their own unassisted exertions, without a single gillie to help them; they assembled their clan, and all partook of the sport, forming a ring, or enclosure, called the Tinchell, and driving the prey towards the most distinguished persons of the hunt. This course would not have suited me, so Ronald and Moy were cooped up in their solitary wigwam, like two moorfowl shooters of the present day'. (8vo1830*PW*, 3.lxx–lxxi)
59.51 Moneira's sullen brook   not identified.
59.59 Katrine's distant lakes   Loch Katrine is about 13 km (8 miles) long in the Trossachs chiefly in SW Perthshire. Scott had visited it on several occasions during the 1790s. About 1.6 km away is Loch Achray, and the mountains of Ben Ledi (876 m), Benmore (1171 m), and Ben Vorlich (1013 m) are prominent features of the surrounding scenery.
60.72 proud Glengyle   there are the ruins of a small fortress at Glengyle, once a Macgregor possession, at the W end of Loch Katrine. Glengyle Water flows into the loch.
60.87 St. Oran's rule   when 'Glenfinlas' was included in *Minstrelsy of the Scottish Border*, Scott made the substance of his footnote into a longer endnote, as follows: 'St Oran was a friend and follower of St Columba, and was buried in Icolmkill. His pretensions to be a saint were rather dubious. According to the legend, he consented to be buried alive, in order to propitiate certain dæmons of the soil, who obstructed the attempts of Columba to build a chapel. Columba caused the body of his friend to be dug up, after three days had elapsed; when Oran, to the horror and scandal of the assistants, declared, that there was neither a God, a judgment, nor a future state! He had no time to make further discoveries, for Columba caused the earth once more to be shovelled over him with the utmost dispatch. The chapel, however, and the

cemetery, was called *Reilig Ouran*; and, in memory of his rigid celibacy, no female was permitted to pay her devotions, or be buried, in that place. This is the rule alluded to in the poem' (2.391).

60.89   Enrick's fight   Enrick is a stream flowing through Glen Urquhart in northern Invernesshire and into Loch Ness. No particular conflict has been identified.

60.89   Morna's death   in the poems of Ossian, Morna avenges the death of her lover, Cadmor, on Duchommar by stabbing him with his sword and is then stabbed by him in turn: see James Macpherson, *The Poems of Ossian and Related Works*, ed. Howard Gaskill (Edinburgh, 1996), 29–30.

61.102   Oban's bay   a semi-circular bay near the seaport of Oban in Argyllshire, protected by the islands of Kerrera and Lismore.

61.104   rocky Colonsay   an island in the Inner Hebrides, roughly 13 km (8 miles) long, which can be reached by sea from Oban. It is also associated with St Columba and St Oran, who are said to have first settled on Colonsay after leaving Ireland.

61.107   lord of Downe   the ruins of Doune Castle, at the SE end of Doune village in Perthshire, stand on a peninsula formed by the river Teith and Ardoch Burn. It was built by Robert Stewart, 1st Duke of Albany (*c.* 1340–1420), and later passed to the crown.

62.134   buskins   half-boots.

63.167   mountain dirk   a Highland dagger or poniard.

63.193–94   Ave-bead ... Pater-noster   two prayers of the Roman Catholic rosary, a string of beads reminding the worshipper of the order and number of prayers to be recited. The Ave Maria ('Hail Mary') is a prayer addressed to the Virgin Mary, while the Paternoster ('Our father') is the Lord's Prayer.

63.195   holy reed   properly, the rood or cross on which Jesus was crucified. Scott presumably adapted the word to rhyme with 'bead' two lines previously.

64.201   high Dunlathmon's fire   the family-seat of Lathmon in the Ossian poems: see James Macpherson, *The Poems of Ossian and Related Works*, ed. Howard Gaskill (Edinburgh, 1996), 469.

64.215–16   Lady of the Flood ... Monarch of the Mine   elemental spirits resembling the group of four featured by Lewis in the 4th edn of his novel *Ambrosio, or The Monk*, 3 vols (London, 1798), 3.21–23, in the context of Theodore telling a group of nuns about four fiends called the Water-King, the Erl-King, the Fire-King, and the Cloud-King. For *Tales of Wonder* Lewis wanted to include a ballad about each.

64.218   St. Fillan's   Scott added a substantial endnote about St Fillan when including 'Glenfinlas' in *Minstrelsy of the Scottish Border*, and further extended it in the 2nd edn of 1803 to read as follows:

> St Fillan has given his name to many chapels, holy fountains, &c. in Scotland. He was, according to Camerarius, an abbot of Pittenweem, in Fife; from which situation he retired, and died a hermit in the wilds of Glenurchy, A. D. 649. While engaged in transcribing the scriptures, his left hand was observed to send forth such a splendour, as to afford light to that with which he wrote; a miracle which saved many candles to the convent, as St Fillan used to spend whole nights in that exercise. The 9th of January was dedicated to this saint, who gave his name to Kilfillan, in Renfrew, and St Phillans, or Forgend, in Fife. Lesley, lib. 7, tells us, that Robert the Bruce was possessed of Fillan's miraculous and luminous arm, which he inclosed in a silver shrine, and had it carried at the head of his army. Previous to the battle of Bannockburn, the king's chaplain, a man of little faith, abstracted the relique, and deposited it in some place of security, lest it should fall into the hands of the English. But, lo! while Robert was addressing his prayers to the empty casket, it was observed to open and shut suddenly; and, on inspection, the saint was found to have himself deposited his arm in the shrine, as an assurance of victory. Such is the tale of Lesley.

But though the Bruce little needed that the arm of St Fillan should assist his own, he dedicated to him, in gratitude, a priory at Killin, upon Loch Tay.

In the Scots Magazine for July, 1802, (a national periodical publication, which has lately revived, with considerable energy), there is a copy of a very curious crown grant, dated 11 July, 1487, by which James III. confirms to Malice Doire, an inhabitant of Strathfillan, in Perthshire, the peaceable exercise and enjoyment of a relique of St Fillan, called the Quegrich, which he, and his predecessors, are said to have possessed, since the days of Robert Bruce. As the Quegrich was used to cure diseases, this document is, probably, the most ancient patent ever granted for a quack medicine. The ingenious correspondent, by whom it is furnished, further observes, that additional particulars, concerning St Fillan, are to be found in *Ballenden's Boece*, Bk 4, folio ccxiii, and in *Pennant's Tour in Scotland*, 1772, pp. 11, 15. (2.425–26).

64.219   Eastern clime   towards the Holy Land but also perhaps as the source of the coming dawn.

64.224   magic change   variations in the tune played.

34.   The Eve of Saint John

Textual Note

'The Eve of Saint John' was intended as a contribution to, and eventually published in, the *Tales of Wonder*, 2 vols (London, 1801) of Matthew Gregory Lewis (1775–1818), 1.137–47. Since Lewis comments on the poem in his letter to Scott of 6 January 1799 (8vo1830*PW*, 3.cv) it must have been composed before the end of 1798. According to Scott's subsequent recollections 'The Eve of Saint John' was his second original ballad, following shortly after 'Glenfinlas': he mockingly described himself as being 'like a pedlar who has got two ballads to begin the world upon' (8vo1830*PW*, 3.lxxii). The publication of Lewis's collection, however, did not take place until January 1801 and in the meantime Scott arranged with James Ballantyne for his poem to appear as a separate, privately-printed publication in Kelso, *The Eve of Saint John. A Border Ballad.* This bears an 1800 title-page, but was published sometime after 22 August in 1799. This Kelso booklet, therefore, is the first publication of 'The Eve of Saint John', but does not necessarily represent the first version produced by Scott for publication.

Of the four surviving early manuscript versions, NLS, MS 818, in Scott's own hand, appears to be a working manuscript. Each leaf measures approx. 23.5 x 18.8 cm, and the two papers employed have watermarks of 'BUDGEN / 1797' and 'MB / 1796'. Although tied with a purple ribbon and with the outside conjugate pair of its sixteen leaves forming a cover, the text, mainly on the rectos, has corrected words and lines and some replacement stanzas are written on versos so that they face the equivalent deleted passages.   Scott's first thought for line 6, for instance, had been 'The Battle's brunt to bear', revised to 'His banner broad to rear', which is the reading of the two other manuscript versions as well as that of the various published texts of the poem. This early version of the poem does not, however, appear to be the direct copy for either of the two early printed versions of 'The Eve of Saint John': it contains two stanzas, for instance, that do not appear in those, and while it differs in various places more from the separate publication than it does from *Tales of Wonder* it combines readings from both.

It seems probable that in various manuscript versions Scott was trying out and experimenting with different readings in individual lines, as their relationship does not appear to be linear or hierarchical. A second manuscript, in the

Harry Ransom Center, Austin, Texas (HRC MS-3753, Container 1.1), consists of seven leaves stitched into a booklet and with the outer two forming a cover with the title on the recto of the first leaf and the verso left blank, the last leaf being blank on both sides. Here the poem, in Scott's hand, has a different title, 'The Baron of Smaylhome An Auld Border Ballad', and is jocularly signed at the end 'Quod Le Seneschal de la Tour' in similar fashion to his manuscript for 'The Fire-King' (BL, Add. MS 39,667, ff. 1–6: see Textual Note to no. 37). With its booklet format and minimal corrections it appears to be a fair copy. Some readings are unique to this manuscript, such as 'gloves of plate' (line 10), while others agree with the later printing in *Tales of Wonder* rather than the first, separate, publication, such as 'I cannot come I must not come' (line 69).

The other two manuscripts are both presentation copies. The first forms part of a booklet in Scott's hand of his 'Ghost ballads', written out for Montagu, the wife of George Abercromby of Tullibody, Clackmannanshire (1770–1843) and daughter of Lord Melville (NRS, GD45/26/107): since it is addressed to her in her married name, the booklet must post-date her marriage in January 1799. The second manuscript, now in the Signet Library, Edinburgh, is a transcription by Scott's wife Charlotte, made for Scott's uncle, Captain Robert Scott of Rosebank (1739–1804), and passed down in his family for many years. The paper on which it is written, measuring approx. 11.5 x 7 cm, bears a 1794 watermark. It imitates a printed book, giving the title of the poem in large Gothic script and even incorporating a small watercolour sketch of Smailholm Tower, the location of the poem. In addition to the provision of different mottoes, and the omission in the Signet Library manuscript of a headnote about Smailholm Tower (superfluous in the case of Robert Scott), there are a number of verbal variations between the two, once more suggesting that the text of Scott's poem in manuscript was relatively fluid even in these presentation copies. This is further confirmed by the copy in Henry Mackenzie's notebook containing transcripts of a number of Scott's poems (NLS, MS 2536, ff. 21–30).

The printing of 'The Eve of Saint John' in the Kelso booklet is likely to have been under Scott's full control, barring accidental printing errors, whereas the version sent to London was subject to Lewis's editorial hand. There are many substantive differences between the two, some of which suggest that individual details of Scott's text were not yet fixed in his own mind, such as whether the Baron whistles for his page 'thrice' (line 27), as in the separate printing, or 'twice', as in *Tales of Wonder*, and whether the wind blew 'wild and shrill' (line 42) as it does in the separate printing or 'loud and shrill' as in *Tales of Wonder*. Other differences can be attributed to Lewis's intervention in the text sent for *Tales of Wonder*, an intrusion that was sometimes (though not invariably) acceptable, since Scott generally respected Lewis's judgement (see Textual Note to no. 21, 'William and Helen'). In his letter to Scott of 6 January 1799 (8vo1830*PW*, 3.cv), Lewis criticises Scott's language and rhymes in a variety of ways: 'Ought not *tore* to be *torn*? *Tore* seems to me not English. In verse 16th, the last line is word for word from *Gil Morrice*. 21st, "*Floor*" and "*bower*" are not rhymes.' Scott sometimes modified his poem to take account of these remarks, and sometimes not. The Baron's acton continued to be described as 'tore' in line 22 and (despite *Gil Morrice*) line 64 still reads 'Ask no bold Baron's leave', though Scott probably did modify the end-rymes of lines 78 and 80. In both the early published versions of the poem the rushes are 'on the stair' and the lady conjures her lover 'to be there', whereas in NLS, MS 818, f. 7 (and presumably in the manuscript Scott had sent to Lewis) the rushes were 'on the floor' and the lady invites her lover 'to come to my bour'. When the poem appeared in the second edition of *Tales of Wonder* (London, 1801), 153–64, 'black Friars' in line 123 was corrected to 'white monks', acknowledging the fact that as Dryburgh Abbey was a Premonstratensian foundation its canons would have worn white habits, and incidentally restoring a reading in the Harry Ransom Center manuscript.

Scott's willingness to defer to Lewis's judgement, at least in some respects, is borne out by the fact that when he included 'The Eve of Saint John' in his *Minstrelsy of the Scottish Border*, 2 vols (Kelso, 1802), 2.309–26, it was the version in *Tales of Wonder* that he chose. He added more specific and personal information at the conclusion to the headnote as follows:

> Brotherstone is a heath, in the neighbourhood of Smaylho'me tower.
> This ballad was first printed in Mr LEWIS's *Tales of Wonder*. It is here published with some additional illustrations, particularly an account of the battle of Ancram Moor; which seemed proper in a work upon Border antiquities. The catastrophe of the tale is founded upon a well known Irish tradition. This ancient fortress and its vicinity formed the scene of the editor's infancy, and seemed to claim from him this attempt to celebrate them in a Border tale.

Scott's additions to the poem for *Minstrelsy* were largely confined to the notes, including substantial accounts of the battle of Ancram Moor and of a reclusive female who lived in the ruins of Dryburgh Abbey in the second half of the eighteenth century (see Appendix below), and to match which the places of retreat of the Baron and his lady were transposed in lines 189 and 191.

From this point onwards the text of 'The Eve of Saint John' was modified only slightly by its author. In the second edition of *Minstrelsy*, 2.335–52, for instance, Scott adjusted stanza 46 (347) to read:

> He laid his left palm on an oaken beam;
> His right upon her hand:
> The lady shrunk, and fainting sunk,
> For it scorch'd like a fiery brand.

As it appeared in the second edition of his *Ballads and Lyrical Pieces* in 1806 (21–38) 'vale' in line 130 was changed to 'dale'. From there the poem was reprinted in the eighth edition of *The Lay of the Last Minstrel* (Edinburgh, 1808), 281–96, cxlvii–cliii, and afterwards passed into Scott's 1820 *Poetical Works* (2.133–54), and the subsequent editions of his collected poems, with almost no variation other than changes of the kind normally associated with the printers. In 8vo1830*PW* (3.231–48), however, there is a reversion to 'vale' in line 130, which is then carried forward into Lockhart's edition of 1833–34 (4.183–99).

However, Scott did continue to develop his notes after the poem had appeared in *Minstrelsy* in 1802. In the second edition of 1803 he corrects his definition of 'vaunt-brace' as armour for the body rather than for the shoulders and arms (2.337), adds the authority of Buchanan to that of Pitscottie on the battle of Ancram (349), gives a more specific location for Kirnetable as now being called 'Ciarntable … at the head of Douglasdale' (350), notes that Mr Haliburton of Newmains was 'the editor's great-grandfather' and corrects the dwelling-place of his companion from 'Sheffield' to 'Sheilfield' (351).

In 1806 in *Ballads* he omits the paragraph from his headnote in which the first publication is given as being in *Tales of Wonder* and replaces 'editor's' with 'author's' to suit the new context of a collection of his own, moving the statement about the Irish origins of his tale to the end of his headnote (22). A new footnote in 1821*PW* provides a more specific account of this in Henry More's *Appendix to the Antidote against Atheism* (3.232) and reinstates Scott's acknowledgement that the poem first appeared in *Tales of Wonder*. Fresh information is supplied about Sir Ralph Evers in Scott's note on the battle of Ancram Moor (3.244). The present text is reprinted from M. G. Lewis's *Tales of Wonder*, 2 vols (London, 1801), 1.137–47 as representing the socialised text at the culmination of Scott's initial creative process. The following emendations have been made:

67.13	days' (18mo1830*PW*) / day's
69.63	say, 'Come (*Minstrelsy* Ed1: say, "Come) / say, come
70.footnote 2	magnificent (*Minstrelsy* Ed1) / magnificient
71.123	white monks they sing (*Tales of Wonder* Ed2) / black Friars sing

Historical Note
Scott was familiar with Smailholm Tower from his extended stays at his grandfather's nearby farm at Sandyknowe in his childhood, from early 1773 to late 1778, and it was the locus of many of his earliest memories. He was understandably vexed therefore when it was vandalised:

> Some idle persons had of late years, during the proprietor's absence, torn the iron-grated door of Smallholm Tower from its hinges, and thrown it down the rock. I was an earnest suitor to my friend and kinsman ... that the dilapidation should be put a stop to, and the mischief repaired. This was readily promised, on condition that I should make a ballad, of which the scene should lie at Smallholm Tower, and among the crags where it is situated. (8vo1830*PW*, 3.lxxi–lxxii)

As one of the earliest of Scott's original compositions, probably composed in 1798, it was naturally influenced by the German poems of Goethe and Bürger, with their spectral appearances, that he was then translating into English verse. It was natural that when M. G. Lewis invited Scott to contribute to his projected collection of poems of diablerie, eventually published in two volumes in January 1801 as *Tales of Wonder* (*Life*, 1.290–92), this should be one of the poems that Scott sent him. The poem itself, while it has a precise historical setting in its reference to the battle of Ancrum Moor on 27 February 1545 (just as Bürger's 'Lenore' does to events following the battle of Prague in May 1757), still has a generic feel of medievalised *Sturm und Drang*. It was only through the development of his notes in subsequent collected editions of his work that Scott, disillusioned with his early enthusiasm for all things Germanic, built up the historical background to his poem and made overt reference to his own family history in the locality.

Explanatory Notes
66.title   Eve of Saint John   St John the Baptist's day is 24 June, his eve being therefore 23 June or Midsummer's Eve when spirits and apparitions were traditionally supposed to be able to cause mischief.
67.1   Baron of Smaylho'me   Smailholm Tower, a peel tower about 8 km (5 miles) W of Kelso, Roxburghshire was built in the 15th or early 16th century by the family of Pringle or Hoppringle. It was only obtained by the Scotts of Harden during the 1640s. Even so, in depicting the Baron Scott is perhaps thinking of William Scott, first Laird of Harden, who died in February 1561 and had in 1535 obtained the lands and barony of Harden from his brother.
67.5   bold Buccleuch   Sir Walter Scott of Buccleuch, who succeeded his father in the family estates in the Scottish borders in 1517 and was killed in an encounter with the hostile Kerr clan in Edinburgh in 1552. His widow features in Scott's first long narrative poem *The Lay of the Last Minstrel* (1805).
67.7   'gainst the English yew   English archers' skill with their long-bows

made of yew was thought to have secured victory in medieval battles such as Agincourt (1415).

67.10 vaunt-brace a form of vambrace, defensive armour for the forearm. Scott's note to this effect was changed in the 2nd edn of *Minstrelsy of the Scottish Border* (2.337) to read 'armour for the body'.

67.17 Ancram Moor a battle taking place in Roxburghshire on 27 February 1545, part of the wasting of Southern Scotland known as the Rough Wooing and motivated by the desire of the English King Henry VIII to marry his son Prince Edward to the Infant Mary, Queen of Scots. When an English army under Sir Ralph Eure and Sir Brian Layton burned both the town and abbey of Melrose Archibald Douglas, Earl of Angus, gathered a Scottish army to pursue the invaders and overtook and defeated them in battle at Ancram Moor.

67.19 Douglas true Archibald Douglas, 6th Earl of Angus (*c.* 1489–1557) had married Margaret Tudor, the elder sister of Henry VIII of England and widow of the Scottish King James IV, in 1514.

67.20 Lord Ivers Sir Ralph Eure, or Evers (1510–45) of Foulbridge in Brompton, Yorkshire, had been Keeper of Redesdale and Tynedale since 1542 and was made Warden of the Middle Marches in 1544. He led many raids into Scotland from Berwick.

67.22 acton a leather jacket, plated with mail.

70.86 Dryburgh an abbey of Premonstratensian monks (Augustinians from Premonstre in France), settled by them in 1150. Its ruins had passed under the control of Scott's great-grandfather, Thomas Haliburton, in 1700.

70.91 mass rite a Requiem Mass is one offered for the dead in the Roman Catholic church. Protestants deny the efficacy of praying for the dead and forbid its practice.

70.103 his shield which would have borne his coat-of-arms, his escutcheon.

70.104 his crest was a branch of the yew a crest is a device once worn by a knight on his helmet but now placed above the shield and helmet in a coat of arms.

71.112 Sir Richard of Coldinghame Coldingham is a village and coastal parish in NE Berwickshire on one of the main routes north from England, and the site of the Priory of Coldingham. Scott's Sir Richard is probably a fictional character, since the feudal lord of Coldingham between 1542 and 1563 was John Stewart, an illegitimate son of James V of Scotland.

71.117 holy Melrose Melrose Abbey near the town of the same name in Roxburghshire was founded by Cistercian monks in 1136, and was well endowed by successive Scottish kings.

71.123 white monks Premonstratensian monks wore white habits. In earlier published versions they were wrongly habited in black, an error corrected in the 2nd edn of *Tales of Wonder*.

71.127 bartizan-seat a bartizan is a battlemented parapet at the top of a castle, especially a battlemented turret projecting from an angle at the top of a tower.

71.131 Mertoun's wood Mertoun House in SW Berwickshire near St Boswells was the seat of the Scotts of Harden, where Scott frequently visited.

71.132 Tiviotdale the area drained by the River Teviot, a way of referring to part of the county of Roxburghshire.

72.149 matin bell the bell summoning monks to matins, an office of the Roman Catholic church originally held at midnight but sometimes recited, as here, at daybreak.

72.163   death-prayer   praying for the dead is considered an important act of charity by the Roman Catholic Church and special prayers are prescribed in favour of a person recently deceased.

73.189   nun in Melrose bower   Melrose Abbey was a Cistercian monastery rather than a nunnery.

Appendix: Scott's Endnotes from *Minstrelsy of the Scottish Border* (1802)

BATTLE OF ANCRAM MOOR

Lord Evers, and Sir Brian Latoun, during the year 1544, committed the most dreadful ravages upon the Scotish frontiers, compelling most of the inhabitants, and especially the men of Liddesdale, to take assurance under the King of England. Upon the 17th November, in that year, the sum total of their depredations stood thus in the bloody ledger of Lord Evers.

Towns, towers, barnekynes, paryshe churches, bastill houses, burned and destroyed	192
Scots slain	403
Prisoners taken	816
Nolt (cattle)	10,386
Shepe	12,492
Nags and geldings	1,296
Gayt	200
Bolls of corn	850

Insight, gear, &c. (furniture) an incalculable quantity.

Murdin's *State Papers*, Vol. I. p. 51.

The King of England had promised to these two barons a feudal grant of the country which they had thus reduced to a desert; upon hearing which, Archibald Douglas, the seventh Earl of Angus, is said to have sworn to write the deed of investiture upon their skins, with sharp pens and bloody ink, in resentment for their having defaced the tombs of his ancestors, at Melrose.—*Godscroft*. In 1545, Lord Evers and Latoun again entered Scotland, with an army consisting of 3000 mercenaries, 1500 English borderers, and 700 assured Scotishmen, chiefly Armstrongs, Turnbulls, and other broken clans. In this second incursion, the English Generals even exceeded their former cruelty. Evers burned the tower of Broomhouse, with its lady, (a noble and aged woman, says Lesly) and her whole family. The English penetrated as far as Melrose, which they had destroyed last year, and which they now again pillaged.——As they returned towards Jedburgh, they were followed by Angus, at the head of 1000 horse, who was shortly after joined by the famous Norman Lesley, with a body of Fife-men. The English, being probably unwilling to cross the Teviot, while the Scots hung upon their rear, halted upon Ancram Moor, above the village of that name; and the Scotish General was deliberating whether to advance or retire, when Sir Walter Scott[1],

---

[1]   The editor has found in no instance upon record, of this family having taken assurance with England. Hence, they usually suffered dreadfully from the English forays. In August, 1544, (the year preceding the battle) the whole lands belonging to Buccleuch, in West Teviotdale, were harried by Evers; the outworks, or barmkin, of the tower of Branxholm, burned; eight Scotts slain, thirty made prisoners, and an immense prey of horses, cattle, and sheep, carried off. The lands upon Kale water, belonging to the same

of Buccleuch, came up at full speed, with a small but chosen body of his retainers, the rest of whom were near at hand. By the advice of this experienced warrior, (to whose conduct PITSCOTTIE ascribes the success of the engagement) ANGUS withdrew from the height which he occupied, and drew up his forces behind it, upon a piece of low flat ground, called Panier-heugh, or Peniel-heugh. The spare horses, being sent to an eminence in their rear, appeared to the English to be the main body of the Scots, in the act of flight. Under this persuasion, EVERS and LATOUN hurried precipitately forwards, and, having ascended the hill which their foes had abandoned, were no less dismayed than astonished, to find the phalanx of Scotish spearmen drawn up, in firm array, upon the flat ground below. The Scots in their turn became the assailants. A heron, roused from the marshes by the tumult, soared away betwixt the encountering armies. "Oh!" exclaimed ANGUS, "that I had here my white goss-hawk, that we might all yoke at once!"—*Godscroft.* The English, breathless and fatigued, having the setting sun and wind full in their faces, were unable to withstand the resolute and desperate charge of the Scotish lances. No sooner had they begun to waver, than their own allies, the assured borderers, who had been waiting the event, threw aside their red crosses, and, joining their countrymen, made a most merciless slaughter among the English fugitives, the pursuers calling upon each other to "remember Broomhouse!"—*Lesly*, p. 478. In the battle fell Lord EVERS, and his son, together with Sir BRIAN LATOUN, and 800 Englishmen, many of whom were persons of rank. A thousand prisoners were taken. Among these was a patriotic *Alderman of London*, READ by name, who, having contumaciously refused to pay his portion of a benevolence demanded from the city by HENRY VIII. was sent by royal authority to serve against the Scots. These, at settling his ransom, he found still more exorbitant in their exactions than the monarch.—*Redpath's Border History*, p. 553. EVERS was much regretted by King HENRY, who swore to avenge his death upon ANGUS, against whom he conceived himself to have particular grounds of resentment, on account of favours received by the Earl at his hands. The answer of ANGUS was worthy of a DOUGLAS. "Is our brother-in-law offended[2]," said he, "that I, as a good Scotsman, have avenged my ravaged country, and the defaced tombs of my ancestors, upon RALPH EVERS? They were better men than he, and I was bound to do no less—and will he take my life for that? Little knows King HENRY the skirts of Kirn-table[3] I can keep myself there against all his English host."—*Godscroft.*

Such was the noted battle of Ancram Moor. The spot on which it was fought is called Lyliard's Edge, from an Amazonian Scotish woman of that name; who is reported, by tradition, to have distinguished herself in the same manner as Squire WITHERINGTON. The old people point out her monument, now broken and defaced. The inscription is said to have been legible within this century, and to have run as follows:

> Fair maiden Lylliard lies under this stane,
> Little was her stature, but great was her fame;
> Upon the English louns she laid mony thumps,
> And, when her legs were cutted off, she fought upon her stumps.
> *Vide Account of the Parish of Melrose.*

chieftain, were also plundered, and much spoil obtained; 30 SCOTTS slain, and the Moss Tower, (a fortress near Eckfer!) *smoked very sore.* Thus BUCCLEUCH had a long account to settle at Ancram Moor.—*Murdin's State Papers*, p. 45, 46.

[2] ANGUS had married the widow of JAMES IV. sister to King HENRY VIII.

[3] Kirnetable is a mountainous tract in Dumfriesshire.

It appears from a passage in STOWE, that an ancestor of Lord EVERS held also a grant of Scotish lands from an English Monarch. "I have seen," says the historian, "under the broad seale of the said King EDWARD I. a mannor, called Ketnes, in the countie of Ferfare, in Scotland, and neere the furthest part of the same nation northward, given to JOHN EURE and his heires, ancestor to the Lord EURE that now is, for his service done in these partes, with market, &c. dated at Lanercost, the 20th day of October, anno regis, 34."—*Stowe's Annals*, p. 210. This grant, like that of HENRY, must have been dangerous to the receiver.

Note 2
There is a nun in Dryburgh bower—cf. line 189.

The circumstance of the nun "who never saw the day," is not entirely imaginary. About fifty years ago, an unfortunate female wanderer took up her residence in a dark vault, among the ruins of Dryburgh abbey, which, during the day, she never quitted. When night fell, she issued from this miserable habitation, and went to the house of Mr HALLIBURTON of Newmains, or that of Mr ERSKINE of Sheffield, two gentlemen of the neighbourhood. From their charity she obtained such necessaries as she could be prevailed upon to accept. At twelve, each night, she lighted her candle, and returned to her vault; assuring her friendly neighbours, that, during her absence, her habitation was arranged by a spirit, to whom she gave the uncouth name of *Fatlips*; describing him as a little man, wearing heavy iron shoes, with which he trampled the clay floor of the vault, to dispel the damps. This circumstance caused her to be regarded, by the well informed, with compassion, as deranged in her understanding; and by the vulgar, with some degree of terror. The cause of her adopting this extraordinary mode of life she would never explain. It was, however, believed to have been occasioned by a vow, that, during the absence of a man to whom she was attached, she would never look upon the sun. Her lover never returned. He fell during the civil war of 1745–6, and she never more would behold the light of day.

These circumstances the editor gives to the public on the best authority. The vault, or rather dungeon, in which this unfortunate woman lived and died, passes still by the name of the supernatural being with which its gloom was tenanted by her disturbed imagination, and few of the neighbouring peasants dare enter it by night.

35. The Gray Brother

Textual Note
The date at which Scott composed 'The Gray Brother' is unknown, and no authorial manuscript appears to have survived: in the headnote to its first publication in the second edition of *Minstrelsy of the Scottish Border* (1803), 3.402–14, Scott says simply that this fragment was written 'several years ago'. Its style and supernatural air are close to that of his earliest original poems, such as 'The Eve of Saint John' (no. 34) and 'Glenfinlas' (no. 33), which also combine the supernaturalism of his favourite German Romanticism with Scottish subject-matter. It was subsequently reprinted in Scott's 1806 *Ballads and Lyrical Pieces* (61–72) and in the eighth edition of *The Lay of the Last Minstrel* of 1808 (315–26, clxiii–clxv), then passing through the portal of his 1820 *Poetical Works* (2.181–96) and the successive lifetime editions of his poetical works and into the Lockhart 1833–34 posthumous edition (4.218–29). There is little sign of

any authorial engagement with the text in these later reprintings, most of the variations between them being of the kind normally associated with the printer, although the change from 'on' to 'to' (line 16) in 8vo1830*PW* (3.437–50) may be authorial. In the 1806 *Ballads* 'The Gray Brother' becomes 'The Grey Brother', some presentational oddities like 'esq.' are corrected to 'Esq.', and the title of Sir James St Clair Erskine is updated to 'Earl of Rosslyn'. Naturally the 'editor' of Scott's headnote to 'The Gray Brother' in *Minstrelsy* becomes the 'author' in that of Scott's own poetry collections. In his headnote in 1821*PW* (3.440), Scott adds a passage providing a classical precedent for the presence of an unclean person inhibiting the performance of a religious duty on the authority of a correspondent, but it drops out of most subsequent editions again.

The present text follows that of the second edition of *Minstrelsy of the Scottish Border*, 3 vols (Edinburgh, 1803), 3.402–14, as best representing the culmination of Scott's original process of composition. The following emendations have been made:

74.headnote	Lasswade (1820*PW*) / Laswade
74.headnote	Abbot of Newbattle (1821*PW*) / abbot of Newbottle
74.headnote	Marquis of Lothian (1820*PW*) / marquis of Lothian
74.headnote	Life of Alexander Peden (1820*PW*) / life of Alexander Peden
74.footnote	Clerk, Esq. (*Ballads*) / Clerk, esq.
75.1	Pope (*Ballads*) / pope
75.2	Saint Peter's (1820*PW*) / saint Peter's
75.5	Pope (*Ballads*) / pope
76.39	Holy Father (*Ballads*) / holy father
78.86	Newbattle's (1821*PW*) / Newbottle's
78.88	Ladye's (*Ballads*) / ladye's
78.95	Until (*Ballads*) / Untill
79.111	Pope (*Ballads*) / pope
80.endnote 1	Sir George Clerk, Bart. (*Ballads*) / sir George Clerk, bart.
80.endnote 2 lemma	*Auchendinny's* (*Ballads*) / *Auchindinny's*
80.endnote 2	Auchendinny (*Ballads*) / Auchindinny
80.endnote 2	Esq. (*Ballads*) / esq.
80.endnote 4	Honourable (*Ballads*) / honourable
80.endnote 4	Lasswade (1821*PW*) / Laswade
80.endnote 4	Lord (*Ballads*) / lord
80.endnote 5	Sir James St Clair Erskine, Bart. (Editorial) / sir James St Clair Erskine, bart.
81.endnote 6	Earl (*Ballads*) / earl

Historical Note

Scott's poem, as his own notes clearly indicate, commemorates his youthful intimacy with the family of John Clerk of Eldin (1728–1812). A close friendship with Eldin's son William was formed by Scott when studying law at Edinburgh University, and, according to Lockhart (*Life*, 1.149–50), the father encouraged Scott's antiquarian bent and made him a welcome guest at the family home. According to the footnote to Scott's headnote John Clerk also related to Scott the legend upon which 'The Gray Brother' was based. The various localities mentioned in this ballad have associations with other friends and acquaintances of Scott's early years as an Edinburgh student, lawyer, and volunteer soldier, people duly commemorated in his annotation to it.

366 COMBINED EDITORIAL NOTES

Explanatory Notes

74.headnote Gilmerton Grange Gilmerton is a high-lying village about 6 km (3¾ miles) SE of Edinburgh and 5 km (3 miles) NW of Dalkeith. The old-fashioned mansion-house is on its south-western edge.

74.headnote Newbattle Newbattle Abbey is the chief feature of the village of Newbattle on the left side of the river South Esk, about 1.5 km (1 mile) SW of Dalkeith. It was founded as a Cistercian monastery by David I of Scotland and became one of the wealthiest medieval abbeys of the Lothians. At the Reformation it passed to the Kerr family, and Mark Kerr became Earl of Lothian in 1606. The owner at the time of writing was William John Kerr, 5th Marquess of Lothian (1737–1815).

74.headnote Life of Alexander Peden many sites in southern Scotland are marked for their association with the Scottish Presbyterian field-preacher Alexander Peden (1626?–86). After Peden's death the events of his life and his prophecies were collected up by Patrick Walker. For Scott's quotation compare the chapbook *The Life and Prophecies of the Reverend Mr Alexander Peden, Late Minister of the Gospel, at New Glenluce, in Galloway. In Two Parts* (Falkirk, 1793), 48–49 (Part II, paragraph 26). It seems likely that Scott himself has interpolated the bracketed glosses 'Peden', 'partition of the cottage' and 'went on'.

74.footnote Essay upon Naval Tactics In 1790 Clerk published the first part of *An Essay on Naval Tactics*, with three further parts published in 1797. It focused on practical tactics of fighting and was critical of the current practice of the Royal Navy.

75.2 Saint Peter's day the feast of St Peter is celebrated on 29 June. Peter was the leader of the Apostles and the popes of the Roman Catholic Church were considered to inherit his spiritual authority over their fellow-believers.

76.13 holiest word presumably referring to the point in the Mass where the bread and wine are supposedly transformed into the body and blood of Christ.

77.46 Eske's fair woods the river Esk flows through Midlothian into the Firth of Forth at Musselburgh. It is composed of the North and South Esk rivers, which come together just below Dalkeith Palace. The stretch of the North Esk that flows though Roslin Glen and Hawthornden is famous for its beautiful scenery.

77.55 banks of Till a river in Northumberland on the banks of which was fought the Battle of Flodden on 9 September 1513 between England and Scotland. James IV of Scotland and many of his nobility were killed and the Scottish army annihilated.

77.66 blast of bugle free (see also Scott's 1st endnote.) Sir George Clerk, 6th Baronet of Penicuik (1787–1867) was the head of the family to which Scott's friends, the Clerks of Eldin belonged.

77.67 Auchendinny's (see also Scott's 2nd endnote.) Auchendinny is a village on the boundary of Lasswade and Glencorse parishes, near where Glencorse Burn flows into the North Esk river. Auchendinny House, to the S of the village, was the home of the Scottish novelist Henry Mackenzie (1745–1831).

77.68 haunted Woodhouselee (see also Scott's 3rd endnote.) Woodhouselee is an irregular mansion of various dates on the eastern slope of the Pentland Hills in Glencorse parish, about 11 km (7 miles) S of Edinburgh and 5 km (3 miles) N of Penicuik. The estate was bought in 1748 by the lawyer and historian William Tytler (1711–92) and inherited by his son, the historian

Alexander Fraser Tytler, Lord Woodhouselee (1747–1813), with whose family Scott was intimate.

77.69 Melville's beechy grove (see also Scott's 4th endnote.) Melville Castle is on the N bank of the North Esk, about 1.5 km (1 mile) N of Lasswade village. It was rebuilt between 1786 and 1798 to a design by James Playfair (1755–94) and famous for its beech trees and pleasure-grounds. It was owned by Scott's patron, the influential Scottish politician and statesman Henry Dundas (1742–1811), who was created Viscount Melville in 1802. His eldest son, Robert Dundas (1771–1851), was Colonel of the Midlothian Cavalry Volunteers as well as MP for Midlothian, and had been a companion of Scott's since his time at Edinburgh High School.

77.70 Roslin's rocky glen (see also Scott's 5th endnote.) Situated between Penicuik and Lasswade on the banks of the North Esk, Roslin is famous for its ruined castle and the collegiate church of St Michael with its profuse sculptures and carvings.

77.71 Dalkeith (see also Scott's 6th endnote.) Dalkeith is a town 10 km (6 miles) SE of Edinburgh on a narrow wedge of land between the North Esk and South Esk rivers, and is the site of Dalkeith Palace. James Douglas, 4th Earl of Morton (c. 1516–81) built the Palace of Dalkeith around 1575. He was one of the original Lords of Congregation and Regent of Scotland for James VI after the assassination of the Earl of Moray until executed for involvement in the murder of Darnley. Dalkeith Palace passed from the Earls of Morton to the Buccleuch family in the mid-16th century, and was largely rebuilt by Anne, Duchess of Monmouth and Buccleuch (1651–1732). At the time 'The Gray Brother' was written it was owned by Scott's patron, Henry, 3rd Duke of Buccleuch (1746–1812), and gave the title of Earl of Dalkeith to the Duke's eldest son, Scott's friend, Charles Scott (1772–1819), subsequently 4th Duke of Buccleuch.

77.72 classic Hawthornden (see also Scott's 7th endnote.) Hawthornden Castle is a three-storey 17th-century mansion formed around a ruined 15th-century tower situated on the edge of a deep gorge by the North Esk river. It was classic as the home of the poet William Drummond (1585–1649). The English poet and dramatist Ben Jonson (1572–1637) visited him there for almost three weeks in the winter of 1618–19 and Drummond recorded their conversations. James Boswell (1740–95) and Samuel Johnson (1709–84) revisited the spot of this meeting during their 1773 tour of Scotland. For the quotation in Scott's endnote see William Collins 'An Ode on the Popular Superstitions of the Highlands of Scotland' (line 212): *Thomas Gray and William Collins: Poetical Works*, ed. Roger Lonsdale (Oxford, 1977), 173, which, however, omits the word 'social'.

78.82 Carnethy's head Carnethy is one of the Pentland Hills on the NE border of Penicuik parish, with a cairn at its top. It is about 576 m above sea level.

78.88 Our Ladye's evening song Mary, the mother of Jesus, was an important figure of devotion in the medieval Roman Catholic Church, which positioned her as having more power than other saints if less than Christ himself. Several feast days were held in honour of her: the Purification (2 February); the Annunciation (25 March); the Visitation (2 July); the Nativity (8 September); and the Conception (8 December). Scott's reference may indicate special commemoration of one of these days, or simply a customary evening recital of the Ave Maria or prayer beginning 'Hail, Mary'.

78.107 shrine of St James the divine the relics of James, one of the three Apostles who witnessed the Transfiguration and Christ's agony in the Garden at Gethsemane, were supposed to be held at Santiago di Compostella in Galicia, Spain. The church was a major centre of international pilgrimage during the Middle Ages, pilgrims being identifiable by a hat with a scallop-shell.

78.108 St John of Beverly John of Beverley, Bishop of York (d. 721) founded a monastery at Beverley in Yorkshire, where he died. King Henry V of England (1386–1422) partly ascribed his victory at the Battle of Agincourt to the intercession of this saint.

79.119 keys of earth and heav'n Jesus declared to Peter, punning upon the meaning of his name, rock, that 'upon this rock I will build my church', and also that he would give him 'the keys of the kingdom of heaven' (Matthew 16.18–19). St Peter is often portrayed holding keys.

36. At Flodden

Textual Note
Unpublished during the author's lifetime, this fragment first appeared, untitled, in Lockhart's *Life*, as an example of lines composed during an 'experimental period' early in Scott's poetic career (1.314). Lockhart attributes it, with other similar items, to 1799, though no manuscript has apparently survived to help to confirm his dating. Clearly the poem is an early effort, however, and was probably written sometime after Scott's first visit to the site of the Battle of Flodden in the summer of 1791 (see Historical Note). It was subsequently included in Cadell's one-volume edition of Scott's poetical works of 1841 as 'Cheviot' (627) and by J. Logie Robertson in *The Poetical Works of Sir Walter Scott* (London, 1904), 699, as 'At Flodden'.

The present text follows that in Lockhart's *Life*, 1.314. Lockhart's quotation marks have been removed, as have the asterisks which precede and follow it there to indicate that the poem is merely a fragment. Otherwise the poem is without emendation. Logie Robertson's title of 'At Flodden', which suggests the poem's links with the later achievement of *Marmion* (1808), has been adopted here.

Historical Note
As Scott recounted in a letter to his friend William Clerk of 26 August 1791 he accompanied his uncle, Robert Scott (1739–1804), that month to Wooler in Northumberland, where they lodged in a farm-house 'in the very centre of the Cheviot hills, in one of the wildest and most romantic situations' (*Letters*, 1.18–20). Excited by his proximity to the scene of many historic battles, Scott's imagination was particularly engaged by that of Flodden fought against the English in 1513: he asked Clerk to suppose the Scottish army of James IV 'posted upon the face of a hill, and secured by high grounds projecting on each flank, with the river Till in front, a deep and still river, winding through a very extensive valley called Milfield Plain', prior to its rashly abandoning this high ground for the engagement itself (1.19). The mention of snow in the poem, on the other hand, may imply that Scott had in mind some other visit, not made in the height of summer, when writing.

Explanatory Notes
82.1 Cheviot's crest Cheviot, at 815 m, is the highest summit in the range of the Cheviot hills extending along the English Border with Scotland, and is itself located in England but only 2 km (1¼ miles) from the Scottish Border.

82.3 scaurs precipices, or steep hills from which the soil has been washed away.
82.6 Bowmont's tide Bowmont Water rises in the Cheviot Hills and flows on the Scottish side of the Border by Kirk Yetholm in NE Roxburghshire before passing into England and joining the River Glen, an 11 km (7 mile) tributary of the River Till in Northumberland.
82.9 Till's sullen bed in contrast to the River Tweed, which it eventually joins near Berwick-upon-Tweed, the Till is a slow-flowing river. Rising in the Cheviot hills, it is the only tributary of the Tweed to flow entirely through England.
82.10 fatal plain the Battle of Flodden, fought on 9 September 1513 between the forces of James IV of Scotland (1473–1513) and those of Henry VIII of England (1491–1547), took place on high ground west of the River Till near Branxton in Northumberland. King James was killed along with many of the Scottish nobility and his army effectively wiped out. The battle forms the climax of Scott's subsequent poem *Marmion; A Tale of Flodden Field* (1808).
82.14 old Ocean's Oceanus is the oldest of the Titans in Greek mythology, the personification of the sea.
82.16 Cutsfeld's wold not identified.

37. The Fire-King

Textual Note
Writing to Archibald Constable on 22 October 1824, Scott recalled the occasion on which he wrote 'The Fire-King' many years previously, 'in one evening after dinner with Heber & Leyden sitting beside me' (*Letters*, 8.409), Richard Heber being in Edinburgh in August 1799. It was written specifically for the *Tales of Wonder* of Matthew Gregory Lewis (1775–1818), and probably sent around the turn of the year, since Lewis's letter to Scott of 3 February 1800 (8vo1830*PW*, 3.cii–cviii) thanks him for the ballad. A manuscript of 'The Fire-King' survives in Scott's hand (BL, Add. MS 39,667, ff. 1–6), undated but presented like many of his early poetry manuscripts as a booklet with an outside cover. It consists of six leaves of unwatermarked paper, each measuring approx. 22.9 x 17.8 cm, the first leaf acting as a title-page complete with motto, in this case from Butler's *Hudibras*: '—"Agrippa kept a Devils Bird / Shut in the Pommel of his Sword"—'. Although bearing text on both rectos and versos, this manuscript is neatly written with minimal punctuation but also minimal alteration. It appears to be a fair-copy manuscript, and has the end-inscription 'Quod Le Seneschal de la Tour / Smaylhome', a cognomen used by Scott in other poems of this time (see Textual Note to no. 34, 'The Eve of Saint John'), and one which derives from his family links to Smailholm Tower.
    Another manuscript, not in Scott's own hand, forms part of a notebook containing transcriptions of Scott's early poems by the Scottish novelist Henry Mackenzie (1745–1831), in NLS, MS 2536, ff. 31–33. While the text of the poem here is very close to that of Scott's own fair-copy manuscript, there are a few variations in wording that suggest this may represent an earlier version of the poem. Line 10, for instance, opens 'What news dost thou bring', and line 81 has 'gateway' rather than 'Arch way'. Quite possibly, however, Scott was simply trying out variations in different early drafts, as he did in composing other poems at this time.
    'The Fire-King' was first published in London in January 1801 in Lewis's *Tales of Wonder* (1.62–69), in a version which differs significantly from that of

Scott's own fair-copy manuscript. It seems probable that Lewis was responsible for a number of the changes, largely designed to improve the scansion and rhyme of the verses, although it is possible that Scott himself made substantial revisions before sending his poem to Lewis in London. The motto was changed to one from an unspecified Eastern Tale, and a headnote added, presumably by Lewis, to indicate that the author was also the translator of *Götz von Berlichingen* and to draw the reader's attention to other poems by Scott in the collection. In general Scott respected Lewis's poetic judgement (see Textual Note to no. 21, 'William and Helen'), and the flow of the poem was arguably improved, for instance, by the substitution of 'this chain be thy fee' for 'our Lady thee see' (line 19), and 'this thou shalt first do' for 'this is the first thing' (line 44). Scott's manuscript refers in lines 123–24 to the 'foul pinions' of 'a Dæmon', which was perhaps too specific to accord with the preceding description of the Fire-King as 'undistinguish'd in form' in line 89: the printed text's 'lightning's red wing' is arguably an improvement. Some ancient-seeming forms such as 'Ladie' and 'groweth' have also been lost in the printed text, perhaps because Lewis objected to the Fire-King's having been removed by Scott from his native land, Denmark, to Palestine in the time of the Crusades (see Historical Note).

Scott must have accepted most of these alterations to his text, for when 'The Fire-King' was reprinted in his *Ballads and Lyrical Pieces* of 1806 (134–42) only one manuscript reading was reinstated: 'Count Albert is prisoner' was preferred to 'Count Albert is taken' in line 32. The odd-seeming indentation of alternate lines in stanza 17 of the poem in Lewis's collection was eliminated in *Ballads*, and lines 17–18 were altered to read 'A fair chain of gold 'mid her ringlets there hung; / O'er the palmer's grey locks the fair chain has she flung'. Other differences are changes of the kind normally associated with the printer. Scott also provided a new headnote in 1806, both explaining the original context of the *Tales of Wonder* and reinforcing the poem's historical background of the Crusades in the Holy Land.

'The Fire-King' was afterwards included in the eighth edition of *The Lay of the Last Minstrel* of 1808 (207–16) and in the subsequent lifetime editions of Scott's *Poetical Works* from 1820 (2.197–206) onwards as well as in the Lockhart 1833–34 posthumous edition (6.319–26), but without any indication of further authorial involvement in the text.

The present text follows that of *Tales of Wonder*, 2 vols (London, 1801), 1.62–69, as representing the socialised text at the culmination of Scott's initial creative process. Lewis's headnote relating specifically to the context of that volume has been omitted, the peculiar indentations in stanza 17 removed, and the following emendations made:

84.32   prisoner (BL MS) / taken
87.127 stripling (*Ballads*) / strippling
87.146 Red-cross (Editorial) / Red-Cross

Historical Note
Lewis planned to include a group of four poems in his *Tales of Wonder*, one for each of his four elemental spirits (for details see the Historical Note to no. 30, 'The Erl-King'). Many years later Scott recalled that Lewis 'was very fond of his idea of four elementary kings' and had 'prevailed on me to supply a Fire King' (8vo1830*PW*, 3.cvi).

Although Lewis was pleased with Scott's contribution, he seems to have felt that its historical setting was a departure from his own northern European legendary conception. In his letter of 3 February 1800 he stated:

It is also objected to, his being removed from his native land, Denmark, to Palestine; and that the office assigned to him in your Ballad has nothing peculiar to the 'Fire King,' but would have suited Arimanzes, Beelzebub, or any other evil spirit as well. (8vo1830*PW*, 3.cviii)

Scott's new headnote when the ballad was included in his own *Ballads* of 1806 reinforces this historical context:

His own ballad was written at the request of Mr Lewis, to be inserted in his "*Tales of Wonder.*" It is the third in a series of four ballads, on the subject of Elementary Spirits. The story is, however, partly historical; for it is recorded, that, during the struggles of the Latin kingdom of Jerusalem, a knight-templar, called Saint-Alban, deserted to the Saracens, and defeated the Christians in many combats, till he was finally routed and slain, in a conflict with King Baldwin, under the walls of Jerusalem. (134)

Scott's note points to the historical figure of Robert of St Albans (d. 1187), an English Knight Templar who converted to Islam in 1185, led an army for Saladin against the Crusaders in Jerusalem, and eventually married Saladin's young relative, in some accounts his niece.

Explanatory Notes
83.8   shell on his hat   pilgrims used to wear cockle-shells or scallop shells on their hats, the symbol of St James of Compostela in Spain.
83.11   Gallilee's strand   Galilee is the northern part of Palestine, the Sea of Galilee being a heart-shaped expanse of water into which the River Jordan flows. The Sea is roughly 19 km (12 miles) long and 11 km (7 miles) wide at its maximum, surrounded by mountains on both sides and with a narrow, shorelike plain where several important towns are located.
83.14   Gilead   a mountainous region E of the River Jordan.
83.14   Nablous   or Nablus, a city in the northern West Bank about 48 km (30 miles) N of Jerusalem.
83.14   Ramah   a Biblical place-name, probably the modern Er-Ram, about 6.5 km (4 miles) N of Jerusalem.
83.15   Mount Libanon   a mountainous region extending along the entire modern country of Lebanon, parallel to the Mediterranean coast. Jerusalem is S of Lebanon.
83.23   Crescent ... Red-cross   the crescent is the symbol of Islam, as the cross is of Christianity. Crusaders in the First Crusade (1096–99) wore red crosses sewn on their clothing, and although the colour changed subsequently English crusaders continued to prefer the red cross of their national saint, St George.
84.30   levin-scorch'd   having been struck by lightning.
84.36   Soldanrie's   the rule of the great Muslim powers of the Middle Ages.
84.40   Soldan's fair daughter   if Count Albert can be identified with Robert of St Albans, who died in 1187, then the Sultan in question would be Saladin, or Salah-al-Din (1137/38–1193), who became Sultan of Egypt in 1169, and later established a unified Muslim state along the E coast of Palestine. He captured Jerusalem from the Crusaders in 1187.
84.46   Curdmans   Saladin himself was a Kurd.
84.50   Frank   a name given in the Middle East to a person from a Western nation.
84.52   Zulema's sake   Zulema, or Selima, is a recognised female Arabic name.

84.55   green caftan, and turban   a caftan is an eastern garment consisting of a full-length tunic girdled at the waist. To take the turban is to convert to Islam. A green turban is mentioned as a distinguishing mark of an emir in Ch. 50 of Edward Gibbon's *The History of the Decline and Fall of the Roman Empire* (1776–88).

85.64   rosary beads   a string of beads in a pattern designed to assist Roman Catholics in keeping count of the recitation of the prayers in the rosary, consisting of 15 sets of ten small beads for *Aves* each preceded by a large bead for a *Pater* and followed by a large bead for a *Gloria*.

86.90   breath ... lightning ... voice ... storm   perhaps an allusion to I Kings 19.11–12, where Elijah is waiting to hear the word of God. A strong wind comes, then an earthquake and then a fire, but God's word is not in these but in the 'still small voice' that succeeds them.

86.93   faulchion blue-glimmer'd   a *faulchion* is a broad sword more or less curved with the edge on the convex side. When a light burns blue, according to popular superstition, this indicates that a spirit is present.

86.101   Paynim   a pagan, the recognised chivalric term for a Muslim.

86.106   sands of Samaar   an area of sand and dunes now in Southern Israel, about 29 km (18 miles) N of Eilat.

86.107   Knights of the Temple   the Knights Templar, founded in 1118, were an armed force of men who had taken monastic orders and were dedicated to the protection of pilgrims in the Holy Land. The name comes from their original residence in the precincts of Solomon's Temple in Jerusalem.

86.107   Knights of Saint John   a military order of monks called the Knights of St John of Jerusalem, founded in 1048 and also known as the Knights Hospitallers, since their duty was to provide lodging and entertainment for pilgrims in the Holy Land.

86.108   Salem's   Salem is Jerusalem. As a result of the First Crusade a European kingdom was founded in 1099, centred on Jerusalem with control of the Jordan valley and a considerable extent of the Mediterranean coast, but most of it (including Jerusalem itself) fell to Saladin in 1187.

86.108   King Baldwin   Scott probably has in mind Baldwin IV (1161–85), who was King of Jerusalem from 1174 until his death, when his nephew, a young child, succeeded as Baldwin V. The child-king died the following year, and in 1187 Guy de Lusignan was King of Jerusalem.

86.114   fence   guard, defence, bulwark.

87.120   *Bonne grace, notre Dame*   *French* Good grace, our Lady.

87.127   casque   armour to cover the head, a helmet.

87.131   Cedron   or Kidron, is the brook flowing through the ravine below the eastern wall of Jerusalem.

87.132   Saracen   that of an Arab, especially a Muslim.

87.133   Ishmaelites   Arabs are thought to be the descendants of Ishmael, Abraham's son by Hagar. Mother and son were driven away into the desert when Abraham's wife Sarah gave birth to Isaac: see Genesis 21.9–21.

87.134   saltier   an archaic spelling of saltire, a cross formed by a bend and a bend sinister crossing one another, like the St Andrews cross that is, among other things, the emblem of Scotland.

87.134   crossletted shield   a shield bearing a cross.

87.136   Bethsaida's fountains   the pool of Bethsaida, or Bethesda, at Jerusalem was resorted to for its healing powers and is the scene of one of the miracles of Jesus (see John 5.2–9).

87.136   Naphthali's head   territory W of the Sea of Galilee and the upper Jordan, associated with the settlement of the tribe of Israel deriving from Naphtali, Jacob's son by the maid Bilhah.

38.   Bothwell's Sisters Three

Textual Note
The incomplete draft manuscript of this poem was discovered by Lockhart after Scott's death among his papers and is now located in NLS, MS 877, ff. 47–50. Written in Scott's earlier hand it consists of four conjugate leaves, each measuring approx. 19.5 x 16 cm and with a watermark of a crest with Britannia. The text, which is untitled, is mainly on the rectos of ff. 47 and 48, with the final two lines only on the recto of f. 49. The first three stanzas contain no revisions, but the density of these increases as the poem proceeds, up to the stuttering and incomplete final stanza. In line 13 'copse wood' is made plural by the addition of a letter 's' in darker ink, while 'with' in line 18, although necessary for the scansion of the line, has been struck out with a horizontal line, these possibly indicating subsequent revision.

Lockhart published an edited version from this manuscript in his biography of Scott (*Life*, 1.305–06), without a title preceding the text (though the running-head is 'BOTHWELL CASTLE—1799', which might be interpreted as referring either to Scott's visit to the castle or a potential title for the poem), adding punctuation and smoothing irregularities of spelling and presentation, but also making a number of verbal alterations, particularly in the poem's final lines. For instance, lines 37–38 in Lockhart read 'And rising at the bugle blast / That mark'd the Scottish foe'. The word 'Scottish' here restores a deletion in the manuscript, but 'rising' has no precedent. The final portion of the manuscript (from line 29) is also reproduced as a facsimile sample of Scott's handwriting in 1799 at the beginning of the first volume of Lockhart's work.

The poem, left unfinished by Scott, did not appear in any of the collected lifetime editions, nor did Lockhart include it in the posthumous collected edition of 1833–34. J. Logie Robertson, however, included a text deriving from Lockhart's biography with the title 'Bothwell's Sisters Three. A Fragment' in his edition of *The Poetical Works of Sir Walter Scott* (London, 1904), 695–96.

The present text follows that of Scott's manuscript in NLS, MS 877, ff. 47–50. In addition to the following listed emendations ampersands have been routinely expanded to 'and', verb forms ending with 'd' to 'ed', and routine apostrophes have been introduced as required. Full stops have also been added at the end of stanzas in lines 20, 28, and 32. Scott's original poem, as previously stated, is untitled, but as lines 27–28 indicate that the tale which is to follow the initial scene-setting before the rule is to be 'the tale ... / Of Bothwell's sisters three', the title used by Logie Robertson has been adopted. The following emendations have also been made:

88.7   o'er (Editorial) / oer
88.7   flood (Editorial) / flodd
88.13   where the copse woods open (MS derived: <the> ↑where↓ copse woods open<ingd>) / where copse wood open
        The deleted 'the' is necessary for scansion, as is the plural of 'woods' to agree with the verb; indeed an 's' has probably been added to the manuscript subsequently.
88.16   O'erlook (Editorial) / Oerlook

88.18   mingled with the (MS mingled <with> the) / mingled the
The deletion of 'with' in the MS is an error, probably made subsequent
to drafting.
88.26   Flung (Editorial) / flung
89.30   bugle (Editorial) / Bugle
89.31   bull (Editorial) / Bull
89.33   St. George's cross o'er (Editorial) / S$^{t.}$ Georges cross oer
89.37   bugle (Editorial) / Bugle
89.41   Aymer (Editorial) / Aymar

Historical Note
Lockhart attributes this unfinished poem to 1799, and it probably does relate
to Scott's visit to Bothwell Castle on the River Clyde in Lanarkshire that year,
although the actual date of composition is uncertain. Scott's hostess at the
modern Bothwell Castle (close to the ruined medieval building), Lady Douglas,
the former Lady Frances Scott (1750–1817), was the sister of Scott's patron,
Henry, 3rd Duke of Buccleuch (1746–1812). She was also a friend of Lady
Anne Hamilton (1766–1846) to whom Scott's poem of 'Cadyow Castle' (see
no. 46) is addressed, Cadzow being about 6 km (3¾ miles) away from Bothwell
Castle itself. Both 'Bothwell's Sisters Three' and 'Cadyow Castle' mention the
wild cattle of Cadzow, and Lady Douglas requested a copy of the manuscript
of 'Cadyow Castle' that Scott had given to Lady Anne (see Textual Note to
no. 46). The Three Sisters of the tale are large isolated stones on the opposite
bank of the Clyde to Bothwell Castle and close to the ruins of Blantyre Priory,
and it seems not unlikely that Scott attempted to write a poem about them
at the request of Lady Douglas, who had made a similar request to Matthew
Gregory Lewis (1775–1818) when he had visited Bothwell. Lewis notes in the
'Advertisement' prefaced to his poem 'Oberon's Henchman; or, The Legend of
the Three Sisters' that during his stay a lady, curious as to 'the cause of their
bearing the above appellation', requested him to account for it in verse and that
the poem, addressed to Lady Douglas, was his response: see *Romantic Tales*,
4 vols (London, 1808), 3.219. Although Lewis's poem was only published in
1808 it was circulating in manuscript much earlier: Scott wrote to Lady Anne
Hamilton on 10 August 1802, 'you do not know how beautiful a poem Mr.
Lewis has written upon Bothwell Castle at Lady Douglas request. In return
for Cadzow, pray ask for the *Three Sisters* which Lewis shewed me in Edinr'
(*Letters*, 1.151). Possibly it was Lewis's performance that prevented Scott from
completing his own legendary story in verse accounting for the stones' name of
the Three Sisters, a story which would have turned to Scottish history rather
than to ghosts for an explanation.

Explanatory Notes
88.3   **Pembroke's ruined towers**   Bothwell Castle, termed Pembroke's
because of its historic associations with Aymer de Valence, 11th Earl of
Pembroke (see note to 89.41–42 below).
88.12   **Blantyre's bowers of green**   in his account of Bothwell Castle in
The Border Antiquities of England and Scotland, 2 vols (London, 1814), Scott
states that the 'craig of Blantyre, with the ruins of the priory upon the top of it,
being immediately opposite, has a striking effect' (1.71). The priory, founded
sometime before 1296, was home to a community of Augustinian canons.
Traces of the orchards by which it was once surrounded may still be found.
88.15   **Bothwell's towers in ruin piled**   Bothwell Castle, one of Scotland's
most spectacular medieval buildings, is located about 16 km (10 miles) SE of

Glasgow by a bend in the river Clyde. The cylindrical keep was built in the 13th century, but further construction interrupted by the Scottish Wars of Independence fought between England and Scotland in the late 13th and early 14th centuries. The castle was rebuilt and enlarged in the 15th century: the present ruin is rectangular with a courtyard surrounded by curtain walls, with its ancient keep surviving and towers at the SE and SW corners. The forces of Edward I of England (1239–1307) invaded Scotland at the start of the Wars of Independence and seized Bothwell Castle, where the English garrison was besieged by the Scots for 14 months in 1298–99 before capitulating. Edward I captured it again in 1301, when it became the headquarters of Aymer de Valence (see note to 89.41–42 below). After the Battle of Bannockburn in 1314 Bothwell Castle was surrendered to the Scots.

88.19–20   Bothwell's banks ... bonny Jean   Bothwell Castle is situated on a high bank overlooking the River Clyde in a gorge below. Scott probably alludes to John Pinkerton's song 'Bothwell Bank', first published in his *Select Scotish Ballads*, 2 vols (London, 1783), 2.131–32. This is the lament of an unnamed Scottish girl for her dead lover. There may also perhaps be a distant allusion in the name Jean (although one of the commonest Scottish female forenames) to Jean Gordon, Countess of Bothwell (1546–1629), divorced by her husband so that he could marry Mary, Queen of Scots, even though she appears to have had no personal connection with Bothwell Castle.

88.28   Bothwell's sisters three   three large isolated stones on the opposite side of the Clyde to Bothwell Castle. The landscape artist Hugh William Williams (1773–1829) had made a water-colour drawing of the stones, now in the Tate (T09838), around 1798.

89.29   Wight Wallace   *wight*, as an epithet, means courageous or valiant, and was commonly applied to Sir William Wallace (d. 1305), hero of the Scottish Wars of Independence, who was captured in early August 1305, taken to London and executed there. The expression features in the abridgement and modernisation by William Hamilton of Gilbertfield (*c.* 1665–1751) of the epic poem on Wallace's life by Blind Hary (b. *c.* 1440, d. in or after 1492).

89.29   Dechmount   Dechmont Hill is on the SW border of Cambuslang parish in Lanarkshire, about 9 km (5½ miles) S of Glasgow. It is 183 m above sea level with a magnificent view of the surrounding countryside.

89.31   wild bull in Cadzow wood   a herd of Scottish wild cattle was kept at Cadzow, about 6 km (3¾ miles) from Bothwell Castle (see Scott's headnote to no. 46, 'Cadyow Castle'). The name is generally spelled 'Cadzow' but pronounced 'Cadyow', as in the title of Scott's poem.

89.33   St. George's cross   the English flag. St George is the patron saint of England, and his cross is red on a white background.

89.40   Norman bow   England had been conquered by forces belonging to the Duke of Normandy at the Battle of Hastings in 1066. The depiction of the battle in the Bayeux Tapestry shows the Norman archers playing an important part in the battle, though they appear to be shooting bows somewhat shorter than the English longbow, the string of their bows being drawn back only to the body rather than to the ear.

89.41–42   Sir Aymer ... Pembroke's Earl   Aymer de Valence, 11th Earl of Pembroke (d. 1324), was a close relation of King Edward I of England. He fought on the victorious English side in the Scottish war at the Battle of Falkirk in 1298. In April 1306 he was appointed English captain of the north after the killing of John Comyn, who was his brother-in-law, by Robert Bruce. He defeated Bruce at Methven in June 1306 but was then defeated by him at

Loudon Hill in May 1307. In August that year he was appointed Keeper of Scotland by the new English king, Edward II (1284–1327).

39. Verses to Lady Charlotte Campbell

Textual Note
What probably represents the first draft of this poem is found in Scott's commonplace book ('Adversaria') in the Abbotsford Library, notable in its earlier parts for the inclusion of a number of poems apparently relating to Williamina Belsches (for more general information on this book, and Scott's relationship with Williamina, see Notes to no. 16, 'To a Lady'). Untitled, it is written there in Scott's hand on two pasted-on leaves, covering pp. 43–44, the first measuring approx. 12.5 x 18.5 cm, and the second approx. 10 x 18.5 cm. A clear sign of Scott being actively engaged in composition is apparent in his deletion of 'A high-sould Chief renownd' in line 3 in favour of 'The high minded famed', in the process of which he seems to have accidentally failed to retain 'Chief' for his replacement. Another, evidently later, autograph manuscript version, with stanza numbering again from 2–4, survives in the Fales Library, New York University (MS 001, Box 153, Folder 32). Comprising two conjugate leaves, each measuring approx. 22.9 x 18.8 cm and watermarked 'J WHATMAN / 1794', this is addressed on the verso of the second leaf to 'Right Honble / Lady Charlotte Campbell'. The text, which is written on the recto of the first leaf only, is without alteration and subscribed 'Castle Street / 1 Novr 1799'. One noticeable feature here is the full integration of the 'Adversaria' commonplace book version's attempted change at line 3, which now reads 'The Chief high-minded, famed in Homers lays'. There are also two verbal changes in the final stanza, with the commonplace book's 'rude lays' now appearing as 'rude verse' (line 14), and 'beauteous brow' becoming 'lovely brow' in the following line.

The poem first appeared in print in the *New Monthly Magazine* for April 1837 (49.468), the same journal having earlier in the year featured a 'Memoir' of Lady Charlotte Campbell (by then Bury) along with an engraved portrait (76–78). This magazine version, which includes the same end-dating and is evidently based on the Fales text, supplies a heading for the first time in 'Verses / Addressed by Sir Walter Scott to Lady Charlotte Bury, / When Lady Charlotte Campbell, / On her giving Sir Walter a small volume of her early Poems'. A contemporary transcript in an unknown hand is also held by the Wordsworth Trust, Grasmere (WLMS A/ Scott, Walter, Sir/ 6), with an extended heading reading 'Lines sent to Lady Charlotte Campbell with a Manuscript Copy of the Author's Poem she having a few days before presented him with a small printed Collection of her own Poetry'. Accompanying this is a note by Gordon Graham Wordsworth, the poet's grandson, stating: 'This poem addressed by Sir Walter Scott to Lady Charlotte Campbell I have not succeeded in finding among his published writings'. This item is indeed missing from all the lifetime collected editions of Scott's poetry as well as the Lockhart 1833–34 posthumous edition.

The present text is based on the autograph manuscript in the Fales Library, New York University (MS 001, Box 153, Folder 32), with a title adapted and truncated from the *New Monthly Magazine* (see above). The following emendations have been made:

89.2   Friendship (Editorial) / Freindship
89.3   Homer's lays, (Editorial) / Homers lays
89.4   gold. (Editorial) / gold

89.6   hero's (Editorial) / heroes
90.16   Druid's (Editorial) / Druids
90.16   Mistletoe (Editorial) / Misletoe

Historical Note
The presence of this item in the Abbotsford commonplace book ('Adversaria'), at a relatively early point, opens up the possibility that it originally formed part of the body of verse addressed by Scott to Williamina Belsches. In particular, in its stress on the riches to be found in ancient poetry, there appears to be a strong affinity to 'To a Lady' (no. 16), apparently one of the earliest Williamina-related pieces. The apportioning of the classical role to the addressee, with Scott adopting the rougher mantle of the Scottish bard, on the other hand might seem more fitting to the circumstances of Lady Charlotte Susan Maria Campbell (1775–1861), whose *Poems on Several Occasions*, mostly in a romantic lyrical style, was published anonymously (as 'By A Lady') in 1797. The youngest child of John Campbell, 5th Duke of Argyll, and the celebrated beauty and hostess Elizabeth Gunning, Lady Charlotte was active in Whig literary circles, and according to Lockhart (*Life*, 1.292) it was at one of her Edinburgh parties in 1798 that Scott first met Matthew Gregory ('Monk') Lewis (1775–1818), then on the look-out for contributions to his *Tales of Wonder* (1801). Scott's subscribing of his verses to Lady Charlotte as from 'Castle Street / 1 Nov.ʳ 1799' also points to a new phase in his own domestic circumstances, after marriage to Charlotte Carpenter late in 1797, the couple setting up home at 19 Castle Street, Edinburgh, in the following year.

Explanatory Notes
89.1   Ilium's   *Ilium* is the Latin name for ancient Troy.
89.3   in Homer's lays   the incident referred to occurs in Homer's *Iliad*, 6.119–211, and involves an exchange between the Greek hero Diomedes and Glaucus, a captain of the Lycian army, allied to the Trojans. Facing each other in battle, Diomedes places a spear in the ground and tells how his ancestors were friends with Glaucus's. As a sign of friendship Diomedes takes off his bronze armour worth nine oxen, and Glaucus, his wits momentarily suspended by Zeus, give Diomedes his golden armour worth 100 oxen.
89.6   Lycian hero's   Glaucus (see previous note).
90.15   Classic *Laurel*   in Greek mythology Apollo, the god of music and poetry, is depicted as wearing a laurel wreath (made from branches and leaves of the bay laurel) on his head. The term survives in the title 'Poet Laureate [i.e. crowned with laurels]'.
90.16   Druid's "magic Mistletoe"   the Druids were supposedly magician-priests of the Celtic tribes in ancient Britain, for whom mistletoe (a parasite growing on oak trees) was a sacred plant.

40.   The Minstrel's Pipe

Textual Note
This verse epistle was first published in Lady Charlotte Bury's *Diary Illustrative of the Times of George the Fourth*, 4 vols (London, 1838–39), 3.292–94, where it is presented as having been sent by the novelist Susan Ferrier (1782–1854) along with a letter to Lady Charlotte positioned as belonging to late 1817. The full title given here is: 'The Minstrel's Pipe, by Sir Walter Scott. / Written on the Occasion of Colonel —— giving him a Pitch Pipe'. According to Ferrier's letter,

the verses had come to her directly from Scott: 'A few evenings ago he gave me
some couplets ... which I transcribe for your perusal, feeling certain that the
slightest production of his muse must give every sensible and feeling mind infi-
nite pleasure' (291). (Since Ferrier in the same letter refers to 'Sir Walter Scott',
and acknowledges his support of her fiction, it is more likely that her letter was
written no sooner than 1819/20, and almost certainly after Scott's commenda-
tion of her as the anonymous author of *Marriage* (1818) at the end of the third
series of his *Tales of my Landlord* (1819).) No original manuscript of Ferrier's
letter or the attached verses has been located. The verses were subsequently
printed from Bury's *Diary* in Grierson's edition of Scott's *Letters* (5.20–21),
where a footnote comments that 'Although transcribed by Miss Ferrier in 1817,
the verses were written before 1800, and I think the colonel referred to was
Colonel John Campbell, Lady Charlotte Bury's first husband, who died in 1800
[*sic*]' (20n). Corson remarks in turn that the piece 'if included at all, should have
been printed in Vol. 1 under 1799' (*N&I*, 142, note to 5.20 (a)). The poem did
not appear in any lifetime collection of Scott's poetry, nor in the posthumous
Lockhart edition of 1833–34; and no subsequent printing has been discovered
other than in the sources mentioned above.

    The present text follows that in Lady Charlotte Bury's *Diary Illustrative of
the Times of George the Fourth*, 4 vols (London, 1838–39), 3.292–94, preserving
the paragraph space within lines 29–44 which is absent in the printing in *Letters*,
5.20–21. The title has been truncated editorially, partly in view of the appar-
ent inappropriateness of the term 'pitch pipe' (a tuning instrument, as used by
choirmasters to give notes to their singers) to a poem about smoking tobacco.
There are no other emendations.

Historical Note
As the footnote in Grierson's edition of the *Letters* (see above) suggests,
the original recipient of this verse epistle was almost certainly Colonel John
Campbell (*c.* 1770–1809), who, after a career in the 3rd Foot Guards, left the
army in about 1799 before becoming a Colonel of the Argyll Militia. In 1796 he
had married Lady Charlotte Susan Maria Campbell, later Bury (1775–1861),
the second daughter of the 5th Duke of Argyll, noted for her beauty, and a
celebrated hostess in Edinburgh during the early years of their marriage. It
was at one of her entertainments, according to Lockhart, that in the summer of
1798 Scott first met Matthew Gregory Lewis (1775–1818) near the start of their
literary collaboration (see *Life*, 1.292). This last connection surfaces in the poem
itself where Scott alludes to Lewis's disapproval of his 'false rhyme(s)' (line 38),
which Lewis had begun pointing out in letters to Scott early in 1799 (see also
note to 91.34–36, below). Early references in the poem also fit well with Scott's
early days as a volunteer cavalryman in the late 1790s (see Historical Note to
no. 32, 'The Rouze of The Royal Edinburgh Light Dragoons'): an involve-
ment which allows him to relate to the recipient both as part-time soldier and
would-be Minstrel. Scott's literary relations with the Lady Charlotte too were
then flourishing, one token of which is the verses beginning 'Of old 'tis said,
in Ilium's battling days' (see no. 39), addressed to her personally from Scott's
new home in Castle Street on 1 November 1799. Though no evidence of the
gift of a pipe has been discovered, the closeness of domestic relations with the
Campbells at this time can be sensed in a letter of Scott's of 1 February 1802:
'Lady Charlotte Campbell ... and Col: Campbell were so good as to scramble
for bread and Cheese with us and between reading reciting and music the time
glided very pleasantly away' (*Letters*, 1.130).

Explanatory Notes

90.3 patriot band alluding to Scott's membership of the Royal Edinburgh Light Dragoons, a volunteer force which he had joined from its foundation in 1797, serving as its Quartermaster and Secretary.

90.8 crested casque referring to the helmets worn by the troopers: see also no. 32, 'The Rouze of The Royal Edinburgh Light Dragoons', note to 55.8–9.

90.13 pipe of simple oat musical pipe made of oat-straw, as traditionally used by shepherds in pastoral poetry.

90.15 war-pipe the bag-pipe, used as an instrument of war by the Highlanders.

91.31 meer-*schaum* referring to a meerschaum pipe, a tobacco pipe having a bowl made of *meerschaum*, a soft white, grey or yellowish mineral resembling hardened clay. Literally, in German *meerschaum* means sea-foam. Two meerschaum pipes, the larger one with tassels of black and gold, were preserved at Abbotsford: see Mary Monica Maxwell Scott, *Abbotsford: The Personal Relics and Antiquarian Treasures of Sir Walter Scott* (London, 1893), Plate 6 and commentary.

91.34–36 Mr. Lewis. … false rhyme Matthew Gregory Lewis (1775–1818), then preparing his *Tales of Wonder* (1801), and whom Scott had first met personally in Edinburgh in 1798 (see also Historical Note). Lewis's subsequent letters to Scott are filled with his objections to incorrect rhyming in Scott's offered contributions. For example, in responding early in 1799 to a version of 'Glenfinlas' (no. 33) sent by Scott: 'I do not despair of convincing you in time, that a *bad* rhyme is, in fact, no rhyme at all' (8vo1830*PW*, 3.cii).

91.39 Halt, La presumably echoing the military command to halt.

91.40 *smoke* a pun involving the alternative meaning of 'to note, or "twig"' (in something).

91.40 Damascus all sham another pun involving the dual meaning of *sham* as a pretence and as a type of tobacco. Compare Lady Hester Stanhope: 'here [in Syria] a species of tobacco grows, known throughout Turkey and the East by the epithet of Gebely (or mountain tobacco), and in England called by the various names of Cham, Sham, or Damascus, all which words have the same meaning, Sham being the Arabic for Damascus' (*Travels*, 3 vols (London, 1846), 1.328).

91.42 got but a *puff* a pun involving the alternative sense of *puff* as constituting 'hot air' or inflated praise.

92.52 Mrs. —— from the rhyme, most obviously 'Mrs Campbell'. If referring to Lady Charlotte (whose title derived from her being a daughter of the Duke of Argyll), Scott is here departing from convention, apparently employing the more familiar nomenclature jocularly.

41. A Song of Victory

Textual Note

This song is in 'The House of Aspen', a prose play Scott wrote around 1799 and intended for the London stage. A number of copies probably existed, so that Scott could garner the opinions of his friends and so that it could be read by John Kemble (1757–1823) and his management team at the Theatre Royal, Drury Lane. Three only of these manuscript copies have apparently survived, two in the Beinecke Rare Book and Manuscript Library, Yale University (GEN MSS 266, numbered respectively 2 and 3). The manuscript referred to in the

Beinecke catalogue as Volume 2, which is apparently the earlier one, though undated, is written in the hand of an amanuensis with corrections by Scott, except for the fifth act, the whole of which is in his hand. This untitled song beginning 'Joy to the victors!' occurs in Act 2 Scene 3, after the successful encounter in battle of Aspen's forces, led by his sons George and Henry, with those of Roderic of Maltingen. It also occurs in the equivalent place in the manuscript referred to in the Beinecke catalogue as Volume 3, which bears a 1799 watermark and is evidently a fair copy made for Scott with some corrections in his own hand. This was once in the library of Dr Thomas Rees (1777–1864), a brother of Owen Rees of Longmans publishing firm, and may well have been sent to him by Scott around 1805 when it was proposed to include 'The House of Aspen' in *Ballads and Lyrical Pieces* published by the firm in 1806 (see Scott's letter to Longmans of 15 November 1805 in *Letters*, 1.269). The song also occurs in the third manuscript, NLS, Acc. 11772, which bears a title-page dating to 1800, and may possibly have been intended as a presentation copy for Lady Charlotte Campbell (for further details about whom see Historical Note to no. 39, 'Verses to Lady Charlotte Campbell'): an inscription in Scott's hand reading 'Charlotte Maria from Walter Scott' survives on a front paste-down and a letter fixed to the front of the manuscript is headed 'Inverary' (the chief seat of the Campbells of Argyll) in Gothic print. The first nine pages of this manuscript, inclusive of a title-page and two pages of Dramatis Personae, are in Scott's hand, as are five lines of the following page, although the remainder of the manuscript is in the hand of an amanuensis.

Scott's letter to Richard Heber of 19 October 1800 (*Letters*, 12.170–71) records the rejection of 'The House of Aspen' by Drury Lane, and the play lay fallow for almost thirty years before Scott offered it to Charles Heath (1785–1848) to make up the total of his promised contributions to Heath's annual, *The Keepsake*. In his journal for 27 February 1829 Scott wrote: 'as he says I am still in his debt I will send him the old drama of the *House of Aspen* which I wrote some thirty years [ago] and offerd to the stage. This will make up my contribution and a good deal more if as I recollect there are five acts. Besides it will save me further trouble about Heath and his annual' (*Journal*, 524–25). From the tone of this entry there was unlikely to be much authorial involvement in revising 'The House of Aspen' in 1829, and indeed the text of this song in *The Keepsake for MDCCCXXX*, ed. Frederic Mansel Reynolds (London, [1829]), 1–66 (25–26), is almost identical to that of the surviving manuscripts, apart from changes of the kind normally associated with the printer. The only potential authorial revision is in line 24 where all three manuscripts have 'triumphant our way' and the published text has 'triumphant away'.

Neither 'The House of Aspen' nor its songs separately were included in either the 8vo or 18mo editions of Scott's *Poetical Works* of 1830, and Lockhart included the songs in his posthumous edition of 1833–34 only within the context of reprinting 'The House of Aspen' (12.363–441), where the text of this song is identical to that of *The Keepsake* apart from two minor variations in punctuation. J. Logie Robertson printed it separately under the title 'A Song of Victory' in his edition of *The Poetical Works of Sir Walter Scott* (London, 1904), 699.

The present text follows that of 'The House of Aspen, A Tragedy', *The Keepsake for MDCCCXXX*, ed. Frederic Mansel Reynolds (London, [1829]), 25–26, without emendation. Logie Robertson's title 'A Song of Victory' has been adopted, given that the 'Song' of the copy-text appears to be simply a stage direction.

Historical Note
'The House of Aspen' is a loose version, rather than a close translation, of *Die Heilige Vehme oder Der Sturtz Der Aspenauer* (The Holy Tribunal, or the Downfall of Aspenauer) by the German writer Leonhard Wächter (1762–1837), under his pseudonym of Veit Weber. It was first published in 1795 as Volume 6 of Weber's *Sagen der Vorzeit* (Tales of Yore), 7 vols (Vienna, 1787–98). (*ALC* shows that Scott possessed this particular volume of Veit Weber's work.) The German original contains no songs, and in general Scott did not add songs to his translations of German plays; but in this instance his intention to offer his work for production in London presumably led him to include the text of three songs in deference to the British taste for songs interspersed in dramas, even in tragedies. This was connected with the legal requirement that any theatre presenting spoken drama had first to be granted a Royal Patent: a common legal subterfuge of the unlicensed theatres was to evade this requirement by including at least five songs in each act of a play, after which it would be classified as a burletta. Audiences therefore expected to hear interspersed songs even in the most solemn plays, and some were included even at patent theatres such as Drury Lane where there was no legal objective to be gained by their inclusion. In Act 2 Scene 3 of 'The House of Aspen' the victorious troops of Aspen sing this song after their victory over the forces of Roderic of Maltingen, anticipating their return home, following the cue given by Henry of Aspen, 'Ere we go, sound trumpets—strike up the song of victory' (*Keepsake*, 25). No indication of a tune for performance is given and presumably Scott expected a suitable one to be chosen by the theatre management.

After Kemble's rejection of 'The House of Aspen' in 1800 and Scott's subsequent turning away from high German Romanticism, he was dismissive of his 'half-mad German tragedy' (*Letters*, 2.495) yet continued to circulate it among his friends, promising to show it to the actress Sarah Smith and sending it to Lady Abercorn and to Joanna Baillie as late as 1808 (see *Letters*, 2.57–58, 89, 495). In the Preface to the published 'The House of Aspen' end-dated 1 April 1829, Scott displays his anxiety that 'there are in existence so many manuscript copies of the following play that if it should not find its way to the public sooner, it is certain to do so when the author can no more have any opportunity of correcting the press, and consequently at greater disadvantage than at present' (*Keepsake*, 2). Scott was correct in assuming that his fame would lead to renewed interest in his early play, for almost immediately after it had been published in *The Keepsake* 'The House of Aspen' was produced in a much-altered version at the Old Surrey Theatre in London on 17 November 1829 with music by Jonathan Blewitt (1782–1853). A lavish Edinburgh production with music by the aspiring young composer John Thomson (1805–41) followed at the Theatre Royal on 17 December: see James C. Dibdin, *The Annals of the Edinburgh Stage* (Edinburgh, 1888), 328–29. There is no indication that Scott himself had any direct connection with this theatrical production other than giving the manager of the Theatre Royal a reluctant consent to its staging. This song was described by a contemporary critic as an impressive finale to the first act of the restructured theatrical version of Scott's drama, the play as a whole being termed a *rifacimento* (recasting) 'though not an opera' of Scott's drama by the manager William Henry Murray (1790–1852):

It opens with a grand burst of warlike exultation, which is sustained for some time with great power, till, by one of those simple, but bold modulations which indicate true genius, a transition is made to a wild and melancholy strain—a sort of lament for the slain and wounded of the victorious band. This part consists of solo passages for a tenor and bass voice, followed by a softly-breathed strain of thrilling and pathetic harmony. The voices die into silence; interrupted sounds, resembling fragments of the military march, are heard from the orchestra, and connected by the low rolling of the drum, during which troops are seen countermarching at a distance, till at length the sounds increase to a full swell of the military instruments, joined again by the voices in a chorus of festive joy, with which the act concludes. This splendid chorus was received, and its repetition called for, with loud acclamations. ('Diary of a Dilettante', *The Harmonicon*, 8: 1 (January 1830), 40–41)

The large-scale musical forces for which this song was evidently set made it unsuitable for drawing-room performance, and probably uncommercial therefore for the kind of separate publication achieved subsequently by 'Rhein-Wein Lied' from the same play (see Historical Note to no. 42).

Explanatory Notes
92.1   sons of old Aspen   the character of the elderly Rudiger, Baron of Aspen, is laid up with injuries during the opening scenes of 'The House of Aspen' and his forces are led by his two sons, George and Henry.
92.10   proud Roderic   Roderic, Count of Maltingen in Bavaria, is an important member of the Invisible Tribunal and a hereditary enemy of the Aspen family in the play. Rudiger has refused him the hand of his ward, Gertrude, in marriage.
92.20   Maltingen   see previous note.
93.23   proud mansion of Aspen   Aspen's seat in the play is the Castle of Ebersdorf in Bavaria, situated about 5 km (3 miles) from the battle that takes place between his forces and those of the Count of Maltingen.
93.33   Love, wine, and song   a variant of the usual 'wine, women and song', a popular expression summarising the joys of a hedonistic life-style.

42.   Rhein-Wein Lied

Textual Note
The history of Scott's 'Rhein-Wein Lied' (Rhine Wine Song) is similar to that of 'A Song of Victory', as it also forms part of 'The House of Aspen', Scott's prose play written around 1799 and intended for the London stage. (For further details of this play see Textual Note to no. 41, 'A Song of Victory'.) 'Rhein-Wein Lied' is not present in what appears to be the earlier of the two manuscripts of 'The House of Aspen' in the Beinecke Library's manuscript Scott collection, GEN MSS 266, Volume 2: at the relevant place in Act 4 scene 3 it is noted that Wickerd sings but without his song being given. However, 'Rhein-Wein Lied' is certainly contemporary, since it does occur in the equivalent place in the Volume 3 manuscript in the Beinecke Scott collection, which bears a 1799 watermark. It is also present in the third surviving manuscript of 'The House of Aspen' in NLS, Acc. 11772.

The text of 'Rhein-Wein Lied', when eventually published in 'The House of Aspen' in *The Keepsake for MDCCCXXX*, ed. Frederic Mansel Reynolds (London, [1829]), 1–66 (48), agrees substantially with that of the Volume 3 manuscript at the Beinecke and with that of NLS, Acc. 11772, apart from changes of the kind normally associated with the work of the printer, except that 'fur' of line 5 in the manuscripts becomes 'furs' in the published text.

Neither 'The House of Aspen' nor its songs separately were included in either the 8vo or 18mo editions of Scott's *Poetical Works* of 1830, while the songs were included in the Lockhart 1833–34 posthumous edition only within the context of reprinting 'The House of Aspen' (12.363–441), where the text of 'Rhein-Wein Lied' is equivalent to that of *The Keepsake* but for the replacement of a semi-colon by a stop at the end of line 8. J. Logie Robertson printed 'Rhein-Wein Lied' separately in his edition of *The Poetical Works of Sir Walter Scott* (London, 1904), 700. If the song was known individually in the nineteenth century it was probably in the form of a musical setting by John Thomson (see Historical Note).

The present text is taken from 'The House of Aspen, A Tragedy', *The Keepsake for MDCCCXXX*, ed. Frederic Mansel Reynolds (London, [1829]), 48. Brackets have been removed from the title, and the typographical error of 'Leid' in the title has been corrected, but otherwise no emendations have been made.

Historical Note
'The House of Aspen' is a loose version, rather than a close translation, of *Die Heilige Vehme oder Der Sturtz Der Aspenauer* (The Holy Tribunal, or the Downfall of Aspenauer) by the German writer Leonhard Wächter (1762–1837), under his pseudonym of Veit Weber: for further details of Scott's creation from this of 'The House of Aspen' see the Historical Note to no. 41, 'A Song of Victory'. 'Rhein-Wein Lied' does not occur in Wächter's original, but in Act 4 of 'The House of Aspen' Wickerd, a follower of the Aspen family, sings it to a group of troopers to beguile the tedium of their night-watch. No indication of a tune for performance is given.

The song is a free adaptation of the final two stanzas of the nine-stanza 'Rheinweinlied' of the German poet and journalist Matthias Claudius (1740–1815), best known for his editorship of and contributions to the periodical *Der Wandebecker Bote* (The Wansbeck Messenger) from 1771 to 1775, a periodical to which Herder, Klopstock and Lessing also contributed. Claudius's words were set to music by the Stockholm-based composer Joseph Martin Kraus (1756–92), known as the Swedish Mozart, and it may be that Scott intended to suggest this tune for performance, as 'Air (Rein wein Lied)' is marked at the head of the song in NLS, Acc. 11772. Claudius's poem is geographically specific, describing the best wine as coming not from other countries such as Hungary, Poland, or Crete, nor from other German mountains such as those of Thuringia, the Ore Mountains, nor the Blockberg. The final two stanzas celebrate the wine grown on the banks of the Rhine as best of all, and the singer urges his comrades to drink it, to rejoice and be cheerful, and to give the wine to anyone who may be sad. It is possible that these stanzas in particular were familiar to English theatre-goers from various English language stage versions. The London playwright and theatrical impresario James Robinson Planché (1796–1880), for instance, concludes his booklet for English tourists in the Rhineland, *Lays and Legends of the Rhine* (Frankfort, 1830), with 'a free translation of part of the celebrated Rhein-wein-lied' (56) in four stanzas, the third of which begins 'The Rhine! the Rhine! Thereon our vines are growing— / For ever bless the Rhine!' (61). Scott himself might have heard a version at a theatre, or have been introduced to it by readers of German among his Scottish friends, such as Henry Mackenzie (1745–1831), James Skene (1775–1864), or the German-born Harriet Scott of Harden (1773–1853). His version of the final stanzas of Claudius's song differs considerably from its German original, most obviously in referring to German troopers and to Saracens.

Soon after publication of 'The House of Aspen' in *The Keepsake* the play was produced both at the Old Surrey Theatre in London and at Edinburgh's Theatre Royal. (For details of both productions see Historical Note to no. 41, 'A Song of Victory'.) A contemporary review of the Edinburgh production with music by John Thomson (1805–41) praised the setting of 'Rhein-Wein Lied' in particular:

The melody of the song, which is exceedingly original, and of a gay and jovial
character, is broken in upon, at each repetition, by a short chorus, full of spirit and
animation. The song was admirably sung by Stanley, and ... was loudly encored.
('Diary of a Dilettante', *The Harmonicon*, 8: 1 (January 1830), 40–41)

Thomson's song was subsequently published as 'The Trooper's Wine-song'
by the musical instrument maker and music seller Paterson & Co of 27 George
Street, Edinburgh, and briefly reviewed ('as clever as it is animated') in *The
Harmonicon*, 8: 1 (March 1830), 126. Its republication as late as 1861 (there is
a copy at BL, H.2727(4)) suggests that Thomson's song achieved a more than
temporary vogue.

Explanatory Notes
93.3   **upon the Rhine they cluster** the Rhine flows from the SE Swiss Alps
through Germany before entering the North Sea in the Netherlands. The
Rhine Valley of Germany (Rheingau), with its steep, hilly vineyards, has a
wine-making tradition going back to Roman times.
93.6   **Saracen**   alcoholic drinks are forbidden to Muslims.

43.   **The Shepherd's Tale**

Textual Note
This unfinished poem did not appear in Scott's lifetime nor in Lockhart's
posthumous collected edition of Scott's *Poetical Works* of 1833–34, but was first
published in Lockhart's *Life*, 1.307–13, from a surviving manuscript, almost
certainly the one now at NLS, MS 876, ff. 1–12. This consists of twelve leaves,
each measuring approx. 19.2 x 15.5 cm, with a watermark of a seated Britannia
in a crowned shield and the date 1798. The text, headed 'The Shepherds Tale',
is on the rectos only, except for f. 9v which has an insertion to go in the text on
f. 10. Although the story is incomplete it is coherently linear so far as it goes,
although with many of the features of a rough draft rather than a fair copy: there
are a number of local revisions and deletions, and the occasional word required
by the sense or the scansion is missing, while only a partial and sometimes
confusing system of punctuation is supplied. The date of composition is not
precisely known, although the watermark date of 1798 provides a *terminus a
quo*. Coleman O. Parsons in his 'Two Notes on Scott', *Notes and Queries*, 164 (4
February 1933), 75–76, argues for a possible date of 1801, assuming that Scott's
reference in a letter to James Currie of 30 July 1801 (*Letters*, 1.121) to a ballad
of the marvellous founded on popular tradition that he had lately begun but
been unable to finish satisfactorily is to 'The Shepherd's Tale'. This is sugges-
tive, but so also is Scott's account in his letter to Richard Heber of 19 October
1800 of a visit from John Leyden, when the two men were deeply engaged both
with traditional lore and with historical and political disputes concerning the
Covenanters: 'we work hard at old Ballads during the forenoon & skirmish in
the Evening upon the old disputes betwixt the Cameronians & their opponents'
(*Letters*, 12.171–72).
    As Parsons points out, Lockhart in producing his version of the poem mis-
read the text and made a number of revisions himself as well as more legiti-
mately adding punctuation, regularising spelling, and supplying a missing word
where one is plainly required. He also implemented a number of pencil revisions
marked by him on the manuscript, probably made when the poem was under
consideration for inclusion in his *Life*.
    The present text is that of Scott's manuscript in NLS, MS 876, ff. 1–12, silently

incorporating Scott's own revisions but ignoring the pencil marks in Lockhart's hand. Although mostly in four-line stanzas, lines 97–108 take the form of two six-line stanzas and this has been retained as reflecting the sequence of ideas at this point in the poem. An apostrophe has been added to the title, and Scott's speech marks have been normalised in line with general editorial principles. In addition to this and to the following listed emendations, ampersands have been routinely expanded to 'and', and verb forms ending with 'd' to 'ed'; routine apostrophes have been introduced as required, as have full stops at the ends of stanzas.

94.1	once, my son, (Editorial) / once my Son
94.2	cavern (Editorial) / Cavern
94.3	persecution's (Editorial) / Persecutions
94.5	slaughter (Editorial) / Slaughter
94.10	troopers (Editorial) / Troopers
94.12	death (Editorial) / Death
94.14	On yon dark (MS derived: MS On the <hill's huge side> ↑yon dark↓) / On the yon dark
94.15	Thro' (Editorial) / Thro
94.16	sunbeam (Editorial) / Sunbeam
94.17	cavern (Editorial) / Cavern
94.21	spell-formed (Editorial) / spell formd
94.27	cavern (Editorial) / Cavern
95.37	arm, (Editorial) / arm
95.44	ocean's (Editorial) / Oceans
95.45	"O in the Oppressor's hour (MS 'O in <the Oppressors day> ↑hour↓') / O in hour An accidental deletion in MS.
95.47	thro' (Editorial) / thro
95.54	welcome (Editorial) / wellcome
95.54	mine." (Editorial) / mine"
95.60	torch's (Editorial) / torches
96.64	thro' (Editorial) / thro
96.75	erne (Editorial) / Erne
96.77	The Wanderer (Editorial) / the Wanderer
96.80	yield. (Editorial) / yeild
96.83	Theirs (Editorial) / Theres
97.93	warlock (Editorial) / Warlock
97.100	spy (Editorial) / spie
97.103	wizard (Editorial) / Wizzard
97.116	o'er (Editorial) / oer
97.117	led (Editorial) / laid
97.117	thro' (Editorial) / thro
97.121	Thro' (Editorial) / Thro
97.124	O'er (Editorial) / oer
98.129	brand: (Editorial) / brand
98.132	eyeballs (MS derived: MS eyes <both> balls) / eyes balls
98.135	pommel (Editorial) / pommell
98.139	wanderer (MS derived: MS wander<d>) / wander
98.140	Thro' (Editorial) / Thro
98.143	armour (Editorial) / Armour
98.147	Thro' (Editorial) / Thro
98.153	thro' (Editorial) / thro
98.155	echoes (Editorial) / Echoes

98.156   the wanderer's steps (MS derived: MS the \<Wanderers measured\> steps) / the steps
99.158   borne (Editorial) / born
99.163   weal, (Editorial) / weal
99.173   Tees, from sea to seas (Editorial) / Tees from Sea to Seas
99.174   bugle (Editorial) / Bugle
99.175   withal (Editorial) / withall
99.176   warders (Editorial) / Warders
99.177   cavern (Editorial) / Cavern
99.180   Sterte up (Editorial) / Sterte up up
99.181   "Woe, (Editorial) / "Woe
99.184   horn?"— (Editorial) / horn"—
100.189   cavern (Editorial) / Cavern

Historical Note

As with the much rougher draft of 'The Reiver's Wedding', written at a similar stage in his poetic career (see Textual Note to no. 47), Scott struggles here to combine somewhat disparate Scottish historical and legendary material into a single story. The persecuted Covenanter of the poem obviously encounters the demonic figure in the cavern during the 'Killing Time' of the 1680s of persecution by government forces led by John Graham of Claverhouse (1648?–89), whose cognomen of 'bloody Clavers' is alluded to in the poem. The legend of the choice of the sword and the horn, on the other hand, is generally associated with the figure of the seer and poet Thomas the Rhymer or Thomas of Erceldoune (fl. late 13th century), as subsequently related by Scott in his *Letters on Demonology and Witchcraft* (London, 1830), 136–37. Scott also brings in the reputed wizard Michael Scott (d. in or after 1235), a mysterious presence in Scott's long narrative poem *The Lay of the Last Minstrel* (1805). Although the whole narrative is related by an elderly shepherd to his son, this framing device appears to have been overlooked after the first stanza.

Explanatory Notes

94.3   persecution's iron days   a reference to the persecution of Scottish Presbyterians between the Restoration of Charles II in 1660 and the accession of William I and III in 1688; more particularly to the 'Killing Time' of the 1680s (see Historical Note).

94.5   Bewlie Bog   within Lilliesleaf parish in NE Roxburghshire. According to the Rev. David Baxter 'the moors in Lilliesleaf parish, from their retired situation, were frequently the resort of numerous conventicles; and for this offence, numbers in this parish appear to have been punished with death, imprisonment, or banishment': *New Statistical Account of Scotland*, 15 vols (Edinburgh, 1845), 3.26.

94.6   wanderer   a Covenanter during the time of persecution, especially one on the run in moors and hills.

94.9   Cheviot edge   the Cheviot at 815 m is the highest summit of the Cheviot Hills, a range of rolling hills along the border between the English county of Northumberland and Scotland, and is only 2 km (1¼ miles) from the Scottish Border.

94.11   the Whitelaw sedge   a place near Dunse, the county town of Berwickshire, about 25 km (16 miles) W of Berwick-upon-Tweed, and originally surrounded on three sides by a morass.

94.23   lourd mell   *lourd* is the past participle of *lief*, while *mell* means to mix with or interfere with, the overall sense being 'I had rather mix with'.

94.24   Clavers   John Graham of Claverhouse (pronounced 'Clavers') was widely known among Presbyterian sympathisers as 'bloody Clavers', because of the system of persecution of the Covenanters, including torture and summary execution without trial, attributed to him.

95.30   faulting   defaulting, failing or guilty of a fault.

95.37   thou battling Lord   God is described as 'strong in battle' in Psalm 24.8 in the metrical psalms of the Church of Scotland.

95.41   Forget not thou thy people groans   the similar plea of 'The congregation of thy poor / do not forget for ever' occurs in Psalm 74.19 of the metrical psalms of the Church of Scotland.

95.42   dark Dunottar's tower   Dunnottar Castle is a ruined medieval fortress on a rocky headland about 3 km (2 miles) S of Stonehaven in Aberdeenshire. A group of Covenanters were imprisoned there for several months in 1685 in a cellar, now known as the Whigs' Vault.

95.49   His widow and his little ones   compare Psalm 109.8–9: 'Let his days be few; and let another take his office. Let his children be fatherless, and his wife a widow.'

95.57   amice   a loose outer garment or cloak.

95.59   dead man's arm   probably a *hand of glory*, the dried and pickled arm of a man who has been hanged and which, when combined with a candle made from the fat of his corpse, was believed to have magic powers. It was variously reputed to be able to undo any lock, to render motionless those whom it shone upon, and to give light only to the holder.

96.65   deadly blue   according to popular superstition when a candle burns with a blue flame this indicates that a spirit is present.

96.71   Vengeance be thine   recalling the opposite instruction in Romans 12.19: 'Vengeance is mine; I will repay, saith the Lord.'

96.75   erne   an eagle.

96.85   Brownie   goblin of shaggy appearance. They are often represented as benevolent spirits connected to a dwelling, only appearing at night to perform work for the inhabitants.

96.87   uneath   difficult, hard, troublesome.

96.92   Halbert Kerr   a legendary figure based on the historical Sir Robert Ker (1569/70–1650) of Cessford, a leading courtier of James VI who was created 1st Earl of Roxburghe in 1616.

97.94   Sir Michael Scott   Michael Scott was widely reputed to be a magician and to have demons at his command in Borders legend. He is a mysterious undead presence in Scott's subsequent long narrative poem *The Lay of the Last Minstrel* (1805).

97.97   Cessford head   Cessford is a settlement in Eckford parish, Roxburghshire, about 10 km (6 miles) NE of Jedburgh and 5 km (3 miles) SW of Morebattle, on the right bank of Cessford Burn. Cessford Castle was the stronghold of the Border Reiver family of the Kerrs of Cessford, ancestors of the Duke of Roxburgh. A large concealed cavern in a steep bank of the burn less than 1 km N of the castle is called Hobbie Kerr's Cave.

97.109   Bowden aisle   Bowden is in Roxburghshire, about 4 km (2½ miles) SE of Melrose. Its ancient parish church was the burial place of the Kerrs of Cessford.

97.111   female guile   Merlin, the magician and advisor of the legendary King Arthur of the Round Table, fell in love with a beautiful woman called Vivien who became his pupil and then used his own magic to trap him, though accounts vary as to the precise details of how.

98.126   barbing   a covering for the breast and flanks of a war-horse.

98.129 brand the blade of a sword.
98.133 gey very, considerable.
98.133 twelve ells an *ell* is a measure derived from the word for 'arm', which in Scotland was generally approx. 95 cm. A lance of twelve ells in length would therefore measure 11.4 metres.
98.135 yare ready, prompt.
98.137 casque military head-piece, a helmet.
98.140 gramarye occult learning, magic or necromancy.
99.163 boot and bale advantage and misery.
99.165 minted feinted, made as if to draw.
99.170 'say shortened form of 'essay', to try.
99.171 brast burst.
99.173 Forth to Tees from the N of Lowland Scotland to the English Borders. The River Forth flows from the Trossachs eastwards past Stirling towards Edinburgh and eventually flows into the North Sea. The River Tees flows eastwards from Cross Fell in the N Pennines into the North Sea near Middlesbrough, County Durham.
99.175 Carlisle's wall Carlisle is the county town of Cumberland, 16 km (10 miles) S of the Scottish Border in NW England.
99.175 Berwick Berwick-upon-Tweed is the northernmost town in England, 4 km (2½ miles) S of the Scottish Border on the east coast at the mouth of the River Tweed.
99.181 caitiff a villain, a despicable wretch.
100.190 glidders small stones.

44. Thomas the Rhymer

Textual Note
Scott's three-part 'Thomas the Rhymer' was first published in Scott's ballad collection *Minstrelsy of the Scottish Border*, 2 vols (Kelso, 1802), 2.244–95, and, according to his letter to Richard Heber (1774–1833) of 10 June 1800, was assembled that summer: 'I have compleated a Ballad of Thos. the Rhymer which Erskine thinks is executed in a right division' (*Letters*, 12.163). As Scott remarks at the end of his headnote in the present volume, the first part was a traditional ballad, the second an assemblage of surviving prophecies and tags concerning Thomas the Rhymer, and the third an entirely original composition of his own. According to Grierson, Scott sent Heber a copy of the third part in his own hand with his subsequent letter of 10 March 1801 (*Letters*, 12.175n), although this copy cannot now be found and no other manuscript of the poem has apparently survived. All three parts of 'Thomas the Rhymer' were first published together in *Minstrelsy* in 1802, with the third following the others, at 2.283–95. Each is typeset with its own headnote, as a separate though related poem, and Scott's headnote of 1802 to the third part recognises that, as a composition of his own, it differs from its predecessors:

> The following attempt to commemorate the Rhymer's poetical fame, and the traditional account of his marvellous return to Fairy Land, being entirely modern, would have been placed with greater propriety among the class of modern ballads, had it not been for its immediate connection with the first and second parts of the same story. (2.285)

Despite Scott's reservations here, however, all three parts continued to be printed together in the lifetime editions of Scott's poetry, not simply in those volumes devoted to *Minstrelsy of the Scottish Border* but also in collections otherwise composed of Scott's poetry alone, such as his *Ballads and Lyrical Pieces* of 1806 (73–133). Even in the Lockhart 1833–34 posthumous edition (4.110–66) all three parts are given. Scott must have had some natural reservations about thus implicitly claiming authorship of all three items, and these are demonstrated by his including only the third part in the second quarto edition of *The Lay of the Last Minstrel* of 1808 (327–43, clxvii–clxviii), which as well as the title poem included those of his poems that had previously appeared both separately and in collections such as Lewis's *Tales of Wonder* and *Minstrelsy of the Scottish Border*.

This new context meant redrafting the headnote, which in this quarto edition of *The Lay of the Last Minstrel* begins with a substantial passage taken from the initial introduction to the three-part poem, though cutting out much of the antiquarian detail from the *Minstrelsy*. Scott also adds the story of Thomas's meeting with a Borders peasant and his introduction of him into the subterranean cave where he must choose between the horn and the sword. Scott had begun a prose romance about Thomas the Rhymer around 1798–99 in which this legend was to feature, and indeed he also recounts it in similar though not identical terms in Appendix I of his General Preface to the Magnum Opus edition of the Waverley Novels: see *Introductions and Notes from the Magnum Opus*, ed. J. H. Alexander with P. D. Garside and Claire Lamont, EEWN 25a (Edinburgh, 2012), 26–29. This amply demonstrates that the rewritten headnote is the work of Scott himself rather than that of an intermediary. Additional material by Scott in these subsequent editions also includes a new endnote about Fairnalie for the second edition of the *Minstrelsy* (2.321).

The verses themselves, however, are substantially unchanged between the first publication of *Minstrelsy of the Scottish Border* and their inclusion in subsequent editions of that and of the various lifetime collections of his own poetical works: the variations are changes of the kind normally associated with the work of the printer. In the posthumous 1833–34 collected edition, Lockhart, presumably on his own authority, inserted a tune for the first part of 'Thomas the Rhymer' (1833–34*PW*, 4. between 116 and 117), but it is unclear if he intended it for the third part also.

In the present edition only the third part of 'Thomas the Rhymer' is included, together with the apparatus Scott designed for its separate publication, since the first two parts properly form part of his antiquarian ballad collection, *Minstrelsy of the Scottish Border*. The text follows that of *The Lay of the Last Minstrel ... With Ballads and Lyrical Pieces*, 8th edn (Edinburgh, 1808), 327–43, clxvii–clxviii, with the following emendations:

104.40   ladie's (*Minstrelsy* Ed1) / ladies'
106.87   pair (*Minstrelsy* Ed1) / pair,

Historical Note
The seer and poet Thomas of Erceldoune (fl. late 13th century) is a largely mythical character based on an historical original, contemporary evidence about whom is very limited. Erceldoune, now Earlston, is a Berwickshire village about 6.5 km (4 miles) NE of Melrose close to the Eildon Hills and where there is still part of the ruins of the Rhymer's Tower. The landowner-bard Thomas was obviously an attractive figure to Scott, who preferred to think that ballads were original compositions by professional minstrels rather than the product of local folk such as small tenant-farmers or agricultural workers and members of their families. Such is the premise on which his first long narrative poem

The Lay of the Last Minstrel, as well as the title of *Minstrelsy of the Scottish Border*, is constructed. 'Thomas the Rhymer' is also motivated by Scott's firm belief that the medieval poem of *Sir Tristrem*, discovered in 1792 by Joseph Ritson (1752–1803) in the Auchinleck Manuscript of the Advocates Library in Edinburgh and edited by Scott in 1804, was the composition of Thomas the Rhymer rather than, as is now generally accepted, a northern English version of a French original.

Explanatory Notes

100.headnote   Alexander the Third of Scotland   the reign of Alexander III (1241–86) was traditionally viewed as a golden age for Scotland, when the country was prosperous and stable. A failed Norse invasion ended with the battle of Largs in 1263, and the accession of the Western Isles to the Scottish crown. Alexander was killed on 19 March 1286 when his horse stumbled and threw him near Kinghorn in Fife. Scott discusses the supposed prophecy by Thomas of his death in his headnote to the 2nd part of 'Thomas the Rhymer' in *Minstrelsy of the Scottish Border*, 2 vols (Kelso, 1802), 2.261–62.

100.headnote   lately republished from an ancient manuscript   Scott's source for his edition of *Sir Tristrem* (Edinburgh, 1804) was the Auchinleck manuscript, compiled about 1330–1340, and now at Adv. MS 19.2.1 in the National Library of Scotland.

101.headnote   "drees his weird"   endures his fate.

101. headnote   Reginald Scott's "Discovery of Witchcraft," edit. 1665   see *The Discovery of Witchcraft ... By Reginald Scot* (London, 1665): ALC. In the supplementary *An excellent Discourse of the Nature and Substance of Devils and Spirits*, whose author is unknown, a man sells his horse to Thomas of Erceldoune and is conducted underground by him to receive payment from a beautiful woman (48): see *Introductions and Notes from the Magnum Opus*, ed. J. H. Alexander with P. D. Garside and Claire Lamont, EEWN 25a (Edinburgh, 2012), 407 note to 28.26.

101.headnote   Dr Leyden's "Scenes of Infancy:"   John Leyden, *Scenes of Infancy: Descriptive of Teviotdale* (Edinburgh, 1803), 71–75: ALC. Scott's ellipsis near the end of the extract indicates the omission of sixteen lines comparing Thomas's sojourn in fairyland to Vathek's incursion to a subterranean hell, Vathek being the protagonist of William Beckford's *[Vathek]. An Arabian Tale* (1786).

103.3   Ruberslaw shewed high Dunyon   (see also Scott's 1st endnote.) Ruberslaw is a rugged, peaked hill rising to about 424 m about 8 km (5 miles) NE of Hawick in Roxburghshire and is a prominent feature of the landscape around the River Teviot. Dunian Hill near Jedburgh is 314 m high.

103.5   Coldingknow   (see Scott's 2nd endnote.)

103.6   palliouns   large and stately tents, pavilions.

103.9   Leader   Leader Water flows through W Berwickshire and NW Roxburghshire until falling into the Tweed to the NE of Melrose.

103.11–12   Caddenhead ... Torwoodlee   (see also Scott's 3rd endnote.) Caddenhead is at the head of Caddon Water, which flows through Stow in Selkirkshire. Torwoodlee is a house in Stow parish associated with the Pringle family on the right bank of Gala Water, about 3 km (2 miles) NW of Galashiels. The ruins of an old tower are close by.

104.14   Learmont's high and ancient hall   that is to say, his family home of the Rhymer's Tower at Ercildoune. Thomas of Learmont or True Thomas are alternative names for Thomas the Rhymer.

104.16   laced in pall   a *pall* is a robe or vestment.

104.37 King Arthur's table round the whole body of stories about the legendary King Arthur, given in Geoffrey of Monmouth's *Historia Regum Britanniae* and in various medieval French romances, was collected and reworked by Sir Thomas Malory (d. 1471), whose prose romance *Le Morte d'Arthur* was published by Caxton in 1485. According to legend, a circular table was made by Merlin for Uther Pendragon, the father of King Arthur, in order to prevent any jealousy about precedence among the 150 knights who were seated at it. These knights of King Arthur's court sought adventures of chivalry and were involved in the quest for the Holy Grail.

104.38 warrior of the lake Lancelot of the Lake, son of King Ban of Brittany, whose cognomen comes from his being stolen by the Lady of the Lake in his infancy. His adulterous relationship with Queen Guinevere was the cause of the disruption of the Round Table and the death of her husband, King Arthur.

104.39 How courteous Gawaine met the wound King Arthur's nephew Gawaine was known as the Maidens' Knight, because of his chivalry. (See Scott's 4th endnote.) A copy of *Fabliaux or Tales, abridged from French Manuscripts of the XIIth and XIIIth centuries, by M. Le Grand, selected and translated into English verse by the late Gregory Lewis Way*, 2 vols (London, 1796, 1800: *ALC*), had been presented to Scott's wife, Charlotte, by Richard Heber, and Scott in returning thanks in his letter of 28 July 1800 praised it highly (*Letters*, 12.166). In 'The Knight and the Sword' (*Fabliaux*, 1.119–42) Gawaine visits by invitation the castle of a knight whom he meets in a wood, and is there not only introduced to his daughter but instructed to take the lady to bed with him. On doing so she warns him that an enchanted sword guards her virtue and that previous knightly visitors, attempting to make love to her, have been killed by the sword. Gawaine has some wounds by the following morning, reflecting his temptation, but by remaining chaste and alive breaks the enchantment and marries the lady. The rest of the story is the same as Bürger's 'Das Lied von Treue', which Scott translated as 'The Triumph of Constancy' (see no. 27).

104.44 Lionelle more normally represented as Lyonesse, was a mythical stretch of land in Cornwall, between Land's End and the Scilly Isles. King Arthur came from this country, which was also reputed to be the birthplace of Sir Tristrem.

105.46 venomed wound in the romance of *Sir Tristrem*, Tristrem the nephew of King Mark of Cornwall kills Moraunt, an ambassador from Ireland demanding tribute, but is himself wounded by Moraunt's poisoned weapon and grows worse and worse. He leaves court by ship and eventually lands at Dublin, where he is nursed by the Irish Queen, who is Moraunt's sister, and falls in love with her daughter Ysonde (a name which is also varied to Isonde, Isolde or Isault). Tristrem returns to Britain and tells his uncle about Ysonde, and King Mark then orders him to request her hand in marriage on his behalf.

105.51 Isolde's lily hand the epithet more properly belongs to Tristrem's wife, Isonde la Blanche Mains, the daughter of King Howel of Brittany, than as applied here to the Isonde who is married to Tristrem's uncle, King Mark of Cornwall. In his edition of *Sir Tristrem* (1804) Scott himself completes the story as 'abridged from the French metrical romance, in the stile of Tomas of Erceldoune' (191). Tristrem is desperately wounded in battle in Brittany and can only be cured by Ysonde of Cornwall (formerly of Dublin), whom he sends a messenger to fetch with the instruction that if she comes the messenger's ship is to carry a white sail and if not then a black sail. Tristrem's wife overhears and tells Tristrem falsely that the sail is black. Tristrem dies in despair and Ysonde of Cornwall on her arrival dies beside his body.

105.54   leech's part   that of a physician or one who practises healing.

105.65   Garde Joyeuse   the estate given by King Arthur to Sir Lancelot for defending Queen Guinevere's honour against Sir Mador. It is sometimes supposed to have been near Berwick-upon-Tweed.

105.67   Avalon's enchanted vale   now identified with Glastonbury in Somerset, but in Arthurian legend the island of blessed spirits where King Arthur was buried.

105.69   Brengwain   the attendant of Ysonde of Cornwall. In *Sir Tristrem* the brother of Sir Tristrem's wife, Ganhardin, falls in love with her.

105.69   Segramore   In Bk 8, Ch. 16, of Malory's *Le Morte d'Arthur* (1485) Sir Segramore and Sir Dodinas le Savage, both Knights of the Round Table, waylay Sir Tristrem and ask him to joust with them both, since from previous encounters with knights of Cornwall they are doubtful of Cornish prowess. Tristrem defeats them both and goes on his way.

105.70   fiend-born Merlin's gramarye   *gramarye* is occult learning or necromancy. The enchanter Merlin, who advised King Arthur, was supposedly the son of a girl seduced by a devil.

106.101   Lord Douglas   the powerful family of Douglas rivalled the Scottish crown in power and influence throughout the medieval period. Hugh Douglas, who contributed to the defeat of a Norse army at the battle of Largs in 1263, succeeded his father as head of the Douglas family in 1276 but died in 1288 and was succeeded by his brother William, who swore fealty to Edward I of England at one time but was at another a companion of Sir William Wallace. He died at York in 1302. Scott may have a generic head of the Douglasses in mind rather than one of these brothers specifically.

107.112   Fairnalie   (see also Scott's 5th endnote.) Fernilee is on the left bank of the River Tweed in Galashiels parish, a little more than 8 km (5 miles) NW of Selkirk, and was once the seat of the Rutherford family.

107.123   sand is run   the image is of an hour-glass, which measures time by the fall of sand from one glass chamber to another.

107.123   thread is spun   the three classical Fates were supposed to control birth, life, and death: Clotho drew the thread of life from her distaff, presiding over birth; Lachesis spun the thread, determining the length of a life; and Atropos severed it.

107.136   Soltra's mountains   Soutra is the most westerly ridge of the Lammermuir Hills, with views from the top over the Lothians and the Firth of Forth to Fife.

45.   Of old, when vassals to their head

Textual Note
This autograph poem survives in the National Records of Scotland [NRS], on a single leaf measuring approx. 18.7 x 11.2 cm, with no visible watermark (GD157/2011/1/18). In a fainter ink, probably in Scott's hand, it is headed 'Dedication'. The stanzas are numbered [1]–4, with the fourth appearing on the verso, and at the end there is a note in another hand stating: 'by Sir Walter Scott to Lord Polwarth's eldest child Charles Walter who died at 9 years old—'. No previous printing of these verses has been discovered.

The present text follows that in NRS, GD157/2011/1/18, with the provision of a title from the first line. Full stops are also supplied editorially at the end of stanzas, while ampersands are expanded in lines 15, 17, 18 and 21. The following emendations have also been made:

110.15   rattle, (Editorial) / rattle
110.16   side— (Editorial) / side
110.17   sires (Editorial) / Sires
110.20   friendship's (Editorial) / freindship's

Historical Note
Charles Walter Scott (1796–1804), to whom these lines are dedicated, was the eldest son of Hugh Scott of Harden (1758–1841) (later 6th Baron Polwarth) and his German wife Harriet Bruhl (1773–1853). Charles Walter was born 1 August 1796, and there is some possibility that Scott's poem was written shortly after that event, in recognition of the arrival of a male heir and prospective future clan leader of the Scotts of Harden. At the same time, there are elements in the poem that suggest a later period in Scott's literary development, and it could be that Scott was adopting a more direct kind of address involving the child himself, to whom he might have been offering tales of Border lore at any point up to his early death in September 1804. Scott had certainly enjoyed an especially close relationship with the parents. In a letter of 23 August 1795, at a highly uncertain moment in his own relationship with Williamina Belsches (see Historical Note to no. 16, 'To a Lady'), he had viewed with excitement the prospect of the 'great marriage' (in September) between 'Scott of Harden, and a daughter of Count Bruhl, the famous chess-player', and the likelihood of their returning shortly to Harden's seat at Mertoun House in the Borders: 'I wish they may come down soon, as we shall have fine racketing, of which I will, probably, get my share' (*Letters*, 1.42). Two years later, it was to the Hardens that Scott naturally turned for support in forwarding his own plans for marriage—as he confided to his wife-to-be Charlotte: 'I went to Mertoun yesterday in order to talk over the most interesting subject which can ever engage me with Mr. and Mrs. Scott ... You will like Mrs. Scott much' (*Letters*, 1.71).

In addition to these personal ties, Scott from an early stage showed a keen interest in his descent from a colourful line of earlier Lairds of Hardens, which included Walter Scott of Harden (*c.* 1550–1629?)—who married Mary, widely-known as 'The Flower of Yarrow'—and his son Sir William Scott (d. 1655), whose exploits were commemorated around 1802 by Scott in his unfinished ballad 'The Reiver's Wedding' (no. 47). Scott's relish for this kind of connection is evident in the account of his 'pedigree' in his Ashestiel 'Memoirs':

> My father's grandfather was Walter Scott ... He was the second son of Walter Scott, first Laird of Raeburn, who was the third son of Sir William Scott, and the grandson of Walter Scott, commonly called in tradition *Auld Wat* of Harden. I am therefore lineally descended from that ancient chieftain whose name I have made to ring in many a ditty, and from his fair dame, the Flower of Yarrow—no bad genealogy for a border minstrel. (*Scott on Himself*, ed. David Hewitt (Edinburgh, 1981), 2)

The 'Memoirs' then proceeds to record a more practical form of indebtedness in the gift of the lease of the remote farm of Sandyknowe to Scott's grandfather by his 'Chief and relative, Mr. Scott of Harden' (4). It was at Sandyknowe that Scott recollected hearing from his grandmother 'many a tale of Wat of Harden' (13) and other border cattle robbers. Wat of Harden's marauding proclivities feature strongly in *Minstrelsy of the Scottish Border* of 1802, both in a long footnote in the Introduction and in action in the ballad 'Jamie Telfer of the Fair Dodhead' (see *Minstrelsy*, 1.cviin–cixn, 104, 109–10). The third stanza in the present piece is particularly evocative of this ballad-collecting phase in Scott's literary career;

while the poem as a whole represents an early experimentation on his part with the role of family Minstrel, later more spectacularly applied in relation to the Scotts of Buccleuch. Scott's continuing closeness to the family at Mertoun House, enhanced by his own residence in the Borders at Abbotsford from 1812, is again evident near the end of his career, when he was called on by Harriet Scott to commemorate in verse the premature death of another of the Harden sons (see no. 131, 'Inscription for the Monument of the Rev. George Scott'). While some uncertainty must remain about its exact date of composition, this piece throws interesting light on a phase in Scott's development when he stood at a cusp between literary antiquarianism and expression of his own 'minstrelsy'.

Explanatory Notes
110.11   Painting ... glowing hand   possibly relating to Mrs Scott of Harden's interests in art. There is a portrait of her in oils painted by Henry Raeburn in 1795, presumably as part of the wedding events. Her own skill as an artist is noted by Scott in writing to her from Naples in 1832: 'I envied your management of the pencil when at Malta, as frequently elsewhere' (*Letters*, 12.44).
110.14   I tell the Raids of border days   referring either specifically to Scott's collection of ballads in *Minstrelsy of the Scottish Border* (1802–03), which had involved successive annual raids to Liddesdale for several years commencing in 1792; or more generally to his own telling of stories about Border history (see also Historical Note).

46. Cadyow Castle

Textual Note
'Cadyow Castle' originated in a visit paid by Scott to Hamilton Palace in Lanarkshire, the mansion of Archibald, 9th Duke of Hamilton, during Christmas 1801. Scott was especially well-acquainted with the Duke's eldest daughter, Lady Anne Hamilton (1766–1846), to whom the poem is addressed, and sent 'the long promised Ballad' to her with his letter of 29 July 1802 (*Letters*, 1.149). This took the form of one of Scott's small presentation booklets, now with this and a subsequent letter to Lady Anne of 10 August in a bound volume in the Berg Collection of the New York Public Library. The booklet consists of four leaves, each measuring approx. 20.2 x 12.5 cm, with no visible watermark, with text in Scott's small neat hand on both sides of the leaves, and is end-dated 'Laswade Cottage / 29 July 1802'. The poem is not fully punctuated but is clearly a fair copy, containing very few corrections and revisions, although the text differs substantially in places from the later version as first published in May of the following year in *Minstrelsy of the Scottish Border*, 2nd edn, 3 vols (Edinburgh, 1803), 3.380–401. It is also noticeable that the poem in this presentation booklet has no headnote or endnotes although Scott's accompanying letter provides a few glosses and some background information about the wild cattle and about Woodhouselee.

Writing to Lady Anne again on 10 August Scott told her that he had 'been endeavouring to render the Ballad rather more worthy of its patroness', explaining that while 'most of the alterations are minute' others 'chiefly regard the arrangement of a verse or two in Bothwellhaugh's Speech' and promising her a fresh copy of the revised poem 'with the notes & illustrations' which his wife Charlotte was then making for her (*Letters*, 1.150 [letter only]). In the meantime, since Lady Anne had told him that their mutual friend Lady Douglas

(1750–1817) wished to have a copy of the poem, Scott includes directions for constructing from her existing copy a revised version of Bothwellhaugh's speech. He writes out the equivalent passage to lines 129–60 in the present text, instructing that her copy should then be followed 'untill you come to the verse immediately subsequent to Bothwellhaughs speech which I have alterd thus', writing out the next stanza (see lines 181–84 in the present text). Unfortunately Charlotte Scott's copy of the complete revised version of 'Cadzow Castle' does not appear to have survived, but the stanzas from Bothwellhaugh's speech in this letter of 10 August are close to the equivalent passage in the published text. In the surviving presentation copy this had consisted of five stanzas only, which are reordered in Scott's letter, some with only a few individual words altered ('an iron grove' became 'a steely grove' in the equivalent of line 149 of the present text, for example), but others completely rewritten. For example, the version in this letter of the equivalent of lines 145–49 in the present text is that of the text in *Minstrelsy*, allowing for routine input by the printer, whereas in the presentation copy they had read:

> "Obsequious at their regents rein
>   Came stout Parkhead & Lochinvar
> And shame! Of all the supple train
>   The lowest bowd ignoble Mar!"

The two stanzas which were added in revision (equivalent to lines 153–60 of the present text) describe the appearance of Regent Murray (or Moray) in the moments preceding his assassination. (As Scott generally terms him Murray this spelling is followed throughout the present Notes, although 'Moray' is the modern spelling adhered to by various historians.)

A third manuscript version of part of Bothwellhaugh's speech forms part of Scott's letter to Anna Seward of 16 August 1802 (see *Letters*, 1.154–55 [minus verses]). The manuscript original in the Berg collection (Scott Letters 1/6) lacks the first page and the text of the remaining leaf is also torn, but it nevertheless provides a text for the equivalent passage to lines 137–76 in the present text that is close to the first printing in *Minstrelsy*. Scott's poem is again accompanied by glosses suited to the recipient, so that he explains to Seward how the name Bothwellhaugh should be pronounced and who Lord Lindesay is. There are also revisions to the two additional stanzas describing Murray. In Scott's letter to Lady Anne, Murray waved a 'steel truncheon' and his brow expressed a 'mingled shade', whereas in the letter to Seward, written less than a week later, Murray waves a 'stout truncheon' and his brow bears a 'passing shade'. As with other copies for friends Scott was possibly trying out alternative versions in passing, since in the text published in *Minstrelsy* Murray has a 'steel truncheon' as in the letter to Lady Anne but his brow bears a 'passing shade' as in the letter to Anna Seward.

There are other differences between the text of the presentation booklet of 'Cadyow Castle' in the Berg collection and the text in *Minstrelsy* in passages not present in Scott's letters to Lady Anne Hamilton and Anna Seward. Many are substitutions of single words, such as the change from 'swift steed' to 'shy steed' (line 44) or from 'hunters band' to 'kindred band' (line 106), but others are more substantial. Lines 29–32, for instance, originally read:

> On Evan's brow, whose chaplet rank
>   Was shagg'd with thorn & tangled sloe,
> The ashler buttress guards the bank
>   With battlements in terraced row.

Publication in the second edition of *Minstrelsy of the Scottish Border* rendered the text of 'Cadyow Castle' more stable. It was afterwards included in *Ballads and Lyrical Pieces* of 1806 (39–60) and in the section of additional poems in the eighth edition of *The Lay of the Last Minstrel* of 1808 (297–314, clv–clxi), before passing through the gateway of the 1820 *Poetical Works* (2.155–80) into the successive lifetime collected editions and into Lockhart's posthumous one of 1833–34 (4.200–17). The poem also continued to be reprinted in the successive lifetime editions of *Minstrelsy of the Scottish Border*. Besides changes of the kind normally associated with the printer there is one clear sign of subsequent authorial engagement, a sentence added in *Ballads* at the start of endnote 12: 'Richard Bannatyne mentions in his journal, that John Knox repeatedly warned Murray to avoid Linlithgow' (60). While this was reproduced in successive editions of Scott's collected poetry it was not included in successive editions of the *Minstrelsy*.

The present text follows that of *Minstrelsy of the Scottish Border*, 2nd edn, 3 vols (Edinburgh, 1803), 3.380–401, as best representing the culmination of Scott's initial creative process in a published text. The following emendations have been made:

111.headnote	Duke of Hamilton (*Ballads*) / duke of Hamilton
111.headnote	Regent Murray (1820*PW*) / regent Murray
111.footnote 2	Sir James Ballenden, Lord Justice Clerk (*Lay* Ed8) / sir James Ballenden, lord justice clerk
112.headnote	Queen Mary (*Ballads*) / queen Mary
112.footnote 1	Archbishop of St Andrews (*Lay* Ed8) / archbishop of St Andrews
112.footnote 1	Duke of Chatelherault (*Ballads*) / duke of Chatelherault
112.footnote 2	Lord John Hamilton (*Ballads*) / lord John Hamilton
113.headnote	Regent's death (1833–34*PW*) / regent's death
116.104	Bothwellhaugh!'" (1822*PW*) / Bothwellhaugh!'"
117.116	Bothwellhaugh! (1820*PW*) / Bothwellhaugh
120.notes subheading	CADYOW CASTLE (*Ballads*) / CADYOW-CASTLE
120.endnote 1	*troop, the* (*Minstrelsy* Ed3) / *troop the*
120.endnote 1	Earl (*Ballads*) / earl
120.endnote 1	Duke (*Ballads*) / duke
120.endnote 1	Queen (*Ballads*) / queen
120.endnote 2	*perflaverint* (Editorial) / *perflaverunt*
120.endnote 2	p. 18 (Editorial) / p. 13
120.endnote 3	Duke (*Ballads*) / duke
120.endnote 3	Queen (*Ballads*) / queen
120.endnote 3	Queen's (*Lay* Ed8) / queen's
120.endnote 3	Marquis (*Ballads*) / marquis
121.endnote 4	*set, since* (*Lay* Ed8) / *set since*
121.endnote 4	Lady Anne (*Ballads*) / lady Anne
121.endnote 4	Honourable (*Lay* Ed8) / honourable
121.endnote 4	College of Justice (*Lay* Ed8) / college of justice
121.endnote 6	*triumph, marched* (*Minstrelsy* Ed3) / *triumph marched*
121.endnote 6	Borders (*Lay* Ed8) / borders
122.endnote 7	Regent (1833–34*PW*) / regent
122.endnote 7	Hamilton Palace (1823*PW*) / Hamilton palace
122.endnote 9	Regent (1823*PW*) / regent
123.endnote 10	*Obseqious* (*Minstrelsy* Ed3) / *Obsequeous*

123.endnote 10   Earl (*Ballads*) / earl
123.endnote 10   Regent (1833–34*PW*) / regent
123.endnote 10   Earl (*Ballads*) / earl
123.endnote 11   Regent's (1833–34*PW*) / regent's
123.endnote 12   Regent (1833–34*PW*)/ regent

Historical Note

At the time of Scott's 1801 visit to Hamilton Palace Cadyow Castle was essentially a garden folly, having been partially reconstructed as such in the course of the eighteenth century. The castle was originally built for James, 2nd Earl of Arran (*c.* 1519–75) between 1500 and 1550, overlooking the park known as Cadyow Oaks containing trees surviving from a medieval hunting park, on the site of an earlier royal castle about 1.5 km (1 mile) SE of Hamilton on a gorge overlooking Avon Water. The sixteenth-century castle was destroyed by John Erskine, 1st Earl of Mar (d. 1572), Regent for James VI, in reprisal for the reception there of Mary, Queen of Scots (1542–87), after her escape from Lochleven Castle in 1568. It was during the short heyday of the castle that Queen Mary's illegitimate half-brother, James Stewart, 1st Earl of Murray (1531/2–70), Regent of Scotland for the infant James VI, was assassinated on 23 January 1570 by James Hamilton of Bothwellhaugh (d. 1581). This was plotted by John Hamilton, Roman Catholic Archbishop of St Andrews (*c.* 1510/11–71), and had wide support among the Hamiltons in general. Bothwellhaugh was the illegitimate nephew of both the Earl of Arran and the Archbishop, who owned the house in Linlithgow in which Bothwellhaugh hid during his ambush of Regent Murray. Although Scott retails the Romantic story about Bothwellhaugh's act of vengeance being in reprisal for brutal treatment of his wife by one of Murray's supporters, leading to her death shortly after childbirth, in fact Bothwellhaugh's wife Isobel outlived her husband. Scott also downplays, perhaps in deference to his Hamilton hosts, the fact that, as Arran's grandfather had married a sister of James III of Scotland, he was for the most part of his life the heir presumptive to the Scottish throne and therefore had a strong political motive for his antagonism to Murray, who opposed his claims. In one view, though clearly not in Scott's, Bothwellhaugh can be viewed as the Hamilton family's hitman.

Explanatory Notes

111.headnote   **river Evan**   an older name for the Avon, a river 38 km (24 miles) in length running from the boundary of East Ayrshire and South Lanarkshire until it joins the Clyde between Hamilton and Motherwell. It flows through a gorge in the pleasure-grounds of Hamilton Palace.

111.headnote   **Caledonian Forest**   the term comes from Pliny the Elder (AD 23–79), who mentions that after the Roman invasion of Britain their knowledge of it did not extend beyond the neighbourhood of the 'silva caledonia', not located but probably in line with the extent of the Roman occupation and therefore north of the River Clyde and west of the River Tay.

111.headnote   **Scottish wild cattle**   generally known as Chillingham wild cattle, since the largest genetically pure herd is kept at Chillingham Castle, about 19 km (12 miles) inland from Bamburgh on the coast of Northumberland. Thomas Bewick listed the herds of these cattle in 1790 in his work on quadrupeds, but did not include Cadzow: for further details see G. Kenneth Whitehead, *The Ancient White Cattle of Britain and their Descendants* (London, 1953).

111.headnote   **Dr Robertson**   the historian William Robertson (1721–93) was moderator of the Church of Scotland and Principal of Edinburgh University as well as an internationally respected historian, who placed his native country of Scotland in a British and European context in his works. For Scott's quotation see *The History of Scotland, During the Reigns of Queen Mary and of King James VI*, 2 vols (London, 1759), 1.435–36: see *ALC*. Allowing for changes of the kind normally associated with the printer, this is accurate, except that 'revenge upon the Regent' has been mistranscribed as 'revenge of the regent', while 'the throng of the people' has been mistranscribed as 'the throng of people'.

111.footnote 1   **Drumlanrig**   an estate near Thornhill in Dumfriesshire, owned at the time of writing by William Douglas, 4th Duke of Queensberry (1725–1810).

111.footnote 2   **Sir James Ballenden**   Sir John Bellenden (d. 1576) had administered the oath of regency to Murray at the coronation of the infant James VI and appeared at his side at the battle of Langside in May 1568. Scott got the name James from his stated source here: see John Spottiswood's *The History of the Church of Scotland*, 3rd edn (London, 1668), 233: see *ALC*.

112.headnote   **burned by Murray's army**   Regent Murray had led a military expedition against the supporters of Queen Mary in SW Scotland in June 1568, known as the 'Raid of Dumfries' and on his route also captured or destroyed the houses of her supporters in Lanarkshire.

112.headnote   **patronage of the family of Guise**   a French princely family, active on the Roman Catholic side in the Wars of Religion. Mary of Guise (1515–60), daughter of Claude of Lorraine, 1st Duke of Guise, was the mother of Mary, Queen of Scots, and acted as regent for her between 1554 and 1560.

112.headnote   **De Thou**   the French historian Jacque Auguste de Thou (1553–1617) published his *Historia sui temporis* (History of his own time) in Latin (his name being rendered as Thuanus) in instalments between 1604 and 1608. Scott's summary derives from Book 46: see *Jac. Augusti Thuani Historiarum Sui Temporis*, 7 vols (London, 1733), 2.768: see *ALC*. In English Bothwellhaugh's response in de Thou's work is thus: 'He replied resolutely that he was not authorised to carry across slaughter from Scotland to France, and that he had done what he had done and punished the one whom he had punished from an urgent sense of his own righteous pain, and that he would never, ever, carry out the revenge of other people for any entreaty or recompense.'

112.headnote   **Gaspar de Coligni**   Gaspard de Coligny, Seigneur de Chatillon (1519–72) was a French nobleman and a Huguenot (Protestant) leader in the French Wars of Religion. Many Huguenots were in Paris for the wedding of the Protestant King of Navarre with Marguerite de Valois, the King's sister, and afterwards on 22 August 1572 Coligny was shot in the street from a house belonging to the Catholic Guise family but escaped with a damaged arm. Fearing reprisals the Catholics carried out a pre-emptive strike on Huguenots in the St Bartholomew's Day Massacre of 24 August, when Coligny was killed.

112.footnote 1   **Duke of Chatelherault**   the Earl of Arran's French dukedom was a reward for his agreement to a French marriage for the infant Mary, Queen of Scots.

112.footnote 2   **Lord John Hamilton**   Lord John Hamilton (1539/40–1604) was the third son of the 2nd Earl of Arran and, despite being a Protestant, a staunch supporter of Queen Mary. He subsequently became 1st Marquess of Hamilton.

113.headnote Blackwood Adam Blackwood (1539–1613) was a Roman Catholic writer who advocated a theory of absolute monarchy, and shortly after the death of Mary, Queen of Scots, published in 1587 *Martyre de la royne d'Écosse*, which described her treatment at the hands of Elizabeth I of England, and included transcriptions of their correspondence, as well as poems attacking Elizabeth. Scott cites this work's account of Murray's assassination from Samuel Jebb, *De Vita & Rebus Gestis Serenissimae Principis Mariæ Scotorum Reginæ*, 2 vols (London, 1725), 2.263: *ALC*. Blackwood's work is given there in French, and the translation is presumably Scott's own.

113.headnote Murdin's State Papers see William Murdin, *A Collection of State Papers relating to Affairs in the Reign of Queen Elizabeth, from the Year 1571 to 1596* (London, 1759), 197: *ALC*. Despite Scott's giving a volume number, the work appears to be in a single volume. Allowing for changes of the kind normally associated with the printer, the quotation is accurate, except that the spelling has been slightly modernised and 'Promyse of Preferment and Reward' has been altered to 'promise of preferment or rewarde'.

114.30 tangling sloe the blackthorn plant, *prunus spinosa*.

114.31 ashler buttress one made of square hewn stone, often used as a facing to rubble or brick wall.

115.45 chief rode on Chatelherault could not have been riding at Cadzow Castle at the time. He had been taken into custody by Murray following Queen Mary's appointment of him as her lieutenant in Scotland on 28 February 1567 and was released only after the murder of Murray.

115.71–72 smoke, / Where yeomen dight the attendants had presumably lit a fire and were preparing a meal for the hunting party: *dight* means to make ready.

116.81 Stern Claud (see also Scott's 3rd endnote.) Lord Claud Hamilton (*c.* 1546?–1621) was in fact the fifth and youngest son of the 2nd Earl of Arran. He had been made commendator of Paisley as a child when his uncle resigned the position to become Archbishop of St Andrews. He played a leading part in forwarding Queen Mary's escape from Lochleven Castle and afterwards accompanied her on her flight into England.

116.82 Pasley's Pasley or Paslay is an older spelling of Paisley, situated 11 km (7 miles) W of Glasgow and 85 km (53 miles) W of Edinburgh. The Cluniac foundation there dates from the later part of the 12th century, though rebuilt in the 14th century.

116.85 Woodhouselee (see also Scott's 4th endnote.) The present Woodhouselee is a mansion in Glencorse parish, about 11 km (7 miles) S of Edinburgh and 5 km (3 miles) N of Penicuik, on the eastern slope of the Pentland Hills. The old Woodhouselee stood at the SE corner of the parish on the left bank of the River Esk near Auchindinny.

116.108 Arran brand a sword belonging to Hamilton, Earl of Arran.

117.128 Linlithgow's crowded town (see also Scott's headnote.) Linlithgow is an ancient royal burgh in West Lothian, close to the border with Stirlingshire and was formerly on the main road between Edinburgh and Stirling.

117.131 Knox the religious reformer John Knox (*c.* 1514–72) was an advisor to Regent Murray, whom he viewed as a leader who had rescued the kingdom of Scotland from disaster. Murray's assassination was a blow to Knox, who preached movingly at his funeral.

117.footnote Spenser the poet Edmund Spenser (1552?–99), best-known for his long romance, *The Faerie Queene* (1590), dedicated to and complimenting Elizabeth I of England.

118.141   Morton (see also Scott's 8th endnote.) James Douglas, 4th Earl of Morton (*c.* 1516–81), was a key political figure during Murray's regency and subsequently (following the death of Lennox in October 1572) became Regent himself.

118.144   Macfarlanes' plaided clan (see also Scott's 9th endnote.) The clan, claiming descent from the ancient Earls of Lennox, occupied the land along the western shore of Loch Lomond in Perthshire.

118.145   Glencairn (see also Scott's 10th endnote.) Alexander Cunningham, 4th Earl of Glencairn (d. 1574/5), was a firm supporter of Murray's regency, and a friend of John Knox.

118.145   Parkhead (see also Scott's 10th endnote.) Parkhead was an estate in Lanarkshire, which the Earl of Morton's natural brother, George Douglas, possessed through his marriage to the heiress Elizabeth Douglas.

118.147   Lindesay's iron eye (see also Scott's 11th endnote.) Patrick Lindsay, 6th Lord Lindsay of the Byres (1521?–89) was Murray's brother-in-law and his firm supporter. His insensibility is indicated by the lack of softness of expression in his eye.

118.155   truncheon a baton symbolising authority, particularly the one borne by a field marshall.

119.177   noble Chatlerault after the battle of Pinkie in September 1547 James Hamilton, 2nd Earl of Arran, was rewarded by the French for agreeing to a French marriage for Mary, Queen of Scots, by the gift of the French duchy of Chatelherault in Poitou and a palace in Paris itself. He was also confirmed in his position as governor of Scotland, with access to crown revenues until the Queen's majority.

119.198   maids, who list these would include Lady Anne Hamilton and her sister Lady Susan, and also potentially Lady Douglas, since all three are mentioned in Scott's letter to Lady Anne of 29 July 1802 (*Letters*, 1.149–50) with his revisions to 'Cadyow Castle' (see Textual Note).

120.endnote 1   lieutenant-general in Scotland after her flight to England in 1568 Mary drew up a paper giving all her interest in the government of Scotland to the Duke of Chatelherault until her return, and on 28 February 1569 she proclaimed him her lieutenant there along with the earls of Huntly and Argyll. As heir presumptive to the Scottish crown he had been named regent for the infant Queen Mary on the death of her father, James V of Scotland.

120.endnote 2   Leslæus Translated this Latin passage reads: 'There is a particular kind of forest bull, that was once frequently found in Scotland, but now only rarely so, truth be told. It has a thick and drooping mane like that of a lion, of a blindingly pale colour. It is fierce and savage, and has an aversion to all humankind, such that whenever people touch it with their hands, or even let it smell their breath, it keeps back from them for many days afterwards. Moreover, such boldness is attributed to this bull, that it will not only furiously throw horsemen to the ground when it is angry, but it will even, when sufficiently provoked, attack everybody indiscriminately with its horns and hooves, and it will wholly disregard attacks made by dogs, even though the dogs we have in our country are very fierce indeed. The meat of this bull is gristly, but most delicious in its flavour. It was once found throughout the very extensive forest that was Caledonia/Scotland, but as a result of human gluttony there remain only three places where it dwells: Stirling, Cumbernauld, and Kincarnia [the last probably being Kincardine on the River Forth].' Scott cites the section 'Regionum & Insularum Scotiae Descriptio' of the Latin history of Scotland by John Lesley, Bishop of Ross (1527–96), a chief supporter of Queen Mary, *De Origine Moribus & rebus gestis Scotorum* (Rome, 1675), 18: *ALC*.

120.endnote 3   Langside   a battle fought at Langside, now part of Glasgow, on 13 May 1568, by supporters of Queen Mary attempting to regain her throne against the Lords of the Congregation led by the Earl of Murray. When Mary's army disintegrated she fled to England.

120.endnote 3   Raid of Stirling   after the battle of Langside Lord Claud Hamilton was declared a traitor and his estates forfeited, while his uncle the Archbishop of St Andrews was hanged at Stirling. On 4 September 1571 Hamilton with a small force of 400 men attempted to surprise the town of Stirling, but they were repulsed after being temporarily successful.

120.endnote 3   ancestor of the present Marquis of Abercorn   James Hamilton (1575–1618), the eldest surviving son of Lord Claud Hamilton, was made Earl of Abercorn in 1606. John James Hamilton, 1st Marquess of Abercorn (1756–1818), and his wife were important patrons of Scott, whose father and brother Thomas served as factors to Abercorn.

121.endnote 4   Lady Anne Bothwell   'Lady Anne Bothwell's Lament' is a well-known Scottish song, in which a mother who has been deserted by her husband or lover sings to her baby. The heroine is sometimes identified with a daughter of Adam Bothwell, Bishop of Orkney (1529?–93). It is included in Thomas Percy, *Reliques of Ancient English Poetry*, 3 vols (London, 1765), 2.194–96 (see *ALC*).

121.endnote 4   Tytler   Scott had been influenced by the lectures of the historian and lawyer Alexander Fraser Tytler (1747–1813) while studying at the University of Edinburgh, and Tytler had subsequently published his *Elements of General History* in 1801. He had inherited the Woodhouselee estate on the death of his father in 1792, and in February 1802 was appointed to the bench of the Court of Session in Edinburgh under the title of Lord Woodhouselee.

121.endnote 5   Birrel's Diary   Robert Birrel (fl. 1567–1605) was a burgess of Edinburgh, whose diary was first published as 'The Diarey of Robert Birrel, Burges of Edinburghe. Containing Divers Passages of Staite, and Uthers Memorable Accidents', in John Graham Dalyell's *Fragments of Scotish History* (Edinburgh, 1798), 18: *ALC*. The spelling in the quotation has been slightly modernised, and the bracketed gloss of 'ditch' added presumably by Scott.

122.endnote 6   Scotish Poems   see 'Ane Tragedie, in Forme of Ane Diallog' in *Scotish Poems, of the Sixteenth Century*, ed. Dalyell (Edinburgh, 1801), 232: *ALC*. The spelling in the quotation has been slightly modernised.

122.endnote 7   carbine ... Hamilton   Palace   for this particular weapon, described as an Italian matchlock hunting carbine with a 0.76 m long rifled hexagonal barrel, see http://www.historicalfirearms.info/post/44080203903/the-first-assassination-with-a-firearm-in-1570. Hamilton Palace was demolished in 1927 and many of its contents sold at auction.

122.endnote 8   murder of David Rizzio   David Rizzio or Riccio (1533–66) was secretary to Mary, Queen of Scots, and was stabbed to death at Holyrood Palace in the presence of the pregnant Queen on 9 March 1566 by her consort, Darnley, and his friends.

122.endnote 8   Darnley   Henry Stewart, Duke of Albany (1545/46–67) was known as Lord Darnley from his barony in Renfrewshire, and was the second husband of Mary, Queen of Scots. He was killed at Kirk o' Field to the south of Edinburgh during the night of 9–10 February 1567, the murder being covered by an explosion at his lodging there. Queen Mary was strongly suspected of being implicated in the death of her husband.

122.endnote 9   Holinshed   Raphael Holinshed (*c.* 1525–80?) published his *Chronicles of England, Scotland, and Ireland* in 1577. It is not clear which edition Scott was quoting from in 1803: for the relevant passage see *Holinshed's Chronicles of England, Scotland, and Ireland*, 6 vols (London, 1807-08), 5.533: *ALC*.

123.endnote 9   *Calderwood's MS. apud Keith*   David Calderwood (*c.* 1575–1650), Church of Scotland minister and historian opposed to James VI and I's attempt to introduce episcopacy in the Church of Scotland. His most important work, *The True History of the Church of Scotland*, was not published until 1678, after his death. Scott cites Calderwood's account from the history of Robert Keith (1681–1757), Bishop of Edinburgh and a Jacobite, whose work is probably the first covering the period from 1542 to 1568 to be based on original research, and contains a collection of supporting documents. For the relevant passage see *History of the Affairs of Church and State in Scotland, from the Beginning of the Reformation to the Year 1568*, Spottiswoode Society, 3 vols (Edinburgh, 1845), 2.817.

123.endnote 9   Melville   Sir James Melville, of Halhill (1535/6–1617) was a diplomat and privy councillor to Mary, Queen of Scots. His autobiography, *Memoirs of his Own Life*, was first published in 1683 and then in a variety of editions during the 18th century, before being produced in a new edition by the Bannatyne Club in 1827. In his account of the battle of Langside, Melville states 'the Regent led the battaill, and the Erle of Mortoun the vantgaird' and that at the start of the encounter 'the rycht wing of the Regentis vantgard put bak and sattil lyk to fle, wherof the maist part wer commons of the barronnye of Ranthrow', until the Laird of Grange told them that their enemies were already turning back and encouraged them to stand fast until he could summon reinforcements: see *Memoirs of his Own Life by Sir James Melville of Halhill MDXLIX–MDXCIII*, Bannatyne Club (Edinburgh, 1827), 201–02.

123.endnote 12   *Spottiswoode*   John Spottiswoode (1565–1639), Archbishop of St Andrews, was an advocate of episcopacy in the Scottish church in the reign of James VI and I. His *History of the Church of Scotland*, though commissioned by King James, was not published until 1655. Spottiswoode relates: 'The Regent had warning given him the same morning, that one did lye in wait for his life, and had the house designed where the man did lurk; but giving small ear unto it, answered, that *his life was in the hands of God, which he was ready to yield at his good pleasure.* Only he resolved to pass out of the Town by the same Gate at which he entered, and to turn on the back of the Town unto the way that led to *Edinburgh*, whither he was purposed. But when he had taken horse, either that he would not seem fearful, or then hindered by the throng of horsemen that attended, and thinking to ride quickly by the house that was suspected, he changed his resolution: but the throng there working him the like impediment, the Murtherer had the occasion to execute his Treachery': *The History of the Church of Scotland*, 3rd edn (London, 1668), 233.

123.endnote 12   *Buchanan*   George Buchanan (1506–82) was attached to the party of Regent Murray and became tutor to James VI of Scotland. His *De Jure Regni* (1579) defended a constitutional monarchy and argued that a bad ruler could be deposed. The account of Murray's assassination in Bk 19 of his Latin History of Scotland, *Rerum Scoticarum Historia*, published in the year of his death, agrees with that of Spottiswoode in emphasising the lack of precaution taken by the Regent despite his having been forewarned of the attempt. In *Ballads* (1806) and subsequent editions of Scott's collected poems, the whole note was prefaced by a sentence reading 'Richard Bannatyne mentions in his journal, that John Knox repeatedly warned Murray to avoid Linlithgow' (60). Bannatyne (d. 1605) was secretary to John Knox, and the Bannatyne Club printed his *Memorials* subsequent to Scott's death: for this allusion see *Memorials of Transactions in Scotland*, Bannatyne Club (Edinburgh, 1836), 290. For details of the Bannatyne Club see no. 116, 'A Bannatyne Garland'.

47. The Reiver's Wedding

Textual Note
On 29 June 1802 Scott wrote to Anna Seward (1742–1809) that he thought of writing a comic ballad on a legend relating to his own ancestor, Sir William Scott, 4th Laird of Harden (d. 1655), but confessed to her on 16 August 'The ballad of the Reiver's Wedding is not yet written' (*Letters*, 1.144–45, 155). Scott never did finish it, and only rough draft manuscript material, representing his attempts to write it, appears to have survived, which is now in the Berg Collection of the New York Public Library. This consists of twelve unnumbered leaves, each measuring approx. 18.4 x 15.2 cm and bearing a watermark of an elaborate crowned shield containing a seated Britannia and 'S 1794'. Of the twelve leaves, bound into a red-leather volume, the ninth and the final two are blank. Scott has written on the rectos only of the others, and the manuscript material bears all the signs of a very rough draft: many individual lines and words have been deleted or inserted, and occasionally a word is missing that seems required by the meaning or the scansion, while one odd couplet is interspersed among the four-line stanzas.

Although stanzas [1]–7 are numbered, there are two fourth stanzas while subsequent stanzas are unnumbered. Scott may have been trying out alternative approaches and had not yet determined which stanza to choose, since neither has been deleted as redundant. However, the repetition for emphasis of the same idea using different wording is characteristic of the ballad and it is possible that eventually both might have been retained. The same is true of the introduction of the Warden's three daughters, which also occurs in two consecutive stanzas (see lines 69–72 and 73–76 of the present text).

Other instances of repetition in this draft manuscript, however, are clearly not ballad-like variations. They appear to consist of an undeleted first attempt followed by a second attempt at conveying the same portion of the narrative: in such cases the coherence of the narrative demands that only one is selected. Although Scott has failed to delete his first attempt, the natural assumption has to be that the second attempt replaces the first, and this is the version included in the present text in two instances. Firstly, following line 20 in the present text, the manuscript supplies three stanzas representing an earlier attempt at the portion of the narrative treated in lines 21–36 of the present text, given below in a reading transcription:

> He blew his bugle sharp & hie
>   Till moss & water rung around
> Three score of Mosstroopers & three
>   Have mounted at that bugle sound
>
> The Michaelmas moon had enterd then
>   And ere she won the full
> Ye might see by her light in Harden glen
>   A bow of kye & a bassend Bull

> And loud & loud in Harden tower
> The quaigh gaed round wi' mickle glee
> For the English Beef was brought in bowr
> And the English ale flowd merrilie

There are also two lines between lines 88 and 89 of the present text, which (although undeleted) appear to represent an abandoned start to the following four-line stanza:

> Her Sisters rode to fair Dumfries
> The bridal sports to see

The narrative proceeds as far as f. 8 of the Berg manuscript, but f. 10, which follows an intervening blank leaf, contains four stanzas that, instead of taking the story forward, represent a different attempt at describing Meg herself and probably belong to another draft of the poem altogether. A reading transcription of the text on this leaf is as follows:

> Her sisters scarfs by gallants gent
> On helm & spear were borne
> But never at tilt or tournament
> Were Margarets colours worne.

> Nor rosy bright was Margarets face
> Nor golden waved her hair
> Nor heaved her breast in snowy grace
> But a leal fast heart was there

> She loved Lord William many a day
> But secret was her pain
> For well she weend that gallant gay
> Would never love again

> She saw him at the border games
> & the painted hall within
> All careless of the loveliest Dames
> That strove his heart to win

Lockhart in his *Life* of Scott states that he had found two copies of the unfinished poem's commencement and prints 'what seems to have been the second one' (1.353–56). Lockhart, however, was a notoriously interventionist editor of Scott's work and it is impossible to tell whether his version has the Berg material as its source or not. Certainly the narrative ceases in Lockhart's version as in the main sequence of the Berg material with Meg seeing some of the Johnston men approaching Lochwood with the captive William Scott, and it is perfectly possible that Lockhart has chosen among alternative lines and stanzas of the Berg manuscript to achieve a smooth narrative flow, also making some changes of his own to what he did use. If based on the Berg manuscript material, the version Lockhart published as the first printing of 'The Reiver's Wedding' represents a somewhat unsatisfactory text.

The present text follows the main narrative sequence in ff. 1–8 of the Berg manuscript, making allowance for Scott's having intended some rhetorical and ballad-like repetition of ideas, but omitting the passages described above as superseded attempts at drafting a portion of the narrative and excluding the material on f. 10 as probably originating in another draft manuscript altogether. Speech marks have been silently regularised, and ampersands have been routinely expanded to 'and'; verb forms ending with 'd' have been interpreted as 'ed', while routine apostrophes and full stops at the ends of stanzas have been silently introduced as required. The following emendations have been made:

124.4	Ladie? (Editorial) / Ladie
124.5	kye (Editorial) / Kye
124.5	herd (Editorial) / Herd
124.7	that ane's ten (Editorial) / that ten
124.9	quo' (Editorial) / quo
124.12	cow? (Editorial) / cow"
124.16	kye (Editorial) / Kye
124.21	bugle (Editorial) / Bugle
124.22	o'er and (Editorial) / oer and
124.24	bugle (Editorial) / Bugle
124.27	moss troopers (Editorial) / Moss troopers
124.28	bugle (Editorial) / Bugle
125.32	bow (Editorial) / Bow
125.32	bull (Editorial) / Bull
125.35	beef (Editorial) / Beef
125.38	braes (Editorial) / Braes
125.44	spur (Editorial) / Spur
125.45	berry (Editorial) / Berry
125.47	ye, my guests, (Editorial) / ye my guests
125.50	three (Editorial) / 3
125.52	men (Editorial) / Men
126.61	gane (Editorial) / Gane
126.66	tho' (Editorial) / tho
126.83	wa' (Editorial) / wa
126.85	gallants (Editorial) / Gallants
126.86	sisters' (Editorial) / Sisters
127.95	maid (Editorial) / Maid
127.97	"Of all (Editorial) / all
127.99	that (Editorial) / that that
127.108	shackled (Editorial) / Shackled

Historical Note

In his letter to Anna Seward of 29 June 1802 Scott described the legend upon which 'The Reiver's Wedding' was to have been based as one which had been repeatedly told to him in early life:

> A certain Sir William Scott, from whom I am descended, was ill-advised enough to plunder the estate of Sir Gideon Murray of Elibank … The marauder was defeated, seized, and brought in fetters to the castle of Elibank, upon the Tweed. The Lady Murray … descried the return of her husband with his prisoners. She immediately inquired what he meant to do with the young Knight of Harden, which was the *petit titre* of Sir William Scott. "Hang the robber, assuredly," was the answer of Sir Gideon. "What!" answered the lady, "hang the handsome young knight of Harden, when I have three ill-favoured daughters unmarried! No, no, Sir Gideon, we'll force him to marry our Meg." Now, tradition says, that Meg Murray was the ugliest woman in the four counties, and that she was called, in the homely dialect of the time, *meikle-mouthed Meg* … Sir Gideon … entered into his wife's sentiments, and proffered to Sir William the alternative of becoming his son-in-law, or decorating

with his carcase the *kindly* gallows of Elibank. The lady was so very ugly, that Sir William, the handsomest man of his time, positively refused the honour of her hand. Three days were allowed him to make up his mind; and it was not until he found one end of a rope made fast to his neck, and the other knitted to a sturdy oak bough, that his resolution gave way, and he preferred an ugly wife to the literal noose. It is said, they were afterwards a very happy couple. (*Letters*, 1.144–45)

As Lockhart points out (*Life*, 1.353), Scott includes other stories relating to the Scotts of Harden in 'The Reiver's Wedding', and alters a number of details in this one. The opening sequence where William Scott's pride is affronted at hearing the cow-herd refer to his one cow, and the presentation at the family table of a dish of spurs as a hint that it was time to replenish the stock of meat by another cattle-raid, had been previously told of William's father, Walter Scott of Harden (*c.* 1550–1629?) by Scott himself: see the footnote in the Introduction to *Minstrelsy* (1.cviii). Furthermore, the bride's father in the traditional story was Sir Gideon Murray of Elibank (*c.* 1560–1621), a neighbouring landowner, whereas in 'The Reiver's Wedding' he is the head of the Johnstone clan of Annandale in Dumfriesshire.

Scott was not the only poet to have found inspiration in this legend, for James Hogg's poem 'The Fray of Elibank' was also based on Scott's telling of it (see *The Mountain Bard*, ed. Suzanne Gilbert (Edinburgh, 2007), 45–51), while subsequently Robert Browning (1812–89) wrote his 'Muckle-Mouth Meg'.

Explanatory Notes
124.title   Reiver's   that of a plunderer or robber, especially someone cattle-raiding.
124.1   bourd   amusement or sport.
124.13   Michaelmas   29 September, the feast of Michael and All Angels.
124.14   fauldfu's lye   the cattle enclosed in a fold or pen, chiefly an outfield part of a settlement where their dung would manure the land.
124.16   kye   cows, rather than a single cow.
125.31   Kirkhope   an area on the left bank of Ettrick Water in Selkirkshire. Kirkhope Tower is 1.6 km (1 mile) NW of Ettrick Bridge and about 11 km (7 miles) from Selkirk.
125.32   bow of kye and a bassened bull   a herd of cows and a spotted or piebald bull.
125.34   quaigh   a shallow drinking-cup with two handles, usually made of staves of wood hooped together.
125.37   Teviot side   Roxburghshire is probably intended. According to John Leyden 'The name of Teviotdale … is not confined solely to the vale of the river, but comprehends the county of Roxburgh': *Scenes of Infancy: Descriptive of Teviotdale* (Edinburgh, 1803), 150.
125.38   Yarrow's braes   the Yarrow flows through Selkirkshire, from St Mary's Loch about 23 km (14 miles) NE until it joins the Ettrick S of Selkirk.
125.43   bowne   preparing, getting ready.
125.46   shente   ashamed, disgraced.
125.53   Falsehope   or Fauldshope, a farm close to the Scott stronghold of Oakwood Tower in the Ettrick valley in Selkirkshire.
125.55   riding turn   a raid made on horseback.
125.56   "*Wat Draw the Sword*"   among clans like the Scotts, where there were likely to be numerous men sharing the same Christian as well as surname, individuals were distinguished by a 'to-name' or nickname.
125.58   Trysting tree   a trysting place is a place of meeting by appointment. Andrew Ogilvie writes of one in the centre of Linton in

Roxburghshire, 'five or six stones form a circle about the size of a cock-pit, called the *Tryst*: Here the parties that made incursions into Northumberland, used to meet; but when those that came first could not wait for the arrival of their companions, they cut with their swords upon the turf, the initials of their names, the head of the letters pointing to the place whither they were going, that their friends might follow them': *The Statistical Account of Scotland 1791– 1799*, 20 vols (Wakefield, 1979), 3.552.

125.60   Lochwood   Lochwood Tower, the home of the head of the Johnstone clan, is about 10 km (6 miles) S of Moffatt in Dumfriesshire. It is probably called 'dark Lochwood' subsequently because it is surrounded by ancient trees.

126.62   Warden's gear   the laird of Johnstone was Warden of the West March for Scotland several times during the later part of the 16th century. The office of Lord Warden entailed keeping the border with England secure and administering March law.

126.71   may   'A May, in old Scottish ballads and romances, denotes a young lady, or a maiden somewhat above the lower class': James Hogg, *Mador of the Moor*, ed. James E. Barcus (Edinburgh, 2005), 33n.

126.81   pranked   dressed up in a showy manner.

126.83   Dundrenan's wa'   Dundrennan Abbey in the village of Dundrennan, about 8 km (5 miles) SE of Kirkcudbright,was founded in 1142 for Cistercian monks rather than for nuns.

126.85   casque   a military head-piece, a helmet.

126.85   gent   noble, well-born, gentle.

126.89   Thirlestane   Thirlestane Castle, about 27 km (17 miles) SW of Selkirk on the left bank of Ettrick Water, was the home of the Scotts of Thirlestane.

127.94   Yarrow to the Tyne   from S Scotland to N England. Yarrow Water is in Selkirkshire, while the Tyne is a river of NE England.

127.98   Teviot to the Dee   from S to N of Scotland. The Teviot flows through Roxburghshire while the Dee is a river flowing mostly through S Aberdeenshire.

48.   On the Death of Simon de Montfort

Textual Note
Scott's 'On the Death of Simon de Montfort' was intended as a contribution to a revised edition of *Ancient Songs, from the Time of King Henry the Third, to the Revolution* (London, 1790), that his antiquarian friend Joseph Ritson (1752– 1803) was preparing towards the end of his life. Unfortunately Ritson, suffering from mental breakdown, barricaded himself into his rooms in Gray's Inn and set fire to his manuscripts shortly before his decease so that the revised work never appeared. Scott's manuscript survived the conflagration because Ritson had previously lent it to a fellow antiquary, Thomas Park (1758/59–1834), by whom it was used, with Scott's permission, in a section of 'Ancient Ballads' included in his new edition of Ritson's *A Select Collection of English Songs*, 3 vols (London, 1813), 2.380–84. Scott had an opportunity for proof correction, since in writing to him on 23 June 1812 (NLS, MS 3883, f. 12) Park enclosed a printed version of the poem asking Scott to add in the blank margin whatever 'you may be inclined to subjoin in the way of illustration or alteration'.

Although also printed in Scott's lifetime as 'Ballad on the Death of Simon de Montfort' in *Blackwood's Edinburgh Magazine*, 17 (April 1825), 484–85, this was as part of a review article of the 1813 edition of Ritson's work, 'Odoherty on English Songs' (480–85), that opens 'I have been tumbling over Ritson's songs listlessly this morning, for want of something better to do'. Scott never included it in any of the editions of his collected poems published during his lifetime, and the 1813 volume thus remains the only authorised printing. Nor does the manuscript Scott sent to Ritson apparently survive.

The present text follows that of 'On the Death of Simon de Montfort, Earl of Leicester, at the Battle of Evesham, 1266', in Joseph Ritson, *A Select Collection of English Songs*, 2nd edn, rev. Thomas Park, 3 vols (London, 1813), 2.380–84. An initial footnote by the volume's editor, keyed to Scott's name as author and thanking him for permission to include the translation in the work, has been omitted since it is clearly the work of Park and not of Scott. The title has been abbreviated, and the unusual-looking indentation of the first two lines of the Chorus (lines 5–6) has also been regularised. Scott's unconventional spelling was clearly designed to suggest the poem's medieval origin and setting, and has not therefore been altered. No emendations have been made.

Historical Note
Park's editorial footnote to 'On the Death of Simon de Montfort' states, 'The Norman-French original, which ought to have accompanied this ballad, cannot now be retraced': Joseph Ritson, *A Select Collection of English Songs*, 3 vols (London, 1813), 2.380. The original ballad was, however, subsequently included in a new edition of Ritson's *Ancient Songs and Ballads, from the Reign of King Henry the Second to the Revolution*, 2 vols (London, 1829: *ALC*), 1.15–18, where it is followed by another English translation (1.18–21) by George Ellis (1753–1815) which an editorial note states was also made at Ritson's request. Both Ellis's and Scott's translations appear to be of the same manuscript of the Norman French ballad, now located in the British Library, Harley 2253, f. 59r–v, and Park indeed mentions in his letter to Scott of 21 March 1812 (NLS, MS 3882, f. 106) that Scott's translation is of 'a Norman French ballad in the [British] Museum'. Though aware that Scott's 'On the Death of Simon de Montfort' more properly belonged in Ritson's *Ancient Songs and Ballads* collection, Park chose to add it to the 'Ancient Ballads' section of *English Songs* he was preparing in 1812, arguing in his letter to Scott of 21 March that 'its insertion there will very nearly accord with your original intention. I represented this circumstance about ten days ago to Mr [Richard] Heber, who approved of my suggestion' (NLS, MS 3882, f. 106). No doubt Park wished to increase the prestige of his edition of *English Songs* by including a ballad translation by a celebrity author. Scott's idiom is reasonably close to that of the original, allowing for the adjustments required by his metre and some minor individual interpretations: for instance, in the third verse of the original de Montfort is not said to be a martyr but only to be like one, and in the fourth verse the original states that Gloucester delivered men to their deaths not that he actually killed them with his sword. Scott takes part of the first verse into the chorus, which in the original consists of four lines only. Most interesting of all perhaps from Scott, as a British author, is that saving England in the original is changed by him to saving '[o]ur native land'.

Scott probably envisaged his work more as a poem than a song for performance, despite its actual and potential inclusion in two of Ritson's song collections. Park in 1813 follows Ritson's original edition of 1783 in giving musical annotation in the third volume for the original airs for the songs wherever possible, but neither the music nor the name of a tune is given for the ballad Scott has translated (3.315) and neither is there any named tune or musical annotation for

the original ballad and Ellis's translation in the 1829 edition of Ritson's *Ancient Songs and Ballads*.
    Simon de Montfort, 8th Earl of Leicester (*c*.1208–65), was an important magnate who pursued personal aggrandisement in conjunction with political reforms. He was a chief mover in the reform movement of 1258–59, directed against the power of Henry III's half-brothers the Lusignans, that drew support from the minor barons, knights, and local freeholders who had been among the chief sufferers from royal misgovernment and the Lusignan influence. Henry's kingship was placed under the control of a baronial council in the Provisions of Oxford of June 1258, and in a reforming parliament the following year concessions were made to under-tenants and others with grievances against their feudal lords. By 1264 England was in a state of civil war, and at a battle at Lewes in Sussex on 14 May that year de Montfort defeated the royal forces and captured both Henry and his heir, the future Edward I. Following the battle the government was assigned to a narrower council of nine, headed by a triumvirate of Montfort himself, the Bishop of Chester, and Gilbert de Clare, Earl of Gloucester. De Montfort encouraged local support for reform by allowing the knights who had been summoned to parliament to nominate their own county sheriffs. However, de Montfort's greediness in acquiring land and the oppressions of his sons led to the Earl of Gloucester deserting him and joining Edward, who had escaped from captivity. At the battle of Evesham on 4 August 1265 de Montfort was defeated and killed, along with his eldest son, Henry. After his death (despite his acquisitive nature) de Montfort's commitment to reform and his religious zeal rapidly gained him the reputation of a saint and martyr. His cult was focused around the battlefield and the abbey at Evesham where he was buried, miracles being reported from both locations within months of de Montfort's death.

Explanatory Notes
128.19   **Edward stoute**   the future Edward I of England (1239–1307) and heir of Henry III. By marriage Simon de Montfort was his uncle and his allegiance shifted between the royal cause and that of the reforming barons. At the battle of Evesham he was at the head of the victorious royalist army, along with the Earl of Gloucester.
129.24   **Becket's fayth**   Thomas Becket (1120?–70), Archbishop of Canterbury, was murdered in his own cathedral church at the supposed instigation of Henry II (1133–89) and posthumously recognised by the church as an important saint and martyr.
129.31   **Sir Hugh Despencer**   Sir Hugh Despenser (*c*. 1223–65) was a middle-ranking baron and supporter of de Montfort, justiciar and keeper of the Tower of London, and a leading figure in the government after the battle of Lewes. He was also killed at the battle of Evesham, reportedly by the thrust of a dagger, and buried with de Montfort at the abbey there.
129.35   **Sir Henry**   Henry de Montfort (1238–65) was the eldest son of Simon de Montfort, and was also killed at the battle of Evesham.
129.38   **Erle Gloster's sword**   Gilbert de Clare, 7th Earl of Gloucester (1243–95), was probably the most powerful man in England except de Montfort himself, who he had joined in May 1263 and by whom he was knighted on the field at Lewes. He was afterwards one of the triumvirate who governed England, but nevertheless resentful of de Montfort's acquisitiveness. After Edward's escape from captivity in May 1265, Gloucester supported him and commanded one of the divisions of the royal army at the battle of Evesham, taking a decisive part in de Montfort's overthrow.

129.50   sackclothe shirt   the original ballad refers rather to a haircloth shirt as a treasure found upon de Montfort's body, a garment worn by ascetics and penitents for the mortification of the flesh.

130.60   infant fair, our noble heir   although a male heir is implied, Simon de Montfort's daughter Eleanor (*c.* 1258–82) appears to have been his heir and she was still a child at the time of his death. She had four elder brothers, but was the last surviving de Montfort, dying in childbirth after her marriage to Llywelyn ap Gruffudd, Prince of Wales.

130.73   losel   one who is lost, a son of perdition, a worthless person.

130.82   Who captive ta'en   those taken prisoner at the battle of Evesham included Simon de Montfort's third son, Guy (*c.* 1244–91/2).

49.   The Recollections of Chastellain

Textual Note
This item was intended as a contribution to a revised edition of *Ancient Songs, from the Time of King Henry the Third, to the Revolution* (London, 1790) that Scott's antiquarian friend Joseph Ritson (1752–1803) was preparing towards the end of his life. It seems probable that Ritson had invited Scott to translate the poem into English during Scott's visit to London during the spring of 1803, when Scott met Francis Douce (1757–1834), since Ritson's letter to Scott of 2 July 1803 comments, 'I shall be, perfectly, satisfy'd with your translation of "The remembrances" of Chastelain; you may wish to run your eye over the manuscript notes, in mister Douce's copy of the edition of 1537, C. P. [*ceteris paribus*(?), all other things being equal] which I should, properly, have given you when here' (NLS, MS 3874, f. 222). Scott sent his poem to Ritson by the hands of the publisher Owen Rees with his letter of 11 September 1803 (*Letters*, 1.199), but unfortunately Ritson, suffering from mental breakdown, barricaded himself into his rooms in Gray's Inn and set fire to his manuscripts shortly before his decease on 23 September, so that the revised work never appeared. Scott clearly kept a copy of his poem, since he was able to send 'Ritson's … copy of Molinet's Remembrances & my translation' for the use of Ritson's nephew, Joseph Frank, with his letter to Robert Surtees of 23 March 1810 (*Letters*, 2.316). It was eventually published, for the first time, in Frank's edition of Ritson's *Ancient Songs and Ballads, from the Reign of King Henry the Second to the Revolution*, 2 vols (London, 1829: *ALC*), 1.157–69, following the French original (1.144–56). Scott's manuscript does not appear to have survived, and the poem was not included in any of the lifetime editions of Scott's poetry nor in the Lockhart 1833–34 posthumous edition.

The present text follows that of Ritson's *Ancient Songs and Ballads, from the Reign of King Henry the Second to the Revolution*, 2 vols (London, 1829: *ALC*), 1.157–69. Frank's footnote (1.157n) has been eliminated, and the English title of the immediately preceding French original is given rather than the actual heading of 'Translation, by Sir Walter Scott, Bart.' (1.157) which is meaningless in isolation. However, as both Ritson and Scott in their earlier correspondence used the usual spelling of the author's name, 'Chastellain', this has been substituted for 'Chatelain' in 'The Recollections of Chatelain' (1.144). In addition to the following listed emendations, routine apostrophes have been silently introduced as required.

131.10   listeners' (Editorial) / listeners
132.54   traitorous (Editorial) / traiterous

134.97	Duke (Editorial) / duke
134.105	King (Editorial) / king
134.113	Master of Saint James's (Editorial) / master of saint James's
134.116	Constable (Editorial) / constable
134.126	comrades' (Editorial) / comrades
135.150	King (Editorial) / king
136.164	church's (Editorial) / churches
136.165	God (Editorial) / god
136.189	Emperor (Editorial) / emperor
137.201	King (Editorial) / king
137.223	God (Editorial) / god
139.273	Queen (Editorial) / queen
139.276	Christian (Editorial) / christian
140.301	Christian (Editorial) / christian
141.322	Christendom (Editorial) / christendom
141.329	Duke (Editorial) / duke

Historical Note

A heading to the French original of Scott's poem in Frank's edition of Ritson's *Ancient Songs and Ballads, from the Reign of King Henry the Second to the Revolution*, 2 vols (London, 1829: *ALC*), 1.144–56, says that this had been 'extracted from the "Faictz et dictz de feu maistre Jehan Molinet ..." Paris, 1531, folio' (144). The ultimate source was thus almost certainly 'Recollection des merveilleuses advenues en nostre temps, commence par tres-elegant orateur Messire George Chastellaine. Et continue par Maistre Jehan Molinet' (Remembrance of the wondrous things that have happened in our time, begun by the highly-elegant orator Milord George Chastellain, and continued by Master Jean Molinet), as printed in leaves cvi to cxiv of *Les faictz et dictz de feu bône memoire maistre Jehan Molinet: contenans plusieurs beaulx traictez, oraisons et champs royaulx comme lon pourra facillimēt trouuer par la table qui sensuyt* ([Paris], 1531). However, Scott was to translate only the first 43 stanzas of the poem, those composed by George Chastellain, running from the verso of leaf cvi to the recto of leaf cix in Molinet's printed work.

Jean Molinet (1435–1507) had entered the service of Charles the Bold, Duke of Burgundy (1433–77) about 1464, becoming secretary to Georges Chastellain (1415–75), the Burgundian court chronicler and poet, and on Chastellain's death succeeding to his post. The whole poem is essentially a verse chronicle of European events (particularly those affecting the Dukes of Burgundy) from 1429 to 1495, Chastellain's portion obviously dealing with events before his death in 1475. Up to 1435 Chastellain had served Philip the Good, Duke of Burgundy (1396–1467), as a soldier, then lived in Paris attempting to improve relations between the Duke of Burgundy and Charles VII of France, before entering Philip's household in 1446 and being engaged in various diplomatic missions on his behalf: his reference to fifteenth-century European events is inevitably both detailed and complex.

Scott was obviously puzzled by Chastellain's wide framework of allusions, writing in the letter of 11 September 1803 to Ritson accompanying his translation that he had been hampered in his work by 'ignorance of the subject' and by want of books and the input of better-informed friends at his country residence of Lasswade:

> The places in which I have found this most puzzling are 1mo The stanza
> commencing with line 116th of the Original. To what historical transaction does
> this allude. ... 2do. The line 281 & the following Stanza What monarchs are here

meant? Is it supposed that they are complimented by the poet for agreeing to hold the states of "Le grant Duc de Virtu" as expressing some real potentate ... Or are we to understand that the expression is that of personification & only means that they were to hold their power of Virtue as their grand Superior & Liege Lord? (*Letters*, 1.200)

Otherwise, he commented that 'tho' the expression may be faulty the meaning is in general clear' (200), but nevertheless stated that he would welcome an opportunity of revision and correction before publication.

Explanatory Notes

131.18   Christentie   Christendom, the Christian domain.

131.20   maid of low degree   Joan of Arc (1412–31), the visionary Maid of Orleans, was sent to relieve the English Siege of Orleans on behalf of the Dauphin of France in the spring of 1429, and when he was subsequently crowned as Charles VII of France in Reims Cathedral on 17 July she was by his side.

131.29   Gallia   Gaul, used to signify France.

131.30   Her death-smoke   on 23 May 1430 Joan was captured at Compiègne by the Burgundian faction, which was allied to the English, and was handed over to them. She was tried by the pro-English Bishop of Beauvais on a variety of charges, including heresy and cross-dressing, and burned at the stake in Rouen on 30 May 1431 when she was about 19 years old.

131.32   martyred maid shall rise   after Joan of Arc's death in 1431 several women posed as her, capitalising on rumours that the Maid of Orleans was still alive. Claude des Armoises, the False Maid of Orleans, acted in collusion with two of Joan's brothers, and appeared to the people of Orleans as Joan in 1436. She was engaged by Gilles de Rais in 1439 to lead his troops, before being eventually exposed as an imposter.

132.33   petty friar   a similar account of this cleric is given by Enguerrand de Monstrelet (*c.* 1400–53), whose chronicle in two books covers the period between 1400 and 1444: see *La Chronique D'Enguerran de Monstrelet*, ed. L. Douët-d'Arcq, 6 vols (Paris: Société de l'Histoire de France, 1857–62), 5.47–48. In 1432 a Benedictine known as the Little Monk, who had been close to Pope Martin V, tried to capture the Castel San'Angelo from Eugene IV, who succeeded to the papacy in 1431. His plot, involving the storage in the fortress of chests containing his supporters, was foiled and he was hanged in Rome and quartered in the marketplace.

132.41   feigned Carmelite   the Carmelite preacher Thomas Couette delivered sermons attacking the failings and vices of the clergy and nobility, sometimes to an audience of 16,000 to 20,000 people, throughout Flanders, Artois, and Amiens around 1428. In 1432 he continued his tirades against the clergy in Italy, and after apparently making some hazardous propositions concerning excommunication was denounced in Rome and burned as a heretic by Pope Eugene IV: see Paul Thureau-Dangin, *The Life of S. Bernardino of Siena*, trans. Baroness G. von Hügel (London and Boston: Medici Society, [n.d.]), 120–21.

132.51   gallant Stuart   James I, King of Scots (1394–1437), was murdered by Sir Robert Graham in the royal lodging of Blackfriars in Perth, as the result of a conspiracy headed by the Earl of Atholl. In the semi-autographical poem attributed to King James, *The Kingis Quair* (Bodleian Library, MS Arch. Selden.B.24), a prisoner falls in love with a beautiful woman on seeing her walking in a garden, this woman being supposedly Joan Beaufort (d. 1445), daughter of the Earl of Somerset, who became Queen to King James.

132.56   vengeance on his foes   Atholl and his principal adherents were rounded up and tortured to death at the instigation of a regency government led initially by the Queen.

132.57 proud Savoy Amadeus VIII (1383–1451), Duke of Savoy, had founded the Order of St Maurice at the Castle of Ripailles on the banks of Lake Geneva, where he and six other knights lived in a quasi-monastic state of celibacy but some luxury. In 1439 the Council of Basel elected him as Pope Felix V in opposition to Pope Eugene IV: he is now regarded as an Anti-Pope.

132.59-60 holy keys ... triple diadem both papal insignia. Two crossed keys symbolises the supreme ecclesiastical authority claimed by the Pope as the successor of St Peter and based on Jesus's words to him in Matthew 16.19. The three-tiered tiara represents the one placed on the Pope's head during his coronation.

132.64 guerdon a reward or recompense.

133.67 Murder'd by a domestic slave Angelotto Fusco, Bishop of Cava, was made a cardinal by Pope Eugenius IV in 1431. Notoriously wealthy and avaricious, he was reputed to have been murdered by a servant.

133.77 female fiend Agnes Sorel (1422–50) was the officially-recognised mistress of Charles VII of France, celebrated for her beauty. Among the fashion trends she started was the wearing of dresses that exposed one breast or both. She had considerable influence over Charles, who gave her among other things the castle of Beauté near Paris for her lifetime.

133.82 money-broker rise Jacques Coeur (1395–1456) was a French merchant and financier who helped to found trade between France and the Levant, and was appointed master of the mint by Charles VII in 1436. In 1450 he was accused of poisoning the king's mistress and of embezzlement, when all his goods were confiscated and he was imprisoned. He escaped in 1455 and reached Rome, but died at Chios the following year taking part in an expedition against the Turks.

133.89 youth of twenty years for an account of a young man who came to Paris in 1446, with degrees in Arts, Medicine, Law and Theology, and speaking Latin, Greek, Hebrew and Chaldean, and Arabic, see *Journal d'un Bourgeois de Paris, 1405–1499*, ed. Alexandre Tuetey (Paris, 1881), 381–82. The unnamed man was equally proficient in learned disputation, the arts of war, music and painting, and people were afraid that when he reached the age of 28 he would become the Antichrist.

134.97 Duke Glo'ster Humphrey, Duke of Gloucester (1390–1447), the youngest son of Henry IV of England, had been protector of England during the minority of Henry VI following the death of Henry V in 1422. He died at Bury St Edmunds on 23 February 1447, a few days after his arrest for treason on 18 February, probably of a stroke although supposedly murdered.

134.106 Sir Giles of Britany Gilles de Bretagne (1420–50), a younger brother of Francois I, Duke of Brittany, was arrested on 26 June 1446 accused of conspiring with the English and murdered, reputedly after a period of attempted starvation, at La Hardouinaie during the night of 25 April 1450. His brother, who ordered his death, died later that year.

134.115-16 Alvarez ... High Constable of Spain Alvaro de Luna y Jarana (1388/90–1453) was the long-term favourite of King Juan II of Castile, High Constable of Castile and Grand Master of the military Order of Santiago, also known as the Order of St James of the Sword. His eventual downfall was engineered by the King's second wife, Isabell of Portugal, and he was beheaded at Valladolid on 2 June 1453.

134.123 shrewd Grecian's not identified.

135.132 Defiled his sister's bed Jean V, Count of Armagnac (1420–73), had two sons by his younger sister Isabelle, before solemnising a marriage with her. He was subsequently convicted by King Charles VII of France of rebellion and incest.

135.133   forged bull   a *bull* is a papal or episcopal mandate. The Count of Armagnac claimed a papal dispensation from Callixtus III, Pope from 1455 to 1458, to marry his sister.

135.138   conquer'd Milan   armed conflict broke out in Milan when its Duke died without a male heir in 1447, eventually resolved by the *condottiero* (mercenary commander) Francesco I Sforza (1401–66) becoming Duke of Milan in 1450 and founding the Sforza dynasty there.

135.145   English race expell'd   in the Hundred Years War between England and France Charles VII of France had reorganised his armies after the Treaty of Tours in 1444, while the English had no clear leadership under their weak monarch Henry VI, so that when the French broke the truce in June 1449 they were able to retake much of Normandy by October, including Rouen. After the decisive French victory at the Battle of Formigny on 15 April 1450 there were no significant English forces left in Normandy, and the French advanced to take over all English possessions in France except Calais.

135.147   three hundred years   Aquitaine had come to the English crown through the marriage of Eleanor of Aquitaine to Henry Plantagenet, Count of Anjou in 1152, he becoming King Henry II of England in 1154.

135.153   Eke   also, in addition.

135.160   glaive   a sword.

136.162   plot of horror dread   Stefano Porcari was a member of a wealthy family of Rome and an admirer of the classical Roman Republic. On the death of Pope Eugene IV in 1447 and before a new Pope could be elected he called on the population of Rome to overthrow papal authority in favour of a republic. The new Pope Nicholas V pardoned him, but he was eventually exiled to Bologna. Towards the end of 1452 he returned to Rome and planned an insurrection against papal rule to begin on 6 January 1453, but the plot was detected and Porcari captured, tried, and hanged at the papal fortress of Castel Sant'Angelo on 9 January 1453.

136.169   Old Ghent   in 1447 Philip, Duke of Burgundy, as feudal overlord imposed an unpopular salt tax on the city of Ghent, which revolted against him in 1449. In 1452 Philip declared war on Ghent, a conflict ended in July 1453 with the surrender of the city after its army had been defeated.

136.178   noble youth   probably a reference to the performance of Jacques de Lalaing (1421–53) at a tournament called the Passage of the Fountain of Tears, when he was not yet thirty. Lalaing had been knighted by Duke Philip of Burgundy and made a member of the Burgundian Order of the Golden Fleece in 1451. His deeds are recorded in the *Livre des Faits des Jacques Lalaing* (Book of the Deeds of Jacques Lalaing), which may have been partly written by Chastellain himself.

136.185   the seat of Constantine   Constantinople, capital of the Byzantine Empire, fell to the Ottoman Turks on 29 May 1453, and Byzantine and Greek scholars fled to the west, especially to Italy. The last Byzantine Emperor, Constantine XI (1405–53), was killed on the day the city fell.

136.190   caitiff miscreants   villainous evil-doers.

137.193   fair Lucrece   probably a reference to Lucrezia d'Alagno (*c.* 1430–79), a noblewoman with whom King Alphonso V of Naples fell in love. He gave her and her family lands, titles, and wealth, and she acted as his *de facto* Queen, the King's attempt to get his marriage to Maria of Castile annulled having failed. The Lucretia of ancient Rome was exemplary for her chastity:

having been raped by a member of the Tarquin family, she killed herself after revealing the fact to her husband.

137.201   King of Hungary   Ladislaus V, King of Hungary (1440–57), was the posthumous child of King Albert, who died in 1439 leaving all his estates to his unborn child. A civil war broke out as a result of disputes about the child's succession. In 1445 the Diet of Hungary appointed the soldier John Hunyadi (c.1406–56) one of seven Captains responsible for state affairs during the minority of Ladislaus, and afterwards sole Regent. Hunyadi was one of the wealthiest landowners in the country and a national hero for his military victories against the Turks, whom he prevented from invading the country, and his birth can only be called lowly relative to that of Ladislaus, who was a Habsburg. Taking advantage of Hunyadi's death in 1456, Ladislaus imprisoned his two sons and executed the elder in March 1457. A rebellion broke out as a result, Ladislaus fled the country, and died suddenly soon afterwards. The Diet of Hungary then elected Hunyadi's surviving son, Matthias (1443–90) as King.

137.205   dight   made ready, ordered.

137.217   first of France's royal line   the French Dauphin, Louis (later Louis XI) fled from his appanage of Dauphiné in 1456, after attempting to pursue an independent foreign policy from that of France and having a French army sent to discipline him. He took refuge for five years at the Burgundian court under the protection of Duke Philip. After Louis' succession to the throne in 1461 he tried to concentrate power in the crown and was resisted by Duke Philip and his allies in the War for the Public Good of 1465.

138.226   firm earth rend   there was a major earthquake in Naples in December 1455, resulting in a huge number of deaths.

138.240   bode some wondrous change   the shock and rage against the English counsellors and commanders viewed as responsible at the end of the Hundred Years War for the loss of England's large territories in France had much to do with the outbreak of civil war in England in the mid-1450s. Professional soldiers and those Englishmen who had sought to settle in France also suffered.

138.242   slaughter over all   an important trigger for the English civil wars between 1455 and 1487 came from the weakness and mental instability of King Henry VI (1421–71), this encouraging the claims to the throne of Richard, Duke of York, another branch of the royal Plantagenet family. The first open fighting between the two factions took place at the Battle of St Albans in 1455.

138.250   Another king they chose   after his crushing victory at the Battle of Towton in 1461, Edward (1442–83), eldest son of Richard, Duke of York, was proclaimed King Edward IV.

138.255   Scotland   after the Battle of Towton (1461) Henry VI, his wife and son, Prince Edward, sought refuge in Scotland at the court of Mary of Gueldres.

139.257   royal fleur-de-lis   the fleur-de-lis is a heraldic lily, the royal arms of France, and here is probably a reference to Charles, Duke of Orleans (1394–1465), nephew to the French king. He had been captured at the Battle of Agincourt (1415) and had been imprisoned by Henry V in the Tower of London. Intermittently a prisoner until 1440, he was then released through the efforts of Duke Philip of Burgundy and died in France.

139.265   crown of Cyprus' isle   Cyprus had been a tributary state of Mameluk Egypt since 1426, when Janus, King of Cyprus, had been taken prisoner by the Sultan of Egypt and had to be ransomed.

139.266   soldan   the supreme ruler of one of the great Muslim powers, particularly the Sultan of Egypt.

139.273   Queen of Cyprus   the reign of Queen Charlotte of Cyprus (1444–87) was particularly unstable, since she had to fight off constant challenges for the crown from her illegitimate half-brother, later James II of Cyprus (c. 1438/40–73). His widow, Catherine Cornaro, sold the island to Venice in 1489.

139.276   fay   faith.

139.279   corsairs   privateers, pirates sanctioned by the country to which their ship belongs.

139.281   Two monarchs whom two kingdoms own   not identified. Scott himself seemed uncertain as to the meaning of this passage, from his letter to Ritson of 11 September 1803 (*Letters*, 1.200).

140.289   Sicilia's monarch   René the Good (1409–80) had the titles of King of Naples, Sicily, and Jerusalem, though effectively controlling only the Dukedom of Anjou and county of Provence. His wife Isabeau was daughter and heiress to the Duke of Lorraine.

140.299–300   Georgian hills and Persian sands ... Armenia   a flattering roll-call of the many ambassadors who visited Charles, Duke of Burgundy and appealed for his support.

140.314   wondrous blazing stars   Halley's comet made one of its appearances in 1456, also the year when the Ottoman Turk invaded Hungary. The then Pope, Calixtus III, ordered special prayers to be said to avert the wrath of God, and was falsely rumoured to have issued a bull excommunicating the comet.

141.325   In fair Mayence, to flames a prey   in 1461 there was a feud between two candidates for the Archbishopric of Mainz in Germany (Mayence being the French name of the city). Diether von Isenburgh was elected by the cathedral chapter with popular support, but Adolf von Nassau was the papal nominee. In October 1462 Adolf, who had been besieging the city, broke in, plundering and firing it, and killing many citizens.

141.329   High Duke   Philip the Good, Duke of Burgundy (1396–1467).

141.330   his son so bold   Charles the Bold, Duke of Burgundy (1433–77).

141.343   MOLINET   a passage linking the poem's account of events that took place before the death of Georges Chastellain in 1475 and those recounted by his successor in the service of the Dukes of Burgundy, Jean Molinet (1435–1507). Ritson plainly intended only to include Chastellain's portion of the poem in his collection, and Scott does not appear to have translated the remainder of the chronicle.

50.   The Battle of Killiecrankie

Textual Note
The manuscript of 'The Battle of Killiecrankie' in Scott's hand is in the Morgan Library, Misc English, MA 869, and consists of two conjugate leaves, each measuring approx. 23.7 x 20.2 cm. It bears a watermark partially obscured by a ribbon reinforcing the fold between the two sheets but possibly reading 'BUTTANSMAW / 1794'. It appears to be a fair copy, with only two authorial revisions, the overwriting of 'Each' with 'The' at the start of line 5 and the alteration of 'dismissd' to 'dispatched' in line 39. In the top right-hand corner of the first of the manuscript's four pages Scott has written an inscription: 'To / A. G. Hunter / of Blackness / from / Walter Scott Esqʳ·', and on the final

page, following the text of the poem, the recipient has added and signed his own note dated 'Novemb.ʳ 11.', stating that the autograph manuscript was a gift from Scott himself 'about six years ago—i.e. 1805'. Alexander Gibson Hunter of Blackness (1771–1812) was partner to the Edinburgh bookseller Archibald Constable (1774–1827) until his retirement from the firm in 1811. His library was sold after his death, in November 1813, by his former partner.

Scott's translation was probably composed some years before 1805, since in his letter to Joseph Ritson (1752–1803) of 11 September 1803 Scott responds to a criticism of some lines in the eighth stanza of his translation. Scott suggests emending a passage equivalent to lines 61–64 of the present text to read:

> He left the boar on Speys bleak shore
> He left the wolf at bay
> The whiggish race like hares to chase
> And course the false Mackay. (*Letters*, 1.200)

Probably, like Scott's 'On the Death of Simon de Montfort' (see Textual Note to no. 48), 'The Battle of Killiecrankie' had been produced as a contribution to a revised edition of *Ancient Songs, from the Time of King Henry the Third, to the Revolution* (London, 1790) that Ritson was preparing towards the end of his life and a version of which was eventually published by Ritson's nephew, Joseph Frank, in 1829.

In a letter to Robert Surtees of 21 February 1807 Scott offered to send his translation to Frank, for his use in a posthumous edition of Ritson's work, presumably from another copy than the one given to Hunter two years earlier. In doing so Scott implied that it had not hitherto been published by Ritson himself. He mentions 'Kennedy's *Praelium Gillicrankiense*, in leonine Latin, which I translated into doggrel verse, at Ritson's instance, and for his collection' (*Letters*, 1.357). Notwithstanding this offer, 'The Battle of Killiecrankie' does not appear to have been published during Scott's lifetime.

It appeared, apparently for the first time, some weeks after Scott's death as one of three 'Reliques of Walter Scott' in *Chambers's Edinburgh Journal* for 29 December 1832, 380–81, evidently printed from the manuscript gifted to Hunter around 1805 since the article cites Hunter's own note. There are a number of misreadings of the manuscript text and lines 7–8 were omitted altogether, presumably because the phrase 'the *Dutch be—t* [beshit] / Their breeches' was regarded as too coarse for publication. (It was probably at this point that an attempt was made to delete these lines in the manuscript with black ink.) It was subsequently published by Alan Lang Strout as a parallel text with the Latin original and with a brief introduction, in 'An Unpublished Ballad-Translation by Scott, *The Battle of Killiecrankie*' in *Modern Language Notes*, 54: 1 (January 1939), 13–18.

The present text follows that of the manuscript itself, incorporating Scott's revisions, but omitting a third line of his heading which comprises the opening words of the Latin original, 'Gramius notabilis colligerat montanos &c'. In addition to the following listed emendations ampersands have been routinely expanded to 'and', verb forms ending with 'd' to 'ed', and routine apostrophes have been introduced as required, as have full stops at the ends of stanzas.

142.3   rout (Editorial) / route
142.4   hand. (Editorial) / hand
142.5   Whig (Editorial) / whig
142.12   mountaineer: (Editorial) / mountaineer

142.18   peer (Editorial) / Peer
142.19   Dunfermline (Editorial) / Dumferline
142.20   down. (Editorial) / down
143.25   Glengarry's (Editorial) / Glengary's
143.29   men (Editorial) / Men
143.36   ran. (Editorial) / ran
143.41   Barra (Editorial) / Bara
143.44   another. (Editorial) / another
143.45   Appin (Editorial) / Appine
143.47   Cannon (Editorial) / Canon
143.52   Whigs (Editorial) / whigs
143.54   Clanranald's (Editorial) / Clanronalds
144.60   flame. (Editorial) / flame
144.63   Whiggish (Editorial) / whiggish
144.67   Highland (Editorial) / highland
144.68   gun. (Editorial) / gun
144.69   you, ye (Editorial) / you ye

Historical Note
Scott's admiration of the Royalist soldier John Graham, Viscount Dundee
(1648?–89), is well-known. Besides portraying him as Claverhouse, the earlier
persecutor of the Covenanters, in his novel *The Tale of Old Mortality* (1816),
Scott in this poem and in no. 122, 'The Bonnets of Bonnie Dundee', also
depicted the end of his career during the 'Glorious Revolution' of 1688–89,
when the Roman Catholic James VII and II (1633–1701) was deposed as king
in favour of his Protestant nephew and son-in-law the Dutch Prince of Orange,
who thus became William I and III (1650–1702). Dundee left Edinburgh with
fifty horse in the spring of 1689, as the Convention of Estates declared for King
William. Between then and his raising the royal standard of James II and VII
at Dundee Law on 16 April he raised little additional support: although many
of the Lowland gentry were thought to be sympathetic, few actually joined
Dundee and his army consisted mostly of small western Highland clans, with
the addition of an Irish battalion commanded by Colonel Cannon. Blair Castle,
at Blair Atholl in Perthshire, about 56 km (35 miles) N of Perth, had been seized
for the Jacobites by the Duke of Atholl's factor, Patrick Steuart of Ballechin.
Blair commanded a key route S to Stirling and N to Inverness, and govern-
ment anxiety to retake it led to the Battle of Killiecrankie on 27 July 1689. On
26 July Dundee held a council of war at Blair, while government forces under
Hugh Mackay (d. 1692), a Highlander who had formerly been in the Dutch
service, moved northwards from Edinburgh. Mackay's troops came through
the Pass of Killiecrankie on the morning of 27 July onto low ground beside the
River Garry while Dundee's army occupied high ground overlooking them
before attacking at sunset. Almost half of those who fought in the exception-
ally bloody battle that ensued were killed, and although it was a victory for the
Jacobite forces, their chieftains suffered disproportionately and Dundee himself
was struck by a bullet and died soon afterwards. Cannon took command of the
surviving Jacobite army, but a battle fought around the cathedral at Dunkeld on
21 August was won by government forces. Although the Jacobite force harried
the Lowlands until a few months after its defeat at Cromdale in 1690, as it split
up into smaller groups it ceased to be effective and the last Scottish Jacobite
outposts had surrendered by 1692. The Battle of Killiecrankie thus signalled the
effective end of a serious Jacobite challenge to the new government of Scotland
of 1689.

The Latin Jacobite poem beginning 'Grahamius notabilis coegerat Montanos' was translated by Scott, as he notes in his letter to Ritson of 11 September 1803 (*Letters*, 1.200), from Alexander Pennecuik's *A Collection of Scots Poems on Several Occasions* (Edinburgh, 1769), 153–54. Pennecuik does not give the name of the author, who is sometimes thought to have been the Aberdeen Latin poet, James Kennedy (fl. 1662–86), who, however, died before Killiecrankie. In James Johnson's *Scots Musical Museum*, 6 vols (Edinburgh, 1787–1803), 2.item 102, the author is said to be Herbert Kennedy, a professor at the University of Edinburgh, of the family of Kennedy of Haleaths in Annandale. According to Andrew Dalzell, in his *History of the University of Edinburgh from its Foundation*, 2 vols (Edinburgh, 1862), Kennedy was appointed Professor of Philosophy in 1684 and was dead by March 1692 when a successor to his post was appointed (2.214, 266). The 56-line Latin original becomes 72 lines in Scott's translation, which carefully reproduces the details of the original. These include the first stanza's 'Cacavere Batavi & Cameroniani' (The Dutch and Cameronians shat themselves), as suppressed by *Chambers's Edinburgh Journal*, and the comparison of Glengarry to Aeneas. Scott, however, removes more remote classical allusions, such as the statement that Cannon was birthed by Bellona to defend his country ('Nam pro tuenda patria hunc peperit Bellona') and the reference to the lord of the Hebrides as Gravidus, one of the titles of Mars. The topographical details in lines 65–66 are Scott's own.

Explanatory Notes

142.1   Graeme   the Royalist commander John Graham, Viscount Dundee (1648?–89).

142.4   Claymore and targe   the characteristic weapons of the Highlander, a two-edged broadsword and a buckler or round shield.

142.7   *Dutch*   the army of the government of William III, the Dutch Prince of Orange (1650–1702), by no means consisted largely of foreigners, but was a mixture of the Dutch battalions (Scottish veterans in the service of the House of Orange), and recent Scottish recruits. Their commander, Hugh Mackay, was also a Scot who had been in the Dutch service before William accepted the crowns of England and of Scotland.

142.9   Herculean   Hercules is the Roman form of Heracles, the prodigiously strong hero of Greek legend.

142.13   twice thy force   estimates of the numbers who fought on each side vary, but the entry for the Battle of Killiecrankie in Historic Scotland's 'The Inventory of Historic Battlefields' (http://data.historic-scotland.gov.uk/data/docs/battlefields/killiecrankie_full.pdf) states that the Jacobites had around 2400 men and that the government forces consisted of between 3500 and 5000 men.

142.15–16   foreign Lord / And stranger race   probably an allusion to the new Dutch king, although an English regiment, the Earl of Huntingdon's Foot led by Colonel Ferdinando Hastings, fought on the government side in the battle.

142.19   Dunfermline   James Seton, 4th Earl of Dunfermline, commanded a troop of horse on the Jacobite side in the battle. He was outlawed in 1690 and served James VII and II at the Court of St Germain until his death in 1694.

142.22–24   Hector gray ... Pitcur   David Halyburton of Pitcur, an estate 5 km (3 miles) SE of Coupar Angus in Forfarshire: he was killed during the battle. Hector, the leader of the Trojan forces during the siege of Troy by the Greeks, was one of the sons of King Priam. In the *Iliad* Homer presents him as noble both in victory and in defeat.

143.25   Glengarry's might   Alastair Macdonell of Glengarry (d. 1724) carried the Stuart banner in the Jacobite line in the battle.

143.27   through fire, who bore his sire   Aeneas, in Bk 2 of Virgil's epic poem *The Aeneid*, escapes from the conquered and burning city of Troy carrying his father, Anchises, upon his shoulders.

143.31–32   sire and son ... Macdonalds of the Isles   Sir Donald Macdonald, 3rd Baronet (d. 1695) of Sleat in Skye, fell ill before the battle, so that his 500 men on the left wing of the Jacobite army were led by his son Donald. Five of the Chief's close relatives were lost in the battle.

143.33   Maclean   Sir John Maclean, 4th Baronet (1670–1716), of Duart and Morvern, the Maclean Chief, fought on Dundee's right in the battle, though he was only 19 years old.

143.37   Lochiel   Sir Ewen Cameron of Lochiel (1629–1719), who had raised about 1000 Highland clansmen for the Jacobite army.

143.40   Blair   Blair Castle, held by the Jacobites, about 5 km (3 miles) NW of the battlefield.

143.41   Barra   Roderick MacNeil of Barra, in the Outer Hebrides, chief of the Roman Catholic MacNeil clan.

143.41   Glencoe   Alexander Macdonald, 12th Chief of the Macdonalds of Glencoe (d. 1692).

143.41   Keppoch   Coll Macdonald, 16th Chief of Clan Keppoch (*c.*1664–1729), known as 'Coll of the cows' for his banditry. On his way to join Dundee he had tried to plunder Inverness, for instance.

143.42   Balloch and his brother   unidentified. Scott's 'Pibroch of Donald Dhu' (no. 92) is in honour of a Balloch, cousin to Alexander MacDonald Earl of Ross and Lord of the Isles (d. 1449).

143.45   Appin   Robert Stewart had succeeded his uncle as Chief of the Stewarts of Appin in 1685, but was still a boy at college, which he abandoned to join his clansmen under the command of John Stewart of Ardshiel, Tutor (guardian and administrator) of the estate of Appin.

143.45   faulchion   specifically a curved broadsword with the cutting edge on the convex side, but generally used to mean any sword.

143.47   Cannon   Colonel Alexander Cannon, the leader of about 300 Irish Jacobites who took part in the battle. He assumed control of the Jacobite forces in Scotland after the death of Dundee.

143.49   he from Hungary   unidentified, though perhaps someone who had seen service under James FitzJames, 1st Duke of Berwick (1670–1734), illegitimate son of James II and VII: the Duke had fought in Hungary against the Ottoman Turks at the Battle of Mohács in 1687.

143.53–54   The tutor ... Clanranald's   Allan, 14th Chief of the Macdonalds of Clanranald, was only sixteen years of age: he fought at Killiecrankie, but his forces were led by the Tutor, Ronald Macdonald of Benbecula.

144.57   Glenmorison   John Grant, 6th Chief of Glenmoriston (1657–1736), was the son-in-law of Sir Ewen Cameron of Lochiel, and fought for the Jacobites at Killiecrankie.

144.59   carbine   a fire-arm shorter than a musket, used by mounted soldiers.

144.64   false Mackay   Hugh Mackay (d. 1692), a Highlander who had been in the Dutch service and now led the forces of William III at Killiecrankie. He had been recalled to Britain in 1688 by James VII and II, but had remained on the Continent in anticipation of the Revolution.

144.65   Tummell's wave   Tummel is the name of a loch and river in N

Perthshire. Loch Tummel is 6.5 km (4 miles) NW of Pitlochry, stretching westward for about 10 km (6 miles). The river which feeds and drains the loch eventually flows into the River Tay about 13 km (8 miles) SE of the loch's eastern end.

51.   The Norman Horse-Shoe

Textual Note
It seems likely that this poem was commissioned by George Thomson (1757–1851), as he claimed, for the first volume of his *A Select Collection of Original Welsh Airs* (Edinburgh, 1809), where it appeared as item 25, even though in the event Scott published it elsewhere several years previously. Thomson's collection had been in preparation for several years, and Haydn's setting of the Welsh air 'Triban Gwyr Morgannwg' (War Song of the Men of Glamorgan) was one of sixty composed by him during 1803 and 1804 for this collection: see M. Ryecroft, 'Haydn's Welsh Songs: George Thomson's Musical and Literary Sources', *Welsh Music History*, 7 (2008), 92–160. It appears that the delay in publication was occasioned by a last-minute decision to acquire settings for the harp for the melodies: see J. Cuthbert Hadden, *George Thomson the Friend of Burns* (London, 1898), 123. By the early autumn of 1803 Thomson was trying to secure lyrics for this work, for instance from Thomas Campbell by 31 August 1803 (Hadden, 201) and from Amelia Opie by 30 September (Hadden, 250). Although the earliest correspondence between Scott and Thomson dates from 1805, Thomson's early records of his outgoing and incoming letters are incomplete and in any case the two men were both in Edinburgh for large parts of the year so that their dealings could easily have been conducted in person. It is not unlikely that Thomson was seeking Scott's assistance at much the same time as approaching other poets for theirs.

The first publication of 'The Norman Horse-Shoe' was as part of a privately-printed 16-page pamphlet issue of the Introduction to *The Lay of the Last Minstrel* produced by James Ballantyne in 1804 'At the Border Press, Holyrood-House', presumably with the object of both advertising Ballantyne's typography and promoting Scott's forthcoming long narrative poem. This Introduction is followed by two 'Songs to Ancient British Airs', of which 'The Norman Horse-Shoe' is the first (11–13). (See the copy of this extremely rare publication in the Mitchell Library, Glasgow, ref. no. 345911.) No acknowledgement to Thomson's work is made in this pamphlet, the name of the Welsh tune is given in English, and Haydn's musical setting is not provided.

The text of these verses in the 1804 pamphlet and in Thomson's collection is identical, apart from minor variations in punctuation and capitalisation attributable to the work of the printer. The headnote, however, while providing the same information in each case, has distinct verbal variations: for instance, the first sentence of the headnote in Thomson's work has 'generally unable' instead of 'usually unable', and the second has 'celebrate a supposed defeat' instead of 'supposed to celebrate a defeat'.

A manuscript version of 'The Norman Horse-Shoe' in Scott's hand survives as the first of two items (the second being no. 52, 'The Dying Bard') in a manuscript headed 'Two Songs in Imitation of the Welch poetry' (NLS, MS 643). This manuscript consists of two pairs of conjugate leaves, each measuring approx. 22.5 x 18.5 cm. Unfortunately, it is not dated and the paper bears no watermark. The two poems each have an explanatory headnote, and while there are a number of deletions and insertions of single words in each, the manuscript appears to be a fair copy and shows signs of having once been sewn into a booklet, suggesting that it may have been a presentation copy of Scott's work rather than copy for a printer. The information in the headnote to 'The Norman Horse-Shoe' is given in a different order to that of the headnote of the 1804 printing, while the text of the poem itself differs from that of 1804 in several places: in the second stanza, for instance, line 9 has 'Chepstow's walls' rather than 'Chepstow's towers', line 13 has 'pennons' rather than 'banners', and line 16 has 'Their Norman' rather than 'The Norman'. It seems probable that this manuscript text is an earlier version of the poem that Scott has subsequently revised and refined for publication.

Before the appearance of 'The Norman Horse-Shoe' in Thomson's 1809 volume it had also been republished in Scott's own *Ballads and Lyrical Pieces* of 1806 (173–75), and in the section of miscellaneous poems in the eighth edition of *The Lay of the Last Minstrel* (Edinburgh, 1808), 247–49, in both cases only with changes of the kind normally associated with the printer. The version included in Scott's *Poetical Works* of 1820 (2.240–42) was probably taken from one of these. 'The Norman Horse-Shoe' was subsequently included in the successive lifetime editions of Scott's collected poems and in the Lockhart 1833–34 posthumous edition (6.363–65), again only with changes of the kind normally associated with the printer. In none of these printings is Haydn's musical setting included.

The text in the present edition is that of the 1804 pamphlet of the Introduction to *The Lay of the Last Minstrel* (11–13), as an early version authorised by Scott for the context of a selection of his own poetry. No emendations have been made.

Historical Note
According to Ryecroft (cited in the Textual Note) the music by Haydn for which Scott's verses were written was based on the version of the traditional Welsh tune 'Triban Gwyr Morgannwg', as found in *Musical and Poetical Relicks of the Welsh Bards*, 2nd edn (London, 1794), 158, by the Welsh harpist and antiquarian Edward Jones (1752–1824). Scott's absorption in the Border warfare between England and Scotland meant that he could easily relate to medieval border skirmishes between England and Wales. His headnote suggests that the conflict he portrays took place sometime during the twelfth century in the vale of Caerphilly in Glamorgan close to its border with Monmouthshire, a county which was sometimes counted as part of England and sometimes as part of Wales, and which is bordered by Gloucestershire.

Explanatory Notes
145.headnote CLARE, Earl of Striguil and Pembroke the Earldom of Pembroke was conferred in 1138 by King Stephen of England (c.1092–1154) on Gilbert de Clare (d. 1148), and in 1185 passed to a female descendant, Isabel de Clare. She married William Marshall who became Earl of Pembroke in 1199.
145.headnote NEVILLE, Baron of Chepstow this Marcher lord has not been identified. The Neville family was generally associated with northern England, and Striguil, which included the manor of Chepstow, was held by the de Clares.
145.headnote Lords Marchers of Monmouthshire the Welsh Marches, which included Monmouthshire, were to some degree independent of both the English crown and of the Principality of Wales. Many castles were built in this frontier region during the 12th and 13th centuries by Norman

lords to defend their territory against Welsh raiders and to demonstrate their power.

145.1 Striguil's bounds Chepstow Castle, on a cliff-top above the River Wye, originally had the Norman name of Striguil, meaning 'river bend'. The castle and its associated Marcher lordship were known as Striguil until the late 14th century.

145.9 Chepstow's towers Chepstow is a town in Monmouthshire adjoining the border with the neighbouring county of Gloucestershire on the River Wye, about 3 km (2 miles) above its confluence with the River Severn, and was a focus of English settlement in the area.

145.14 Rymny's stream the River Rhymney flows through a glacial valley in SE Wales, through Cardiff and into the Severn estuary: it formed the boundary between Glamorgan and Monmouthshire.

145.15 Caerphili's sod Caerphilly is at the S end of the Rhymney valley. The castle there was begun by Gilbert de Clare, 7th Earl of Gloucester and 6th Earl of Hertford (1243–95) in 1268.

145.20 Severn's tide the estuary of the River Severn, which empties into the Bristol Channel, has a noted tidal bore, whereby the high tide sends a funnel of water upstream against the river current. In the spring, when the largest bores occur, this can be at a speed of up to 25 km (16 miles) per hour and causes a rapid rise in the level of the water.

146.26 Cambrian Welsh, pertaining to Wales.

146.32 Fairies' emerald ring a circle of grass of a darker colour than the grass around it. The colour is caused by the presence of fungi, but traditionally is supposed to be produced by fairies when dancing.

52. The Dying Bard

Textual Note

The textual history of 'The Dying Bard' in many ways parallels that of 'The Norman Horse-Shoe' (see Textual Note to no. 51). It seems likely that it was commissioned by George Thomson (1757–1851), as he claimed, for the first volume of his *A Select Collection of Original Welsh Airs* (Edinburgh, 1809), where it appeared as item 6, even though in the event Scott published it elsewhere several years previously. Thomson's collection had been in preparation for several years, the delay in publication apparently occasioned by a last-minute decision to acquire settings for the harp for the melodies, and Thomson was probably seeking Scott's assistance at much the same time he was approaching other poets for theirs, by the early autumn of 1803.

The setting by Joseph Haydn (1732–1809) of the Welsh air 'Dafydd y Garreg-Wen' (David of the White Rock) was one of sixty composed by him during 1803 and 1804 for Thomson's Welsh song collection: see M. Ryecroft, 'Haydn's Welsh Songs: George Thomson's Musical and Literary Sources', *Welsh Music History*, 7 (2008), 92–160. In Thomson's work the title of Scott's lyrics is 'The Last Words of Cadwallon', but the engraved tune on the facing page is headed 'The dying Bard to his Harp'.

The first publication of 'The Dying Bard' was as part of a privately-printed 16-page pamphlet issue of the Introduction to *The Lay of the Last Minstrel* produced by James Ballantyne in 1804 (for details see the Textual Note to no. 51, 'The Norman Horse-Shoe'). No acknowledgement to Thomson's work is made in this pamphlet, the name of the Welsh tune is garbled as 'Daffydz Gawgwen', and Haydn's musical setting is not provided.

The text of these verses in the 1804 pamphlet and in Thomson's collection is identical, apart from routine printing changes, the different title, and a slightly different headnote, which in Thomson's work covers the verses written by the Rev. George Warrington to the tune as well as Scott's, which themselves are printed below Warrington's on the same page. This headnote, presumably by Thomson, names the dying bard as Dafydd y Garreg Wen, whereas Scott in his own headnote (the bard of his poem being named as Cadwallon) understandably does not.

'The Dying Bard' is the second of two items (following 'The Norman Horse-Shoe') in Scott's manuscript headed 'Two Songs in Imitation of the Welch poetry', in NLS, MS 643 (for details of which see the Textual Note to no. 51, 'The Norman Horse-Shoe'). The manuscript text of 'The Dying Bard' differs from that of the 1804 pamphlet in various ways, most obviously in consisting of three 8-line stanzas rather than six 4-line stanzas, but also in the wording of several lines: for instance, lines 11–12 here read 'But where is the Harp shall resound with their name / And where is the Bard who gives heroes their fame'. Lines 17 and 21 in this version both say 'farewell Dinas-Emlinn' where the 1804 pamphlet firstly has 'adieu, silver Teivi' and secondly 'adieu, Dinas-Emlinn', this suggesting that the manuscript text may be an earlier version of the poem that Scott has revised and refined for publication.

Before the appearance of Scott's poem in Thomson's 1809 volume as 'The Last Words of Cadwallon' (item 6) it had also been republished as 'The Dying Bard' in his own *Ballads and Lyrical Pieces* of 1806 (176–77) and in the section of miscellaneous poems in the eighth edition of *The Lay of the Last Minstrel* (Edinburgh, 1808), 250–52. In both these texts line 18 reads 'bards that have been' rather than 'bards who have been'. The poem was also reprinted from Thomson's work, and with an abbreviated version of Thomson's headnote, as 'The Last Words of Cadwallon' in Scott's *Miscellaneous Poems* (Edinburgh, 1820), 108–10.

This dual publication history of the same poem under different titles inadvertently led to its appearance under both titles in Scott's *Poetical Works* of 1820 (2.243–45 and 10.194–96), and under both titles it duly passed from there into successive lifetime editions of Scott's collected poetry without there being any substantial differences, apart from titles and headnotes, between the two items. Lockhart, however, in the posthumous 1833–34 edition chose to include it once only, as 'The Dying Bard' (6.366–67). George Thomson had previously republished it from his earlier collection, though this time adopting the title of 'The Dying Bard', in *The Select Melodies of Scotland*, 5 vols (Edinburgh, 1822–23), 1.item 49, with Scott's consent.

Scott's original title was almost certainly 'The Dying Bard'. This is the title in the surviving manuscript, while Thomson's letter to Scott of 30 March 1805 (BL, Add. MS 35,266, ff. 59v–60v) raises an objection to one expression in 'your Dying Bard', which was obviously by then in his possession. It was also called 'The Dying Bard' in early printings largely under Scott's own control. The present text follows that of the 1804 pamphlet of the Introduction to *The Lay of the Last Minstrel* (14–16), as an early version authorised by Scott for the context of a selection of his own poetry. However, it emends the garbled Welsh name of the air given there to the more correct 'Dafydd y Garreg-Wen'.

Historical Note
The inspiration for Scott's poem was evidently the legend of the dying bard that accompanied the Welsh tune sent to him in Haydn's setting by George Thomson. The composer of 'Dafydd y Garreg-Wen' (David of the White Rock)

was the Welsh harpist David Owen (1711/12–41), who had supposedly composed it on his death-bed, the White Rock being the name of the farm near Porthmadog in Caernarfonshire where he lived. In Scott's day there were no generally accepted words to this tune, the ones now known as 'David of the White Rock' being added subsequently by the Welsh poet and collector of folktunes, John Hughes, known as Ceiriog (1832–87). Scott's dying bard, however, does not seem to be a man of the eighteenth century but of the Middle Ages: in death he goes to join other medieval Welsh bards and his name recalls that of 'Cadwallo', which occurs in 'The Bard' of Thomas Gray (1716–71), a poem in which a Welsh bard defies the forces of Edward I of England (1239–1307). There are also distinct resemblances to the Ossian poems of James Macpherson (1736–96), which provide a proto-Romantic account of Scottish Gaelic heroes and bards of the Dark Ages.

Explanatory Notes

146.1   Dinas Emlinn   probably Dinas, near Newcastle Emlyn in Carmarthenshire. Dinas is the ancient Welsh word for a fort, and survives as such in various Welsh place-names. Emlyn was one of the cantrefs (ancient land-divisions theoretically consisting of a hundred settlements) of Dyfed, an ancient district of Wales, bordering on the river Teifi.

146.3   Teivi   the river Teifi at 122 km (76 miles) is the longest river flowing entirely in Wales, from its sources in the Cambrian mountains to its estuary at Cardigan. For much of its length it forms the boundary between Ceredigion and Caernarfonshire.

146.3   Cadwallon   a name best known as that of Cadwallon ap Cadfan (d. 634), King of Gwynedd until his death in battle against Oswald of Northumbria near Hexham in 634. Scott presumably adopts the name for that of his generic Welsh bard, who must have lived after the 12th-century Welsh bards he hopes to join in death.

146.10   Prestatyn's side   now the name of a Welsh seaside resort, Prestatyn here may suggest the coastal settlement in Denbighshire, historically in Flintshire.

146.14   white bosom … dark hair   compare, for instance, the description of Braghéla in *Fingal*, 'lovely with her raven-hair is the white-bosomed daughter of Sorglan': James Macpherson, *The Poems of Ossian and Related Works*, ed. Howard Gaskill (Edinburgh, 1996), 62.

147.19   Lewarch   probably Llywarch ap Llywelyn (fl. *c.*1180–*c.*1220), the chief court poet of Gwynedd. Thirty of his works survive, totalling 1780 lines.

147.19   Meilor   probably Meilyr Brydydd (fl. 1081–1137), among the first of the professional Welsh medieval poets whose work can be approximately dated. His son Gwalchmai and two grandsons were also known as poets.

147.19   Merlin the old   Merlin or Myrddin was a Welsh poet supposedly flourishing in the 6th century. He features in an 11th-century Welsh poem, 'The Dialogue of Myrddin and Taliesin', which connects him with Dyfed.

147.20   Taliessin   the Welsh poet Taliesin supposedly flourished in the 6th century. A famous 14th-century manuscript called the Book of Taliesin, now in the National Library of Wales (Peniarth MS 2), contains poems reputedly by him.

53.   The Bard's Incantation

Textual Note

This poem was first published under Scott's name in *English Minstrelsy*, ed. Scott, 2 vols (Edinburgh, 1810), 2.192–96, along with an initial footnote stating it to have been 'Written under the threat of invasion, in the autumn 1804'. It was then rapidly reprinted, as 'From The English Minstrelsy', in the *Edinburgh Annual Register, for 1808*, 1: 2 (Edinburgh, 1810), xxi–xxiii, before entering the collected editions with the *Poetical Works* of 1820 (12.126–30), at which point Scott's first footnote about an 1804 composition was elevated into a sub-heading to the poem. This formulation continued, with only very minor alterations to the text, up to the posthumous Lockhart edition of 1833–34 (8.357–60), which itself adds a new introductory footnote stating in brackets that 'This poem was first published in the "English Minstrelsy," 2 vols. Edin. 1810.' Along with the sub-heading, this would appear to confirm a fairly straightforward pattern of composition in 1804 followed by publication in 1810.

This situation is complicated, however, by J. G. Lockhart's account of Scott's having composed the poem during a 'fiery ride from Gilsland to Dalkeith' at a moment of crisis when rumours of invasion by France spread like wildfire through the Border country (*Life*, 2.71–72). Even disregarding the improbability of such a ride from Gilsland (a village and spa on the border of Cumberland and Northumberland, some 25 km (16 miles) NE of Carlisle), this version of events contains a number of inconsistencies. Lockhart's narrative places it as Scott and his wife were returning from their visit to Wordsworth in Grasmere, an event which occurred in August 1805 (see Historical Note to no. 55, 'Hellvellyn'). The most notable false alarm on the Borders, which led to a widespread muster-ing of volunteer troops in the South of Scotland, was triggered by the lighting of beacons as first witnessed in Kelso on the evening of 31 January 1804 (*Kelso Mail*, 2 February 1804; see also *The False Alarm: A Narrative of the Lighting of the Border Beacons in 1804* (Jedburgh, 1865)). Scott himself later gave a vivid account of the incident in a Magnum note to *The Antiquary* (*Introductions and Notes to the Magnum Opus*, ed. J. H. Alexander, with P. D. Garside and Claire Lamont, EEWN 25a (Edinburgh, 2012), 153–55), but without mentioning any involvement of this kind by himself; and indeed residence at Gilsland with his wife at such a time of year would have been unlikely.

The chronology is further disturbed by two anonymous printings of the poem prior to 1810, both similarly annotated apart from the initial note about 1804. The first of these appears, under the heading 'The Highland Bard's Incantation. / From the Gaelic', in *The Poetical Register, and Repository for Fugitive Poetry, for 1805* (London, 1807), 478–80, subscribed there 'Thomas the Rhymer. / Cot below the Cairn, Sept. 19, 1805'. Under the editorship of Richard Alfred Davenport (1776/7–1852), *The Poetical Register* offered an annual compilation of shorter verse, much but not all of it appropriated from current periodical literature. 'Thomas the Rhymer' itself is a not unlikely pseudonym for Scott at this period (the inclusion of the definite article is characteristic of his usage), especially in the wake of the publication of his edition of *Sir Tristrem* in May 1804; just as the fictional 'Cot below the Cairn' might well allude to Scott's new home at Ashestiel, to which he was then moving (see *Letters*, 12.258–59). The other earlier printing discovered is in *The Spirit of the Public Journals, for 1806* (London, 1807), 128–30. Under the main heading of 'Gaelic Ode', this notes a derivation 'From the Oracle'. Here, moreover, the verses (which retain the title 'The Highland Bard's Incantation') are preceded by the following letter, purportedly from the author to the original editor:

Sir,

I am induced, by the high reputation of your paper, to offer for insertion the enclosed free translation of an original Gaelic Ode, composed in a remote district of the Northern Highlands of Scotland. I have ventured to modify, and, in some instances, altogether to suppress, the wild imagery and periphrastic expression of the original; but I fear my translation will be thought very feeble by the enthusiastic admirers of the ancient language of Caledonia. It will, doubtless, afford pleasure to your patriotic readers to see, that the flame which has burst forth so gloriously in the metropolis glows with equal ardour among our distant mountains. I only fear that you may object to receiving this Poem, from its similarity to so many compositions of merit upon the same noble theme. This similarity is at present unavoidable. But I have little doubt that the hero of Corsica, to whom we are indebted for the present subject of the British muse, will speedily, in his great generosity, and at his own proper expense, furnish her with an opportunity to exchange the themes of hope and exhortation for those of victory and triumph:

    Carmina tum melius, cum venerit ipse, canemus.

In this confidence I remain, Sir,
        Yours, &c.
           THOMAS THE RHYMER.
   Cot below the Cairn

Though possibly spurious, the above letter echoes Scott in a number of ways: including its scathing depiction of Napoleon as 'the hero of Corsica' and the concluding Latin quotation (from Virgil's *Eclogues*). The most obvious identity of the 'The Oracle' is *The Daily Advertiser, Oracle, and True Briton*, a pro-government newspaper which appeared under that fuller title between 1804 and 1807. (However a trawl through its numbers has led to no sighting of the piece there.)

In view of the early printings above there is a fair possibility that the song originated during a brief renewal of invasion fears in late summer 1805, with Lockhart (encouraged by the dating in *English Minstrelsy*) later mingling in his account events more properly relating to 1804. Perhaps significantly, Wordsworth in a letter to Scott of 7 November 1805 appears to allude to difficulties experienced by Scott on his return from Grasmere, exacerbated by his wife's situation: see *The Early Letters of William and Dorothy Wordsworth (1787–1805)* (Oxford, 1935), 540. According to the *Caledonian Mercury* for Thursday, 15 August 1805:

The long meditated invasion of this country is, as it is now believed, to be immediately attempted. The preparations of the French for this purpose is immense; and it is reported that Bonaparte was at Boulogne last week to hasten the sailing of his large flotilla. In the mean time, every preparation is making to give them a warm reception, as we have little fear of the result of such an attempt.

The papers received this morning abound with proofs of the activity and bustle among all description of our defenders, particularly among the volunteers in their respective districts.

A month later, however, this crisis had abated, the *Mercury* on 12 September remarking that 'the Continental war [i.e. Napoleon's decision to engage in a land war] has banished any idea of invasion'. If indeed Scott did compose his poem during this last emergency, then he might well have been left with a feeling of its having become somewhat outdated as the crisis subsided. It is also interesting to note in view of the poem's Highland theme a temporal proximity to Scott's extensive review of the *Report of the Committee of the Highland Society of Scotland, appointed to inquire into the Nature and Authenticity of the Poems of Ossian* for the July 1805 issue of the *Edinburgh Review* (6.429–62). Perhaps significantly, too, it is in autumn 1805 that one first catches glimpses of Scott's ambition to write the long Highland poem that was eventually to emerge as *The Lady of the Lake* (1810) (see, for example, *Letters*, 12.278–79).

Compared with its complex publication history, and the shift in 1810 to the shorter title of 'The Bard's Incantation', the text of the poem remained remarkably stable. The main substantive verbal change occurs in the *English Minstrelsy*'s substitution of 'fierce Hengist's strain' for what had previously appeared as 'the Saxon train' at line 53, indicating Scott's creative involvement at that stage. Apart from this the variants noted are of the kind normally associated with the printer, and there is no clear sign of any authorial input after 1810. (The 1833–34 Lockhart posthumous collected edition text actually runs together the first two stanzas, presumably through misinterpreting a page break in its copy text.)

The present text follows that in *English Minstrelsy*, 2 vols (Edinburgh, 1810), 2.192–96, the first fully authorised printing and evidently the last in which Scott was creatively involved, with the following emendation:

148.45   car (*Spirit of the Public Journals, for 1806*) / car,

Historical Note

Notwithstanding remaining uncertainties about the exact date of composition (see Textual Note), this poem evidently originated in response to a threatened invasion from France. After the collapse of the Peace of Amiens in May 1803, Napoleon assembled the Grande Armée on the northern coast of France, posing a threat that receded in October 1804 after a successful attack on the French flotilla in Boulogne Bay, but which was still capable of reigniting at flash points in the following year, the prospect of invasion only fully abating with Nelson's victory at Trafalgar in late October 1805. Patriotic anti-invasion songs and poems flourished at this time, one of the best-known ones being James Hogg's 'Donald Macdonald', whose anti-French tirade is delivered by an archetypal Highland trooper (see Peter Garside, 'The Origins and History of James Hogg's "Donald Macdonald"', *Scottish Studies Review*, 7: 2 (Autumn 2006), 24–39). As in Hogg's song, Scott's poem sets out to re-channel earlier forms of patriotic Scottish resistance into a larger British context. Notwithstanding indications of a Gaelic origin in the early periodical printing of the poem, no such source text has been discovered. A more general indebtedness to the Bardic tradition in later eighteenth-century poetry, and especially the Ossianic literature of James Macpherson (1736–96), is however apparent throughout.

Explanatory Notes

147.1   Forest of Glenmore   in Strathspey, in the NE Highlands, between the River Spey and the Cairngorm Mountains. According to John Grigor, *Arboriculture* (Edinburgh, 1868), 168: 'In the end of the last century the forest of Glenmore was considered the finest in the country. His Grace the Duke of Gordon about that time sold the principal part of the timber to Mr. Osbourne, an eminent wood-merchant in Hull, who finished felling it in 1804. The timber was floated to Speymouth, and principally employed in naval purposes. One of the finest frigates built there of this timber for his Majesty's service was named "The Glenmore".'

147.6   troubled lake   if a specific location is intended, possibly Loch Morlich, now forming part of the Glenmore Forest Park, and situated 8 km (5 miles) NW of Cairn Gorm and 7 km (4½ miles) SE of Aviemore.

147.8   shelvy strand   shore having shelves or dangerous sandbanks.

148.21   spectre with his bloody hand   as partly indicated by Scott's 1st footnote on this page, *làmh dearg* is Gaelic for 'red hand'. For the spectre, see his later note to *Marmion* (1808): 'The forest of Glenmore, in the North Highlands, is believed to be haunted by a spirit called *Lham-dearg*, in the array of an ancient warrior, having a bloody-hand, from which he takes his name.' (Note VIII to Canto Third in *Marmion*, ed. Ainsley McIntosh, EEWSP 2 (Edinburgh, 2018), 244; see also her note to 244.1–8 (459)). A further note, to *The Lady of the Lake* (1810), envisages 'A goblin dressed in antique armour, and having one hand covered with blood' ('Notes to Canto Third', lvi).

148.27   Lochlin   signifying in Gaelic culture Scandinavia, or more specifically Norway. Compare *The Lay of the Last Minstrel* (1805): 'Stern Lochlin's sons of roving war, / The Norsemen, trained to spoil and blood, / Skilled to prepare the raven's food' (Canto 6, stanza 22). The term Lochlin appears frequently in James Macpherson's *Fingal; An Ancient Epic Poem* (London, 1762): see also *A Legend of the Wars of Montrose*, ed. J. H. Alexander, EEWN 7b (Edinburgh, 1995), 151 motto (and note). It also features in Scott's review of the *Report of the Committee of the Highland Society of Scotland on the Poems of Ossian* for the *Edinburgh Review* (July 1805): 'Magnus falls, and is bound. Fingal generously spares his life, and offers him his choice, either to return to Norway in safety, or again try his fate in battle. Magnus vows never again to lift his sword against his generous conqueror; and with his departure to Lochlin the poem concludes' (6.438).

148.30   Skilled to prepare the raven's food   the raven was revered by the Vikings, for whom the bird was associated with war and death. The bodies of doomed opponents, sometimes with entrails exposed, were supposedly offered to the ravens after battle as a reward. For the proximity of this and the preceding two lines to equivalents in Scott's *The Lay of the Last Minstrel*, see previous note.

148.32   Largs and Loncarty   as Scott's 2nd footnote on this page indicates, two battles in which according to tradition Scots forces defeated the Norsemen. At the battle of Largs in 1263 an attempt by the King of Norway to reassert sovereignty over the Western seaboard of Scotland was thwarted by an indecisive engagement, leading to the departure of the Norwegian fleet, an event later magnified by partisan historians into one of international importance. Luncarty is the site, some 7 km (4½ miles) N of Perth, of a battle in which the Scots defeated the Danes. The battle occurred during the reign of Kenneth III, probably around the year 990, and was similarly applauded by later historians. 'Loncarty' was an acceptable alternative spelling in Scott's day: see, for example, *The Peerage of Scotland* (London, 1767), 61.

148.44   Albion's weal   *Albion* is an archaic name for the island of Great Britain, also used sometimes for both England and Scotland separately (*Alba* in Scottish Gaelic denotes Scotland).

148.45   Coilgach   variant form of Calgacus, a Celtic chieftain who according to the historian Tacitus fought the Roman army at the battle of Mons Graupius in northern Scotland in AD 84. Tacitus accords to him a rousing speech prior to the battle in favour of freedom (*Agricola*, 29–38), though both this as well as Calgacus himself are possibly Tacitus's own invention. The battle of Mons Graupius subsequently became a matter of obsessive enquiry for Scott's fictional character Jonathan Oldbuck in *The Antiquary* (1816): see *The Antiquary*, ed David Hewitt, EEWN 3 (Edinburgh, 1995), 461–62 (note to 28.21–26).

148.48   died on Aboukir   referring to Sir Ralph Abercromby (1734–1801), veteran Scottish general, who died of his wounds after the otherwise successful engagement with the French at the Battle of Alexandria on 21 March 1801, following a landing of British forces at Aboukir [Abu Qir] Bay in Egypt earlier that month.

149.53 fierce Hengist's strain Hengist and Horsa figure in Anglo-Saxon history as brothers who led the Germanic armies that conquered the first territories in Britain in the 5th century. Compare Scott's 'Introduction' to *Sir Tristrem* (Edinburgh, 1804): 'For ages after the arrival of Hengist and Horsa, the whole western coast of Britain was possessed by the aboriginal inhabitants' (xxxv).

54. The Maid of Toro

Textual Note
An early and incomplete version of 'The Maid of Toro' was included by Scott in his prose drama of 'The House of Aspen', written around 1799, where it is sung by Gertrude, at the request of her aunt's husband, Rudiger of Aspen, as they wait anxiously for the sons of the household to return from battle. Distressed by the thought that the fate of the heroine may be her own, Gertrude breaks off her song after twenty lines. Scott hoped that his play might be produced for the London stage, which is no doubt the reason why a number of songs were included, and it was in fact under consideration for production at the Drury Lane theatre in London in 1800. Clearly a number of copies would need to be made for that purpose, and from his correspondence it is evident that Scott also sent copies as gifts or loans to his friends at various times subsequently: it can be deduced, for instance, that he sent a manuscript copy to Joanna Baillie in 1808 (*Letters*, 2.57–58) and one to Lady Abercorn in 1811 (*Letters*, 2.495). There are apparently now only three copies of the original play surviving, two at the Beinecke and one as NLS, Acc. 11772. (For further details of these manuscripts see the Textual Note to no. 41, 'A Song of Victory'.) The text of the song later entitled 'The Maid of Toro' is substantially the same in both Beinecke manuscripts, but the second manuscript is more fully punctuated and also has 'and' in several places where the first manuscript uses an ampersand. The first manuscript includes a number of deletions and revisions, where the second has only the final reading: in line 8, for instance, the first manuscript reads '<Restore me my love> ↑My Frederic restore↓' where the second has simply 'My Frederic restore'. NLS, Acc. 11772 has one variant in the third stanza: line 18 reads 'guardian' where the Beinecke manuscripts have 'lover'. There is no indication of the tune to which an actress performing the role should sing this song in any of the manuscripts.

Scott also extracted the song from its dramatic context to include it in a booklet of poems presented to Lady Charlotte Campbell (Aberdeen University Library, WS C2), the outside leaves of which bear the watermark 'T STAINS / 1799' and which is apparently dated 16 January 1805, although it is possible that the year is in fact 1801. In this manuscript, as in 'The House of Aspen', the lost lover is called Frederic and the song ends after twenty lines. Slight variations in wording, such as 'came' in line 9 and 'brave' in line 19 where the Beinecke manuscripts both have 'were' and 'bold', may be due to Scott's recalling the poem from memory or simply to his testing out possible alternatives.

Scott revised the song substantially, completing the third eight-line stanza, for publication in William Whyte's *A Collection of Scottish Airs*, 2 vols (Edinburgh, 1806–07), 1.item 37. His letter to James Ballantyne of 2 October 1805 (*Letters*, 1.260) refers to contributing 'Hellvellyn' (see no. 55) to Whyte's publication and it seems likely that 'The Maid of Toro' was revised for Whyte at much the same time. The lover's name is changed to Henry, a syllable shorter than Frederic and a number of other words are altered and new ones introduced, presumably to accommodate the poem's rhythm to that of the tune in Haydn's musical setting on the facing page. In line 4, for instance, 'Sighed to the breezes' was revised to 'Sorely sighed to the breezes'.

'The Maid of Toro' was then reprinted, without musical notation or other indication of the tune, in Scott's 1806 *Ballads and Lyrical Pieces* (178–79) and in the section of other poems in the eighth edition of *The Lay of the Last Minstrel* of 1808 (253–54), without any variation other than changes of the kind normally associated with the printer. In similar fashion, it passed into *Poetical Works* of 1820 (2.246–47) and the subsequent lifetime collected editions of Scott's poetry, followed by the Lockhart 1833–34 posthumous edition (6.368–69). It was additionally printed in its original incomplete version within 'The House of Aspen' itself in *The Keepsake for MDCCCXXX*, ed. Frederic Mansel Reynolds (London, [1829]), 28–29, and when the drama was included in Lockhart's posthumous edition of Scott's collected poetry (12.399).

The present text follows that of *A Collection of Scottish Airs*, 2 vols (Edinburgh, 1806–07), 1.item 37, but provides opening and closing speech marks for Eleanor's prayer in lines 5–8 and for the soldier's speech in lines 17–20 in accordance with all of the collected lifetime editions of Scott's poems.

Historical Note
It was presumably after his breakthrough success with *The Lay of the Last Minstrel* early in 1805 that Scott was approached by William Whyte for lyrics for his musical publication *A Collection of Scottish Airs* (1806–07). Scott had recently invested heavily in the printing firm headed by James Ballantyne, who was the printer of Whyte's collection, and Ballantyne almost certainly acted as intermediary between Whyte and Scott. Writing to Ballantyne on 2 October 1805, Scott was gratified by Ballantyne's approval of 'Hellvellyn' (see no. 55, also contributed to Whyte's collection). He added 'I hope Mr. White understands that he is not to give the words to any publication unless a musical one, and that he is satisfied with them' (*Letters*, 1.260), thus demonstrating his own concern to retain control of his lyrics for inclusion in future editions of his own poems.

William Whyte was an Edinburgh music-seller and music publisher, whose premises between around 1799 and 1809 were 'at the sign of the Organ' at 1 South Andrew Street: see Charles Humphries and William C. Smith, *Music Publishing in the British Isles*, 2nd edn (Oxford, 1970), 332. In forming *A Collection of Scottish Airs* he followed very closely the precedent set by fellow Edinburgh music editor George Thomson (1757–1851) in assembling a number of traditional Scottish song melodies and employing the most famous German composers of the day to arrange these with introductions and musical settings for performance in drawing-rooms and at concerts. Thomson had commissioned musical settings for the earlier volumes of *A Select Collection of Original Scottish Airs* from Ignace Joseph Pleyel (1757–1831) and by 1800 was also receiving musical settings from Joseph Haydn (1732–1809). Whyte's deliberate rivalry with Thomson's enterprise is shown by his also engaging Haydn in 1802–03 to make 65 arrangements of Scottish tunes for his similarly-titled song-book. Thomson was hurt by Haydn's undertaking the work: see *Grove's Dictionary of Music and Musicians*, ed. J. A. Fuller Maitland, 5 vols (New York, 1911), 5.518.

Thomson had enlisted Robert Burns to write lyrics for the earlier volumes of his collection, a move copied by Whyte's engagement of Scott to write new lyrics to suit Haydn's music, as emphasised by the mention of 'two original songs, from the elegant pen of Mr Walter Scott' in the prefatory Advertisement to his first volume, dated 1 March 1806. The implicit comparison was strengthened by the fact that several of the tunes accompanying Scott's words in Whyte's collection were previously associated with verses by Burns in Thomson's work. The air for which Haydn made his musical setting here, for instance, is named as 'Captain O'Kain', for which Burns had written his song beginning 'The small birds rejoice in the green leaves returning' and known as 'The Chevalier's Lament', published in the 1799 volume of Thomson's *Select Collection of Original Scottish Airs*, item 97 (Kinsley, no. 220).

Although the terms of Whyte's payments to Scott are unknown, they were probably handsome ones since Thomas Campbell, writing of his declining an offer to write song lyrics for Thomson's work to his friend John Richardson in 1805, remarked that 'my time would be lost in attempting to do any thing, unless I got such terms as Scott has got from Whyte': see William Beattie, *Life and Letters of Thomas Campbell*, 3 vols (London, 1849), 2.64–65.

Explanatory Notes

149.1   lake of Toro   'The House of Aspen' is set in Germany, but no specific location has been identified.

55. Hellvellyn

Textual Note
This song was first published as item 16 in the first volume (1806) of William Whyte's *A Collection of Scottish Airs*, where the text in letterpress is accompanied by a musical notation based on the air 'Erin-gobragh' [*Éirinn go Bràch*] incorporating the first stanza. (For further information on Whyte and his collection, see Historical Note to no. 54, 'The Maid of Toro'.) Scott apparently sent the text for Whyte's consideration shortly after having returned to Edinburgh in the wake of an excursion to the Lake District, during which he had climbed the mountain Helvellyn in the company of William Wordsworth. A letter of Scott's to James Ballantyne of 2 October 1805 expresses pleasure at Ballantyne's approval of this piece, while adding: 'I hope Mr. White understands that he is not to give the words to any publication unless a musical one, and that he is satisfied with them' (*Letters*, 1.260). An autograph fair copy also survives in Edinburgh University Library (CLX-A-63 E90.122). Consisting of a single sheet measuring 23.7 x 19.7 cm, and with a 'C & S / 1801' watermark, this closely matches the wording in Whyte's publication (including the headnote), and may have been used as a copy-text. In comparison, the printed version supplies a standard punctuation system, while raising initial capitals in several instances ('Pilgrim', 'Prince', 'Chief', 'People'). The piece next featured in *Ballads and Lyrical Pieces* (1806), 178–80, as one of a small section of 'Songs', with only a few minor alterations in punctuation, most notable of which is the replacement of the three exclamation marks in the first half of the third stanza with two semi-colons and a final question mark. It subsequently appeared in the eighth edition of *The Lay of the Last Minstrel* (1808) (where 'dim-lighted hall' in line 26 uniquely mutates to 'dimlighted-hall'), before entering into the collected *Poetical Works* beginning with the edition of 1820 (2.248–50). Apart from a further incursion of question marks in the first half of the third stanza, and the representation of 'desart' as 'desert' in line 37, the

text in the posthumous Lockhart edition of 1833–34 (6.370–2) remains close to the earliest printings.

The present text follows the letterpress in *A Collection of Scottish Airs*, 2 vols (Edinburgh 1806–07), 1.item 16, the first authorised printing and the one nearest to the surviving manuscript, with the following emendation:

152.33   Lover of Nature (EUL MS) / lover of nature

Historical Note
Scott's excursion to the Lake District, accompanied by his wife Charlotte, evidently took place in August 1805, and involved visits to Robert Southey in Keswick and William Wordsworth at Grasmere. It was while staying with Wordsworth at Dove Cottage that the two poets, accompanied by the chemist and inventor Sir Humphry Davy (1778–1829), undertook the ascent of Helvellyn, the third highest peak (at 950 m) in the Lake District, overlooking Ullswater to the east and the present Lake Thirlmere to the west. As Wordsworth later recalled:

> We ascended from Paterdale & I could not but admire the vigor with which Scott scrambled along that horn of the mountain called 'Striding Edge'. Our progress was necessarily slow & beguiled by Scott's telling many stories & amusing anecdotes as was his custom. Sir H. Davy would have probably been better pleased if other topics had occasionally been interspersed & some discussion entered upon; at all events he did not remain with us long at the top of the mountain but left us to find our way down its steep side together into the Vale of Grasmere where at my cottage Mrs. Scott was to meet us for dinner. (*The Fenwick Notes of William Wordsworth*, ed. Jared Curtis (London, 1993), 176)

It was on this excursion that Scott probably first heard of the fate of Charles Gough (1784–1805), a tourist and artist, who had set off earlier in April to walk over the mountain, and whose skeletal remains, attended by his dog, had only recently been discovered, after what was assumed to have been a fatal fall from a ridge of the mountain: see *The Unfortunate Tourist of Helvellyn and his Faithful Dog: Charles Gough* (Grasmere, 2003). Both Wordsworth and Scott subsequently wrote poems based on the incident, Wordsworth's 'Fidelity', also composed in 1805, focusing especially on the dog's role as an expression of the benevolent force of nature. Neither poet touched on a more carnivorous explanation for the fleshless state of the body and the dog's survival, though such an interpretation was being offered in the *Carlisle Journal* as early as 27 July 1805 (*Unfortunate Tourist*, 11).

Explanatory Notes
151.5   Striden-edge   Striding Edge, a sharp-topped ridge on the SE side of Helvellyn.
151.5   Red-tarn   Red Tarn, small lake in a deep glacial cove, on the E flank of Helvellyn, overlooked by Striding Edge from the SW.
151.6   Catchedicam   variant form of Catstye Cam, an outlying fell NE of Helvellyn, further encircling the Red Tarn.
152.27   scutcheons   shield-like devices with armorial bearings, here especially those of a deceased person.

56.   A Health to Lord Melville

Textual Note
This song was first performed at a dinner to celebrate the acquittal of Lord Melville held in the Assembly Rooms, George Street, Edinburgh on Friday, 27 June 1806. According to a letter from Scott to Lady Abercorn, the following day, though it had only been 'scratched down' on the 'morning of the day of the meeting' a few copies had already been printed, one of which he hoped to enclose with his letter (*Letters*, 1.304). This situation is confirmed by another letter of 28 June, to Colonel Robert Dundas, in which a printed broadside of this item was included, though Scott was obliged to transcribe another song of his sung at the dinner (see NLS, MS 855, ff. 1–2; also Textual Note to no. 57, 'The Lawyer and the Archbishop of Canterbury'). No manuscript of the present song apparently exists, though two early broadside copies, evidently printed close to the time of the occasion, survive in the National Library of Scotland. Both are in the form of a booklet, with a leaf size measuring approx. 22 x 13.8 cm, paginated [1]–4, the header reading 'A / HEALTH TO LORD MELVILLE; / BEING / AN EXCELLENT NEW SONG', this being followed by a three-line epigraph from Shakespeare (as in the present text), while the tune is named as Carrickfergus. Further examination however reveals small, but significant, differences. NLS, L.C.1268(136), part of a collection originally formed by James Maidment, bears the colophon 'Edinburgh: Printed by James Ballantyne and Co.' The first two lines of the second stanza here read: 'What were the Whigs doing, what measures pursuing, / When PITT quelled Rebellion, gave Treason a string?' In contrast the copy at MS 933, ff. 52–53, has no colophon, and here at stanza 2, lines 1–2, reads: 'What were the Whigs doing, when boldly pursuing; / PITT banished Rebellion, gave Treason a string?' It is worth noting that this copy, the text of which is partly obscured through tearing, is bound after a letter to J. G. Lockhart from W. Imlay of 26 February 1834, enclosing the same. An explanation for the differences between the two copies can apparently be found in a further copy of the broadside held in the Berg Collection, New York Public Library, which bears corrections in Scott's hand. Here the underlying text, matching MS 933, is altered at stanza 2, lines 1–2, to the wording as in L.C.1268(136), suggesting that Scott at some later point desired this alteration to be made to what from the circumstances had presumably been a rushed first impression. Scott can also be seen here italicising 'petty' at line 52; as well as introducing two small footnotes.

One remarkable feature of subsequent editions of the song is that all effectively bypass the changes made by Scott in the Berg proof and in part incorporated in L.C.1268(136). Another early printing, in the form of a single leaf broadside, and with the colophon 'Printed in the Herald Office, Glasgow' (NLS, R.B.m.294(4)), clearly follows the text as in MS 933, though at one point misspelling 'O'CONNOR' at line 13 as 'O'CONNER'. The song also appeared after a short gap in the *Scots Magazine* for September 1806 (68.693–94), with minor changes in punctuation, under the title 'Health to Lord Melville', and with a bracketed preamble intimating that inclusion had come as a result of external pressure: 'None of our readers are probably ignorant of the occasion on which these verses were sung, or of the author by whom they are written. They are inserted here at the request of several respectable subscribers.' Here again the crucial lines read: 'What were the Whigs doing, when boldly pursuing; / PITT banished Rebellion, gave Treason a string?' This in turn (with the addition of a guiding comma after 'when') is the version given in J. G. Lockhart's *Life* (2.106–09), which for the first time fills in the names at line 75 to read 'GRENVILLE and SPENCER'. Lockhart in passing expresses his regret 'that this piece was inadvertently omitted in the late collective edition of his poetical works' (106); and, indeed, it appears not to have been reprinted in any of the collected sets of Scott's poetry up to and including the posthumous edition of 1833–34.

The present text follows the printed broadside NLS, L.C.1268(136), as including changes subsequently made by Scott to the original broadside version, and so representing the completion of the initial creative process. Two small annotations introduced by Scott in the broadside held in the Berg Collection, New York, are incorporated in the Explanatory Notes below. The following emendation has also been made to the text:

155.52   *petty* (Berg MS) / petty

Historical Note

This is one of two songs by Scott written for and performed at a dinner held in the Assembly Rooms in Edinburgh in 1806 celebrating the acquittal of Henry Dundas, 1st Viscount Melville (1742–1811), after a trial before the House of Lords where he had stood charged of misappropriating public funds. Melville's lengthy political career had seen him hold high office in London, while effectively managing the patronage system in his native Scotland, leading to him being named pejoratively by opponents 'King Harry the Ninth'. The trial, which opened to great excitement on 29 April 1806 in Westminster Hall, also coincided with the brief Whig coalition 'Ministry of All the Talents' (1806–07), which led to significant changes among office holders in Scotland. Scott's keen political involvement, in mostly resisting these changes, was sharpened further by feelings of personal indebtedness to Melville and his family. As he wrote to George Ellis on 20 February: 'He was the architect of my little fortune, from circumstances of personal regard merely; for any of my trifling literary acquisitions were out of his way. My heart bleeds when I think on his situation' (*Letters*, 1.280). News of Melville being found innocent on all charges on 12 June helped galvanise Tory opinion when it reached Edinburgh. As the *Caledonian Mercury* reported on Thursday, 19 June: 'on account of the acquittal of Lord Melville, several houses and shops were brilliantly illuminated in Edinburgh, the New Town, George's [*sic*] Square &c. Some of them had the words "Melville and Innocence" beautifully displayed.' Over 500 guests attended the celebratory dinner, held on the evening of Friday, 27 June, at a guinea-and-a-half a head, and at which, according to the *Mercury* of the following day, 'Many excellent songs were sung, and suitable music ... given by Gow's musicians, and the several military bands now in this city and neighbourhood'. Scott's two 'squibs', as he informed correspondents, met 'with most exceeding good approbation', having been 'hollow[ed] forth' by James Ballantyne 'with the voice of a Stentor' (*Letters*, 12.285; 1.305). In particular the tribute to the recently-deceased William Pitt (see lines 18–20, and note to 153.20), as he told Lady Abercorn, 'drew tears from many of the jovial party to whom it was addressed' (*Letters*, 1.304). Less appealing, in the minds of some neutral as well as Whig observers, were the following words (line 79) concerning Charles James Fox, Pitt's long-standing Whig opponent, whose current ill-health was to lead to his own death later that year.

Explanatory Notes

153.motto   see *Macbeth*, 5.5.5–7.

153.Air   Irish folk song, named after a settlement in Northern Ireland, 17 km (10½ miles) NE of Belfast.

153.12 PITT William Pitt, the Younger (1759–1806), Tory statesman, Prime Minister 1783–1801 and 1804–06.

153.12 quelled Rebellion most obviously referring to the suppression of rebellion in Ireland in 1798, as orchestrated by William Pitt's Tory administration.

153.12 gave Treason a string in addition to the repression of radical activity at home and rebellion in Ireland (see previous note), possibly referring more specifically to mutinies in the Navy at Spithead and the Nore, suppression of the latter leading to its alleged ringleader and 24 seamen being hanged from the yardarm.

153.13 ARTHUR O'CONNOR (1763–1852), United Irishman and later general in Napoleon's army. Arrested in 1798 while travelling to France with other supporters of the Irish cause, but acquitted with the help of evidence of his good character given by members of the Whig circle at his trial. Pitt's fury at not being able to convict O'Connor led to a duel with the Foxite Whig MP and Irishman George Tierney: see Edward Royle, *Revolutionary Britannia? Reflections on the Threat of Revolution in Britain, 1789–1848* (Manchester, 2000), 33. O'Connor was subsequently imprisoned at Fort George in Scotland, but released in 1802 under condition of banishment.

153.14 DESPARD Colonel Edward Marcus Despard (1751–1803), last man in Britain to be sentenced to be hung, drawn and quartered for high treason. Evidence presented in Court suggested Despard, a former officer and colonial official, planned with his conspirators to assassinate George III and seize strongpoints in London as a prelude to a larger uprising in the city. Execution (in modified form) took place on 21 February 1803 before an estimated crowd of 20,000. On a previous occasion, when he was detained in prison under the suspension of habeas corpus, Whig politicians, notably Sir Francis Burdett (1770–1844), had agitated strongly for his release. As Scott wrote in a letter of 6 March 1803: 'his fate was deplored & howled over by Sir Frances [*sic*] Burdett & other reforming members of the house of commons: the first act of this worthy & oppressed patriot upon his liberation was to organize the murder of his Sovereign' (*Letters*, 1.178).

153.16 PITT and MELVILLE the political partnership between William Pitt and Henry Dundas (see Historical Note) was long-standing, dating back to the formation of Pitt's first administration in 1783–84, and finding renewed strength during Pitt's last period of office in 1805 and 1806.

153.20 Pilot that weather'd the storm echoing the 1802 song in praise of William Pitt's patriotism by George Canning, first sung at a dinner to celebrate Pitt's birthday after his resignation as Prime Minister in 1801: 'No!— here's to the Pilot that weather'd the storm' (line 4): see *English Minstrelsy*, ed. Scott 2 vols (Edinburgh, 1810), 2.199–201. Pitt had since died in January 1806. Compare *Marmion*, Introduction to Canto First, line 102: see *Marmion*, ed. Ainsley McIntosh, EEWSP 2 (Edinburgh, 2018),12, 372 (note to 1.102); also 'Essay on the Text' there, 310, for William Rose's comment to Scott in 1807 that the phrase had become 'hackneyed at Taverns by public singers'.

154.21 the Blues annotated by Scott in the Berg copy of the broadside as: '1st Regt Edinburgh Volunteers'. The Royal Edinburgh Volunteers were established in 1794 and Lord Melville, who played a leading part in parliament in the formation of such forces, had officially joined at a ceremony in 1795. The uniform included a blue coat. There is a portrait of 'Henry Dundas, Viscount Melville, in the Uniform of the Royal Edinburgh Volunteers' in John Kay's *A Series of Original Portraits and Caricature Etchings*, 2 vols (Edinburgh, 1838), 1 pt 2, (no. CXVII, facing 288).

154.29   Blue Grenadier   probably relating to the Grenadier Company of the Edinburgh Volunteers, to which Scott's brother Thomas had belonged (see *Letters*, 1.37).

154.31   turn us adrift   perhaps referring to movements to disband volunteer corps, the Volunteer Act and Provisional Cavalry Act being allowed to lapse by the government in 1806. See *Letters*, 1.314, for comments by Scott about the possible 'breaking up' of his own Royal Edinburgh Volunteer Light Dragoons.

154.33   blue bonnet   blue flat-topped round cap, considered a distinguishing Scottish appendage. For Scott's well-known song 'Blue Bonnets o'er the Border', see *Marmion*, ed. Ainsley McIntosh, EEWSP 2 (Edinburgh, 2018), 430 (note to 5.698).

154.43   CORNWALLIS cashier'd   apparently referring to Charles Cornwallis, 1st Marquess of Cornwallis (1738–1805), veteran British general who had commanded the British forces during the American War of Independence, surrendering at Yorktown in 1781. In 1798 he was appointed Commander-in-Chief in Ireland, and oversaw the response to the 1798 Irish rebellion. He was chief signatory to the Peace of Amiens with France in 1802, after which he withdrew into private life until being recalled as Governor General of India in 1805, dying shortly after arrival there. No evidence has been found of his ever being cashiered (i.e. dismissed from service, often after a court martial), though in the looser sense of being ignored or overlooked this might relate to his apparent retirement from military affairs after 1802.

154.44   Cape call'd a bauble   the Cape of Good Hope, on the southern tip of Africa, was of vital importance as a port for ships passing between Asia and Europe. The British Cape Colony, originally secured by an expeditionary force in 1795, after French troops had captured the Dutch republic, was returned to the Dutch by the Peace of Amiens of 1802. In 1806 a second expedition recaptured the colony, and it remained in British hands until the establishment of the Union of South Africa in 1910.

154.50   SIR DAVID and POPHAM   Sir David Baird (1757–1829), British lieutenant-general, commanded an army which landed at the Cape of Good Hope in January 1806, defeating the Dutch at the battle of Blaauwberg; Sir Home Riggs Popham (1762–1820), naval commander, who co-operated with Baird in occupying the Cape. Both were implicated in the same year in an unsuccessful attack on the River Plate in South America, assuming tacit support from a Pittite government, but for which they were censured on their return to London in 1807.

155.52   *petty* Statesman   with *petty* perhaps signifying smallness in significance in addition to the more modern sense of 'trivial-minded'. Compare David Hume, the philosopher, in a letter of 1767: 'I am now, from a Philosopher, degenerated into a petty Statesman' (see E. C. Mossner, *The Life of David Hume*, 2nd edn (Oxford, 1980), 533).

155.53–54   Beer-tax … Pig-iron duty   when war with France broke out in 1793 the government first took out loans, but as it continued turned more to taxes, initially on luxury items, then increasingly on common consumer goods. 'Small beer tax' and 'Iron Tax' (the latter crossed out) both feature on a list held out in a John Gillray cartoon '"The Friend of the People" and his Petty-New-Tax-Gatherer paying John Bull a visit'. William Pitt's introduction of an income tax in 1799 was partly an attempt to rationalise the system. A Pig Iron Duty Bill was being debated in the House of Commons in April/May 1806. The name 'pig iron' apparently originated in the early days of iron-ore reduction when the output of the blast furnace was cast into 'pigs'—a mass of iron roughly resembling the shape of a reclining pig.

155.53   as if W—— had brew'd it   alluding to the Whig politician and brewer, Samuel Whitbread (1764–1815): see also no. 57, 'The Lawyer and the Archbishop of Canterbury', especially note to 156.21.

155.61   Our King   George III (1738–1820), a focal point for Tory loyalist sentiments, notwithstanding increasing mental derangement through illness.

155.61   our Princess   most possibly, in the circumstances, Princess Caroline of Brunswick-Wolfenbüttel (1768–1821), who married the Prince of Wales (later George IV) in 1795, followed by separation in 1796. Whereas the Prince of Wales was closely associated with the Whig party, Princess Caroline at this time continued to enjoy the support of George III. Scandal attaching to her private life led to a setting up of an official commission ('delicate enquiry') in 1806; inevitably associated with the new Whig administration, this began in May 1806 and concluded in July 1806 by clearing the Princess though reporting that her general behaviour was questionable. Scott expressed his pleasure at meeting her during a visit to London in early spring 1806: 'She is an enchanting princess … and I cannot help thinking that her prince must labour under some malignant spell when he denies himself her society' (*Letters*, 1.285; see also 12.281). Alternatively, Princess Charlotte Augusta (1796–1817), the only child of Caroline and the Prince of Wales, who would have been ten at the time of the song.

155.71   Auld Reekie   'Old Smokey': nickname for Edinburgh, particularly the Old Town, over which a pall of smoke used to hang. Scott himself annotates this as 'Edinburgh' in the Berg copy of the broadside.

155.74   law-book, nor lawyer   alluding to the attempted intervention by John Clerk, Lord Eldin (1757–1832), the new Whig Solicitor-General for Scotland, in advising the Edinburgh Lord Provost that it was illegal and contrary to public safety to encourage an illumination of windows following news of Melville's acquittal: see Henry Cockburn, *Memorials of His Time* (Edinburgh, 1856), 218–19.

155.75   G——LLE and Sp——R   William Wyndham Grenville, Baron Grenville (1759–1834), and George John Spencer, 2nd Earl Spencer (1758–1834): respectively Prime Minister and Home Secretary during the Whig 'Ministry of All the Talents' of 1806–07. Scott in these lines can be seen favourably distinguishing old-style aristocratic Whigs from their reformist associates.

155.78   the Brewer   see note to 155.53 above.

155.79   Tallyho to the Fox   the metaphor of fox-hunting, as punningly applied here to the Whig politician Charles James Fox (1749–1806), was deemed especially offensive by some contemporaries.

57.   The Lawyer and the Archbishop of Canterbury

Textual Note

This is the second of two songs by Scott performed at the dinner to celebrate the acquittal of Lord Melville held in the Assembly Rooms, George Street, Edinburgh on Friday, 27 June 1806 (see also no. 56, 'A Health to Lord Melville'). A printed broadside version, with stanzas numbered 1–6, survives as NLS, MS 1036, f. 50. Consisting of a single sheet, measuring approx. 32 x 19 cm, and without a visible watermark, this is headed 'NEVER BEFORE PRINTED. / WRITTEN ON THE OCCASION OF / LORD MELVILLE'S ACQUITTAL, / 1806.' A manuscript version in Scott's hand is also to be found in NLS, MS 877, ff. 205–06, comprising two leaves (measuring approx.

26.5 x 21 cm), probably conjugate though tipped in, and with no visible water-mark. Headed 'The Lawyer and the Bishop / To the tune of "King John & the Abbot of Canterbury"', a number of substantive variants from the broadside version indicate that this MS represents an earlier version than the printed song. Individual differences include 'Justice' rather than 'Chief Justice' at line 7 and 'Quoth' not 'Said' (line 14). In stanza 4 moreover the second line reads 'And beheld it as blank as the brow of an ass', while the fourth has 'But from thence-forth the Lawyer was *Non est inventus*' compared with 'But the Lawyer thence-forward was non est inventus'. The NLS MS version also contains an additional verse after the fifth stanza, which reads:

> The party now find themselves in the wrong Box
> Though they thanked the Committee & voted with Fox
> They've found out the difference twixt merit & jaw
> And the damnable odds betwixt *Justice* & *Law*

Derry down &c (f. 205v)

An equivalent of this stanza is also found in another (single leaf) manuscript, measuring approx. 25 x 19.7 cm and with a 'C & S / 1801' watermark, now in the Berg Collection, New York Public Library. In this version, the first line reads: 'I'll tell you a story a story so merry'. In the case of the second line to stanza 4 also the wording has been altered to match that found in the ver-sion in NLS, MS 877. Quite possibly, then, the Berg MS represents an earlier draft state, though allowance should be made for Scott sometimes reverting to alternative forms when writing out copies. Immediately after the event he was certainly keen to disseminate the song among friends and political sympathisers. In a letter to Lady Abercorn, probably of 28 June, now in the Morgan Library (Accession MA 427/2), Scott provided a transcript of the 'trifling song which was sung with *immense approbation*' at the meeting (compare *Letters*, 1.304 [letter only]). This mostly parallels the wording as found in the corrected Berg MS, albeit beginning 'Come listen brave Boys to a story so merry', and like it includes the additional stanza beginning 'The party now find themselves in the wrong box'. A transcript of the song, along with a printed copy of 'A Health to Lord Melville', was also sent on 28 June to Colonel Robert Dundas, Melville's son, a communication which now only exists in full in the form of a copy (NLS, MS 855, ff. 1–2). Beginning 'I'll tell you a story a story so merry', this in turn in its main body approximates other manuscript versions and includes the additional stanza. Another manuscript version, in Scott's best hand, is also to be found as a single sheet (approx. 28.2 x 17.5 cm; 'C & S / 1801' watermark) in a folder in the Morgan Library (Misc.English, MA 1861), the first line here reading 'Come Listen Brave boys to a story so merry', and with the additional stanza in place. In view of these circumstances, it seems most likely that the bulk of surviving manuscripts reflect the song as it was actually sung at the dinner, and that the broadside version, being published at a later point, deliberately left out the penultimate stanza for prudential reasons, and more particularly for its direct mention of the Whig politician Charles Fox (see also Explanatory Note to 156.27).

This song was not included in any of the collected editions of Scott's poetry, nor, unlike 'A Health to Lord Melville', did it feature subsequently in J. G. Lockhart's *Life* of Scott. An extended eight-stanza version, however, was pub-lished in *The Court of Session Garland*, ed. James Maidment (Edinburgh, 1839), Supplement, 5–12. The source given is 'a Manuscript Volume compiled by the late Mr. William Hume or Home, who, for many years of his life, was Clerk to the first Lord Meadowbank' ([3]). Here the first five stanzas and the last generally match the above manuscript versions, but the sixth (as below) is entirely new, while the seventh contains substantive differences:

> If a tradesman crave pay ere his work it is done,
> Or committee ask thanks ere their cause it is won;
> You may judge of them both in the very same way,
> And believe both your money and thanks thrown away.
>
> The party now find themselves in a fine stew,
> But must be contented to *drink* as they *brew*;
> For we've found out the diff'rence 'twixt merit and jaw,
> And the damnable odds between Justice and *Law*. (12)

The Lord Meadowbank referred to above is identifiable as Allan Maconochie (1748–1816), Advocate from 1773 and raised to the Bench in 1796, who was later in 1808 to help Scott in founding the *Edinburgh Annual Register* (see *Letters*, 2.136). Considering its content, it is not unlikely that Scott's song enjoyed an extended currency among Tory members of the Scottish legal establishment, where some of the above augmentations might feasibly have originated.

The present text is based on the surviving broadside (NLS, MS 1036, f. 50), which, though evidently printed sometime after the dinner, probably represents most fully the wording as it finally settled down. At the same time, it restores the omitted sixth stanza, as found in all surviving manuscript versions, the copy-text here being NLS, MS 877, as quoted above. The main title provided matches that found in the Berg manuscript. The following emendations have also been made:

156.19	from thenceforth the Lawyer was (NLS, MS 877) / the Lawyer thenceforward was
156.19	*Non est inventus* (NLS, MS 877) / non est inventus
156.23	Plumer (Editorial) / Plummer
156.26	box, (Editorial) / Box (NLS, MS 877)
156.27	Committee and voted (Editorial) / Committee & voted (NLS, MS 877)
156.27	Fox, (Editorial) / Fox (NLS, MS 877)
156.28	merit and jaw, (Editorial) / merit & jaw (NLS, MS 877)
156.29	Justice and Law. (Editorial) / *Justice* & *Law* (NLS, MS 877)
156.30	down. (Editorial) / down &c (NLS, MS 877)

Historical Note

Like its companion 'A Health to Lord Melville' (no. 56), this song concerns the unsuccessful impeachment of Henry Dundas, 1st Viscount Melville (1742–1811), before the House of Lords in 1806, though with greater specificity regarding the actual trial and personalities involved. There is also an underlying affinity to the old English folk-song, 'King John and the Bishop' (Child, 45), in which a rapacious King John, covetous of the Bishop of Canterbury's wealth, compels him on pain of death to answer three impossible questions: a stratagem only circumvented through the help of a shepherd. A version of the song as 'King John and the Abbot of Canterbury' featured in Thomas Percy, *Reliques of Ancient English Poetry*, 3 vols (London, 1765; see *ALC*), 2.302–07, where it is described as having been 'chiefly printed from an ancient black-letter copy, "To the tune of Derry down"' (302). In Scott's updating, according to Maidment's account, the present-day Archbishop is applauded for standing up against a particularly virulent speech made during the trial by Lord Ellenborough, Lord Chief Justice of the King's Bench: 'His Lordship having spoken with that violence which he sometimes indulged in, was answered by the Archbishop of Canterbury, in a temperate but energetic manner, and so effectually, that he attempted no reply' (*Court of Session Garland*, 6). At the dinner in Edinburgh celebrating Melville's acquittal, the Archbishop of Canterbury was one of the first names to be toasted (*Caledonian Mercury*, 28 June 1806).

Explanatory Notes

156.2   Archbishop of fair Canterbury   Charles Manners-Sutton (1755–1828), appointed Archbishop of Canterbury in 1805, partly through George III's personal intervention, and a firm upholder of High Church and Tory principles.

156.3   full bottom   alluding to the full-bottom wig, as used by judges for criminal trials up to the 1840s, now worn only as ceremonial dress.

156.5   Derry down   refrain, the meaning of which is now uncertain, commonly used in the choruses of popular songs from the 16th century onwards. Compare Scott's footnote concerning its ancient origins in *Ivanhoe*, ed. Graham Tulloch, EEWN 8 (Edinburgh, 1998), 150n. The traditional English tune of 'Derry Down' was published in the 18th century to lines beginning 'Goody Bull and her daughter together fell out', and was supposedly played at the surrender of the British troops at Yorktown in 1781.

156.6   very great hall   Westminster Hall, housing the Law Courts in London.

156.7   Chief Justice, some Law   referring in punning style to Edward Law, 1st Baron Ellenborough (1750–1818), appointed in 1802 as Chief Justice of the King's Bench, and elevated to the peerage at the same time. He voted to convict Lord Melville on six of the ten articles of impeachment faced in 1806.

156.13   hang, quarter, or draw   the old penalty in English law for high treason involved live disembowelling and dismemberment of the body.

156.16   Lauderdale   James Maitland, 8th Earl of Lauderdale (1759–1839). He returned to politics in 1806 with the formation of the new Whig coalition, and was created 1st Baron Lauderdale of Thirlestane in the British peerage. Becoming Lord Keeper of the Great Seal of Scotland, he hoped to purge Scotland of Lord Melville's influence, though his tenure of the post proved short-lived. In several manuscript versions of the poem his name is disguised (as 'L—d—rd—le', etc.).

156.16   tablet of brass   possibly alluding to the Mosaic tablets of the law, but here with 'brass' (impudence, bare-faced effrontery) substituting for stone.

156.19   *Non est inventus*   *Latin* he or she has not been found. Used of sheriffs returning to a process requiring the arrest of a defendant, when the latter is not found in their jurisdiction.

156.21   Whitbread's lost all his *hops*   referring to Samuel Whitbread (1764–1815), radical Whig politician and brewer, and again involving a pun (with 'hops' suggesting both political ambitions and the use of the flower of the hop plant to flavour beer).Whitbread led the parliamentary campaign that ended in a vote to impeach Melville on 25 June 1805 and in the House of Lords was the main manager on the committee representing the Commons at the trial. While many fellow-members remained silent, Whitbread made significant interventions during the proceedings, though later suffering ridicule for lapses of taste and judgement in his concluding speech of 16 May 1806.

156.22   wormwood   an exceedingly bitter herb, as used to help make the spirit *absinthe*. There is a story that the plant got its name as a result of its having grown up in the tracks of the serpent expelled from Eden.

156.23   Plumer   Sir Thomas Plumer (1753–1824), barrister, judge, and politician, who served as leading Counsel for the defence at Lord Melville's trial, gaining credit for his skillful cross-examination of witnesses; appointed Solicitor General in 1807. The name of Plumer (as 'Plomer') is only found in NLS MS 877 among the surviving manuscript versions cited above, Scott here intervening to alter the previous reading of 'For when to the peers the fair question was put' to the state found in the printed broadside.

156.24   mere butt   another double meaning, based on a butt being a target for ridicule or mockery and also a cask or barrel for storing beer.

156.26   in the wrong box   proverbial (out of place; awkwardly situated): see *ODEP*, 924.

156.27   voted with Fox   Charles James Fox (1749–1806), veteran Whig statesman and Foreign Secretary in the present Administration. He is listed as one of the managers in the committee representing the House of Commons at the trial, but does not appear to have taken a prominent part in the proceedings.

157.31–32   Prelate ... true Presbyterians   the Archbishop of Canterbury is head of the episcopalian Church of England, whereas most of the attendants at the dinner are likely to have been members of the Church of Scotland, itself organised along presbyterian lines (government of the church by a series of church courts of which one is the Presbytery).

58.   The Monks of Bangor's March

Textual Note
The song-collector and editor George Thomson (1757–1851) invited Scott to write words for a Beethoven setting of the Welsh tune 'Ymdaith Mwnge' (Monks March) in his letter of 12 June 1806:

> The monks march, *supposed* to have been played before the monks of Bangor in Flint shire, when they marched to Chester, to assist the prince of Powis with their prayers, against the invasion of the king of Northumberland about the beginning of the seventh century. This supposition respecting the Air is probably without any foundation, and as it suggests nothing almost for the Poet to build on, it were best I conceive that you should take the subject which may occur to your own imagination, only making the scenery and localities Welsh. (BL, Add. MS 35,266, f. 90)

In spite of Thomson's reservations Scott chose to adopt the legend, promising in early July that he would send Thomson some verses 'before I leave town' (*Letters*, 1.310), at the end of the current legal term. A subsequent letter to Thomson, also undated but presumably written later that month, mentions that William Erskine (1768–1822) 'who is just leaving me takes charge of a few verses for the Monks March' (*Letters*, 1.295). This original manuscript does not appear to have survived, though in a subsequent undated letter, endorsed by Thomson 'Oct 1806', Scott encloses a fair copy, including a headnote and footnote, stating that he has 'added another stanza to the Monks of Bangor' and that his own friends 'think the Monks improved by wanting the double rhymes' (BL, Add. MS 35,263, f. 276). This fair copy (ff. 277–78) is still with the letter, headed 'The Monks of Bangor', and written on a double sheet of paper with a watermark 'J BUDGEN / 1806', each leaf measuring approx. 24.7 x. 20.2 cm. It is in the handwriting of an amanuensis, possibly Scott's wife Charlotte, presumably written at Scott's direction as copy for the printer. In the accompanying letter Scott also asks to see a proof 'in case any minute alterations may yet occur to me' (f. 276) and presumably also to ensure that the song was printed correctly.

Two further manuscript versions of the verses have survived, the first of which forms part of Scott's letter to Lady Abercorn of 24 October 1806 (Morgan, MA 427/34) and has several differences in wording from the fair copy sent to Thomson. For instance, line 13 has 'holy band', while the third stanza begins with the present lines 21–22 and reverses the present lines 17 and 18, the first of which has 'anthems' instead of 'masses'. There is no headnote or footnote here, although Scott provides some background information in the letter itself and also glosses the Latin refrain for his correspondent. Possibly this letter was written before Scott prepared his fair copy manuscript for Thomson. Another manuscript version was sent to Lady Abercorn, part of a presentation copy of Scott's ballads written out by Charlotte Scott and dated by her to 1807 on the title-page outside wrapper (Senate House Library, University of London: Sterling MS S.L.V.24, ff. 8–10). This includes Scott's headnote and footnote and follows the wording of the fair-copy manuscript with only minor variations in spelling and punctuation and was almost certainly derived from it.

Scott's verses were first published in the third volume of Thomson's *A Select Collection of Original Welsh Airs* (Edinburgh, 1817), as item 62. It appears that the delay in publication of the first volume of this work was occasioned by a last-minute decision to acquire settings for the harp for the melodies, and that sales were so poor as to delay the subsequent production of the other two volumes: see J. Cuthbert Hadden, *George Thomson the Friend of Burns* (London, 1898),123–26. Apart from routine changes of the kind normally associated with the printer, there are a number of differences from Scott's manuscript more likely to be the result of Thomson's editorial hand as an intermediary or of Scott's own revisions in proof. The title, for instance, has been altered from 'The Monks of Bangor' to 'The Monks of Bangor's March', 'Alrid' becomes 'Olfrid', and the tune is 'supposed to have been played at' the monks' procession rather than being 'said to refer to' it. In line 11 the 'Maiden-mother' becomes the 'virgin-mother'. The refrain has been italicised and also indented.

'The Monks of Bangor's March' was included in Scott's *Miscellaneous Poems* of 1820 (117–20), where lines 35 and 36 are reversed, presumably accidentally since they are in their original order in his *Poetical Works* of the same year (10.206–09) and in subsequent lifetime editions of Scott's collected poems. Otherwise the poem was reprinted only with changes of the kind normally associated with the printer. A degree of slippage, however, is evident in the refrain to the fourth stanza acquiring an extra syllable in *Miscellaneous Poems* as '*Sing O miserere Domine!*', an error which persists down to Lockhart's posthumous edition of 1833–34 (11.342–44). Also in some, though not all, editions, 'thy ruins' in line 34 becomes 'the ruins'. 'The Monks of Bangor's March' was also reprinted by Thomson from the 1817 third volume of *A Select Collection of Original Welsh Airs* in his subsequent quarto compilation set of *The Select Melodies of Scotland*, 5 vols (Edinburgh, 1822–23), 4.item 48, with no sign of renewed authorial involvement.

The present text follows that of item 62 in the third volume of George Thomson's *A Select Collection of Original Welsh Airs* (Edinburgh, 1817). In line 11 'virgin-mother' has been emended editorially to 'Virgin-mother' (1820*PW*), since the Virgin Mary is clearly intended.

Historical Note

The massacre of the monks of Bangor around 613 is told by the Northumbrian monk and historian Bede (673/4–735) in his *Historia ecclesiastica gentis Anglorum*, the history of the English church he had completed by 731. Thomson, in referring to this tradition as associated with the tune for which he requested lyrics by Scott in his letter of 12 June 1806 (see Textual Note), added that the link was 'probably without any foundation'. Scott may not have heard the tune before composing his lyrics, since in the same letter Thomson (though offering to call and hum it over to Scott if he wanted to hear it) stated that Scott might 'write with perfect success without looking at the Music, merely observing what I have said of the general character & measure' (f. 91). As a metrical model for Scott to write his lyrics he wrote out the opening lines of Burns's 'Robert Bruce's March to Bannockburn' (Kinsley, no. 425), a poem with a medieval martial subject, and further informed Scott that the present tune was 'Maestoso' (majestic).

The tune of 'Ymdaith Mwnge' had been published by Edward Jones in *Musical and Poetical Relics of the Welsh Bards* (London, 1784), 67, which was probably the source of the air Thomson sent to Beethoven. The English Morris dance tune, 'Monks March', popularly associated with George Monck, 1st Duke of Albemarle (1608–70), who fought on the Cromwellian side in the English Civil War, bears no resemblance to it.

Explanatory Notes

157.headnote ETHELFRID, or OLFRID Æthelfrith, King of Northumbria (d. *c.* 616) succeeded to the throne of Bernicia in 592, and in 604 to that of the joint Northumbrian kingdom of Deira and Bernicia which he ruled until his death. He was the dominant ruler in northern England, and his campaign in Wales was intended to secure territory in the west and to cut off the Welsh from the British peoples in the north.

157.headnote BROCKMAEL in fact the ruler of Powys killed in the battle of Chester was Selyf ap Cynan (d. 616), known as Sarffgadau, or Serpent of Battles. Brochfael, possibly one of his kinsmen, was the guard assigned by the prince to the monks of Bangor and other clerics assembled to pray for a British victory.

157.headnote monastery of Bangor Bangor is in Caernarfonshire in N Wales on the coast near the Menai strait. A monastic establishment was founded, perhaps on the site of the present cathedral, by the Celtic saint Deiniol (d. 584) in the 6th century.

157.headnote put the monks to the sword According to Bede, in Bk 2, Ch. 2 of his ecclesiastical history, when Æthelfrith understood that the monks were assembled to pray for the victory of his opponents, he said, 'If they are praying to their God against us, then, even if they do not bear arms, they are fighting against us, assailing us as they do with prayers for our defeat' and ordered that they should be killed first. Bede states that about 1200 men who had come to pray were killed and only 50 escaped: see *Bede's Ecclesiastical History of the English People*, ed. Bertram Colgrave and R. A. B. Mynors (Oxford, 1969), 141.

157.6 Cestria's *Cestria* is the Latin name for Chester, walled city on the River Dee in Cheshire, England, close to the Border with Wales. It is about 112 km (70 miles) E of Chester.

157.7 sylvan Dee the River Dee is about 110 km (68 miles) long and flows through parts of both England and Wales, often forming the boundary between the two countries. It rises in Snowdonia and flows E through Chester entering the sea between Wales and the Wirral peninsula in England.

157.8 *O miserere Domine!* Latin for 'Lord have mercy upon us', a phrase deriving from the opening of Psalm 51, and which appears in the Roman Catholic mass as 'Kyrie Eleison'.

158.footnote WILLIAM of MALMESBURY William of Malmesbury (b. *c.* 1090, d. in or after 1142) was a historian and Benedictine monk of the order's ancient foundation at Malmesbury in Wiltshire. In Scott's quotation here, from Bk 2, Ch. 47 of his De *Gestis regum Anglorum*, William describes the ruins of a typical Benedictine foundation at Bangor: 'So many half-destroyed walls, so many distortions of the cloister, such a large and disorderly pile of broken stone as you would hardly see anywhere else.' For the Latin wording see *De Gestis regum Anglorum*, ed. William Stubbs, 2 vols (London, 1887–89), 1.47. However, in Bk 2, Ch. 2 of his *Historia ecclesiastica gentis Anglorum* Bede describes the clerics of Bangor as disputing with Augustine the date of Easter: see *Bede's Ecclesiastical History of the English People*, 135–39. Since this was an important point of dispute between the Roman and Celtic churches, the passage supports the idea that the monastery may rather have been a typical Celtic enclave, with a series of wattle and daub buildings covering a large extent of ground.

59. On Ettrick Forest's Mountains Dun

Textual Note
Scott's lyrics 'On Ettrick Forest's Mountains Dun' were first published as item 227 in the fifth volume of the folio edition of *A Select Collection of Original Scottish Airs* produced by George Thomson (1757–1851) and published in Edinburgh in June 1818, but were written more than ten years previously. On 12 June 1806 Thomson wrote to Scott, requesting him to write words to two Welsh airs, one of which entitled 'Conset y Siri' was in a musical setting by Haydn and subsequently used to accompany Scott's 'Hunting Song' instead (see Textual Note to no. 64):

> The other air is of a *light & cheerful* cast, & is called the *Sheriff's fancy*; it requires 8 lines in the stanza, & of the 8 syllables measure … You may write with perfect success without looking at the Music, merely observing what I have said of the general character & measure of each Air; however, should you desire to hear the Airs, I shall call at your convenience, & hum them over to you. (BL, Add. MS 35,266, f. 91r)

In replying in July, Scott sent Thomson the first twelve lines of his 'The Lamentation of the Faithful Wife of Asan Aga' (see Textual Note to no. 23), offering if they suited the tune to make them the start of a war-song (*Letters*, 1.310). Thomson, however, declined the offer the following day on the grounds that 'the sheriffs tune is rather of a lively cast, it is at least tranquil, & not serious enough for the war song' (BL, Add. MS 35,266, f. 98). Subsequently Scott sent verses to the other Welsh tune and promised in a postscript 'If these answer I will forthwith finish "the Sheriffs fancy"' (*Letters*, 1.296). By October Scott was able to send a revised version of his verses for the air, asking Thomson to 'destroy the foul copy which you have', and requesting to see the song in proof 'in case any minute alterations may yet occur to me, and also to ensure their being correctly printed' (*Letters*, 1.327).

Three manuscripts of these verses survive. The first, at the Harry Ransom Center, Austin, Texas (MS -3753, Container 1.2), is written in Scott's own hand on both sides of a leaf of unwatermarked paper measuring approx. 26.7 x 20.3 cm. This is clearly a rough draft with a number of second thoughts and revisions: for instance, line 3 reads 'And seek the heath-<birds> ↑fowls↓ lonely brood'. The second is a fair copy among George Thomson's incoming correspondence (BL, Add. MS 35,263, ff. 279–80), presumably the one accompanying Scott's October letter and therefore written on his instruction (although not in his own hand but that of an amanuensis), on a double sheet of paper each leaf of which measures approx. 24.7 x 20.1 cm with no visible watermark, and bearing after the title the information 'To a Welch Tune so called'. The third forms part of a presentation booklet of Scott's poems written by his wife Charlotte at his desire as a gift to his friend Lady Abercorn, which is dated '1807' on the title-page and the pages of which bear the watermark 'MAGNAY & PICKERING / LONDON / 1804' (University of London Library, Sterling MS S.L.V.24, ff. 11–12). The three manuscript versions agree with one another substantially, except for the third line where the version sent to Thomson has 'heath-birds', rejected for 'heath-fowls' in the rough draft of the Ransom Center, which the presentation copy also prefers. The presentation copy also has 'chiefs of yon' in line 6 for 'chiefs of yore', presumably a simple transcription error, and the stanzas are numbered in the rough draft and the version sent to Thomson but not in the presentation manuscript. Each of these early manuscript versions of the poem, however, has a second stanza omitted from the verses as first published, here cited from the version sent to Thomson:

II.
'Tis blithe in Ettricke forest fair
From the brown fern to rouse the hare
And blithe with buxsome hoop and hollo
To bid the gallant Greyhounds follow
And blithe o'er Newark hill to fly
While the grey tower returns our cry
The brake, the brook she vainly tries
Doubles in vain and screaming dies

The reason for its omission remains unclear. It is possible that Thomson, who included Scott's lyrics on a page beneath another set of verses, simply made the cut to fit Scott's verses into the available space. On the other hand, in his letter of 12 June 1806 (cited above) he had declared, 'I care not how *long* your Songs are', suggesting a minimum length of three or four stanzas for each. It is as likely perhaps that Scott himself eventually chose to make the cut: the poem progresses more economically without it, while the omitted verse undercuts the otherwise light-hearted tone by emphasising the sufferings of the victim of the sheriff's sport ('and screaming dies'). His October letter to Thomson does ask for a proof to be sent to him and when the poem was included in Scott's *Poetical Works* of 1820 (10.197–99) the verse was not reinstated.

The verses as printed in Thomson's 1818 volume have a new title taken from the opening words of Scott's lyrics, instead of 'The Sheriff's Fancy' (another tune having been substituted for the one with that title). The printed text also has 'heath frequenting brood' instead of 'heath-birds lonely brood' in the third line, and a printing error gives 'sportman's gun' in the second line for 'sportsman's gun'. An explanatory headnote provides a personal sporting context to the reader, and two footnotes reference place-names. Scott may have provided the contextualising headnote and footnotes himself since they also occur in 1820*PW* (with the headnote becoming an initial footnote, and the footnote on Alwyn updated to record the death of its owner), as does the reading 'heath-frequenting brood'. However, Thomson's italicisation of '*midnight* tide' in line 17 is omitted there. The musical setting was not provided, nor indeed, named when the verses were included in 1820*PW*. In correcting the printing error in the second line, however, 1820*PW* introduced another, with 'bear the sportman's gun' becoming 'hear the sportsman's gun'.

Subsequently the poem was included in successive lifetime editions of Scott's collected poetry and in the Lockhart 1833–34 posthumous edition (11.334–35) with only the kind of further changes attributable to the work of the printer. The present edition follows the text of the fifth volume of *A Select Collection of Original Scottish Airs* of 1818 (item 227), substituting for the words 'The Same Air' the name of the tune from the head of the page. The headnote and footnotes are retained, while the following emendations have been made:

159.1	Forest's (1820*PW*) / forest's
159.2	sportsman's (BL MS) / sportman's
159.3	heath-frequenting (1820*PW*) / heath frequenting
159.17	midnight (BL MS) / *midnight*
160.32	Forest (*MiscPoems*) / forest
160.footnote 1	Somerville (1820*PW*) / Sommerville

Historical Note
The inspiration for Scott's poem most obviously derives from the title of the Welsh tune for which it had been written, 'Conset y Siri', in English 'The Sheriff's Fancy', which was the title used in all three of Scott's manuscript versions. Scott had been appointed Sheriff-Depute of Selkirkshire in 1799, and the poem celebrates his sporting activities with local landowners there, particularly with the agricultural improver John Southey Somerville, 15th Lord Somerville (1765–1819). Mention of the houses of Alwyn and Ashestiel (see notes to 160.27 and 160.28 below) locates the poem firmly in the south of Scotland. It was very likely for this reason that Thomson was reluctant to put it with the music of another country in the second volume of his *Select Collection of Original Welsh Airs* published in 1817: Scott's 'Hunting Song' (see no. 64), which was used for the tune of 'Conset y Siri' there, could relate to any nation. Thomson, no doubt reluctant to omit any of Scott's contributions to his project, subsequently found a Scottish tune to which it was well suited in rhythm and mood so that it could be included instead in the fifth volume of *A Select Collection of Original Scottish Airs*. Thomson printed Scott's verses beneath those he had already had set to this traditional tune, 'I Canna Come Ilka Day to Woo', as arranged by Haydn, and beginning 'Now bank and brae are clothed in green'. Although Thomson names Burns as the author of these lines, they were in fact by Richard Gall (1776–1801) who had sent them to James Johnson for his *Scots Musical Museum* with Burns's name attached.

Explanatory Notes
159.1   Ettrick Forest's mountains dun   Ettrick Forest is a hilly district, not forested in Scott's day but largely given over to sheep, comprising the area around the valleys of the Ettrick and Yarrow waters in Selkirkshire. Dun describes a colour that is a dull or greyish brown.
159.9   Tweed   the Tweed is one of the largest rivers in SE Scotland, part of which forms the border with England, and is joined by Ettrick Water to the N of Selkirk.
159.17   midnight tide   salmon fishing in the Borders was generally undertaken in boats at night. Armed with torches and pronged spears the fishermen in the boat would try to impale on their spears the fish as they swam towards the surface, attracted by the light of the torches. Scott gives a detailed description of such a party in *Guy Mannering*, ed. P. D. Garside, EEWN 2 (Edinburgh, 1999), 136–38.
159.24   Genii   genies or djinn were supernatural creatures in Arabian and Islamic mythology, supposed to be made of a smokeless and scorching fire.
160.27   ALWYN'S lordly meal   a dinner hosted by Lord Somerville at

his house at Alwyn, also known as the Pavilion, overlooking the Tweed near Melrose and with a view of Melrose Abbey. Somerville had purchased it in 1805, and adapted the existing stable buildings of the previous owners (who had planned but not built a mansion on the site) to form a two-storey, five-bay 'shooting-box' there.

160.28   Ashesteel   Scott had moved to his country home of Ashestiel, near Clovenfords in Selkirkshire in 1804, not long before these verses were composed.

60.   The Palmer

Textual Note
'The Palmer' first appeared as item 41 in the second volume of William Whyte's *A Collection of Scottish Airs*, published in Edinburgh on 8 July 1807, and there seem to be no grounds for disbelieving Whyte's assertion there that it was 'written for this work'. A surviving manuscript in Scott's hand (BL, Add. MS 12115, f. 3) consists of a single leaf of paper measuring approx. 25.3 x 20 cm without watermark and the poem itself is undated. Scott has written on both sides of the paper, as he commonly did in rough-drafting, and makes minor changes in wording in lines 5, 13, and 34. For the first of these, for instance, the manuscript reads 'No outlaw <comes to> seeks your castle gate'. Two red pencil notes in another hand, however, provide a page reference and a direction to the printer: 'Page 41 / Written for this work by Walter Scott Esqr' and 'As the air only takes in *four* lines the Song must be [illegible word] in that way'. This suggests that it was the manuscript given to Whyte for publication. A letter of April 1816 accompanying this manuscript (ff. 4–5), from Scott to Archibald Park (1770–1820), brother of the explorer Mungo Park (1771–1806), opens 'I have great pleasure in sending you the enclosed': most likely Scott reclaimed his manuscript of 'The Palmer' from James Ballantyne, the printer of Whyte's collection, and later gave it to Park in response to a request from him for an autograph.

'The Palmer' was also included in a presentation booklet of Scott's poems made by his wife Charlotte at his request for the Marchioness of Abercorn (Senate House Library, University of London: Sterling MS S.L.V.24, ff. 6–7), which is dated 1807 on the first leaf, simulating a printed title-page. This appears, however, to have been copied from Whyte's collection despite some minor variations in punctuation and the odd transcription error: most noticeably the poem is divided into four-line stanzas and omits the repetitive 'O's at the end of lines, needed to fit the rhythm to the music but omitted from the text-alone version in Whyte's printed work (see below).

'The Palmer' is carefully presented in Whyte's collection as quality free-standing poetry as well as lyrics for singing to an accompanying tune. The five eight-line stanzas of the BL manuscript become ten four-line stanzas to suit the tune, but the rather clumsy and repetitive ending of every second line with the syllable 'O' to suit the musical rhythm is eliminated, and instead a note at the head of the self-standing poem reads '(In singing this Ballad, the Interjection O must be added to every second and fourth line, as in the verses engraved with the Music.)' Otherwise Scott's manuscript is fairly straightforwardly transformed into print with the usual variations of spelling and punctuation resulting from the printer's work, except that 'our Ladys' in line 11 becomes 'our lady's', and 'Or' at the start of line 15 becomes 'Oh'. These changes are clearly production errors, since the palmer is referring to the Virgin Mary and it appears highly unlikely that in a song already overloaded with the syllable O/Oh Scott would have added another unnecessarily.

'The Palmer' was reprinted in *The Vision of Don Roderick, and Other Poems* in 1811 (135–38), with only changes of the kind normally associated with the printer, though line 11 has 'Our Lady's' and line 15 begins with 'Or'. It was then included in Scott's *Poetical Works* of 1820 (12.109–11), and afterwards in the subsequent lifetime collected editions of his poetry as well as the Lockhart 1833–34 posthumous edition (8.361–62), again with only the usual kind of printing changes. In no version subsequent to that in Whyte's collection is there any music given, or indeed any indication of a tune to which 'The Palmer' might be sung.

The present text follows that of William Whyte's *A Collection of Scottish Airs*, 2 vols (Edinburgh, 1806–07), 2.item 41, as best representing the culmination of Scott's original creative impulse. The following emendations have been made:

160.11   Our Lady's (BL MS derived: our Ladys) / our lady's
160.15   Or (BL MS) / Oh

Historical Note
An approach to Scott to become a contributor of lyrics to *A Collection of Scottish Airs*, produced by the Edinburgh music publisher William Whyte, was probably made through the work's printer, James Ballantyne, during the summer of 1805. Scott had contributed two items to the first volume published in 1806, and he contributed four to the second volume published in Edinburgh on 8 July 1807. Whyte's collection deliberately rivalled the similar one of George Thomson (1757–1851), employing Joseph Haydn (1732–1809) for the musical settings of Scottish tunes, a number of which were associated with the songs of Burns (for further details see Notes to no. 54, 'The Maid of Toro'). Haydn's musical setting on the facing page to Scott's poem 'The Palmer' names the tune as 'O open the door'. This tune was firmly associated with Burns, who had modelled his own song on one in the *New and Complete Collection of the most favourite Scots Songs* by the composer Domenico Corri (1746–1825), published in 1783 (2.30: see Kinsley, no. 403 and commentary). In Burns's song the appeal is made by a male lover to his false mistress, who opens the door eventually only to see his corpse on the threshold, repent, and die by his side. In Scott's song the dramatic situation is closer to that of *The Lay of the Last Minstrel* (1805), with an old man from an ancient world seeking shelter: however, where his plea is granted in Scott's long narrative poem, here it is denied and it is implied that his ghost will haunt the refuser.

Explanatory Notes
160.9   Palmer   a pilgrim returned from the Holy Land, potentially carrying a palm branch as a token of this.
160.13   pardons   remissions from the penalties of committing various sins, subsequently regarded by Reformation theologians as licences to sin.
160.14   reliques   an object such as a body part, item of clothing, or article of personal use that remains as a memorial of a departed saint or martyr and was often thought to have miracle-working power.
161.21   Ettrick's   Ettrick Water is a river rising from the SW extremity of Selkirkshire and flowing roughly 52 km (32 miles) NE until it joins the Tweed near Selkirk.
161.33   Ranger   a forest officer or game-keeper.

61. Wandering Willie

Textual Note
'Wandering Willie' first appeared, with musical annotation, as item 45 in the second volume of William Whyte's *A Collection of Scottish Airs*, published in Edinburgh on 8 July 1807, headed 'written for this work'. The subject-matter of Scott's song points to a composition date subsequent to the British naval victory of Trafalgar on 21 October 1805, although there is no indication of date on the only surviving manuscript of the poem in Scott's own hand (NLS, MS 876, f. 14B), which is on a single leaf of paper measuring approx. 19.9 x 12.5 cm and bearing a partial watermark of a crowned shield. Although the text's being written on both sides of the paper and the presence of a few deletions and insertions suggest that this is not a fair copy, this draft is remarkably close to the poem as first published. A second contemporary manuscript exists in the hand of Scott's wife, Charlotte, part of a presentation copy of her husband's poems made at his direction as a gift to Lady Abercorn (1763–1827), the paper of which bears a watermark 'MAGNAY & PICKERING / LONDON / 1804', and which is dated 1807 by Charlotte on a simulated title-page (Senate House Library, University of London, Sterling MS S.L.V.24). Barring a few transcription errors, the text of the poem here (ff. 2–3) agrees substantially with both Scott's draft manuscript and with the printed copy. One noticeable feature of both manuscripts is that the poem consists of five eight-line stanzas rather than the ten four-line stanzas of the published version, a difference that is almost certainly accounted for by the music in Whyte's collection, to which only four lines could be sung for each verse.

'Wandering Willie' was subsequently reprinted in Scott's *The Vision of Don Roderick, and Other Poems* (Edinburgh, 1811), 144–47, without any reference to a musical setting. Changes of the kind normally associated with the work of the printer perhaps include the superfluous alteration in line 16 of 'ere' (previously) to 'e'er' (ever), although 'e'er' is repeated in the poem's subsequent reprinting, with no evidence of further authorial involvement, in Scott's *Poetical Works* of 1820 (12.117–20) and the other lifetime collected editions of his poetry as well as in the Lockhart 1833–34 posthumous edition (8.367–69). None of these subsequent publications revert to the eight-line stanza of the poem as represented in the manuscripts or provide a musical setting.

The present text follows that of Whyte's *A Collection of Scottish Airs*, 2 vols (Edinburgh, 1806–07), 2. item 45, as best representing the culmination of Scott's initial creative processes. No emendations have been made.

Historical Note
An approach to Scott to become a contributor of lyrics to *A Collection of Scottish Airs*, produced by the Edinburgh music publisher William Whyte, was probably made through the work's printer, James Ballantyne, during the summer of 1805. Scott contributed two items to the first volume published in 1806, and he contributed four to the second volume published in Edinburgh on 8 July 1807. Whyte's collection deliberately rivalled the similar one of George Thomson (1757–1851), employing Joseph Haydn (1732–1809) for the musical settings of Scottish tunes, a number of which were associated with the songs of Burns (for further details see Notes to no. 54, 'The Maid of Toro'). Burns's version of 'Wandering Willie' had appeared in the first volume of Thomson's *A Select Collection of Original Scottish Airs* in 1793 (item 2) with a setting by Ignace Joseph Pleyel (1757–1831). Burns had based his version on the traditional song ('Here awa', there awa', here awa' Willie') as found in David Herd's *Ancient*

and Modern Scottish Songs, 2nd edn, 2 vols (Edinburgh, 1776: *ALC*), 2.140 (see also Kinsley, no. 396 and commentary). The song in Herd's collection voices a woman's satisfaction at the return of her lover, while Burns's song rather expresses her yearning for a still absent one. She hears the winter's storms and longs for the summer when her lover may return to her, and expresses anxiety about his faithfulness in absence. Scott's song combines elements of both, as a song of reunion that yet emphasises the anxiety and doubts about the lover's safety and faithfulness during his absence, with topical reference to the great British naval victory of Trafalgar.

Explanatory Notes
162.4   banned it   cursed it.
162.16   Inch Keith   a rugged and stony triangular-shaped island in the Firth of Forth, situated between Kinghorn on the N shore and Leith on the S shore.
162.18   great victory   the culminating British naval victory against Napoleonic France and its ally Spain was fought on 21 October 1805 off Cape Trafalgar in Spain, after which the British Royal Navy controlled the seas even though Napoleonic France had military supremacy on land. National hero Admiral Horatio Nelson (1758–1805) was killed in this battle.
163.32   leal   loyal or faithful, constant in friendship or in love.
163.38   Holland   the Dutch were long-standing naval rivals to Britain, but during the time of the Batavian Republic (1795–1806), when Holland was a vassal state of revolutionary France, the Dutch navy was crushingly defeated by British naval forces under the command of Admiral Adam Duncan (1731–1804) at the battle of Camperdown in October 1797.

62.   The Maid of Neidpath

Textual Note
'The Maid of Neidpath' was first published, headed 'written for this work', in the second volume of the Edinburgh music publisher William Whyte's *A Collection of Scottish Airs* (item 54), issued on 8 July 1807. A surviving manuscript in Scott's hand (NLS, MS 876, ff. 13–14) consists of two leaves, each measuring approx. 26.1 x 16.9 cm and bearing the watermark 'D & AC / 1806', and appears to be a fair copy since the text is written on one side of the paper with only one substantive alteration ('life's <time> extremity' in line 3) and a scriptorial error of 'and hedless gaze' in line 25. Although this manuscript bears no signs of having been used as printer's copy it is close to the text in Whyte's collection, apart from changes of the kind normally associated with the printer, and the addition after 'a house in Peebles' of 'belonging to the family' in the printed headnote. The poem also features in a presentation copy made by Charlotte Scott of her husband's poems by his direction for Lady Abercorn, and dated '1807' by Charlotte. The text of 'The Maid of Neidpath' in this presentation booklet (Senate House Library, University of London, Sterling MS S.L.V.24, ff 4–5) also agrees with Scott's own manuscript, apart from a few incidental transcription errors. The probable dating of the two manuscript versions thus tends to support Whyte's claim that Scott's poem was written specifically for his work.
    'The Maid of Neidpath' was afterwards published in Scott's *The Vision of Don Roderick, and Other Poems* (Edinburgh, 1811), 139–43, after which it passed into Scott's *Poetical Works* of 1820 (12.112–16) and the subsequent lifetime

editions of his collected poetry and into the posthumous Lockhart edition of 1833–34 (8.363–66). Apart from changes of the kind normally associated with the printer there are only two variations in the text of these editions, both originating in the 1820 *Poetical Works* (12.112–16) and followed in three of the succeeding collected editions only. In the final sentence of the headnote 'instance' replaces 'incident' and in line 31 'hardly' replaces 'scarcely': in both cases the new word seems less apt than the old, and is probably a production error.

The present text of Scott's verses is that of the first printing in Whyte's *A Collection of Scottish Airs*, 2 vols (1806–07), 2.item 54, as best representing the culmination of Scott's original creative process. The following emendations have been made:

163.headnote	Fleur d'Épine (Editorial) / Fleur d'Epine
164.1	lovers' (*Don Roderick*) / lovers
164.2	lovers' (*Don Roderick*) / lovers

Historical Note
The legendary story on which Scott based 'The Maid of Neidpath' had evidently been told to him by James Hogg (1770–1835) and William Laidlaw (1779–1845) at the time they were collecting materials for the third volume of his *Minstrelsy of the Scottish Border* (1803). In his letter to Scott of 7 January 1803 Hogg, at Laidlaw's instigation, sent Scott a version of the traditional song 'Tushielaw's Lines' along with a prose summary of the love-affair it was supposed to commemorate between a Scott of Tushielaw and a 'daughter to the Earl of March some say Morton': see *The Collected Letters of James Hogg*, ed. Gillian Hughes and others, 3 vols (Edinburgh, 2004–08), 1.33–38. Although Scott did not include 'Tushielaw's Lines' in *Minstrelsy* he clearly remembered the story when he was approached by William Whyte for lyrics for his musical work (for further details see Notes to no. 54, 'The Maid of Toro').

In keeping with his deliberate rivalry of the similar collection of George Thomson (1757–1851), the Edinburgh music publisher William Whyte had likewise employed the famous German composer Joseph Haydn (1732–1809) to create settings of traditional Scottish melodies for his publication, and had chosen a number of tunes associated with the work of Thomson's premier lyricist Robert Burns. This does not appear to be the case here, however. Scott's words must have been intended for the Haydn setting of the song beginning 'Shepherds, I have lost my love; / Have you seen my Anna?'. Although in T&B, no. 21Ab, this is stated to be a Burns song, it does not appear in Kinsley and had earlier been published in *Vocal Music or the Songster's Companion* (London, 1775), 28–29. While 'The Maid of Neidpath' approximates rhythmically to the lyrics of this song, Whyte must have considered it less fitted to Haydn's musical setting than the original words, the first verse of which was printed under the relevant lines of the musical notation in his work. Reluctant to lose the prestige of Scott's contribution, however, he also printed Scott's poem on the facing page above the original song lyrics, here entitled 'Anna'.

Explanatory Notes
163.headnote   Neidpath Castle, near Peebles   Neidpath Castle is situated high on the N bank of the River Tweed, about 1.5 km (1 mile) W of Peebles and overlooking the town. During the first half of the 18th century it was the summer home of the Earls of March.
163.headnote   Tushielaw   a place long associated with the Scott clan, situated on the left bank of Ettrick Water where it is joined by Tushielaw

Burn, about 24 km (15 miles) SW of Selkirk. Its ruined tower was associated with Adam Scott, known as the 'King of Thieves', who was executed by James V of Scotland in 1529.

163.headnote   Count Hamilton's "Fleur d'Épine"   Anthony Hamilton (1644/5?–1719) was a member of a Scottish Catholic family, born in Ireland but spending much of his life in France and writing primarily in the French language. He succeeded to the French title of Count on the death of his brother George, who had served Louis XIV as a soldier. Scott edited Hamilton's *Memoirs of Count Gramont* in 1811. *L'histoire de fleur d'épine*, a set of tales satirising popular imitations of the *Arabian Nights Entertainments*, was published in Paris in 1730. At one point in its complicated plot the health and looks of the eponymous heroine, Fleur d'Épine, have declined greatly while she is staying with the wicked widow of the Seneschal. With this in mind, she refuses to see her lover, Tarare, when he calls on her, but the widow admits him anyway, telling Fleur the caller is the Caliph to whom they cannot refuse admission. Tarare fails to recognise her, calling out her name and then enquiring of her where Fleur d'Épine is to be found. She breaks down altogether, hiding her face, and he leaves, feeling disgruntled.

63.   Address Written for Miss Smith

Textual Note
This poetic address was written for the benefit night at the Edinburgh Theatre Royal on 8 August 1807 of the young Irish actress Sarah Smith (1783?–1850), a visiting star performer from London's Covent Garden Theatre. Scott evidently sent it to her from Ashestiel with his letter of 4 August 1807, only a few days before the occasion for which it was intended:

> I send you the promised lines; which indifferent as they are have proved better than I durst venture to hope considering that I have been obliged to postpone the task of writing them till this morning. The idea is better than the execution, but I comfort myself that many better lines have wanted the advantages which your recitation will give mine. (*Letters*, 1.372)

A surviving manuscript in Scott's hand consists of a single sheet of unwatermarked paper measuring approx. 19.9 x 12 cm (NLS, MS 894, f. 87) and written on both sides. This appears to be a rough draft since it contains a number of deletions and additions. Among the changes made in the course of composition 'tragic art' was altered to 'Thespian art' (line 19), and 'No stranger asks a boon' to 'No stranger ever sued' (line 30). There is also a deleted couplet reading 'No merit seem his toils to claim / But calling on his patrons name' (subsequently replaced by lines 15–16 of the present text). This manuscript was probably not the one sent by Scott to Miss Smith with his letter, however, since it differs substantially from the first printing of the poem in the annual *Forget Me Not for 1834*, ed. Frederic Shoberl (London, 1833), 197–98. It seems probable that this first printing was based on the fair-copy manuscript sent by Scott to Miss Smith, which does not appear to have survived. Lines 15–16 for instance, appear to rethink the deleted manuscript couplet, while in the manuscript the equivalent to lines 21–22 in *Forget Me Not* reads 'And when the mimic scene is done / Dare scarcely hope your favour won'. Similarly, the manuscript lines equivalent to lines 25–26 in *Forget Me Not* read 'Land long renowned for Beautys charms / And poets lays & <warm> heroes arms'. In this light the manuscript now in the NLS is almost certainly an initial draft, subsequently revised by Scott before sending the address to Miss Smith with his letter. Lockhart in the posthumous edition of Scott's poems of 1833–34 (10.367–68), reprints the text from the *Forget Me Not* with only minor variations in punctuation, presumably originating with the printer.

The present text follows that of the *Forget Me Not for 1834*, ed. Frederic Shoberl (London, 1833), 197–98, though a prefatory note added by the editor of the *Forget Me Not* has been omitted. Scott's surviving manuscript provides no title, and the one given in the *Forget Me Not* of 'Address, Written for Miss Smith, (now Mrs. Bartley)' has been adapted editorially to reflect his composing the poem for the unmarried Miss Smith in 1807. Otherwise no emendations have been made.

Historical Note

An advertisement for the Edinburgh Theatre Royal in the *Caledonian Mercury* of 23 July 1807 announces that Miss Smith had been engaged 'to perform at this Theatre a few Nights only'. This appears to have been her first appearance in Edinburgh, although she performed there again in 1812: see James C. Dibdin, *The Annals of the Edinburgh Stage* (Edinburgh, 1888), 251, 266. Scott describes her as 'a powerful and striking actress' in a letter to Matthew Weld Hartstonge of 30 June 1812 (*Letters*, 3.454). Her first appearance in Edinburgh on 25 July 1807 was as Portia in *The Merchant of Venice*, and she played a number of other tragic parts before taking the role on her benefit night of 8 August of Madame Clermont in a new play entitled *Adrian and Orrila; or, A Mother's Vengeance* (Dibdin, 251).

Scott had been introduced to Miss Smith by 'the Buccleuch ladies' as he told Anna Seward in a letter of 11 August 1807, adding that she was a person for whom he had 'an especial regard as a very good and pleasing Girl with high talents for her profession in which she is now second to Mrs. Siddons alone' (*Letters*, 1.375). In the letter enclosing the address for her benefit night he also invited her to visit him at Ashestiel on her way southwards after the conclusion of her Edinburgh engagement (*Letters*, 1.372), an invitation which was thankfully accepted. The friendship was continued over the following years, with Scott giving Miss Smith a copy of *Marmion* and the actress in turn seeking his advice about dramatising his narrative poems for the Dublin Theatre (*Letters*, 2.29, 410–13, 471).

Explanatory Notes

165.19   Thespian art   art of acting. The semi-legendary Greek poet Thespis is said to have introduced an actor into performances which had previously been given by a chorus alone and was regarded by later Greek authors as the father of tragedy.

165.23   from sister climes   alluding to Miss Smith's engagement at the Covent Garden Theatre in London.

165.24   Wallace   Sir William Wallace (d. 1305), an early champion of Scottish attempts to resist the domination of England.

166.29   Caledonian plain   the Scottish lowland belt in which Edinburgh is situated.

64.   Hunting Song

Textual Note

In November 1806, a box of papers left at his death by the engraver and antiquary Joseph Strutt (1749–1802) had been passed to Scott by publishers John Murray and Archibald Constable with a view to his examining their suitability for publication: see Constable to Murray, 18 November 1806, in Thomas Constable, *Archibald Constable and his Literary Correspondents*, 3 vols (Edinburgh, 1873), 1.354. Chief among these was the manuscript of a historical novel set in Elizabethan England and entitled *Queenhoo-Hall*, only partly finished. According to a subsequent letter to Murray of 8 December (Constable, 1.357) Scott thought well of the work, Constable writing that 'he has a person busy at work transcribing the difficult parts of the MS., and we believe where any slip or deficiency occurs he supplies it himself'. Constable also mentioned that Scott would probably not wish to be publicly recognised as its editor. Scott, who indeed was referred to in the prefatory 'Advertisement' to the novel not as its editor but as the editor's 'literary friend', also had to write a conclusion to draw the plot to a hasty end. According to his letter to Robert Cadell of 15 September 1828, this consisted of 'from p. 43 to p. 79 being the two last chapters of the work' (*Letters*, 10.501), that is the fourth and fifth chapter of the fourth volume as printed, the former including a four-stanza, 32-line song (given without music or any indication of the tune) beginning 'Waken lords and ladies gay'. In an undated letter to James Ballantyne, printer of *Queenhoo-Hall*, Scott wrote 'I wish you would see how far the copy of Queenhoo-Hall, sent last night, extends, that I may not write more nonsense than enough' (*Letters*, 2.109), this suggesting that the conclusion was written not long before publication of the novel in London in June 1808. Otherwise it is not possible to supply a precise date of composition for the song, first published in Joseph Strutt, *Queenhoo-Hall. A Romance*, 4 vols (Edinburgh, 1808), 4.47–48.

In the context of *Queenhoo-Hall* no title for the song was necessary, but when it was subsequently included in *English Minstrelsy*, 2 vols (Edinburgh, 1810), 1.264–66, again anonymously, a title was required and it was called 'Hunting Song'. It was reprinted with Scott's name several months afterwards in the poetry section of the *Edinburgh Annual Register for 1808*, 1: 2 (1810), xxviii. Any differences between these versions are of a kind normally associated with the work of the printer, but an error was introduced into line 11 of the *EAR* text when 'streaming' became 'steaming'.

The song collector George Thomson (1757–1851) had previously invited Scott in a letter of 12 June 1806 (BL, Add. MS 35,266, ff. 90r–92v) to supply lyrics for a Welsh air entitled 'Conset y Siri' (The Sheriff's Conceit or Fancy), set for him by Beethoven. Initially Scott sent a fragment of 'The Lamentation of the Faithful Wife of Asan Aga' (see Textual Note to no. 23) with his letter of 23 July (BL, Add. MS 35,263, f. 272), offering to finish that should Thomson think it suitable. When Thomson rejected this as too serious for the tune, Scott then sent 'On Ettrick Forest's Mountains Dun' (see Textual Note to no. 59). Thomson evidently refused this also, perhaps because he had requested in his letter of 24 July 1806 that the scene of Scott's song should be in North Wales (BL, Add. MS 35,266, f. 98). Finally Scott wrote in a subsequent letter to Thomson of 16 November 1809: 'I make you welcome with the Ballantynes' consent, which I dare say you can obtain, to use in your publication a hunting song ... which I gave them for a little miscellany which J. Ballantyne is now printing' (*Letters*, 2.271–72). This is clearly a reference to the poem as it appeared in *English Minstrelsy*. 'Hunting Song' was duly published, with the music for 'Conset y Siri', in the third volume of Thomson's *A Select Collection of Original Welsh Airs* (Edinburgh, 1817), item 73. Scott's letter implies that he had no direct authorial involvement in this version of 'Hunting Song', which nevertheless differs markedly from previously-published versions. Thomson himself was probably responsible for the changes, most of which were clearly made to fit the words more precisely to the tune. For instance, at the start of the second line 'On' becomes 'Upon' and in line 23 'You shall see' becomes 'You soon shall see', in both cases providing an extra syllable for a musical note. Twice Scott's couplets are entirely rewritten: for instance, in lines 5–6 Scott's 'Hounds are in their couples yelling, / Hawks are whistling, horns are knelling' becomes 'The eager hounds in chorus cry, / The swelling horns salute the sky'.

Scott presumably made no objection to Thomson's revisions, but when 'Hunting Song' was included in his own *Poetical Works* of 1820 (12.121–23) it was the earlier version that was used, presumably taken from *EAR* since 'streaming' in line 11 is 'steaming' here too, an error that persisted in most subsequent editions of Scott's collected poetry, and also in Lockhart's posthumous edition of 1833–34 (8.370–71). Otherwise the lifetime editions of Scott's collected poetry reprint 'Hunting Song' with only the usual kind of printers' variations.

When Thomson included 'Hunting Song' in *The Select Melodies of Scotland*, 5 vols (Edinburgh, 1822–23), 3.item 47, with the tune, however, he naturally reprinted the version revised to suit that. It was also included as part of Scott's conclusion to *Queenhoo-Hall* in an appendix to the Magnum Opus edition of the Waverley Novels, 48 volumes (Edinburgh, 1829–33), 1.lxviii, with only the kind of changes from the 1808 novel normally associated with the work of the printer.

The present text is that of *Queenhoo-Hall. A Romance*, 4 vols (Edinburgh, 1808), 4.47–48. The title of 'Hunting Song', first given in *English Minstrelsy*, has been added, but no other emendations made.

Historical Note
The original context for 'Hunting Song' in Joseph Strutt's novel was an English Tudor deer-hunt organised by Lord Boteler, the owner of Queenhoo-Hall at Tewin in Hertfordshire, for his guests and neighbours. Lord Boteler's servants and huntsmen, having previously located the deer, would drive it past the local gentry stationed along the animal's route, and the gentry would shoot arrows and finally close in with swords or knives. The song is sung underneath the guests' chamber-windows by Peretto and his two attendant minstrels with a chorus of rangers and falconers. As George Thomson clearly realised, however, there is nothing in the song to indicate that this antiquated deer-hunt could not have taken place equally well in Wales. It is only in Thomson's song-collections that there is any indication of a named tune for singing 'Hunting Song' and its association there with the Welsh tune of 'Conset y Siri' appears to be largely arbitrary, created after two previous Scott poems had been rejected as not ideally suited to the tune and the song-collection in which it was to appear.

65.   War-Song of Lachlan

Textual Note
A first draft of the 'War-Song of Lachlan' forms part of an undated letter to Mrs Marianne Maclean Clephane (Castle Ashby Archive, FD 1357), sent from Scott's London lodgings in Half Moon Street in April 1809. In introducing it Scott wrote:

> On my return home before dinner, finding I had half an hour good, I employd it in an attempt to versify the Macleans song. No English rhythm would suit the structure of the original so I fear singing the lines at least to *its own tune* is out of the question.

It seems possible from this letter that Scott had heard the Gaelic original sung by one of Mrs Clephane's musical daughters and received from them an English prose translation of the words which served as the basis for his own poem. In his letter Scott's poem is headed 'War Song of the Macleans / Imitated from the Gaelic' and contains a number of corrections and revisions in the third and final stanza, particularly in the last four lines: line 21, for instance, reads 'And <who> ↑woe↓ to <all> ↑him↓ who stops to gaze'.

From Scott's letter to one of the daughters, Margaret Clephane, of 27 October 1810, this song was subsequently earmarked as a potential contribution to *Illustrations of Northern Antiquities*, of which only one volume was published in Edinburgh in 1814, consisting chiefly of poems in 'ancient Gothic dialects'. According to its prefatory Advertisement, the editors' researches into 'the Poetry of the Celtic Dialects' was postponed to future consideration (v), and it was with this never fully realised strand of the work in mind that Scott presumably thought of offering his verses from the Gaelic:

> I think of giving them my song of the Clans which I will most willingly attempt to enlarge by Saxonising those you are so good as to recommend to me. I have I believe three already Macleans Warsong and the Coronach over Sir Lachlan and the farewell to Mackenneth. (*Letters*, 2.398–99)

What Scott here terms 'Macleans Warsong' was published, apparently for the first time, in 1820 with the title 'War-Song of Lachlan', in Scott's *Poetical Works* of that year (12.154–56), where the text shows a number of changes from the manuscript sent to Mrs Clephane. In the first two stanzas these are mostly single word changes: 'feasted' in line 2 becomes 'parted', 'bold Sir Lachlan' in line 5 'valiant Lachlan', 'battle' in line 9 'ocean', 'former' in line 12 'bloody', while 'Full far' in line 13 was changed to 'For wide'. In the third stanza, as well as a change from 'The' to 'Our' at the start of line 18 and the adoption of 'face' (a deleted reading in the manuscript) instead of 'brave' in line 23, line 21 has been refigured entirely from 'And woe to him who stops to gaze' to 'Woe to the bark whose crew shall gaze'.

'War-Song of Lachlan' then passed through the successive lifetime editions of Scott's collected poems and into Lockhart's posthumous collected edition of 1833–34 (8.395–96), with only the kind of changes normally associated with the work of the printer.

The present text follows that in *Poetical Works* of 1820 (12.154–56), but hyphenates 'Clan-Gillian' in line 9 to match the other instances in the text.

Historical Note
Scott's friend, Mrs Marianne Maclean Clephane (1765–1840) was the daughter of the 7th Maclean Chieftain of Torloisk in Mull, and she and her musical daughters, Margaret (1793–1830) and Anna Jane (b. 1798), told Scott various stories about the Maclean clan to which they were proud to belong and introduced him to the relevant Highland music. Scott's letter to Mrs Clephane of April 1809 (see Textual Note) refers to 'the Macleans' song', and Corson states that 'Margaret Clephane's literal translation from the Gaelic was expanded by Scott into his *War-song*' (*N&I*, 49: note to 2.189(e)). It would appear, however, that two different sets of Gaelic words were associated with the same tune, for Margaret Clephane, sending 'a translation of the words of the Gaelic coronach of Sir Lauchlan Maclean (the hero of the war song)' in a letter to Scott of 7 August 1809, notes that the song has 'become so popular as to be the coronach of the clan' (NLS, MS 3878, ff. 104–06). 'Coronach on Sir Lauchlan, Chief of Maclean' was subsequently included in Scott's notes to the third canto of *The Lady of the Lake* (Edinburgh, 1810), lxii, where Scott himself states that the 'tune is so popular, that it has since become the war march, or Gathering of the clan'. The coronach laments the chief's death and praises his ancestry, without

the lament of the female singer for her lover that opens 'War-Song of Lachlan' and which Scott in his headnote suggests is also present in the original Gaelic song. This original Gaelic song and its tune have not been identified. Although when he composed his lines in April 1809 Scott may have had this tune in mind, he admitted in his accompanying letter to Mrs Clephane that he had failed to adopt the rhythm of that tune in composing his verses and that as a result 'singing the lines at least to *its own tune* is out of the question' (Castle Ashby Archive, FD 1357). Nor do his verses seem to have been associated with any other tune during his lifetime.

The hero of Scott's lines is Sir Lachlan Mor Maclean of Duart (1558–98), who succeeded his father as the Maclean Chief in 1575. He commanded a fighting force of 3000 men and was engaged in a blood feud with the rival MacDonald clan that had an international dimension because of the involvement of both clans in Ulster politics. The forces of Elizabeth I of England were attempting to put down the Irish rebellion of Hugh O'Neill, 2nd Earl of Tyrone (*c*. 1550–1616), and Lachlan Mor (who was knighted in 1596) could have tipped the balance either way. He was consequently courted by both sides and promised a financial subsidy by the English crown, which was never in fact paid. Sir Lachlan was killed in Islay on 5 August 1598, and the cost of maintaining such a large fighting force generated serious debts for future generations of the family.

Explanatory Notes
168.6   galley   the Highland galley or *birlinn* was a wooden boat, influenced by the design of the Viking longship. It had a single mast with a square sail and also between twelve and forty oars, depending on its size. The galley was commonly used in the Hebrides and Western Highlands from the Middle Ages onwards.
168.9   Clan-Gillian   (see also Scott's footnote.) The Macleans traced their descent from a leader called Gilleain-na-Tuaighe, or Gillean of the Battle Axe, a descendant of the Irish Kings of Dalriada, who had fought against the invading Norwegians at the Battle of Largs in 1263.

66.   Prologue to *The Family Legend*

Textual Note
Scott's prologue to the play of *The Family Legend* by his friend, Joanna Baillie (1762–1851), was probably written on 21 January 1810, since his letter to the Marchioness of Abercorn of that date describes the lines as 'written within this hour' (*Letters*, 2.286; Morgan, MA 427/28). Although Scott mentions enclosing her a copy it is no longer with the original letter and has not apparently survived. The prologue was subsequently included with Scott's name in the first print edition of *The Family Legend*, published by Ballantyne in Edinburgh on 28 April 1810, and repeated in a second printing published on 15 September, virtually unaltered, except that in line 21 the spelling of 'groupe' is altered to 'group'. Scott mentions seeing proofs for the first printing in his letter to Baillie of 30 March 1810 (*Letters*, 2.319).

In due course Scott's prologue was then included in his own *Poetical Works* of 1820 (12.145–47), and the successive lifetime editions of his collected poems, with only the kind of changes normally associated with the work of the printer. For instance, 'expiring summer's' in line 1 becomes 'expiring Summer's' (1820*PW*) while in some later editions 'should' in line 39 becomes 'shall'. The present text is that of the first printing of *The Family Legend* (Edinburgh, 1810), iii–iv, with the title emended editorially from 'Prologue. Written by Walter Scott, Esq.'. The following emendation has also been made:

169.19   were (1820*PW*) / was

Historical Note

When Scott intervened decisively in the takeover by Henry Siddons (1774–1815) of Edinburgh's Theatre Royal in 1809 it was with the object of providing drama superior to what he termed 'the garbage of melo-drama and pantomime' (*Letters*, 2.118), and he regarded Joanna Baillie as 'the best dramatic writer whom Britain has produced since the days of Shakespeare and Massinger' (*Letters*, 2.29). She was also Scottish by birth, and Scott specifically aimed to foster a native dramatic tradition begun with John Home's *Douglas* in 1756. Scott had been in London in the spring and early summer of 1809, and on his return to Edinburgh in June he brought the manuscript of Baillie's *The Family Legend* back with him to be staged in Edinburgh, where he was extremely active in promoting its success in every possible way, even superintending rehearsals at the theatre.

Besides his own prologue the play was also to be supported by an epilogue written by veteran Scottish author Henry Mackenzie (1745–1831), and incidental music was to consist predominantly of Scottish airs in keeping with its historical subject-matter of a sixteenth-century feud between two Highland clan chiefs. The first performance was originally planned for 22 January 1810 (the day after his prologue was written), but the indisposition of the actress taking the leading female role caused its postponement to 29 January. Scott's prologue was spoken by the actor Daniel Terry (1789–1829), who played Argyll: see James C. Dibdin, *The Annals of the Edinburgh Stage* (Edinburgh, 1888), 261–62. Terry's delivery of the Prologue, according to the *Scots Magazine* for February 1810, was over-expressive: 'Mr T. should remember, that there is a difference between reciting and acting; that the vehemence and impetuosity which are well suited to the one, are out of place in the other' (72.107). The *Edinburgh Evening Courant* of 3 February judged both prologue and epilogue 'worthy of their authors', while the *Edinburgh Annual Register* in its article on 'Scottish Drama' thought Scott's prologue written 'with a romantic nationality of allusion to the subject of the tragedy, a loveliness of imagery, and a glow of feeling strongly characteristic of the bard of chivalry' (2: 2 (1811), 398). The positive reception given to his lines is also demonstrated by the existence of two manuscript copies by contemporaries (NLS, MSS 6366, f. 5, and 6390, f.11).

Explanatory Notes

169.9   Caledon   more usually Caledonia, is the ancient Roman name for Scotland, used poetically by Scott and others.

169.12   Acadia's   (see also Scott's footnote.) Referring to a former French settlement, ceded to Britain in 1713, and which forms part of the provinces of Nova Scotia and New Brunswick.

169.18   mossy cairn   a pyramid of loose stones as a memorial marking a grave, the site of a murder, or sometimes a boundary.

169.27   She, within whose mighty page   the first volume of Baillie's *Plays on the Passions* of 1798 included 'Basil' and 'De Montfort', the latter produced in London with the stellar actors John Philip Kemble (1757–1823) and Sarah Siddons (1755–1831) in 1800. A second volume had been published in 1800.

169.32   Mull's dark coast   the island of Mull in NW Argyllshire is separated from the mainland by the Sound of Mull and Firth of Lorn, and has an irregular coastline with rocky cliffs and indentations as well as many adjacent islets and insulated rocks.

170.34   fatal rock   in the central scene of *The Family Legend* Helen, the daughter of Argyll and wife of Maclean, is abandoned by her husband's orders on a rock in the sea between the NW coast of Argyllshire and the Isle of Mull to drown when the rock is submerged at high tide.

67.   Lines Addressed to Ranald Macdonald

Textual Note
These lines were originally written by Scott in an album once kept at the inn on the island of Ulva, during his tour in the Highlands and Western Isles of Scotland in July 1810, though the album itself apparently no longer exists: for further details, see H. B. de Groot, 'Scott, Hogg, and the Album in the Inn on Ulva', *Studies in Hogg and His World*, 14 (2003), 93–99. A manuscript transcription survives in NLS, MS 876, f. 15, headed 'Lines on Mr. Macdonald of Staffa by W Scott, left in the Book at the Inn where the Travellers put their names after visiting the Island of Staffa 1810', and in a hand apparently not Scott's own. The first known printing appeared in the *Edinburgh Advertiser* newspaper of 12 October 1810, accompanied by a short preamble stating: 'The following Lines, from the pen of Mr Walter Scott, are to be found, in his handwriting, in the Album at Ulva. They are addressed to Ranald Macdonald Esq., the Laird of Staffa.' Subsequent printings, presumably from this source, featured in the October 1810 numbers of both the *Gentleman's Magazine* and *European Magazine*. The poem was also anthologised in *The Poetical Register, and Repository of Fugitive Poetry for 1810–1811* (London, 1814), 231, under Scott's name and with the title of 'Lines Addressed to Ronald Macdonald, Esq. Laird of Staffa. Written in the Album, at Ulva'. The next significant printing is found in the *Monthly Magazine* for 1 November 1812 (34.309–10), in the form of a letter dated 20 August 1812 to the editor from one J. T. Mayne of Trowbridge, who had visited Ulva the previous autumn, and was evidently unaware of any earlier printing. Variants in the *Monthly Magazine* (some of which might plausibly originate from a superior transcription of Scott's hand compared with these earlier printings) include 'Clan-Ranald' instead of 'Clanronald' at line 2, 'chieftain spirit' not 'chieftain's spirit' (line 9), 'Pausing while' not 'Pausing, as' (line 10), and 'reign' rather than 'rest' (line 12). Unlike other printings, however, it creates a line space and indentation before the final four lines of the poem. A degree of fallibility however is suggested by the introduction of 'Taffa' for 'Jaffa' at the end of the penultimate line.

   In spite of such airings in periodical form, this poem failed to enter the official canon during Scott's lifetime, not appearing in any of the collected editions until the posthumous Lockhart *Poetical Works* edition of 1833–34 (10.356). The text here, under the title 'Lines, Addressed to Ranald Macdonald, Esq., of Staffa' parallels that in both the transcript in MS 876 and the *Monthly Magazine* in opting for 'Clan Ranald' (line 2), 'Chieftain' (line 9), 'Pausing while' (line 10), and 'reign' (line 12) though it is alone in introducing 'Atlantic [thunder']' for 'Atlantic's' at line 7. Along with the MS transcript it prefers 'heart' to 'breast' in the final line. At the same time, it prints 'Staffa' at the end of the penultimate line, causing further repetition, as well as omitting a whole line ('All thou lov'st …') immediately above that. A footnote also offers an incorrect date in stating the lines to have been written 'in the Album, kept at the Sound of Ulva Inn, in the month of August, 1814'.

The present text is based on that in the *Monthly Magazine*, 34 (1812), 310, as arguably the most accurate first-hand transcription from the original album. As the poem there lacks a heading, a title has been adopted from the *Poetical Register* for 1810–11 in modified form. The present text differs in closing up the line break before the final four lines, though the indentation of line 12 (also found in MS 876) is preserved. The three following emendations, commonly found in other versions and more probably reflecting Scott's original inscription, have also been made:

170.1   Macdonald (*Poetical Register*) / Mac-Donald
170.14   Warmer (*Edinburgh Advertiser*) / For warmer
170.14   Jaffa (*Edinburgh Advertiser*) / Taffa

Historical Note
Writing to Joanna Baillie (1762–1851) on 19 July 1810, Scott described how he had passed over the narrow stretch of water separating the islands of Mull and Ulva, accompanied by pipers, and was now fully established as the guest of the laird at Ulva House: 'Our friend Staffa is himself an excellent specimen of Highland chieftainship; he is a cadet of Clan Ranald, and Lord of a cluster of isles on the western side of Mull' (*Letters*, 2.361). Reginald (or Ranald) Macdonald of Staffa (1778–1838), later Sir Reginald Macdonald Steuart-Seton, had inherited his estate in 1800 as the eldest son of the second wife of Colin Macdonald of Boisdale, who had bought Ulva in 1785. Reginald Macdonald of Staffa, a friend of Scott's and fellow member of the Faculty of Advocates, became renowned for his hospitality and adoption of the manners of a Highland Chief, drawing many visitors to Ulva, several of whom like Scott set out from there to nearby Iona and Staffa (famous for its Fingal's Cave). He also endeavoured to promote the kelp industry on Ulva, by which according to Scott he 'has at once trebled his income and doubled his population while emigration is going on all around him' (*Letters*, 2.361). Scott at the same time touched on a potential fallibility in his host ('The habit of solitary power is dangerous ... and this ardent and enthusiastic young man has not escaped the prejudices incident to his situation' (2.361)); and in fact by 1817, notwithstanding an advantageous-seeming marriage, Macdonald of Staffa had effectively lost possession of the island, though continuing as its titular lord and playing a prominent role in Highland Society activities in Edinburgh.

Explanatory Notes
170.1   Staffa   territorial appellation of Reginald Macdonald of Staffa (see Historical Note), whose property included Staffa, the small island in the Inner Hebrides 8 km (5 miles) SW of Ulva.
170.2   Clan-Ranald   Clan Macdonald of Clanranald, also known as Clan Ranald, a branch of Clan Donald, one of the largest Scottish clans. Clan Ranald actively supported the Jacobite cause during the 1715 and 1745 Risings. Alexander Macdonald of Boisdale, grandfather of Reginald Macdonald, was a half-brother of the 16th chief of Clan Ranald.
170.9   chieftain spirit   possibly alluding to the spirit of a Highland chieftain taking the form of the eagle. Clan chiefs are entitled to wear three eagle feathers behind the crest badge worn on their bonnets, and clan chieftains entitled to two feathers.
170.14   Jaffa   ancient port city now in Israel, famous for its association with

biblical and other mythological stories. The site of a famous battle between
Richard I and Saladin during the Crusades, and more recently stormed by
Napoleon during his campaign against the Ottoman Empire in 1799.

68. The Battle of Sempach

Textual Note
Scott wrote to Margaret Clephane (1793–1830) on 27 October 1810 that, while
confined to the house with a cold at Ashestiel, he had been 'brushing the jackets
of some old Swiss ditties upon the battles of Sempach, Morat and other encoun-
ters with the Knights of Austria and Burgundy' (*Letters*, 2.399); and his transla-
tion of 'The Battle of Sempach' probably dates to this time. The earlier of two
manuscripts in Scott's hand consists of two leaves, probably conjugate, of paper
measuring approx. 27 x 20 cm with an 1805 watermark, now in NLS, MS 877,
ff. 200–01. The poem here consists of nineteen four-line stanzas only, but each
line is equivalent to two lines of the published text. The number of deletions and
insertions suggests that this is a rough draft, perhaps written soon after Scott
had acquired the copy of the first edition of *Des Knaben Wunderhorn* (*ALC*) that
was presumably his source and had been published in Heidelberg between 1806
and 1808. As Duncan Mennie argues in 'A MS Variant of Sir Walter Scott's
Battle of Sempach', *Beiblatt zur Anglia*, 49 (1938), 57–63, this is a more literal
and perhaps less polished version of the German original than the text as first
published in *Blackwood's Edinburgh Magazine*, 2 (February 1818), 530–32. In
this earlier text Scott includes, for example, in the heifer's speech about the
foreign nobleman attempting to milk her (see lines 113–20), the homely detail
that his pitcher was broken in the attempt. The second and later manuscript
is among the Blackwood Papers, in NLS, MS 4940, ff. 1–6, and consists of six
leaves, each measuring 24.4 x 19.3 cm with a watermark consisting of an elabo-
rate crowned shield and a date of 1813. The text is mostly written on the rectos,
but with some notes on the versos keyed to the text of the poem by asterisks.
There is also a substantial headnote and it is evident that this is Scott's fair-
copy manuscript sent as a contribution to *Blackwood's Edinburgh Magazine*. A
pencil note in another hand between the headnote and the poem itself, obviously
intended for the compositor, reads 'leave 5 or 6 lines'. Scott must have made a
number of changes in proof, adding a sentence about the death of Leopold III
to the end of the headnote, for instance, and also two stanzas concerning this
event to the poem itself (lines 105–12). He also rephrases line 76 from 'And to
his friends he said' to read 'Who to his comrades said'.
    After appearing in *Blackwood's Edinburgh Magazine* 'The Battle of Sempach'
was reprinted in Scott's 1820 *Poetical Works* (11.212–26) with a few adjustments
to suit the new context, such as the replacement of 'The verses inclosed' at the
start of the headnote by 'These verses' and some minor rephrasing such as 'the
Austrian men-at-arms' for 'the Austrian gentry' and 'the German chivalry' for
'the German men-at-arms' in its final paragraph. In line 28 of the poem itself,
for instance, 'He gives a penance' is revised to read 'He deals a penance'. Not all
of the changes seem due to authorial revision: in line 107, for instance, 'Konig's
field' is miscorrected to 'Konigsfield', creating an odd single-word amalgam of
English and German; while in line 120 the foreign nobleman comes to 'range'
rather than 'rule' the cow's field. Other differences are more clearly the work of
the printer. Similarly, none of the variations in the text in subsequent collected
editions of Scott's poetry are of a kind that can be readily attributed to the
author. Inevitably, errors creep in to some printings, such as 'mounted bull' for

'mountain bull' in line 103, which occurs in 1822*PW* and subsequent editions until corrected in 8vo1830*PW*. The text of the Lockhart posthumous collected edition of 1833–34 (6.332–42) largely follows 8vo1830*PW*, giving the reading 'Mountain Bull', for instance, but also repeating an error there of 'main and tail' in line 66.

The present text is that of *Blackwood's Edinburgh Magazine*, 2 (February 1818), 530–32, as best representing the culmination of Scott's initial creative process. The following emendations have been made:

172.11–12	"On Switzer … and old." (1820*PW*) / On Switzer … and old.
172.24	woe (Blackwood MS) / wo
172.28	drear. (Blackwood MS) / drear."
173.37	stalwart (Blackwood MS) / stallwart
174.57	Confederates (*MiscPoems*) / confederates
174.61	throbb'd (*MiscPoems*) / throb'd
174.63	Confed'rates (*MiscPoems*) / confed'rates
175.94	Lion's (Blackwood MS Lions) / lion's
175.100	thrust (Blackwood MS) / thurst
175.101	Lion (1821*PW*) / lion
175.103	Mountain Bull (1821*PW*) / mountain bull
175.107	König's (Editorial) / Konig's
	The German word for 'king' is König.
175.116	plain. (1820*PW*) / plain."
176.119	borne (1820*PW*) / born
176.130	And, glad the meed to win, (1820*PW*) / And glad the meed to win;
176.142	stunn'd (1820*PW*) / stun'd

Historical Note

The Old Swiss Confederation, between the Wäldstetten (forest cantons) of Uri, Schwytz, and Unterwalden, is generally considered as originating with the Federal Charter of 1291, formed for mutual defence of their rights against Austrian rule in northern and eastern Switzerland. Lucerne was included as a fourth member of the Confederation in 1332, and by 1353 the four town cantons of Zurich, Glarus, Zug, and Bern had also been admitted. In 1386 Duke Leopold III of Austria (1351–86), supported by the local nobility, attempted to curb the growing power of the Swiss Confederates but was defeated and killed at the battle of Sempach, 14 km (8½ miles) NW of Lucerne. According to tradition Arnold von Winkelried grasped as many Austrian pikes as he could, ensuring his own death but opening a way for his comrades into the Austrian ranks. This was followed two years later by the battle of Näfels, 50 km (31 miles) SE of Zurich, at which the Swiss Confederation finally cast off Austrian domination.

Scott had almost certainly become interested in the history and legends surrounding the battle of Sempach long before making this translation. His friend James Skene of Rubislaw (1775–1864), who had been partly educated at Frankfurt in Germany, revisited the continent in 1802 during the short-lived Peace of Amiens. It was then, presumably, that he acquired the copy of *Schweizerische Volkslieder mit Melodieen* (Zurich, 1788), inscribed 'J. Skene. Bern 1802' and 'Walter Scott / from James Skene', that he gave to Scott (*ALC*). 'Schlacht den Sempach. Ein Schweizer-Ballade' (The Battle of Sempach. A Swiss Ballad) is the first item in this collection of songs (4–5) and recounts the events of the first part of Scott's poem, the heroic death of Arnold von Winkelried and the consequent Swiss victory, but does not continue with the escape and death of the fleeing Austrian nobleman and his squire that follows.

Scott's source for his poem, which he declares in his headnote to be a literal translation, is rather 'Die Schlacht bei Sempach' (The Battle at Sempach) in the well-known German folk collection made by J. A. von Arnim and Clemens Brentano, *Des Knaben Wunderhorn*, 3 vols (Heidelberg, 1806–08), 1.349–53, which Scott also owned (*ALC*). Scott's poem is indeed a close, if not quite a literal, translation of this German original. As Duncan Mennie points out in 'A MS Variant of Sir Walter Scott's *Battle of Sempach*' (cited in the Textual Note), Scott makes the bull and not the cow attack the foreign nobleman who seeks to milk her and omits her knocking over the milking-pail, and he is also confused about the geography of the ballad, making the Austrian army approach Sempach from Willisau in the west and from Zurich in the east at the same time. (The German ballad mentions Sursee, a settlement on the N end of Lake Sempach, rather than Zurich.)

When Scott first made his translation in 1810 it was apparently for his own amusement rather than with a view to publication. Probably he came across this manuscript several years later at a time when he wanted to offer support for the newly-formed *Blackwood's Edinburgh Magazine*. At the time of its inception in 1817 *Blackwood's* was assumed to be much the same as older miscellany magazines, combining some original and some reprinted material, and Scott, like many other established writers who made early contributions to it, had no idea of contributing new or specially-written material. Although he revised and extended his old draft, clearly he did not check its geographical accuracy.

Explanatory Notes

171.headnote **Albert Tchudi, denominated the Souter** Scott conflates the author of this ballad with the source given for it in the well-known German folk collection made by J. A. von Arnim and Clemens Brentano, *Des Knaben Wunderhorn*, 3 vols (Heidelberg, 1806–08), 1.349: 'Von Halb Suter Tschudi. I. 529'. Von Arnim and Brentano refer the reader to the *Chronicon Helveticum*, a history of the early Swiss Confederation by Aegidius Tschudi (1505–72), for the ballad attributed to 'Halb Suter' (half shoemaker), the Swiss craftsman-poet who was reputed to have fought for the Confederation in 1386: see *Chronicon Helveticum*, 2 vols (Basel, 1734–36), 1.529–33.

171.headnote *Meistersinger* the members of the guilds of Meistersinger had to compose and perform *Meistergesang*, a form of poetry set to music and sung solo, and which was either religious (to be sung at the *Singschule* in church) or secular (sung as part of the ensuing celebrations in the tavern afterwards). Members of these guilds were generally citizens and respected craftsmen, and Hans Sachs (1494–1576), one of the best-known *Meistersinger*, was a shoemaker by trade. Scott's use of the term *Meistersinger* here is somewhat anachronistic, since they appear to have developed only in the course of the 15th century.

171.headnote **Collins** see 'Ode to Fear' (1746), lines 32–33, in *Thomas Gray and William Collins: Poetical Works*, ed. Roger Lonsdale (Oxford, 1977), 140. The Greek tragic poet Aeschylus (525–456 BC) is supposed to have fought for his country against the Persians at the battles of Marathon and Salamis.

171.headnote **Winkelried** the heroic Winkelried, like William Tell, is more of a legendary Swiss than an historical figure. The story of the deed attributed to him at the battle of Sempach probably began 50–90 years after the battle, but the name of Winkelried associated with it does not occur until the early 16th century. Tschudi in his *Chronicon Helveticum* terms the hero a man of Unterwalden of the Winkelried family. The most plausible candidate is the historical Erni Winkelried, of the Winkelried family of Stans, who witnessed a document dated 1 May 1367, according to the Swiss historian Hermann von Liebenau (1807–74), though he appears to have survived the battle.

171.headnote called "The handsome man-at-arms," this may relate not to the Habsburg Duke Leopold III (1351–86) who was killed at the battle of Sempach, but to an earlier ruler of Austria of the house of Babenberg, the Margrave Leopold II (1050–95), known as 'Der Schöne' (The Beautiful).

172.1 linden trees the German name for lime-trees, which bear strongly-scented small white flowers in June and July and are particularly attractive to bees, who are often so intoxicated by the nectar that they fall to the ground stunned. In ancient Germany courts were often held underneath linden trees, since they are supposed to unearth the truth and help to restore peace and justice.

172.5 Willisow Willisau is a medieval town E of Lake Sempach at the foot of the Napf mountain and close to the border between the cantons of Lucerne and Bern.

172.11 carles husbandmen, or men of the people.

172.13 clarion a shrill-sounding trumpet with a narrow tube.

172.14 Zurich on the lake in the German original Sursee at the N end of Lake Sempach.

172.21 rede counsel or advise.

172.21 shrive to gain absolution from sin by performing penance, part of the process of making one's confession to a priest.

172.23 Helvetian Latin for Swiss, so-called for the Helvetii, a people mentioned by Julius Caesar at the start of his commentary of 51 BC on the Gallic war.

172.31 partizan a long-handled spear.

173.41 Hare-castle (see also Scott's 1st footnote on this page.) The German original has 'Hasenburg', meaning hare-castle, as in the poem itself rather than in Scott's gloss.

173.46 Oxenstern the German original has Ochsenstein.

173.52 wain a wagon or cart.

174.58 pray'd to God aloud known to be a general habit of the Swiss forces before entering into battle. See also Scott's subsequent account of the battle of Morat of 1476 in *Anne of Geierstein*, ed. J. H. Alexander, EEWN 22 (Edinburgh, 2000), 373.

174.59 his rainbow interpreted as a covenant existing between God and his people, from the rainbow that appeared to Noah and his family after the Flood in Genesis 9.13–17.

174.65 Austrian Lion (see also Scott's footnote.) The first syllable of the name Leopold is the Latin word for a lion.

174.69 Lance, pike, and halberd a *lance* is a weapon consisting of an iron or steel head on a long wooden shaft, held by a horseman in charging at full speed; a *pike* is a weapon consisting of a long wooden shaft with a pointed metal head; a *halberd* is a weapon combining a spear and an axe mounted on a wooden shaft five feet or more in length.

175.103 Mountain Bull (see also Scott's footnote.) The arms of the canton of Uri include a bull's head.

175.107 König's field the monastery of Königsfelden (King's Field) was founded by Agnes, Queen of Hungary and her mother at the place, near Brugg in Switzerland, where her father Albert I, Duke of Austria had been assassinated in 1308.

176.121   stour   a tumult or uproar; a contest in battle.
176.126   Hans Von Rot   not identified. *Rot* is the German word for the colour red.
176.130   meed   reward or recompense.
176.131   shallop   a dinghy, or small rowing-boat.
177.157   wight   here probably a noun signifying a man or human being, rather than an adjective meaning courageous or valiant. In the equivalent passage *Des Knaben Wunderhorn* simply describes him as unforgotten and as a man of Lucerne.

69.   The Poacher

Textual Note
'The Poacher' was first published as 'Fragment First. The Poacher', one of three poetical imitations appended to an anonymous article, 'The Inferno of Altisidora', *Edinburgh Annual Register, for 1809*, 2: 2 (1811), 582–99. The others were of Thomas Moore (1779–1852) and of Scott himself, while this was an imitation of George Crabbe (1754–1832), Scott telling James Ballantyne in his letter of 23 October 1810, 'The subject of Crabbe is "The Poacher" a character in his line but which he has never touched'. Scott also mentioned planning a series of such imitations: 'I think the imitations will consist of Crabbe, Southey, W. Scott, Wordsworth, Moore and perhaps a ghost story for Lewis. I should be ambitious of trying Campbell' (*Letters*, 1.412). Scott's periodical essay was not itself republished in his lifetime, although it was included, without the three poems, in Kenneth Curry's *Sir Walter Scott's Edinburgh Annual Register* (Knoxville, 1977), 119–32, and more recently, with the three poems, in Walter Scott, *The Shorter Fiction*, ed. Graham Tulloch and Judy King, EEWN 24 (Edinburgh, 2009), 1–20.
   The poem, called simply 'The Poacher', was afterwards included in Scott's *Poetical Works* of 1820 (11.173–81). Although largely presented as self-standing, this and Scott's imitation of Moore from 'The Inferno of Altisidora' (see no. 70, 'Song') were preceded by a half-title denoting them to be fragments which originally appeared in the *Edinburgh Annual Register* for 1809. Otherwise most of the changes are of the kind normally associated with the work of the printer. There are two verbal changes which might just be authorial, though both are within the remit of intermediaries working in the printing-house: 'O'er court and custom-house' in line 7 becomes 'O'er court, o'er custom-house', and the repetitive-seeming 'had had the same' in line 121 becomes 'had done the same'. (A change from 'prompt for desperate hand' to 'prompt from desperate hand' in line 67 was more likely to have resulted from a printer's error.) 'The Poacher' then passed through the successive lifetime editions of Scott's collected poetry and into the Lockhart posthumous collected edition of 1833–34 (6.375–81) without further evidence of authorial involvement.
   The present text follows that of 'The Inferno of Altisidora', *Edinburgh Annual Register, for 1809*, 2: 2 (1811), 591–95, as best representing the original period of composition, omitting the words 'Fragment First' in the title as in the lifetime editions of Scott's collected poetry. No other emendations have been made.

Historical Note
The three imitations of contemporary poets appended to 'The Inferno of Altisidora' seem, on one level, to put Scott in the vanguard of a contemporary vogue for poetic parodies during the 1810s. The brothers James Smith

(1775–1839) and Horace Smith (1779–1849), for instance, had a popular success in 1812 with their *Rejected Addresses; or, The New Theatrum Poetarum*, a collection purporting to consist of unsuccessful entries for a competition to choose an inaugural ode to celebrate the reopening of London's Drury Lane Theatre after the fire of 1809. Closer to home, in 1816 Scott's friend James Hogg (1770–1835) was to publish his own ingenious volume of poetic parodies, *The Poetic Mirror*. Scott was, however, anxious to distinguish his imitations from parody, writing in his letter to Ballantyne of 23 October 1810, 'understand I have no idea of parody but of serious anticipation if I can accomplish it' (*Letters*, 1.412), thus implying that his objective was to predict a poem that the author might come to write himself.

In 1810 Crabbe had published *The Borough* (1810), a long poem consisting of twenty-four verse-letters describing the various professions, trades, poor people, amusements and institutions of East Anglian towns such as Aldeburgh and Ipswich. A number of reviewers, including Francis Jeffrey in the *Edinburgh Review*, 16 (April 1810), 30–55, criticised Crabbe's stern view of life and his depraved characters, notable amongst whom is Peter Grimes, an abuser of apprentice-boys who is haunted by visions of the spirits of his deceased father and the dead apprentices just as Scott's poacher's sleep is disturbed by dreams of his past murder of a gamekeeper. Scott had similar reservations about Crabbe's poetry in general, writing to Charles Kirkpatrick Sharpe on 13 January 1809, 'He has, I think, great vigour and force of painting; but his choice of subjects is so low, so coarse, and so disgusting' (*Letters*, 2.149). Scott himself judged his imitation of Crabbe a good one (*Letters*, 2.525), while Crabbe himself, when he read the anonymous verses, is said by Lockhart to have exclaimed 'This man, whoever he is, can do all that I can, and *something more*' (*Life*, 2.352).

'EEWN 24' when found at the end of the following Explanatory Notes indicates that these are reprinted, by kind permission of the editors Judy King and Graham Tulloch, from Walter Scott, *The Shorter Fiction*, EEWN 24 (Edinburgh, 2009).

Explanatory Notes

177.3–4 sage ... rights of man a probable allusion to Thomas Paine (1737–1809), who, in his *Rights of Man* (1791–92), supported the French Revolution. (EEWN 24)

177.6 true Indian shawls intricate, tapestry-woven wool shawls from Kashmir in India were luxury items. From the beginning of the 19th century imitations were produced at Paisley near Glasgow, now known as Paisley shawls. Imitation Indian shawls were also advertised as 'the invention of an eminent House in London' as early as 1802: see *Saint Ronan's Well*, ed. Mark Weinstein, EEWN 16 (Edinburgh, 1995), 474 (note to 167.5).

177.7 his shoe who flings throwing a shoe at a person or institution is an expression of contempt.

177.8 bilks cheats, avoids paying.

178.14 buckskin'd justices i.e. magistrates wearing the buckskin breeches of a country squire. (EEWN 24)

178.15 Wire-draw the acts that fix for wires the pain i.e. draw out inordinately the laws fixing the penalties for poaching. (EEWN 24)

178.22 one poor Easter chace the annual 'common hunt' held in Epping Forest on Easter Monday, during which a loosed deer was pursued by large crowds of Londoners; possibly instituted in 1226, it lasted until about 1882. (EEWN 24)

178.23–24 as free ... the Parisian train following the storming of the

Bastille on 14 July 1789, French peasants flocked to every chateau, burning hunt registers, and forcing their masters to sign away their feudal rights; when the National Assembly ratified the annulment of feudal privileges on 4 August, peasants all over France began hunting the game in the parks and forests for themselves (see Erich Hobusch, *Fair Game: A History of Hunting, Shooting and Animal Conservation*, trans. Ruth Michaelis-Jena and Patrick Murray (New York, 1980), 188). Chantilly, about 40 km (25 miles) from Paris, was the site of the magnificent chateau of the dukes of Condé, with its old and extensive hunting forest; it was razed during the Revolution. (EEWN 24)

178.25   musquet, pistol, blunderbuss   a *musquet*, or musket, is a hand-gun carried by infantry; a *pistol* is a small fire-arm to be fired with one hand; and a *blunderbuss* is a short gun with a wide bore, firing many pellets, and designed to be effective at short range without a precise aim.

178.26   field-pieces   light cannons for use on a field of battle.

178.27   leveret's heart   that of a young hare, usually within a year of birth.

178.28   covey   a brood or hatching of partridges.

178.29   *La Douce Humanité*   French gentle humanity. Edmund Burke in his *Letter to a Noble Lord* (1796; see *ALC*) described those who planned to rise against their unsuspecting masters as having 'nothing but *douce humanité* in their mouth': *The Writings and Speeches of Edmund Burke*, Vol. 9: *The Revolutionary War: Ireland*, ed. R. B. McDowell (Oxford, 1991), 175. (EEWN 24)

178.32   Seine   the river which flows through Paris entering the English Channel at Le Havre.

178.32   *vive la liberté!*   French long live freedom! (a catchcry of the French Revolution). (EEWN 24)

178.33   But mad *Citoyen*, meek *Monsieur* again   on 19 June 1790 the National Assembly in France abolished both nobility and the associated titles; as a consequence the form of address 'monsieur' was replaced by 'citoyen' (citizen). Napoleon, as emperor, restored titles of nobility in 1808, and the addressive 'monsieur' came back into use. (EEWN 24)

178.34   With some few added links resumes his chain   for Scott, Napoleon's empire was more oppressive than the monarchy which, after an interval of republican rule, it had replaced. (EEWN 24)

178.46   dingle   deep dell or hollow, usually closely wooded.

179.50   charcoal's smothering steam   burning charcoal produces small soot particles which can aggravate lung complaints. In a closed environment burning charcoal will increase the amount of carbon monoxide in the atmosphere, poisoning any inhabitants.

179.54   wattles   rods or stakes, interlaced with twigs and branches.

179.57   Conqueror's   William I, Duke of Normandy and King of England (1027/8–1087), known as 'William the Conquerer' for his successful invasion and conquest of England in 1066. William loved hunting and created large areas of royal forest in England, of which the New Forest is the best known.

179.61   that shrouds the native frore   i.e. that shelters the frore (freezing) American Indian. (EEWN 24)

179.62   Labrador   the Labrador peninsula is in northern Canada, bordered to the S and W by Quebec province.

179.72   crow   an abbreviation for crow-bar, a metal bar with a bent end for levering.

179.72   crape   a mask made of a thin black material.

179.77   sweeping net   large fishing-net capable of enclosing a wide area. (EEWN 24)

179.footnote   an antique stirrup ... "The Red King."   William II (called Rufus; born *c.* 1060; ruled 1087–1100), was killed on 2 August 1100 while hunting in the New Forest, probably by an arrow from one of his companions, Walter Tyrrell. 'The Red King' is an original ballad on the death of William II by William Stewart Rose (1775–1843), English poet and translator and a friend of Scott's, which appeared along with his translation of *Partenopex de Blois* in the volume of the same name (London, 1807). Stanza 40 tells how 'still, in merry Lyndhurst-hall, / Red William's stirrup decks the wall'. Scott and Rose made 'a long circuit through the forest' on horseback together in April 1807 (*Letters*, 12.105). Referring to this visit, Lockhart quotes from Rose's 'Gundimore': 'Here Walter Scott has woo'd the northern muse; / Here he with me has joy'd to walk or cruise; / And hence has prick'd through Yten's Holt, where we / Have called to mind how under greenwood tree, / Pierced by the partner of his "woodland craft," / King Rufus fell by Tyrrell's random shaft' (*Life*, 2.119). (EEWN 24)

180.83   higgler's evening cart   a *higgler* is a carrier who trades with country dwellers for poultry or dairy produce, exchanging for these a range of petty goods from the shops in town.

180.96   wold   a plain, a piece of open country.

180.102   grouse or partridge massacred in March   i.e. outside the shooting season. The Act of 1773 (13 Geo. III, c. 54), in force in Scott's time, determined the close season for game birds, which for grouse was 10 December–12 August, and for partridge 1 February–1 September. (EEWN 24)

180.104   no wicket in the gate of law   i.e. no small door set within the bigger gate through which simple access could be given to a secure place. (EEWN 24)

180.111   Edward Mansell   a very different character of this name appears in *The Fortunes of Nigel* as the 'punctilious old soldier and courtier' Sir Eward Mansel, who is himself possibly based on the Edward Mansel (d. 1595) knighted by Queen Elizabeth in 1572: see *The Fortunes of Nigel*, ed. Frank Jordan, EEWN 13 (Edinburgh, 2004), 335.13 and note. The baronetcy expired in 1750. (EEWN 24)

181.115   chords   the strings of a musical instrument.

181.125   robs the warren or excise   i.e. steals game birds from the enclosures in which they have been bred, or smuggles liquor thus stealing from the state by not paying excise duty. (EEWN 24)

181.133   the revenue baulked, or pilfered game   i.e. tax evasion (probably through smuggling) and poaching. (EEWN 24)

181.134   Flesh   to initiate in or give a taste for bloodshed or warfare.

181.138–39   Around the spot ... midnight round   according to tradition, on the anniversary of William Rufus's death his ghost follows the trail of blood which flowed from his body as it was transported to Winchester for burial. (EEWN 24)

181.142   bittern's   a *bittern* is a bird related to the heron which utters a boom during the mating season.

181.142   sedges   coarse, grassy plants growing in wet places.

181.143   wading moon   the moon when apparently moving through clouds or mist.

181.148   Malwood-walk   formerly an administrative area of the New Forest in Hampshire. (EEWN 24)

70. Song

Textual Note

'Song' was first published as 'Fragment Second', one of three poetical imitations appended to an anonymous article by Scott, 'The Inferno of Altisidora', *Edinburgh Annual Register, for 1809*, 2: 2 (1811), 582–99. (For further details see Notes to no. 69, 'The Poacher'.) This song is an imitation of those of the Irish poet and song-writer Thomas Moore (1779–1852). As 'Song' rather than as 'Fragment Second' it was afterwards included in Scott's *Poetical Works* of 1820 (11.182–83) with modifications to suit its new publication context. In 'The Inferno of Altisidora', for instance, the verses are a casualty of their function as a tennis-ball in a match between a pair of demons: they end with a line of asterisks and a note, 'The rest was illegible, the fragment being torn across by a racket stroke' (595). The asterisks and note were removed in the changed context. Although largely presented as self-standing, however, this and Scott's imitation of Crabbe from 'The Inferno of Altisidora' (see no. 69, 'The Poacher') were preceded by a half-title denoting them to be fragments which originally appeared in the *Edinburgh Annual Register* for 1809. Other differences from the *EAR* text, such as the change from an exclamation mark at the end of line 4 to a full stop and the substitution of 'fashion'd' for 'fashioned' in line 9, are of the kind normally associated with the printer's work. And while the apparently more substantive change from 'ardours' to 'ardour' in line 7 could be authorial it could equally well be a printing error.

'Song' passed subsequently through the successive lifetime editions of Scott's collected poems and into Lockhart's posthumous edition of 1833–34 (6.382) with no evidence of further authorial involvement.

The present text follows that in 'The Inferno of Altisidora', *Edinburgh Annual Register, for 1809*, 2: 2 (1811), 595, but adopts the title given for its subsequent inclusion in lifetime editions of Scott's collected poems. The final line of asterisks and the footnote have also been omitted since the present context is that of a collected edition of Scott's poetry rather than that of his original essay.

Historical Note

The three imitations of contemporary poets appended to 'The Inferno of Altisidora' on one level would appear to put Scott in the vanguard of a contemporary vogue for poetic parodies during the 1810s, although Scott himself took pains to distinguish his imitations from parody: for further details see Notes to no. 69, 'The Poacher'. Francis Jeffrey's denunciation of Moore as a licentious poet in reviewing his *Epistles, Odes, and other Poems* in the *Edinburgh Review*, 8 (July 1806), 456–65, led to an attempted duel, much ridiculed in newspapers, which pretended that the ammunition was to consist of paper pellets, a charge perhaps giving an extra edge to Scott's depiction of Moore's poem as ammunition used in a tennis game between literary devils, one of whom was Jeffrey himself: see *The Shorter Fiction*, ed. Graham Tulloch and Judy King, EEWN 24 (Edinburgh, 2009), 234–35 (note to 9.33).

The present love-song reflects the mildly erotic nature of Moore's verse from his first collection, *Poetical Works of the late Thomas Little* (1801) onwards. Scott admired Moore but, as King and Tulloch indicate in EEWN 24 (176), he expressed some concern about the moral effects of Moore's amatory poetry on young people, and it seems likely that he had particularly in mind the highly successful *A Selection of Irish Melodies*, the first two numbers of which were published with music by William Power of Dublin in 1808, a third and fourth number appearing in 1810 and 1811 respectively. In 'Believe me, if all those endearing young charms' in the second number (98–102), the poet tells his mistress that he will still love her after her youthful attractions have faded away with time. Scott's 'Song' imagines a reunion of the lover with his mistress after this change has indeed taken place and the ultimate fulfilment of his promise.

Explanatory Notes
182.9   **fay's**   a fairy's.
182.11   **at gaze**   a steady intent look, in this case presumably like the falcon's at its prey.

71.   The Vision of Triermain

Textual Note
'The Vision of Triermain' was first published as 'Fragment Third. The Vision of Triermain', one of three poetical imitations appended to an anonymous article by Scott, 'The Inferno of Altisidora', *Edinburgh Annual Register, for 1809*, 2: 2 (1811), 582–99. (For further details see Notes to no. 69, 'The Poacher'.) This third poem was an imitation of Scott himself. Unlike the other two imitations attached to Scott's article, 'The Vision of Triermain' was not reprinted in Scott's lifetime, almost certainly because two years later he had decided to use it as the nucleus of a full-length narrative poem for separate publication, *The Bridal of Triermain*, which was published in Edinburgh on 9 March 1813, also anonymously.

No manuscript of 'The Vision of Triermain' has apparently survived, and Scott's manuscript of *The Bridal of Triermain* in the Morgan Library, MA 451.1, does not contain the equivalent lines, for at the end of the 'Introduction' to the longer poem Scott has written the instruction 'Take in as in Register' (f. 7), suggesting that the printed text in the *Edinburgh Annual Register* was the copy-text used by the printer for the equivalent section of the longer poem: see *The Bridal of Triermain, or, The Vale of St John* (Edinburgh, 1813), 15–26. Scott must either have enclosed a marked-up copy of his *EAR* lines, however, or revised the text of 'The Vision of Triermain' in proof, since there are various revisions in the lines as they appear in *The Bridal of Triermain*, apart from the normal variation in punctuation and spelling originating in the work of the printer. In *The Bridal of Triermain* 'Glaramara's distant' in line 37 of the present text, for instance, becomes 'Skiddaw's dim and distant', while 'Whither or where / Has she gone' in lines 49–50 becomes 'What time or where / Did she pass', 'nether earth' in line 100 is altered to 'middle earth', and 'the red deer-hair' in line 126 becomes 'fern and deer-hair'. More substantial changes occur in the final lines of 'The Vision of Triermain' in order to adapt it to the context of the longer poem, so that the 'druid sage' of line 124 becomes the 'hoary sage' in *The Bridal of Triermain*, since the vision must now relate to a Christian context. From line 130 the verse paragraph then concludes:

> Then sprung young Henry from his selle,
> And greeted Lynulph grave,
> And then his master's tale did tell,
>   And then for counsel crave.
> The Man of Years mused long and deep,
> Of time's lost treasures taking keep,
> And then, as rousing from a sleep,
>   His solemn answer gave.
>   (*The Bridal of Triermain*, 26)

In 'The Vision of Triermain' Scott's lines read very differently without the context of the multiple time-frames provided in *The Bridal of Triermain*. The longer poem's Introduction opens with the successful present-day wooing of the landed heiress Lucy by a man named Arthur of lower social station, in the course of which Arthur tells her of the magical wooing of the legendary King Arthur's daughter by the medieval Roland de Vaux of Triermain, and of the distant events of that daughter's conception and birth and of the ages-long enchanted sleep into which she is put by the wizard Merlin. The original context of Scott's prose article also tends to define the reading of 'The Vision of Triermain' as imitation or parody more than as a short unfinished poem by Scott himself.

The present text is based upon that of *Edinburgh Annual Register, for 1809*, 2: 2 (1811), 596–99, and substantially therefore agrees with that in 'The Inferno of Altisidora' in the volume of Scott's *Shorter Fiction*, ed. Graham Tulloch and Judy King (EEWN 24). The heading 'Fragment Third' has been omitted, but the asterisks at the end have been retained since the poem ends with young Henry (and the reader) awaiting the response of the sage to Roland de Vaux's enquiry. The following emendations have also been made:

183.2   Triermain (*Bridal*) / Tiermain
184.50   brow, (*Bridal*) / brow

Historical Note
The three imitations of contemporary poets appended to 'The Inferno of Altisidora' seem, on one level, to put Scott in the vanguard of a contemporary vogue for poetic parodies during the 1810s, although Scott himself took pains to distinguish his imitations from parody: for further details see Notes to no. 69, 'The Poacher'. After his outstanding run of success with *The Lay of the Last Minstrel* (1805), *Marmion* (1808), and *The Lady of the Lake* (1810), Scott seems to have been testing out anonymously in this fragment one idea for a future narrative poem. As Tulloch and King point out in their EEWN edition of Scott's *Shorter Fiction*, 'The Vision of Triermain' is in many respects from the same poetic mould as *The Lay of the Last Minstrel* (1805), a tale of magic and of the Border between England and Scotland. In the event Scott's next long narrative poem, *The Vision of Don Roderick* (1811), was to be set in Spain; but in the same year, 1813, when he afterwards produced *Rokeby* under his own name, he also published *The Bridal of Triermain* anonymously. In 'The Vision of Triermain' therefore Scott tested out the possibility of a return to the imaginative territory of his first major success as a poet.

The note EEWN 24 when found in the following Explanatory Notes indicates that these are reprinted, by kind permission of the editors Judy King and Graham Tulloch, from Walter Scott, *The Shorter Fiction*, EEWN 24 (Edinburgh, 2009). Within these notes *Poetical Works* refers to Lockhart's posthumous edition of 1833–34.

Explanatory Notes
183.title   Triermain   a castle about 4 km (2½ miles) W of Gilsland in N Cumbria, known to Scott from his time in Gilsland in the autumn of 1797 when he met his wife. Medieval in origin (its exact date is unknown), it was described as partly 'fallen down and decayed' in 1580. In Scott's time substantial ruins remained but a further portion collapsed in 1832: see W. T. McIntire, 'Triermain Castle', *Transactions of the Cumberland and Westmorland Antiquarian and Archaeological Society*, new series 26 (1926), 247–54. (EEWN 24)

183.20 Plantagenet name given by later historians to the descendants of Matilda and Geoffrey of Anjou who ruled England 1154–1399, with reference to Geoffrey's badge, a sprig of broom (in Old French, *plante geneste*). The first three of these kings (Henry II, Richard I and John) are, however, sometimes termed the Angevins, the name Plantagenet being reserved for their successors, ending with Richard II. (EEWN 24)

183.23 Sir Roland de Vaux King and Tulloch speculate that Scott may have obtained the name Roland de Vaux either from his pre-publication hearing of Coleridge's 'Christabel' (1816) or from independent reference to a common source, William Hutchinson's *The History of the County of Cumberland*, 2 vols (Carlisle, 1794), 1.55 (see 'Essay on the Text', EEWN 24, 99). They refer to several historical figures of the Middle Ages, as follows: 'Ranulph de Vaux granted the fief of Triermain within his barony of Gilsland to his son Roland in the 1190s. It was held by Roland's descendants, many also called Roland, until the male line died out in the reign of Edward IV' (see 'Historical Note', EEWN 24, 177).

183.25 pricking riding on horseback, using spurs.

184.37 Glaramara's distant head rocky mountain ridge rising to a height of 783 m about 4 km (2½ miles) S of Borrowdale in Cumbria. Despite its height it would not be visible from Triermain and in later editions it was replaced by the nearer and higher Skiddaw. (EEWN 24)

184.53 eagle-plume this indicates noble descent in Scotland, where a clan chief wears three such feathers, a chieftain two, and gentlemen of the clan one.

184.55 Richard de Brettville a fictitious character, although a Richard de Bretevill is mentioned in relation to a London property in the late 12th century (see Derek Keene and Vanessa Harding, *Historical Gazetteer of London before the Great Fire* (Cambridge, 1987), 355–56). (EEWN 24)

184.67 Philip of Fasthwaite a fictitious character and place, although Scott introduced a similar name for a farm in *Waverley*, ed. P. D. Garside, EEWN 1 (Edinburgh, 2007), 300.40 and note, locating it on Ullswater. The name, especially its suffix, is characteristic of the region; though no such actual location has been discovered, there is a Finsthwaite Parish at the S end of Lake Windermere. (EEWN 24)

185.76 the sack of Hermitage Hermitage Castle, Roxburghshire, 10 km (6 miles) NE of Newcastleton. Begun in the 13th century and much modified over time, it was, as a major Border castle, often attacked. (EEWN 24)

185.79 Nine-stane Hill the Nine-Stane Rig, a prehistoric stone circle, stands on a hill about 2 km (1¼ miles) NE of Hermitage Castle. (EEWN 24)

185.85 Lyulph's tow'r a small modern Gothic castle, built on the ruins of an existing peel tower above the northern shore of Ullswater by the Duke of Norfolk in 1780. He belonged to the Howards of Greystoke in Cumbria and named it after Lyulph (Ligulf), the father of the first baron of Greystoke from whom he was descended. (Some authorities give Ligulf's name as Sigulf.). (EEWN 24)

185.88 druid one of an order of men among the ancient Celts of Britain and Gaul who, according to Caesar, were priests, but in native Irish and Welsh legends are magicians.

185.90 Arthur's and Pendragon's *Arthur* was a legendary Romano-British king of the late 5th or early 6th centuries, who became a hero in the pseudo history of the kings of Britain (*Historia Regum Britanniae*) by Geoffrey of Monmouth in the 12th century, whereas *Pendragon* was a title given to an ancient British or Welsh chief holding or claiming supreme power. According to legend, Uther Pendragon was the father of Arthur. (EEWN 24)

185.91   Dunmailraise   according to legend, a cairn on Dunmail-Raise, a high point on the road between Thirlmere and Grasmere in Cumbria, marks the spot where Dunmail, king of Cumbria, was buried after being defeated in battle in 945, supposedly by Edmund, King of the Saxons, and Malcolm I, King of Scots. (EEWN 24)

185.95   Helvellyn's cliffs   Helvellyn is the third highest peak in the Lake District (at 950 m); it overlooks Ullswater to the east and Thirlmere to the west. (EEWN 24) Scott's poem of that name (see no. 55) was written following his climbing of it with Wordsworth in 1805.

185.96   sigil   an astrological sign, having mystic power.

185.100   nether earth   from below the surface of the earth, often indicating hell.

186.106   blessed rood   the cross on which Jesus was killed, as a symbol of the Christian faith.

186.111   Irthing's mead   river flowing W through northern Cumbria to join the Eden SE of Carlisle. (EEWN 24)

186.112   Kirkoswald's verdant plain   town beside the Eden about 12 km (7½ miles) N of Penrith in Cumbria. (EEWN 24)

186.113   Eden   river flowing N through Cumbria to the Solway Firth. (EEWN 24)

186.114   red Penrith's Table Round   a prehistoric earthwork near Eamont Bridge just S of Penrith in Cumbria, known as King Arthur's Round Table although it substantially predates the legendary King Arthur. Scott in a later note recorded the conjecture 'that the enclosure was designed for the solemn exercise of feats of chivalry' (*Poetical Works*, 11.34). Many of the buildings of Penrith are constructed of the local red sandstone: according to Camden the name, 'if derived from the British language', means '*Red Head* or *Hill:* for the soil and the stones of which it is built are of a red colour' (William Camden, *Britannia*, trans. Richard Gough, 2nd edn, 4 vols (London, 1806), 3.246: *ALC*). Camden's *Britannia* was written in Latin and first published in 1586. (EEWN 24)

186.116   Mayburgh's mound and stones of pow'r   prehistoric earthwork with standing stones just S of Penrith. Only one stone remained when the poem was written but Scott noted later that 'Two similar masses are said to have been destroyed during the memory of man' (*Poetical Works*, 11.35). (EEWN 24)

186.118   Eamont's   river flowing out of Ullswater to join the Eden near Penrith. (EEWN 24)

186.119   Ulfo's lake   Ullswater in Cumbria; the name is derived from 'Ulf's lake' (see Eilert Ekwall, *The Concise Oxford English Dictionary of Place-Names* (Oxford, 1936), *Ullswater*). (EEWN 24)

186.126   red deer-hair   perhaps dried deergrass, *trichophorum cespitosum*, a grass-like, tufted plant found in boggy areas in Northern England and in Scotland.

186.130   selle   a saddle.

72.   Epitaph, Designed for a Monument

Textual Note

This epitaph memorialising the poetess Anna Seward (1742–1809) and her family forms part of a monument which still stands in the cathedral at Lichfield, Staffordshire. Originally positioned in the north transept of the Cathedral, it was later moved to its present position near the north-west entrance. Scott's verses in block capital letters and without any indentation occupy the second and larger of two plaques beneath the main design of the memorial. No autograph manuscript has apparently survived. However, an unpublished letter of Scott's to William Hayley of 12 March 1811 (John Work Garrett Library, The Sheridan Libraries, Johns Hopkins University: in a copy of John Forster, *The Life of Charles Dickens* 2nd edn (London, 1872), Vol. 2, Part 1, #19) includes a full transcript of the final lines provided, minus punctuation but otherwise closely approximating the text as found on the monument (see also below). For further details concerning the origins and nature of the monument itself, and an earlier shorter autograph draft version of the verses, see Historical Note.

The poem first appeared in print as 'Epitaph' in the *Edinburgh Annual Register, for 1809*, 2: 2, 643–44, first published in Edinburgh on 1 August 1811, ascribed to Scott, and with the following extensive sub-header: 'Designed for a Monument to be erected in Lichfield Cathedral, agreeably to the Bequest of the late Miss Anna Seward, to designate the Burial Place of her Father, the Rev. Thomas Seward, a Canon of that Cathedral, in which she herself is interred.' The text in the *Register* reveals a number of variants compared with the monument inscription. Punctuation is fuller, with an influx of semicolons and consequent loss of three question marks, and 'would you' is replaced by 'wouldst thou' (see line 7). A fresh paragraph is also introduced by indentation after line 6. There are also four more substantive changes: with 'is' being substituted for 'lies [smother'd]' at line 11, 'anthems' for 'chorus' (line 12); 'wept' for 'mourn'd' (line 14), and the unpunctuated 'our sorrows say' becoming 'let friendship say' surrounded by commas in the penultimate line. One possibility is that Scott rewrote the poem for publication, another that an intermediary was more than usually involved, though the punctuation and occasional differences in spelling (for example 'show'd' not 'shew'd) are most likely routine work by the printer. The next printing is found in *The Vision of Don Roderick, and Other Poems* (Edinburgh, 1811), 163–64, first published in Edinburgh on 1 January 1812. Here interestingly the wording reverts to 'chorus' and 'mourned' at lines 12 and 14, as if Scott was recalling an earlier version, though 'is' and 'let friendship say' remain at lines 11 and 15 (the latter for the first time followed by a concluding end-of-line dash). This printing is close in its wording to the autograph transcript in Scott's letter to William Hayley (see above), the one verbal variant in the latter ('paens' instead of 'chorus' in line 12) being unique to that version. In the *Vision* printing the shorter sub-heading 'Designed for a Monument in Lichfield Cathedral, at the Burial Place of the Family of Miss Seward' is also established for the first time. It is this state of the poem that was evidently taken up by the various collected sets of Scott's poetry, beginning with the 1820 *Poetical Works* (12.135–36), which introduces a number of small printing changes, while through a space after line 6 effectively creating a two-stanza poem. The printing in the Lockhart posthumous 1833–34 *Poetical Works* (8.377–78) gives the 'Edinburgh Annual Register, 1809' as its source, though the wording follows that in the preceding collected sets, with the usual slight changes attributable to the printer. It differs however in having no kind of break after line 6, the lines running on unhindered as in the original monument inscription.

The present text follows without emendation the version found in the 'Miscellaneous Poems' section of *The Vision of Don Roderick, and Other Poems* (Edinburgh, 1811), 163–64, the first to appear in print in an edition of Scott's poetry and the closest both to the transcript in Scott's letter of 12 March 1811 to William Hayley (see above) and to the original inscription as found on the Monument at Lichfield Cathedral.

Historical Note
Familiarly known as 'the Swan of Lichfield', Anna Seward had continued to reside in the Bishop's Palace after the death of her father, the Rev. Thomas Seward, Canon Residentiary at the Cathedral, in 1790. From the first publication of *Minstrelsy of the Scottish Border* (1802), Seward had been engaged with Scott in a regular and lengthy correspondence, taking in a variety of mainly poetical issues, including Scott's early original verse, the Ossian controversy, and contemporaries such as Southey, Wordsworth, Burns and Hogg. Seward's ballad 'Rich Auld Willie's Farewell' was published in the third volume (1803) of the *Minstrelsy*, while other pieces communicated to Scott included her epitaph for John Saville, vicar-choral at the Cathedral, a married man with whom she had been involved in a relationship considered by some to be scandalous. (The epitaph, notwithstanding, was engraved on a tablet at Seward's expense, and is now found in the south transept of the Cathedral.) Scott in turn sent Seward pre-publication extracts from *The Lay of the Last Minstrel* and *Marmion* for her opinion. The two poets finally met in Lichfield in May 1807, when Scott stayed two days, and was able to experience at first hand the ambience of a town whose literary offspring included Samuel Johnson, David Garrick, and Erasmus Darwin. Though impressed by Seward's appearance and good nature, Scott's letters to friends suggest that he found the intensity of her attentions somewhat demanding; and he had already been careful prior to his visit to warn her not to expect too imposing a figure: 'you would expect to see a person who had dedicated himself much to literary pursuits, and you would find me a rattle-sculled half-lawyer ... half-educated—half-crazy, as his friends sometimes tell him; half everything' (*Letters*, 1.325).

Seward's last letter to Scott, written days before her death on 25 March 1809, describes her increasing mental incapacity while anxiously outlining plans for the posthumous publication of her work.

These are set out in greater detail in a long and complicated will, which makes Scott her literary executor, and assigns to him the task of editing her poetry. This obligation was communicated to Scott by Charles Simpson, one of the executors of the will, on 9 April 1809: 'I am very glad Mrs Seward has left you the publication of her Poetical Works & Juvenile correspondence' (NLS, MS 865, f. 138r). In a postscript to the same letter Simpson added that Seward by the terms of the will had left Scott £100, presently held in Navy Annuities, and payable in two years. As early as 13 May that year, Southey was reporting rumours that 'Scott has a legacy of 100*l.*, for which he is expected to write her epitaph' (*Selections from the Letters of Robert Southey*, ed. John Wood Warter, 4 vols (London, 1856), 2.137); though in Simpson's letter, as in the will itself, the suggestion that the legacy represented any kind of fee is not apparent.

Most probably Scott heard of details concerning the monument at a later point. In Seward's will this features prominently at the beginning, immediately after her request for 'a frugal and private Funeral':

> I will that my hereafter appointed Executors and Trustees commission one of the most approved Sculptors to prepare a Monument for my late Father and his Family of the value of Five hundred pounds and that with the consent of the Dean and Chapter they take care the same be placed in a proper part of Lichfield Cathedral. (Staffordshire Record Office, LD262/1/35).

The proposal that Scott should write the inscription is made explicit in a letter from Charles Simpson of 1 October 1809: 'Mrs Seward left 500 for a Monument for her fathers family & herself—May we beg an Inscription in English—& a design for the Monument. The Inscriptions in our Cathedral are very bad with few exceptions' (NLS, MS 865, f. 144r). Scott's reply of 25 October is headed by the following twelve-line draft version:

> To him who asks why o'er this tablet spread
> In female grace the willow droops her head?
> Why on her branches silent and unstrung
> The sculptors hand a marble harp has hung?
> Oer what quenchd lamp yon mourner seems to sigh?
> For whom yon Cherub points a brighter sky?
> What poets flame has smothered here in dust?
> What Christian hopes the Rising of the Just?
> Lo! one brief line an answer sad supplies
> Honourd, beloved and mournd, here **Seward** lies
> Her worth her warmth of heart our sorrows say
> Go seek her genius in her living lay.

In the main letter Scott offers the verses as 'simpler and better than any thing which after several attempts I have been able to achieve', adding however that as he had left Simpson's letter describing the design of the monument in Edinburgh he could not be sure of its accuracy with regard 'to the emblems of the sculptor'. This also reveals Scott's assumption that the tribute was to be for Anna alone. More eulogy might have been thrown into the description, 'but it seemd better taste to leave it to be inferrd from the propriety of the emblems, the regret of her friends and the value of her literary remains' (Berg Collection, New York Public Library; printed with minor inaccuracies in *Letters*, 2.393–94). In a response of 29 November, quoting directly from the will, Simpson duly corrected Scott on the matter, at the same time clarifying the nature of the design: 'For this reason we thought Filial Piety weeping over the Ashes of her Parents would take in the whole & the Willow & Harp suspended Emblematical of her Genius. There is no Cherub' (NLS, MS 3879, f. 270r). It might be appropriate too if the final two lines were omitted: 'If her fame does not survive we cannot perpetuate it on a Tombstone' (f. 270v). He also indicated how an additional prose inscription, commemorating Seward's father, mother, and sister, and preceding Scott's verses, might help alleviate any problem. No further communication on this issue has been discovered, though a letter from Simpson of 30 March 1811, announcing the availability of Scott's £100 legacy, expresses pleasure at the eventual outcome: 'The Epitaph you so kindly furnishd is much approved & admired & the work in the hands of Bacon for completion' (NLS, MS 3880, f. 75v).

The main design of the monument as sculpted by John Bacon (1777–1859) is much as indicated in Charles Simpson's letter to Scott of 29 November 1809. The full-length figure of a bare-breasted woman in classical drapes is seated with a scroll in her right hand and with her head in her left hand in a gesture of despair, the elbow resting on a coffin. Behind her is a drooping willow tree, on whose branches hangs a harp. Two plaques are underneath this tableau: the first describing Seward's family, much as suggested by Simpson; the second containing the text of Scott's epitaph as extended to sixteen lines, without any ascription. Some of the difficulties faced by Scott are confided in his letter to William Hayley of 12 March 1811:

> The attempt was by no means an easy one to me nor have I succeeded at all to my satisfaction—there is I think nothing more embarrassing for you must be grave & yet somewhat poetical, kind yet not flattering, moral & not dull and above all you must tell the name whether it be Seward or Higginbottom, otherwise says Dr. Johnson what information does your epitaph communicate. After having much ponderd I e'en dip'd (as my betters have done before me) into the commonplaces of poetry and like a man diving for a wig, brought up the following lines ... (John Work Garrett Library, John Hopkins University: insert in Bib #2098795).

As a whole Scott may be said to have succeeded in his aim to avoid excessive eulogy, in contrast with the more effusive manner employed by Seward in her lines on Saville, as well as in several other elegiac tributes, to Garrick and Captain Cook among others, which are likely to have been familiar to Scott as Seward's editor at the time of writing.

Explanatory Notes

187.6   domestic charities   Thomas Seward (1708–90) became a resident of Lichfield in 1754, occupancy of the Bishop's Palace in the Close being available to him as a result of the Bishop residing elsewhere. Here he helped develop an active social and literary circle. Amongst more familial charities was his adoption with his wife of Anna's younger foster sister, Honora Sneyd, whose mother had died when she was six years old. Thomas Seward's 'active benevolence' is recognised at the beginning of a 'Biographical Sketch of the late Miss Seward', published in the *Gentleman's Magazine*, 79 (April 1809), 378–79.

187.8   willow droops   the (weeping) willow tree is a traditional symbol of mourning, and sometimes used for making mourning garlands. Compare Psalm 137.2: 'We hanged our harps upon the willows in the midst thereof.'

187.10   minstrel harp   the harp as conventionally associated with poetry. In this context, Scott is possibly also reflecting Seward's regard for Scotland as a 'classic ground' for poetry: see, for example, her letter to Scott of 20 June 1806, in *Letters of Anna Seward*, 6 vols (Edinburgh, 1811), 6.276. The harp features in such a way in Seward's extempore lines on the poems of Ossian, in a letter of 1762 given by Scott as a specimen of her 'Literary Correspondence' in *The Poetical Works of Anna Seward*, 3 vols (Edinburgh, 1810), 1.lvii: 'Sweet was the harp, and lofty was its tone, / To which the bards of Scotia's ancient race / Warbled, in notes majestic, soft, and full, / The tales of other times'.

187.12   chorus of the just   probably alluding to 'justified' Christians in Heaven, and also reflecting the idea of a 'heavenly choir'.

187.15   warmth of heart   compare Scott's letter to Mrs Clephane of 5 February 1809, discussing Seward's illness: 'She has a warm enthusiastic feeling of poetry, and an excellent heart, which is a better thing' (*Letters*, 2.163).

73.   The British Light Dragoons; or, The Plain of Badajos

Textual Note

This is one of three songs contributed by Scott to George Thomson's *A Select Collection of Original Irish Airs*, Vol. 1 (Edinburgh, [1814]), as first issued with a Preface dated March 1814. The musical notation (item 28), headed ''Twas a Marechal of France' and with the words of the first stanza interspersed, occupies page 65; while the letterpress wording of the whole song, under the title 'The British Light Dragoons; or, The Plain of Badajos', is found on the following page. The composer of the designated air 'The Bold Dragoon' is not known, though the arrangement is by Beethoven. Scott's song was originally submitted in a communication endorsed by Thomson 30 April 1811, now in the Thomson Papers in the British Library (Add. MS 35,264, ff. 12–13). In his accompanying letter Scott refers to having hit on the suitability of his subject to one of the airs suggested by Thomson, with words beginning 'There was an ancient fair', on finding an account of the cavalry engagement at Campo Mayor in a newspaper at Bankhouse Inn (a staging-post on the Edinburgh–London road, on the right bank of Gala Water), on his way from Edinburgh to Ashestiel (f. 13; *Letters*, 2.483). In another letter, with a May 1811 postmark, Scott returned a revised version of the song sent to him by Thomson, remarking that 'The lines cannot be better cut down than you have done it yourself', his only proviso being that Thomson may have mistaken the pattern in some octosyllabic lines (f. 15; *Letters*, 2.484–85). Comparison between Scott's original draft and Thomson's revised transcript shows that the changes made, with musical considerations no doubt in mind, are for the most part localised and efficient, the most prominent difference being a reduction of the original eight (or more) syllables in the fourth line in each verse to just six (so that for instance 'His Eclaireurs of Corps d'armée' in line 4 becomes 'And boasted corps d'armée'). Both MS versions also include a fifth stanza, omitted in the printed version. In Scott's original draft (deletions and insertions included) this reads:

> Their squadrons formed to front, their sabres then they drew
> And as ↑if↓ their ranks were spider-webs they broke the Frenchmen
> > through
> > Still as they <strive> ↑struggled↓ to form again
> > Our <horsemen> ↑merry-men↓ rode them down amain
> For they fought <with> like stout dragoons with their long swords boldly
> > riding
> > > Whack fal de ral &c (f. 12v)

Thomson's version, as well as opting for 'strove' rather in 'struggled' in line 3 (half-restoring a deletion in Scott's original), characteristically cuts down the fourth line; 'we' is also subsequently preferred to 'they' in the fifth line:

> Their squadrons form'd to front, their sabres then they drew
> And as if their ranks were spider-webs they broke the Frenchmen through
> > Still as they strove to form again
> > We rode them down amain!
> For <they> ↑we↓ fought like stout dragoons with their long swords boldly
> > riding
> > > Whack fal de ral &c. (f. 14v)

No explanation has been found for the omission of this verse, though it is perhaps worth noting that inclusion would have required an additional page for the letterpress wording.

Scott's letters to Thomson indicate a preference for his name not being attached to a 'rough effusion, which can have no effect unless when sung, and which I have studiously kept thin of poetry in hopes of giving it a martial and popular cast' (*Letters*, 2.483). An attribution to 'Walter Scott, Esq.' nevertheless appears above the letterpress text in *A Select Collection of Original Irish Airs*, and one could scarcely expect Thomson to have hidden such a prize contributor. Scott's reservations, however, no doubt influenced the absence of this item in all collected editions of his poetry, prior to the posthumous Lockhart *Poetical Works* of 1833–34 (10.357–59). Headed there 'The Bold Dragoon [in the singular]; or, The Plain of Badajos', a footnote observes how 'It was first printed in Mr George Thomson's Collection of Select Melodies, and stands in vol. vi of the last edition of that work' (357n). Reference to *Thomson's Collection of the Songs of Burns, Sir Walter Scott [etc.]*, the additional sixth volume [1825] to his *Select Melodies of Scotland*, shows that the letterpress lead title there (in keeping with the tune) has similarly transmuted to 'The Bold Dragoon' (item

59). Evidently this served as the Lockhart copy-text, to which his edition adds a slightly fuller punctuation system, but without any mention of a musical component. The Lockhart note also claims that the song was written 'shortly after the battle of Badajos, (April, 1812,) for a Yeomanry Cavalry dinner'. The misdating of a battle actually fought one year earlier (see Historical Note) hardly inspires confidence, and no evidence has been discovered of such a celebration.

The present text is based on the letterpress in Thomson's *A Select Collection of Original Irish Airs*, Vol. 1 (Edinburgh, [1814]), 66, though the full refrain as in stanza 1 is taken from the preceding musical notation there. It also restores the missing fifth stanza as found in both Scott's original manuscript and Thomson's revised transcript, as possibly omitted in the printed version on the grounds of available space. Thomson's transcript is preferred here on the basis that this corresponds more fully with the other verses and like those had met with Scott's tacit approval. The following emendations have been made to the Thomson transcript in the case of this stanza as found in BL, Add. MS 35,264, f. 14v:

189.26   drew, (Editorial) / drew
189.27   through, (Editorial) / through
189.30   riding. (Editorial) / riding

Historical Note
The event celebrated in this song took place on 25 March 1811 during the Peninsular War, when the 13th Light Dragoons accompanied by Portuguese cavalry charged French forces outside Campo Maior forcing them to retreat over the Spanish border to Badajoz, where the assault was eventually repulsed. A positive account of the action, from the *London Gazette*, featured in the *Morning Post* and *Caledonian Mercury* on 22 and 25 April respectively, and it is probable that Scott's song was triggered by such an account. According to the *Morning Post*: 'A great number of the French were sabred, as were the gunners belonging to sixteen pieces of cannon that were taken upon the road, but afterwards abandoned. ... The enemy's loss is estimated at 5 or 600 men killed, wounded, or prisoners; great numbers of horses and mules were taken, together with one howitzer and some ammunition waggons.' A later account of the engagement in the *Edinburgh Annual Register* for 1811 highlighted a single incident in which a Corporal Logan of the 13th Light Dragoons had sabred and killed Colonel Chamorin, a distinguished French officer, whose death was mourned on the field of battle by a French captain during a truce on the following day: 4: 1 (1813), 'History of Europe', 271–72. Both this and the preceding accounts tend to obscure a bitter row that subsequently broke out in the British command, with the Duke of Wellington accusing the 13th of behaving like 'a rabble', and Brigadier-General Long protesting that the French would have been forced to surrender had the British heavy brigade been brought up. There is no evidence however of Scott being aware of such complications when writing his song, the exuberance of which expresses something closer to delight at a rare triumph by British against French cavalry in spite of being outnumbered. Nor, notwithstanding the singular title later adopted for the piece, is there any hint of Scott being aware at this point of the heroics of Corporal Logan, the poem rather dealing with the dragoons collectively.

The nominated tune of 'The Bold Dragoon' seems to have been especially popular, and was reportedly one of the tunes played in Parliament Hall at the dinner in honour of George IV during the royal visit to Edinburgh in 1822: see John Prebble, *The King's Jaunt* (London, 1988), 316. A comic version to a tune of that title, and with words beginning 'There was an ancient fair', is included in *A Collection of the most favorite Comic Songs: Sung at the Theatres Royal and Public Meetings* (London, [1811]), 19–20. Similar words are also found in a number of contemporary Broadside Ballads, not uncommonly under the title of 'Mrs. Flinn, and the Bold Dragoon'. Here the engagement is of a libidinous nature, involving a dragoon and a lascivious older lady, and the refrain of 'Whack row de row' is marked by sexual innuendo. Knowledge of this dimension would no doubt have added further relish to those singing or listening to Scott's adaptation for more bellicose purposes.

Explanatory Notes

188.1 Marechal of France *French* military Marshal. The French commander in Portugal during 1810–11 was Maréchal André Masséna (1758–1817), though there is no evidence that he directly participated in the actions described in the song. Masséna was subsequently relieved of his post, marking the end of his career as a military commander.

188.4 corps d'armée *French* army-corps. Designed as independent military groups, these initially gave forces under Napoleon a considerable advantage. 'Each corps d'armée formed a complete army within itself, and had its allotted proportion of cavalry, infantry, artillery and troops of every description. ... [it] might vary in number from fifty to eighty thousand men, and upwards; and the general of such a body exercised the full military authority over it, without the control of any one excepting the Emperor himself': Scott, *Life of Napoleon Buonaparte*, 9 vols (Edinburgh, 1827), 6.108–09.

188.8 Campo Mayor Campo Maior, fortified town in Portugal, close to the Spanish border, some 20 km (12½ miles) NW of Badajoz in Spain. The town had been occupied by the French shortly before the arrival of the British/Portuguese force sent to relieve it.

188.9 fricassee from the French, referring to meat, especially chicken or veal, browned lightly, stewed, and served in a sauce made with its own stock.

188.10 peste! morbleu! mon General *French* plague! confound it! my General.

188.footnote glacis in military engineering, an artificial slope from a fortress which exposes attackers to the defenders' missiles (from the Old French, *glacer* 'to slide').

189.21 sous'd swooped down, descended with speed and force; as used of the actions of a hawk.

189.22 Long, de Grey, and Otway Brigadier-General Robert Ballard Long (1771–1825), appointed commander of the British and Portuguese cavalry in the army of Marshal Sir William Beresford (see also note to 189.35) shortly before the action at Campo Maior; Colonel (later General) Sir Loftus William Otway (1775–1854), commander of the Portuguese cavalry brigade at Campo Maior; Major-General (then Colonel) George De Grey, commander of the 3rd Dragoon Guards Heavy Cavalry Brigade, killed at a subsequent siege of Badajoz. All three feature positively in early newspaper reports of the action.

189.29 amain with force, vigorously.

189.35 Beresford Sir William Carr Beresford (1768–1854), appointed Marshal of the Portuguese army in 1809, and commander of Wellington's southern wing in Spain in 1811. Vindicated by Wellington after the action of Campo Maior, though critics claimed that he had been slow in giving orders and allowed the enemy to escape.

189.38 Wellington Arthur Wellesley (1769–1852), commander-in-chief of the British expeditionary force during the Peninsular War from 1809, in which year he was created Viscount Wellington (later Duke of Wellington in 1814).

189.40   eagles that to fight he brings   referring to the figure of an eagle on a staff (following the practice of Roman imperial legions) as carried into battle as regimental standards by the Grand Armée of Napoleon Buonaparte during the Napoleonic Wars. Their capture by opposing forces was highly prized.

74.   On the Massacre of Glencoe

Textual Note
In a letter of 14 November 1809 (BL, Add. MS 35,267, ff. 4v–5r) the Scottish song collector George Thomson (1757–1851) invited Scott to write the words to 'two beautiful Irish Airs' sent to him by a friend in Cork, which he would, if the invitation was accepted, send 'with a stanza under each to shew you the *measure* of verse necessary'. In a subsequent undated letter he further requested that the names and localities of the songs should be Irish (BL, Add. MS 35,267, ff. 6v–8v). Scott was slow to supply the verses and after several reminders Thomson noted on 23 May 1811 that he had sent Scott in addition a Highland air, one 'called by Gow, Lord Balgonie's favourite', adding a further note that in July he had asked Scott to write verses 'on the Subject of the massacre of Glencoe, to be the measure of [Thomas Campbell's] Hohenlinden' (BL, Add. MS 35,267, f. 20r). By July of the same year Scott wrote that he had 'Glencoe' 'finished in the rough' (*Letters*, 2.506).

Scott's manuscript of 'Glencoe' (BL, Add. MS 35,264, ff. 34–36) was probably sent to Thomson in November 1814, for on 24 November Thomson expressed enthusiastic approbation of it, suggesting at the same time a number of corrections. Some of these were adaptations to the rhythm of the tune: he asked Scott to 'throw the emphasis upon the second syllable of the third line of the first stanza' as with the other stanzas, suggesting that 'Down the dark bosom of Glencoe' might become 'Adown the dark wood of Glencoe' in line 3. Considerations of personal taste alone, however, seem to have determined his objections to such expressions as 'The mist wreath has the mountain crest' and 'faithless butchery' (BL, Add. MS 35,267, ff. 33v–34v). Thomson seems to have returned Scott's manuscript to him for correction, since (BL, Add. MS 35,264, f. 35v) Scott has added a new stanza (equivalent to lines 17 to 24 in the present text) to it and also responded to Thomson's criticisms, pointing out, for instance, that there is no word in Glencoe and suggesting either 'Far down the desert of Glencoe' or 'Far down the dale of dark Glencoe' as a replacement for line 3 and agreeing to think of something better than 'faithless butchery'.

In a letter of 2 December (BL, Add. MS 35,267, ff. 33v–34v) Thomson praises the additional stanza while pointing out that 'plied' in the fifth line of it is echoed by 'ply' in its last, and he agrees that 'Far down the desert of Glencoe' is 'quite the thing', though reiterating his earlier objection to 'The mist wreath has the mountain crest' which Scott had simply ignored and which indeed survived into the published text. A copy of the revised text in Thomson's hand (BL, Add. MS, 35,264, ff. 52–55) accompanied this letter, and Scott has marked it with further corrections. In the final line of the new stanza, for instance, he has replaced 'ply' with 'tend' in the present line 24, but has changed 'ruthless cruelty' to 'ruthless butchery' (line 36) reinstating a word to which Thomson had formerly objected. This copy is headed 'Page 11' and 'written for this work / By Walter Scott Esq', indications that it may have been intended as copy for the printer.

The text as published in the first volume of Thomson's *A Select Collection of Original Irish Airs* is that of this revised manuscript version with the kind of changes normally associated with the printer. There are also two changes in wording, by which 'gar' in line 27 became 'gave' and 'last notes' in line 41 became 'best notes', and the title has been altered from 'Glencoe' to 'On the Massacre of Glencoe'. It is possible that these alterations were made in proof by Scott, particularly as, in a note to Thomson added to his original autograph manuscript, he had written 'other little corrections can lie over till the proof sheet' (BL, Add. MS 35,264, ff. 33–36). Scott's verses were not however set to the Scottish tune for which they had been originally written, as Thomson's headnote indicates:

> This Air, (No. 5.) which was communicated, without a name, by a Friend in Ireland, is so remarkable for its simple and pathetic character, that it might pass for a Highland LAMENT. No music could be better suited to the following sorrowful tale of truth which the Poet has indited for it. (11)

Probably the actual tune supplied is one of those 'Irish airs' mentioned by Thomson in his letter to Scott of 14 November 1809 (see above). No evidence of when and why the substitution was made has been found, and presumably at a fairly late date Thomson, lacking the right words for his Irish air, simply shifted Scott's verses with the same rhythm from his Scottish to his Irish collection to fill the gap, even though it created the anomaly of verses with obviously Scottish subject matter accompanied by an Irish tune, a feature for which this headnote provides a somewhat lame justification.

'On the Massacre of Glencoe', with a musical setting by Beethoven for voice accompanied by piano and violin, was first published in Edinburgh as part of the first volume of Thomson's *A Select Collection of Original Irish Airs* (11 letterpress; 12–13 musical notation) in April 1814. It was also included, after Scott's death, with a different musical setting by Beethoven, as item 298–99 [*sic*] in the sixth volume of Thomson's *The Melodies of Scotland* (Edinburgh, 1841), a note by Thomson stating that Beethoven's music was here first published. Thomson had complained to Beethoven that some of his settings were too difficult for Edinburgh performers and asked for revisions in nine of those Beethoven had prepared for him, and in his reply of 19 February 1813 Beethoven, while declining to revise them, had agreed instead to provide new music: see J. Cuthbert Hadden, *George Thomson the Friend of Burns* (London, 1898), 325–26. Thomson therefore had two settings by Beethoven of the same tune for 'Glencoe', and, having used the second one in his 1814 collection, Thomson must have decided belatedly in 1841 to publish the first setting by this prestigious composer as well.

'On the Massacre of Glencoe' appeared subsequent to first publication in Scott's *Poetical Works* of 1820 (12.141–44) without a musical setting or the name of the air being given, and with only changes of the kind normally associated with the work of the printer. It then passed in similar fashion through successive lifetime editions of Scott's collected poetry, and into Lockhart's posthumous collected edition of 1833–34 (8.382–86).

The present text follows that of the first volume of *A Select Collection of Original Irish Airs* (Edinburgh, [1814]), 11, as best representing the socialised text at the culmination of Scott's initial creative process. The headnote has been removed, as it is obviously the work of Thomson and not that of Scott himself. Following a pattern set for successive editions of Scott's collected editions by the 1820 *Poetical Works* (12.141–44), speech marks have been used to distinguish the enquiry made in the first stanza from the Harper's answer in the rest of the song, while the final line has been given single speech marks as a speech within a speech. Otherwise no emendations have been made.

Historical Note
In August 1691 William III (1650–1702) offered the Highland clans who had supported the former king a pardon on condition that they took the oath of allegiance to him in front of a magistrate before January 1692, and the exiled Stuart King James VII and II (1633–1701) eventually gave his consent to them to do so. Through no fault of his own Alastair MacIain Macdonald, 12th Chief of Glencoe, was late in taking the oath, but advantage was quickly taken by John Dalrymple, Secretary of State for Scotland and Lord Advocate (1648–1707), who, together with the rival Campbell clan chief, Archibald, 10th Earl of Argyll (d. 1703), persuaded King William to sign an order of extirpation against the Macdonalds of Glencoe, which was duly passed on to the military command in Scotland. A party of soldiers under Captain Robert Campbell of Glenlyon was billeted on the Macdonalds of Glencoe, ostensibly to collect taxes, and hospitably received by them, but during the early morning of 13 February 1692 the Campbell soldiers turned upon their hosts, murdering Macdonalds including the Chief himself, while many more died of exposure afterwards when their homes were burned.

Explanatory Notes
190.title   Glencoe   a narrow and desolate mountain glen about 16 km (10 miles) long through which the River Coe runs in N Argyllshire. From the entrance on the E at Rannoch Moor it forms a U-shape with the pass of Glencoe about half-way along and ends by opening out into Loch Leven near the village of Glencoe.
190.11   erne   the eagle.
190.22   snood   a ribbon bound around the brow and tied underneath the hair at the back of the neck, worn by young unmarried women, and a symbol of virginity.
190.23   distaff   a cleft stick on which wool or flax was wound for spinning, used as a symbol of woman's work more generally.
191.40   southron   southerner, including Lowland Scots as well as English people and indicating the wider political agency implicit in the actions of the Campbell soldiers.
191.48   Revenge for blood   an allusion perhaps to the blood feuds of clan society, where an affront to any member of a clan would be deemed to create an obligation to revenge it on all the other members. The massacre was a key episode in the feud between the Macdonalds and the Campbells.

75.   Lines Written in Susan Ferrier's Album

Textual Note
The original manuscript of these verses appears in Susan Ferrier's autograph album, numbered '13' amongst other poems, letters, and drawings by various distinguished people. The verses are subscribed by Scott 'Ashestiel [or Ashesteel] 13 October 1811', and underneath Ferrier has written 'Lines written by Walter Scott while the carriage was waiting to convey my Father & me from Ashestiel'. A microfilm containing the contents of the album, the original of which is still in the possession of Susan and David Irvine, descendants of Susan Ferrier's sister Jane Graham, is held in the National Library of Scotland (Mf. MSS 414). A pencilled transcript of the poem, taken from the autograph album, can also be found at NLS, MS 1750, ff. 111–12. In her subsequent 'Recollections of Visits to Ashistiel [*sic*] and Abbotsford', published posthumously in the liter-

ary magazine *Temple Bar* for February 1874, Ferrier enlarges on the circum-
stances of its inclusion there at the end of a brief visit by herself and her father:

> The night preceding our departure had blown a perfect hurricane; we were to leave
> immediately after breakfast, and while the carriage was preparing Mr. Scott stepped
> to a writing-table and wrote a few hurried lines in the course of a very few minutes;
> these he put into my hand as he led me to the carriage; they were an allusion to the
> storm, coupled with a friendly adieu, and are to be found in my autograph album.
> (40.329)

The magazine also prints the text of the poem, evidently for the first time, this
having not previously featured in any of the collected editions of Scott's verse.
Scott's original manuscript, as preserved in the microfilm, is evidently written
on both sides of a single leaf, and reveals only a handful of alterations made in
the course of composition (for example the substitution of 'beauty' for a repeti-
tive 'wonder' at line 17); it is also untitled as well as unpunctuated. To this the
printed version adds a conventional punctuation system while regularising some
spellings.

The present text follows the printed version in *Temple Bar*, 40 (February
1874), 329–30, while editorially supplying the title, and with the following
emendations:

192.20   Minstrel's (MS: Minstrels) / minstrel's
192.21   birks (MS) / birk
192.29   storms (MS) / storm
192.end-date   Ashestiel (MS?) / *Ashistiel*
                The MS lettering is unclear.

Historical Note
At the time of the visit, Susan Edmonstone Ferrier (1782–1854) had acquired
none of the literary fame which followed from the success of her first novel
Marriage in 1818, and which in turn led to Scott's nominating its author as
his successor when supposedly withdrawing from the genre himself at the end
of the third series of *Tales of My Landlord* (1819). Her father, James Ferrier
(1744–1826), as a Principal Clerk of Session, however, was a close colleague
of Scott's and chief intermediary in the protracted negotiations which led ulti-
mately in 1812 to Scott's receiving remuneration for his own Clerkship as a
result of his predecessor's at last agreeing to accept a pension (see *Letters*, 2.461;
3.1). It was in a letter of 18 September 1811 thanking Ferrier for his 'kind exer-
tions' that Scott invited father and daughter to visit him at his country residence
at Ashestiel:

> And now, my dear sir, Mrs. Scott and I make a joint petition, that if the weather be
> favourable in the beginning of October … Miss Ferrier and you would look in upon
> us for a quiet day or two. We will take great care to give Miss Ferrier a comfortable
> and well air'd room, and as we are near Melrose and some other shewplaces, I would
> fain hope we might make the time glide pleasantly away. (*Memoir and Correspondence
> of Susan Ferrier 1782–1854* (London, 1898), 237)

In the event, the weather proved to be 'infamous' (*Letters*, 3.10); and October
also found Scott in a frenzy of activity making plans for his recently-purchased
estate at Abbotsford, which at one point was narrowly saved from flooding
by the Tweed (3.12). As Susan Ferrier recalled: 'the weather was too broken
and stormy to admit of our enjoying any of the pleasant excursions our more
weather-proof host had intended for us' ('Recollections', 329). The resultant
impromptu verse epistle mirrors in some respect the Introduction to Canto

First in *Marmion* (1808), in looking beyond present anxieties to prospects in a more favourable season.

Explanatory Notes

191.4   summer bower   compare *Marmion* (1808), 'Introduction to Canto First': 'The daisy's flower / Again shall paint your summer bower' (lines 45–46); *Marmion*, ed. Ainsley McIntosh, EEWSP 2 (Edinburgh, 2018), 10.

191.6   tardy shocks   a *shock* is a group of sheaves of grain placed upright and supporting each other in order to permit drying and ripening. Here *tardy* suggests that these have been left out too long in view of the inclement season.

192.16   our cot   Scott refers familiarly to Ashestiel—actually a fairly substantial building rented by him from 1804 to 1812—as his 'cottage': a term also applied initially to its planned replacement at Abbotsford and reflecting a more general tendency at the time to describe country vacation residences in this way.

192.19–20   Melrose grey ... Minstrel's lay   alluding to Scott's *Lay of the Last Minstrel* (1805), and the famous lines there concerning Melrose Abbey (Canto 2, stanza 1).

192.21–22   Yarrow's birks ... rural song   referring to the pastoral song tradition of the Yarrow Valley, then considered as a kind of classic ground for such poetry; as well as perhaps more specifically to 'The Braes of Yarrow' by William Hamilton of Bangour (1704–54), and its repeated fourth line 'Puing the birks [plucking the birch] on the braes of Yarrow'. Compare also no. 19, 'Unpued on Yarrow's braes'.

192.29   Tweed   Ashestiel overlooks the river Tweed, some 10 km (6 miles) upstream from Scott's eventual home at Abbotsford. It was (and still is) an unusually remote place, 'eight miles from the nearest markettown [*sic*] and four from the nearest neighbour', as he described it to Lady Abercorn (*Letters*, 1.311).

76.   The Return to Ulster

Textual Note

The song-collector George Thomson (1757–1851) approached Scott on 14 November 1809 to write words for some Irish melodies (see Textual Note to no. 74, 'On the Massacre of Glencoe'), and Scott agreed to do this on 16 November (*Letters*, 2.271). Sending the tunes the following month, Thomson noted of the air by Carolan (see Historical Note) that it was 'fitted either for the wild, the grand, or the pensive, as seemeth good to the Muse' (BL, Add. MS 35,267, ff. 6v–8v). Scott was slow to fulfil this commission and it was almost two years later, on 28 November 1811, that he wrote to Thomson, 'I send you the *prima cura* [first draft] of the Irish song, reserving corrections till I know how you like it and how it suits the music. I am apt to write eleven instead of twelve syllables in this measure, which does well enough for metrical rhythm, but not for musical' (*Letters*, 3.24). Thomson replied enthusiastically on 2 December, 'I like the Irish Song extremely ... It will suit the Music perfectly. Will you have the goodness to put a note at the foot of the song, for the sake of those unacquainted with the localities of it?'. He enclosed his own transcription of Scott's lyrics for him to correct, preferring this 'in case I should be mistaken about any particular word' (BL, Add. MS 35,267, ff. 33v–34r).

On the transcription Thomson noted 'it so happens that *eleven* syllables suit the music better than twelve'. A comparison of Scott's manuscript (BL, Add. MS

35,264, ff. 44–45) with Thomson's transcription (BL, Add. MS 35,264, ff. 48–51) reveals a number of revisions, beyond the normal changes associated with the transmission of manuscript into print. Thomson shortened several lines from twelve syllables to eleven by removing a word, or substituting a single syllable word for a disyllabic one. For instance, in line 35 'endure' becomes 'bear'. Revisions in Scott's hand made on Thomson's transcription before returning it include changing 'Lofty' to 'High' (line 10), 'And avoided mine eye, while she lent me her ear' to 'And listed my lay while she turnd from mine eye' (line 26), and in the following line substituting 'too a vision' for 'form of my fancy'. The assumption must be that where he did not revise Thomson's transcription Scott accepted his alterations. 'The Return to Ulster' was first published in *A Select Collection of Original Irish Airs*, Vol. 1 (Edinburgh, [1814]), 1 (letterpress) and 2–3 (musical notation).

Subsequently 'The Return to Ulster' appeared, without a musical setting or indication of the tune, in Scott's *Poetical Works* of 1820 (12.137–40), then passing into the various collected poetry editions of Scott's lifetime and into Lockhart's posthumous collected edition of 1833–34 (8.379–81) without any alteration besides the normal changes associated with the work of the printer. Thomson reprinted the song with the music in *The Select Melodies of Scotland*, 5 vols (Edinburgh, 1822–23), 3.item 42, again without any sign of further authorial revision.

The present text follows that of *A Select Collection of Original Irish Airs*, Vol. 1 (Edinburgh, [1814]), 1, as best representing the culmination of Scott's initial creative process. A superfluous opening speech mark at the start of the final line has been omitted, but otherwise no emendations have been made.

Historical Note
The tune named for 'The Return to Ulster' as 'Young Terence Macdonough', also known as 'Lament for Terence MacDonough', is by Turlough Carolan (1670–1738), often considered to be Ireland's foremost national composer and in whose honour a harp festival is held each year at Keadue in County Roscommon. Blinded by smallpox at the age of eighteen, he travelled on horseback with his harp throughout Ireland composing songs for patrons. Thomson's setting was commissioned from Beethoven. As indicated above, when asking Scott to write lyrics Thomson supplied a metrical pattern and provided an indication of the melody's mood. He clearly anticipated that Scott would not be able to read the music himself, nor in all probability have an opportunity of getting it played or sung over to him. Indeed, a letter of Scott's, dated 2 December 1811 in Thomson's endorsement and which enclosed the corrected transcript, states 'I will call one morning to hear the melodies' (*Letters*, 3.47; BL, Add. MS 35,264, ff. 46–47). Scott added a footnote on Fingal's standard to the corrected transcript but, in response to Thomson's request for notes on the song's locations, commented that such details seemed 'scarce worth mentioning'. Thomson had also supposed that the 'wanderings' of the narrator in the opening lines referred to foreign parts and was therefore puzzled by the Irish place-names given, to which Scott responded, 'The sounds he refers to are those he has heard since his return as if a man returned from India should say I have again heard the sounds of the Tweed & Teviot & of the falls of Clyde' (BL, Add. MS 35,264, ff. 48–49).

Explanatory Notes
193.2 Lagan the River Lagan, about 86 km (54 miles) long, forms the boundary between County Antrim and County Down in Northern Ireland before falling into the sea at Belfast.

193.2   Bann   the Bann is the longest river in Ulster, running from its SE corner NE for about 129 km (80 miles).

193.3   Clanbrassil   in *Gaelic* Clann Bhreasil, the name of a Gaelic territory in what is now County Armagh.

193.4   Tullamore   in a note on the corrected draft of the poem (BL, Add. MS 35,264, ff. 48–49) Scott described Tullamore as 'a seat of Lord Clanbrassil remarkable for its cascades'. Tollymore, now a Forest Park, at the foot of the Mourne mountains in County Down was owned by James Hamilton, 2nd Earl of Clanbrassil (1730–98), and after his death without children passed to his sister. The river Shimna runs through the estate, which has many fine trees and garden follies.

193.12   Eden   garden in which Adam was placed by God before the fall of man in Genesis 2.15. The word signifies delight or pleasure.

193.17   Ultonia's   Ultonia was a former Irish province and kingdom, subsequently settled by English and Scottish Protestants. In 1920 it was divided, with six counties forming Northern Ireland and three forming part of the Republic of Ireland.

193.19   Fion   an Irish Gaelic name meaning 'fair' or 'white'. Fionn mac Cumhail, the mythical hunter-warrior of Irish myth, ate an enchanted salmon which made him wise, and fought against a giant together with his son Oisin and grandson Oscar. The Scottish version of his name, Fingal, is used in the Ossian poems of James Macpherson (1736–96).

193.21   harp of green Erin   Erin is the ancient name for Ireland, which is often symbolised by a harp.

193.footnote   *Sun-beam* of Macpherson   Fionn mac Cumhail features in the Ossian poems of James Macpherson. In Bk 4 of *Fingal* Macpherson wrote, 'We reared the sun-beam of battle; the standard of the king': see *The Poems of Ossian and Related Works*, ed. Howard Gaskill (Edinburgh, 1996), 87.

77.   Prologue to *Helga*

Textual Note

Scott's prologue was composed for the first performance on 22 January 1812 at Edinburgh's Theatre Royal of a play entitled *Helga, or The Rival Minstrels* by Sir George Steuart Mackenzie (1780–1848). Scott's autograph manuscript in NLS, MS 912, ff. 24–25, appears to be a working draft since it is substantially unpunctuated and contains numerous deletions and insertions as Scott tested out the wording of various lines. Line 19, for instance, reads 'Twas then that <bounded> ↑wafted↓ from <the boundless North> ↑a distant <a frozen> sky↓'. A second manuscript exists among copies of others of Scott's and Henry Mackenzie's theatrical prologues and epilogues among the Mackenzie papers in NLS, MS 6390, ff. 16–17, but this is not in Scott's own hand. Another Scott autograph manuscript, noted in the National Register of Archives for Scotland (NRAS, 200/12), cannot now be found. The prologue was printed, together with Henry Mackenzie's epilogue, in the *Caledonian Mercury* of 25 January 1812, and in the *Scots Magazine*, 74 (February 1812), 134–35, shortly after the first Edinburgh performance of the play. These printings of Scott's contribution probably represent the performance text, as adapted in-house and recorded by the press, and differ substantially from Scott's manuscript. For instance, in them the third line reads 'Tragic and comic muse before him came' and two lines are added between lines 26 and 27, 'While smoke and steam through frozen skies are tost, / And central earthquakes shake a land of frost—'. It seems unlikely that Scott himself played any part in the changes for performance.

The present text follows Scott's autograph manuscript (NLS, MS 912, ff. 24–25), since the versions published in Scott's lifetime were periodical texts outside his control. In addition to the following listed emendations ampersands have been routinely expanded to 'and', verb forms ending with 'd' to 'ed', and routine apostrophes have been introduced as required.

194.2   plann'd (Editorial) / plan'd
194.2   campaign: (Editorial) / campaign
194.4   Farce, Pastoral, Opera, (Editorial) / Farce Pastoral Opera
194.8   played. (Editorial) / playd
194.10   Man, monster and machine, (Editorial) / Man monster & machine
194.12   phrase, (Editorial) / phrase
194.12   ass: (Editorial) / ass
194.13   camel (Editorial) / Camel
194.14   rear. (Editorial) / rear
195.16   Theatric (Editorial) / theatric
195.26   glaciere (Editorial) / Glaciere
195.26   fire. (Editorial) / fire
195.30   arose: (Editorial) / arose
195.32   O'er (Editorial) / Oer
195.32   day. (Editorial) / day
195.34   sung. (Editorial) / sung
195.36   again: (Editorial) / again

Historical Note
The success at Edinburgh's Theatre Royal of Joanna Baillie's *The Family Legend* at the start of 1810 must have bolstered Scott's hope, in encouraging Henry Siddons (1774–1815) to take the management of the Edinburgh Theatre Royal, that it might support a national drama freed of 'the garbage of melo-drama and pantomime' of the previous regime (*Letters*, 2.118). Trouble was taken to present Sir George Steuart Mackenzie's new play, *Helga, or The Rival Minstrels* as a worthy successor to it, the *Edinburgh Evening Courant* of 18 January 1812 declaring that 'if Helga be as successful as the Family Legend, there can be no doubt but we shall find many gentlemen of literary abilities willing to come forward to assist the drama of the country'. Icelandic scenery was painted by J. F. Williams and, as with Baillie's play, Scott and Henry Mackenzie wrote a Prologue and Epilogue for it.

Sir George Steuart Mackenzie was a baronet, geologist and antiquary, who had visited Iceland in 1810 and, as well as forming an impressive collection of mineralogical specimens, subsequently published *Travels in the Island of Iceland during the Summer of MDCCCX* (Edinburgh, 1811). His play is based upon the plot of *Gunnlaugs ok Skald-Rafni Saga*, as summarised in a lengthy footnote (30–32) to an essay by Henry Holland on Icelandic history and literature in this book. Unfortunately, Mackenzie's play was unsuccessful, the first-night audience rendering the whole tragedy ludicrous. Scott himself reported to Joanna Baillie that 'even those who went as the authors friends caught the infection and laughd most heartily all the while they were applauding' (*Letters*, 3.101). Initially, according to the *Caledonian Mercury* of 25 January, Sir George hoped to revise it for a second performance, but ultimately decided to withdraw his play. Scott's letter to Baillie contains no mention of the prologue as his own composition, although it seems to have been widely known as his work. Very probably Scott wished to dissociate himself from Mackenzie's play, and this may also be the reason why this prologue was not printed in the successive lifetime editions of his *Poetical Works* nor in the Lockhart 1833–34 posthumous edition.

Explanatory Notes

194.2   Our stage-director   Henry Siddons had taken the management of the Theatre Royal, Edinburgh in 1809. He is also the 'Chief Theatric' of line 16.

194.3   The Tragic Muse, the Comic   the nine muses, daughters of Zeus and Mnemosyne, were identified with individual arts and sciences, Melpomene being the muse of tragedy and Thalia the muse of comedy. For the 1811–12 season Henry Siddons had moved the theatre back from Leith Walk to the Shakespeare Square building, which had statues of Comedy and Tragedy on the roofline: see James C. Dibdin, *The Annals of the Edinburgh Stage* (Edinburgh, 1888), 265.

194.12   In Hamlet's phrase   *Hamlet*, 2.2.397.

194.13   Car, camel, war-horse   typifying the novelties offered in Regency Christmas and New Year theatrical shows.

194.13   water-dog   a holiday entertainment advertised as an 'Aquatic Melo Drama' was performed at the Theatre Royal on 23 December 1811 (see the *Caledonian Mercury* of that date), entitled *The Caravan; or, The Driver, and his Dog Carlo*, for which the last scene was to include 'Real Water for the Dog'.

194.14   Bluebeard's elephant   following the success of the seasonal Christmas holiday extravaganza by George Colman, *Blue-Beard; or Female Curiosity* (1798), the French fairy-tale 'Bluebeard' of Charles Perrault (1628–1703) was generally given an Eastern setting for seasonal end-of-year melodramas or pantomimes, with stuffed figures of horses, elephants and camels appearing on stage.

195.16   young Ammon's voice   an oracular voice, the temple of Jupiter Ammon of Libya being famous for its oracle, once consulted by Hercules.

195.17   Athenians of the North   citizens of Edinburgh, whose neo-classical monuments imitated those of ancient Athens.

195.31   historic lay   perhaps an allusion to the source of Mackenzie's play in an Icelandic saga. Sagas are histories describing events that took place among Icelandic families in the 10th and 11th centuries, although these were in fact prose narratives.

195.33   In monarchs' halls   like Thomas Percy (1729–1811) Scott believed that ballads and other forms of early poetry were originally the creation of single bards or minstrels employed by a king or chieftain, a theory supported by the treatment of Icelandic Scalds in Mackenzie's book and in *Helga*.

195.36   Runic rhymes   ancient poetry written using an alphabet in use among the Gothic tribes of northern Europe.

195.38   Our wandering bard   Edgar, depicted as a renowned Icelandic minstrel, is the hero of *Helga, or The Rival Minstrels*, and prior to the action of the play has defeated his rival Haco in a poetic contest at the court of Sweden.

78.   For the Anniversary Meeting of the Pitt Club of Scotland, 1814

Textual Note

Probably the earliest surviving printing of this song is found in the form of an apparently unique copy of a broadside, now held by Edinburgh University

Library (Special Collections, De.1.13). Headed '*For the Anniversary Meeting of the PITT CLUB of Scotland*, 1814', and measuring approx. 32.5 x 19.5 cm, it contains the text of the song on one side only. A tear down the left-hand side suggests possible detachment from a larger document, though there is the fully visible watermark of 'C WILMOTT / 1810'. The text of the song also appears as the second item, along with nine others, in an undated 16-page pamphlet, *Songs Sung at the Anniversary Dinner of The Pitt Club of Scotland, May 28, 1814*, printed by James Ballantyne in Edinburgh. It is presumably to this pamphlet that Scott is referring in the postscript of a letter of 3 June to Matthew Weld Hartstonge: 'they have published the songs together—I send two copies' (*Letters*, 3.449). The fullness of the heading for each individual song there, and dissimilar print fonts used for separate items, suggest that Ballantyne might have recycled existing settings of each in haste to assemble the pamphlet.

According to Scott's letter to Hartstonge, this proved less successful than 'For A' That' (no. 79), the second of his two songs for the event, when performed: 'The serious song did not tell very well as indeed both its length and the slowness of the tune were an objection, it was however well enough received' (*Letters*, 3.449). It nevertheless proved to be a lasting favourite at the Club, and was performed regularly in succeeding meetings, if sometimes in truncated form. (Versions in two later surviving collections of *Songs Sung* printed by Ballantyne, one for the 1816 meeting and the other without a date, have only the first three stanzas.) Evidence of its popularity at the time is also found in a number of contemporary transcripts, one by Susan Ferrier (Edinburgh University Library, Dk.3.8.10), another by an unidentified hand fastened into a copy of the eighth edition (1808) of *The Lay of the Last Minstrel* (Glasgow University Library, BD 19-a.11), the latter of which also includes several variants ('autumn' not 'Harvest', line 23; 'Warriors' not 'Heroes', line 35).

Excluding several contemporary newspaper reports, the next significant printings occurred in the *Scots Magazine*, 76 (July 1814), 536, and the *Edinburgh Annual Register, for 1813*, 6: 1 and 2 (1815), cccxl—both of which acknowledge Scott as the author. Apart from minor printing changes, neither differs significantly from the original version. The first substantive change occurs with the 1820 *Poetical Works* (12.226–28), where in line 6 'accept' is changed to 'take', possibly in an effort to improve scansion. This is followed by succeeding editions of the *Poetical Works*, which themselves make only minor changes of the kind normally associated with the work of the printer. The last substantive change occurs in the Lockhart posthumous 1833–34 set (11.309–11), where in line 29 'and' is substituted for 'or', leading to an arguably less forceful 'success and disaster'. None of the above-mentioned texts supply music, or give any other indication of tune.

The present text follows the broadside '*For the Anniversary Meeting of the PITT CLUB of Scotland*, 1814', EUL, De.1.13, as probably representing the first authorised printing, and without emendation.

Historical Note
This is one of two songs by Scott as performed at the inaugural dinner of the Pitt Club of Scotland held in the Assembly Rooms in Edinburgh on Saturday, 28 May 1814. Newly instituted on 20 May that year, the Pitt Club of Scotland followed the procedure of the London Pitt Club (founded 1793, reconstituted 1808) in commemorating the birthday of the statesman and patriot William Pitt the Younger (1759–1806). A large number of Pitt Clubs throughout Britain were founded in 1813–14, encouraged by the mounting allied successes against Napoleon, which were viewed by Tory supporters as vindicating the severe

measures introduced by Pitt in the earlier days of the war against France. According to the report in the *Caledonian Mercury* on 30 May 'about 500 noblemen and gentlemen' attended the Edinburgh dinner, at which a succession of toasts were given and songs performed: 'The singing certainly surpassed that at any former public meeting of the same description in Scotland; and a great many new songs, written for the occasion, were sung.' Prior to his return to Edinburgh for the summer legal term, Scott had responded with increasing delight to the news of the Duke of Wellington's victory at Toulouse, ending the Peninsular War, the Allies' occupation of Paris, and Napoleon's abdication. On 30 May, only days after the dinner, the 1st Treaty of Paris between the Allies and France was signed, bringing an apparent close to a sequence of almost uninterrupted hostilities over more than twenty years. As a whole the song offers a valuable insight into Scott's jubilant response to unfolding military and political events, at a time when he was rapidly completing his first novel, *Waverley*, published early in July of the same year.

Explanatory Notes

196.2   Marengo   the battle of Marengo, fought between the French and Austrian armies, in Piedmont, Italy, on 14 June 1800. The defeat of the Austrians, with some 8000 taken prisoner and 6500 dead or wounded, led to their suspending operations in Italy and strengthened the position of the victorious Napoleon as First Consul of France. It also threw into disarray British plans to aid the Austrians, and seriously undermined the Allies' coalition against France. According to John Ehrman, 'The spring and summer of 1800 may be said to have witnessed the nadir in the British management of the war': *The Younger Pitt: The Consuming Struggle* (London, 1996), 372.

196.4   closed in his anguish the map of her reign   compare Scott in *The Life of Napoleon Buonaparte*, 9 vols (Edinburgh, 1827): 'Even Pitt himself, upon whose declining health the misfortune made a most unfavourable impression, had considered the defeat of Marengo as a conclusion to the hopes of success against France for a considerable period: "Fold up the map", he said, pointing to that of Europe, "it will not be again opened for these twenty years".' (4.289). Other accounts associate this with Pitt shortly before his death early in 1806 on hearing news of the defeat of the Austrian and Russian armies at the battle of Austerlitz and the ensuing armistice which left large parts of Europe in the hands of the French.

196.11–13   sow it in sorrow ... reap in their gladness   compare Psalm 126.5.

196.25   HIS grey head   referring to King George III (1738–1820), who having suffered various bouts of illness, had become blind and permanently deranged from 1811, though retaining a large degree of popularity, especially among Tory supporters.

196.28   his SON   George IV (1762–1830), who had become Prince Regent in 1811. According to newspaper reports, the first two toasts at the dinner were to The King and The Prince Regent.

197.37   WELLINGTON'S cup   Arthur Wellesley, 1st Duke of Wellington (1769–1852), commander of the victorious British forces during the Peninsular War, and created Duke in 1814. Toasted as The Duke of Wellington at the dinner.

197.38   DALHOUSIE   George Ramsay, 9th Earl of Dalhousie (1770–1838), commander of the 7th Division during the later stages of the Peninsular War under Wellington, appointed Lieutenant-General in 1813. Dalhousie had been granted the freedom of the City of Edinburgh alongside Scott at a dinner given by the Lord Provost on 5 January 1814 (see *Edinburgh Annual Register, for 1814*, 7: 1 and 2 (1816), 'Chronicle', iv–v).

197.38 GRÆME General Sir Thomas Graham, 1st Baron Lynedoch (1748–1843), veteran of the wars with France, and likewise engaged as a commander in the Peninsular War under Wellington. The final toast at the dinner, according to the *Caledonian Mercury* of 30 May, was to 'The Earl of Dalhousie, Lords Niddry, and Lyndock [*sic*], whose warlike exertions have so much redounded to the honour of themselves and of Scotland'.

79. For A' That an' A' That

Textual Note
No surviving copy of this song as a single broadside has been discovered. However, the text of the song features anonymously as the eighth of ten items in *Songs Sung at the Anniversary Dinner of The Pitt Club of Scotland, May 28, 1814*, printed by James Ballantyne shortly after the event. It then appeared, along with Scott's other anniversary 'Song' on the occasion (see no. 78), and similarly attributed to him as author, in the *Scots Magazine* for July 1814 (76.535). Here at line 25 'choke' is changed to 'chock', and 'sleight' at line 29 becomes 'slight', making the internal rhyme more visible; the apostrophe is also shifted at line 36 to create 'father's' rather than 'fathers''. Otherwise, apart from some minor changes to punctuation and the raising/lowering of initial letters, the text follows that found in Ballantyne's compilation. Unlike Scott's other song this was evidently not taken up by the *Edinburgh Annual Register*, possibly as a result of Scott having second thoughts about its suitability for his established canon. In turn, this song was not included in any of the collected editions of Scott's *Poetical Works* until the posthumous 1833–34 edition (10.360–61), where a footnote describes it as having been 'Sung at the first meeting of the Pitt Club of Scotland; and published in the Scots Magazine for July, 1814'. This final version contains one substantive change compared with the earlier texts, with 'They ca'd America, that' (line 34) being changed to 'America they ca' that', perhaps in an effort to improve rhythm and/or sense, though some of the import of the original is lost in the process.

The present text follows that in *Songs Sung at the Anniversary Dinner of The Pitt Club of Scotland, May 28, 1814*, 13–14, as representing the first surviving authorised printing, and without emendation.

Historical Note
This is the second of two songs attributable to Scott that were performed at the anniversary dinner of the Pitt Club of Scotland on 28 May 1814. According to his letter to Matthew Weld Hartstonge of 3 June it went down better with the audience than its more 'serious' companion: 'The other had an excellent effect' (*Letters*, 3.449). In addition to its greater jauntiness, the words as well as probably the accompanying tune would have been recognisable as bearing a similarity to Robert Burns's song of the same title (Kinsley, no. 482), perhaps now most famous for its line 'A Man's a Man for a' that'. Here Scott can be seen boisterously, and somewhat unashamedly, transferring Burns's original democratic sentiments into more loyalist and militaristic terms, creating in the process something of a jingoistic parody. The range of events celebrated in this song is also extended in the final full stanza to encompass Britain's recent and ongoing war with America in addition to the Allies' recent triumph over Napoleon. No direct indication of a prescribed tune has been discovered, though the air

suggested by the title was a common one, with previous Jacobite associations: see, for example, 'Though Geordie reigns in Jamie's stead', in Joseph Ritson, *Scotish Songs*, 2 vols (London, 1794: *ALC*), 2.102–05. For further information on the tune, a variant of 'Lady Macintosh's Reel' from Robert Bremner's *A Collection of Scots Reels* (1759), 52, see Commentary to Kinsley no. 84 (3.1160).

Explanatory Notes
197.3   leilfu'   lawful, just.
197.4   bear the grie   win the prize. A direct echo of Burns's 'For a' That': 'Shall bear the gree, and a' that' (line 36).
197.4   for a' that   in the sense of 'in spite of that'.
197.7   Fleur-de-lis   *French* flower of the lily, a traditional emblem of the French monarchy, and replacing the revolutionary tricolour after the restoration of the House of Bourbon in 1814.
197.10–13   Rose ... Shamrock ... Thistle   national emblems respectively of England, Ireland, and Scotland.
197.12   Wellington made bra' that   alluding to the Anglo-Irish origins and military successes of Arthur Wellesley, 1st Duke of Wellington (1769–1852), who was himself born in Ireland.
197.14   misca'   disparage, slander.
197.15   shelter'd in her solitude   at the end of the 18th century, Holyroodhouse in Edinburgh had provided a home for the Comte d'Artois, younger brother of the executed Louis XVI of France, later crowned Charles X after the restoration of the Bourbons.
198.17–19   Austrian Vine ... Prussian Pine ... Spanish Olive   Austria, Prussia, and Spain, alongside the United Kingdom, were partners in the Sixth Coalition against France (1812–14), which finally led to Napoleon's defeat and exile on Elba. The three countries are characterised by prominent agricultural products.
198.18   Blucher's sake   referring to Gebhard Leberecht von Blücher (1742–1819), Prussian Field Marshal, who led his army in the campaign to defeat Napoleon in 1813–14, then later in support of Wellington at the battle of Waterloo in 1815.
198.21–24   Russia's Hemp ... his gra-vat   hemp had been cultivated in Russia for a long time, and was a major source for the ropes employed in shipping. In 1807 Napoleon signed a treaty with Russia to cut off imports to Britain, but the Czar failed to enforce the treaty and an illegal trade continued. Napoleon's unsuccessful invasion of Russia was partly intended to cut off the supply to Britain, and the Royal Navy was dependent on Russian hemp to stay afloat during the war with the United States in 1812. The term 'gravat', as well as referring to a neckcloth, was used figuratively for the hangman's noose (often preceded by 'hempen'); the spelling, as opposed to 'cravat', is a peculiarly Scottish one.
198.27   Devil's Elbo'   the Devil's Elbow was a name used for the dungeon vaults in Edinburgh Castle, whose occupants included those accused of treason as well as soldiers captured during the Napoleonic Wars.
198.35   coward plot her rats had got   the American declaration of war in 1812 was partly a response to British Orders in Council that attempted to prohibit American trade with France, a measure that was deeply unpopular with British merchants such as cotton manufacturers. The 'rats' mentioned here refer not only to rodents, but deserters from a cause, among these in this case probably Whig opponents of the war whose views were voiced, for instance, in the *Edinburgh Review*.

198.37 **top-gallant high** on a square-rigged vessel, the top-gallant sail is that on the highest mast or *top-gallant mast*; here signifying a warship at full speed. More broadly this stanza refers to British naval successes during the Anglo–American War of 1812–14.

198.40 **kames in hand to claw that** a *kame* in Scots is a comb or rake: applied here in the sense of administering a severe drubbing.

80. Pharos loquitur

Textual Note
This item was originally written by Scott in the Visitor's Album at the Bell Rock Lighthouse on 30 July 1814, near the beginning of a tour of inspection taking in the northern and western isles of Scotland on the Lighthouse Yacht, embarked on shortly after the publication of his first novel *Waverley*. According to Robert Stevenson (see also below), in *An Account of the Bell Rock Light-House … Drawn up by Desire of the Commissioners of the Northern Light-Houses* (Edinburgh, 1824): *ALC*: 'They [the Commissioners] breakfasted in the library, when Sir Walter, at the entreaty of the party, upon inscribing his name in the *album*, added the interesting lines, of which the reader will find a fac-simile on the second title-page' (419). The album in question cannot now be located. However, as Stevenson's comment above suggests, a plate containing a facsimile of the original in Scott's handwriting is found (under an engraved drawing of the lighthouse itself) facing page 64 in the *Account of the Bell Rock Light-House*. The text here is unpunctuated and without marks of alteration, the latter element possibly suggesting an element of tidying up on the engraver's part; though it is unlikely that Stevenson, who sought Scott's approval with proofs of the volume's Dedication to the King (see NLS, MS 785, f. 3), would have allowed any significant interference. At least two alternative versions of the lines were apparently in circulation prior to the publication of the *Account*. A manuscript volume titled 'Reliques of Rank and Ability &c., collected MDCCCXIV', now in private hands, contains a punctuated version verbally identical to that in the *Account*, apart from the appearance of 'wide' rather than 'wild' ('wide shelves') in the second line: see William Zachs, *'Breathes There A Man': Sir Walter Scott 200 Years Since Waverley* (Edinburgh, 2014), 26–27. In the summer of 1817 the French marine engineer Charles Dupin (1784–1873) also visited the Bell Rock Lighthouse, and saw Scott's verses in the album there, subsequently offering both a transcript and 'une imitation très-libre [a very free imitation]' of his own in French (*Mémoires sur la marine et les ponts at chaussées de France et d'Angleterre* (Paris, 1818), 95–96; reprinted in *Two Excursions to the Ports of England, Scotland, and Ireland 1816, 1817, and 1818* (London, 1819), 40). It was apparently from this source that the verses were extracted in various periodicals, including the *Caledonian Mercury* of 30 November 1818. Apart from the addition of punctuation, the lowering of the initial letters in 'Night' and 'Seaman', and the substitution of 'hails … sails' for 'hail … sail' at the ends of the final two lines, Dupin's text matches that of the 1824 facsimile. While the poem was not reprinted in any of the lifetime editions of Scott's poetry, it did feature in the Lockhart posthumous set of 1833–34, 10.[355], as the first of a sequence of 'Occasional Pieces, not contained in any former edition'. The presence there as a footnote of an extract from Stevenson's *Account* suggests strongly that the latter's facsimile provided the copy-text, to which that edition adds conventional punctuation.

The present text is based on the facsimile in *An Account of the Bell Rock Light-House* (Edinburgh, 1824), facing p. 64, with the following emendations:

199.2   keep. (Editorial) / keep
199.4   night, (Editorial) / Night
199.5   seaman (Editorial) / Seaman
199.6   sail. (Editorial) / sail

Historical Note
Situated out at sea some 40 km (25 miles) E of Dundee and 20 km (12½ miles) SE of Arbroath, the Bell Rock Lighthouse was considered one of the greatest engineering feats of its day. Previously the largely-submerged reef on which it stood, also known as the Cape Rock or Inch Cape, had proved an exceptional hazard to ships navigating the eastern coast of Scotland, either forcing them too far inland or outward towards the exposed North Sea, and in stormy weather effectively closing off the Firths of Tay and Forth. According to legend a fourteenth-century Abbot of Aberbrothick (Arbroath) had caused a warning bell to be placed on the rock, though this lasted for only a year before it was taken by a Dutch pirate. This story was the foundation of a quasi-supernatural poem 'The Inchcape Rock' (1803), by Robert Southey (1774–1843), which Scott can be found transcribing from memory in 1809 (see *Letters*, 2.227), and which was published anonymously in the *Edinburgh Annual Register, for 1810* (1812).

Navigational difficulties in Scott's own time were exacerbated by wartime conditions, with a gale lasting three days in December 1799 destroying over 70 ships around the Scottish coastline, and the warship HMS *York* running aground on the Bell Rock with all hands lost. The construction of the lighthouse, in the face of initial apathy from the Northern Lighthouse Commissioners and against apparently insuperable physical odds, was largely propelled through the efforts of Robert Stevenson (1772–1850), grandfather of the novelist Robert Louis Stevenson (1850–94), with construction proper beginning in 1807 and the oil-fed beacon being lit for the first time in 1811. Stevenson as engineer and chief executive to the Northern Lighthouse Board also served as the main guide to the Commissioners on the inspection voyage of the northern lighthouses in summer 1814, which Scott eagerly joined as a guest. Scott's admiration for the Bell Rock Lighthouse, both in terms of its sublime effect and practical efficiency, is recorded in the entry for 30 July, a day after having set sail from Leith, in his Diary of the voyage:

> Waked at six by the steward: summoned to visit the Bell-Rock, where the beacon is well worthy attention. Its dimensions are well known; but no description can give the idea of this slight, solitary, round tower, trembling amid the billows ... You enter by a ladder of rope, with wooden steps, about thirty feet from the bottom, where the mason-work ceases to be solid, and admits of round apartments. ... Breakfasted in the parlour. (*Life*, 3.137).

Lockhart's footnote at this point reiterates the point that that it was at breakfast that Scott on request had 'penned immediately the lines', citing the 1833–34 *Poetical Works*, whose own source is Robert Stevenson's *Account* of 1824. In his later MS 'Reminiscences' (1850) of the voyage Stevenson gave a fuller version of events following breakfast:

> This over the Album was produced for signatures—but when it came to Sir Walter Mr [William] Erskine laid his hand upon the page and said 'Now Scott, you must give us some thing more than Walter Scott'—he wished to decline for the present and rather seemed uneasy at the proposal and rising from the table he looked out of the window for two or three minutes and again took his seat Erskine still remonstrating— when Sir Walter at last took the pen and with a somewhat grave expression wrote the ... lines (NLS, MS 3831, pp. 9–11).

Granted that Scott was extemporising under pressure, it is not impossible that his mind turned to the recently-published decasyllabic couplets of Southey's poem, the images of doomed sailors and dark forces at work depicted there now countered at least in part through the 'lustre' of Enlightenment scientific achievement.

Explanatory Notes

199.title 'Pharos loquitur' in *Latin* signifies 'the lighthouse speaks' or 'the lighthouse is speaking'. Scott would also have been aware of the Lighthouse of Alexandria, a tower built on the island of Pharos, and one of the Seven Wonders of the Ancient World. Pharos was also the name of a floating vessel used during the construction of the lighthouse, and was also adopted as the name for a new yacht built for the Northern Lighthouse Commissioners in 1816 (*Account of the Bell Rock Light-House*, 115, 419).

199.2 wild shelves the Bell Rock consisted of a sandstone reef extending about 1400 feet, mostly lying underwater.

199.3 ruddy gem compare Scott's description of the Light at Bell Rock in a letter to his wife Charlotte of 30 July 1814: 'It consists of three or four most immense brilliant lamps combined with reflectors. Two of these shine through coloured glass-shades one of these shades is of a dark red and the other a brilliant red—The whole machine moves round by Clock work so that turning slowly round the Sailors see first a bright white light then a bright red one then a dark red one' (NLS, MS 1551, f. 164r).

199.6 strike … sail lower or take down sail(s) (in fear of a storm, or sometimes as a sign of surrender).

81.   Epistle to His Grace the Duke of Buccleuch

Textual Note

The original letter addressed to 'His Grace / The Duke of Buccleuch & Queensberry / &c &c &c / Dalkeith House / Edinburgh', and comprising this verse epistle, is held in the National Records of Scotland [NRS], GD224/32/1/19. It consists of two sheets of paper, each folded to make a 4-page booklet, and of which only five pages carry the text of the poem, the individual leaves measuring approx. 25.2 x 20.1 cm. Each sheet bears the watermark 'J WHATMAN / 1810', and there are two postmarks, one illegible and the other dated 23 August 1814. The letter is endorsed in another hand 'Poetical letter / from Walter Scott / 1814'. The text of the epistle appears to have been written spontaneously and contains only local alterations, most apparently made in the course of composition, with Scott in the third line for instance immediately opting for 'isles' in place of 'land'. Punctuation throughout is limited, with a preference for dashes over more conventional marks, though some care has evidently been taken at points to prevent the reader misconstruing meaning. Scott adds his name (as 'W. Scott') at the foot of the first main part of the epistle, which itself may have been written in stages; while the following 'Postscript' is subscribed 'Kirkwall Orkney 13 Augt 1814'.

Scott's lines did not appear in any of the lifetime collected editions of poetry, nor in the posthumous Lockhart set of 1833–34. The first known printing (minus the original footnotes) is found in 1837 in Lockhart's *Life* of Scott (3.279–83), where a fuller punctuation system is supplied. There are also a number of substantive verbal differences, in some of which the hand of Lockhart might be suspected. In the third line, for example, Scott's original 'where Dawn at morning weaves' is changed to 'where dewy Morning weaves', presumably in an effort to remove an assumed tautology. It was this version of the text which was followed in later collections of Scott's verse, such as the one-volume *Poetical Works* of 1841 (641–42), and which is still in place in J. Logie Robertson's *The Poetical Works of Sir Walter Scott* in 1904 (719–22). A transcript of the autograph letter, with only very minor deviations from the original, subsequently appeared in the Grierson edition of Scott's *Letters* (3.481–85).

The present text is based on the autograph letter in NRS, GD224/32/1/19. Ampersands however have been routinely expanded, verb forms ending with 'd' normally interpreted as 'ed', apostrophes supplied as required, and full stops provided at the end of verse paragraphs where absent. No attempt has been made to provide a full range of punctuation, however, granted the sense remains clear, and in particular a number of rhetorically implied questions have been left unmarked. The signature 'W. Scott' after the main part of the epistle has been removed; while the title (matching that used in Logie Robertson) has been supplied editorially. The following emendations have also been made:

199.date	8 August (Editorial) / 8th. Augt
200.25	Lady, (Editorial) / Lady
200.32	colonnade (Editorial) / colonade
200.34	cormorant. (Editorial) / cormorant
201.51	vessel's (Editorial) / vessell's
201.57	heaven: (Editorial) / heaven
201.footnote	off (Editorial) / of
202.83	comrades (Editorial) / comerades
202.84	cabin-skylight (Editorial) / cabbin-skylight
202.85	rays, (Editorial) / rays
202.87	trimm'd (Editorial) / trimd
202.96	Scalloway-bay: (Editorial) / Scalloway-bay
202.100	whale. (Editorial) / whale
203.116	those. (Editorial) / those
203.120	Bowhill. (Editorial) / Bowhill
203.140	hanged. (Editorial) / hanged

Historical Note
These lines were composed during a tour of inspection by the Northern Lighthouse Yacht in the summer of 1814, which Scott had joined as a guest at Leith on 29 July, visiting the Bell Rock Lighthouse off Arbroath a day later, where his 'Pharos loquitur' inscription was written (see no. 80 and Notes). Sailing further northward, the vessel anchored at Lerwick, the capital of the Shetland Islands, on 4 August, with Scott making various excursions on the following three days, including a rowing-boat trip to the adjacent small islands of Bressay and Noss, and an inland journey to Scalloway on the opposite side of the main island. After dinner on 8 August the Lighthouse Yacht arrived back at Lerwick, and it was probably after the party had reassembled on board for a late evening departure that Scott commenced his epistle. Between 9 and 11 August the vessel was at sea, on a journey southwards to Orkney, during which Scott again suffered the effects of the Sumburgh Rost (a dangerous tidal stream) off the southernmost tip of Shetland, and at which point possibly the main part of the Epistle was concluded. He then witnessed from offshore the dissection of a mass of beached whales along the coast of the small island of Sanday, as the boat proceeded towards Kirkwall, capital of the Orkney Islands, where it reached harbour early in the morning of 12 August. The above and immediately

following occurrences are also recorded in some detail in the Diary that Scott wrote during the trip, which subsequently formed five chapters in Lockhart's *Life* (see 3.134–277), and a number of overlaps indicate that its record of the visits to Shetland and the Orkney Islands was written collaterally with the Epistle to Buccleuch. Scott's somewhat unflattering account of Kirkwall in the Epistle ("Tis a base little burgh both dirty & mean': see line 137), matches the commencement of his Diary entry for 12 August: 'Upon landing we find it but a poor and dirty place, especially towards the harbour' (*Life*, 3.184). This initial disappointment is mitigated in the Diary by the antiquarian interest of the Cathedral and Earl of Orkney's Palace (see also notes to 203.139 and 203.140 below), which the Epistle in contrast passes over hurriedly. Scott expressed disappointment in finding no letters for him from Edinburgh at Kirkwall (*Life*, 3.188), and it seems likely that the Epistle was brought to a close quickly in order to find a means of conveyance before the Lighthouse Yacht set sail again early on 14 August.

Explanatory Notes
199.1–2 Chieftain … true minstrel Scott is jointly addressing Charles William Henry Scott, 4th Duke of Buccleuch (1772–1819), as his clan leader, and the Duke's wife, Harriet Katherine Townshend (1773–1814), as her supposed Minstrel. Scott had intended to dedicate his forthcoming poem *The Lord of the Isles* (1815) to the Duchess, but was shocked to hear of her death on returning from the cruise: see *Letters*, 3.502.
199.4 chaplet string of beads or wreath.
199.10 *cradle* of the Cape of Noss as Scott's footnote describes, a device consisting of ropes and a small wooden chair for carrying men and sheep over the chasm. The Isle of Noss, 'a detached and precipitous rock, or island' (*Life*, 3.150) is separated by a narrow sound from Bressay, close to Lerwick to the E, and has cliffs rising to 183 m.
199.14 sea mew the common gull.
200.25 Lady, the worst thy presence alluding to the charitable works of Harriet, Duchess of Buccleuch (see also note to 199.1–2). Compare James Hogg's lament on her death near the end of his poem *The Pilgrims of the Sun* (1815): 'She comes not now our land to bless, / Or to cherish the poor and the fatherless, / Who lift to heaven the tearful eye / Bewailing their loss—and well may I!': *Midsummer Night Dreams and Related Poems*, ed. Jill Rubenstein (Edinburgh, 2008), 50.
200.28 proud Drumlanrig to my humble home Scott is contrasting Drumlanrig Castle, 28 km (17½ miles) NW of Dumfries, acquired by the Duke of Buccleuch in 1810 and which was undergoing extensive improvements, with his own home at Abbotsford, purchased in 1811, and as yet consisting mainly of the original farmhouse.
200.41 industrious Dutchman traditionally Dutch sailing vessels had arrived every summer to fish the rich herring grounds off Shetland. See Samuel Hibbert, *A Description of the Shetland Islands* (Edinburgh, 1822), 499–500. As Scott's footnote suggests, the victory of the allies over Napoleon in spring 1814 had alleviated a situation whereby the Dutch had been effectively blockaded from the trade.
200.42 Brassa's shore Bressay is an island 10 km (6 miles) long which lies slightly E of Lerwick, providing a natural breakwater for Lerwick's harbour: a customary rendezvous for the Dutch ships (see Hibbert, *Shetland Islands*, 499).
200.44 Lerwick the chief town of Shetland. It is 35 km (22 miles) NE of Sumburgh Head, itself at the southernmost tip of Shetland.

200.46 Wellington victory by Arthur Wellesley, 1st Duke of Wellington (1769–1852), at Toulouse on 10 April 1814 had brought an end to the Peninsular War, leading to the first Treaty of Paris between the allies and France at the end of the following month.

200.footnote schuyt a Dutch flat-bottomed boat.

201.47 Greenland tar referring to sailors on whaling ships from ports such as Hull and Dundee, which regularly called at Lerwick, where islanders joined them for expeditions to Greenland and the Davis Straits. The presence of 'nine fine vessels … lying in the harbour' was noted by Scott in his Diary entry from Lerwick of 4 August, as too the unruly behaviour of their non-islander crewmembers onshore (*Life*, 3.142).

201.52 captive Norse-man the presence of 'a Norwegian prize lying in the Sound of Lerwick, sent in by one of our cruisers', is noted retrospectively in Scott's Diary entry for 11 August (*Life*, 3.179). Ships were occasionally captured during the conflict between Denmark-Norway and the British navy during the Napoleonic wars, the last major fight taking place in July 1812, and with two Danish vessels being taken that August.

201.66 Latian belonging to Latium, region in central Italy in which the city of Rome was founded and grew to be the capital of the Roman Empire.

201.76 Scald minstrel of the ancient Scandinavians.

201.77 Fair-haired Harold Harald Harfagri (Harfagri means 'fair hair'), first king of all Norway, who conquered the Shetland Islands in 875.

201.80 Mousa's castled coast Mousa is an island in Dunrossness parish, Shetland, near the E coast of the mainland, about 18 km (11 miles) S of Lerwick, and 16 km (10 miles) NE of Sumburgh Head. Scott describes a visit to the 'Pictish fortress' (Broch) there in his Diary entry for 9 August (*Life*, 3.166–67).

201.81 Sumburgh-rost as Scott's footnote indicates, a tidal race below Sumburgh Head, at the extreme S of the mainland of Shetland. The drastic effect of this on the return voyage from Shetland is recorded in Scott's Diary entry of 10 August (see *Life*, 3.170–71).

202.82 bald disjointed lines compare *1 Henry IV*, 1.3.64.

202.89 bolt sprit pole or spar extending forward from a vessel's prow.

202.93 Kraken fabulous sea monster. Hibbert comments that the 'kraken or horven, which appears like a floating island, sending forth tentacula as high as the masts of a ship' is a monster sometimes recognised in the seas around Shetland (*Shetland Islands*, 565). The Duke of Buccleuch had humorously requested one in a letter to Scott of 27 July 1814: 'If indeed you happen to meet with a tolerably sized Craken we should like to have it preserved for us in spirits' (NLS, MS 3885, f. 144v). The Duke's attention to such a creature had perhaps been drawn by *The Lay of the Last Minstrel* (1805): 'Of that sea-snake, tremendous curled, / Whose monstrous circle girds the world' (Canto 6, stanza 22: and Note). Scott's investigation of 'a report (January was two years) of a kraken or some monstrous fish being seen off Scalloway' appears in his Diary entry for 7 August (see *Life*, 3.161). It concludes: 'This for the Duke of Buccleuch' (162).

202.96 Scalloway-bay Scalloway is on the W coast of Shetland, 10 km (6 miles) SW of Lerwick, and anciently the capital of Shetland.

202.100 morse walrus.

202.100 sea-horse alternative name for a walrus.

202.100 grampus popular name for marine creatures, remarkable for the spouting and blowing which accompanies their movements.

202.101   thing that is not   echoing Jonathan Swift's *Gulliver's Travels* (1726), where in the language of the Houyhnhnms 'the thing which is not' is the closest equivalent for 'to lie'. See the Master Houyhnhnm's response in hearing Gulliver's account of human warfare: 'in recounting the numbers of those which have been killed in battle, I cannot but think that you have said *the thing which is not*' (Bk 4, Ch. 5).

202.102   Mr Scott   probably John Scott of Scalloway (1756–1833). His conversation with Scott is recorded in the Diary entry for 7 August (*Life*, 3.160–62).

202.104   Scotts of Scotstarvit   a family settled in Fife without direct lineal connection with the Border Scotts. The best-known bearer of the designation was Sir John Scot of Scotstarvit (1585–1670), author of *The Staggering State of the Scots Statesmen for One Hundred Years, viz. from 1550 to 1650*, an exposure of the wiles and misfortunes of statecraft that circulated in manuscript until it was eventually published in Edinburgh in 1754 (*ALC*). Scott notes in his Diary how the family of Mr Scott (see previous note) had made 'many enquiries after the state of the Buccleuch family, in which they they seemed to take much interest' (*Life*, 3.161).

202.112   Neptune's dominion   Neptune was the Roman god of water and of the sea.

202.114   kettle of fish   in the Border country used to describe a meal of fish cooked in a boiling vessel outdoors, at a boating excursion or picnic. Also a proverbial expression indicating a muddle or awkward state of affairs (*ODEP*, 421).

203.115   night-caps or hose   knitting was a traditional craft in the Shetland islands, and the export of stockings a mainstay of the economy.

203.120   lake at Bowhill   Bowhill is a country house and estate 5 km (3 miles) W of Selkirk, belonging to the Buccleuch family since the mid-18th century. The 4th Duke (see note to 199.1–2) was actively involved in planting and landscaping the grounds; there are now two lakes at Bowhill.

203.121–22   whales ... two hundred and fifty   the same incident features in the Diary entry for 11 August (*Life*, 3.180–81), which describes 'no less than the carcasses of two hundred and sixty-five whales, which have been driven ashore in Taftsness bay, now lying close under us'. Scott also described the spectacle, viewed off the coast of the island of Sanday, in a letter of 13 August addressed from Kirkwall to his wife Charlotte: 'The day before yesterday we might have seen 250 whales lying upon the beach of Tressness bay but the wind did not serve to go in—we saw the people *flinching* that is cutting them to pieces—this shoal of monsters were all destroyd by seven boats which chased them on shore a few days ago' (*Letters*, 12.126).

203.124   Triffness and Liffness   Triffness is presumably Scott's representation of Tres Ness, a headland on the E coast of the island of Sanday (see also note to 203.129). Liffness possibly relates to the Bay of Lopness, closer to the NE tip of Sanday.

203.127   shoal of leviathans   *leviathan* in Jewish mythology is a sea-serpent (see Job 41); but often used, as here, to refer to a whale.

203.128   lee-beam   used to describe the side of a ship away from the wind.

203.129   Sanda   the island of Sanday, some 40 km (25 miles) NE of Kirkwall.

203.130   *flinching*   cutting up and slicing the fat from; to slice the blubber of a whale (see also note to 203.121–22).

203.134   Wilson   probably Captain James Wilson, previously commander of the floating-light and landing-master during the construction of the Bell Rock

Lighthouse, as mentioned in Robert Louis Stevenson, *Records of a Family of Engineers* (London, 1912), 148. See also Scott's footnote.

203.135   Kirkwall   chief town of the Orkney Islands.

203.136   once called it *fair*   in *The Lay of the Last Min*strel (1805): 'Still nods their palace to its fall, / Thy pride and sorrow, fair Kirkwall!' (Canto 6, stanza 21).

203.139   Church   of St Magnus Cathedral, dominating the skyline at Kirkwall. Described in some detail by Scott in his Diary entry for 12 August (see *Life*, 3.186–88).

203.139   prelate harangued   possibly referring to Robert Reid (d. 1558), appointed to the diocese of Orkney in 1541, and one of the greatest bishops of St Magnus Cathedral; also diplomat, Lord President of the Court of Session, and founder of the University of Edinburgh. Scott in his Diary entry for 12 August refers to him while describing the Bishop's Palace and its tower: 'This was built by Bishop Reid ... and there is a rude statue of him in a niche in the front' (*Life*, 3.185).

203.140   Earl that was hanged   Patrick Stewart, 2nd Earl of Orkney (*c.* 1566/7–1615), whose Palace was erected early in the 17th century, a short distance S of St Magnus Cathedral. He was sentenced to death and executed by the maiden, an early form of guillotine, in 1615 at the Mercat Cross, Edinburgh. The ruins of the Palace are described in Scott's Diary entry of 12 August (see *Life*, 3.185–86). In the autograph letter Scott leaves a marker for a footnote after 'Earl', though none can be found there.

203.142   a peak   in a vertical position: used to describe a ship drawn directly over the anchor.

82.   Farewell to Mackenzie

Textual Note
The first known printing of 'Farewell to Mackenzie' was in 1820 in Scott's *Poetical Works* (12.148–50), but it must have been written at least ten years previously. Lockhart in his posthumous edition of Scott's collected poems of 1833–34 (8.390) mistakenly dates it to 1815, presumably because a second part, 'Imitation of Farewell to Mackenzie' (see no. 83) commemorates the death of Francis Humberston Mackenzie, 1st Baron Seaforth (1754–1815) on 11 January 1815. 'Farewell to Mackenzie' does lead naturally into 'Imitation of Farewell to Mackenzie', which opens 'So sung the old Bard' and was clearly designed to be read immediately afterwards. It is for this reason that 'Farewell to Mackenzie' directly precedes 'Imitation of Farewell to Mackenzie' in the present volume, where otherwise it would logically appear earlier in the volume's chronological sequence.

Margaret Clephane in a letter to Scott of 21 October 1810 had expressed her delight in Scott's intention of 'learning Gaelic this winter', adding 'do not flatter yourself that I shall forget to send you translations of our family songs in the hopes of seeing them adorned by your English verse' (NLS, MS 3879, ff. 219–21). In a letter to her of 27 October 1810 Scott refers to 'Farewell to Mackenzie' as one among a number of Gaelic songs of which he had obtained a prose translation from her and subsequently versified, and which he then had it in mind to contribute to a future volume of *Illustrations of Northern Antiquities* (for further details see Textual Note to no. 65, 'War-Song of Lachlan'). He wrote:

> I think of giving them my song of the Clans which I will most willingly attempt to enlarge by Saxonising those you are so good as to recommend to me. I have I believe

three already Macleans Warsong and the Coronach over Sir Lachlan and the farewell to MacKenneth. (*Letters*, 2.398–99)

No manuscript appears to have survived. After its inclusion in *Poetical Works* of 1820 'Farewell to Mackenzie' passed through the successive lifetime editions of Scott's collected poems and into the posthumous Lockhart edition of 1833–34 (8.390–91), with only the kind of changes normally associated with the work of the printer.

The present text follows that of the 1820 *Poetical Works* (12.148–50), the first known printing of the poem, but corrects the error of '1718' in the headnote to '1719'.

Historical Note

Scott's friend, Mrs Marianne Maclean Clephane (1765–1840), was the daughter of the 7th Maclean Chieftain of Torloisk in Mull, and she and her musical daughters, Margaret and Anna Jane, introduced Scott to various Highland songs and legends, of which the 'Farewell to Mackenzie' was one. Unfortunately this tune, described by Scott as a boat-song, has not been identified.

William Mackenzie, 5th Earl of Seaforth (d. 1740), was a Roman Catholic Jacobite, who took part in the 1715 Jacobite Rising, after which he escaped to France, having been attainted and his lands forfeited. By the terms of the Treaty of Utrecht of 1713, which concluded the War of the Spanish Succession, the new Bourbon King of Spain, Philip V, had agreed to abstain from exercising Spanish influence in Italy. However, this condition was broken in 1718 when Spain seized Sardinia and Sicily. Britain, as a guarantor of the Utrecht settlement, then retaliated by attacking the Spanish fleet near Messina upon which Spain declared war on Britain. In March 1719 an invasion force of 29 Spanish ships with 5000 soldiers was dispatched from Cadiz, but the Spanish fleet was shattered by a storm near Cape Finisterre: however, a tiny diversionary force of 300 Spanish infantrymen in two Spanish frigates did reach Scotland under the command of the Jacobite George Keith, 10th Earl Marischal (1692/3?–1778). They were reinforced by a small group of Jacobite exiles from France, including Seaforth, who sailed from Le Havre and met up with the two Spanish ships at Stornaway on Lewis. The Jacobite forces made their headquarters at the Mackenzie stronghold of Eilean Donan Castle on a small island at the head of Loch Alsh but without the support of the two frigates, which had returned to Spain before the arrival of a Royal Navy squadron in the loch. Seaforth moved most of his forces towards Inverness, leaving only around 50 men to garrison Eilean Donan (which was eventually blown up by the Royal Navy). General Joseph Wightman (d. 1722) issued from Inverness to block this Jacobite advance, and about 19 km (12 miles) from Eilean Donan Castle at the Battle of Glenshiel on 10 June 1719 government forces routed the alliance of Spanish and Jacobite troops. Seaforth fought at the head of 200 men on the left of the Jacobite force and was badly wounded in the arm, escaping to France after the battle only with difficulty and leaving his tenants to be burned out by government forces. From his headnote Scott envisages the song as marking Seaforth's departure from Scotland after the failing of this abortive 1719 Rising.

Explanatory Notes

204.headnote   galley   the Highland galley or *birlinn* was a wooden boat, influenced by the design of the Viking longship. It had a single mast with a square sail and also between twelve and forty oars, depending on its size. The galley was commonly used in the Hebrides and Western Highlands from the Middle Ages onwards.

204.headnote   jorrams, or boat-songs   according to Scott, these were 'usually composed in honour of a favourite chief. They are so adapted as to keep time with the sweep of the oars, and it is easy to distinguish between those intended to be sung to the oars of a galley, where the stroke is lengthened and doubled as it were, and those which were timed to the rowers of an ordinary boat': see *The Lady of the Lake* (Edinburgh, 1810), 'Notes to Canto Second', xxxiii.

204.1   Mackenneth   the Mackenzies, who held land in Kintail in the S of Wester Ross, were called 'the children of Kenneth' from an Irish ancestor of that name, who is supposed to have settled in Scotland around 1261.

204.2   Lochcarron, Glenshiel, and Seaforth   all places in the Mackenzie heartlands in SW Ross-shire. Lochcarron is a coastal district, taking its name from the salt-water loch of that name; Glenshiel is the narrow valley of the River Shiel, which flows from the mountain Sgurr Fhuaran (see note to 205.23 below) towards the Atlantic into Loch Duich; Seaforth Loch is a projection of the sea on the E coast of the Isle of Lewis, which gave the title of Earl to the Chief of the Mackenzies.

204.11   gunnel   or gunwale, the uppermost planking which, in a large ship, covers the timber-heads and reaches from the quarter-deck to the forecastle on either side.

204.11   bonnail   (see also Scott's footnote.) Or *bonaillie*, a word derived from the French *bon* (good) and *aller* (go), meaning God speed or farewell. A drink taken with, or a toast to, a friend when about to part with him, expressing the wish that his journey may be prosperous.

205.21   from streamer to deck   all the sails of a vessel from the flag or pennant streaming in the wind at the head of the mast down to the lowest portion immediately above the deck, or planked floor of the ship.

205.23   Skooroora   Sgurr Fhuaran (or Scour Ouran), a mountain of 1068 m, one of the Five Sisters of Kintail, which stretch E from the head of Loch Duich.

205.23   Conan's glad vale   the River Conan in SE Ross-shire is formed by the confluence of the Sheen and the Meig and flows E from Contin parish into the head of Cromarty Firth S of Dingwall. The expression 'glad vale' perhaps suggests the supposedly ancient Gaelic poems published by James Macpherson (1736–96) and his imitators: see, for example, 'But they were beams that shone in the glad vale, only for a little': 'Manos: a Poem', in John Smith, *Galic Antiquities: Consisting of a History of the Druids ... and A Collection of Ancient Poems, translated from the Galic of Ullin, Ossian, Orran, &c.* (Edinburgh, 1780), 257: *ALC*.

83.   Imitation of Farewell to Mackenzie

Textual Note
No manuscript material for this item has apparently survived, and it was first published undated in 1820 in Scott's *Poetical Works* (12.151–53). Allusions in the poem itself, however, imply that it was composed between the death of Francis Humberston Mackenzie, 1st Baron Seaforth (1754–1815) on 11 January 1815, which it commemorates, and the remarriage of his daughter, Mary Elizabeth Frederica Mackenzie (1783–1862), formerly Lady Hood, to James Alexander Stewart of Glasserton on 21 May 1817, as she is referred to in the closing lines as a widow. While the poem suggests that some time has elapsed since Seaforth's death, no Highland bard having come forward with a

memorial poem, it echoes comments made on the event in Scott's correspondence of January 1815 so closely as to imply a composition date not long after that event. In his letter to the Marchioness of Stafford of 21 January 1815, for example, Scott, giving Seaforth his traditional title of Caberfae (see Historical Note), wrote:

> The last days of poor Caberfae were really heaviness and sorrow—an indistinct perception of the heavy loss he had sustained in his sons death, which was frequently exchanged for an anxiety about his health, and wonder why he did not see him—so it is a mercy that the curtain is dropd. All the Highlands ring with a prophecy that when there should be a deaf Caberfae the clan and chief shall all go to wreck, but these predictions are very apt to be framed after the event. ... I trust Lady Hood will be soon home. She will have hard cards to play from the involved state of the property; but with her excellent sense and noble spirit much may be done ... (*Letters*, 4.22)

Lady Hood, who had accompanied her husband, the admiral Sir Samuel Hood (1762–1814), to India, returned home after his death and by July 1815 was dining with Scott in Castle Street (*Letters*, 4.29; Corson, *N&I*, 110, note to 4.29(a)). Given that the poem's conclusion addresses itself to Lady Hood, it seems not unlikely that Scott wrote it for her shortly after her return to Scotland, although unfortunately no correspondence between them has been found for the year 1815. Lockhart, in the posthumous 1833–34 edition of Scott's *Poetical Works*, states that this lament was written 'shortly after the death of Lord Seaforth' (8.392).

Although Scott's second stanza implies that he has come forward, for want of a public lament for Seaforth from a Highland bard, no publication of these verses has been traced previous to 1820. After publication in the 1820 *Poetical Works* this lament passed through the successive lifetime collected editions and the posthumous Lockhart collected edition of 1833–34 (8.392–94), with only the kind of changes normally associated with the work of the printer.

The present text follows that of Scott's *Poetical Works* of 1820 (12.151–53), where it is titled 'Imitation of the Preceding Song' and follows immediately after 'Farewell to Mackenzie' (no. 82): the title here has been accordingly adjusted editorially to read 'Imitation of Farewell to Mackenzie'. No other emendations have been made.

Historical Note
In 1808 Scott described Lady Hood as 'a great friend of ours a daughter of Seaforths and an enthusiastic Highlander of course' (*Letters*, 2.132). He also referred to the deceased Francis Humberston Mackenzie, 1st Baron Seaforth, in his letter of 21 January 1815 (cited in the Textual Note), as 'Caberfae', or *caber feidh* (meaning 'stag's antlers'), a traditional Gaelic name for the Mackenzie Chief. It was therefore natural that Scott should envisage a memorial poem for him in terms of Highland tradition, especially as it was, partly at least, addressed to his daughter. Some years previously Scott had made an English language poetic version of a Gaelic lament for the loss to his clan of an earlier Mackenzie Chief, on his going into foreign exile after the abortive Jacobite Rising of 1719 (see no. 82, 'Farewell to Mackenzie'), and the opening words of the present poem indicate that it partly represents a sequel to that, making sense only when read after it or with the earlier poem firmly in mind.

In keeping with the genre of a lament or memorial poem, Scott's verses elide negative aspects of Seaforth's character and history of which his correspondence reveals him to have been well aware. Seaforth's extravagance and improvidence, for instance, led him to mismanage his estates and he was in desperate straits financially before his death, the sale of substantial parts of his lands being only averted temporarily by financial gifts from his tenants, who were reluctant to see them pass out of the family. Scott's letters also dwell gloomily on the state of mental and bodily paralysis that preceded Seaforth's death at Warriston near Edinburgh, and which Scott perhaps (remembering the death of his own father) already feared for himself.

Explanatory Notes

205.1 So sung the old Bard a reference to the Gaelic lament versified by Scott as 'Farewell to Mackenzie' (see no. 82), which precedes this poem in all lifetime editions of Scott's collected poetry, as in the present volume.

205.3 Albyn the Gaelic name for Scotland. Alexander Campbell's collection of Scottish music of 1816–18, for example, to which Scott contributed, is entitled *Albyn's Anthology*.

205.6 Mackenzie, last Chief of Kintail Chief of Kintail, from the family estates in a mountainous area of the NW Highlands, was a traditional title for the heads of the Mackenzie clan, who did not bear the title Earl of Seaforth before the 17th century. On the death of Seaforth his estates passed by entail to his eldest daughter, Lady Hood, but the chieftainship of the Mackenzie clan was disputed by a male cousin, Mackenzie of Allengrange.

205.7 Minstrel Scott himself, editor of *Minstrelsy of the Scottish Border* (1802–03) and author of *The Lay of the Last Minstrel* (1805).

205.15 Son of Fitzgerald the Mackenzies were supposedly descended from a Colin Fitzgerald of Ireland who supported the Scottish king Alexander III (1241–86), assisting him at the Battle of Largs (1263) to repel an attempted invasion of Haakon IV of Norway and being rewarded with the lands of Kintail.

206.19 thy talents Mackenzie was considered a man of intellectual ability and extensive attainments. Besides military service in the 1790s he had, as MP for Ross-shire, supported Pitt's government against revolutionary France and later served as Governor of Barbados. The title of Earl of Seaforth had been forfeited by attainder in 1716, and his title of Baron Seaforth was gained by his own political services. He was made a fellow of the Royal Society in 1794, and was a patron of the painters Sir Thomas Lawrence and Benjamin West.

206.20 deaden'd thine ear and imprison'd thy tongue at the age of 12 an attack of scarlet fever left Mackenzie permanently deaf, and for a while also deprived him of speech.

206.25 Thy sons Seaforth had four sons as well as six daughters, but only his third son, William Frederick Mackenzie (born in 1791), survived into adulthood. He became MP for Ross-shire in 1812 but died unmarried on 25 October 1814 after a sudden illness.

206.31 thou, gentle Dame Seaforth's eldest daughter, Lady Hood, who inherited the encumbered Seaforth estates on the death of her father although the title became extinct.

206.32 cares of a Chief the Seaforth estate was entailed on Lady Hood, who would bear the traditional responsibility of the clan Chief for the people who lived there.

206.34 thy husband Mary Elizabeth Frederica Mackenzie had married Admiral Sir Samuel Hood in November 1804 at Bridgetown in Barbados, during her father's term as Governor there. In 1812 he was appointed naval commander-in-chief for the East Indies, his wife accompanying him to India. He died of malaria at Madras on 24 December 1814.

84. The Dance of Death

Textual Note
Scott seems to have composed at least the opening of 'The Dance of Death' shortly after his visit of August 1815 to the site of the battlefield of Waterloo. His companion, John Scott of Gala, recalled that on a subsequent excursion from Paris to Malmaison Scott repeated to him 'the commencement of the wild and imaginative poem, in which the fatal choosers of the slain are supposed to select their victims from the ranks of the combatants on the night before the battle': see John Scott, *Journal of a Tour to Waterloo and Paris, in company with Sir Walter Scott in 1815* (London, 1842), 206. An undated manuscript in Scott's hand of 'The Dance of Death' survives in the Berg Collection, New York Public Library, consisting of five leaves in a leather-bound volume with gold tooling, each leaf measuring approx. 25.2 x 20.7 cm, the paper having a watermark of 'JOHN DICKINSON & CO / 1810'. The text is on the rectos of the leaves only, as is characteristic of Scott's fair-copy manuscripts, and is also unpaginated. There are a number of corrections by Scott: for instance, the first line reads '<Dawn> ↑Night↓ and <Darkness> ↑Morning↓ were at meeting' and line 65 '<shadowy> ↑phantom↓ band'. Overall, however, the manuscript is clear and legible while the inscription 'E A R' in another hand at the top right-hand corner of the first leaf suggests that this was used as copy for the *Edinburgh Annual Register* (see below).

It seems possible that Scott had originally intended 'The Dance of Death' as one of his promised contributions to the song-collection *Twelve Vocal Pieces* of the composer John Clarke Whitfeld (1770–1836). In his letter to Whitfeld of 6 January 1817 Scott enclosed an unnamed poem: 'after much hesitation I could not think it likely to answer your purpose & so gave it to the Edin: Ann: Register with a view to try something else. My printer however who is very musical shewed it to Braham, & from the said Braham's anxiety to get it argued that it is of some value with a view to Music' (*Letters*, 4.352). Perhaps Whitfeld did not consider the poem suitable for his collection, despite the opinion of the celebrated tenor John Braham (1777?–1856) and its containing an inset song of the spirits, and it was apparently never set to music by him. Scott had previously sent the poem to John Ballantyne with a letter of 20 October 1815:

> I send you the poems for Register which I shall be glad to see in proof as I have hardly had time to look over the Dance. There could be no objection to having a few quartos of that by the way & I should like at any rate to have a few separate 8vo copies for my freinds [*sic*] ... (*Letters*, 1.494)

One of these copies Scott may have promised to his friend J. B. S. Morritt (*Letters*, 4.101–02), but if any were printed separately they do not appear to have survived.

'The Dance of Death' was duly published in the *Edinburgh Annual Register, for 1813*, 6: 1 and 2 (Edinburgh, 1815), cccxxxv–cccxxxix. Scott evidently made a few corrections in proof, so that at the start of line 47, for instance, the manuscript reading 'Oft came the clang' becomes 'The frequent clang'. He also added an end-date, '*Abbotsford, October 1*, 1815'. The poem was afterwards included, without the end-dating, in Scott's 1820 *Poetical Works* (12.209–19) and the subsequent lifetime collected editions of his poetry, with only changes of the kind normally associated with the work of the printer. Some textual corruption also occurred, such as 'Make space' for 'Makes space' in line 101 (1821*PW*, 10.62). 'The Dance of Death' was also included, with no evidence of further authorial involvement, in Lockhart's posthumous collected edition of 1833–34

(11.297–303), two of his footnotes appearing to indicate, however, that he then had access to Scott's manuscript.

The present text follows that in the *Edinburgh Annual Register, for 1813*, 6: 1 and 2 (Edinburgh, 1815), cccxxxv–cccxxxix, as the first printing of the poem, with the following emendations:

208.36   foemen's gore (1821*PW*) / foemens' gore
211.141   man. (1821*PW*) / man."
211.148   Highland (1820*PW*) / highland

Historical Note
Scott had visited the site of the Battle of Waterloo near Brussels in August 1815, about six weeks after the battle itself, moving on afterwards to Paris, where he stayed until early September before returning home to Abbotsford. At the time of his visit traces of the battle itself were plainly visible, as he later described in his *Paul's Letters to his Kinsfolk* (Edinburgh, 1816), even though most of the bodies of the dead had been burned or buried:

> Bones of horses, quantities of old hats, rags of clothes, scraps of leather, and fragments of books and papers strewed the ground in great profusion, especially where the action had been most bloody. … Letters, and other papers, memorandums of business, or pledges of friendship and affection, lay scattered about on the field—few of them were now legible. Quack advertisements were also to be found where English soldiers had fallen. Among the universal remedies announced by these empirics, there was none against the dangers of such a field. (198–200)

'The Dance of Death' embodies several details from Scott's personal observation or from his conversations with local people and combatants. These include the storm of the preceding night, and his detailed knowledge of the terrain.

Explanatory Notes
207.2   Waterloo   Scott's poem is set during the night that preceded the Battle of Waterloo on 18 June 1815, the decisive contest that defeated the French army and ended the Napoleonic Wars. The battlefield is located 15 km (9 miles) S of Brussels, and about 2 km (1¼ miles) from the small town of Waterloo.
207.6   heights of Mount Saint John   Scott explains the relative positions of the British and French armies on two lines of facing heights in *The Life of Napoleon Buonaparte*, 9 vols (Edinburgh, 1827), 8.474–75: 'On the opposite chain of eminences, a village called La Belle Alliance gives name to the range of heights. It exactly fronts Mont St Jean, and these two points formed the respective centres of the French and English positions. … Behind the heights of Mont St Jean, the ground again sinks into a hollow, which served to afford some sort of shelter to the second line of the British. In the rear of this second valley, is the great and extensive forest of Soignes, through which runs the causeway to Brussels'.
207.9   thunder-clap   'The night, as if the elements meant to match their fury with that which was preparing for the morning, was stormy in the extreme, accompanied by furious gusts of wind, heavy bursts of rain, continued and vivid flashes of lightning, and the loudest thunder our officers had ever heard' (*Paul's Letters*, 125–26).
207.12   levin-light   a flash of lightning.
207.14   bivouack   a temporary encampment of soldiers under improvised shelter or none.
207.19   such a tide and hour   three o'clock in the morning is known as the

witching hour, when supernatural beings such as witches, demons and ghosts are thought to have most power. It is also sometimes referred to as the devil's hour, perhaps because it is an inversion of the time of Christ's redeeming death. Waterloo was fought only a few days before the summer solstice.

207.22   gifted ken   *ken* as a Scots noun means knowledge, comprehension, or insight. This phrase indicates that the Highland soldier Allan has the gift of second-sight, whereby he is able to see future or distant events taking place as though they were present. Scott also refers to him in line 23 as a prophet.

207.27   Albyn's   the Gaelic name for Scotland. Alexander Campbell's collection of Scottish music of 1816–18, for example, to which Scott contributed, is entitled *Albyn's Anthology*.

207.28   Allan   a characteristic Highland Christian name.

207.29–30   for many a day … follow'd   in typifying Highland loyalty to an hereditary chief, Allan is possibly intended to recall Ewen McMillan, the foster brother of John Cameron (see next note), who attended him throughout his life and buried his body with his own hands during the great storm that preceded the Battle of Waterloo, although it was afterwards disinterred for reburial at Kilmallie in Scotland.

208.33–34   grandson of Lochiel … Fassiefern   Colonel John Cameron (1771–1815), son of Sir Ewen Cameron of Fassiefern. He was one of the original officers of the 92nd Regiment of Gordon Highlanders, which was partly raised with the help of his father, and served with them in Corsica, Gibraltar, Egypt, and the Spanish peninsula. He was mortally wounded by a shot from a sniper in the upper storey of a wayside house as he advanced with his men at Quatre Bras on 16 June 1815, and buried during the great storm of the night preceding the battle of Waterloo. Scott wrote the inscription on his monument in Kilmallie churchyard. Fassiefern is a place in the vicinity of Lochiel, and the celebrated Jacobite Sir Ewen Cameron of Lochiel (1629–1719) was Col. Cameron's great-great-grandfather.

208.37   native lake's wild shore   that of Loch Eil, a sea-loch opening into Loch Linne near the town of Fort William, and from which the Cameron chief is called Lochiel.

208.38   Sunart   a sea-loch in Argyll, winding 31 km (19 miles) E from the N of the Sound of Mull to within 8 km (5 miles) of Loch Linnhe. Alternatively, the district in N Argyll between Loch Sunart and Loch Shiel.

208.38   high Ardgower   or Ardgour, is the district on the W shore of Loch Linnhe in Argyll. Its Gaelic name, *Aird Ghobhar*, means 'height of the goats'.

208.39   Morvern   a peninsula in NW Argyll, extending SW between Lochs Sunart and Linnhe to the Sound of Mull.

208.40   Bennevis   Ben Nevis, immediately SE of Loch Eil at Fort William, and at 1345 m the highest mountain in Great Britain.

208.41   bloody Quatre-Bras   the battle fought at the strategic cross-roads of Quatre-Bras on 16 June, two days before Waterloo, between Wellington's army and French forces under Marshal Ney.

208.47   courser's hoof   that of a charger, or horse for charging in battle.

208.60–61   Scotland's James … Flodden's fatal plain   James IV of Scotland (1473–1513) was killed fighting against an English army at the Battle of Flodden in Northumberland on 9 September 1513. According to legend, while the King was in Edinburgh preparing to march S into England a voice was heard at midnight at the market-cross summoning by name various Scottish noblemen and gentlemen to appear before the speaker's master within 40 days, those named being subsequently killed in the battle. This ghostly summons features in the fifth canto of Scott's long narrative poem *Marmion* (1808).

208.63 Chusers of the Slain   in Scandinavian mythology the Valkyries or handmaids of Odin, known as the Choosers of the Slain, rush into battle mounted on swift horses and holding drawn swords, selecting those destined for death. These heroes were subsequently conducted by them to Valhalla.

209.82 They do not bend the rye   describing his visit to the battlefield of Waterloo, Scott regretted that at that time 'the plough was already at work in several parts of the field', wishing that the land containing the bodies of the dead had for a time been left fallow, adding, however, 'But the corn which must soon wave there will be itself a temporary protection to their humble graves, while it will speedily remove from the face of nature the melancholy traces of the strife of man' (*Paul's Letters*, 201).

209.90 trampled paste   in *Paul's Letters* Scott describes the 'tall crops of maize and rye ... trampled into a thick black paste, under the feet of men and horses' as an obvious sign of the recent battle (200).

210.105 cuirassier   a mounted soldier wearing a cuirass, or piece of body-armour reaching down to the waist and consisting of a breast-plate and back-plate buckled together. Scott described the French cuirassiers at Waterloo as displaying 'an almost frantic valour. They rallied again and again, and returned to the onset, till the British could recognise even the faces of individuals among their enemies. ... In this unheard-of struggle, the greater part of the French heavy cavalry were absolutely destroyed' (*Life of Napoleon Buonaparte*, 8.488).

210.108 broad-sword's weight   that of a cutting sword with a broad blade.

211.139 welkin's thunders   those of the sky, of the arch of the apparent heavens.

211.146 stark   stiff, rigid, unyielding.

211.151 picquet-post   a picket is an outlying post of soldiers, sent to watch for the approach of an enemy or for enemy scouts.

211.152 watch-fires   fires maintained during the night for the use of parties on watch.

211.end-date   this is unlikely to be the actual date of completion, since Scott's letter to John Ballantyne of 20 October 1815 (*Letters*, 1.494), accompanying his undated manuscript of 'The Dance of Death', suggests that he had finished writing it only shortly before sending.

85. Saint Cloud

Textual Note

Two manuscript versions of this poem, composed near the end of Scott's stay in post-Waterloo Paris in 1815, have survived. The first is a fair copy in Scott's hand, now held in the Harry Ransom Center, Austin, Texas (HRC MS -3753, Container 1–3). End-dated 'Paris Sepr 5. 1815', and consisting of two mounted leaves measuring approx. 23.5 x 18.5 cm, this contains two verbal alterations by Scott, substituting 'silence' for 'absence' and 'moonless' for 'midnight' at lines 18 and 23. The other MS version was sent as an enclosure in a letter to Lady Alvanley (1758–1825), Scott's companion with her two daughters on the occasion described in the poem, shortly after he had returned to his hotel in Paris. According to the containing letter, which now only exists in the form of a later copy: 'The enclosed came into my head last night during two or three hours that that I happened to lie awake ... That your Ladyship may not withhold your sympathy I send you and the young Ladies the melancholy fruits of my broken rest' (*Letters*, 4.90). The text of the enclosed poem, which is omitted from the Grierson edition of the *Letters*, is written in the same unknown hand on two leaves with an 1831 watermark (NLS, MS 855, ff. 10–11). Its heading, 'Lines written on a beautiful Summer's Evening spent at St. Cloud 12 Augst 1815', has led to a degree of uncertainty about the date of composition. However, close inspection of this MS copy indicates that the '12 Augst 1815' dating has been added later, and possibly in yet another hand. Furthermore Scott was not in a position to make an excursion to St Cloud at that date: according to the Journal kept by Robert Bruce, one of his travelling companions, only arriving in Paris having left Chantilly on 14 August (NLS, MS 991, f. 15r). Additional evidence also indicates that the excursion to St Cloud applied at the British embassy for his return passport on 7 September: see John Scott of Gala, *A Journal of a Tour to Waterloo and Paris, in company with Sir Walter Scott in 1815* (London, 1842), 205–09. In this respect, the end-dating of the Texas MS places it close to the circumstances described in the poem, with Scott perhaps making his own copy after drafting that for Lady Alvanley. The Alvanley version contains a number of verbal variants compared with the Texas MS, with 'Glade' not 'shade' at line 13, 'empty' rather than 'broken' urns (line 14), 'sat us on' rather than 'sate upon' (line 17), 'As' instead of 'While' (line 23), and 'Their' instead of 'The' at the beginning of line 30. Though uncertainties remain about the precise order of composition, the two verbal alterations within the Texas MS suggest that Scott was still creatively engaged while making that version.

The first known printing of the poem, in the 1820 *Poetical Works* (12.157–59), matches closely the Texas MS, as well as adopting its heading and end-dating (as 'PARIS, *Sept.* 5, 1815'), indicating strongly that it provided the copy text. The one substantive verbal variant there, 'arms' rather than 'urns' at line 14, most probably results from simple misreading. Otherwise the main changes consist in the addition of a conventional punctuation system and the raising and lowering of the initial capitals in isolated cases, of a kind normally associated with the printer. Subsequent lifetime editions alternate between 'arms' and 'urns', before eventually stabilising with 'urns' in the posthumous 1833–34 Lockhart edition (11.295–96). This version however differs in placing its 'Paris, 5th September, 1815' dating at the head in brackets; and also, somewhat remarkably, by providing footnotes in which the two words changed in the Texas MS ('absence' and 'midnight') are given as actual MS readings. A third footnote also states that 'These lines were written after an evening spent at Saint Cloud with the late Lady Alvanley and her daughters, one of whom was the songstress alluded to in the text'.

The present text follows that of the 1820 *Poetical Works*, 12.157–59, the first known authorised printing, with the following emendations, both matching the two surviving manuscript versions:

212.14   urns (Texas MS) / arms
212.27   Music's (Texas MS) / music's

Historical Note

As suggested above, the visit with Lady Alvanley and her two daughters which led to this poem evidently took place near the beginning of September 1815, shortly before Scott returned home from his excursion to France. According to Scott of Gala's account the party first took in Malmaison, famous for its association with the Empress Josephine, then in the afternoon moved on to St Cloud, the 'favourite abode' of Napoleon himself:

On the evening of our visit, the fine view from the terrace was seen to great
advantage, lighted as it was by a rich autumnal sunset. ... We dined at the Hotel, and
returned from our agreeable day's excursion at a late hour. One of the ladies of the
party was a good musician, and favoured us with several very pleasing songs, both at
Malmaison and St. Cloud. (*Journal of a Tour to Waterloo and Paris*, 208–09)

For Scott, the second location in particular would have been filled with histori-
cal reverberations. It was from the palace at St Cloud that Napoleon staged the
coup d'état which led to the overthrow of the French Directory in 1799. Before
the Revolution it had served as a main royal residence, traditionally associated
with the cadet Orléans family, and was given by Louis XVI as a gift to Marie
Antoinette, who supposedly had a considerable input into the design of the
gardens. Most recently, as observed by Scott in his own *Paul's Letters to his
Kinsfolk* (Edinburgh, 1816), 352–53, it had been briefly occupied as a defensive
position by French forces after the defeat at Waterloo, prior to the capitulation
marked by the Convention of St Cloud, signed there on 3 July 1815. Affording
panoramic views of the Seine and Paris, the park was renowned for its artificial
cascade, with water tumbling down towards the river through formal parterres.
In letters to his wife Charlotte, Scott reported on the pleasure he had received
from the company of Lady Alvanley while in Paris, someone who (he was later
to recollect) had gone out of her way to help them as a virtually unknown couple
visiting London in 1799 (*Letters*, 12.146, 148; 8.482). It has not been possible to
identify which of the two daughters was the songstress, though the mesmeris-
ing effect of her intimate musical performance, in such a setting, and against a
backdrop of recent cataclysmic events, suffuses the poem as a whole.

Explanatory Notes
211.title St Cloud is now an affluent suburb some 10 km (6 miles) W of
the centre of Paris. The chateau was first built in 1572, and destroyed in the
Franco–Prussian war in 1870.
212.9–10 drum's deep roll ... bugle referring to the Last Post, then
known as Setting the Watch. Compare Scott's account, observed slightly
earlier during his visit to Paris, in *Paul's Letters to his Kinsfolk* (1816): 'the
distant roll of the drums, and the notes of that beautiful point of war which is
performed by our bugles at the setting of the watch' (292). See also *Waverley*
(1814): 'The trumpets and kettle-drums of the cavalry were next heard to
perform the beautiful and wild point of war appropriated as signal for that
piece of nocturnal duty, and then finally sunk upon the wind with a shrill
and mournful cadence' (*Waverley*, ed. P. D. Garside, EEWN 1 (Edinburgh,
2007), 238.4–7). The effect on the present occasion is suggested by a report
in the *Caledonian Mercury* of 26 January 1828 of Scott's conversation with the
musician Ignaz Moscheles (see also Historical Note to no. 124): 'Sir Walter
chanced to allude to the effects of the various martial sounds which reached
his ears, when the evening watch was set of the Allied troops in Paris, after the
battle of Waterloo. Seated on a small eminence near the village of St Cloud,
amidst the calm of a French summer's night, he described the mingling
sounds, in the distance, of the instruments of almost all the nations in the
world, rising in strange and wild harmony around, as producing an effect upon
him such as he should never forget.'
212.11 Hulan Polish light cavalry with lances, sabres, and pistols, though
the term was later used to describe lancers in the Russian, Prussian, and Austrian
armies. Troops of this description served throughout the Napoleonic wars.
212.11 Hussar term used of a number of types of light cavalry, originating
in the Hungarian army in the 15th century. Hussar regiments served in both

the French and British armies during the Napoleonic wars, though Scott clearly has in mind here the Allied occupying troops. Compare *Paul's Letters to his Kinsfolk*: 'The hussar uniforms of Austria are very handsome, particularly those of the Hungarians, to whose country the dress properly belongs' (365).

212.13 Naiads in Greek mythology a type of water nymph, presiding over fountains, wells, springs, streams, brooks and other bodies of fresh water. A River God and Naiad are among the statues adorning the fountain at St Cloud.

86. Romance of Dunois

Textual Note
Scott visited the site of the Battle of Waterloo near Brussels in August 1815, moving on to Paris, where he stayed until early September. He probably translated 'Romance of Dunois' from a French manuscript original during his time in Paris or soon after his return to Scotland. No authorial manuscript of his translation appears to have survived. On 20 October 1815 Scott wrote to John Ballantyne 'I send you the poems for Register' (*Letters*, 1.494), and 'Romance of Dunois' appeared anonymously in the *Edinburgh Annual Register, for 1813*, 6: 1 and 2 (1815), cccxxxix, published in Edinburgh on 11 January 1816. It was also included in Scott's pseudonymous account of his foreign tour, *Paul's Letters to his Kinsfolk* (Edinburgh, 1816), 210. This was first published in Edinburgh only slightly later, on 25 January, and was also in an advanced state of preparation by October 1815. Although the poem appeared first in the *Edinburgh Annual Register*, it seems probable that Scott wrote it as part of *Paul's Letters*, from which he then extracted it for periodical publication. One copy of *Paul's Letters* (BL, c.28.g.4) contains an earlier state of sheet O (pp. 209–24) which includes 'Romance of Dunois' marked with corrections in Scott's hand. Scott's interventions include both the correction of a number of routine errors (for instance, the removal of a second and superfluous full stop at the end of the poem, and the replacement of 'Isobel' by 'Isabel' in line 11) and also some new revisions to his poem. 'And' in line 7 is altered to 'Where', and 'battle to his sword' becomes 'conquest to his arm' in line 9. 'Soldier's prayer' in line 3 is changed to 'soldier's prayer', this last small correction going through to the text in *Paul's Letters* but not that of the *Edinburgh Annual Register*.

Besides the usual variations in punctuation and spelling between the printings in the journal and in *Paul's Letters* resulting from work at the printing-house, the contextualising headnote in the *Edinburgh Annual Register* was unnecessary in *Paul's Letters* and does not appear there. The poem was openly acknowledged as Scott's work by being included in his own *Poetical Works* of 1820 (12.220–21).

'Romance of Dunois' was soon set to music by the Cambridge musician John Clarke Whitfeld (1770–1836), who had previously set a number of songs from Scott's narrative poems. Whitfeld's letter to Scott of 5 January 1812 (NLS, MS 3882, ff. 20–21), for instance, indicates that Scott had sent him songs from *Rokeby* (1813) previous to publication, extracting a promise that Whitfeld's musical settings should not be published before first publication of that poem. In the present case, however, it seems likely that Whitfeld first saw 'Romance of Dunois' in the *Edinburgh Annual Register*, and then wrote to Scott seeking permission to set it to music, for in his reply to Whitfeld of 22 February 1816 Scott wrote, 'You are heartily welcome to the song from the French, and to another which is in a work called "Pauls letters" if you think it worth while; and as they are my own property I have it in my power to authorize you to publish them as composed for your work' (*Letters*, 4.179). 'Romance of Dunois' was eventually published by Whitfeld as a glee for three voices with a piano accompaniment as the twelfth item in the second volume of his *Twelve Vocal Pieces* (London, [1817]), 2.14 (letterpress), 80–87 (musical notation). Scott's headnote is reprinted as a footnote and, besides differences in punctuation and capitalisation attributable to work undertaken in the printing-house, there are also three differences in wording: in the first line 'brave' becomes 'bold'; 'Where' becomes 'And' at the start of line 7; and 'conquest to his arm' becomes 'battle to his sword' in line 9. Interestingly, the last two variations agree with the earlier version of the poem in Sheet O of the BL copy of *Paul's Letters*, discussed above.

When the poem was subsequently included in Scott's *Poetical Works* of 1820 (12.220–21) the three variations of Whitfeld's publication were not adopted, suggesting that this was not used as copy for this collected edition. Probably *EAR* provided this, since 1820*PW* includes the headnote whereas the text in *Paul's Letters* does not, although the variations between both earlier versions and 1820*PW* are slight and of the kind that could have originated in the work of the printer. 'Romance of Dunois' was then reprinted, again with only this kind of change, in the successive lifetime editions of Scott's collected poetry and in Lockhart's posthumous edition of 1833–34 (11.304–05). The replacement of 'with clay and with blood' by 'with clay and blood' in the headnote and of 'beloved' by 'be loved' in lines 8 and 16 in some of these later editions probably resulted from carelessness at the printing-house.

'Romance of Dunois' was also included by George Thomson (1757–1851) in *The Select Melodies of Scotland*, 5 vols (Edinburgh, 1822–23), 5.item 11, with a musical setting by the Edinburgh composer George Farquhar Graham (1789–1867). After November 1821 Thomson acted on a general permission to set any Scott verses he chose to music in his publications (see Scott's letter to Thomson of November 1821, BL, Add. MS 35,265, ff. 96–97), Scott as a result having no direct influence over the appearance of his work in subsequent editions of Thomson's song-collections.

The present text follows that of the *Edinburgh Annual Register, for 1813*, 6: 1 and 2 (1815), cccxxxix, as best representing the culmination of the original creative process and as a text which includes the contextualising headnote created for the poem when published outside *Paul's Letters to his Kinsfolk*. The following emendation has been made:

213.3   soldier's (BL *Paul's Letters*) / Soldier's

Historical Note
In *Paul's Letters to his Kinsfolk* (Edinburgh, 1816) Scott recalls how 'a manuscript collection of French songs, bearing stains of clay and blood, which probably indicate the fate of the proprietor' was given to him as a souvenir of the Battle of Waterloo 'by a lady, whose father had found it upon the field of battle' (209). The lady concerned was apparently the wife of Pryse Lockhart Gordon (1762–1845), a resident of Brussels whom Scott had visited during his tour: see Gordon's *Personal Memoirs*, 2 vols (London, 1830), 2.336–37. This notebook collection, together with other Waterloo relics collected by Scott, is still at Abbotsford. Scott printed three poems in the original French from it in his anonymous *Paul's Letters* (216–18) as well as his own translations (210–13). The translations were presented there as having been obtained 'by meeting at Paris with one of our Scottish men of rhyme' (209). 'Romance of Dunois', the first of these, is described by Scott as 'a common and popular song in France' (212). Both the words and music were written by Hortense de Beauharnais (1783–1837), step-daughter to Napoleon and the wife of his brother Louis Buonaparte

(1778–1846), who was appointed King of Holland by Napoleon in 1806. At the Bourbon restoration in 1814 she was granted the title of Duchess of Saint-Leu at the instigation of Alexander I of Russia. A plate of this poem, entitled 'Le beau Dunois' and with its musical setting, was included in an unpaginated appendix of her 'Romances' in *Mémoires sur Madame la Duchesse de St Leu* (London, 1832). Scott's claim to have produced a literal translation from the French poem he prints in *Paul's Letters* is for the most part justified, although it is Scott that has Dunois mistreating his sword, where the French simply says he carved his oath of honour into the stone but without specifying a tool ('Il grave sure la pierre le serment de l'honneur', 216). In the third stanza the speech of Dunois's lord simply begins 'Puisque tu fais ma gloire je ferai ton bonheur' (Since you have made my glory, I shall make your happiness', 216).

Neither in the French original nor in Scott's translation do the circumstances of the Dunois of the song correspond to those of the historic French hero of that name. The song envisages Dunois as a crusader who wins an Isabel for his bride, whereas the well-known French hero Jean d' Orléans, comte de Dunois (1402–68), was a French military commander and diplomat who played an important part in France's final victory over the English in the Hundred Years War. An illegitimate son of the Duke of Orleans, Dunois served his cousin the dauphin, later Charles VII of France, and although he married twice both his wives were named Marie.

There is no resemblance between the original French tune by Hortense de Beauharnais and those composed by either Whitfeld or Graham (for details see above). The inclusion of Scott's verses in these British song-collections was presumably due rather to Scott's popularity as a poet than to any possible celebrity of its French original, a popularity also signalled by the inclusion of 'Romance of Dunois' in a contemporary commonplace book now in the National Library of Wales at Aberystwyth (Penty Park Deeds & Documents, no. 101).

Explanatory Notes
213.2 orisons   prayers.
213.3 **Queen of Heaven**   the Virgin Mary, mother of Christ.
213.13 **holy knot**   the bond of marriage effected by the religious and legal ceremony, which in the Roman Catholic church is also a sacrament.

87. The Troubadour

Textual Note
'The Troubadour' was first published as the translation of a French original from the notebook of a French officer who had fallen at Waterloo in Scott's anonymous *Paul's Letters to his Kinsfolk* (1816), 211–12. It seems to have been composed at much the same time as 'Romance of Dunois' (see no. 86), during or shortly after Scott's visit to Brussels and Paris in August and early September 1815. No manuscript by Scott appears to have survived, but some trace of an earlier version than the published text exists in the form of a copy of *Paul's Letters* (BL, c.28.g.4) containing an earlier state of sheet O (pp. 209–24). This includes 'The Troubadour' marked with revisions in Scott's hand: 'helmed head' becomes 'helm on head' in line 9; 'While' in line 11 is changed to 'As'; and 'minstrel's burthen' is altered to 'minstrel-burthen' in line 12. The rhyming lines 18 and 20 as printed in this sheet read 'Where axes clash'd and swords were swung,' and 'Was heard the lay the minstrel sung:' before correction to the reading of the published text, while in the final line 'a valiant Troubadour' was

altered to 'the valiant Troubadour'. All of Scott's corrections are implemented in the published text.

'The Troubadour' was subsequently included in Scott's *Poetical Works* of 1820 (12.222–24) with no evidence of further authorial involvement, and in the same way passed into the successive lifetime editions of his collected poems and into Lockhart's posthumous edition of 1833–34 (11.306–07) with only changes characteristic of the printer's work.

When Scott gave permission for the composer John Clarke Whitfeld (1770–1836) to set 'Romance of Dunois' to music in his letter of 22 February 1816 he also made him welcome to use 'another which is in a work called "Pauls letters"' if you think it worth while' (*Letters*, 4.179), but Whitfeld evidently did not set 'The Troubadour' to music. It was, however, included by George Thomson (1757–1851) in his *Select Melodies of Scotland*, 5 vols (Edinburgh, 1822–23), 4.item 9, set to a tune composed by Thomson himself and with musical accompaniments by his fellow Edinburgh song-collector Robert Archibald Smith (1780–1829). In the appendix volume to his subsequent five-volume folio edition of 1826 (item '2d 125') Thomson included 'The Troubadour' to his own air once again, but this time with 'Symphonies and Accompaniments' provided by the German Romantic composer Carl Maria von Weber (1786–1826). From November 1821 Thomson acted on a general permission to set any Scott verses he chose to music in his publications (see Scott's letter to Thomson of November 1821, BL, Add. MS 35,265, ff. 96–97) and as a result Scott had no direct influence over the appearance of his work in subsequent editions of Thomson's song-collections. There is no evidence of any direct involvement on Scott's part in the inclusion of 'The Troubadour' in Thomson's work.

The present text follows that in *Paul's Letters to his Kinsfolk* (1816), 211–12, as best representing the culmination of the initial creative process, without emendation.

Historical Note

In *Paul's Letters* Scott printed three French poems, with his own translations of them, taken from a manuscript collection given to him as a souvenir of the Battle of Waterloo (for details see the Historical Note to no. 86, 'Romance of Dunois'). The second of these poems is 'The Troubadour', which Scott supposed, like the 'Romance of Dunois', to be 'a common and popular song in France' (*Paul's Letters*, 212), though having no prior knowledge of it himself. In the third edition of the work, published later that year, he noted that 'Paul has since learned that these two romances were written by no less a personage than the Duchesse de St Leu' (222n). This title was granted at the Bourbon restoration in 1814 to Hortense de Beauharnais (1783–1837), step-daughter to Napoleon and the wife of his brother Louis Buonaparte (1778–1846), who was appointed King of Holland by Napoleon in 1806. The poem was not, however, included in the appendix of her 'Romances' in *Mémoires sur Madame la Duchesse de St Leu* (London, 1832).

Scott's poem is a rather loose translation of the French original (titled 'Romance de Troubadour') as given in *Paul's Letters* (216–17), particularly of the first verse which might be literally translated 'Burning with love, as he left to go to war, / the troubadour, enemy of sorrow, / thought about his young shepherdess in this way, / every morning while singing this refrain'. In the following lines the original talks about dying for love and honour rather than fighting for them. The French also has nothing about splintering lances in the third verse or shields in the fourth verse, while the second has the troubadour in a military encampment or his tent rather than marching.

Explanatory Notes
214.title   Troubadour   troubadours were lyric poets, living in southern France from the 11th to the 13th centuries, who sang songs of love and gallantry in Provençal.
214.19   falchion-sweep   the action of a broad curved sword with the blade on the convex side.
214.26   glaive   a lance or spear.
214.28   stave   a verse of a song, an expression derived from the name for the set of lines drawn for musical notation.

88.   Song of Folly

Textual Note
These lines seem to have been composed at much the same time as 'Romance of Dunois' (see no. 86), during or shortly after Scott's visit to Brussels and Paris in August and early September 1815. No manuscript appears to have survived and they were first published as his translation of a French original from the notebook of a French officer who had fallen at Waterloo in *Paul's Letters to his Kinsfolk* (Edinburgh, 1816), 212–13. One copy of *Paul's Letters* (BL, c.28.g.4) contains an earlier state of sheet O (pp. 209–24) which includes these lines marked with a few minor revisions in Scott's hand: 'in a season' in the opening line is altered to 'on a season'; 'And though' in line 9 is revised to 'Though thus'; and in line 11 'And Constancy' becomes 'Fidelity'. All these corrections were duly implemented in the published text.

The poem was subsequently included in Scott's *Poetical Works* of 1820 (12.225) with no evidence of further authorial involvement, except for the removal of the final line of asterisks that indicate the conclusion of the French original is indecipherable (see Historical Note), and the addition of the title of 'From the French'. Afterwards it passed into the successive lifetime editions of Scott's collected poems and into Lockhart's posthumous edition of 1833–34 (11.308), similarly with only changes of the kind normally associated with the printer. The change from 'his wife' to 'a wife' in line 7 in editions from 1825*PW* (10.64) onwards is probably due to carelessness at the printing-house.

The present text follows that of *Paul's Letters to his Kinsfolk* (Edinburgh, 1816), 212–13, as that of the first printing. The title (from the French one of 'Chanson de la folie') has been added editorially and the final line of asterisks has been removed, but otherwise no emendations have been made.

Historical Note
In *Paul's Letters to his Kinsfolk* (1816) Scott printed three French poems, with his own translations of them, taken from a manuscript collection given to him as a souvenir of the Battle of Waterloo (for details see Historical Note to no. 86, 'Romance of Dunois'). The present poem is the third of these, and Scott remarks in *Paul's Letters* that the notebook contained 'another verse of this last song, but so much defaced by stains, and disfigured by indifferent orthography, as to be unintelligible' (213). The author of this French original has not been identified.

Scott's poem is a reasonably accurate translation of the French original in *Paul's Letters* (218), though arguably he is a little more severe in his judgement of Cupid/Love than the original poet. The French calls Love a 'fripon' (rogue) for his bigamy, but also implies that his 'double galanterie' is understandable as both ladies are very beautiful. The two offspring, which are Fidelity and Folly in Scott's version, are 'the lover' and 'Pleasure' in the original. Scott was aware that in this context 'L'amant' (the lover) in the penultimate line of the French original does not make sense, for he footnotes this '*Ita* [thus] in MS.'

Explanatory Notes
215.1   Cupid   the Roman god of love, usually represented as a beautiful winged boy.

89.   The Lifting of the Banner

Textual Note
The words of this song—followed by another by James Hogg (1770–1835) as the Ettrick Shepherd—first officially appeared in *The Ettricke Garland; Being Two Excellent New Songs on the Lifting of the Banner of the House of Buccleuch, at the Great Foot-ball Match on Carterhaugh, Dec. 4, 1815* (Edinburgh, 1815), [3]–5. Comprising an eight-page pamphlet (leaf size 24.5 x 14.5 cm), with the opening cover serving as a title-page and bearing a vignette illustration of the Buccleuch banner along with other emblems, this was specially printed by James Ballantyne for the occasion. No full autograph manuscript for Scott's piece has been discovered. However letters sent to Mrs Marianne Maclean Clephane and to her daughter Margaret, by then Lady Compton, contain early drafts of the opening sections. In his letter to Lady Compton, dated 12 November 1815, inviting her to provide 'some good rattling tune', Scott offered as a prompt the first stanza and the chorus, written 'extempore as they occur' (*Letters*, 4.125–26). Examination of the original letter in the archives of the Northampton family at Castle Ashby (FD 1357) indicates that Scott was indeed actively engaged as he wrote, with 'From' being altered to 'Oe'r' as the opening word, and the second word in the second line finally settling down as 'beacon' after the prior deletion of both 'summons' and 'signal'. In the letter to Mrs Clephane (*Letters* 4.124; original also at Castle Ashby), where Scott provides the same portion of text but on a separate page, the situation is reversed at the beginning with Scott deleting 'O'er' in favour of 'From', while in the second line the text oscillates between 'summons' and 'signal' before arriving at the form found in the printed version. Though undated (apart from docketing as November 1815), this second letter appears to be slightly later than the one sent to Lady Compton. Whatever the case, the composition of both songs in *The Ettricke Garland* must have been accomplished in some haste. Scott's request for assistance from Hogg was sent via a letter to the Duke of Buccleuch of 19 November (*Letters*, 4.127–28), Hogg meeting the challenge with a draft version of his 'To the Ancient Banner of the House of Buccleuch', as sent to Scott in a letter on 24 November: *The Collected Letters of James Hogg*, ed. Gillian Hughes and others, 3 vols (Edinburgh, 2004–08), 1.258–60. Both versions in the *Ettricke Garland* are end-dated similarly, Scott's as from '*Abbotsford, Dec. 1, 1815*', Hogg's on the same day from his home at Altrive Lake. The production of the pamphlet itself must also have been conducted at speed. As early as 2 December 1815 the *Caledonian Mercury* in anticipating the match was able to print full versions of both songs under the heading 'Foot-ball Match'. Collation of Scott's song here against *The Ettricke Garland* reveals only minor presentational differences, indicating that the newspaper had already purchased the *Garland* or been provided with advance copy for promotional reasons.

Scott's song was reprinted on numerous occasions. A report of the event in the *Edinburgh Weekly Journal* for 13 December 1815, which copies both songs from the pamphlet, has been claimed as Scott's own work, largely as a result of Lockhart's statement in providing a large extract that such was supplied to 'Ballantyne's newspaper' by 'the Sheriff of the Forest' (*Life*, 3.391, 395–97). However, James Ballantyne's proprietorship of the *Journal* only commenced in 1817, and the account given there does not entirely match the extract provided by Lockhart, which might potentially have been taken from an assortment of contemporary papers, including the London ones. While Scott's authorship of the core account is a moot point, there can be little doubt that the two poems reached a wider audience through this medium. The song, along with Hogg's, also featured in the *Scots Magazine* for December 1815 (77.935–36), with some slight variants; then again verbatim in the *Edinburgh Annual Register, for 1813*, 6: 1 and 2, cccxli–cccliii, published in Edinburgh on 11 January 1816. Variants in the *Scots Magazine*, almost certainly the work of the printer, include the Scoticisation of 'with' as 'wi'' in line 5, and the replacement of 'our' with 'the' (to read 'the pleasure') at line 31. The song entered the collected editions with the *Poetical Works* of 1820 (12.229–32), under the extended title of 'Song, on the Lifting of the Banner of the House of Buccleuch, at a Great Foot-Ball Match on Carterhaugh', and yet again without any signification of a tune. It is here that the spelling 'Ettricke' is first normalised to 'Ettrick', the end signature and dating also at this point being discarded. In parallel the piece featured under the title of 'From the Brown Crest of Newark, &c.' in George Thomson's *Select Melodies of Scotland*, 5 vols (Edinburgh, 1822–23), 2.item 2, with an air attributed to Nathaniel Gow and the harmony to Beethoven. In the collected sets of Scott's poetry, the text of the song continued to be printed regularly, with only minor printing changes, up to the Lockhart posthumous 1833–34 edition (11.321.4), where it appears with the following footnote: 'This song appears with music in Mr G. Thomson's Collection—1826. The foot-ball match on which it was written took place on December 5, 1815, and was also celebrated by the Ettrick Shepherd' (312n).

The present text follows that in *The Ettricke Garland* (Edinburgh, 1815), [3]–5, without emendation.

Historical Note
The grand football match commemorated in this song took place at Carterhaugh, a level area near the confluence of Yarrow Water and Ettrick Water, some 4 km (2½ miles) SW of Selkirk. While there is some uncertainty in contemporary documents about the exact date, with James Hogg for example in his *Songs* (Edinburgh, 1831), 262, opting for 5 December, the greater probability is that the match and its surrounding ceremonies took place on Monday, 4 December 1815, as declared in the extended title of *The Ettricke Garland* (see Textual Note). That such was the original intention is apparent in Hogg's letter to Scott of 16 November from the Duke of Buccleuch's residence at Bowhill:

> the great match at Ball is finally settled to take place at Carterhaugh on *Monday the fourth of Decr*. I never was so much excited with the prospect of any thing I wish no lives may be lost. The two parishes of Yarrow and Selkirk are to be matched against each other Lord Hume as I understand to head the Yarrow shepherds against you and the *other* Souters of Selkirk. I hope at all events to see you then. (*Collected Letters*, ed. Hughes, 1.256)

If less clear initially about the precise nature of the contestants, there can be no doubt that Scott was a prime mover in a scheme which foreshadows his later orchestration of public events such as George IV's visit to Edinburgh in 1822. As he had already written to Mrs Clephane on 12 November:

there is a terrible match at football to be played at Carterhaugh in December by the parish of Ettrick against the parish of Yarrow, backed by the Duke and the Sheriff—so the whole glens are to be raised by beacons as of yore. We are to hoist the old pennon of the house of Buccleuch a curious banner with the arms and war cry of the family and clan painted upon it, and I am soliciting Lady Compton to help me to a good air for a ballad to be called and entitled 'The lifting of the Banner'. (*Letters*, 4.123)

In the event, the sides facing each other were the Sutors of Selkirk (after the old song, and comprising the inhabitants of the town) and the shepherds of Yarrow and Ettrick, the latter headed by the Earl of Home. Carterhaugh, in addition to its traditional association with the ballad of 'Tamlane' (see *Minstrelsy*, 2.242–44), would have been an especially redolent historical location for Scott, overlooked as it was by Newark Castle (an old stronghold of the Douglas family) and close to Philiphaugh, where the Marquis of Montrose's royalist forces had been surprised and defeated in 1645. The ceremonies prior to the contest were presided over by the Duke of Buccleuch. No direct record survives of the tune connected to Scott's piece, though Lady Compton apparently enclosed one in a letter to Scott of 18 November, somewhat apologetically noting its similarity to the song 'Johnny MacGill', which she felt might be used alternatively in its own right (NLS, MS 3886, f. 233r). According to Scott's response of 12 December, while there was not enough time 'to train a ballad singer or two to sing our joint minstrelsy upon the field', her contribution had nevertheless been 'much admired by all who had an opportunity of hearing it' (*Letters*, 4.141). (This music as written by Lady Compton and her sister Anna Jane Clephane was later copied into Mrs Charlotte Hope-Scott's MS 'Book of Border Ballads', still at Abbotsford.) The match itself evidently resembled a mixture of handball and the present-day rugby scrum, with the two rivers representing the goals. After the first game had been won by the Selkirk men, the Yarrow/Ettrick shepherds were augmented through a body from Galashiels changing sides, leading to a victory for the latter decided mainly by force of numbers: see *Transactions of the Hawick Archaeological Society* (1871), 107–13. A third game was proposed between a hundred men selected from each side, but encroaching darkness prevented this taking place. While Scott and his family retired to a grand ball at Bowhill (*Letters*, 4.143), fights reportedly broke out fuelled by resentment amongst the Selkirkers over the shift of allegiance by the Galashiels men before the second match, a defection laid by some at Scott's own door and by one account causing a lingering resentment (*Transactions*, 109–10). Scott's more upbeat post-mortem comments by contrast point to the rechannelling of old animosities and creation of a spirit of unison: as had no doubt been the original design in what might be counted as one of the earliest modern appropriations of sport as a means of social engineering.

Explanatory Notes
215.1   Newark   Newark Hill (440 m), 7 km (4½ miles) W of Selkirk, above the junction of Ettrick Water and Yarrow Water, overlooking Bowhill. Compare Scott's account of 'Newark Castle' in *Border Antiquities*, 2 vols (London, 1814): 'A fine back ground is formed by Newark hill, which rises at a little distance, and adds greatly to the effect of the landscape' (1.66).
215.5   Banner   the Buccleuch banner, still owned by the Buccleuch family, is a pennon-shaped flag, bearing both stars and crescents, as well as a stag *trippant* surmounted by an earl's coronet and the words 'A Bellendaine' (the war-cry of the Buccleuchs), on a field azure.
215.6   over Ettricke eight ages and more   by tradition the designation

of Buccleuch derived from an early ancestor having come to the king's rescue while hunting in 'Buck Cleugh' about 3 km (2 miles) above the junction of Rankle Burn and Ettrick Water. In actuality the lands of Buccleuch and Bellenden in Selkirkshire appear to have come into the possession of the family during the 13th century. In Scott's own day the Dukes of Buccleuch owned extensive lands in both Ettrick and Yarrow, including James Hogg's tenancy at Altrive Lake.

216.10   her crescents   referring to the crescents ornamenting the Buccleuch banner (see note to 215.5).

216.12   Flowers of the Forest   an allusion to the ancient Scottish folk tune lamenting the defeat of James IV by the English at Flodden in 1513. Words were later added, notably Jean Eliot's lyrics in 1756. Eliot's version was included by Scott in *Minstrelsy*, 1.274–78. The term Forest also alludes to the traditional name of Ettrick Forest, still commonly used after the deforestation caused by sheep since the 16th century.

216.14   stripling's weak hand   Scott's eldest son, Walter, then 14 years old, delivered the Buccleuch banner on horseback to Lady Anne Scott, eldest daughter of the 4th Duke of Buccleuch. As Scott recalled to his friend J. B. S. Morritt: 'Your friend Walter was banner-bearer dressd like a forester of old in green with a green bonnet and an eagle feather in it and as he was well mounted and rode handsomely over the field he was much admired by all his clansmen and the spectators who could not be fewer than two thousand in number' (*Letters*, 4.146).

216.19   contention of civil dissension   echoing civil disturbances that had broken out in 1815 as a result of agitation for reform and repeal of unpopular legislation such as the Corn Laws, culminating in the two Spa Fields meetings held in London on 15 November and 2 December.

216.20   HOME, DOUGLAS, and CAR   names of leading clans on the Scottish Borders (with Kerr spelt here as Car), each of whom had at times in the past feuded with the Scotts as with each other, while on other occasions banding against the English as a common foe.

216.21   ELLIOT and PRINGLE   two further reiving Border clans, once mortal enemies.

216.34   Borough and Landward   the town and the country. The phrase is commonly found in Scots Law.

216.35   herd's ingle-nook   herdsman's or shepherd's chimney corner.

90.   Lullaby of an Infant Chief

Textual Note
Scott evidently first sent this song to the wife of John Norman Macleod, 24th Chief of Macleod (1788–1835), in response to her supplying him with the Highland tune of 'Cadil gu lo' (see Historical Note), although no manuscript has survived. In the early months of 1816, in the interest of the editor and song-collector Alexander Campbell (1764–1824), Scott was soliciting contributions towards Campbell's *Albyn's Anthology* and it seems likely that Mrs Macleod had sent him this melody in response to such an appeal. However, before *Albyn's Anthology* appeared Scott's song was included by the actor Daniel Terry (1789–1829) in his drama *Guy Mannering; or, The Gipsey's Prophecy: A Musical Play, in Three Acts* (London, 1816), 27, first performed at London's Theatre Royal, Covent Garden on 12 March 1816, and printed shortly afterwards. In adapting it for the London theatre an English refrain beginning 'Oh! rest thee, babe' was

substituted for the Gaelic one, and the second verse of the song provided for Campbell was also omitted. Soon afterwards it was published, with a footnote acknowledging its previous inclusion in Terry's play, in Alexander Campbell, *Albyn's Anthology*, 2 vols (Edinburgh, 1816–18), 1.22–23. Although the first volume of *Albyn's Anthology* was not published until July 1816, Scott referred to the music for his song as 'already printed' for Campbell's work in his letter to Terry of 18 April 1816 and expressed his intention of asking Campbell to publish his words anonymously there (*Letters*, 4.217–18). Accordingly Scott's name was not given at the head of 'Lullaby of an Infant Chief' in Campbell's work, or in the index to the volume. Scott was almost certainly motivated by a wish to dissociate this song from his novel *Guy Mannering* (1815), which had been published anonymously, even though, as he told Terry in his letter of 18 April, 'I cannot see what earthly connexion there is between the song and the novel, or how acknowledging the one is fathering the other' (218).

The text of Scott's song in *Albyn's Anthology* was then implicitly acknowledged by its author by being reprinted in his 1820 *Poetical Works* (10.174–75), though without a musical setting. The first instance of 'baby' (though not the subsequent ones) is spelled 'babie' (line 1) and there are also other changes of the kind normally associated with the work of the printer. The footnote was revised for the new context, Scott referring to 'my friend Mr Terry's' in a publication of his own work rather than simply 'Mr Terry's' and omitting the name of the composer of the music to the stage version of the song. Scott's poem was subsequently printed in the various lifetime editions of his collected poems and in the posthumous Lockhart collected edition of 1833–34 (11.317–18), without other changes than those normally associated with the work of the printer.

'Lullaby of an Infant Chief' was also included in George Thomson's *The Select Melodies of Scotland*, 5 vols (Edinburgh, 1822–23), 2.item 31. However, from 1821 Thomson acted on a general permission to set any Scott verses he chose to music in his publications (see Scott's letter to Thomson of November 1821, BL, Add. MS 35,265, ff. 96–97), and consequently Scott had no direct influence over the appearance of his work in any subsequent editions of Thomson's song-collections. Minor variations in wording and the omission of the Gaelic refrain were almost certainly made by Thomson in order to fit Scott's words to music (see Historical Note).

For his national song project Campbell created a substantial musical and textual apparatus for the Gaelic-derived items, in this case involving the original Gaelic words to the song and a literal translation, which Scott dispensed with in creating a version appropriate to a collection of his own poetry and which seems equally inappropriate, therefore, to the present volume. The present text thus follows that of Scott's *Poetical Works* of 1820 (10.174–75). 'Gadil' in the name of the air has been corrected to 'Cadil', as in *Albyn's Anthology*, but no other emendations have been made.

Historical Note
The tune of 'Caidil gu lo', described as 'Sleep on till day. A Skye Air', was published by Patrick MacDonald as item 157 in *A Collection of Highland Vocal Airs* (Edinburgh, 1784), 26. According to Scott's letter to Daniel Terry of 18 April 1816 (*Letters*, 4.218), the tune was given to him by the wife of John Norman Macleod, 24th Chief of Macleod. Scott had visited the couple at Dunvegan in 1814 and Mrs Macleod had presented him with a purse made by herself, Scott in return sending her husband a presentation copy of *The Lord of the Isles* (1815). The words Scott wrote to fit this tune he sent to Mrs Macleod, and in his letter to her of 3 March 1815 (*Letters*, 4.38–39) he mentions that his

eldest daughter, Sophia, sang the song. Probably Mrs Macleod had originally sent with the Highland tune the Gaelic words generally sung to it, for these are included in the editorial notes in *Albyn's Anthology*, along with a rough translation into English. From this it seems clear that the refrain of 'cadil gu lo' originally formed part of a love-song for a 'youth who went away in the evening' (*Albyn's Anthology*, 1.22) and not part of a lullaby for the infant of a Highland chieftain.

According to a footnote in *Albyn's Anthology* (1.22n), the tune to which Scott's words were sung in Terry's *Guy Mannering; or, The Gipsey's Prophecy*, which opened at London's Theatre Royal at Covent Garden on 12 March 1816, was composed by John Whitaker (1776?–1847). The equivalent note in Scott's *Poetical Works* of 1820 (10.174n) remarks that the words were there 'adapted to a melody somewhat different from the original'. In this musical play, Miss Bertram sings it to Colonel and Miss Mannering as a song which is 'said, from a very ancient period, to have been sung in our family to soothe the slumbers of the infant heir' (*Guy Mannering; or, The Gipsey's Prophecy*, 27). Writing to Anna Jane Clephane in May Scott noted that 'Caduil gu la has taken immensely in Covent Garden' (*Letters*, 4.180). There were therefore two, albeit related, melodies in circulation along with different versions of Scott's words, a scholarly-antiquarian one and a theatrical hit, although they shared a title and Scott by 1820 seemed equally happy for his name to be associated with either.

Scott's words were set to an entirely different tune, composed by Leopold Kozeluch (1747–1818), in George Thomson's *The Select Melodies of Scotland*, 5 vols (Edinburgh, 1822–23), 2.item 31. Thomson adapted Scott's words to suit Kozeluch's pre-existing music, in particular omitting the lullaby's refrain. In successive reprintings in various editions of his collected poems, however, Scott preferred to continue footnoting Terry's 1816 stage play rather than either Campbell's or Thomson's musical works.

That three melodies were associated with Scott's song in his lifetime and with his consent may be one reason why Lockhart did not add music to 'Lullaby of an Infant Chief', as he did for some other songs, in the posthumous collected edition of Scott's poetry of 1833–34 (11.317–18).

91. Jock of Hazeldean

Textual Note

'Jock of Hazeldean' was first published in Alexander Campbell's *Albyn's Anthology*, 2 vols (Edinburgh, 1816–18), 1.18, with musical notation following on page 19. In his letter to Lady Compton of 6 February 1816, describing his promised contribution to Campbell's work, Scott gives her the words of the first stanza, adding 'I will make out the legend' (*Letters*, 4.172), that is, complete the story. A surviving manuscript version in Scott's hand, end-dated 'Abbotsford 24 July', forms part of a small red leather-bound autograph album once belonging to Lady Frances Shelley (Morgan, Acc. 500). Unfortunately no year is given, but it is probable that Scott's contribution to Lady Shelley's book was made during her visit to Abbotsford in the summer of 1819. This manuscript version differs from the published text of *Albyn's Anthology* in several respects, most obviously in its Scots being much diluted: in the first stanza, for instance, 'weep ye' is 'weep you' (line 1), 'ye sall' is 'you shall' (lines 4, 5), 'Sae' is 'So' (line 6), and 'loot' is 'let' (line 7). It is likely that Scott, writing out his verses from memory, consciously or unconsciously adapted them to their English recipient. There are, however, more substantial variations in wording, most strikingly in line 28 which in the manuscript reads 'The bridal hour is near'; but this is clearly a presentation manuscript and not a preliminary draft for the published text.

Scott's verses of 'Jock of Hazeldean' were subsequently published in his *Poetical Works* of 1820 (10.171–73) with a headnote stating, 'The first stanza of this ballad is ancient. The others were written for Mr Campbell's Albyn's Anthology' (171). Corson supposes that Scott may have tried to write 'the song which eventually became *Jock of Hazeldean*' for the Scottish song-collector George Thomson (1757–1851) around 1811. This is on the basis of a mention of 'Lord Langley' in a letter to Thomson of May that year and that the rejected suitor is referred to in the second stanza of 'Jock of Hazeldean' as 'lord of Langley-dale' (*N&I*, 71–72, note to 2.491(d)). There seems no reason, however, to doubt Scott's own statement in his headnote in the 1820 *Poetical Works* that the song was written for Campbell's work and at no point does he refer to a completion of the ancient fragment forming the first stanza as 'Lord Langley'. Apart from the addition of a headnote in 1820 the only differences from the text of *Albyn's Anthology* appear to be the work of the printer. The alteration in line 17 from 'O' chain o' gold' to 'A chain o' gold' is probably the result of textual corruption. 'Jock of Hazeldean' was included in the successive lifetime editions of Scott's collected poetry and in the Lockhart posthumous collected edition of 1833–34 (11.315–16) with no evidence of further authorial involvement in the text.

The popularity of 'Jock of Hazeldean' meant that other Scottish song-collectors were anxious to include it in their works. George Thomson printed 'Jock of Hazeldean' 'by express permission' as item 7 in the third volume of the five-volume edition of his *Select Melodies of Scotland* of 1822–23, giving the traditional air Campbell had collected with a new and more elaborate musical setting by an unspecified composer. Thomson subsequently included the piece in the Appendix volume of the 1826 folio edition of his work (5.item 231) with new 'Symphonies and Accompaniments' by the Austrian composer Johann Nepomuk Hummel (1778–1837). However, from 1821 Thomson acted on a general permission to set any Scott verses he chose to music in his publications (see Scott's letter to Thomson of November 1821, BL, Add. MS 35,265, ff. 96–97) and Scott had no direct influence over the appearance of his work in subsequent editions of Thomson's song-collections. Robert Archibald Smith (1780–1829) afterwards included Scott's words with a more straightforward, simple accompaniment of his own in the second edition of *The Scotish Minstrel*, 6 vols (Edinburgh, [1828]), 5.80. Perhaps Smith had not obtained formal permission to include Scott's verses in his work, since he makes no acknowledgement to Scott as he does to song-writers like James Hogg and Robert Tannahill in the Preface. There is no sign of Scott's authorial hand in the texts of 'Jock of Hazeldean' in any of these later song collections.

In the case of this Borders air no elaborate Gaelic context was provided for the reader in *Albyn's Anthology*, 2 vols (Edinburgh, 1816–18), 1.18, so that this first authorised publication was well-suited to Scott's subsequent incorporation of the song into his own collected poetry. It is therefore the copy-text here, and no emendations have been made.

Historical Note

The composer and writer Alexander Campbell (1764–1824) had been employed by Scott's mother to teach her sons music, while Scott himself paid him in 1817 to teach theory of music to his daughters, Sophia and Anne. In his letter to Lady Compton of 5 February 1816 Scott describes Campbell as 'a regular musician with a good deal of taste, a furious highlander, and I believe a very good man' (*Letters*, 4.171). With the help of a grant from the Highland Society of Scotland Campbell travelled hundreds of miles through the country collecting tunes for his *Albyn's Anthology*, 2 vols (Edinburgh, 1816–18). Scott involved himself heavily in its production, writing the prospectus, securing permission for it to be dedicated to the Prince Regent, providing a frontispiece, enlisting his correspondents both as subscribers and contributors, and writing new words to a number of the tunes. In his letter to the composer John Clarke Whitfeld (1770–1836) of 22 February 1816, responding to a request for words to Whitfeld's music, Scott expresses a wish that Whitfeld 'were near me to suggest tunes and hum them over till my stupid ear had got some hold of them', adding that he proceeded in this way when writing songs for 'an old Highland acquaintance who fell back in the world', surely Alexander Campbell (*Letters*, 4.179). From this it appears that Scott's lyrics were far more closely linked to a particular tune when writing for Campbell than they were in his songs for George Thomson.

Anxious to promote Campbell's interest, Scott set out to make this historical and scholarly work one that would also have a popular appeal for drawing-room and professional singers. He told Lady Compton, 'It is a great card for him to have good words' (*Letters*, 4.172), and he was correspondingly vexed when Campbell 'stuff'd in some execrable trash of his own which he calls poetry' (*Letters*, 4.246). 'Jock of Hazeldean' certainly did become popular. For example, it was taken up by the actress Catherine Stephens (1794–1882), who performed it regularly: see, for instance, 'Second Yorkshire Musical Festival', *Harmonicon*, 3 (October 1825), 177. The popularity of Scott's words in his lifetime is also shown by their republication in collections by George Thomson and Robert Archibald Smith (see Textual Note). In the twentieth century the song was a key item in the repertoire of the celebrated folk-singer Jean Redpath.

Campbell recorded that he collected the tune together with the words of the first verse in the course of a tour in the Scottish Borders. During this tour he visited the sisters of his friend Thomas Pringle in Jedburgh, '[t]he oldest of whom communicated the admirable & now popular air of "Jock of Hazlegreen," or Hazeldean': see 'Notes of my Third Journey to the Borders', EUL, La.II.378/2, p. 10. He must have communicated this to Scott, who gave the words of the existing stanza to Lady Compton in his letter of 6 February 1816, describing the tune as 'most beautiful and to me an entirely unknown Scottish air' (*Letters*, 4.171). Although Scott did not know it, the tune had been previously published under different guises for many years; and, under the title of 'Lashley's March', it has been dated by John Glen back to a publication of 1652: see *Early Scottish Melodies* (Edinburgh, 1900), 39–41. Child (no. 293) records the entire ballad as 'John of Hazelgreen' in five different variants, some of which post-date Scott's popular song and were probably influenced by it. Child's 'Version A' apparently derives from a manuscript transcribed by C. K. Sharpe for Scott himself, although the first stanza of this version is not the same as that of Scott's 'Jock of Hazeldean', and it is probable that either Scott did not recognise it as related to the stanza supplied by Campbell, or that he saw it after making his contribution to *Albyn's Anthology*. As Charles G. Zug III argues, it seems likely that Scott himself replaced 'Hazle-green' with 'Hazeldean', a name that he identified with Hassendean in Roxburghshire: see '"Jock of Hazeldean": The Re-Creation of a Traditional Ballad', *Journal of American Folklore*, 86 (April to June 1973), 152–60. In this way Scott localised the story and, in giving the heroine's unwanted suitor lands in Northumberland and County Durham, turned it into an account of a cross-Border love-affair. The original story is not particularly localised, and the male speaker's attempt to marry the girl to his son is successful when, after resisting his gifts and blandishments, it is revealed to her that he is in fact the father of young Hazlegreen.

Explanatory Notes

219.title   Scott refers to the 'estate of Hazeldean, corruptly Hassendean' in a Note to Canto 1 of *The Lay of the Last Minstrel* (Edinburgh, 1805), 221. Hassendean is a former Scott stronghold on the left bank of the River Teviot opposite Cavers, in Roxburghshire.

219.11   chief of Errington   the Errington family owned Walwick Grange on the bank of the North Tyne close to Hadrian's Wall at Warden, about 3 km (2 miles) W of Hexham in Northumberland.

219.12   Langley-dale   situated 8 km (5 miles) N of Barnard Castle in County Durham.

219.19   managed hawk   a hawk trained to hunt in the sport of falconry.

219.20   palfrey   a small saddle-horse for a lady.

92.   Pibroch of Donald Dhu

Textual Note

'Pibroch of Donald Dhu' was first published as 'Pibroch of Donuil Dhu' in Alexander Campbell's *Albyn's Anthology*, 2 vols (Edinburgh, 1816–18), 1.89. An early manuscript version survives in the form of two unwatermarked leaves, each measuring approx. 19.6 x 12.5 cm, the second of which seems to have been constructed from two pieces, suggesting that the paper was possibly torn from a notebook (NLS, Acc. 13426). A note in another hand starting at the foot of the recto of the second leaf reads 'This is the *prima cura* [first draft] of the Pibroch. It was written at the Clerk's table while Jeffrey was pleading the case of Sir W^m v Lady Cunninghame Feb. 9 1816. The names of two of the Counsel are mentiond from what reason I know not'. (Scott has apparently jotted down in a different pen-stroke the names of two of the lawyers involved.) In this manuscript Scott's verses consist of only four eight-line stanzas with a number of revisions and corrections, and these include eight lines unique to this version. The second stanza opens

> Come o'er the lake's <wild> broad wave
> Come from the wildwood
> None may be absent save
> Woman and childhood

while the third stanza opens

> Blaze out our pennon brave
> Let the gale shake it
> Come like the oceans wave
> When the winds wake it

Scott mentioned in a letter to Lady Abercorn of 14 June 1816 that he had recently been writing two or three songs for Alexander Campbell and that 'One of them is the only good song I ever wrote—it is a fine Highland Gathering tune called *Pibroch an Donuil Dhu* that is the Pibroch of Donald the Black' (*Letters*, 4.284). The manuscript original of this letter (Morgan, MA 427/64) continues with a draft of the song in Scott's hand that differs substantially both from the earlier manuscript and from the subsequently published version. Where the NLS manuscript has 'Dirk targe and bonnet plume / Glance o'er the heather' this manuscript reads 'Wide waves the eagle plume / Blended with heather', as in all published versions (see lines 35–36 of the present text). In the version contained in Scott's letter to Lady Abercorn he seems to have experimented with a high degree of repetition in each verse, probably to mimic the return of the basic melody in the successive variations of the pibroch form (see also Historical Note).The first verse of twelve lines begins here with lines 1–4 as published and ends with lines 5–8, while lines 9–12 as printed are sandwiched between them. The second verse opens 'Pibroch of Donald Dhu &c as in the first stanza' and ends 'Come away come away &c'. Scott begins the third stanza 'Pibroch of Donald Dhu &c', but then seemingly abandons his experiment, since the fourth and fifth stanzas consist each of eight lines only, as in the NLS manuscript and all the subsequent separately-published texts. The version sent to Lady Abercorn, otherwise closer to the published text, is thus far from a fair copy, and it also shows a number of deletions and corrections.

When first published in *Albyn's Anthology*, 2 vols (Edinburgh, 1816–18), 1.89, Scott's words consisted of five eight-line stanzas without an explanatory headnote, perhaps because the musical notation that preceded them (82–88) itself provides the context of a pibroch and variations. However, when Scott came to include his verses as 'Pibroch of Donald Dhu' in his *Poetical Works* of 1820 (10.176–79), without Campbell's music, he clearly needed to provide material illustrating that musical context and did so in a headnote, giving the supposed historical background for the tune, the words accompanying the Gaelic base melody, and an English translation of them. In addition 'bares one' in line 16 was corrected to 'bears one', this orthographic error having been pointed out by John Wilson Croker in a letter to Scott of 19 July 1816 (NLS, MS 3887, ff. 94–95), the only one of a number of suggestions in this letter to have been actually taken up. Immediately under the title Scott noted that his verses were written for *Albyn's Anthology*, the following line then providing the name of the tune. Scott's verses afterwards appeared in the successive lifetime editions of his collected poems, and in Lockhart's posthumous collected edition of 1833–34 (11.319–21), with only changes of the kind normally associated with the work of the printer.

'Pibroch of Donald Dhu' was also reprinted 'by express permission' by George Thomson (1757–1851) in his *Select Melodies of Scotland*, 5 vols (Edinburgh, 1822–23), 3.item 4. However, from 1821 Thomson acted on a general permission to set any Scott verses he chose to music in his publications (see Scott's letter to Thomson of November 1821, BL, Add. MS 35,265, ff. 96–97) and Scott had no direct influence over the appearance of his work in subsequent editions of Thomson's song-collections. Using the same basic tune, Thomson had it set with new symphonies and accompaniments, and Scott's verses were preceded by the historical part of his headnote in his 1820*PW*. Robert Archibald Smith (1780–1829) afterwards included Scott's words under their original title of 'Pibroch of Donuil Dhu', without a headnote and set to the same tune with a more straightforward, simple accompaniment of his own, in the second edition of *The Scotish Minstrel*, 6 vols (Edinburgh, [1828]), 6.25. Perhaps Smith had not obtained formal permission to include Scott's verses in his work, since he makes no acknowledgement to Scott as he does to song-writers like James Hogg and Robert Tannahill in the Preface. There is no sign of Scott's authorial hand in the texts of either of these later song collections.

A substantial Gaelic context was provided for this song in *Albyn's Anthology*, notably musical notation that made clear the pattern of a pibroch and variations for the reader. Scott adapted his verses for a collection of his own poems by altering the title from 'Pibroch of Donuil Dhu' to the anglicised (and now more generally known) 'Pibroch of Donald Dhu' and adding a headnote that explained the historical background as well as giving the Gaelic words to the basic theme of the pibroch. The present text follows that in the *Poetical Works* of 1820 (10.176–79) as the earliest version prepared by Scott for an edition of his collected poems. The statement that the verses were written for *Albyn's Anthology* has been omitted, but otherwise no emendations have been made.

Historical Note
During 1816 Scott was heavily involved in assisting Alexander Campbell (1764–1824) with his Scottish song-collection *Albyn's Anthology* (for information on this collection and Scott's participation in it see Historical Note to no. 91, 'Jock of Hazeldean'). Campbell's work still represents a significant piece of scholarship for its inclusion of *piobaireachd* (pipe-music) songs and for its information about early publications of Scottish music, the result of his having travelled hundreds of miles collecting through the Highlands and Isles. His manuscript record of a tour made between 23 July and 23 October 1815 (EUL, La.III.577) shows that he then collected 122 pieces of music, some directly noted down by himself and others from the collections of people he visited along the way. These Gaelic songs in particular would probably have had only a restricted circulation were it not for Scott's attempts to make the work one that would also have a popular appeal for drawing-room and professional singers, in particular by writing his own words for the traditional melodies Campbell had collected. Scott may well have had in mind the tremendous commercial success achieved by the national song project of Thomas Moore (1779–1852), *Irish Melodies*, which began publication in 1808 and by the time it was concluded in 1834 ran to ten volumes and a supplement.

The pipe-tune for which Scott wrote 'Pibroch of Donald Dhu' is associated, perhaps arbitrarily, with the Battle of Inverlochy of 1431, which was fought after Alexander MacDonald, 12th Earl of Ross and Lord of the Isles (d. 1449), had been imprisoned by James I of Scotland. A force of Highlanders led by Donald Balloch, Alexander's cousin, defeated Royalist forces led by the Earls of Mar and Caithness, and it is estimated that more than a thousand men were killed in the battle, including the Earl of Caithness. Balloch then went on to ravage the country of Clans Cameron and Chattan because of their loyalty to the king. The tune was first published by Campbell in *Albyn's Anthology*, he having obtained it in September 1815 during a visit to the collector and editor of Highland bag-pipe music Niel MacLeod of Gesto (c. 1754–1836) in Skye. Campbell's music manuscript of 'Pioberach Dhomnuill Duibh, or Cameron's Gathering', dated 'Gesto Sky 29th Septr 1815', is among a bound volume of his surviving manu-scripts and correspondence (EUL, La.II.51, ff. 172–76), and his title associates it with the Cameron rather than Macdonald clan. He noted that this version was 'as taught by the MacCrimmons of Sky to their Pupils' (f. 172), the well-known MacCrimmons (or Mackrimmons) being hereditary pipers to the MacLeods of Dunvegan in Skye. In a note to the tune of 'MacGregor's Gathering' in *Albyn's Anthology*, 1.90, Campbell recorded obtaining the tunes for both 'Pibroch of Donald Dhu' and 'MacGregor's Gathering' at the same time and in the same way, by a 'tedious and exceedingly troublesome' process that involved translat-ing MacLeod's *canntaireachd* (a system of verbal notation where melody notes were represented by vowels and grace-notes by consonants) into conventional musical notation. A pibroch (*Piobaireachd*, literally piping) is a piece of formal music for the bagpipe, an extended composition in which a melodic theme is reworked in a series of elaborate formal variations. In Campbell's musical setting the words of Scott's lyrics are preceded by the melody and the Gaelic words associated with it, and individual verses are interspersed with the variations (1.82–88).

Explanatory Notes

220.title   a pibroch (piping-music) for Donuil Dhu (*Gaelic* for Donald the Black), presumably intended by Scott to signify Donald Balloch, cousin to Alexander MacDonald, Lord of the Isles (see Historical Note). Alexander Campbell, however, gives the name of the tune he collected as 'Pioberach Dhomnuill Duibh, or Cameron's Gathering' (EUL, La.II.51, ff. 172–76). An early chief of the Camerons of Lochiel, who supported the MacDonalds at the battle of Harlaw in 1411, was called Domhnall Dubh, or Donald the Black, but Scott apparently linked the tune to the Battle of Inverlochy of 1431 because of the mention of Inverlochy in the Gaelic original.

220.headnote   Earls of Mar and Caithness   Alexander Stewart, Earl of Mar (*c.* 1380–1435), was a prominent government political leader and magnate in the north of Scotland. He had previously commanded the government forces at the Battle of Harlaw in 1411. Alan Stewart, the Earl of Caithness who was killed at the Battle of Inverlochy, was the second son of Walter Stewart, Earl of Atholl (early 1360s–1437). Alan had been granted his father's earldom of Caithness in 1430 and given a major role in King James I's campaign against the Lord of the Isles.

220.headnote   words of the set, theme, or melody   these are taken from the start of Campbell's musical setting in *Albyn's Anthology*, except that the Gaelic spelling of 'Inbhirlochi' is approximated to the usual Lowland form of 'Inverlochy'.

220.4   Clan-Conuil   evidently referring to the MacDonald clan, although the name is usually associated with the McConnells, who have a common ancestry with the MacDonalds.

221.19   Leave the corpse   compare the passage of the fiery cross in Canto Third of Scott's *The Lady of the Lake* (1810), where in order to answer the immediate summons of their chief various clan members abandon both a funeral and a wedding.

221.24   Broad swords and targes   a Highland broadsword is a cutting sword with a broad blade, while the *targe* is a small, round shield.

221.35   eagle plume   mark of high rank in a clan, where the chief was entitled to wear three eagle feathers, and his chieftains two.

93.   Nora's Vow

Textual Note

There appears to be no surviving manuscript material for 'Nora's Vow', which was first published with Scott's name in Alexander Campbell's *Albyn's Anthology*, 2 vols (Edinburgh, 1816–18), 1.21, alongside the traditional tune as arranged by Campbell himself (20) and with the original Gaelic words to the tune and a translation of them beneath Scott's verses. 'Nora's Vow' was afterwards included in Scott's 1820 *Poetical Works* (10.180–82), without the musical setting (although the tune itself is named) and without the original Gaelic song and its translation, although a new headnote was provided (see also below), and Scott also stated beneath the name of the tune that his song had been written for Campbell's collection. Otherwise the only changes are of the kind that can be

attributed to the work of the printer, with the possible exception of the substitu-
tion of 'water-lily's' for 'water-lilies' in line 25. From there it passed through
the successive lifetime editions of Scott's collected poetry and into the Lockhart
posthumous edition of 1833–34 (11.322–24) with only changes of the kind nor-
mally associated with the work of the printer.

'Nora's Vow' was also reprinted 'by express permission' by George Thomson
(1757–1851) in his *Select Melodies of Scotland*, 5 vols (Edinburgh, 1822–23),
1.item 36. In a letter of November 1821, Scott refused to write any new songs
for Thomson's work (BL, Add. MS 35,265, ff. 96–97). In his reply Thomson
wrote, 'since no hope now remains of an original song from you for *the Deuks
dang o'er*, I cannot deny myself the pleasure of uniting Nora's Vow to that very
pretty air; for I have sung them together till I am in raptures with them' (BL,
Add. MS 35,268, f. 71). As his letter indicates, Thomson put Scott's words to
another Scottish tune, 'The Deuks dang o'er my daddie', as arranged by the
Czech composer Leopold Kozeluch (1747–1818).

'Nora's Vow' required substantial adaptation for publication without musical
notation in the new context of Scott's own *Poetical Works* of 1820. The original
Gaelic words for the traditional Highland tune and a translation of them were
important to Campbell's ethnographic purposes, but were surplus to require-
ments here. Instead Scott provided a summarising headnote, distinguishing
between his own poem and the traditional song, while a courteous acknowledge-
ment to *Albyn's Anthology* was also made.

The present text follows that of Scott's 1820 *Poetical Works* (10.180–82),
as the earliest version prepared by him for an edition of his collected poems.
Scott's headnote has been preserved, but the statement that the song was first
written for *Albyn's Anthology* has been omitted. Otherwise no emendations have
been made.

Historical Note
During 1816 Scott was heavily involved in assisting Alexander Campbell (1764–
1824) with his Scottish song-collection *Albyn's Anthology* (for general informa-
tion on this collection and Scott's participation in it see the Historical Note to
no. 91, 'Jock of Hazeldean', and for its significance for Highland music see the
Historical Note to no. 92, 'Pibroch of Donald Dhu').

'Nora's Vow' was developed by Scott from a Gaelic original, 'Oran Gaoil'
(A Love Song) which Campbell printed, along with an English version, at the
bottom of the page in *Albyn's Anthology* underneath Scott's lyrics and which
begins 'Cha teid mis a chaoidh' (1.21), which is also the name of the tune. This
original is in three stanzas with a refrain, and the sole speaker is a girl who lays
down in each some impossible circumstance in which she would willingly go to
'the Earl's young son': respectively, the moving of a mountain, the swan build-
ing her nest on the cliffy rock, and the salmon-trout making three leaps in the
lamb-fold. Campbell rather than Scott, who was not a fluent Gaelic speaker,
must have supplied this material, which is merely summarised in the headnote
to Scott's *Poetical Works* of 1820 (see Textual Note). Scott's four stanzas give
the girl a name, provide her with an older and more worldly-wise interlocutor in
Callum, and add a dramatic and comical conclusion in the change of mind that
leads to her wedding her previously-despised suitor. In other words a traditional
song is turned into one ideally suited for drawing-room entertainment of the
kind provided by Thomas Moore's *Irish Melodies* (1808–34). The subsequent
popularity of Scott's lyrics is shown by Thomson's adoption of them in his
1822–23 collection of *Select Melodies of Scotland* (see Textual Note).

Explanatory Notes
222.title   Nora's   the name Nora is particularly associated with Ireland.
222.headnote   Red Earl's son   Campbell's English version has 'Earl's young son' for the Gaelic 'óg an Iarla' ruaidh' (the son of the Red Earl), so here Scott renders the Gaelic more literally than Campbell has done. The medieval Irish magnate Richard de Burgh, 2nd Earl of Ulster (b. in or after 1259–1326), was known as the Red Earl. He was a close ally of Edward I of England, and his daughter Elizabeth was married to Robert I of Scotland.
222.9   Callum   a common Gaelic male name, a variant of Malcolm.
222.19   Awe's fierce stream   the Awe is a river of central Argyllshire, running from the NW of Loch Awe 8 km (5 miles) NW to Loch Etive. As it leaves the loch it rushes through a narrow and deep gorge called the Pass of Brander.
222.20   Ben-Cruaichan   Ben Cruachan is a mountain of 1100 m filling the space between Loch Awe and the upper reach of Loch Etive.
222.20   Kilchurn   a rocky elevation at the influx of the confluent Orchy and Strae rivers to Loch Awe, and the site of an ancient stronghold of the Macgregors, although the present ruins are those of a castle whose keep was built by Sir Colin Campbell in 1440.
223.30   Highland brogue   a Highland shoe made of untanned hide.

94.   MacGregor's Gathering

Textual Note
Although the composition date of 'MacGregor's Gathering' is unknown and no manuscript version has apparently survived, it seems probable that Scott wrote it in the spring of 1816 at much the same time as he was working on its companion piece 'Pibroch of Donald Dhu' (see no. 92). It was first published in Alexander Campbell's Scottish song-collection, *Albyn's Anthology*, 2 vols (Edinburgh, 1816–18), 1.90, with notes apparently by Campbell and followed by Campbell's musical notation (91–97).
'MacGregor's Gathering' was subsequently included in Scott's own *Poetical Works* of 1820 (10.183–85), without musical notation although the name of the tune is given as well as a note to say that it was written for *Albyn's Anthology*. Scott also supplied a footnote translation of '*Thain' a Grigalach*' as 'The MacGregor is come', and a brief headnote on the tune and the severe treatment of the clan. The spelling of 'Gregalich' in the refrain was also changed to 'Gregalach'. Scott's verses then passed through the successive lifetime editions of his collected poetry without any other changes than those normally associated with the work of the printer, and similarly into the Lockhart posthumous edition of 1833–34 (11.325–27), where the spelling of the Gaelic word was changed once more, this time to read 'Grigalach'.
'MacGregor's Gathering' was also included by Robert Archibald Smith (1780–1829), set to the same tune with a more straightforward, simple accompaniment of his own, in the second edition of *The Scotish Minstrel*, 6 vols (Edinburgh, [1828]), 6.78–79. Smith uses the spelling 'Gregalich', and as his text begins with the refrain in full it follows the text written underneath Campbell's musical setting in *Albyn's Anthology* rather than the text-only version there. There is no sign of any involvement by Scott in this later song collection, and perhaps Smith had not obtained formal permission to include Scott's verses in his work, since he makes no acknowledgement to Scott as he does to song-writers like James Hogg and Robert Tannahill in his Preface.

'MacGregor's Gathering' required some adaptation for publication without musical notation in the new context of Scott's own collected poems. Scott added a new headnote and omitted the detailed and somewhat cumbersome annotation by Campbell on his source for the tune and the historical background to the legal proscription of the Campbell clan. The present text follows that of Scott's 1820 *Poetical Works* (10.183–85), as the earliest version prepared by him for the different context of an edition of his collected poems and one which includes his own headnote. The statement that the verses were written for *Albyn's Anthology* has been omitted, and the following emendation has also been made:

223.1   mist's (*Albyn's Anthology*) / mists

Historical Note
During 1816 Scott was heavily involved in assisting Alexander Campbell (1764–1824) with his Scottish song-collection *Albyn's Anthology* (for general information on this collection and Scott's participation in it see the Historical Note to no. 91, 'Jock of Hazeldean', and for a brief account of Campbell's Highland collecting tour and its significance for Highland music see the Historical Note to no. 92, 'Pibroch of Donald Dhu'). Scott had been aware since the 1790s at least of the legendary figure of Rob Roy MacGregor and the attempted suppression of the MacGregor clan. He owned a copy of *The Highland Rogue: or, the memorable actions of the celebrated Robert Macgregor, commonly called Rob-Roy* (London: 1723: *ALC*), while his narrative poem *The Lady of the Lake* (1810) was set in the Trossachs and Loch Lomond area associated with Rob Roy. In December 1817 he would also publish the novel *Rob Roy*.

The pipe-tune for which Scott wrote his words was taken down by Campbell in September 1815 during a visit to the collector and editor of Highland bagpipe music Niel MacLeod of Gesto (*c.* 1754–1836) in Skye. He noted that this version was 'as performed by the celebrated Macrimmons of Skye' (*Albyn's Anthology*, 1.90), the MacCrimmons (or Mackrimmons) being hereditary pipers to the MacLeods of Dunvegan in Skye. The 'tedious and exceedingly troublesome' collecting process involved translating MacLeod's *canntaireachd* (a system of verbal notation where melody notes were represented by vowels and grace-notes by consonants) into conventional musical notation. Campbell apparently later sent the manuscript of his own music notation of this tune to Sir John MacGregor, 1st Baronet of Lanrick (1745–1822) with a letter of 25 July 1816: see 'Thain a' Grhiogaireach.—The MacGregors' Gathering', *Celtic Monthly*, 3 (January 1895), 79.

A pibroch (*Piobaireachd*, literally piping) is a piece of formal music for the bagpipe, an extended composition in which a melodic theme is reworked in a series of elaborate formal variations. In Campbell's musical setting individual verses of Scott's lyrics are interspersed with the formal variations (1.91–97), the Gaelic words to the basic melody being given above the treble clef line at the start. The final two lines of Scott's stanzas are an obvious imitation of these and of the rhythmical patterning of the pibroch melody.

Explanatory Notes
223.2   nameless   an act of the Privy Council of Scotland of April 1603 abolished the name MacGregor and ordered those who had hitherto borne it to take some other surname. A subsequent act of the Council of 1613 introduced the death penalty for those who were formerly called MacGregor who should assemble in groups of more than four: see *Rob Roy*, ed. David Hewitt, EEWN 5 (Edinburgh, 2008), 527, note to 170.27–28.

223.3 Gregalach Campbell explains 'Gregalich' as 'the Hebridean mode of pronouncing *Gregarich*, substituting the letter l for r': *Albyn's Anthology*, 1.90. *Gregarich* is the Gaelic designation of the MacGregor clan.

223.5 signal for fight, that from monarchs we drew the battle-cry of the MacGregors is *Ard-Coille* (High Forest), but Scott is perhaps rather alluding to the chief's motto of *S rioghal mo dhream*, meaning 'Royal is my race', alluding to the clan's supposed descent from the Pictish King Kenneth I (d. 858), known as Kenneth Macalpine.

223.9 Glen Orchy's proud mountains Glenorchy is a large Highland parish of an alpine character in the Lorn district of Argyllshire, long associated with the MacGregor clan. The Orchy, flowing through it, runs (under the name of the Tulla) 17 km (10½ miles) from the Perthshire boundary to Loch Tulla, and from there as the Orchy SW for 43 km (27 miles) to Loche Awe.

223.9 Coalchuirn the 5-story keep of Kilchurn Castle, a ruin even in Scott's day, was built by Sir Colin Campbell in 1440. Once a stronghold of the Macgregors, it is situated on a rocky elevation at the influx of the Orchy into Loch Awe, 4 km (2½ miles) NW of Dalmally.

223.10 Glenstrae and Glenlyon the Strae in Glenorchy flows 13 km (8 miles) SW to join the Orchy about 1 km above Kilchurn Castle. The Lyon flows roughly eastwards from Loch Lyon 48 km (30 miles) along the narrow valley of Glenlyon, eventually falling into the Tay.

224.17 pursue us with beagles as Campbell explains, an Act of the 1625 Parliament of Charles I required the members of the MacGregor clan to report annually to the Privy Council and provide cautions for their good behaviour. If they failed to do so they were declared outlaws and could legally be apprehended or killed. Campbell states that 'their enemies became so bold and callous, that they actually employed blood-hounds, called by the natives "*Coin-dubh*," (black dogs) to hunt them': *Albyn's Anthology*, 1.90.

224.25 Loch Katrine the setting of Scott's poem *The Lady of the Lake* (1810), a large loch bordering both SW Perthshire and Stirlingshire, about 1.5 km (1 mile) at its widest, and curving about 13 km (8 miles) SE.

224.26 Ben-Lomond a mountain 974 m high, extending along the E side of the upper part of Loch Lomond towards Loch Katrine.

224.27 Craig Royston a cavern at the E side of Loch Lomond, known as Rob Roy's Cave.

95. Verses, Composed for the Occasion

Textual Note

Scott's original manuscript containing these verses survives in The New York Society Library as part of a collection of papers (Call No. Z–L S431 C6) mainly relating to their composition for a dinner held on 19 December 1816 by Edinburgh's Lord Provost for the Russian Grand Duke Nicholas. They were originally owned by Robert Johnston (1771?–1833), a contemporary of Scott's at the Edinburgh High School, afterwards grocer on the North Bridge, and a long-serving Bailie of the city. The holograph manuscript (no. 2) is on a single leaf, measuring approx. 26.9 x 19.1 cm, pasted into a leather-bound volume and consequently with no visible watermark. Untitled, it contains the wording of the whole song, largely unpunctuated and with a minimum of internal alteration. Between the second and third stanzas, however, Scott had originally written 'To which the following lines may be added if it is thought necessary', before the deletion of this note either by Scott or another hand. The collection also contains a short undated note by Scott (no. 4) reading: 'Dear Sir / The Inclosed is quite right—Print as many copies as you like only don't give up your author / WS'. Most probably this was addressed to Johnston and relates to what appears to be a proof of the wording of the song, also in the same collection (as no. 7). The holograph poem itself is followed by a short account (no. 3) of the surrounding circumstances by Johnston, headed 'Edinburgh 29 June 1831':

> The foregoing verses were composed by Sir Walter Scott Bar[t] on occasion of the Arch Duke Nicolas of Russia, visiting Edinr—He is now the Emperor. He was invited to dinner on Monday [*sic*] the 19 December 1816 with Sir William Arbuthnot Bar[t] then Lord Provost of Edinr, to which dinner all the Rank around was invited. It was thought right that some compliment should be paid to the Royal Guest; a piece of Music was selected, with which he was likely familiar, "God Save the Emperor"— but words applicable to the occasion were required; I waited on my old school fellow on Sunday betwixt Sermons, & during the Evening received the original Copy of the lines, here preserved—The whole company joined in giving them to Sir Walter, who was present, but maintained his usual Silence—

The proof copy in the New York Society Library collection lacks any heading, but supplies punctuation to the manuscript wording, as well as rendering the name of [Czar] Alexander in the first line in capital letters. The next reference to a printed version by Scott occurs in an undated note to John Ballantyne: 'As you are a collector of my fugitives I send you a trumpery thing to the tune of God preserve the Emperor Francis sung at the Provosts Gala with good approbation. Give no copies' (NLS, MS 863, f. 182; *Letters*, 1.512). Corson, who dates this about 22 December 1816, assumes that Scott must have been referring here to the manuscript before it was printed, on the grounds that otherwise there would be no need to say give 'no copies' (*N&I*, 35–36, note to 1.512(e)). However, the presence of a four-page booklet containing the song (ff. 180–81) alongside Scott's note to Ballantyne within the same bound volume in NLS indicates that Scott had actually sent printed copy of the song as performed at the dinner. This includes the following full title for the piece, set in a variety of different fonts: 'Verses, Composed for the Occasion, and adapted to Haydn's celebrated air, "God Save the Emperour Francis", And sung by a Professional Band, after the Dinner given by the Lord Provost to the Grand Duke Nicholas of Russia, and his Suite, at Charlotte Square, 19th December 1816'. Another copy of the same booklet, in unbound form, survives as NLS, Abbot 111(6). With print only occupying the first page, the page dimensions are 20 x 12.3 cm (full sheet 20 x 24.6 cm), and there is no visible watermark. Compared with the proof version, the most significant change (apart from the addition of its extensive heading), is the placing of 'Illustrious Stranger' in the final stanza in capital letters, matching those used for Alexander in the first stanza. According to an article headed 'Hymn for the Czar' in *Chambers's Edinburgh Journal* for 29 December 1832, which includes the verses, the company at the dinner 'receiv[ed] copies ... on a printed slip' (381). At the time the song featured in a number of contemporary accounts in newspapers and other periodicals, including the *Caledonian Mercury* of Saturday, 21 December 1816, and *Scots Magazine* for January 1817 (79.74–76). In a letter of 1817, forming part of the New York Society Library collection (no. 6), Scott asks Johnston if he could supply Lord President Hope and his wife with 'two copies of the song', having not retained any himself. Johnston subsequently in 1819 presented Scott with a mounted copy of the verses exhibiting 'beautiful ... penmanship' (*Letters*, 5.489), and a framed glazed print of the verses still survives at Abbotsford.

This song did not appear in any collected editions of Scott's verse until the posthumous set of 1833–34 (10.365–66), which supplies a full title comparable to that in the original printing. Here, however, the three stanzas are run on together, without any indentation of alternate lines; while in line 21 'Foemens' has mistakenly become 'Freemen's'. An accompanying footnote states: 'Mr, afterwards Sir William Arbuthnot, the Lord Provost of Edinburgh, who had the honour to entertain the Grand-Duke, now Emperor of Russia, was a personal friend of Sir Walter Scott's; and these *Verses*, with their heading, are now given from the newspapers of 1816' (10.365n).

The present text follows the original broadsheet version of 1816, as found at NLS Abbot 111(6), with a truncated title and the following emendation:

225.21   Foemen's (*Scots Magazine*) / Foemens

Historical Note
According to contemporary accounts, the dinner in honour of Grand Duke Nicholas (1796–1855), was hosted by Sir William Arbuthnot (1766–1829), Lord Provost of Edinburgh, in his residence at 16 Charlotte Square, Edinburgh, on the afternoon of Thursday, 19 December 1816. As the *Caledonian Mercury* reported on 21 December 1816:

> On the desert [*sic*] being removed, the health of the King was drunk, accompanied by "God save the King", sung by an excellent professional band. The Lord Provost then proposed the health of the Emperor Alexander: upon which the following verses, composed for the occasion, were sung by the band, adapted to the celebrated air of Dr Haydn's "God save the Emperor Francis"; all of which, and particularly the allusion in the last verse, were received by the company with much applause.

Czar Alexander had played a major part in the coalition that finally defeated Napoleon the previous year at Waterloo, in the wake of which Scott went on to witness in Paris 'about 15000 Russians pass in review' before the Czar and other dignitaries (*Letters*, 4.95). According to Lockart, the two had met then at a dinner given by the Earl of Cathcart, at which Scott had somewhat awkwardly worn his volunteer uniform (see *Life*, 3.369). The visit of the Czar's younger brother Nicholas to Edinburgh, while apparently in private terms less appealing to Scott (see *Letters*, 4.315), offered an alternative opportunity to recognise on behalf of Scotland both Russia's wartime contribution and her leading position in the new world order.

The 'celebrated air' nominated in the original extended title in German is 'Gott erhalte Franz den Kaiser', a tune composed in 1797 by Joseph Haydn (1732–1809), from lyrics by Lorenz Leopold Haschka (1749–1827), originally as an anthem to Francis II, Emperor of the Holy Roman Empire and later of Austria. The music was afterwards employed in a variety of contexts, and is the tune of the national anthem of Germany.

Explanatory Notes
224.1   brave ALEXANDER   Alexander I (1777–1825), Emperor of Russia from 1801 to 1825. During the Napoleonic wars he had switched allegiances, joining Britain in 1805 in the War of the Third Coalition, but then forming a treaty with Napoleon in 1807 in the aftermath of the Battle of Austerlitz, this alliance in turn collapsing in 1810. His resistance of Napoleon's invasion of Russia in 1812 proved a decisive factor in France's first defeat at the hands of the allies in 1814.
224.6   Tyrant overthrown   Napoleon I (1769–1821), Emperor of the French, finally defeated at the Battle of Waterloo in 1815.
225.11   Of the land of foemen master   Russian troops played a major part in the occupation of France after Waterloo (see also Historical Note).

225.13   just resentment victor   in negotiating the surrender of Paris in 1814 Alexander had offered generous terms to the French, disregarding a desire to avenge the depredations inflicted on his country. See Scott's 'History of Europe, 1814': 'I do not come to retaliate these injuries. I am at peace with France, and it is with Napoleon alone that I am at war' (*Edinburgh Annual Register, for 1814*, 7: 1 and 2 (1816), 268).

225.17   ILLUSTRIOUS STRANGER   referring directly to Grand Duke Nicholas (1796–1855), the Czar's brother, afterwards Emperor of Russia from 1825 to 1855. His rule was marked by its reactionary nature, cultivation of a large military force, and engagement in numerous wars, culminating in the Crimean War (1853–56), with disastrous results.

96.   The Search After Happiness

Textual Note

'The Search After Happiness' was first published anonymously in no. 5 of John Ballantyne's weekly paper *The Sale-Room*, for 1 February 1817, 33–39, and Scott probably wrote it not long before publication. On 1 January he wrote to Ballantyne of his imminent return to Edinburgh from Abbotsford on Friday, 3 January, promising to bring copy for the first three issues of *The Sale-Room* with him, and half-promising a future issue in more light-hearted mood ('Look early out for a light No. 4' (*Letters*, 1.507)). Before the end of the month he was corresponding about specific details of the poem with James Ballantyne, Scott's printer and the confidential reader of his literary work (see also Historical Note). No manuscript has apparently survived.

The poem was reprinted in August that year, again anonymously and as '*From the Sale-Room*', in the *Edinburgh Annual Register, for 1815*, 8: 1 and 2 (1817), cclviii–cclxvi, without evidence of further authorial involvement. However, when it was subsequently included in Scott's own *Poetical Works* of 1820 (10.217–38), some authorial changes appear to have been made in addition to the kind of adjustments normally associated with the work of the printer. A new footnote was provided to *couroultai* ('See Sir John Malcolm's admirable History of Persia', 222), while in line 146 'if worn warm' was altered to 'if taken warm'. Line 265 was redrafted to remove the coarse expression 'Kiss my breech', John Bull's rude speech to the Sultaun being amended to '"Kiss and be d——d," quoth John, "and go to hell!"'. No doubt what was acceptable in a weekly paper was less so in a volume. The poem afterwards passed through the successive lifetime editions of Scott's collected poems and into Lockhart's 1833–34 posthumous collected edition (11.352–66) with no further signs of authorial intervention.

The present text follows that in *The Sale Room* of 1 February 1817, 33–39, as best representing the culmination of the original process of composition. Some unusual indentation given to lines 204–15 has been removed, and a single opening speech mark at the start of line 221 has been corrected to a double one, but no other emendations have been made.

Historical Note

The use of travellers from eastern countries to satirise European society was a well-established literary trope, notable examples including Montesquieu's *Persian Letters* (1721) and Goldsmith's *The Citizen of the World* (1762), while Byron's Turkish tales in verse, such as *The Giaour* (1813) and *The Bride of Abydos* (1813), fostered contemporary interest in the Islamic world. Scott's interest in the post-Waterloo settlement of Europe can only have been intensified by his time in Paris during the autumn of 1815, when he observed the interactions of the natives of that city with their recent conquerors from Britain, Prussia, and Russia and wrote about them in *Paul's Letters to his Kinsfolk* (1816). Two recent publications may also have reinforced Scott's interest in oriental tales: *The Arabian Nights Entertainments*, ed. Jonathan Scott, 6 vols (London, 1811: *ALC*); and Henry Weber's *Tales of the East*, 3 vols (Edinburgh, 1812: *ALC*). 'Story of the First Lunatic' in Jonathan Scott's work (6. 31–44) is alluded to specifically in lines 64–66 of 'The Search After Happiness' (see Explanatory Notes). In its reworking of Italian comic verse 'The Search After Happiness' bears a strong resemblance to Byron's *Beppo* (1818) as well as to his masterpiece *Don Juan* (1819–24). Having apparently been a leader in the field of Italian-style comic verse in Britain with 'The Search after Happiness', it is perhaps surprising that Scott did not pursue the form further. By 1817, however, he had become deeply engaged in writing novels. He may also have been hampered by his own reputation: while Byron's work was known to be *risqué*, Scott's acknowledged poems were reputedly decorous enough for any young lady. Scott's correspondence with his literary advisor James Ballantyne shows some concern over this poem's propriety. Scott directs Ballantyne in a letter probably of 29 January 1817, for instance, to substitute the exclamation 'Poffaredio' for 'Cazacco' in line 193 on the grounds that the latter word has 'rather a licentious derivation though constantly used' (*Letters*, 4.427). In another letter Scott is clearly vexed by a further demand from Ballantyne for rewording, perhaps of line 265 which was subsequently bowdlerised for volume publication:

> This is the second time that you really make me spoil my verses but as you are determined on the thing you may read
> Keep what you list quoth John &c.
> Nearer I will not come & I think it spoils the simplicity of the thing altogether—I have no notion of that fastidious sort of delicacy nor do I meet it among good society. (NLS, MS 2525, f. 85)

It may be that Scott foresaw too many potential irritations of this kind had he continued to write in a similar vein.

Explanatory Notes
225.2 Bandello's laughing tale   Matteo Bandello (*c.* 1480–1562) was the author of a collection of *novelle*, or tales, published in 1554 and 1573, several of which were reused by Shakespeare and other Jacobean playwrights.
225.4 Giam Battista   (see also Scott's footnote.) Giovanni Battista Casti (1724–1803) wrote *Le Novelle Galanti* (Gallant Tales) in the *ottava rima* metre. In 'La camicia dell' uomo felice' (The Happy Man's Shirt), a king's son appears to be dying without a cause and the king's astrologer tells him that a cure can be effected by exchanging the prince's shirt for that of a truly happy man. Eventually the king finds a happy peasant, but unfortunately he does not have a shirt. Scott owned a copy of *Novelle di Giambatista Casti*, 3 vols (Paris, 1804: *ALC*), in which this metrical tale appears in Vol. 1, pp. 27–51.
225.6 canorous   musical, singing, melodious.
225.footnote   *La Camiscia Magica*   *Italian* The Magic Shirt. This precise title cannot be identified, that used by Giovanni Battista Casti in his *Novelle* being 'La camicia dell' uomo felice' (see note to 225.4).
226.11 Sultaun Solimaun   a sultan is the king or chief ruler of a Muslim country (one which professes Islam), while Solimaun is a variant of Solomon, the name of an ancient King of Israel renowned for his wisdom.

226.19   Monarch who can amble round his farm   an allusion to King George III (1738–1820), popularly known as 'Farmer George', whose court set an example of duty, respectability and propriety to his subjects.

226.22   a Prince will bid the bottle pass   an allusion to the future King George IV (1762–1830), from 1811 Prince Regent because of the insanity of his father. Although notorious for his dissipated life-style, the Prince Regent was an outstanding patron of the arts and sciences and a particular friend to Walter Scott.

226.28   Serendib   an Arab name for Sri Lanka, from the ancient Tamil name Cerentivu.

226.31   Pegasus   the winged horse on which Bellerophon tried to fly to heaven, the name being used to signify the inspiration of a poet.

226.32   Rennell   originally in the service of the East India Company, the cartographer James Rennell (1742–1830) produced his standard *Bengal Atlas* in 1780, followed by other maps of India and various geographical treatises.

226.33   Captain Sindbad's map   a jocular warning of the fictionality of what follows, since Sindbad the sailor visited magical places, meeting with monsters and supernatural phenomena. In the *Arabian Nights Entertainments*, a collection of ancient Oriental tales introduced into Europe by Antoine Galland in a French translation (12 vols, 1704–07), Sindbad tells the adventures of his seven voyages in the course of seven days to a poor porter who carries goods through the city. On each of these days he holds a feast for his friends and relations and gives the porter a sum of money.

226.38–39   Long: and Co., / Rees, Hurst, and Orme   the publishing house of Longman, Hurst, Rees, Orme and Brown of Paternoster Row in London published the orientalist Jonathan Scott's six-volume edition of the *Arabian Nights Entertainments* in 1811: *ALC*. They had also published Scott's poetry.

227.48   Mollah   a Muslim title for a man learned in theology and sacred law.

227.49   Degial, Ginnistan   the Dajjal (or Liar) in Islam is a false messiah, whose object is to deceive humanity. Ginnistan is the land of the Jinn, supernatural creatures mentioned in the Koran.

227.55   Burton   Robert Burton (1577–1640), author of the encyclopaedic *Anatomy of Melancholy*, first published in 1621 and extended in several subsequent editions up to a posthumously-published one of 1651. Burton defines the different kinds of melancholy and their causes and symptoms in the first part of his work, while dealing with cures in the second.

227.64   Mahazzim al Zerdukkaut   Scott probably encountered this phrase in the 'Story of the First Lunatic', *The Arabian Nights Entertainments*, ed. Jonathan Scott, 6 vols (London, 1811), 6.31–45: *ALC*. The merchant hero is bathed by eunuchs who afterwards bring him 'mahazzim al zerdukkaut' to rub himself with (36). In his note, Jonathan Scott explains that he does not know what this is, but supposes it to be 'compound of saffron, yolk of eggs, or of yellowish drugs' (414).

227.66   Munaskif al fillfily   In 'Story of the First Lunatic' (see previous note) 'munnaskif al fillfillee' is also brought to the merchant hero after his bath (6.36) and Jonathan Scott glosses it as a compound 'of peppers, red, white, and black' (6.414).

227.73   a bowstring or a sabre   the string of a bow was used in Turkey for strangling offenders, while the sabre is a sword with a curved blade.

227.75   leeches   physicians.

227.footnote   D'Herbelot   the life-work of the French orientalist Barthélemy d'Herbelot de Molaineville (1625–95) was his *Bibliothéque orientale* *ou dictionnaire universel contenant tout ce qui regarde la connoissance des peuples de l'Orient* (1697), which is based on an existing Arabic bibliography and contains the substance of a large number of Arabic and Turkish compilations and manuscripts.

227.footnote Receipts of Avicenna The *Canon of Medicine*, by the prolific Islamic scholar Ibn Sina, or Avicenna (*c.* 980–1037), is a famous medical encyclopedia, first translated into Latin by a Gerard of Cremona in the 13th century, reputedly by order of the Holy Roman Emperor Frederick II (1194–1250), and used as a standard medical textbook in many European universities up to the 18th century.

228.79 Tatārs Tatars or tartars are Turkic-speaking Mongolian people, particularly the Turkic Muslims of Ukraine and Russia.

228.83 Malcolm the diplomat and administrator Sir John Malcolm (1769–1833), primarily associated with India, also served in Persia. He explains that 'Coroultai is the name by which this assembly of the Tartar nobles is called' in his *History of Persia*, 2 vols (London, 1815), 1.410n: *ALC*.

228.87 Omrahs (see also Scott's footnote.) Lords of a Muslim court.

228.88 like Sempronius in Bk 21, Ch. 53 of his *History of Rome* Livy describes how, during the Second Punic War, Tiberius Sempronius Longus (*c.* 260–210 BC) argued in favour of an immediate attack against Carthaginian forces in Italy led by Hannibal, against the advice of his fellow-commander Scipio. Sempronius then led his forces into the major Roman defeat of the Battle of the Trebia of December 218 BC.

228.91 Tambourgi drummers. The word may have been familiar to Scott from Byron's song set in Albania beginning 'Tambourgi! Tambourgi! thy 'larum afar / Gives hope to the valiant, and promise of war!': see Canto 2 of Byron's *Childe Harold's Pilgrimage* (London, 1812), 97–100.

228.95 bold Lootie a man engaged in marauding or looting, from the Hindi word 'Luti'.

228.103 Double assessment, forage, and free quarters the doubling of a tax based on the value of property; the provision of supplies; and the obligation to give free board and lodging to troops.

228.104 fearing ... as China-men the Tartars most obviously indicated by the erection of the Great Wall of China in an E–W line along the country's northern frontier.

228.107 reverend Convocation from the name of a provincial synod in the Church of England, called together to debate on ecclesiastical matters.

228.108 turban green mentioned as a distinguishing mark of an emir in Ch. 50 of Edward Gibbon's *The History of the Decline and Fall of the Roman Empire* (1776–88).

228.109 Imaum the officiating priest of a Muslim mosque.

228.110 Santon a European word for a Muslim monk or hermit.

228.110 Fakir a Muslim religious mendicant or beggar.

228.110 Calendar a member of a Persian or Turkish order of mendicant dervishes, religious men who have taken vows of poverty and an austere life.

229.113 Kiosque a light, open pavilion or summer-house.

229.118 Sheik Ul-Sofit a *sheikh* is the chief of an Arab family or tribe. Possibly Scott intends a reference to the title Sheikh al-Islam, an honorific title used for outstanding Islamic scholars and also referring to the governor of religious affairs in the Ottoman Empire.

229.138 *Sympathia magica* Latin sympathetic magic. Scott provides a lengthy note on cures by sympathetic magic to Canto 3 of *The Lay of the Last Minstrel* (London, 1805), 256–60.

230.160   Rais   (see also Scott's footnote.) The captain, who was also often the owner, of a Muslim ship or galley.

230.162   call'd The Happy   *Arabia Felix* was the name given by the Romans to the southernmost province of the three into which they divided the Arabian peninsula.

230.163   Mokha   a port on the Red Sea coast of Yemen.

230.165   where Judæa weeps beneath her palm   an image best known from its use on coins issued by the Roman Emperor Vespasian and the two sons who succeeded him. It refers to Jerusalem after the razing of the Jewish temple there in AD 70.

230.166   Nubian   Nubia was an ancient African empire in what is now southern Egypt and northern Sudan, in the region of the river Nile.

230.168   Copt   a member of an Egyptian Christian sect.

230.169   Bruce his goblet fill'd at infant Nile   the African traveller James Bruce of Kinnaird (1730–94), believing himself to have discovered the source of the River Nile, called to his Greek companion Strates to drink the health of King George III in 'a large cup made of a cocoa-nut shell, which I procured in Arabia, and which was brim-full': *Travels to Discover the Source of the Nile in the Years 1768–73*, 5 vols (Edinburgh, 1790), 3.599: see *ALC*.

230.173   dolimans   wearers of a Turkish dolman, a full-length loose robe with narrow sleeves and an opening in front.

230.174   Giaours   infidels, non-Muslims and especially Christians.

230.177   drink good wine   alcohol is forbidden to Muslims.

230.177   Ramazan   Ramadan is the Islamic holy month when the Koran was revealed, and believers engage in strict fasting during daylight hours.

231.181   eagle-banners   an eagle, as the bird of Jove, was borne on the military standards of the Roman Empire.

231.185   not half the man he once had been   although the settlement of European territory agreed at the Congress of Vienna (1814–15) mostly restored its former territory to the papacy, Avignon and Comtat Venaissin remained part of France.

231.188   vengeful claws of Austria   (see also Scott's 2nd footnote on this page.) By the settlement of European territory after the ending of the Napoleonic Wars agreed at the Congress of Vienna (1814–15), Austria gained Venice and much of northern Italy.

231.189   Great Devil   (see also Scott's 3rd footnote on this page.) Fra Diavolo (Brother Devil) was the name given to Michele Pezza (1771–1806), the famous Neapolitan guerrilla leader who resisted French occupation of Naples and subsequently became the subject of Daniel Auber's 1830 opera of that name. Scott seems to have transferred his legend further south in Italy and to post-Napoleonic times.

231.191   Giovanni Bulli   an Italian variant of John Bull, a name for the stereotypical Englishman.

231.192   tramontane   dwelling beyond the mountains, that is the Italian alps.

231.192   buck   a dandy, a dashing male.

231.193   Poffaredio   normally *poffare dio* (*Italian*: literally, God can do), an exclamation of wonder and mild irritation meaning 'Is that possible?'.

231.198   Monsieur Baboon   a common name for a Frenchman. Scott refers to Louis XVIII, the recently-restored Bourbon monarch of France, as 'Louis Baboon' in his letter to Southey of 26 September 1824 (*Letters*, 8.376).

231.203   a recent hiding   the Battle of Waterloo of 18 June 1815 was the crushing French defeat that ended the Napoleonic Wars.

231.207 *comme il faut* *French* correct in behaviour and etiquette (literally, as it is necessary).

231.208 *Vive le Roi* *French* Long live the King: currently Louis XVIII, the Bourbon monarchy in France having been restored after the Napoleonic wars.

231.209 Nappy Napoleon Buonaparte (1769–1821), Emperor of the French from 1804 to 1815. He had been banished to the island of St Helena following the Battle of Waterloo.

231.212 herring-pool an ocean, in this case the English Channel and North Sea dividing Britain from mainland Europe.

231.footnote 4 Slang Dictionary various English slang dictionaries had appeared from the mid-16th century. Scott owned and frequently referred to Francis Grose's *A Classical Dictionary of the Vulgar Tongue*, 3rd edn (London, 1796): *ALC*.

232.218 lace and lawn to conceal some of the bosom otherwise revealed by the bodice of a woman's dress, the neckline would be edged with a piece of frilled lace or fine linen.

232.224 Ma foi! il s'est tres joliment battu *French* my faith! he fought very prettily.

232.225 m' entendez vous? *French* do you know what I mean? (literally, do you hear me?).

232.226 son-gun a designation implying contempt or jocular familiarity, and supposedly originating from the days when women were allowed to live on naval ships. Births would take place behind a canvas screen erected near the midship gun, and if paternity was uncertain the child was entered in the log as 'son of a gun'.

232.227 Vellington Arthur Wellesley, 1st Duke of Wellington (1769–1852), the victorious British general of the Battle of Waterloo (for which, see note to 231.203).

232.231 sterile farms and unsold goods Britain was currently enduring a post-war agricultural and industrial slump.

232.233 beat the Devil's tattoo drumming with his fingers, as a sign of impatience or annoyance.

232.237–39 "Never to grumble ... pay too much." (see also Scott's footnote.) These lines are slightly adapted from Daniel Defoe, *The True-Born Englishman. A Satyr* (London, 1700: see *ALC*), 57.

233.247 Frangistan (see also Scott's footnote.) A Persian expression, meaning literally 'Land of the Franks' but referring to Western Europe in general.

233.252 cursed war and racking tax with the Napoleonic following the French Revolutionary War Britain had been almost continually at war with France between 1792 and 1815. In order to meet the spiralling costs, parliament sanctioned the introduction of income tax in 1799, which was particularly resented by merchants and manufacturers.

233.257 break the yard commit burglary, one term for which in British law is breaking and entering.

233.260 guinea a gold coin worth 21s, or £1-1s. (£1.05).

233.265 Kiss my breech an only slightly less vulgar version of the insulting 'Kiss my arse', the breech meaning the buttocks, that part of the body covered by a man's breeches. For volume publication in editions of Scott's collected poems the expression was eliminated, the line then reading '"Kiss and be d—d," quoth John, "and go to hell!"' (1820*PW*, 10.233).

233.266 sister Peg previously used for Scotland when John Bull signified England. See, for instance, Adam Ferguson's satire against William Pitt the

Elder, *The History of the Proceedings in the Case of Margaret, commonly called Peg, only lawful sister to John Bull, Esq.* (London, 1761): *ALC*.

233.269   *doucely*   steadily, sedately.

233.270   **erst ... needy slattern**   dirt and slovenliness were depicted as national characteristics of the Scottish people in, for instance, Elizabeth Hamilton's novel *The Cottagers of Glenburnie* (1808).

233.278   **her warlike joys**   Scots had been mercenary soldiers for centuries, but perhaps Scott alludes more specifically to the Jacobite Risings of 1715 and 1745–46, which had produced a number of popular songs.

234.281   **cat-and-doggish**   always snapping and quarrelling.

234.283   **the main chance**   profit or money, perhaps from the game of hazard where the first throw of the dice is called the main.

234.284   **a long grace ... a northern jargon**   alluding to the puritanical Presbyterian Church of Scotland, and to the Scots language.

234.286   **made his leg**   bowed respectfully.

234.291   **Her dram, her cake, her kebbock**   the common Scottish refreshments of a drink of whisky, an oatcake, and some cheese.

234.293   **her absent bairns**   Scottish soldiers and administrators serving in India and the Middle East, where commodities such as tea and spices were obtained and traded.

234.295   *nitmugs*   nutmegs, seeds of an evergreen tree native to the East Indian islands, used as spices and in medicines.

234.296   *speerings*   information obtained by inquiry.

234.296   **our Mungo Park**   Mungo Park (1771–1806) was a native of Selkirkshire in the Scottish Borders and author of the best-selling *Travels in the Interior Districts of Africa* (London, 1799): see *ALC*. The details of his death on an expedition to trace the course of the River Niger had to be pieced together from various records. Additional stories about Park were afterwards picked up by subsequent European travellers in Africa. Scott had been friendly with Park before his second and final departure for Africa in January 1805.

234.297   **sark**   shirt.

234.309   *brose*   a dish of oatmeal or pease-meal made with boiling water or hot milk, and with salt or butter added.

235.314   **verdant Erin**   Erin is an ancient name for Ireland, also known as the Emerald Isle for its lush vegetation.

235.316   **Paddy**   sometimes Paddywhack (see line 344), a generic name for an Irishman, probably from the popularity of the name Patrick, that of the patron Saint of Ireland.

235.323   **wigwam**   originally a tent or hut of native Americans, but extended to similar structures among native tribes in other parts of the world and often used jocularly or pejoratively.

235.324   **middlemen**   in Ireland a person who leases land and sub-lets it again at an advanced rate.

235.325   **screw'd his rent up to the starving place**   compare *Macbeth*, 1.7.60–61: 'But screw your courage to the sticking-place / And we'll not fail'. The general non-residence of Irish landowners on their estates encouraged the proliferation of middlemen extorting the maximum profit from a half-starved peasant tenantry for themselves and the landlord.

235.334   **a bonus of imputed merit**   if a believer repents of sin, he is forgiven by God not through his own merit but through that earned by Christ's sacrifice on the cross. In the Roman Catholic Church receiving Christ in the Eucharist forgives venial sins, while for forgiveness of mortal sins a

Catholic must go to confession and receive absolution from a priest before receiving communion.

235.341 **will he nill he**   whether he will or not.

235.342 **Shilela**   or Shillelagh, an Irish cudgel made of blackthorn or oak.

235.344 **the odds that foil'd Hercules**   Hercules, the son of Zeus and Alcmena in Greek mythology, was a hero of superhuman physical strength, after whom the constellation of Hercules (also known as the Kneeler) was named. According to legend Hercules fought two giants named Alebion and Bergion in Liguria in NW Italy, and when their combined strength proved too much for him he kneeled to pray to his father Zeus for help. Only with divine assistance did he win. The odds that foiled Hercules could therefore be interpreted as two to one, but in this context probably implies fighting against gigantic forces.

235.346 **Ub-bubboo**   a stock exclamation of a stage Irishman.

97. Mr Kemble's Farewell Address

Textual Note
Scott's letter to Mrs Clephane of 23 March 1817 (*Letters*, 4.421) indicates that this poem was written only shortly before that date (see also Historical Note). There is no manuscript material for 'Mr Kemble's Farewell Address' in Scott's hand. A poem of 56 lines was printed in the *Scots Magazine*, 79 (April 1817), 296, with 20 lines (lines 9–28) omitted by Kemble in performance marked by inverted commas, but it is not clear who supplied the magazine with this copy. A shortened version of 36 lines, with a necessary adjustment in line 29 from 'This must not be' to 'But years steal on' (presumably made so as to include the basic idea of the omitted section) was published as part of the report on the conclusion of Kemble's theatrical career given in *The Sale-Room* of 5 April 1817, 105–12 (111–12) and also in the *Caledonian Mercury* of that date. A third early printing of the 36-line version can be found in *An Authentic Narrative of Mr. Kemble's Retirement from the Stage* (London, 1817), 76–77, a commemorative pamphlet produced to mark Kemble's subsequent retirement from the London stage on 23 June 1817 and the public dinner to him given by admirers a few days later on 27 June. It is clear from Scott's letter of 5 May 1817 to the actor George Bartley that he had been approached to write an address marking Kemble's retirement from the London stage also, but had politely declined, 'as from the literary talents belonging to the names which you enumerate you must certainly be considered as having Moses & the Prophets on your side of the border and cannot need assistance from our northern regions' (*Letters*, 4.441). Thomas Campbell obliged, but Scott's earlier address was also included in the commemorative London pamphlet, one of the poems, presumably, that the title-page announces as having been 'selected from various periodical publications'. A contemporary manuscript copy in another hand (NLS, MS 10279, ff. 194–95) of the 36-line version has also survived, almost certainly copied from *The Sale-Room* since it includes the following paragraph of comment given there.

In the performance context to give only the lines spoken by Kemble on the occasion was appropriate, but when Scott included the poem in his collected *Poetical Works* of 1820 (10.213–16) he chose to give the full 56-line version of the poem. This was then included in the subsequent lifetime editions of Scott's collected poems and in Lockhart's posthumous collected edition of 1833–34 (11.348–51) with only changes of the kind normally associated with the work of the printer.

The present text follows that of 1820 *Poetical Works* (10.213–16), as representing Scott's 56-line poem authorised for publication as part of his collected poetry, without emendation.

Historical Note

Scott first met the celebrated tragic actor John Philip Kemble (1757–1823) and his wife during the Easter holidays of 1807 at Bentley Priory at Stanmore in Middlesex, the country house of the Marquess of Abercorn, a welcome interlude from his business in London of petitioning the government on behalf of the Clerks of Session. Kemble became a friend and visited at Ashestiel as well as Scott's Edinburgh home in Castle Street, and Scott was also on familiar terms with other members of Kemble's famous theatrical family, including his even better-known sister, Sarah Siddons (1755–1831), and her son Henry (1774–1815), who was manager of the Edinburgh Theatre Royal from 1809 until his death, when his brother-in-law, William Henry Murray (1790–1852), succeeded him. Kemble was also widely known as a studious, scholarly actor and was clearly sympathetic to Scott's efforts to raise the tone of the Edinburgh theatre. When due to retire from the stage in 1817 it was natural both that Kemble should take a formal farewell of his appreciative Edinburgh audience and that he should invite Scott's participation. Writing to his old friend Mrs Clephane on 23 March 1817 Scott expressed his particular appreciation of Kemble's acting 'the Roman Patrician' roles such as Coriolanus, Brutus, and Cato, as well as expressing some annoyance, given his current ill-health from gall-stones, about the process of producing a poetic farewell for the celebrated actor:

> He made me write some lines to speak when he withdraws and he has been here criticizing and correcting till he got them quite to his mind, which has, I think, rather tired me, for he would not make the alterations on the broad ground that as he was to speak them, he had a title to please himself, but dragd me into the land of metaphysics and rythmical harmony where I am not at present very equal to follow him. (*Letters*, 4.421)

Kemble's final Edinburgh performance (as the eponymous hero of *Macbeth*, Shakespeare's Scottish play) took place less than a week later, on 29 March 1817, when he recited a shortened version of Scott's poem in costume at the end of his performance. According to the report in John Ballantyne's weekly paper, *The Sale-Room* of 5 April 1817, they were delivered:

> with exquisite beauty, and with an effect that was evidenced by the tears and sobs of many of the audience. His own emotions were very conspicuous. When his Farewell was closed, he lingered long on the stage, as if unable to retire. The house again stood up, and cheered him with the waving of hats and long shouts of applause. (112)

Scott's poem, with its appropriate classical allusions, was clearly much admired, being copied out by at least one contemporary admirer (see Textual Note).

Explanatory Notes

236.1   war-horse, at the trumpet's sound   compare Job 39.25, where the horse 'saith among the trumpets, Ha, ha; and he smelleth the battle afar off, the thunder of the captains, and the shouting'.

236.15   the taper, wearing to its close   to burn the candle within the socket is to be on the verge of death (see *ODEP*, 100).

236.29   higher duties   as a Roman Catholic Kemble would be aware of the necessity for spiritual preparation for death.

236.31   like the Roman in the Capitol   Julius Caesar was assassinated in the Capitol in March 44 BC. According to Plutarch's account in the *Life of Julius Caesar* Tillius pulled Caesar's toga down from his neck as a signal for his assassination to begin, but Caesar, when he subsequently saw Brutus among his assassins, pulled it over his head.

237.38   younger men   a covert allusion perhaps to the spectacular debut at the Drury Lane theatre on 26 January 1814 of the charismatic actor Edmund Kean (1787–1833) as Shylock, which had also been an important role for Kemble.

237.44   immortal Shakespeare's magic wand   perhaps an allusion to Prospero's breaking of his magic staff and forswearing his art at the conclusion of Shakespeare's *The Tempest*.

237.49   O favour'd Land   Scotland.

237.56   Friends and Patrons, hail, and FARE YOU WELL!   'Hail and farewell' (ave atque vale) are the final words of Poem 101 of Catullus, in which the Roman poet addresses the ashes of his dead brother.

98. The Foray

Textual Note

'The Foray' was solicited from Scott by the composer John Clarke Whitfeld (1770–1836) in 1815 and first published, as written expressly for that work, in Whitfeld's collection of *Twelve Vocal Pieces*, 2 vols (London, [1817]), 1.item 1. Scott's manuscript forms part of his letter to Whitfeld of 18 April 1817 (now in the Berg Collection, New York Public Library: Scott Letters Vol. 1/4), in which Scott mentions his own haste in composition: 'As I wish to send it immediately I have not taken time to read it over so I will be obliged to you if you will give me an opportunity of seeing it in print.' Nevertheless there is only a single revision in line 8 of this manuscript version, which originally began 'The tramp of the steed', and one indication of hesitation over the choice of the word 'march' in line 16 which is preceded by a deleted 'f'. Scott's verses achieved a very smooth transition into print in Whitfeld's collection, with only those changes normally associated with the work of the printer. Scott's verses on page 3 were set to music by Whitfeld (18–24) in a spirited style, for voice with a straightforward keyboard accompaniment and an introductory four bars marked 'Bagpipe', probably an indication of its Scottish credentials and a direction to the drawing-room keyboard player to simulate that instrument, rather than one to play the passage on an actual set of either Border or Highland bagpipes. So far as is known, Scott had no specific tune in mind in composing his verses, but simply provided Whitfeld with some poetry which he might subsequently set to music as he chose for inclusion in his collection.

'The Foray' then passed without musical accompaniment into the 1820 edition of Scott's *Poetical Works* (10.204–05) with only those changes normally associated with the work of the printer, although some apparent errors were made. In the first line 'the steers on our board' became 'our steers on the board', in line 3 'be gone' was changed to 'begone' (although line 18 retains 'be gone'), and in line 17 'and' has been omitted. From here it passed through the successive lifetime editions of Scott's collected poems and into Lockhart's posthumous collected edition of 1833–34 (11.340–41), also with only the kind of changes normally associated with the printer. In some of these later editions, however, a mistaken attempt at consistency resulted in 'be gone' becoming 'begone' in line 18 (see, for instance, 8vo1830*PW*, 10.105) to match the earlier mistaken occurrence in line 3.

'The Foray' was also included in two further musical collections published in Scott's lifetime. Robert Archibald Smith (1780–1829) set Scott's verses to the air of 'Baddich na brigan' in *The Scotish Minstrel*, 6 vols (Edinburgh, 1821–24), 1.70–71, a tune quite different from the one Whitfeld composed for it. There is no evidence that Scott himself played any part in its publication there, and in the Preface to his collection Smith significantly thanks a number of other lyricists, such as James Hogg, but makes no mention of Scott. It was also included in 1831 in the five-volume collection of George Thomson's *Melodies of Scotland* (Edinburgh, 1831), 3.item 129, Scott's verses appearing underneath those of Sir Alexander Boswell's 'Argyle is my Name', which were set to the Scottish tune 'Bannocks o' Barley Meal' as arranged by Haydn. However, from 1821 Thomson acted on a general permission to set any Scott verses he chose to music in his publications (see Scott's letter to Thomson of November 1821, BL, Add. MS 35,265, ff. 96–97), and consequently Scott had no direct influence over the appearance of his work in any subsequent editions of Thomson's song-collections.

The present text follows that in *Twelve Vocal Pieces*, 2 vols (London, [1817]), 1.item 1, as best representing the culmination of Scott's initial creative process, without emendation.

Historical Note

John Clarke Whitfeld, Professor of Music at the University of Cambridge, set a number of Scott lyrics to music. Scott's letter to Whitfeld of 10 January 1809, for instance, thanks him for sending a copy of his song-settings from *Marmion* (*Letters*, 2.147). On 29 July 1810 Whitfeld wrote to Scott, 'O! that you would write *for me* a little story, in the style of Alice Brand [in *The Lady of the Lake*]' (NLS, MS 3879, ff. 151–52). Scott evidently thought well of Whitfeld, arranging for him to receive extracts from *Rokeby* (1813) for setting to music in advance of the poem's publication, although with the proviso that Whitfeld's songs were not to appear in advance of the narrative poem itself: see the letter to Scott from Whitfeld of 28 March 1813 (NLS, MS 3884, ff. 112–13). In a letter of 24 April 1815, Whitfeld requested Scott to write some pieces specifically for a collection he intended to publish (NLS, MS 3886, ff. 135–36). Scott agreed but took time to fulfil his promise, which Whitfeld reminded him of in a letter of 28 October 1816 (NLS, MS 3887, ff. 121–22). On 6 January 1817 Scott, assuring him that he had 'been silent, but not at all thoughtless of your request', gave permission for Whitfeld to include 'Romance of Dunois' from *Paul's Letters to his Kinsfolk* (*Letters*, 4.352: see no. 86) and also enclosed a copy of another unnamed poem, possibly 'The Dance of Death' (see no. 84), which Whitfeld did not apparently set to music. Scott eventually redeemed his promise in full by his letter of 18 April 1817, which included his copy for 'The Foray' (see Textual Note), and on 11 May 1817 Whitfeld was able to tell Scott that his collection was at long last published (NLS, MS 3888, ff. 67–68).

'The Foray' was undoubtedly just the kind of thing Whitfeld must have been hoping for, a dramatic evocation of the sixteenth-century Border raids from Scotland into England that form such a notable feature in Scott's first successful narrative poem, *The Lay of the Last Minstrel* (1805).

Explanatory Notes

237.1   last of the steers   in a note to Canto 4 of *The Lay of the Last Minstrel* (1805) on his own Border raiding ancestry, Scott explains how the cattle captured by Scott of Harden, 'served for the daily maintenance of his retainers, until the production of a pair of clean spurs, in a covered dish, announced to the hungry band, that they must ride for a supply of provisions' (277–78).

238.10 beacon a bonfire laid in a conspicuous situation and lit to indicate a threatened invasion or celebrate an event of national importance.

238.11 Warder's dull eye that of a watchman on a tower, or a soldier guarding an entrance.

238.20 Teviot the River Teviot rises on the border of Dumfriesshire and flows NE through this region, eventually flowing into the River Tweed SW of Kelso. Alternatively, Scott may intend to refer to Teviotdale, the area drained by that river.

99. Epistle to His Grace the Duke of Buccleuch, at Drumlanrig Castle

Textual Note

These lines appear at the head of a letter of Scott's to the Duke of Buccleuch and Queensberry, undated and without a postmark, now in the National Records of Scotland [NRS], GD224/32/1/41. The document as a whole is written on two leaves, each measuring approx. 25.3 x 20.2 cm, with the watermark 'VALLEYFIELD / 1809', and is endorsed in another hand 'July—W. Scott / Duke of Buccleuch / 1817'. The prose letter, which begins 'My dear Lord', follows the verses and gives notice that Scott and his party expect to arrive 'by the time you are calling for coffee', this being end-dated 'Sanquhar Inn / two o'clock'. The verses were subsequently printed in Lockhart's *Life* (4.81), headed 'July 30, 1817', and the whole published from the original source in Grierson's *Letters* (4.471–72), dated '[July, 1817]'. Secondary sources however suggest that the letter was most likely transmitted, probably by hand, on Saturday, 19 July (see also Historical Note).

The verses did not appear in any of the lifetime editions of Scott's poetry, though they do feature in the one-volume *Poetical Works* of 1841 (667), where the additional punctuation (including the use of dashes at the end of lines) matches the version in Lockhart's *Life*. The present text follows the original manuscript in NRS, GD224/32/1/41, with the expansion of two ampersands in the penultimate line. The title has been supplied editorially.

Historical Note

These lines describe part of a journey undertaken by Scott, accompanied by his wife, daughter Sophia and close friend Adam Ferguson (1771–1855), after the rising of the Court of Session in Edinburgh for the summer vacation in 1817. It first involved a short stay with his old colleague Hector Macdonald Buchanan (d. 1828) at his home Ross Priory on the southern edge of Loch Lomond, from where Scott (then researching his novel *Rob Roy* (1818)) branched out on a day's excursion to the braes of Glen Falloch. Evidently the original plan had been to set out straight for the Duke of Buccleuch's palace at Drumlanrig after a stay of several days; but this was forestalled by illness at Ross, resulting in Scott and his party engaging in a kind of self-imposed quarantine by taking an excursion round Ayrshire beforehand (see *Letters*, 4.470, 472). Lockhart's account of this part of the journey includes a visit to Glasgow (*Life*, 4.80–81), though Scott in his own letters make no mention of this, and the present lines may be taken to suggest that he went straight from Ross to Greenock: see *Rob Roy*, ed. David Hewitt, EEWN 5 (Edinburgh, 2008), 354. The first five lines in the verses in fact seem to indicate (as they rhythmically reflect) a series of overnight stops

at staging posts along the way, ending at Sanquhar inn, with Scott apparently
writing from there early in the afternoon on 19 July to announce his intended
arrival at Drumlanrig that evening. After a stay of about a week there, Scott's
excursion was completed by a return to Abbotsford on 26 July (*Letters*, 4.479).

Explanatory Notes
238.1 Ross Ross Priory, on the S shore of Loch Lomond, about 15 km
(9 miles) N of Dumbarton, home of a branch of the Buchanan family. The
present house, remodelled in a Gothic style, was complete in 1816.
238.1 Ben-Lomond distinctive peak (974 m) in the Scottish Highlands,
situated on the E shore of Loch Lomond.
238.2 Greenock extensive seaport town in Renfrewshire on the S shore at
the mouth of the River Clyde, about 37 km (23 miles) W of Glasgow.
238.3 Largs town and parish in N Ayrshire situated on the Firth of Clyde,
about 20 km (12½ miles) SW of Greenock, and enjoying some of the facilities
of a spa resort at that time.
238.3 Northmen a drilling referring to the battle of Largs in 1263, when
an attempt by the King of Norway to reassert sovereignty over the Western
seaboard of Scotland was thwarted by the Scots. Relics of the battle seen
there were described by Sophia Scott in a letter of 3 August to her governess:
'We went from Ross to Drumlanrig round by Greenock and Largs, at which
last place we walked over the ground where the battle against the Danes was
fought; the remains of immense cairns of stones mark the battle': *Letters,
hitherto unpublished, written by members of Sir Walter Scott's family*, ed. P. A.
Wright-Henderson (London, 1905), 41–42.
238.4 Ardrossan town and parish in Ayrshire, about 18 km (11 miles) S of
Largs and 50 km (31 miles) SW of Glasgow, with lodging houses for visitors
and popular for sea-bathing by 1830. See also next note.
238.4 harbour ... shilling the construction of a harbour at Ardrossan
was projected by Hugh Montgomerie, 12th Earl of Eglinton (1739–1819),
with the object of providing a port for Glasgow, the work being authorised by
an Act of 1805 (which also covered a canal to Glasgow). Funds were obtained
from shareholders, with over £100,000 being spent on the project, much
of it supplied by the Earl himself. By 1807 a pier had been completed, but
recommendations for a wet dock faltered as a result of planning uncertainties,
and the scheme was further disrupted through the Earl's death in 1819.
238.5 Old Cumnock town and parish, about 40 km (25 miles) SE of
Ardrossan and 26 km (16 miles) E of Ayr, standing at an important crossroads.
Distinct from New Cumnock, which was created as a separate parish in 1650.
238.6 Sanquhar town and parish, near the head of Nithsdale in
Dumfriesshire, about 24 km (15 miles) SE of Old Cumnock and 15 km (9
miles) NW of Drumlanrig (see next note). A mining centre in Scott's time.
238.7 Drumlanrigg Drumlanrig Castle, in Upper Nithsdale, about 28 km
(17½ miles) NW of Dumfries. After the death of the 4th Duke of Queensberry
(1725–1810), it had been acquired by Charles William Henry Scott, 4th
Duke of Buccleuch (1772–1819), who embarked on an ambitious programme
to restore the estate after the depredations of its previous owner. As Scott
observed after his arrival in a letter from Drumlanrig of 24 July to Joanna
Baillie: 'The late Duke of Queensberry cut down the magnificent woods
which once surrounded Drumlanrigg but there are already five hundred acres
replanted and the Duke proposes to extend them to upwards of a thousand'
(*Letters*, 4.474–75).
238.7 we anchor perhaps intentionally echoing Scott's earlier verse epistle

to the 4th Duke of Buccleuch (see no. 81), written in Summer 1814 from the Lighthouse Yacht at Shetland and Orkney.

100. Mackrimmon's Lament

Textual Note
Scott appears to have written 'Mackrimmon's Lament' in the autumn of 1817 for publication in the second volume of the collection *Albyn's Anthology* made by the Edinburgh musician Alexander Campbell (1764–1824). In a letter to Scott of 29 September 1817 Campbell thankfully acknowledges the 'admirable Lyrics which you sent to me just now adapted to the favourite pibroch, or rather Bagpipe Lament, "cha till mi tuille"' (NLS, MS 3888, ff. 185–86). A manuscript of Scott's verses, with a headnote, in his own hand, survives in the Scott Manuscript Collection of the Brotherton Library, University of Leeds, written in a four-page booklet of paper with a watermark 'VALLEYFIELD / 1809' and addressed 'To Miss Buchanan / Cambusnan'. Cambusnan has not been located, but possibly Scott meant Cambusmore near Callander in Perthshire, where he had often visited his friends the Buchanans. The text of the poem itself matches that of the early printed versions of 'Mackrimmon's Lament' and probably derives from one of them. It thus appears to be a presentation copy of the poem rather than either a rough draft or a fair copy intended for the printer. The headnote of the manuscript, however, differs from the one in *Albyn's Anthology*, suggesting that Scott adapted the printed headnote to suit the recipient of his manuscript. Gaelic words included in the headnote in *Albyn's Anthology* are not present and the translation of them is a more literal one than that provided in the printed version, while the manuscript headnote reads 'the West Highlands' rather than 'the West Highlands, and Isles'.

'Mackrimmon's Lament' was first published in *Albyn's Anthology*, 2 vols (Edinburgh, 1816–18), 2.57, following Campbell's notation of the music (54–56). This first publication included a number of footnotes, subsequently omitted when 'Mackrimmon's Lament' was included, without musical notation, in Scott's 1820 *Poetical Works* (10.191–93). 'Mackrimmon's Lament' then passed through successive lifetime editions of Scott's collected poems with only the kind of changes normally associated with the work of the printer, and similarly into Lockhart's posthumous collected edition of 1833–34 (11.332–33).

The present text follows that of Scott's 1820 *Poetical Works* (10.191–93), as the earliest version prepared by him for an edition of his collected poems, this omitting Campbell's substantial annotation and substituting a single note translating the Gaelic name of the tune. A missing closing speech mark has been supplied at the end of the poem, but otherwise no emendations have been made.

Historical Note
The expedition during which the Macleod piper was killed is undated in the account given by the headnote to this poem, though it clearly took place during the Jacobite Rising of 1745–46 (see Explanatory Notes). Instead of historical specificity, however, 'Mackrimmon's Lament' seems to evoke a timeless archaic Gaelic world reminiscent of the Ossian poems of James Macpherson (1736–96). Along with this a number of details about Dunvegan in Skye and the Macleod family derive from Scott's own visit there during his sea-voyage of 1814, while the ending of the lament evokes the Highland Clearances, with which the tune was associated by Scott's time. Scott's own lyrics formed part of his efforts to assist Campbell with *Albyn's Anthology*. (For further information on this collection and

Scott's participation in it see Historical Note to no. 91, 'Jock of Hazeldean', and for a brief account of Campbell's Highland collecting tour and its significance for the work see Historical Note to no. 92, 'Pibroch of Donald Dhu'.)

It is unclear when and where Campbell wrote down the already well-known tune of 'Cha till mi tuille', whether on his journey collecting Highland music for his publication undertaken from July to October 1815 or at another time. His musical notation is that of a song rather than of a pibroch (a bagpipe melody with a subsequent pattern of variations), and thus contrasts with his notation for the music accompanying Scott's 'Pibroch of Donald Dhu' (no. 92) and 'MacGregor's Gathering' (no. 94). The tune had previously been published with variations as 'Cha till mi tuille. Never more shall I return. A Bagpipe Lament' in Patrick MacDonald, *A Collection of Highland Vocal Airs* (Edinburgh, 1784), 41. A manuscript in *canntaireachd* form (a system of verbal notation where melody notes were represented by vowels and grace-notes by consonants) dating from 1797 can be found in NLS, MS 3714, no. 56, the first volume of the Campbell Canntaireachd manuscript collection. For a detailed account of the tune's history prior to the publication of Scott's poem, and for the influence of Scott's poem itself on subsequent folk versions of the song, see V. S. Blankenhorn, 'Traditional and Bogus Elements in "MacCrimmon's Lament"', *Scottish Studies*, 22 (1978), 45–67.

Explanatory Notes
239. headnote   Mackrimmon   the Mackrimmon or MacCrimmon family were hereditary pipers to the Macleods of Dunvegan in Skye, and the lament, while written in the voice of Donald Ban (Donald the Fair-haired) MacCrimmon, was supposedly composed by his half-brother Malcolm. Donald Ban MacCrimmon is supposed to have foreseen his own death in 1746. The lament exists both as a song called 'Cha till mi tuille' and in pibroch form.
239.headnote   distant and dangerous expedition   Norman Macleod of Dunvegan (1705–72), Chief of the Macleod clan, adhered to the government side during the Jacobite Rising of 1745–46. His piper was reputedly the only fatal casualty at the Rout of Moy of 16 February 1746, when government forces under the command of John Campbell, 4th Earl of Loudoun (1705–82), attempted to capture Prince Charles Edward Stuart, who had been staying at Moy Hall, the home of the Mackintosh chief about 16 km (10 miles) SE of Inverness. Loudoun's night-march failed after five Jacobites panicked Loudoun's soldiers, creating by the noise they made the false impression that they were a large force ready to ambush them.
239.headnote   emigrants from the West Highlands and Isles   Scott concluded his notice of the *Culloden Papers* for the *Quarterly Review* by regretting the contemporary emigration from the Scottish Highlands of a population from which the British army had in recent times drawn so many recruits: 'The children who have left her will re-echo from a distant shore the sounds with which they took leave of their own—*Ha til, ha til, ha til, mi tulidh!*'—"We return—we return—we return—no more!"': see *Quarterly Review*, 14 (January 1816), 333. This article was cited in the footnotes to *Albyn's Anthology*, though not ascribed there to Scott.
239.1   Macleod's wizard flag   on his visit to Dunvegan Castle in August 1814 Scott had been shown a flag supposedly given to a Macleod chief by the Queen of the fairies, and described it in his journal of his tour aboard the Lighthouse Yacht as 'a pennon of silk, with something like round red rowan-berries wrought upon it'. When produced in battle it was supposed to multiply the numbers of the Macleods (*Life*, 3.227–28).

239.1 gray castle Dunvegan Castle on Skye, the base of the Macleod chiefs, is situated on a rocky headland with the sea on three sides of it, being approached on the fourth by a bridge over a narrow ravine. Scott had slept in a reputedly haunted room in Dunvegan Castle on the night of 23 August 1814: see *Letters on Demonology and Witchcraft* (London, 1830), 399–401.

239.3 broad-sword …target and quiver a Highland broadsword is a cutting sword with a broad blade, while the *targe* (or target) is a small, round shield. A quiver would contain a bowman's arrows.

239.9 Quillan the Quillan mountains within view of Dunvegan Castle were known as Macleod's Dining-Tables, according to Scott: see *Letters on Demonology and Witchcraft* (London, 1830), 400.

239.10 Dun an ancient name for a hill-fort, a component in the place-name of Dunvegan.

239.13 *Banshee*'s wild voice Scott subsequently described the Irish Banshie as a 'household fairy, whose office it is to appear, seemingly mourning while she announces the approaching death of some one of the destined race', adding that several 'families of the Highlands of Scotland anciently laid claim to the distinction of an attendant spirit, who performed the office of the Irish banshie' (*Letters on Demonology and Witchcraft* (London, 1830), 351–52). See also note 6 to Canto III of *The Lady of the Lake*, 2nd edn (Edinburgh, 1810), 346–47.

239.14 pall of the dead for a mantle those possessing the second-sight would perceive a shroud partially enveloping the person of anyone about to die. According to Martin Martin in *A Description of the Western Islands of Scotland*, 2nd edn (London, 1716: *ALC*): 'When a Shroud is perceiv'd about one, it is a sure Prognostick of Death: The time is judged according to the height of it about the Person … and as it is frequently seen to ascend higher towards the head, Death is concluded to be at hand within a few days, if not hours, as daily experience confirms' (302).

101. Donald Caird's Come Again!

Textual Note

'Donald Caird's Come Again!' must have been written in response to a request from the musician Alexander Campbell (1764–1824) for words to the tune of 'Malcolm Caird's Come Again' for *Albyn's Anthology*. He obtained this tune at the house of Scott's close associate William Laidlaw on 11 October 1816 (for further details see Historical Note), and Scott's verses were almost certainly written between that date and the publication of the second volume of Campbell's collection, which came out in February 1818. 'Donald Caird's Come Again!', for which no manuscript has apparently survived, first appeared in *Albyn's Anthology*, 2 vols (Edinburgh, 1816–18), 2.83, with footnotes evidently provided by Campbell and following Campbell's musical notation (80–82).

Scott subsequently included these verses in his 1820 *Poetical Works* (10.186–90), without Campbell's notes or music notation. Various routine printing changes took place including regularisation of spelling and punctuation: the word previously spelled as both 'widdie' and 'woodie', for example, was standardised to 'wuddie' (lines 48, 56) and some obvious errors were corrected, such as 'bots' for 'bolts' (line 57). A glossing footnote 'Caird signifies Tinker' was added, simplifying a similar note provided by Campbell in his publication. At the same time fresh errors were introduced, such '*the shirra*' for '*the Shirra*' (line 51). In line 60 the variation to 'Donald Caird's loose again' of the repeated phrase 'Donald Caird's come again' was overlooked, while the variation from 'and glen' to 'or glen' in lines 11 and 15 also suggests carelessness in printing.

'Donald Caird's Come Again' was subsequently reprinted in the successive lifetime editions of Scott's collected poems and in Lockhart's posthumous edition of 1833–34 (11.328–31) with only the kind of changes normally associated with the work of the printer, these including some further instances of minor textual slippage, such as the probably unintentional Anglicisation of 'weel' as 'well' in line 42 (1821*PW*, 10.97).

George Thomson (1757–1851) included 'Donald Caird's Come Again!', professedly 'by express permission', in his *Select Melodies of Scotland*, 5 vols (Edinburgh, 1822–23), 3.item 29. This almost certainly alludes to the general permission upon which Thomson acted from 1821 to set any Scott verses he chose to music in his publications (see Scott's letter to Thomson of November 1821, BL, Add. MS 35,265, ff. 96–97) and there is no evidence of direct involvement by Scott in this reprinting. Thomson did not set Scott's words to the tune collected by Campbell, but used a new one composed and arranged by himself.

The present edition follows Scott's text as first published in *Albyn's Anthology*, 2 vols (Edinburgh, 1816–18), 2.83, but omits Campbell's remarks on the tune and his source, retaining only the initial definition of 'caird' subsequently adapted as a footnote in 1820*PW*. The following emendations have been made:

240.6   Hieland (1820*PW*) / hieland
241.35   Lawland (1820*PW*) / lawland
241.45   kebbuck (1833–34*PW*) / kebbeck
242.57   bolts (1820*PW*) / bots

Historical Note
During 1816 Scott was heavily involved in assisting Alexander Campbell with his Scottish song-collection *Albyn's Anthology*, 2 vols (Edinburgh, 1816–1818), not least by his composition of suitable verses to be sung to the tunes collected and arranged for it (for further information on this collection and Scott's participation in it see Historical Note to no. 91, 'Jock of Hazeldean'). The tune of 'Malcolm Caird's Come Again' had been previously recorded by the Aberdeenshire laird George Skene (1695–1756) in his 1717 manuscript book (NLS, Adv. MS 5.2.21, ff. 18v–19). In his article 'Exploring the Skene Manuscripts of 1717 and 1729', *Common Stock: The Journal of the Lowland and Border Pipers' Society*, 16: 2 (December 2003), 45–51, Iain MacInnes argues that this tune as recorded by Skene was probably for a Northumbrian rather than Highland bagpipe, such tunes representing a north-eastern piping tradition with clear affinities to that of the Borders and Lowlands. Campbell's 'Notes of my Third Journey to the Borders' records that on 8 October [1816] he arrived at the house of Scott's friend William Laidlaw (1779–1845), where on Friday, 11 October 'in the evening James Cockburn a native of Banffshire appeared, an itinerant Piper & wool-gatherer he had three varieties of bellows-pipes—one an Irish pipe he performed but indifferently—I pricked down his sett of "Malcolm Caird's come again"' (EUL, La.II.378/2, p. 2). In his notes in *Albyn's Anthology* Campbell describes Cockburn as from 'the How-o'-Buchan', near Peterhead, and the tune as 'a dancing-measure, or slow Strathspey' (2.83). In describing the conduct of an itinerant Highland worker in the rural Scottish Borders, Scott's lyrics partly reflect the circumstances of Campbell's informant and there is also perhaps a sly reference to Scott himself as a Borders magistrate in the reference

to '*the Shirra*' in line 51. The Scots language used also reinforces the Borders setting.

Explanatory Notes

240.title   Donald Caird's   in the title of the tune the tinker's forename was Malcolm, also a Highland name. *Caird* is the Scots word for a tinker, so Donald was perhaps chosen as equally generic, being the name for a typical or stage Highlander.

240.3   burgh   a borough, a town with privileges conferred by charter and which has a municipal corporation.

240.6   Hieland fling   a traditional Highland solo dance characterised by precise steps on one spot, with curved arms sometimes raised and sometimes angled downwards with hand on hip. It demonstrates the dancer's strength, stamina, and agility.

240.8   Fleech   to coax, flatter, or entreat.

240.9   Hoop a leglen   put an iron band around a pail used for milking, in order to strengthen it and hold its wooden staves together.

240.9   clout   patch or repair.

240.10   crack a pow   break the scalp or skull of an opponent.

241.17   wire a maukin   snare a hare.

241.19   Leisters kipper   catches salmon by means of a pronged spear, the fish then being kippered or preserved by smoking.

241.20   moor-fowl   the red grouse.

241.21   Water-bailiffs, rangers, keepers   a *water-bailiff* is an official responsible for the enforcement of by-laws relating to fishing; a *ranger* is a keeper of a royal park or hunting-ground; and a (game)*keeper* is employed on a landed estate to prevent poaching.

241.23   bountith   a bounty, or a gift specified as an addition to money-wages from an employer.

241.24   mell   mix with, come together (in combat) with.

241.27   Gar   make.

241.29   gill   Scottish measure of liquids, used for drinks such as whisky, equivalent to a fourth of a pint in England, but a much larger measure in Scotland.

241.30   hostler-wife   the landlady of an inn.

241.32   bends a bicker   to have a drink, from the action of turning up the cup or tankard in order to drink from it.

241.34   cantle of the cawsey   middle of the road or street, the dominant position.

241.41   Steek the amrie   close or shut up the pantry or cupboard.

241.41   kist   chest.

241.42   gear   goods or property.

241.43   orra   spare or superfluous.

241.44   Where Allan Gregor fund the tings   to find something where the Highlandman found the tongs (that is, by the fireside) is a proverbial expression for pretending that an object has been found and picked up when it has in fact been stolen: see *ODEP*, 257; Ramsay, 123. The name Allan Gregor is presumably used as another generic one for a Highlander.

241.45   Dunts of kebbuck   lumps of cheese.

241.45   taits of woo'   tufts or small bundles of wool.

241.46   Whiles … whiles   at one time, and at another.

241.47   Webs or duds   lengths of woven cloth or clothes.

241.48   'Ware the widdie   beware of the withy, or gallows-rope.

241.51   Shirra   Sheriff, the chief local judge of a Scottish county. Scott had been appointed Sheriff of Selkirkshire in 1799.

242.53   doom   sentence, or legal judgment.

242.54   Craig to tether, legs to airn   throat to be tied by a rope, legs to be chained by iron.

242.63   Justice   local magistrate, the presiding judge of a court.

102.   The Sun upon the Weirdlaw Hill

Textual Note

Scott's 'The Sun upon the Weirdlaw Hill' was written at the request of George Thomson (1757–1851) to accompany a musical setting by Beethoven and first published in the fifth volume of the folio edition of *A Select Collection of Original Scottish Airs* (Edinburgh, 1818), item 215. The date when Thomson made his initial request is unknown, but on 9 March 1818 Scott referred to his own delay in responding as the result of illness. The verses, he noted, 'have been, in truth, written for months, but I hoped always to find some subject which should smell less of apoplexy' (*Letters*, 5.105). His accompanying manuscript entitled 'Sunset' (BL, Add. MS 35,265, f. 12) contains some deletions and revisions and also differs from the published text in a few places in addition to its different title: for instance, line 6 reads 'Bears the bright hues that ever it bore', while the second stanza refers to Melrose's 'sacred pride' (line 12). It seems likely that, according to his usual practice, Thomson returned Scott a revised transcript of his verses which were then subject to Scott's further revision in proof, though neither a revised transcript nor proofs appear to have survived. In Thomson's work Scott's lyrics are entitled 'The Sun upon the Weirdlaw Hill' while the air only is named 'Sunset'. Thomson's headnote states that he has renamed the tune 'Sunset' in honour of Scott's lyrics.

However, when 'The Sun upon the Weirdlaw Hill' was included in Scott's *Poetical Works* of 1820 (10.200–01), a work under his own control, Scott in effect intervened in a current dispute about the authorship of the tune signalled by Thomson in his 1818 headnote and in his renaming of the tune. Scott in 1820 implies his conviction that Alexander Campbell, editor of *Albyn's Anthology*, was its composer. The Edinburgh composer and musician Nathaniel Gow (1763–1831) had called the air 'Lord Balgonie's Favourite', claiming an ancient origin for the tune, but Scott chose to revert in naming it to Campbell's original title of 'Rimhin aluin 'stu mo rùn' (see Historical Note). In addition a new headnote states categorically that while Scott's poem was composed for Thomson's work the air was 'composed by the Editor of Albyn's Anthology'. The text of the poem itself shows only the kind of changes normally associated with the work of the printer, and it was reprinted in similar fashion in the successive lifetime editions of Scott's collected poetry and in Lockhart's posthumous collected edition of 1833–34 (11.336–37). The change of title to 'The Dreary Change' as found in J. Logie Robertson's edition of *The Poetical Works of Sir Walter Scott* (London, 1904), 742, is not matched by any of the lifetime collected editions, none of which include the musical setting by Beethoven.

The present text follows that of the fifth volume of the folio edition of *A Select Collection of Original Scottish Airs* (Edinburgh, 1818), item 215, as the first printing of 'The Sun Upon the Weirdlaw Hill', but with the name of the air emended from 'Sunset' to 'Rimhin aluin 'stu mo rùn' in accordance with the correction made in 1820, while the original headnote is naturally excluded as being the work of Thomson rather than of Scott. Otherwise there are no emendations.

Historical Note

In the letter to Thomson of 9 March 1818 accompanying his verses (*Letters*, 5.105) Scott wrote, 'I had a sincere belief they were the last lines I should ever write', a reference to the excruciatingly painful attacks of stomach cramps due to gallstones he had suffered throughout 1817 and which only began to abate in the early months of the following year. Scott's illness was widely known among his friends and colleagues, and had greatly altered his appearance for the worse. The reduced diet and blistering imposed on him as treatment no doubt also contributed to the languor and lassitude Scott expresses in 'The Sun upon the Weirdlaw Hill', and to his sense of personal disenchantment with a much-loved landscape, that of the Ettrick valley in Selkirkshire in the Scottish Borders.

Thomson's headnote to the song in his collection (5.item 215) reveals a current dispute about the origin of the melody he had sent to Beethoven for musical arrangement:

> This Melody, which the Editor has called Sun-set, from the admirable verses with which it is here united, made its first appearance in Gow's collection of Strathspeys and Reels some twenty years ago, and has since been published by different persons, both with and without verses. Mr Gow tells the Editor that he got it from Mr Dalrymple of Orangefield, who had it of a Gentleman from one of the Western Isles, as a very old Highland production; and as such the Editor sent it to Beethoven. But how uncertain is the history of Melodies! It has very lately been published in Albyn's Anthology as a composition of the Editor of that collection.

Nathaniel Gow (1763–1831) had included the tune as 'Lord Balgonie's Favourite' in his publication of his father Niel Gow's *A Fourth Collection of Strathspey Reels* (Edinburgh, [1800]), 36, terming it an ancient air, the tune then achieving a wider circulation as the one to which the popular song of 'Gloomy winter's now awa'' by Robert Tannahill (1774–1810) had been published in 1808. In 1816, however, Alexander Campbell (1764–1824) published the tune to accompany Gaelic words beginning 'Rimhinn aluin 'stu mo rùn' (the English title being 'Come, My Bride') in the first volume of his *Albyn's Anthology* (Edinburgh, 1816), 66–68, claiming it as an early composition of his own from 1783, first published as a single sheet publication in 1791 or 1792 and dedicated to the Rev. Patrick Macdonald of Kilmore. Controversy over the authorship of the melody persisted for many years in the apparent absence of a copy of Campbell's early publication, which, however, was later unearthed by John Glen. In his *Early Scottish Melodies* (Edinburgh, 1900) Glen firmly attributes the composition to Campbell, arguing that Thomson's history of it 'is nothing more than an attempt to cover the fraud committed by Nathaniel Gow' (239–40). Thomson's retitling of the tune as 'Sunset', like his headnote, avoids a definitive pronouncement as to its authorship. The disputed authorship may also lie behind Thomson's subsequent reprinting of 'The Sun Upon the Weirdlaw Hill' in *The Melodies of Scotland*, 5 vols (Edinburgh, 1831), 5.item 215, with new music composed in 1830 by Johann Nepomuk Hummel (1778–1837).

Explanatory Notes

242.title Weirdlaw Hill Weirdlaw or Wardlaw Hill is on the left bank or NW of the River Ettrick and at 594 m one of the highest summits in this area.

242.10 Tweed's silver current about 4 km (2½ miles) N of Selkirk,

Ettrick Water falls into the Tweed, one of the largest rivers in SE Scotland, part of which forms the border with England.

242.12   Melrose   near the town of Melrose in Roxburghshire by the Tweed are the spectacular ruins of Melrose Abbey, a Cistercian abbey founded by David I of Scotland in 1136 and begun by monks from Rievaulx Abbey in Yorkshire. Scott had celebrated the ruins in *The Lay of the Last Minstrel* (1805).

243.17   broken board   painting on wooden panels was popular up to the 16th century when the use of cheaper, flexible canvas gradually superseded it in Europe. With age wooden panels tend to crack and warp, especially if kept in environments that are insufficiently humid.

243.23   Araby's or Eden's   a garden of a traditional Arabian design originating in Persia surrounded by a wall and containing four channels of water meeting at a central fountain or pond and representing the four rivers of Paradise. Eden or Paradise was the home of Adam and Eve before the fall of man: see Genesis 2. 8–15.

103.   Farewell to the Muse

Textual Note
Scott's words for 'Farewell to the Muse' were first published in the fifth volume of the folio edition of George Thomson's *A Select Collection of Original Scottish Airs* (Edinburgh, 1818), item 217. The date when Thomson sent Scott the music for the song, in a setting by Beethoven, is unknown, but on 9 March 1818 Scott referred to his delay in responding as a result of his recent illness, noting of the two songs he then enclosed, 'they have been, in truth, written for months, but I hoped always to find some subject which should smell less of apoplexy' (*Letters*, 5.105). His accompanying manuscript (BL, Add. MS 35,265, f. 13) contains very few deletions and revisions but differs from the published text in a few places: line 10, for instance, ends 'darken my day', while the final line opens 'Farewell thou Enchantress'. It seems likely that, according to his usual practice, Thomson returned Scott a revised transcript of his verses which were then subject to Scott's further revision in proof, though neither a revised transcript nor proofs have apparently survived. It seems reasonable to conclude, then, that the printed verses in Thomson's work represent an agreed version of Scott's lines for publication.

Subsequently 'Farewell to the Muse' was included in Scott's collected *Poetical Works* of 1820 (10.210–11). Apart from the kind of changes normally associated with the work of the printer, 'Explore' was substituted for 'Seek out' at the start of line 4. A note at the head of the song, 'The Air composed by George Kinloch, Esq. of Kinloch', was also omitted, perhaps because no actual name was given to the tune by Thomson but perhaps also from a dislike of Scott's name being linked to that of a notorious radical (see Historical Note).

'Farewell to the Muse' was then reprinted in the successive lifetime editions of Scott's collected poetry and in Lockhart's posthumous collected edition of 1833–34 (11.345–46) with only the kind of changes normally associated with the work of the printer. 1821*PW* and many of its successors change 'those enchantments' in line 21 to 'thy enchantments', but this is probably a case of textual corruption. In none of these collected editions of Scott's poetry is Beethoven's musical setting included, Lockhart in his posthumous edition merely footnoting that the tune was composed by George Kinloch of Kinloch. Thomson's *A Select Collection of Original Scottish Airs*, 5 vols (Edinburgh, 1822), 5.item 30, simply reprints both lyrics and tune from his earlier work, naming the tune as 'Kinloch'.

The present text follows that in the fifth volume of the folio edition of George Thomson's *A Select Collection of Original Scottish Airs* (Edinburgh, 1818), item 217, as representing the culmination of the original phase of composition. No emendations have been made, except the removal of Thomson's headnote concerning authorship of the tune.

Historical Note

In his letter of 9 March 1818 accompanying 'Farewell to the Muse' and 'The Sun upon the Weirdlaw Hill' (*Letters*, 5.105) Scott wrote of his recent ill-health, which had led him to doubt the continuance of his capability as a poet (see Historical Note to no. 102, 'The Sun upon the Weirdlaw Hill'). Together such factors must have accounted for the melancholy mood of these lyrics.

By contrast, Beethoven's musical setting is distinctly lively, the resulting mismatch no doubt the result of Thomson sending the composer tunes without any previously existing words and of Scott's limited ability to interpret written music. The melody was attributed by Thomson to the Scottish radical landowner George Kinloch of Kinloch in Strathmore (1775–1833), a progressive landlord regarded by Scott as a class traitor for his support of the political reform movement in the early nineteenth century. After the Peterloo massacre in Manchester in August 1819 Kinloch addressed a public meeting in Dundee to protest against such an outrage and to urge that the people of Britain should have a voice in elections to the House of Commons. A warrant was issued for his arrest for sedition and, convinced that he would be sentenced to transportation to Australia, he fled to Paris and was declared an outlaw: in 1823 he was pardoned and able to return to Kinloch. The tune of 'Farewell to the Muse' is still widely attributed to him, but it also bears more than a passing resemblance to that of the Northumbrian folk-song 'Blow the Wind Southerly'.

Explanatory Notes

243.3   lated   that is, belated, coming late or overtaken by the coming of night.

243.5   numbers   verses, signified by their rhythm or metrical feet.

243.18   warrior lay stretch'd on the plain   a reference to the final canto of Scott's poem *Marmion* (1808) where, after taking part on the English side in the Battle of Flodden (1513), the fatally wounded Lord Marmion is given a drink of water by his erstwhile captive and intended bride, Clara de Clare, although she fetches the water in his helmet rather than in a goblet.

104.   Epilogue to *The Appeal*

Textual Note

Scott's epilogue was evidently composed not long before the first performance at Edinburgh's Theatre Royal of *The Appeal*, a tragedy by Scottish novelist John Galt (1779–1839), for Scott only sent it to the actress who was due to speak it, Harriet Siddons (1783–1844), on that very day of 16 February 1818. In his accompanying letter Scott apologises for the delay, gives her permission to make 'any alterations you please', and requests that he should not be named as the author (*Letters*, 5.82). Unfortunately, the manuscript that once accompanied this letter (the original of which is in the Berg Collection, New York Public Library) does not appear to have survived.

The Epilogue was first published as 'By a Friend of the Author' in *The Appeal: A Tragedy, in Three Acts* (Edinburgh, 1818), 53–54, but acknowledged as Scott's work by its inclusion in his *Poetical Works* of 1820 (10.239–41). This version alters 'Alarming neighbours' in line 19 to 'Tremendous neighbour', and, presumably to avoid the consequent repetition of 'tremendous', then substitutes 'tempestuous' for that word in line 22. (Other changes, however, can almost certainly be attributed to the printer.) In addition, Scott revised his second footnote about the buildings on the North Bridge to refer specifically to the projected law-suit concerning them instead of stating the reasons for and against their removal (see note to 245.22). The Epilogue subsequently passed into the successive lifetime collected editions of Scott's poems and into the posthumous Lockhart collected edition of 1833–34 (11.367–68) with only minor variations of a kind normally associated with the work of the printer.

The present text is taken from *The Appeal* of 1818 (53–54), as the text which reflects the moment of composition and first performance most clearly. The poem was there attributed to a friend of the author of *The Appeal*, an ascription irrelevant to the present volume and which has therefore been omitted. Otherwise no emendations have been made.

Historical Note

Galt's tragedy, based upon an Irish murder trial, had initially been published under the title of 'The Witness' as the first item in his collection of plays rejected for representation at the London theatres, the *New British Theatre* of 1814. Scott's friend, William Erskine (1768–1822), later Lord Kinedder, had read this play on a London visit, and on being introduced to Galt advised him to enlarge and revise it and promised his assistance in getting it produced in Edinburgh: see Galt's *Literary Life and Miscellanies*, 3 vols (Edinburgh, 1834), 1.170–71. Scott had known Galt since 1812 at least, but expressed the view that he wrote 'the worst tragedies ever seen' (see *Letters*, 3.146n), although subsequently appreciating Galt's Scottish novels. His request that his authorship should remain unknown, plus the arch tone and local and topical reference of the Epilogue itself, contrast with that of his prologue for Joanna Baillie's *The Family Legend* in 1810 (see no. 66, 'Prologue to *The Family Legend*'), indicating Scott's expectation that Baillie's play would achieve classic status and that Galt's would not. It seems likely that Scott agreed to write the Epilogue mostly out of general goodwill, because of the involvement of his friend Erskine in the production, and to oblige the actress who was to deliver it, his friend Harriet Siddons. *The Scotsman* of 21 February 1818 ('Theatre') pronounced that the play 'contains much beautiful poetry; but it is not a good tragedy', and noted that the announcement that it was to be performed again was received with mixed approbation and censure. The *Caledonian Mercury* of 19 February had made a similar report, also noting that the Epilogue, 'which was smart and lively, was spoken by Mrs Henry Siddons with great spirit and effect, and seemed to soften the asperity of some of those harsher critics who were disposed to pronounce a sentence of instant condemnation'.

Explanatory Notes

244.1   old Æsop   Æsop, the traditional composer of Greek moral fables about animals, is said to have lived in the 6th century BC and to have been a slave. Scott has in mind the fable of 'A Cat and Venus', in which a young man in love with a cat begs Venus to change her into a woman. When they go to bed together Venus introduces a mouse into the room. 'The new-made woman, upon this temptation, started out of the bed, and directly made a leap at the mouse; upon which Venus turned her into a puss again': 'Fable 52. A Cat and Venus', *Æsop's Fables* (York, [1792?]), 41–42: see *ALC*.

244.5 my bridegroom lawyer the Epilogue was spoken by Harriet Siddons in the character of Ariette, the daughter of the Chief Magistrate Helgert, and betrothed to Ethelstane who is joined with her father in the commission as a Judge. Ethelstane suspects that his father was murdered by Ariette's father and supports a trial even though Helgert's accuser appears to be a madwoman. The conscience-stricken Helgert confesses at the end of the play and is led off to imprisonment and, presumably, eventual execution.

244.7 Hymen's mystic knot Hymen is the Greek god of marriage, often depicted as a young man carrying a torch and wearing a garland of flowers.

244.10 New Jail (see also Scott's footnote.) The Calton Jail was erected to the E of Princes Street in 1817, on the site presently occupied by St Andrews House, the Scottish government building on Regent Street. The Theatre Royal was in Shakespeare Square, between the Calton Jail and the North Bridge, then the chief thoroughfare between Edinburgh's Old and New Towns.

245.22 Up or down? (see also Scott's footnote.) A report headed 'North Bridge Buildings' in the *Edinburgh Evening Courant* of 23 February 1818 reported on a meeting of a committee of the inhabitants of Edinburgh about these buildings held at the Royal Exchange Coffee-house on 12 February. Its 14 members included the painter Alexander Nasmyth (1758–1840), the meeting being chaired by Sir James Ferguson. After sending a letter of protest to the Lord Provost and declaring their intention to take legal advice on the matter, the committee called for a subscription to cover the costs of a potential lawsuit and agreed to publish all relevant correspondence in the newspapers. Scott's footnote was revised in 1820*PW* to read: 'At this time the public of Edinburgh was much agitated by a law-suit betwixt the magistrates and many of the inhabitants of the city, concerning the range of new buildings on the western side of the North Bridge; which the latter insisted should be removed as a deformity' (10.240).

245.23 Scylla and Charybdis Scylla is a shoal of rocks opposite Charybdis, a whirlpool on the coast of Sicily: together they signify the difficulty of negotiating between two dangers.

245.25 who lives at Rome the Pope must flatter an allusion to the proverb 'It is hard to sit in Rome and strive against the Pope': see *ODEP*, 737.

105. The Maid of Isla

Textual Note

Scott's words for 'The Maid of Isla' were first published in the fifth volume of the folio edition of George Thomson's *A Select Collection of Original Scottish Airs* (Edinburgh, 1818), item 209. The date when Thomson sent Scott the music for the song, composed by Beethoven, is unknown, but on 9 March 1818 Scott referred to his delay in responding as a result of his recent illness, adding 'I keep the "Maid of Isla" that I may hear it played over, and I will send you some words to it if I then like it: it has some local associations which always makes the task light to me' (*Letters*, 5.105). He must have sent his lyrics shortly afterwards, since Thomson replied enthusiastically two days later after having received in 'The Maid of Isla' what he referred to as 'in every feature, a perfect Beauty' (BL, Add. MS 35,268, f. 19v). Scott's manuscript (BL, Add. MS 35,265, ff. 50–51), without date or postmark, has a number of deletions and corrections, mostly of single words or short phrases though three lines were deleted at the start of the third and final stanza. Presumably Thomson then sent Scott a revised transcript of the poem for correction according to his usual practice since, although this has not apparently survived, there are a number of differences between Scott's manuscript and the song as printed in Thomson's work, even apart from the changes normally associated with the work of the printer. In Scott's manuscript, for instance, line 4 reads 'War with the ocean gallantly' rather than 'Contend with ocean gallantly'. It seems reasonable to conclude, then, that the printed verses in Thomson's work represent an agreed version for publication.

'The Maid of Isla' passed subsequently, minus its musical setting but with the name of the air and an acknowledgement that the song was written for Thomson's collection, into Scott's collected *Poetical Works* of 1820 (10.202–03), with a number of changes, some of which may possibly be authorial: in the first line 'yon cliff' becomes 'the cliff', while in line 12 'her way' becomes 'away', readings which then persist through the various lifetime editions of Scott's collected poetry. Other changes seem to be the effect of textual corruption: for instance, in line 11 1820*PW* has 'storm-clad', an error corrected in later lifetime collected editions so that 'storm-cloud' duly appears in Lockhart's posthumous collected edition of 1833–34 (11.338–39). Thomson also reprinted 'The Maid of Isla' in his subsequent five-volume edition of *The Select Melodies of Scotland*, 5 vols (Edinburgh, 1822–23), 5.item 8, from his earlier collection.

The present text of 'The Maid of Isla' follows that of the fifth volume of the folio edition of Thomson's *A Select Collection of Original Scottish Airs* (Edinburgh, 1818), item 209, as best representing the culmination of the initial creative process. No emendations have been made.

Historical Note
In some respects it is surprising that Thomson requested Scott to write new words to the tune of 'The Maid of Isla' since that tune was already identified with another of his contributors, Sir Alexander Boswell of Auchinleck (1775–1822). Boswell's 'The Maid of Isla' is a verse dialogue of eight four-line stanzas which alternate a male and female lover. Willie tells his Mary on the day before their wedding that he has lost his sheep, cows, and house and assumes that she will no longer wish to marry him; and then, after she maintains her promise, reveals that this was simply a device to test the sincerity of her love. As 'The Lass of Isla' Boswell's version was published anonymously at the start of the nineteenth century with music by Nathaniel Gow (1763–1831) as a separate song-publication by the Edinburgh music-publishing firm of Gow and Shepherd from the premises at 16 Princes Street they occupied between 1801 and 1810, and again published anonymously in 1803 in Edinburgh as 'Ah Mary sweetest maid' in the sixth and final volume of James Johnson's *Scots Musical Museum* (item 529), though the tune there is another setting to that of the earlier separate song-publication. Boswell's lyrics also appeared as 'The Maid of Isla' without the tune in his own anonymous *Songs, Chiefly in the Scottish Dialect* (Edinburgh, 1803), 1–3, a publication which he declared on the leaf following the title-page was prompted by several of his songs having been published without the author's permission and 'with alterations which he did not consider as improvements'. In a footnote Boswell declared that the tune was 'a reel of the island of Isla' as supplied by Lady Charlotte Campbell (1775–1861). Although Boswell's authorship was unacknowledged initially, the song was referred to as his work throughout the nineteenth century and beyond: see, for instance, John Glen, *Early Scottish Melodies* (Edinburgh, 1900), 222–23. The assumption must be that, having obtained a musical setting from Beethoven, Thomson would be

unlikely to secure Boswell's consent to publish his lyrics in a setting other than that of Nathaniel Gow and therefore sought alternative verses for the tune from Scott.

Explanatory Notes
245.title   Isla   or Islay, an island in Argyllshire, the chief one of the southernmost group of the Hebrides. Its shores are swept by rapid tidal currents with short cross billows that make it dangerous for sailors to approach.
245.sub-title   Gaelic   no Gaelic original has been identified, and Scott's description (also present in his manuscript, though absent from 1820*PW*) may imply no more than that his lyrics have an elevated Ossianic mood in keeping with the air, originally a Strathspey tune.
245.3   skiff   a small sea-going boat adapted for rowing as well as sailing.
245.6   leeward deck   the deck on the side facing away from the wind, the sheltered side of the boat.
246.24   Allan Vourich   Clan Vourich has the surname of Macpherson, one of its best-known chiefs being the celebrated Jacobite Ewen Macpherson of Cluny (1706–64).

106.   I, Walter Scott of Abbotsford

Textual Note
These lines are to be found facing the title-page of a copy in the Abbotsford Library of the original edition of Walter Scott [of Satchells], *A True History of Several Honourable Families of the Right Honourable Name of Scot* (Edinburgh, 1688), given to Scott, as an inscription in it records, by his publisher Archibald Constable (1774–1827) on 26 March 1818. Lockhart states that Scott received the copy at breakfast and on 'rising from table' immediately wrote his own lines in the book (*Life*, 1.63–64n). The date of composition, therefore, is probably within a few days of that of Constable's inscription. There is also a copy, in Scott's own hand, on a slip of paper, measuring approx. 4.4 x 17.2 cm, mounted on a board frame, in NLS, Acc. 12370. Scott was perhaps recalling the verses from memory in the latter since there are a few minor differences from the book inscription. Most of these relate to punctuation but the first line has the reading 'a poor scholar & no soldier', while the fifth line reads 'Medeas or Jasons golden fleeces'. The book inscription was not included in any of the lifetime editions of Scott's collected poetry nor in the Lockhart 1833–34 posthumous edition. Lockhart did, however, include it in his *Life* (1.64n), with the stop and dash at the end of the third line becoming a semi-colon and some additional punctuation and normalisation of spelling.

The present text follows the original lines in the Abbotsford Library copy of Walter Scott [of Satchells], *A True History of Several Honourable Families of the Right Honourable Name of Scot* (Edinburgh, 1688). A title has been supplied from the opening words, and the following emendations made:

246.1   I, (Editorial) / I
246.2   and (Editorial) / &
246.5   Jason's (Editorial) / Jasons

Historical Note
Walter Scott of Satchells (1613–in or after 1688), author of *A True History of Several Honourable Families of the Right Honourable Name of Scot*, was the son

of Robert Scott of Satchells in Roxburghshire and his wife, a daughter of Sir
Robert Scott of Thirlestane. After a long military career he had returned to
Scotland by 1654 and at the age of 73 began his metrical work which recounts
notable incidents in the history of the extended Borders family of Scott in its
first part, while the second part ('Satchels's Post'ral') comprises various shorter
poems dedicated to and supplicating individual members of the clan for finan-
cial assistance. By his own admission he was barely literate and hired schoolboys
to write to his dictation.

According to Lockhart, Scott had been familiar with Satchells's work from
his earliest childhood, commenting on Constable's gift of a copy of the original
edition, 'This is indeed the resurrection of an old ally' (*Life*, 1.63n). From this
it seems likely that he had come across the work at his grandfather's house at
Sandyknowe. The volume included a poetical address to the contemporary
Scott of Raeburn, a family from whom Scott was descended, and quotations
from it occur in several of Scott's own works, such as *The Lay of the Last
Minstrel* (1805). Scott's lines mimic the self-description of Satchells on the title-
page of the volume as:

Capt. WALTER SCOT,
*An old Souldier, and no Scholler,
And one that can Write nane,
But just the Letters of his Name.*

Explanatory Notes

246.1   poor scholar   Scott lamented his own comparative lack of
knowledge of classical languages (especially Greek), attributing it to habits of
desultory reading and lack of application in his youth (see, for example, *Life*,
1.40–43).

246.1   no soldier but a soldier's lover   despite the lameness which
debarred him from any kind of military career Scott had been an enthusiastic
member of the Royal Edinburgh Volunteer Light Dragoons as a young man,
and took great pride in the military career of his elder son Walter.

246.3   the twenty-four letters   although by modern reckoning there are 26
letters in the alphabet, formerly these would be counted as only 24 since *i* and *j*
and *u* and *v* were considered interchangeable.

246.4   golden pieces   coins consisting entirely or mostly of gold. During
Scott's lifetime the most common gold coins in circulation in Britain were
the guinea (£1-1s.) and the half-guinea (10s. 6d.). In various individual
supplicatory poems in the second part of his work, Scott of Satchells indirectly
appeals to his wealthy clansmen for financial assistance.

246.5   Jason's and Medea's golden fleeces   in classical Greek mythology
Jason sailed on the ship *Argo* with fifty of the chief heroes of Greece to Colchis
to recover the Golden Fleece, with its supposedly magical qualities, having
many adventures on the way. In Colchis the King agreed to surrender the
Fleece to Jason provided he could perform three apparently impossible tasks.
Jason accomplished them with the help of the King's daughter Medea, an
enchantress who had fallen in love with him and who returned with him
and the other Argonauts to Iolcos with the Golden Fleece. The legend is
repeatedly mentioned by Satchells in the second part of his work, including his
address to the Laird of Raeburn, presumably because the wealth of the Scott
clan substantially resulted from wool.

107. My Mither is of Sturdy Airn

Textual Note

This poem was evidently composed by Scott as a compliment to his host following a visit to the country house of Francis Gray, 14th Lord Gray (1765–1842), who recalled the circumstance in a letter to Scott of 7 July 1818:

> I take the liberty to send you over the German which is inscribed on a Mineralogical nick-nack and which you were so good as translate impromptu at dinner one day, but said you would give it a different meaning in other verses. (NLS, MS 3889, f. 138)

No manuscript of Scott's verses appears to have survived, but they were printed privately by Lord Gray with the imprimatur 'PRINTED at GRAY HOUSE Sept. 1st. 1818' on one side of a single sheet of unwatermarked paper, measuring 22.0 x 13.9 cm, a copy of which survives in EUL, La. III. 831. Lord Gray seems to have had it reprinted several years later, since another copy end-dated 19 November 1823, on a single sheet of unwatermarked paper, measuring 23.0 x 19.1 cm, exists in NLS, F.7.d.5. The only difference in the lines, besides the end-dating, is the addition of an elaborate printed frame for the verses in the later printing. It was also embedded in a poem, 'L'Envoie', on three leaves following the title-page of the privately-printed and unpaginated *Catalogue of the Gray Library, Kinfauns Castle* (Perth, 1828), presumably the work of the compiler, David Morison, employed by Lord Gray to assist him in the work of creating the catalogue. In 'Fytte. ii' of 'L'Envoie' Scott's lines are inset in smaller type, to distinguish them from the larger poem, being further demarcated as 'Penned by that pleasing Master hande, / Knowne, loved and honoured through ye lande'; and apart from giving the 'Silver' of earlier versions as 'silver' this exactly reprints the earlier text (f. 2 following title-page).

Scott's poem in the present edition follows the earliest known text as printed by Lord Gray in September 1818 (EUL, La. III. 831). A title has been supplied editorially from the first words of the poem, and the imprimatur of Lord Gray has been omitted.

Historical Note

Lord Gray was a keen antiquarian, Vice-President of the Royal Society of Edinburgh from 1815 to 1823 and President of the Society of Antiquaries of Scotland from 1819 to 1823, and presumably his friendship with Scott was the result of mutual antiquarian interests. He presented a copy of the catalogue of his library made in 1828 to Scott (*ALC*). A headnote supplied evidently by Lord Gray in his first printing of this poem provides a description of one of the curios Scott had seen at his home (see Textual Note):

> The first Verse is a literal translation of a German Motto, engraved round a Dish of curious Workmanship, containing a little Figure, holding on his head, a small Tray with a bit of Silver Ore in it, and several other Minerals scattered in the dish which is of Copper richly gilt. The two other Verses are in compliment to Lord Gray's Family.

Unfortunately, no image of this dish or record of its German inscription appears to be extant, Victorian travellers to Kinfauns Castle recording no more of this artefact than is contained in this headnote. The present Kinfauns Castle, 5 km (3 miles) SE of Perth, was designed for Lord Gray by Robert Smirke (1780–1867) and built between 1822 and 1826 on the site of its medieval predecessor. The Gray House of Lord Gray's imprimatur was another mansion owned by him, built in 1715, and located 8 km (5 miles) NW of Dundee.

Explanatory Notes

246.1–4   My Mither ... gold   supposedly a literal translation of the original German inscription on Lord Gray's dish. Scott's use of Scots words such as *Mither* (mother), *airn* (iron), and *Bairn* (child) perhaps signifies that the original inscription was in a German dialect.

108.   Lines on the Caledonian Canal

Textual Note

These lines were evidently first published in Britain in *Two Excursions to the Ports of England, Scotland, and Ireland 1816, 1817, and 1818 ... with a Description of the Breakwater at Plymouth, and of the Caledonian Canal* (London, 1819), translated from the French of Charles Dupin. They appear there immediately below Dupin's own 'Lines on the Caledonian Canal', written in French, as an 'Imitation of the above, by the MODERN BARD OF CALEDONIA' (98–99). This attribution, which to contemporaries would most obviously have suggested Scott, is also found at the end of an Introduction by the book's translator: 'Our best thanks are due to the elegant version of M. Dupin's lines ... with which we have been favoured by the MODERN BARD OF CALEDONIA' (viii). The same account of Dupin's excursions, apparently using similar sheets, also featured as part of the first volume of *New Voyages and Travels: Consisting of Originals, Translations, and Abridgements*, 9 vols (London, [1819–1823]), likewise published by Sir Richard Phillips (1767–1840). The verses also appeared in Phillips's *Monthly Magazine* for June 1819 (47.442–43), though this time with a direct author attribution: 'Mons. Dupin wrote some lines on the Caledonian Canal, which, to oblige the editor of the Journal, Mr. Walter Scott has obligingly anglicized' (442). Apart from very minor changes by the printer the texts are identical. Scott apparently never publicly acknowledged his authorship, and these verses have not previously appeared in any collected edition of his poetry. The author's identity nevertheless was fully revealed in later works by Dupin, such as *Force commerciale de la Grande Bretagne* (1824): 'l'illustre Walter Scott n'a pas dédaigné d'en écrire une imitation qui fait oublier l'original [the illustrious Walter Scott has not disdained to write an imitation which overshadows the original]' (2.162). Dupin also noticeably treats the authorship as a given in a letter to Scott of 1 June 1824, offering him a presentation copy of his *Force commerciale* (NLS, MS 3898, f. 192r).

The present text follows that in *Two Excursions to the Ports of England, Scotland, and Ireland 1816, 1817, and 1818* (London, 1819), 98–99, without emendation.

Historical Note

In all, five trips to installations in the British Isles were undertaken by the French marine engineer, mathematician, and later politician, Charles Dupin (1784–1873), the second of these reaching its northerly point at the Caledonian Canal, the engineering feat celebrated in his original verses in French (see above). Dupin left London on 22 July 1817, proceeding through Hull, Sunderland, and Berwick, then travelled through the Borders to Edinburgh, which he hails as 'the Athens of the north': 'It is a literary phenomenon extremely remarkable' (*Two Excursions*, 38). No mention is made of any direct encounter with Scott either at Abbotsford or in Edinburgh, though several modern commentators assume that a meeting took place, and Scott is hardly likely to have been unreceptive to a persuasive young Frenchman with literary pretensions. Visiting the Bell Rock Lighthouse, as he moved further northward, Dupin came across Scott's verses in the album there (see no. 80, 'Pharos loquitur'), and subsequently offered both a transcript and 'une imitation très-libre [a very free imitation]' of his own in French (*Mémoires sur la marine et les ponts et chaussées de France et d'Angleterre* (Paris, 1818), 95–96: *ALC*; *Two Excursions*, 40). Dupin's description of the Caledonian Canal is the most extensive in the whole account, effectively forming a dissertation on its own. Under the direction of the engineer Thomas Telford (1757–1834), and authorised by an Act of Parliament in 1803, this represented an ambitious scheme to link the NW and NE coasts of Scotland, a stretch of some 100 km (62 miles) including interconnecting lochs, thereby avoiding the dangerous sea route round Cape Wrath and Orkney. Not completed until 1822, the canal failed to realise the original commercial expectations, partly owing to the new steam-powered boats being too big to use it. In late 1817, however, the works would have been at their most impressive, especially with the near-completion of the chain of eight locks known as Neptune's Staircase. Dupin's original poem, which appeared on its own in the first French accounts of his journey, is in twelve rhyming alexandrine couplets, reminiscent in some respects of Racine, whose well-structured dramas Dupin elsewhere defended from the assaults of doctrinaire romanticism: see Robert Fox, 'From Corfu to Caledonia: The Early Travels of Charles Dupin, 1808–1820' in *The Light of Nature*, ed. J. D. North and J. J. Roches (Dordrecht, 1985), 303–20 (p. 313). Scott's version, while mainly following the sense of the original, is more reminiscent of the Augustan verse of Dryden and Pope. How it first came into Dupin's possession or that of his English publisher is not clear. In reversing the situation found in the case of the Bell Rock verses, the lines may have originated in a direct appeal from Dupin. Alternatively they might have been sent in response to an invitation from Sir Richard Phillips or his staff, though the radical Whig Phillips makes an unlikely contact for Scott at this time.

Explanatory Notes
247.7   adamantine   'adamant' was a name applied by the ancients for various hard substances, including an imagined rock with fabulous properties. Here it indicates a geological formation which is hard and unyielding. Compare 'The Vision of Don Roderick' (1811), 'Conclusion', stanza 3: 'An adamantine barrier to his force!'.
247.16   iron frames   as Dupin noted of the lock gates: 'The gates are framed of cast-iron, in great bars, covered over with strong oak planks, fastened by screw-bolts with nuts' (*Two Excursions*, 93).
247.18   basins eight   referring to the eight locks commonly called 'Neptune's Staircase', at Banavie, near Fort William, just N of Loch Linnhe. According to Dupin's account: 'This majestic chain of locks was finished with the exception of the gates, in 1817, and will be completed in less than a year' (*Two Excursions*, 92).
247.22   NEPTUNE'S STAIRS   named after Roman god of freshwater and the sea; see also Historical Note.
248.28   Roman arms had fail'd   alluding to the Roman legions' failure to establish themselves northward beyond the Antonine Wall, running through the Central Belt of Scotland.

109.   The Noble Moringer

Textual Note
According to Lockhart (*Life*, 4.259–60), Scott told him during a visit to
Abbotsford 'towards the end of the spring vacation' of 1819 that he had trans-
lated the German ballad of 'The Noble Moringer' as a test of the possible
impairment of his intellectual powers while suffering from gall-stones. Scott
asked his daughter Sophia to fetch the manuscript, which had been written
'partly by her and partly by Mr [William] Laidlaw', and he then proceeded
to read it to Lockhart and to John Ballantyne. James Skene (1775–1864) tells
a similar story in which the poem was 'a short ballad of Bürger': see *Memories
of Sir Walter Scott*, ed. Basil Thomson (London, 1909), 70. Scott may have
chosen to prove his skills on more than one occasion during his illness, or
Lockhart may have seen a manuscript of 'The Noble Moringer' in Sophia's
hand and mistakenly believed that this was the test poem: a note by her on the
verso of the final leaf of what appears to be the only surviving manuscript ver-
sion reads 'The noble Moringer in Papas handwriting, I copied it for him to
preserve the original'. Scott's adaptation of the ending of the German original
to meet the conventions of contemporary politeness (see Historical Note) also
perhaps renders Lockhart's story suspect, since if Scott were merely aiming
to test his skills his objective would presumably be a translation as close to the
original as possible.
    This surviving manuscript in Scott's hand, in NLS, MS 876, ff. 22–29, con-
sists of eight conjugate leaves, each page measuring approx. 26.2 x 20.5 cm and
with a watermark 'BANK MILL / 1813'. The leaves have been folded and
stitched to make a booklet, which shows signs of damage with the upper right-
hand corner of ff. 22–25 torn away and f. 26 having been torn and reattached.
It must have been written after the death of the Countess of Balcarres in 1816,
since she is referred to as deceased in the headnote. The text, on the rectos only,
is in Scott's own hand throughout, with numbered stanzas and an introductory
headnote. Despite its containing a number of his corrections and revisions, it
appears to be a fair copy. Most changes are of single words or brief phrases,
though on one occasion Scott has replaced two full lines. Possibly the copy for
the poem's first publication in the *Edinburgh Annual Register, for 1816*, 9: 1 and
2 (Edinburgh, 1820), ccccxcv–ccccci, may have consisted of the transcription
of NLS, MS 876, ff. 22–29 that Sophia Scott records having made in order 'to
preserve the original' manuscript.
    There are several differences between the NLS manuscript in Scott's hand
and the text in *EAR*. In the penultimate line, for instance, the 'warder bold'
becomes the 'warder kind' and in line 41 Marstetten's heir is now 'fiery, hot and
young' rather than 'fiery rash and young'. The poem then passed into Scott's
collected *Poetical Works* of 1820 (11.227–48) and into the subsequent lifetime
editions of his collected poetry and Lockhart's posthumous collected edition of
1833–34 (6.343–59), with only the kind of changes normally associated with the
work of the printer. Some textual corruption also occurred, such as the substi-
tution of 'burning gold' for 'burnish'd gold' (line 138) in 1820*PW* (11.244), an
error which persists in many of the subsequent collected editions, including that
of 1833–34.
    The text of 'The Noble Moringer' here is taken from *Edinburgh Annual
Register, for 1816*, 9: 1 and 2 (Edinburgh, 1820), ccccxcv–ccccci, as the first
authorised printing representing the culmination of the initial creative pro-
cess. Square brackets have been removed from the headnote, and the following
emendations have been made:

248.headnote *Sammlung Deutscher Volkslieder* (Editorial) / Sammlung
        Deutschen Volkslieder
254.126   meed (MS) / mead

Historical Note
In apparently selecting 'The Noble Moringer' from the collection *Sammlung Deutscher Volkslieder* (see note to 248.headnote, below) as a translation exercise during his illness in 1819, Scott reverted to the favourite subject-matter of a knight returning from the Crusades (compare, for instance, *The Betrothed*, ed. J. B. Ellis with J. H. Alexander and David Hewitt, EEWN 18a (Edinburgh, 2009)). It may well also have appealed to him for its repetitions and formulaic patterning, reminiscent of his favourite Border ballads. Scott turned the seven-line stanzas of the German original into four-line stanzas rhyming aabb, while his own repetition of phrases such as 'It was the noble Moringer' recall the repeated stanza introduction of ''Er sprach' or 'Da sprach' of the German. Scott's translation follows the German poem closely until its conclusion, with only minor changes of detail. For instance, the 'boding vision' (line 54) in Scott's poem which warns Moringer of the imminent remarriage of his wife is specifically an angel from heaven in the German ballad, and although the miller asks God to comfort the soul of his supposedly dead lord he does not, as in Scott, promise a gift to the priest to that end. Scott departs substantially from the original in his conclusion however, presumably with publication in mind and perhaps feeling that the misogynism of medieval times would be unacceptable to a polite Regency readership. Moringer forgives the erring squire and gives him his daughter as a bride with the future inheritance of his estate both in the German original and in Scott's translation, but in the German original he is far from forgiving his wife as he does in Scott's poem and although he tells the squire to take the young bride and leave him the old one, he promises in the poem's final line 'Ich will ihr selber gerben die Haut' (I will tan her hide for her).

Explanatory Notes
248.headnote Sammlung Deutscher Volkslieder see *Sammlung Deutscher Volkslieder mit einem Anhange Flammländischer und Französischer nebst Melodien*, 3 vols (Berlin, 1807: *ALC*). 'Der edele Moringer' (the German original of 'The Noble Moringer') is item 44 at 1.102–15, with an editorial endnote at 1.391–93. The first volume of this work contains text only, while the other two contain printed music for some items, though not for 'Der edele Moringer' itself.
248.headnote Chronicle of Nicolaus Thomann cited as the source for item 44 in *Sammlung Deutscher Volkslieder*, 1.391–93. The chaplain of Weissenhorn, Nicolaus Thoman (*c*. 1457–1545), worked for 62 years on his Chronicle.
248.headnote Saint Leonard in Weisenhorn Weissenhorn is a town in Bavaria in Germany, about 22 km (13½ miles) SE of Ulm. Scott anglicises the German name of Leonhard, the saint to whom the medieval chapel there was dedicated.
248.headnote Professor Smith of Ulm Professor Smith (Schmidt, in German) has not been identified. His opinion on the date of 'Der edele Moringer' is given in the editorial endnotes in *Sammlung Deutscher Volkslieder*, 1.392–93. He had contributed 'Das Lied von dem edeln Moringer' from Thoman's Chronicle to *Bragur: Ein litterarisches Magazin der Deutschen und Nordischen Vorzeit*, 3 (1794), 402–15, and expressed his views on the date of the poem in his endnote there (414–15).

248.headnote   Haigh-hall in Lancashire   in his notes of 1831 to *The Betrothed* (1825) Scott gives further details of this Lancashire legend and relates that the stained-glass window depicting it is no longer extant: see *Introductions and Notes from The Magum Opus: Ivanhoe to Castle Dangerous*, ed. J. H. Alexander with P. D. Garside and Claire Lamont, EEWN 25b (Edinburgh, 2012), 381–83.

248.headnote   late Countess of Balcarras   the heiress of the Bradshaigh estate and of Haigh Hall, Elizabeth Dalrymple, wife of Alexander, 6th Earl of Balcarres, had died on 10 August 1816.

249.1   old Bohemian day   Bohemia was a kingdom in the Holy Roman Empire, which was subsequently incorporated into the Austrian Empire before becoming part of the independent state of Czechoslovakia after World War I. It is presently part of the Czech Republic.

249.3   halsed   an archaic word for embraced.

249.6   Saint Thomas-land   presumably the Holy Land is intended, although the apostle Thomas was widely associated with India in the Middle Ages, the supposed scene of his missionary work after Pentecost. The phrase 'Sankt Thomas Land' is in the German original.

249.7   fay   an archaic word for faith.

249.8   seven twelvemonths and a day   the original German ballad has simply seven years. In law a year and a day was the period of time which in certain matters determines a right or liability. For instance the Crown formerly had the right to hold the land of felons for a year and a day, and if a person wounded did not die within a year and a day their assailant was not guilty of murder.

249.22   Chamberlain   a chamber attendant of a lord, or sometimes the steward who receives his rents.

249.23   miniver   plain white fur, more specifically that of the ermine in its winter coat.

250.30   rede   advice or counsel.

250.40   Our Lady dear was guarded by Saint John   after the Resurrection the apostle John, following Jesus's words to him on the cross (see John 19.27), is supposed to have taken the Virgin Mary as his adopted mother, a comparison which emphasises the generational difference between the young heir of Marstetten and Moringer's lady.

251.51   top-sails   the uppermost sail, or pair of sails, of a ship.

252.80   palmer   a pilgrim who had returned from the Holy Land.

252.87   Saint Martin's tide   the feast day of St Martin of Tours is on 11 November, commonly the time in England for hiring servants and for killing cattle for meat during the winter. It was also one of the Scottish Quarter Days, and when presumably the miller's accounts with his customers would be settled.

254.122   shalm   a *shalm* or *shawm* is an early form of the oboe.

255.161   falchion   a sword, more specifically a curved broad-sword that has the cutting edge on the convex side.

110.   Epitaph on Mrs Erskine

Textual Note

This sonnet-length epitaph was written at the request of Scott's close friend and literary adviser William Erskine, Lord Kinedder (1768–1822), to mark the death of his wife Euphemia on 20 September 1819. The call for 'a few lines for a plain Tombstone' was made in the form of a letter of 7 October, which Erskine intended should be left in Scott's hand as they parted from a meeting in Edinburgh:

> I make this request with great reluctance not I assure you from the slightest doubt of your wish to oblige me but from a consciousness that the task is much more difficult than it is generally supposed to be. … It would gratify me more than I can tell, that the last and permanent tribute to the companion of my happiest years should be paid by my own dearest friend.
> I shall give you this when we are about to part today, and beg that no answer may be made to it. (NLS, MS 3890, f. 191r)

The letter is docketed in Scott's hand 'W. Erskine About the Epitaph Alas!'. While Scott made a number of general observations to other friends regarding the sadness of the situation, no mention of the circumstances of the burial is found in his correspondence, and the manuscript containing the epitaph has not been located. A large square mausoleum, identifiable as relating to Lady Kinedder, survives in the old Cemetery at Saline, in Fife, though this is ruinous, and a frame on the far internal wall where a plaque might have been inserted is empty. The verses were first printed in Scott's *Miscellaneous Poems* (1820), and appeared regularly without significant alteration in the various lifetime collected editions, commencing with the *Poetical Works* of 1820 (10.212). In the posthumous Lockhart collected edition of 1833–34 (11.347), a footnote states: 'Mrs Euphemia Robison, wife of William Erskine, Esq. (afterwards Lord Kinedder,) died September, 1819, and was buried at Saline in the county of Fife, where these lines are inscribed on the tombstone.'

The present text follows that in the *Miscellaneous Poems* (1820), [147]–48, without emendation.

Historical Note
Mrs Euphemia Erskine was the only daughter of John Robison (1739–1805), Professor of Natural Philosophy at the University of Edinburgh, 1774–1805. She married William Erskine in 1800, the couple residing at Nether Kinneddar House near Saline, approx. 8 km (5 miles) NW of Dunfermline. Scott first heard of her death through a letter from William Wordsworth of Wednesday, 22 September 1819, in which Wordsworth describes how she had 'expired at Lowood Inn on the banks of Windermere on Monday morning' (NLS, MS 3890, f. 170: *Letters*, 5.491n). In writing to other correspondents Scott expresses doubts about the medical advice which had proposed a visit to the Lakes for the purposes of recuperation, while at the same time showing concern for the surviving partner's state of mind (see, for example, *Letters*, 5.500–01, 6.2–3). However, there may have been an additional reason for the couple seeking solace in the Lake District. Euphemia's admiration for Wordsworthian poetry is referred to in Scott's answer to Wordsworth: 'Of her taste in literature it was no slight evidence that she was a great admirer of your writings' (*Letters*, 5.492). Such literary interests are more generally described in the pamphlet *Sketch of the Life and Character of the Late Lord Kinedder* (Edinburgh, 1822), commemorating her husband, in which Scott himself evidently had a hand:

> To manners the most amiable and gentle, she united a strength of understanding, a taste for literature, and a degree of general information, rarely met with in one of her sex. These qualities served to draw still closer the ordinary ties of conjugal affection, and rendered Mrs Erskine the intelligent and constant friend and companion of her husband. Their tastes were so congenial, that he took a great pleasure in reading to her, and listened with much satisfaction to her observations and criticisms—

particularly on all works of imagination, poetry, or the Belles Lettres, which constituted their favourite studies. (7–8)

Considering that William Erskine was often the first on whom Scott called when seeking guidance over his own literary career—for example, whether to resume *Waverley* in 1810 (see *Waverley*, ed. P. D. Garside, EEWN 1 (Edinburgh, 2007), 378–79)—it is not improbable that some of the advice offered came from her direction, as Scott might have had in mind when writing the Epitaph. At the same time the stress on simplicity, especially in the opening lines, sensitively reflects William Erskine's plans for a 'plain Tombstone', while the poem as a whole shows signs of more generally echoing the 'unadorned' language of Wordsworth's lyric poetry.

111. For Mrs Siddons's Farewell to Dublin

Textual Note
Scott wrote these lines in answer to an appeal from Harriet Siddons for a farewell address for her closing performance night at Dublin's Theatre Royal, and they form part of his letter to her of 4 July 1821, now in the Berg Collection, New York Public Library. This consists of two conjugate leaves, each measuring approx. 22.6 x 18.7 cm and with a watermark 'E & S / 1799'. The first leaf contains Scott's verses while the second has Scott's accompanying letter on the recto and the address panel on the verso. It has been folded for the post and addressed 'For / Mʳˢ Henry Siddons / Theatre Royal / Dublin / Ireland' and above that 'To be forwarded to Mʳˢ Siddons / directly'. The letter bears a postmark of 5 July 1821.

Scott's manuscript is plainly a draft written in a hurry since, as well as being largely unpunctuated, it also contains his revisions and corrections. Line 11, for instance, reads 'It wakes <some> ↑each↓ sorrow chills <some> ↑each↓ genial fire<s>', while in line 14 'such word' was originally 'this word'. The address must have reached Mrs Siddons too late to be used on the occasion for which it was intended and it was never published in Scott's lifetime, although when Scott subsequently wrote an address for the same actress's retirement in Edinburgh he reworked some of his earlier ideas for that occasion (see no. 129, 'Farewell Address for Mrs Siddons').

No printing has been discovered and the present text is based upon Scott's manuscript. A suitable title has been added, and, in addition to the following emendations, verb forms ending with 'd' have been routinely expanded to 'ed', while routine apostrophes have been introduced as required.

257.4   broken! (Editorial) / broken
257.6   Friendship (Editorial) / Freindship
257.8   dies. (Editorial) / dies
257.10   Farewell. (Editorial) / Farewell
257.11   sorrow, (Editorial) / sorrow
257.14   unmoved— (Editorial) / unmoved
257.18   claim? (Editorial) / claim
257.19   Genius, (Editorial) / Genius

Historical Note
On 18 January 1821 Henry Harris, who held the patent for the Theatre Royal in Dublin, opened his new building on Hawkins Street, the first major nineteenth-century Irish theatre and on a grander scale than any of its Dublin predeces-

sors: for details see Christopher Morash, *A History of Irish Theatre 1601–2000* (Cambridge, 2002), 77–79. Naturally, Harris wished to provide an attractive and lucrative opening season for his splendid new theatre and among the visiting actors he secured for it was the female star of Edinburgh's Theatre Royal company, Harriet Siddons (1783–1844). Mrs Siddons was free to take up the offer of a short summer engagement in Dublin, since the Edinburgh season had closed on 11 June and the theatre there would not reopen for the summer months until 30 July: see James C. Dibdin, *The Annals of the Edinburgh Stage* (Edinburgh, 1888), 296–97. She acted in Dublin between 18 June and 7 July in a series of her favourite Shakespearean roles (Juliet, Rosalind, Portia) and leading parts in standard eighteenth-century repertoire plays (such as Mrs Oakley in George Colman's *The Jealous Wife*). She also took the leading female role, Calanthe, in the first performances of a new tragedy, *Damon and Pythias*, by John Banim (1798–1842). This was the most successful play of Harris's opening season and concerned itself with the rule of a tyrant given power by a corrupt senate, interpretable as a commentary on the state of Ireland following the 1801 Act of Union.

Mrs Siddons proved to be extremely popular with the Dublin audience. The *Caledonian Mercury* of 25 June 1821 quoted an enthusiastic *Dublin Evening Post* notice of her Rosalind in *As You Like It*, which among other high praise called her 'the life of every scene in which she appeared'. Scott had probably heard of this report, for he wrote in a letter to his son Walter of 27 June, 'I am happy to see Mrs. Siddons has been so well received in Dublin and am very sorry you are not there to shew her some attention and civility' (*Letters*, 6.483). At her benefit night in Dublin on 4 July, Mrs Siddons delivered an address written by 'a Gentleman of this City' (*Freeman's Journal*, 3 July 1821), and she had clearly requested Scott to write one for her closing performance on 7 July. Scott acceded, but the performance of his promise was delayed, according to his letter accompanying the address, by his having been 'out of town and out of tune', through grief for the death on 16 June of John Ballantyne (1774–1821) and the distraction of a visit from his sister-in-law, Mrs Carpenter, following her return from India. Scott perhaps hardly expected a letter written in Edinburgh on 4 July to reach Dublin within three days, concluding it 'I hope in heaven these lines will come in time'. On arrival in Dublin it had to be forwarded from the theatre to Mrs Siddons's lodgings at a bookseller's in Grafton Street, where it probably reached her almost as she left the city.

Explanatory Notes

257.1   prompter's bell   Scott's address was to be spoken in front of the lowered curtain at the end of the evening's performance, since the ringing of the prompter's bell was a signal for the raising and lowering of the stage curtain at theatres.

257.15   from the genial land I part   advertisements, such as that in *Freeman's Journal* of 7 July 1821, emphasised that Mrs Siddons's performance at the Theatre Royal Dublin that evening was to be 'her Last Appearance in this Kingdom'.

257.19   Fair Isle to Genius   Scott had already commented on the 'warmth of heart and feeling' of the Irish as favourable to the reception of poetry in a letter to the actress Sarah Smith (1783?–1850) of 4 October 1810 (*Letters*, 2.384).

112.   The Death of Don Pedro

Textual Note
The date of composition of 'The Death of Don Pedro' is unknown, although
it is likely to have been subsequent to Scott's acquisition in the spring of 1819
of C. B. Depping's collection of Spanish Romances that contains the Spanish
original (see also Historical Note). Scott's translation was first published anony-
mously in his son-in-law, J. G. Lockhart's edition of Cervantes's *The History
of the Ingenious Gentleman, Don Quixote of La Mancha*, trans. Motteux, 5 vols
(Edinburgh, 1822), 1.312–14. Not long afterwards Lockhart included it as
'translated by a friend' in his *Ancient Spanish Ballads: Historical and Romantic*
(Edinburgh, 1823), 89–94, but it was not until this work was reprinted in an
unpaginated and handsomely illustrated edition by John Murray of London in
1841 that this friend was identified as 'the late Sir Walter Scott'. A headnote to
the poem in the original edition of *Ancient Spanish Ballads* was revised from the
containing endnote in the 1822 edition of *Don Quixote*, but both are presumably
the work of Lockhart himself. The poem in *Ancient Spanish Ballads* was clearly
set from a copy of *Don Quixote*, since it follows the printing there in all details,
except for the provision of two additional guiding commas, one after 'this' in
line 11 and one after 'That' in line 12. No manuscript of 'The Death of Don
Pedro' appears to have survived, and the poem was not included in any of the
lifetime collected editions of Scott's poetry, nor in Lockhart's posthumous col-
lected edition of 1833–34.
   The present text follows that in *The History of Don Quixote of La Mancha*,
trans. Motteux, ed. J. G. Lockhart, 5 vols (Edinburgh, 1822), 1.312–14, as the
first printing of Scott's translation. Lockhart's surrounding annotation has been
omitted, and the following emendations have been made to include the two
helpful guiding commas from *Ancient Spanish Ballads*:

258.11   this, (*Ancient Spanish Ballads*) / this
258.12   That, (*Ancient Spanish Ballads*) / That

Historical Note
Lockhart states that during his adolescence Scott acquired 'as much Spanish
as served for the Guerras Civiles de Granada, Lazarillo de Tormes, and, above
all, Don Quixote' (*Life*, 1.130). By the end of 1808 Scott was contemplating
an edition of Miguel de Cervantes's *Don Quixote* (1605, 1616), writing to the
London publisher John Murray on 15 November that he had 'many references
by me for the purpose' of annotation (*Letters*, 2.126). It is possible that he was
then aware of the Spanish original of 'The Death of Don Pedro', but more
likely that his interest was ignited by the acquisition in the spring of 1819 of
a copy of C. B. Depping's *Sammlung der besten alten Spanischen Historischen,
Ritter- und Maurischen Romanzen* (Leipzig, 1817) (*ALC*), which contains this
ballad in Spanish, though with the German title of 'Heinrich von Trastamara
bringt König Pedro um's Leben' (209). As he wrote enthusiastically to Southey
on 4 April 1819 (in the wake of a visit by the American scholar and Hispanicist
George Ticknor (1791–1871) to Abbotsford):

> Have you seen decidedly the most full and methodized collection of Spanish
> romances (ballads) published by the industry of Depping (Altenburgh and Leipsic),
> 1817? It is quite delightful. Ticknor had set me agog to see it, without affording me
> any hope it could be had in London, when by one of these fortunate chances which
> have often marked my life, a friend, who had been lately on the Continent, came
> unexpectedly to inquire for me, and plucked it forth *par manière de cadeau*. (*Letters*,
> 5.339–40)

By the autumn of 1821, however, Scott had abandoned his old intention of creating a new edition of *Don Quixote*, explaining in a letter to his Edinburgh publisher Archibald Constable of 30 September, 'I meant to do it myself and made some progress but Lockhart being a much better Spaniard and having more time I gave him my materials' (*Letters*, 7.16). In his Introduction to *Ancient Spanish Ballads* (1823) Lockhart acknowledged Depping's collection as the source of '[b]y far the greater part of the following translations' (viii) and also noted that 'a considerable number of the *historical* ballads in this collection' had already appeared in the previous year's edition of *Don Quixote* (xxvii).

King Pedro of Castile (1334–69), known variously as The Cruel and as The Just, was challenged in the Castilian Civil Wars (1366–69) by his illegitimate half-brother Enrique or Henry (1334–79). Henry had been given the title of Count of Trastámara and large grants of land in the NE of the Spanish peninsula by their father, King Alfonso XI, and had further improved his position by his marriage to Juana Manuel, an heiress and legitimate descendant of King Alfonso X. He deposed his brother in 1366, and Pedro fled to English-held Gascony where he enlisted the support of the English under Edward, the Black Prince (1330–76), but after successfully regaining power in 1367 failed to honour his commitments to the English. Henry returned from exile in France and with French military support defeated Pedro at the Battle of Montiel on 14 March 1369. Pedro fled to the nearby castle of Montiel, from which he was lured into a trap by the promise of negotiations. In conference in his own tent on 23 March 1369 Henry inflicted multiple stab wounds on Pedro, murdering him and thus securing power as Henry II of Castile. In 'The Monk's Tale' in Chaucer's *The Canterbury Tales* Pedro is referred to as a noble, worthy Spanish king betrayed and piteously slain by his brother, while the contemporary Spanish chronicler Pero López de Ayala, who served Henry II, depicts Pedro as an exceptionally cruel and vicious ruler.

Scott's translation is a faithful rendering of the Spanish original, including the same details with only such variations as result from the difference of language and maintenance of poetic form. For instance, a literal translation of lines 13–16 might read 'And in that fierce struggle / Only one witness was to be found / The sword page of Enrique / Who, from outside, watches events'.

Explanatory Notes

258.1   King Pedro   see Historical Note. There was a traditional alliance between Castile and Plantagenet England, the object of which was to keep French territorial ambitions in check. King Pedro was to have married Joan, daughter to Edward III of England, who died of the Black Death in 1348 on the way to her marriage in Castile.

258.14   Don Henry's page   Scott's translation forms part of one of Lockhart's endnotes for his edition of *Don Quixote*, a note which relates that Don Pedro was captured as he attempted to escape from the castle of Montiel and taken before his brother, when the two engaged in personal combat: 'Henry drew his poniard and wounded Pedro in the face, but his body was defended by a coat-of-mail; and in the struggle which ensued, Henry fell across a bench, and his brother being uppermost, had well nigh mastered him, when one of Henry's followers seizing Don Pedro by the leg, turned him over, and his master gaining the upper-hand, instantly poniarded him. Froissart calls this man the Vicomte de Roquebetyn, and others the Bastard d'Anisse' (1.311).

113.   Carle, now the King's Come!

Textual Note

This item was first printed in the form of two anonymous four-page pamphlets, one for each part of the song, the individual pages of which measure 20.5 x 12 cm. Copies of these original pamphlets, issued to mark George IV's visit to Scotland in the second half of August 1822, can be found in the National Library of Scotland, the Bodleian Library, and at Harvard University (see also below). A holograph manuscript now held by the Morgan Library (Scott 25, Accession MA 451.2), in a bound volume of Scott MSS once the property of the publisher Robert Cadell, contains the text of Part First of the song, written on two leaves (ff. 57–58) each measuring approx. 24.6 x 19.5 cm, with the watermark 'FELLOWS / 1807'. A number of small changes made in the course of writing, such as the deletion of 'Hamilton' in favour of 'premier Duke' at line 37, suggest that Scott was still actively engaged. Also noticeable is the deletion at two separate points of complete stanzas, one of which is immediately replaced sequentially, the other finding an equivalent on the final verso (which also provides one entirely new stanza). Apart from these changes, and an almost complete absence of punctuation, the wording generally matches the printed pamphlet. A proof of Part First with Scott's corrections also survives in NLS, F.5.f.17(2), facsimile samples of which are provided by Ruff (no. 174, fig. 19/20). In the case of the 14th stanza (lines 57–60), where Scott's interventions are most obtrusive, 'Auld Pentland's' at the start is replaced by 'King Arthur's', 'from' in the next line becomes 'in', and 'light up your crests' in the following one is changed to 'behold my crest'. (Since this represents one of the stanzas replaced in the manuscript, and which had originally begun there with 'Brave Arthur's', one might possibly trace here ongoing uncertainties as to where the beacon fires meant to announce the King's arrival were to be situated.) Elsewhere Scott changes 'England's' to 'England' (line 9), alters the spelling 'rokely' to 'rokela' (13), Scoticises 'down' and 'crown' to 'doun' and 'croun' (37, 38), and substitutes 'yon' for 'your' (47): all of which changes are carried through into the final printed pamphlet. At the head of the first page Scott has also written: 'To be thrown off on ordinary tea-paper such as is used for *ballant*s'—an instruction reflected in the rough 'broadsheet' quality of the end product.

The date of the song's composition and first printing can be surmised from a number of parallel events. The overall anticipation rather than retrospective description of events there places it somewhere after 22 July, when Scott finally became sure that the visit would take place (see *Letters*, 7.213), and before 14 August when the Royal Yacht finally entered the harbour at Edinburgh's port of Leith. This can be further narrowed down by comparison with the publication of *Hints Addressed to the Inhabitants of Edinburgh* (Edinburgh, 1822), nominally by 'an old Citizen', but evidently Scott's work, which closely parallels the song in outlining coming events, naming personnel, and advising on behaviour. At one point here Scott quotes at length a letter 'from one of the Edinburgh Newspapers of last week', one 'not ... from the pen of any ordinary newswriter' (18), and again palpably his own work. The publication also ends with a verbatim version of Part First of the song, stating it to have already been 'circulated on the occasion' (29). The letter incorporated in *Hints* first appeared in the *Edinburgh Weekly Journal* on 31 July, while the pamphlet itself was advertised in the same paper as 'this day published' on 7 August. Both parts of the song featured in the *Edinburgh Evening Courant* (as by 'a celebrated Bard') and the *Edinburgh Weekly Journal* on 12 and 14 August respectively, each without material differences from the pamphlet text. Even before that, on 10 August the *Caledonian Mercury* carried an advertisement for music to accompany the song; while an announcement in the same paper on 12 August for a performance of the 'National Opera' of *Rob Roy* states that 'In the course of the evening MR MACKAY will sing the National Ballad of CARLE, NOW THE KING'S COME'. From all this evidence, it seems likely that composition took place somewhere between 22 July and 7 August, with the second part possibly being completed fractionally later; and that the text of both parts was in circulation in print by 12 August, the source-text for the newspaper versions most probably being the printed pamphlets.

Versions of the song proliferated in a variety of contexts during and in the aftermath of the King's Visit. Prominent here are a number of London and English provincial newspapers, with Part First for example featuring in *The Examiner* for 11 August and the *Leeds Mercury* on 17 August. One interesting feature of these printings is the addition in the case of Part First of a handful of small explanatory footnotes, glossing for example 'premier Duke' as 'Hamilton', and (like the song) in one instance seemingly anticipating events ('There is to be a bonfire on the top of Arthur's seat'). On Thursday, 15 August, the *Morning Chronicle* in London printed a version of Part Second, attributing it directly to 'Sir Walter Scott'. In this case there are a number of significant variants compared with the wording found in the original pamphlet, though the latter is carried through without significant alteration in other papers as well as periodicals such as the *Gentleman's Magazine*, which featured the first part in its number for August 1822, and the second part in that for September. Most immediately apparent in the *Morning Chronicle* version are the opening lines, which now read 'She toom'd her quaigh of mountain dew, / It rais'd her heart the higher too, / Because it came from Waterloo' (compare lines 73–75). Other verbal variants include 'I'll hae a braw new snood o' smoke' instead of 'And lace with fire my snood o' smoke' at line 111, 'vanquish'd foeman's' rather than 'falling Despot's' (line 118), and 'wild flowers' instead of 'blossoms' (line 146). The two stanzas beginning 'Lord, how the pibrochs groan!' (lines 129–32) and 'I'll shew him wit' (lines 161–64) are moreover omitted. Similar variants are apparent in the case of the second part of the full text of the song provided in Robert Mudie's *A Historical Account of His Majesty's Visit to Scotland* (Edinburgh, 1822), 48–53, where Scott once more is named as author, and which adds a number of sizeable additional footnotes of its own to the text as a whole. The same variant text is also followed in the song as included in *The Royal Scottish Minstrelsy* (Leith, 1824), [1]–11, an anthology of 'loyal effusions' occasioned by the King's Visit. No specific explanation for these changes has been discovered, though one possibility is that an alternative copy-text of Part Second was issued in the rush to disseminate materials, while some smaller changes might have occurred more naturally through the process of transmission.

The song was not included in any of the collected editions of Scott's poetry until the posthumous Lockhart edition of 1833–34 (10.369–80), where the text largely follows that of the original pamphlets, with an assortment of changes to punctuation and spelling of the kind that can be attributed to the printer. At the same time, it provides an arguably more conventional spelling of proper names in the case of Montagu, Buccleuch, Rosebery, and Huntly (see lines 29–30, 50, 121). This version also carries over a number of footnotes from earlier printings, including those in Mudie's *Historical Account*, while making sizable additions apparently of its own. Lastly, the footnotes include three alleged alternative MS readings, though, on examination, the two of these that appear in Part First match stanzas that are actually deleted in the surviving holograph manuscript in the Morgan Library (see above), this suggesting a degree of disingenuousness on the editor's part.

One final element in the gestation of this Song is revealed in the copy of the original pamphlets in the Houghton Library, Harvard University (EC8. Sco.86.822ac), which at the end includes an additional stanza and note relating to it, both in handwriting and signed 'A S':

> O whar shall I find a Bard, a Bard,
> To pay him honour & regard?
> For auld Sir Walter's wrought ower hard
> Carle, now the King's come

This verse concluded the Song as it stood in the original MS. but was afterwards struck out by Sir Walter, probably because he found that the authorship was no secret—The third line was abundantly true.

The handwriting in both the stanza and note can be identified as that of Anne Rutherford Scott (b. 1802), Scott's niece and in his later life amanuensis, and it is possible that the addition was written on the pamphlet sometime after the event when she was working with materials at Abbotsford. While it might be tempting to add the stanza to the present edited version, as almost certainly by Scott, it is unlikely that he ever would have authorised the public appearance of such a self-reflecting detail even if a semblance of anonymity had been maintained. In some respects, this flourish bears a resemblance to expressions of exhilaration or relief at completion found at the end of manuscripts of other works by Scott, including some of his novels.

The present text follows that of the original pamphlet versions of the song, as representing the only printing known to have been authorised by Scott, and for which he had examined proofs. The following emendations have been made:

259.13	Reekie (MS) / Reikie
260.29	Montagu (1833–34*PW*) / Montague
260.30	Buccleuch (1833–34*PW*) / Buccleugh
261.50	Rosebery (MS) / Roseberry
263.121	Huntly (1833–34*PW*) / Huntley
264.147	you— (1833–34*PW*) / you

Historical Note

A clear prototype for this item can be found in the Jacobite drinking song, 'Carle, an' the King Come'. Scott had already jubilantly quoted from it in the wake of the rediscovery of the Scottish Regalia (an event he had effectively orchestrated himself), in writing to John Wilson Croker on 14 February 1818:

> It should not be omitted though it does not appear in the minutes that the Commissioners adjourned to my house and got about *half fou* [i.e. half drunk] to celebrate the joyful day and wash the dust out of their throats. I am always harping on an event which would make us still gayer
>
> > Cogie and the King come
> > Cogie an' the King come
> > I'se be *fou* and ye's be toom
> > Cogie an' the King come.
>
> With which scrap of a loyal legend I rest ever yours … (*Letters*, 5.278)

The same lines can be found also written in pencil, probably in Scott's hand, at the end of proof sheets of Part First of the song, with a reference to James Hogg's *Jacobite Relics* (1819), in which another version appears: see first series, ed. Murray Pittock (Edinburgh, 2002), 39–40. Though the origins of the original song are uncertain, it was probably in circulation at the time of the Jacobite Rising of 1715 (when the exiled Stuart King James VIII and III made a brief appearance in Scotland), and became more fully assimilated into the Scottish musical scene later in the century. A modified version beginning 'Peggy, now the King's come' is sung by Mause in Allan Ramsay's *The Gentle Shepherd* (1725), 2.3; the same also featuring in his *Tea-Table Miscellany* (see 11th edn, 1750, 2.202), with 'Carle and the King come' as the nominated tune. It was recorded too with a musical notation in James Johnson's *Scots Musical Museum*, 6 vols (Edinburgh, 1787–1803), 3.item 239, where the 'Old Words' are also given, with a main chorus matching Scott's own. The air had likewise appeared in a number of earlier eighteenth-century Scottish collections, and must have been well-known in Scott's time. Robert Chambers in *The Songs of Scotland prior to Burns* (Edinburgh, 1880) recalls how Scott in preparing his own song 'got his old music-master, Alister [*sic*] Campbell, to play over the air ... and when he had got its strain into his head (which Alister told me a few days after was no easy matter), he scribbled a long series of verses anticipating the doings of the royal visit' (52).

Considering that the song was completed and printed in a narrow space prior to the King's arrival (see Textual Note), and that Scott found himself almost single-handedly acting as Pageant-master for the event, it is a credit to his acumen and powers of persuasion that so much of what is anticipated was matched in the performance. Part First, mirroring in some respects Gaelic verse calling for a gathering of clans, is much concerned with nominating the leading Scottish nobility and office-holders, many of whom Scott was still actively canvassing, as well as outlining their ceremonial roles. It also anticipates events such as the removal of the Regalia from the Castle to the Palace at Holyrood, the sighting of the royal flotilla as it entered the Firth of Forth, and the procession from Leith through the gates of Edinburgh to the Palace. Part Second carries on in the same vein, while bringing in a larger body of the citizenry, with a view to later events such as the procession to the Castle lined with onlookers, a military display at Portobello, two levees at Holyroodhouse (one specifically for the ladies), and a grand banquet at Parliament House. It is here, too, that Scott's concern to involve Highlanders, real and otherwise, comes most fully into view (see lines 125–32). As his *Hints Addressed to the Inhabitants of Edinburgh* (Edinburgh, 1822) advises: 'Those who wear the Highland dress must ... be careful to be armed in the proper Highland fashion,—steel-wrought pistols, broadsword, and dirk. It is understood that Glengarry, Breadalbane, Huntly, and several other Chieftains, mean to attend the levee with *their tail on, i.e.* with a considerable attendance of their gentlemen followers' (16). Notoriously, George IV himself was set to appear at the same levee decked in just such costumery. As a whole, however, and notwithstanding persistent assertions since concerning Scott having 'tartanised' Scotland, an appreciably larger body of national life was involved, as the following notes indicate.

Explanatory Notes
259.title   Carle   man, fellow. An alternative derivation might be found in 'carol', in the sense of singing.
259.sub-title   Auld Spring   old lively dance-tune.
259.2   bang'd the South   beaten the South, effectively England, where the monarch had mostly resided since the Union of the Crowns in 1603.
259.3   de'il a Scotsman's die of drouth   not a Scotsman will die of thirst.
259.10   Ireland had a joyfu' cast   referring to George IV's earlier state visit to Ireland in 1821.

259.13   Auld Reekie   'Old Smokey', familiar name for Edinburgh, and alluding to the pall of smoke often covering the tenements of its crowded Old Town.

259.13   rokela gray   a *rokelay* is a short cloak worn by women; its greyness here reinforcing the sense of enveloping smoke (see previous note).

259.15   weary time away   *weary* in the sense of dispiriting, vexatious. George IV was the first British monarch to visit Scotland for 171 years, since Charles II in 1651.

260.17   skirling frae the Castle Hill   *skirling* in the sense of making a shrill noise or screeching, and probably alluding to the noise of bagpipes. The Castle Hill refers to the approach to the Castle up from the High Street of Edinburgh, including an esplanade, and not the Castle itself.

260.18   Carline's   *carline* in Scots denotes a woman, often old, and sometimes with supernatural qualities. Here serving as a personification for Edinburgh.

260.19   Canon Mill   or Canonmills, district of Edinburgh, in a low hollow N of the New Town, deriving its name from a mill established in medieval times, and once containing a loch, progressively drained during the 18th and 19th centuries.

260.22   busk   make ready, equip.

260.22   weapon-shaw   or 'weapon-showing' involved the mustering of any group of Scottish men to determine whether they were properly armed. Medieval wappenshaws normally occurred when the Scottish feudal host was being raised either to resist English cross-border invasions, or to attack the northern counties of England; but on the present occasion a display of martial loyalty within a larger British context is clearly posited. Compare *The Tale of Old Mortality*, ed. Douglas Mack, EEWN 4b (Edinburgh, 1993), 14–16, for Scott's account of the traditional wappenshaw.

260.25   Newbattle's ancient spires   Newbattle Abbey, about 11 km (7 miles) SE of Edinburgh and 1.5 km (1 mile) S of Dalkeith. Originally founded in 1140 by monks from Melrose Abbey, it had been inhabited as a family residence since the 16th century, and was remodelled in a castellated style in the later 18th century. George IV paid a special visit, and the King's Gate there was erected in his honour.

260.26   Bauld Lothian   William Kerr, 6th Marquess of Lothian (1762–1824), Lord Lieutenant of Midlothian, and proprietor of Newbattle Abbey (see previous note).

260.29–30   Montagu ... young Buccleuch   Henry James Scott-Montagu, Lord Montagu of Boughton (1776–1845), 3rd son of the 3rd Duke of Buccleuch, and co-guardian to the 5th Duke, Walter Francis Montagu Douglas Scott (1806–84) during his minority. A regular correspondent of Scott's, Montagu resided chiefly at Ditton Park, near Slough in Buckinghamshire, close to Windsor Castle, and served as an important intermediary regarding the King's intentions earlier in 1822. The King chiefly resided at Dalkeith House, belonging to the Buccleuch family, during his visit.

260.31   some that I may rue   Charles William Henry Scott, 4th Duke of Buccleuch (1772–1819), and his wife Harriet (1773–1814), parents of the present young Duke, had been Scott's personal friends and patrons.

260.33   Haddington   Charles Hamilton, 8th Earl of Haddington (1753–1828), Lord Lieutenant of Haddingtonshire from 1804 to 1823, and hereditary keeper of Holyrood Park. For Scott's familiarity with 'the old peer of Haddington', see, for example, *Letters*, 8.287.

260.34 causeway paved part of a street or path: here presumably referring chiefly to that of the High Street of Edinburgh.

260.37 premier Duke Alexander Douglas Hamilton, 10th Duke of Hamilton (1767–1852), whose Dukedom was the first in Scotland other than titles given to members of the Scottish royal family. He was first in order of precedence in the procession that carried the Regalia of Scotland from the Castle to the palace at Holyrood, shortly before the royal visit, and acting as hereditary Keeper of the palace was first amongst the nobility to kiss the King's hand on his arrival there.

260.38–39 yonder craig … lang sleep referring to the removal of the Scottish Regalia from Edinburgh Castle (see also previous note), where it had been secreted since the Union of 1707, prior to the rediscovery orchestrated by Scott in 1818.

260.41 Athole John Murray, 4th Duke of Atholl (1755–1830), chief of the Clan Murray, and a main target of Scott's as a source of Highlanders for the celebrations. In actuality the Duke, though attending himself, was somewhat hesitant in providing more clansmen for the spectacle: see John Prebble, *The King's Jaunt* (London, 1988), 214 and passim.

260.43 Morton, shew the Douglas' blood George Douglas, 16th Earl of Morton (1767–1827), Lord Lieutenant of Fife from 1808 to 1824. Scott here emphasises his ancestry in the once pre-eminent Douglas family of Scotland.

260.45 Tweeddale George Hay, 8th Marquess of Tweeddale (1787–1876), was one of the first of the Scottish nobility to greet George IV on his entry to Holyroodhouse (see Prebble, 252). Previously he had served as a staff officer in the Peninsular War, was appointed a Knight of the Thistle in 1820, and was to become Lord Lieutenant of East Lothian in 1824.

260.46 Hopetoun John Hope, 4th Earl of Hopetoun (1765–1823), a veteran soldier of the wars against France, and Captain-General of the Royal Company of Archers, who ceremonially guarded George IV during the visit. The King's host at Hopetoun House immediately prior to his return.

260.47 Clerk Sir George Clerk, 6th Baronet of Penicuik (1787–1867), MP for Midlothian 1811–32.

260.47 bugle breath according to a footnote to the song in Robert Mudie's *A Historical Account of His Majesty's Visit to Scotland* (Edinburgh, 1822), 50n (and reproduced in the posthumous 1833–34 collected edition, 10.371n): 'The Baron of Pennycuik is bound by his tenure, whenever the King comes to Edinburgh, to receive him at the Harestone (in which the standard of James IV. was erected when his army encamped on the Boroughmuir, before his fatal expedition to England), now built into the park-wall at the end of Tipperlin Lone, near Boroughmuir-head; and, standing thereon, to give three blasts on a horn.' A similar account is given by Scott himself in endnote 1 to 'The Gray Brother' (no. 35); see also Scott's Note X to Canto Fourth of *Marmion*, ed. Ainsley McIntosh, EEWSP 2 (Edinburgh, 2018), 252. No evidence of this ceremony being re-enacted during George IV's visit has been discovered.

261.49 Wemyss Francis Wemyss Charteris Douglas (1772–1853), known as the Earl of March from 1810 to 1826, but created Baron Wemyss in 1821, and later in 1826 obtaining a reversal of the attainder of the earldom of Wemyss, becoming the 8th Earl. From 1821 to 1853 he served as Lord Lieutenant of Peeblesshire.

261.50 Rosebery … Dalmeny shades John Archibald Primrose, 4th Earl of Rosebery (1783–1868), who commissioned the building of Dalmeny House on the southern coast of the Firth of Forth some 10 km (6 miles)

NW of Edinburgh, this providing an alternative to the ancestral residence at nearby Barnbougle Castle. Completed in 1817 in a Gothic Tudor-revival style, Dalmeny House stands in wooded parkland.

261.51   Breadalbane   John Campbell, 4th Earl of Breadalbane, later 1st Marquess (1762–1834), whose family seat was at Taymouth Castle, on the southern bank of the Tay 2 km (1¼ miles) NE of Kenmore, rebuilt in a Gothic style. One of the Highland 'Chieftains' Scott was insistent should bring clansmen to the celebrations (see *Hints Addressed to the Inhabitants of Edinburgh*, 16; Prebble, 165, 208, 215, 240).

261.51   belted plaids   Highlanders wearing a piece of tartan plaid, secured by a belt buckled tight round the body.

261.53–54   stately Niddrie … Minden   Andrew Wauchope of Niddrie-Merschell, born in 1735, who fought as a Captain in the 1st Dragoon Guards at the Battle of Minden in 1759 during the Seven Years War: see James Paterson, *Genealogy of the Family of Wauchope of Niddrie-Merschell* (Edinburgh, 1858), 83–84. An early footnote attached to the poem describes him as 'Wanchope of Niddrie, a noble looking old man, and a fine specimen of an antient Baron' (see, for example, *Gentleman's Magazine*, August 1822, 164n).The mansion-house of Niddrie-Merschell stood in the vicinity of Craigmillar Castle, about 5 km (3 miles) SE of Edinburgh.

261.57   King Arthur's grown a common crier   referring to Arthur's Seat, the striking peak (250 m), S of Holyroodhouse, Edinburgh, the name of which has been suppositiously connected to the legendary King Arthur. A bonfire was lit on its summit as a signal on the arrival of the royal yacht at Leith and sustained during the King's visit. As Scott had previously noted at the end of *Hints Addressed to the Inhabitants of Edinburgh*, 28: 'all classes have been invited to send materials to the Duke's Walk, for the purpose of having an immense bonfire on the summit of Arthur's Seat.' The 'common crier' alludes to the crier of a city or town, who announced public news on the streets.

261.58   Fife and far Cantire   Fife is the county (once known as a kingdom) N of the Firth of Forth on the eastern coast of Scotland; Cantire, or Kintyre, is a long peninsula protruding southwards from W Argyllshire. In Scottish geographical terms thus denoting from coast to coast.

261.59   my crest of fire   the outline of Arthur's Seat (see note to 261.57) has been likened to that of a lion. Compare *The Heart of Mid-Lothian*, ed. David Hewitt and Alison Lumsden, EEWN 6 (Edinburgh, 2004), 156.22–23 ('Arthur's Seat, like a couchant lion of immense size').

261.61   Saint Abb   St Abb's Head, rocky promontory 1.5 km (1 mile) N of the village of St Abbs, in Berwickshire, on the SE coast of Scotland towards the approach to the Firth of Forth. There was a signal station there in Scott's time.

261.62   Tantallon and the Bass   Tantallon Castle, set on high rocks on the E Lothian coast, 4 km (2½ miles) E of North Berwick; the Bass Rock, an island rising out of the sea off the same coast, roughly parallel with Tantallon.

261.63   Calton, get out your keeking-glass   referring to the Calton Hill Observatory, on the hill of that name at the E end of Princes Street in Edinburgh, the foundation stone of which was laid in 1818, leading to completion in 1822. It became the Royal Observatory as a result of George IV's visit. A *keeking-glass*, in Scots normally referring to a looking-glass or mirror, presumably alludes to a telescope; though it was not until the 1830s that funding allowed the installation of major instruments.

261.66   ta'en a dwam   fainted, swooned.

261.67 Oman Charles Oman (d. 1825), first tenant of the extensive Waterloo Hotel, in Waterloo Place, Edinburgh, which was opened in 1819 and included three dining rooms and a large ballroom. During the visit it housed several members of the King's suite as well as a number of visiting Scottish notables. Compare *Hints Addressed to the Inhabitants of Edinburgh*: 'The whole of the Waterloo Hotel has been engaged for the use of his Majesty's suite' (13).

261.68 Cogie a *cog* in Scots is a container for food and drink, made of wood with metal hoops, sometimes (as indicated here) used for holding liquor.

261.71 I'se be fou, and ye's be toom I'll be full (of drink), and you'll be empty.

261.73 Hawick gill a measure of ale or spirits equivalent to half an Imperial pint. Compare the popular song 'Andro and his cutty Gun': 'And well she loo'd a *Hawick* gill'.

261.73 mountain dew whisky, used especially if illicitly distilled.

261.74 Heised up raised or lifted up.

261.74 Auld Reekie's see note to 259.13.

261.75 minded her of Waterloo led her to recollect the Battle of Waterloo; in which the British-led allied forces in 1815 had finally defeated Napoleon. Waterloo Place, Waterloo Bridge, and the Waterloo Hotel (see note to 261.67) in Edinburgh were all named in honour of the victory, and plans were in place in 1822 for a National Monument to the fallen upon Calton Hill, though a shortfall in subscription meant that it was never completed.

262.82 dirdum noise, uproar.

262.83 Saint Giles's jowing bell the tolling bell of St Giles' Cathedral (the High Kirk in Edinburgh). The Great Bell there was cast in 1460, in the time of James II of Scotland.

262.85 trusty Provost Sir William Arbuthnot (1766–1829), Lord Provost of Edinburgh 1815–17, 1821–23. Scott had consulted with him about the arrangements for the visit from an early stage. During the celebrations he offered the King the keys to the city at the entrance of the gateway to Edinburgh, and officiated at a number of other public occasions.

261.86 Good Town's a sobriquet for Edinburgh.

262.87 waur than you been made a Knight worse men than you (possibly with a suggestion of lower social rank) have been knighted. On 24 August Arbuthnot (see note to 262.85) hosted a grand dinner in Parliament Hall, during which the King reportedly asked if he would object to being made a Baronet, with Arbuthnot kneeling before him and kissing his hand. Authorisation of the award, however, appears to have been secured somewhat earlier. Lord Provosts were traditionally knighted, but not as baronets.

262.91 warstle wrestle in prayer, pray earnestly for.

262.95 dinna pike a plea don't pick a quarrel (more *literally*, a lawsuit).

262.97 burgher's bairn apprentice.

262.98 dunts thumps, knocks (so as to produce a dull sound).

262.98 clanks on airn strikes or beats on iron.

262.99 oon oven.

262.99 winds the pirn referring to the action of loading a weaver's bobbin with yarn.

262.101 Blanket Blue standard of the incorporated trades of Edinburgh. This was to be displayed during the King's procession between Holyroodhouse and the Castle, as outlined by Scott in his letter to the newspapers, subsequently quoted in *Hints Addressed to the Inhabitants*. See, for example, the *Edinburgh Weekly Journal* of 31 July: 'Along the High Street, as far as the Lawn Market, the incorporated Crafts are to be drawn up on both sides, displaying, as in ancient times, their banners, and disposed under their various Deacons; the whole under the command of the Deacon Convenor, with the Blue Blanket, which is said to have seen the Holy Wars' (compare *Hints*, 19). A substantial footnote later appeared with the version of the song in Robert Mudie's *Historical Account of His Majesty's Visit to Scotland* (1822), 51n–52n, outlining the tradition that 'this standard was used in the Holy Wars by a body of crusading citizens of Edinburgh', while providing a 'real history' in its representing a gift from James III of Scotland in gratitude for being released from imprisonment in the Castle. The same note was replicated in the posthumous Lockhart collected edition of 1833–34 (10.375n–76n).

262.105   downa loup, and rin and rave   don't leap, run, and act wildly. One of Scott's concerns prior to the visit was that the onlookers would break rank and crowd after the King. See, for example, *Hints Addressed to the Inhabitants*: 'If the crowd become for a moment unsteady or tumultuous—if once they break their front rank, that is, the line of the constituted bodies—if ever they begin to shoulder, and press, and squeeze, and riot—the whole goodly display will sink at once into disorganization and confusion' (20–21).

262.107   keep the causeway   appear with pride and self-assertion; for the more literal meaning of *causeway*, see note to 260.34.

263.109   Sir Thomas   Sir Thomas Bradford (1777–1853), British officer, commander-in-chief in Scotland 1819–25. Salutes from the batteries on the Castle rock were a regular feature during the celebrations.

263.110   Pentland   the Pentland Hills, on the SW border of modern Edinburgh, stretching in that direction for about 32 km (20 miles).

263.110   dinnles   trembles, vibrates.

263.111   snood o' smoke   a *snood* was a fillet or ribbon bound round the brow and tied at the back under the hair, worn especially by young unmarried women.

263.113–14   Melville ... bands of blue ... Louden lads   Robert Saunders Dundas, 2nd Viscount Melville (1771–1851), statesman, manager of Scotland, and a confidante of the King's during the visit, was Colonel of the Royal Midlothian Yeomanry Cavalry, whose uniforms were coloured navy blue, scarlet, and silver. ('Louden lads' means Lothian lads.) At the turn of the century they had amalgamated with Scott's old regiment, the Royal Edinburgh Volunteer Light Dragoons. A squadron rode at the head of the procession which marked the King's entry into Edinburgh. During the visit the King also paid a special visit to Melville Castle, 1.5 km (1 mile) NE of Lasswade, near Edinburgh, where the Midlothian Cavalry were drawn up on the lawn: see William Beattie, *Scotland Illustrated*, 2 vols (London, 1838), 1.135.

263.115   Elcho   Francis Wemyss, Lord Elcho (1796–1883); succeeded as 9th Earl of Wemyss in 1853. Evidently a key member in the Midlothian Cavalry: 'There is a new Edinburgh squadron under Lord Elcho very fine young men & good horses' (*Letters*, 6.109).

263.115   Hope   Sir John Hope of Pinkie, 11th Baronet (1781–1853), Major of the Midlothian Cavalry Volunteers. Pinkie House is at Musselburgh, East Lothian. Not to be confused here with Sir John Hope (1765–1836), who in 1822 was Colonel of the 92nd Highlanders.

263.115   Cockburn   Captain Robert Cockburn, commander of the Edinburgh troop of the Midlothian Cavalry escorting the Royal Carriage during the visit (see *Hints Addressed to the Inhabitants*, 11–12).

263.117   bluidy braes   referring to the extensive casualties on the field of the Battle of Waterloo (see also note to 261.75).

263.118–19   falling Despot's praise ... gallant Greys   the Scots Greys were heavy cavalry, whose charge at Waterloo, and capture of one of the French Imperial Eagles, had become legendary in Scott's time. A footnote in the posthumous Lockhart 1833–34 collected edition states that: 'Bonaparte's exclamation at Waterloo is well known: "Ces beaux chevaux gris, comme ils travaillent!" [Those beautiful grey horses, how hard they work!]' (10.377n). The Scots Greys were on duty throughout the King's visit.

263.121 Cock of the North, my Huntly George Gordon, Marquess of Huntly, later 5th Duke of Gordon (1770–1836), British general. Scott refers to 'Huntly the Cock of the North' in a letter to Lord Montagu of January 1821 (*Letters*, 6.329). This title was originally used in relation to Earls of Huntly in the 15th and 16th centuries, in reference to the pre-eminence of the Gordon family in NE Scotland. The tune 'Cock of the North' has long been a march of the Gordon Highlanders.

263.122 Forty-twa 42nd Regiment of Foot (Black Watch), of which George Gordon, Marquess of Huntly (see previous note) was Colonel from 1806 to 1820.

263.123 waes my heart woe is my heart, alas.

263.125 canty Celts Highlanders (supposedly of Celtic origin), *canty* here being used in the sense of lively, cheerful, pleasant. More specially referring to the Celtic Society, founded in Edinburgh in January 1820 to foster Highland dress and culture, and of which Scott was Vice-President.

263.127 still some plaids and kilts after the Jacobite Rising of 1745 the wearing of Highland dress, tartan and the plaid (forerunner of the kilt), was forbidden and remained proscribed until 1782. During the visit George IV famously appeared at a levee in dressy Highland garb, variously interpreted as an act of rapprochement or as a ludicrous self-indulgence, according to political bias.

263.129 pibrochs piping tunes, music for the Highland bagpipe.

263.130 MacDonnell's ta'en the field Alexander Ranaldson Macdonell of Glengarry (1773–1828), who is sometimes claimed as a model of Fergus Mac-Ivor in Scott's *Waverley* (1814); the subject also of a large canvas in oils by Sir Henry Raeburn (1756–1823), painted in about 1810 and now in the National Galleries of Scotland (NG 420). He forcefully played the part of the Highland chief during the King's visit accompanied by his flamboyantly dressed following.

263.131 MacLeod John Norman Macleod, 24th Chief of Macleod (1788–1835). One of the first to whom Scott wrote summoning him with his clansmen to the event: 'Do come and bring half-a-dozen or half-a-score of Clansmen, so as to look like an Island Chief as you are' (*Letters*, 7.213). Scott had previously visited MacLeod at Dunvegan, Skye, in 1814.

263.131 branking ower the fell prancing over the moor-hills.

263.133 each Archer spark referring to the Royal Company of Archers, under the leadership of the Earl of Hopetoun (see note to 260.46). Formed in the late 17th century, and receiving official recognition by a Royal Charter in 1704, this company performed the role of a bodyguard during the proceedings, dressed for the occasion in green tartan and bonnets with long feathers (see Prebble, 91–92; *Hints Addressed to the Inhabitants*, 13–14).

263.137 Young Errol William George Hay, 18th Earl of Erroll (1801–46). Scott anticipated a large part for him in the proceedings: 'The Sword of State will … be carried by the young Earl of Errol, Lord High Constable of Scotland. In virtue of this high office, Lord Errol ranks as the first of Scottish subjects' (*Hints Addressed to the Inhabitants*, 23).

263.138 Panie-Morarchate A footnote in the posthumous Lockhart

1833–34 collected edition observes: 'In more correct orthography, *Banamhorar-Chat*, or the Great Lady, (literally *Female Lord*) *of the Chatte*; the Celtic title of the Countess of Sutherland' (10.378n). Elizabeth, Marchioness of Stafford (1765–1839) was Countess of Sutherland in her own right, her Gaelic title meaning roughly 'The Great Lady of the Cat'. Scott used the title, again spelt differently, in a Journal entry of 13 December 1825: 'Letter from Lady Stafford, kind and friendly after the wont of Banzu-Mohr-ar-chat' (*Journal*, 35). During the preparations for the King's visit she sought Scott's assistance in securing the honour of carrying the Sceptre for her second son, Francis Leveson-Gower, afterwards 1st Earl of Ellesmere (1800–57), following a hereditary right of the Earls of Sutherland.

263.139   Knight Mareschal Sir Alexander Keith of Dunnottar and Ravelston (1780–1832), appointed Knight Marischal in 1819 in the wake of the rediscovery of the Scottish Regalia in 1818. Scott envisaged a high-profile role for him during the visit, especially in the procession to the Castle to claim and then escort the Regalia to Holyroodhouse: 'The Knight Marischal (who represents the ancient and illustrious house of the Earls Marischal, and possesses their estates, the title of Earl having been forfeited in 1715) will ride, according to the old custom, on horseback, attended by six esquires in rich costumes of scarlet and gold' (*Hints Addressed to the Inhabitants*, 23).

264.141   cummer Leith Leith, the port of Edinburgh and a separate burgh, depicted here as a woman gossip (*cummer*).

264.141   mis-set put out of humour. Referring presumably to delays experienced while anticipating the King's arrival, the last of which involved him staying on board the day the Royal Yacht entered port.

264.143   handsel present, celebratory gift.

264.145–46   daughters ... blossoms strew events during the visit involved a special levee in the King's Drawing-room for the ladies, as well as a grand ball in the Assembly Rooms and a Caledonian Hunt Ball.

264.149   propine gift, tribute.

264.151   ne'er a groat's in pouch familiar expression denoting a lack of funds. A *groat* is silver coin worth 4 pence Scots (0.14p).

264.157   mason-work referring to Edinburgh's architecture, involving Scottish stonework.

264.158   Babel clay the Tower of Babel was built of bricks baked from clay: see Genesis 11.3. Possibly intimating a difference between the Scottish city's stone buildings and the bricks used in many London ones.

264.161   lair learning; alluding to the intellectual credentials of Edinburgh as the 'Athens of the North'.

264.165   Sir John, of projects rife Sir John Sinclair, 1st Bart. of Ulbster (1754–1835), lawyer and agriculturalist, whose extensive projects included the first *Statistical Account of Scotland*, published in 21 volumes between 1791 and 1799. Sinclair apparently lobbied Scott during the preparations with the prospect of securing a peerage for his contribution; but, in spite of being allowed a special interview with the King at Holyrood, this was not forthcoming (see Prebble, 92, 274).

114.   Lines added to the King's Anthem

Textual Note

These additional lines to the British National Anthem first appeared in print in the Edinburgh newspapers as part of their reports on George IV's visit to the

Theatre Royal in Edinburgh on the evening of Tuesday, 27 August, during his state visit to Scotland in 1822, featuring in the *Edinburgh Weekly Journal* on 28 August, then in the *Caledonian Mercury* and *Edinburgh Evening Courant* on the following day. As the paper most closely associated with Scott—its proprietor being the printer James Ballantyne—the *Edinburgh Weekly Journal* may possibly have enjoyed special access in its reportage, in addition to providing copy for its rivals. The same verse is also quoted in Robert Mudie's *Historical Account of His Majesty's Visit to Scotland* (Edinburgh, 1822), 277, though again without any mention of an author. It was subsequently anthologised in *The Royal Scottish Minstrelsy: Being a Collection of Loyal Effusions Occasioned by the Visit of His Most Gracious Majesty George IV to Scotland* (Leith, 1824), 229, in this last instance acquiring a header including a direct attribution to Scott: 'Lines added to the King's Anthem, ascribed to Sir Walter Scott, Bart. And sung at the Theatre while His Majesty was about to retire'. None of the above versions differ textually, apart from very minor variations in punctuation.

The present text follows that in *The Royal Scottish Minstrelsy* (1824), 229, without emendation, and with a title truncated from the heading there.

Historical Note
Scott evidently had a large hand in the organisation of the King's visit to the Theatre Royal, then managed by his close associate William Henry Murray (1790–1852), whose production of a dramatisation of Scott's novel *Rob Roy* was the main event of the evening. According to the majority of newspaper reports, it was after the final falling of the curtain that the national anthem was sung by the cast with the additional stanza in place. The overall effect, however, might not have fully satisfied Scott, sitting in a box near to the King's. In particular, the *Edinburgh Weekly Journal* regretted that it had been 'totally lost upon the audience, by being sung in parts, in place of being legibly delivered by one distinct and intelligible voice'. It would be hard to exaggerate the significance of the moment for Scott in historical terms. At the height of the Jacobite Rising in September 1745, another stanza had been temporarily added to the anthem, and sung by the cast at Drury Lane Theatre in London, with the concluding lines: 'May he sedition hush, / And like a torrent rush / Rebellious Scots to crush! / God save the King!': see Richard Clark, *An Account of the National Anthem Entitled God Save the King!* (London, 1822), 8. With George IV on the point of returning home to England, on 29 August, Scott would no doubt have been conscious of reversing this earlier situation, while offering a final reprise to the larger displays of rechannelled loyalism he had stage-managed throughout the King's Visit (see also Notes to no. 113, 'Carle, now the King's Come!').

Explanatory Notes
265.6 latest accents *accent* in the sense of musical intonation, but possibly also alluding to the distinctive Scottish speech now being heard. The same term had been used by Scott earlier in 1822 ('Winds bear the accents forth') when hesitantly proffering four additional lines to the Anthem, having been sounded out about a contribution to Dr William Kitchiner's *Loyal and National Songs of England* (1823): see *Letters*, 7.107. The lines did not appear in Kitchiner's volume.

115. Epilogue

Textual Note

According to a letter from Scott to Constable of 22 October 1824 this Epilogue was 'never spoken but written for some play afterwards withdrawn in which Mrs H: Siddons was to have spoken it in the character of Queen Mary' (*Letters*, 8.407). The surviving manuscript in Scott's hand (EUL, La. IV.1.17) is written on a single leaf of paper, measuring approx. 25.2 x 19.8 cm, and bearing the watermark 'A COWAN / 1822'. In sending this to the antiquary David Laing (1793–1878) as an autograph poem with an accompanying letter of 22 October 1824 Scott described it as 'a prima cura [first draft]. I never wrote any thing over clean as it is calld' (*Letters*, 8.407). This manuscript is indeed far from being a fair copy, since it includes several deletions and additions by Scott representing his revisions in the course of writing. Line 22, for instance, reads 'The <waggon> loads of tapestry which <she> ↑that poor Queen↓ wrought—'.

After the play for which the Epilogue was composed failed to be staged by the Theatre Royal this manuscript was apparently left lying on the author's hands until late October 1824, when it was transcribed to serve as copy for the *Literary Souvenir*, an annual published by the London firm of Hurst, Robinson, and Co. Scott's own publisher, Archibald Constable, their business associate, wrote to Scott on 7 October reminding him that he had agreed to become a contributor (NLS, MS 868, ff. 84–85), and Scott responded on 22 October with a transcript of the poem (NLS, MS 743, ff. 234–35) and a covering letter, stating 'It is at your service if you think it worth while to insert it' (*Letters*, 8.407). Remembering at this time that he had promised to send David Laing an autograph manuscript he wrote to Laing on the same day: 'I inclose an autograph containing I believe the only unprinted lines I have in the world. Constable wanted them for some purpose or other so I send him the copy & you the autograph' (*Letters*, 8.407). The manuscript sent to Constable with his letter of 22 October 1824 (NLS, MS 743, ff. 234–35) is not in Scott's own hand, and while Scott's accompanying letter was transcribed into several other copy-books belonging to the publishing firm (NLS, MS 854, ff. 199–200; NLS, MS 854, ff. 237–38; NLS, MS 32117, ff. 341–42), the poem was not transcribed along with it. A further copy of Scott's letter to Constable in NLS, MS 877, f. 269 does include the poem, but this is not in Scott's hand either. The 'prima cura' sent to David Laing with Scott's letter to him of 22 October therefore seems to be the only extant manuscript of the poem in Scott's own hand.

The transcription sent by Scott to Constable on 22 October as copy for the *Literary Souvenir* is an accurate representation of the autograph manuscript sent to David Laing, with the single verbal exception of having 'on' for 'upon' in line 30, but it has its own more extensive system of punctuation that represents 'every' as 'ev'ry', gives ampersands as 'and', and introduces further capitalisation, such as 'Old Tradition' in line 17. It is impossible to determine which of these changes result from the writing habits of the copyist and which have been made by Scott's direction. Constable duly wrote to Hurst and Robinson on 29 October, enclosing Scott's letter:

> You will receive inclosed a letter from Sir Walter Scott with the Epilogue which he has been so kind as send for the use of your literary Pocket Book. It is very beautiful and I hope will be correctly printed, when copied for the press I request it may be returnd to me as I wish to preserve the document entire. (Morgan, MA 431, f. 109)

Constable also wrote to Scott himself, on 5 November, acknowledging receipt of the poem and asking his permission 'to include it in the Octavo edition of The

Poetical Works now going to press' (NLS, MS 3899, ff. 191–92). In the event, however, it was not included in the *Poetical Works* published in August 1825, perhaps to avoid compromising the exclusivity of the *Literary Souvenir* contribution published only a few months earlier.

Scott's Epilogue was evidently a late addition to the 1825 *Literary Souvenir*. The annual was advertised as 'In a few days will be published' in the *Literary Gazette* for 30 October 1824 (704) and reviewed in the same magazine for 13 November (721–23). Constable's anxiety that it should be printed correctly in the letter with which he transmitted the poem to London on 29 October may itself imply that there would not be time to send Scott a proof. The offhand 'if you think it worth while to insert it' from Scott in his letter of 22 October also suggests a certain lack of involvement on the author's part.

The printing in the *Literary Souvenir* is upon the whole a faithful interpretation of the transcription of Scott's manuscript, tidied up and fully punctuated by the annual's editor and printer. Two interventions, however, require explanation. First, the couplet in lines 33–34 has been omitted, probably by accident. Although annual editors sometimes shortened a contribution to fit the page, in the present case there was ample room for the inclusion of this couplet and no obvious reason for its omission. The second alteration, the omission of 'which' before 'that poor Queen' in line 22, is more comprehensible. As noted above, Scott made a number of changes to this line in his autograph manuscript and it seems likely that he had not realised that his failure to delete the redundant 'which' makes the line too long and causes the reader to stumble. There are other signs of Scott's haste or carelessness in this manuscript, such as 'besow' for 'bestow' in line 23. The poem was not included in any edition of Scott's *Poetical Works* before Lockhart's posthumous one of 1833–34 (11.374–75). This restores the couplet omitted in the *Literary Souvenir* (lines 33–34), but otherwise shows only the kind of variation normally associated with the work of the printer.

The present text is based upon the only printing in Scott's lifetime, in the *Literary Souvenir for 1825* (London, [1824]), 373–74. The missing couplet from Scott's manuscript has been reinstated, and the following emendations made:

265.2   copy-book (EUL MS) / Copy-book
265.12   Pinkie's field (EUL MS Pinkies field) / Pinkie's Field
266.32   Mary (EUL MS) / Mary.
266.33–34   Mary [new line] That unto ... *sesamum!* [new line] In history (NLS
            MS 743: EUL MS is unpunctuated) / Mary. [new line] In history
            Literary Souvenir omits this couplet: see Textual Note.
266.40   Rose (EUL MS) / rose

Historical Note
Harriet Siddons (1783–1844) was the widow of the actor and manager of the Edinburgh Theatre Royal, Henry Siddons (1774–1815). After the death of her husband in 1815, the theatre was managed for her by her brother, William Henry Murray (1790–1852). Scott, as one of the theatre's trustees and shareholders, was anxious to support the venture, his ambition being to provide an improved theatre for Scotland (see also Historical Note to no. 66, 'Prologue to *The Family Legend*'). Besides the part she herself played in Scott's plans for an Edinburgh theatrical revival, Mrs Siddons was also a personal friend, Scott describing her to Lady Abercorn on 22 December 1810 as 'a very pleasant as well as a very amiable person' (*Letters* 2.414). Scott wrote several verses for Harriet Siddons to speak on stage, some in response to her direct request.

It is unclear which play these lines were originally intended for, but Queen Mary was a popular heroine of the Scottish stage. A play entitled *Mary Queen of Scots* had been produced at Edinburgh's Theatre Royal on 28 December 1809, and when Sarah Siddons made her farewell appearances on the Edinburgh stage in March 1812 Mary, Queen of Scots was one of the roles she chose to perform: see James C. Dibdin, *The Annals of the Edinburgh Stage* (Edinburgh, 1888), 261, 266. Scott's own novel about Queen Mary, *The Abbot*, was published in September 1820, but it was not until 4 July 1825 that a dramatisation of it was performed at the Edinburgh's Theatre Royal, the *Caledonian Mercury* of 2 July announcing in an advertisement that 'On Monday will be produced a New Melo-Dramatic Entertainment in Two Acts, founded upon a portion of the Historical Novel, entitled "The Abbot," and called Mary, Queen of Scotland, or the Castle of Loch Leven'. Since the paper on which Scott's autograph manuscript is written has an 1822 watermark it post-dates the publication of *The Abbot*. Scott's lines may have been intended for an earlier projected dramatisation of *The Abbot* than that of July 1825, but it is as likely that the play for which this Epilogue was written had no direct connection with Scott's novel.

Explanatory Notes

265.2   Seneca's Morals   the *Moral Letters* of the Roman poet Lucius Annaeus Seneca (4 BC–AD 65), addressed to his friend Lucilius, was his most popular work and frequently anthologised.

265.2   copy-book   a book containing lines of writing for pupils to copy, characterised by its moral or improving sentiments.

265.9–10   two ages gone, / A third wanes fast   Scott's numerical precision perhaps suggests that he intends an age in the restricted sense of a century, like the French *siècle*.

265.10   Mary filled the throne   Mary Stuart (1542–87) was Queen of Scots from 1542 to 1567.

265.12   Pinkie's field   a Scottish defeat by the English of 10 September 1547, fought on the River Esk near Musselburgh, when as many as 15,000 Scots were casualities and which led to English occupation of much of SE Scotland. French assistance to repel the English was given on condition that Mary was sent to France, where she married the Dauphin in 1558.

265.12   fatal Fotheringay   after detention in England from 1568 Mary was executed on 18 February 1587 on the authority of her cousin Elizabeth I of England, at Fotheringhay Castle, a little to the N of the market town of Oundle in Northamptonshire.

265.15   learned quarrel   there was fierce controversy in the 18th century about the authenticity of the so-called Casket Letters, which Queen Mary allegedly wrote to James Hepburn, Earl of Bothwell, and which indicate her complicity in the murder of her second husband, Henry Stewart, Earl of Darnley. William Robertson's *History of Scotland During the Reigns of Queen Mary and James VI* (1759) portrays Mary as a tragic heroine, whereas the fourth volume of David Hume's *History of England* (1759) regards her as a foolish and stubborn woman. More recently George Chalmers's *Life of Mary Queen of Scots* (1818) had adopted Robertson's side of the dispute.

265.16   poet plants his laurel   Scott may have in mind the play *Maria Stuart* (1800) by the German author Friedrich Schiller (1759–1805), or closer to home James Hogg's *The Queen's Wake* (1813), which recounts a poetic contest at Mary's court on her return to Scotland from France in 1561.

266.20   Mary's picture, and of Mary's cell   a number of pictures claim to be portraits of Mary, Queen of Scots, many of them inauthentic.

The best-known picture of her is probably the one by François Clouet at Holyrood Palace in Edinburgh (RCIN 403429). Mary was firstly imprisoned in Lochleven Castle in Scotland, and after her escape from there in 1568 at locations in England including Sheffield Castle, Wingfield Manor, Tutbury, and Fotheringhay.

266.22 loads of tapestry Mary was an expert needlewoman whose work is still on display at locations such as Hardwick Hall in Derbyshire, the family home of the Countess of Shrewsbury, whose husband was Mary's keeper for Elizabeth I between 1569 and 1584.

266.27 three wedlocks Mary was married to the French Dauphin Francis in April 1558 but he died in December 1560, only a few months after becoming King of France. She then married her first cousin, Henry Stewart, Earl of Darnley (1545/6–67), in July 1565, who was murdered by a group of conspirators at Kirk o' Field near Edinburgh on 10 February 1567, perhaps with her connivance. She was married for the third time in May 1567 to James Hepburn, 4th Earl of Bothwell (1534/5–78), who was generally believed to be heavily involved in Darnley's murder.

266.30 Duncan Targe lays hand on his claymore the name suggests a generic Highland warrior, since a *targe* is a shield, but perhaps also that of a specific character in the preceding play. A claymore is the two–edged broadsword, the characteristic weapon of a traditional Highland warrior. To many Scots Mary had become a national icon, to be vigorously defended.

266.33 all and some an expression signifying collectively and individually.

266.34 *open sesamum!* the magic phrase used by Ali Baba to open the door of the robbers' den in the *Arabian Nights*. See 'The Story of Ali Baba, and the forty Thieves destroyed by a slave', in *Tales of the East*, ed. Henry Weber, 3 vols (Edinburgh, 1812: *ALC*), 1.402–14. *Sesamum* is Latin for the grain *sesame*. See also *Waverley*, EEWN 1, ed. P. D. Garside (Edinburgh, 2007), 615 (note to 347.30).

266.38 bait ... fly the audience of the theatre whose attention must be captured by the actors and their play is likened to a trout that must be angled for by the fisherman.

116.   A Bannatyne Garland

Textual Note
These verses were originally written to celebrate the inauguration early in 1823 of the Bannatyne Club, a bibliographical society devoted to the printing of rare Scottish literature and historical records. According to Lockhart they were composed for the Club's first dinner, 'that of March 9, 1823', and sung there by James Ballantyne, with the other members heartily joining in the choruses (*Life*, 5.261). However the 'Minutes' of the Club, recorded by David Laing as Secretary, place the first general meeting at Barry's Hotel, 8 Princes Street, on Thursday, 27 February. A pencilled endnote there, again by Laing, also records that 'The publick business of the Club being concluded, the Members present celebrated the first Anniversary of the Club by dining together—Sir Walter Scott in the Chair' (NLS, MS 2046, pp. 5–9). These details of time and location are confirmed in *Notices Relative to the Bannatyne Club* (Edinburgh, 1836), in a Prefatory Notice by its editor James Maidment, who also describes the convention of completing publications of the society 'in time to be shewn as "Ane New-Yere Gift", or at farthest when the Court sits [i.e. mid-January]'. Maidment

continues: 'And first in order comes the "Bannatyne Garland, No. 1"', from the pen of the Magician Knight of Abbotsford, which was sung at their first meeting to the tune of "Four bottles more"!' (3–4).

A copy of *A Bannatyne Garland, Quhairin the President Speaketh*, held in the National Library of Scotland (H.22.f.7(6)), consists of eight leaves measuring 20.3 x 12.8 cm, in green glossy paper covers, the title-page and main text of the verses all in black-letter Gothic type (a convention carried on in later such 'garlands' by other members, some of which are found bound together in the containing NLS volume). Proofs of the same *Bannatyne Garland*, bearing corrections evidently by Scott, also survive at G.A.Scott.8°754(126) in the Bodleian Library (along with similar proofs of the second such garland, by Patrick Fraser Tytler). While some of Scott's attention is drawn by failures in the Gothic lettering, there are a number of more substantive alterations, all of which are carried through into the final printed version. At line 24, the text originally stood as 'I can't call that worthy so candid as learn'd' before being altered to 'I cannot quite call him so candid as learn'd'. Similarly, 'from' is altered to 'of' to read 'secure of Exchequer' (line 46), 'Savient' is corrected to 'Sapient' (50), and 'his Bishops' becomes 'the Bishops' (51). According to T&B, no. 169A, the pamphlet was 'Printed 22 November 1823 in Edinburgh', in a run of 40 copies, though no source for this information is provided.

For this and other reasons it would be wrong to assume automatically that the pamphlet Garland represents exactly the text as presented at the dinner. In view of the rush to embody the Club in February 1823, it is possible that an earlier version was sung there. That dinner too might just possibly have taken place after the second meeting of the Club, recorded in the Club's Minutes as being held on 8 March 1823, at which a number of decisions apparently alluded to in the verses were made. Some support for this conjecture is found in the text (titled 'The Bannatyne Club') as given in the posthumous Lockhart 1833–34 edition (11.377–80), the first collected set to reprint this item. Here noticeably line 46 reads as in the Bodleian proofs rather than the printed *Garland*, suggesting the use of an earlier copy text. Lockhart's dating of 9 March in the *Life*, albeit one day later than that given in the Club's Minutes for the second meeting, could also be taken as an indication of his having privileged material to hand. In other respects, a small number of other variants in the 1833–34 edition (such as a dissonant 'sour' rather than 'sore' at the end of line 31) might have originated through errors in transmission.

The present text follows that in the original pamphlet *A Bannatyne Garland*, as the first surviving printed version, and one which carried Scott's direct approval. Apart from the representation of the original black letter of the main text in a more orthodox font, this is reproduced without emendation.

Historical Note

The Bannatyne Club under Scott's Presidency involved a number of his close friends and associates from the main Scottish institutions in a convivial though nationally significant enterprise. As he wrote the antiquary Robert Pitcairn on 22 January 1823: 'I have long thought that a something of a Bibliomaniacal Society might be formed here for the prosecution of the important task of publishing dilettante editions of our National Literary Curiosities' (*Letters*, 7.315–16). Mirroring in some respects the activities of the more aristocratic Roxburghe Club (which in that same year Scott had joined as 'the Author of Waverley'), it was named after the Edinburgh merchant George Bannatyne (1545–1607/8), the compiler *c.* 1568 of a large manuscript anthology containing some of the most significant works of medieval and early renaissance Scottish poetry. Eventually acquired by the Advocates Library in 1772, it had provided a rich source for a succession of printed editions by literary antiquarians, whose names, mounting input, and various limitations are recounted progressively in the song, with Scott in the process apparently allowing himself an element of licence with regard to the actual level of engagement of some of these with the Bannatyne materials (see *Letters*, 10.494). The growing number of volumes involved echoes the source song, usually known as 'One Bottle More' ('Assist me, ye lads, who have hearts void of guile'), in which the final verse ascends to the prospect of 'twelve bottles more': see *The Edinburgh Musical Miscellany*, 2 vols (Edinburgh, 1792–93), 2.218–19. The tune of this song is attributed to the blind Irish harper Turlough Carolan (1670–1738), another of whose airs was used by George Thomson for Scott's 'The Return to Ulster' (see Historical Note to no. 76).

Explanatory Notes
266.2 sage Bannatyne George Bannatyne, Edinburgh merchant and compiler of the Bannatyne Manuscript. See also Historical Note above.
267.7 Allan Ramsay poet and editor (1684–1758), whose *The Ever Green: Being a Collection of Scots Poems, Wrote by the Ingenious before 1600*, 2 vols (Edinburgh, 1724: *ALC*), was the first published work to draw heavily on the Bannatyne Manuscript.
267.8 hortus *Latin* garden.
267.12 ways were not ours alluding to what were perceived to be Allan Ramsay's slipshod editorial standards compared with those aspired to by the Club. Ramsay freely adapted the Bannatyne texts to suit the tastes of his own audience, altering spelling and versification, and interpolating material of his own.
267.17 Lord Hailes Sir David Dalrymple, Lord Hailes (1726–92), judge and historian, who published *Ancient Scottish Poems* (Edinburgh, 1770: *ALC*), taken from the Bannatyne Manuscript. In his Preface, Hailes draws attention to his predecessor Ramsay's inexact editorial methods, vouchsafing that his own reader 'will find the language, versification, and spelling, in the same state as they were in 1568' ([v]). As Scott himself was later to point out, however, he was not immune to overlooking errors himself, an egregious example being reference to 'one Ballantine [*sic*]' at the beginning of the Preface: see 'Memoir of George Bannatyne', in *Memorials of George Bannatyne* (Edinburgh, 1829), 23–24.
267.18 every letter in the Preface to *Ancient Scottish Poems*, Hailes is at pains to describe how individual letters in the manuscript have been interpreted in his edition in print ([v]–vi).
267.20 castrated Banny 'The editor of this collection has excluded the indecent, and omitted the unintelligible poems' ('Preface', *Ancient Scottish Poems*, vii). Scott himself remarks: 'The publication is an excellent specimen of Bannatyne's Collection, though the severe delicacy of Lord Hailes's taste has excluded some curious matter' ('Memoir of George Bannatyne', 24).
267.23 John Pinkerton's referring to the historian and antiquary (1758–1826), editor of *Ancient Scotish Poems, Never Before in Print*, 2 vols (London, 1786: *ALC*), and *Scotish Poems, Reprinted from Scarce Editions*, 3 vols (London, 1792: *ALC*). Neither of these publications noticeably exploits the Bannatyne materials, the first being indebted primarily to the Maitland manuscript, held in Cambridge and the other main source for early Scottish poetry. Pinkerton in his correspondence does however refer to transcripts of the Bannatyne Manuscript, and there is evidence of his having later privately published an

edition of Sir David Lindsay's *Ane Pleasant Satyre of the Thrie Estaitis* utilising that source: see *The Literary Correspondence of John Pinkerton, Esq.*, 2 vols (London, 1830), 1.148, 165.

267.25 rail'd at the plaid ... claymore Pinkerton was well-known for his at times virulently hostile attitude to Scottish history and especially its Gaelic components. See also next note.

267.28 Celt and Goth In *An Enquiry into the History of Scotland Preceding the Reign of Malcolm III* (London, 1789: see *ALC*), Pinkerton elaborated the theory that the Goths were the master race, and the Celts (identifiable with the Gaels or Highlanders) inferior: a distinction with strong racial overtones which encouraged an intense level of controversy amongst antiquaries.

267.30 Nebuchadnezzar Biblical king, humbled by God by being made to eat grass for seven years (see Daniel 4.1–37).

267.31–32 diet too acid ... Little Ritson Joseph Ritson (1752–1803), antiquary and editor, among whose publications can be counted *An Essay on Abstinence from Animal Food, a Moral Duty* (London, 1802: *ALC*). His antiquarian literary works include *Scotish Songs*, 2 vols (London, 1794: *ALC*), though no direct mention of Bannatyne can be found there. Scott nevertheless surmised to David Laing in 1828: 'I suppose Pinkerton & Ritson both rummaged the Bannatyne' (*Letters*, 10.494). Ritson's irascible nature and sometimes eccentric-seeming stance on editorial matters led him into intemperate arguments with fellow-antiquaries, Scott being one of the few of his correspondents not to have openly fallen out with him.

267.35 Gothic Yeditour's according to a note in Lockhart's posthumous 1833–34 collected edition, 'The Yeditour' was the name given by John Clerk of Eldin to describe James Sibbald (1747–1803), whose *Chronicle of Scottish Poetry from the Thirteenth Century to the Union of the Crowns*, 4 vols (Edinburgh, 1802: *ALC*), makes extensive use of the Bannatyne Manuscript. Sibbald had begun his career as a bookseller and editor by purchasing the Edinburgh Circulating Library, which had formerly belonged to Allan Ramsay, and where Scott as a young man had borrowed books. According to the note in Lockhart's edition, 'The description of him here is very accurate' (11.379n2).

267.37 honest Gray-steel referring to David Herd (1732–1810), editor of *Ancient and Modern Scottish Songs, Heroic Ballads &c.* (Edinburgh, 1769), later reissued in expanded two-volume form in 1776: *ALC*. According to a note in the posthumous 1833–34 collected edition, 'He was called Greysteel [*sic*] by his intimates, from having been long in unsuccessful quest of the romance of that name' (11.379n3). Compare Scott to David Laing on 3 October 1824: 'I am glad you think of Sir Graysteel which from whatever reason has been at one time very popular in Scotland. It puts me in mind of poor David Herd to whom we used to give that chivalrous title' (*Letters*, 8.386). Laing's *Early Metrical Tales, including the history of Sir Egeir, Sir Gryme, and Sir Gray-Steill* was published in Edinburgh in 1826. Extracts from the 1711 printed version of the romance had been given earlier in George Ellis's *Specimens of Early English Metrical Romances*, 3 vols (London, 1805), 3.299–346: *ALC*. The nickname might have also partly derived from Herd's physical appearance. As Scott wrote to another correspondent, in 1825: 'I can tell you many funny tales of Graysteel ... He was a fine figure with a real Scotch face of the harsh but manly & intelligent cast & a profusion of grey hair' (*Letters*, 9.245).

268.41 our Thirty and One according to the second resolution passed at the first meeting of the Club, 'the numbers of its Members shall be limited; and at no time shall exceed the number of Thirty-One' (NLS, MS 2046, p. 8).

268.43 Trade and the Press original members of the Club included the bookseller Archibald Constable, and the printer and (then) newspaper proprietor James Ballantyne.

268.46 secure of Exchequer or Jury i.e. subject neither to taxation nor the law of libel. One of the earliest members of the Club was Sir Samuel Shepherd (1760–1840), at that time Lord Chief Baron of the Exchequer in Scotland.

268.50 King Jamie the Sapient and Sext King James VI and I (of England), whose reputation for learned wisdom led to his facetious naming as 'the wisest fool in Christendom'. 'The History of King James the Sixth, from a collection of the more ancient and perfect manuscripts which can be obtained' is the second item in a list of publications agreed at the second meeting of the Bannatyne Club on 8 March 1823 (NLS, MS 2046, p. 11). This eventually appeared in 1825 as the 13th publication by the Club.

268.51 Bob of Dumblaine and the Bishops apparently referring to the first item in the proposed list of publications at the second meeting of the Club, described there as '"The lives of the Bishops of Dunkeld" by Alexander Myln, Abbot of Cambuskenneth, from the Original Manuscript in the Advocates Library'. This was published under a Latin title later in 1823, as the first full publication by the Club. More generally 'Bob o' Dunblane' is a traditional Scottish weaving song and tune, referring to courtship and marriage, but also open to more scurrilous interpretation.

268.52 tome miscellaneous also included in the list of publications proposed at the second meeting of the Club was 'The Bannatyne Miscellany— to be published in Annual Volumes'. *The Bannatyne Miscellany*, Vol. 1, edited by Scott and David Laing, was completed in 1827.

268.55 your subscriptions according to the resolutions passed at the Club's first meeting, subscriptions were to be set at 4 guineas (£4.20) annually. This was meant to underpin the publications of the Club as a joint effort, as opposed to the Roxburghe Club whose volumes were financed individually by members.

117. To Mons. Alexandre

Textual Note

An autograph manuscript held by the Houghton Library, Harvard University (MS Autograph File 'S'), almost certainly represents the original poem as handed by Scott to the French ventriloquist Nicholas Marie Alexandre Vattemare (1796–1864), after a short visit to Abbotsford in April 1824, during which he had impressed Scott's family and other guests with his conjuring tricks. According to a report in the *Edinburgh Weekly Journal* of 28 April 1824:

> This ingenious foreigner was on a visit at Abbotsford some days since; and, having chanced to mention to his distinguished host that he kept a sort of Album, or Scrap-book, in which were reposited various tributes which had been paid to his talents by so many eminent individuals of the countries he had visited, Sir Walter stept aside, while the carriage was getting ready for his guest's departure, and immediately presented to him the following good-humoured and characteristic lines.

The text of the poem, which is untitled, is written on one side of a single leaf of paper (22 x 18.9 cm), with Scott's signature and seal added and subscribed 'Abbotsford / 23 April'. The address of the recipient ('Mons.ʳ Alexandre / Caledonian Theatre / Edinr') has been pasted (presumably from elsewhere) near

the left hand foot of the document. The text incorporates a conventional punc-
tuation system, though much of this appears to be in a darker ink, and may well
have been added later, most probably by James Ballantyne in preparing copy for
his compositors. A facsimile version, based on Scott's original holograph (but
minus the seal), can also be found in NLS, MS 3581, f. 119. The first printing (as
'To Mons. Alexandre') appeared on 28 April in the *Edinburgh Weekly Journal*,
as then edited by Ballantyne, with Scott's name and dating from Abbotsford at
the foot, and punctuation closely matching that on the Houghton MS. It then
featured in the *Caledonian Mercury* of the following day, accompanied by a simi-
lar preamble. It was subsequently reprinted in the *Edinburgh Annual Register,
for 1824*, 17: 2 (1825), 265–66, again as 'To Mons. Alexandre', and once more
subscribed with Scott's name and dated 'ABBOTSFORD, *23d April*'. The text
in the *Register* matches that in the original manuscript and newspaper print-
ings, though minor differences include the raising of the initial letter in 'old' in
the first line and the removal of italicisation in 'you' and 'one' at lines 3 and 11.
The piece eventually entered the collected *Poetical Works* with the posthumous
Lockhart edition of 1833–34 (10.363–64), accompanied by two footnotes, the
first explaining the circumstances of composition, and the second its previous
appearance in the *Edinburgh Annual Register*. Again, the text remains virtually
unchanged, though the lower-case 'old' in the first line and the italicised '*you*' at
line 3 are restored, and there are some minor shifts in punctuation.

   The present text is based on the version in the *Edinburgh Annual Register, for
1824*, 17: 2 (1825), 265–66, as the earliest non-newspaper printing and the first
over which Scott potentially had control, with the following emendations:

268.1	old (MS) / Old
268.3	folks (MS) / folk
268.3	*you* (MS) / you
268.5	Arch-deceiver (MS) / arch deceiver
268.10	screw. (MS) / screw,
269.11	*one* (MS) / one
269.15	verse, (MS) / verse!
269.end-date	April 1824 (Editorial) / *April*

Historical Note
At the time of his visit to Abbotsford in 1824, Vattemare (see above) was per-
forming as Monsieur Alexandre at the Caledonian Theatre at the head of Leith
Walk in Edinburgh to capacity crowds, his success there leading to a run of
performances through April and May. According to the account of Alexandre's
performances in the *Caledonian Mercury* of 22 April, the multifariousness of
guises adopted was an outstanding feature:

> At times the dialogue goes on so rapidly—question, answer, reply and rejoinder
> follow in such quick succession—that the spectator imagines he hears two or three
> persons speaking at once. He also entertains his auditors with a brawl among the
> domestic animals of his master's family; where dogs of various species, snapping,
> barking, and howling, cats mewing, hissing, and spitting, pigs grunting and
> squeaking, hens kackling, the cock crowing, and the old woman alternately scolding
> at the brutes, and soothing an infant whom their noise has set a squalling, present a
> scene at once noisy, ludicrous, and diverting. Mr Alexandre, besides, imitates with
> equal success the sawing and planing of wood, drawing of corks, decanting of liquors,
> striking fire with flint and steel, frying of eggs, tuning of an instrument, &c. &c.

   Scott's knowledge of Vattemare and his activities evidently preceded these
performances. On 30 May 1821 Lord Montagu had sent a letter of recom-

mendation on his behalf, stating that Vattemare had 'married into a starving Emigrant family' and spoke hardly any English, but strongly advising 'your inviting him to your Home even as a visitor, for I think his occasional introductions of his art even more entertaining than his regular exhibitions' (NLS, MS 3892, f. 142v–43). This would have made him seem an eminently suitable guest for Scott and the French-speaking Lady Scott, though there is no evidence that any consequent invitation by Scott to Vattemare at this earlier point was actually taken up (see also *Letters*, 6.460–61n). Nor is it likely Scott personally witnessed the Edinburgh stage performances in 1824, which only commenced on Monday, 19 April, since he was in attendance at the Jedburgh Circuit Court immediately prior to Vattemare's arrival at Abbotsford (see *Letters*, 8.261–69). In the event, Vattemare appears to have adapted one of his main tricks to the immediate domestic situation, as described at first hand by William Berwick, the painter, then also a guest of the Scotts:

> He began his wonderful imitations by setting to work to plane the French polished dining-tables. The attitude, the action, the noise, the screeches and hitches at knots, throwing off the shavings with his left hand, were all so perfect that Lady Scott screamed in alarm, 'Oh! My dining-table,—you are spoiling my beautiful table, it will never be got bright again,' &c. (*Life and Letters of William Berwick*, ed. Thomas Landseer, 2 vols (London, 1874), 1.248)

A further insight into Vattemare's activities in 1824 can be gained from James Hogg's story 'Scottish Haymakers' in which Hogg, Alexandre, Scott, and the painter Alexander Nasmyth and others take an excursion from Edinburgh, during which the ventriloquist displays his powers in a country inn: *Contributions to Annuals and Gift-Books*, ed. Janette Currie and Gillian Hughes (Edinburgh, 2006), 78–84.

Explanatory Notes
268.2 two visages proverbial: 'Never carry two faces under one hood' (Ray, 214; *ODEP*, 850). Compare *Rob Roy*, ed. David Hewitt, EEWN 5 (Edinburgh, 2008), 92.3–4.
268.5 Arch-deceiver traditionally the devil, but more generally one who orchestrates deception.
269.14 Sheriff Scott was appointed Sheriff-Depute of Selkirkshire in 1799, and held the position until his death.
269.16 Riot Act an Act of Parliament of 1714 authorising local authorities to declare any group of twelve or more people to be unlawfully assembled, and thus have to disperse or face punitive action. In Scotland this could be made by the local Sheriff, and involved reading out the wording of the original Act.

118. Epilogue to *Saint Ronan's Well*

Textual Note
It seems probable that Scott's Epilogue to the dramatisation of his novel *Saint Ronan's Well* (1824) was written shortly before the benefit night of Edinburgh's Theatre Royal manager William Henry Murray (1790–1852) on 5 June 1824, the occasion on which it was first performed. Of two surviving manuscripts the first is now located in the Manuscript File of the Howard Gotlieb Archival Research Center of the University of Boston (N334). This consists of two unwatermarked leaves measuring approx. 20 x 25 cm with text written in Scott's hand on three pages and the final one blank, apart from a note in another hand reading 'Sir Water's [*sic*] Scott's / Epilogue to / St Ronan's Well'. While legible

and reasonably clean, the manuscript includes a number of revisions by Scott so that, for instance, in line 44 Scott has originally written 'auld warld stories' and then substituted 'clavers' for the last word. There are also obvious signs of haste, so that line 2, for instance, has a word missing and reads 'And lend yon muckle a whack—', a deficiency rectified subsequently by a blue pencil insertion in another hand (perhaps that of a printer) of 'ane' above the line. As with many of Scott's manuscripts the punctuation is incomplete. A second manuscript, in NLS, MS 877, ff. 267–68, is in another hand and appears to be copied from the account of the performance published in the *Edinburgh Weekly Journal* of 9 June 1824, since it includes the title and date of the newspaper and repeats its headnote to the poem. This consists of two leaves, each measuring approx. 33.5 x 20.6 cm with no visible watermark. A bracketed note states 'Will Murray says this is genuine', suggesting that sometime after Scott's death his authorship of the poem was verified by reference to the Theatre Royal manager. This possibly represents an initiative by J. G. Lockhart when considering the poem for inclusion in the posthumous 1833–34 *Poetical Works* (see also below).

The *Edinburgh Weekly Journal* text differs in a number of ways from that of the Boston manuscript, and probably represents the verses as adapted for actual stage performance, as Barbara Bell and John Ramage argue in 'Meg Dods—Before the Curtain', *International Journal of Scottish Theatre*, 1: 2 (2000), available at https://ijosts.ubiquitypress.com/articles/248/. The stage-direction, for instance, substitutes 'a town's officer' for the 'Stage-keeper', and Meg's Scots is exaggerated in various places so that, for instance, the repeated 'Wheres' in the third stanza becomes 'Whar's'. A few words are also altered, so that in line 4 'bauld' becomes 'proud' and in line 24 the old-fashioned 'lanthorn' is modernised to 'lantern'.

'Epilogue to *Saint Ronan's Well*' was not printed in any of the lifetime collected editions of Scott's poetry, but was included in the Lockhart 1833–34 posthumous edition (11.369–73) following the version in the *Edinburgh Weekly Journal*.

The present text is based on that of the manuscript in the Howard Gotlieb Archival Research Center of the University of Boston (N334), as representing Scott's composition before alteration in performance. In addition to the following listed emendations ampersands have been routinely expanded to 'and', verb forms ending with 'd' to 'ed', routine apostrophes have been introduced as required, as have full stops at the ends of stanzas.

269.headnote	Meg Dods, (Editorial) / Megg Dodds	
	The character is 'Meg Dods' in Scott's novel.	
269.1	right, (Editorial) / right	
269.2	muckle ane (Editorial) / muckle	
269.8	Wi' (Editorial) / Wi	
269.8	wi' the Guard (Editorial) / wi the guard	
269.10	Laing. (Editorial) / Laing	
269.12	sic (Editorial) / sick	
269.13	Tolbooth (Editorial) / tolbooth	
269.13	ee'noo? (Editorial) / ee'noo	
269.14	blue? (Editorial) / blue	
269.15	Doo? (Editorial) / Doo	
269.16	Weigh House? (Editorial) / weigh house	
270.21	Wi' (Editorial) / Wi	
270.24	Wi' (Editorial) / Wi	
270.31	gane, (Editorial) / gane	

270.36	caa'd (Editorial) / caa d
270.37	Meg! (Editorial) / Meg
270.43	"And wha may ye be" (Editorial) / And wha may ye be?
270.44	"That … here?" (Editorial) / That … here
270.45	Troth, (Editorial) / Troth
270.48	Dods. (Editorial) / Dodds
271.62	sentry (Editorial) / centry
271.65	ventri- — (Editorial) / ventri= —
271.66	caa'd?— -loquister. (Editorial) / caa'd— =loquister
271.67	Weel, Sirs, (Editorial) / Weel Sirs

Historical Note

Among the Edinburgh Theatre Royal's most successful and lucrative productions were various dramatisations of Scott's novels, so it is not surprising that, seeking a crowd-pulling novelty for his benefit night on 5 June 1824, William Murray should have decided to stage a play based upon Scott's recently-published *Saint Ronan's Well*. Scott himself had actively forwarded a dramatisation by his friend Daniel Terry (1789–1829), having arranged for his printer James Ballantyne (1772–1833) to send Terry printed sheets of the novel in advance of publication (see *Letters*, 8.113); but the version staged by Murray was the work of James Robinson Planché (1796–1880), the stock author at London's Covent Garden Theatre at this time. As Barbara Bell and John Ramage indicate in 'Meg Dods—Before the Curtain' (cited in the Textual Note) the chief comic part in this play was that of Meg Dods, the elderly landlady of the St Ronan's Inn, so that the play had the considerable drawback of containing no part for the Edinburgh Theatre's star comic actor Charles Mackay (1787–1857), whose previous triumphs had included Bailie Nicol Jarvie in *Rob Roy*. In the event Mackay played Meg Dods in drag, Scott praising him to Terry for the way in which he 'kept his gestures and his action more within the verge of female decorum than I thought possible' (*Life*, 5.317–18). Scott's Epilogue was intended to be spoken at the end of the evening and addressed directly to the Edinburgh audience, just as the traditional manager's address of thanks would have been. Murray's advertisements emphasised that it was 'Written expressly for this Occasion' (see the *Caledonian Mercury* of 31 May 1824), and it must have been successful in performance, since an advertisement for a performance of *Saint Ronan's Well* during the succeeding autumn in the *Edinburgh Dramatic Review* of 23 November 1824 (new series 1.24) noted, 'At the End of the Play, Mr Mackay will deliver the Address in the character of Meg Dodds, which was last season attended with so much applause'. In its review in the same issue, however, the *Edinburgh Dramatic Review* pronounced that 'there is not a parish in Scotland, in which we could not pick up some hedge-poet who could produce a much better thing' (1.23).

Explanatory Notes

269.1 gaitlings a variant of 'getling', an opprobrious word for a child, or more generally for a knave or vagabond.

269.2 yon muckle ane possibly a comic reference to the presence on stage of the theatre's manager, William Murray. Bell and Ramage explain in 'Meg Dods—Before the Curtain' (cited in the Textual Note) that the manager himself would be expected to give the final address to the audience on his benefit night, to thank the audience for their support during the past season and to request their continuing patronage.

269.6 causey causeway, the paved or cobbled part of a street.

269.8 Tolbooth Edinburgh's 16th-century Tolbooth was situated at the NW corner of St Giles' Kirk on the High Street, and was the city's main gaol. From 1785 it was also the site of public executions, before being demolished in 1817. The title of Scott's novel *The Heart of Mid-Lothian* (1818) alludes to a popular name for the prison.

269.8 Guard Edinburgh's Town Guard was a peace-keeping body under the control of the city's Provost, constituted earlier but confirmed by an act of 1690 and disbanded in 1817, although their Guard House, to the W of Hunter Square, had been previously demolished in 1785. The body, consisting mostly of veteran Highlanders dressed in a red uniform and bearing an old-fashioned weapon known as a Lochaber axe, had become something of a joke. The Town Guard occupied the whole of the ground floor of the Tolbooth.

269.10 Jamie Laing according to Lockhart, 'James Laing was one of the Depute-Clerks of the city of Edinburgh, and in his official connexion with the Police and the Council-Chamber, his name was a constant terror to evil-doers. He died in February, 1806' (1833–34*PW*, 11.370).

269.11 water-hole Lockhart (1833–34*PW*, 11.370) glosses this as 'The Watch-hole', the meaning of which is unclear. It may perhaps refer to one of the city's points of supply of clean water to the inhabitants, which before the water of Crawley Spring at Glencorse in the Pentland Hills was brought to the city in 1822 was obtained from two reservoirs, one on Castle Hill and one located near Heriot's Hospital on the south side of the Old Town: see Mary Cosh, *Edinburgh: The Golden Age* (Edinburgh, 2003), 120.

269.14 Auld Claught 'Claught' seems to have been a nickname for the Town Guard: see Robert Chambers, *Traditions of Edinburgh*, 2 vols (Edinburgh, 1825), 2.297n.

269.15 John Doo according to Lockhart, 'John Doo, or Dhu—a terrific-looking and high-spirited member of the Town Guard, and of whom there is a print by Kay, etched in 1784' (1833–34*PW*, 11.370). This etching can be found in John Kay, *A Series of Original Portraits and Caricature Etchings*, 2 vols (Edinburgh, 1838), 1 pt 1 (no. XC, facing 216).

269.16 Weigh House according to Lockhart this was demolished in connection with the Scott-orchestrated visit of George IV to Scotland in 1822: 'The Weigh-House, situated at the head of the West Bow, Lawnmarket, and which had long been looked upon as an encumbrance to the street, was demolished in order to make way for the royal procession to the Castle, which took place on the 22nd of August, 1822' (1833–34*PW*, 11.370).

269.17 Deil ha'et the devil have it, an exclamation of irritation or annoyance.

269.18 playhouse the Theatre Royal building in Shakespeare Square at the junction of Edinburgh's New and Old Towns was opened on 9 December 1769: see James C. Dibdin, *The Annals of the Edinburgh Stage* (Edinburgh, 1888), 152.

270.24 lass and lanthorn perhaps an allusion to Mackay's celebrated role of Bailie Nicol Jarvie in the dramatisation of Scott's *Rob Roy*, since in that novel Jarvie is escorted to Glasgow Tolbooth to call upon Frank Osbaldistone by his servant girl Mattie, who holds a lantern to light their way: see *Rob Roy*, ed. David Hewitt, EEWN 5 (Edinburgh, 2008), 179.

270.25 in the public line in Scott's novel Meg Dods is the landlady of the old-fashioned inn at St Ronan's that preceded the fashionable Tontine Hotel.

270.26 howffs favourite haunts or meeting-places, often public houses.

270.26 lang syne long since, long ago.

270.31 Fortune's a celebrated tavern on the W side of the Old Stamp

Office Close, High Street, opened by John Fortune in the 1750s, the meeting-place of many convivial clubs and where the Commissioners to the General Assembly of the Church of Scotland held their levees. The tavern was so famous that Old Stamp Office Close was sometimes known as Fortune's Close: see Stuart Harris, *The Place Names of Edinburgh Their Origins and History* (Edinburgh, 1996), 475. The date when this tavern closed has not been established, though Marie W. Stuart states that the proprietor's son Matthew was one of the New Town's first hotel-keepers: see *Old Edinburgh Taverns* (London, 1952), 57, 172. There is an entry for Matthew Fortune of the Caledonian Tontine and Coffee Room at 5 Princes Street in the *Edinburgh and Leith Postal Directory for 1796–97*, 94, but none for his father.

270.31 Hunter's a tavern situated in the now-demolished Writer's Court off the High Street, opposite to St Giles' Kirk. There is an entry for James Hunter, vintner, Star and Garter, Writers Court in the *Edinburgh and Leith Postal Directory for 1800–01*, 121. This was the sign of the tavern owned by Clerihugh in Writer's Court, scene of the High Jinks of Counsellor Pleydell: for further details see *Guy Mannering*, ed. P. D. Garside, EEWN 2 (Edinburgh, 1999), 552 (note to 202.32).

270.32 Bayle's Bayle's Tavern was at 1 Shakespeare Square, in the vicinity of the Theatre Royal at the N end of the North Bridge, on the corner of Leith Street and Bridge Street: see *Chronicles of the Canongate*, ed. Claire Lamont, EEWN 20 (Edinburgh, 2000), 385 (note to 14.9–10). There is an entry for John Bayle, vintner, of 1 Shakespeare Square in the *Edinburgh and Leith Postal Directory for 1800–01*, 64. The premises had been opened by Bayle in 1793 and were taken over by Charles Oman in 1803: see Marie W. Stuart, *Old Edinburgh Taverns* (London, 1952), 81–83. The building itself appears to have been demolished in 1815.

270.33 splice a brace to have a double ration of alcohol, from the naval expression 'splice the mainbrace', originally an order to make a difficult and strenuous repair to a ship's rigging, an operation normally rewarded on completion with a double allowance of rum.

270.36 hottle hotels were a fairly recent development in Edinburgh. Colonel Mannering visiting the city in the early 1780s, for instance, finds none: see *Guy Mannering*, ed. P. D. Garside, EEWN 2 (Edinburgh, 1999), 550 (note to 200.13–14).

270.37 hoddle bustle about, walk with quick short steps.

270.38 glegg alert, wide-awake, pert and impudent.

270.41 chield a man, a fellow.

270.41 makes a leg makes a deep bow, with the right leg drawn back.

270.43 speir ask, enquire.

270.44 clavers gossip, idle or foolish talk.

270.49 west of Currie Currie is a village about 10 km (6 miles) SW of Edinburgh on the Water of Leith. The geographical location of the spa-town is also imprecise in Scott's novel *Saint Ronan's Well*, although often identified with Innerleithen in Peeblesshire about 48 km (30 miles) S of Edinburgh.

270.52 crouse bold, confident, happy, lively.

271.57 drowth thirst.

271.58 dramock a mixture of raw oatmeal mixed with cold water, here as a type of plain and unluxurious food.

271.63 far frae rent-free largely through Scott's influence the actor Henry Siddons (1774–1815) had acquired the patent for the Theatre Royal Edinburgh in 1809, and this was due to expire after 21 years in 1830. Strictly speaking Siddons (and subsequently his widow) did not pay rent but an annual instalment of 2000 guineas (£2100) of the purchase money, so that the theatre would become their property at the end of this time: see Mary Cosh, *Edinburgh: The Golden Age* (Edinburgh, 2003), 572. According to the *Edinburgh Dramatic Review*, 9 (7 June 1824) Mrs Siddons and her brother 'from the profits of the concern … have already cleared off L.20,000 of *debt*, sunk L.14,000 in the purchase of property, and are amassing thousands yearly' (112). The journal therefore resented this implication of straitened financial circumstances.

271.64   lone sister   Murray had managed Edinburgh's Theatre Royal in the interest of his sister, Harriet Siddons (1783–1844), after the death of her husband in 1815.

271.65–66   ventri- … -loquister   a topical allusion to the recent performances given to capacity crowds by the French ventriloquist Nicholas Marie Alexandre Vattemare (1796–1864) during April and May 1824 at the Caledonian Theatre at the head of Leith Walk in Edinburgh: for further details see Historical Note to no. 117, 'To Mons. Alexandre'. Vattemare also visited Scott at Abbotsford in April.

271.68   bairns   children.

271.70   failyie   a formal warning of a penalty in case of non-compliance with an order.

271.72   *Bailyie*   a town magistrate.

119.   Beam forth fair opening Dawn

Textual Note
This autograph poem survives in the National Records of Scotland [NRS], on a single leaf measuring approx. 22.5 x 17.1 cm, with no apparent watermark (GD224/32/5). It is subscribed by Scott 'Bowhill 13 Nov^r / 1824', and endorsed at the bottom in another hand 'written by Sr Walter Scott—by the request of R. M. Par[?]'. There is also a separate cover, with two further endorsements in hands other than Scott's, the first reading "Lines written by Sir Walter Scott—at Bowhill 1824', the other (at right angles) '13 Nov. 1824 Lines written by Sir Walter Scott Bart. to be put below a Transparency at the end of a room for a Servants Ball at Bowhill'. The event referred to was retrospectively mentioned in the *Edinburgh Advertiser* of Tuesday, 29 November 1825, in an article mainly concerning a subsequent birthday dinner in honour of the young Duke of Buccleuch at Dalkeith on 26 November 1825, at which the Chair (William Tait, Esq. of Pirn) is described as quoting the same lines: 'His Grace seemed a nobleman of the greatest promise. And he could not help giving the lines made *ex tempore*, on a similar occasion, by our greatest national poet, in allusion to the Duke.' Apart from this one instance, no evidence has been discovered of any printing prior to the present text, which follows the manuscript in NRS, GD224/32/5, without alteration, apart from the provision of a title from the first line, and the addition of a concluding full stop.

Historical Note
Scott's lines were reportedly written to serve as an ornament at a Servants' Ball late in November 1824 held at Bowhill, the Buccleuch family residence close to Selkirk, and which would have coincided with the 18th birthday of the young 5th Duke, Walter Francis Montagu Douglas Scott (1806–84), who had succeeded to his titles in 1819 while a pupil at Eton. Writing to Lord Montagu, the Duke's co-guardian during his minority (then to the age of 21), Scott on 18

November 1824 reported how 'I was three times up at Bowhill coursing as my young Chief was very keen about a little match of greyhounds which we had together. He is really a fine youth active bold and courteous' (*Letters*, 8.429). It is likely that Scott provided the lines during one of these visits, for the purposes of a transparency, comprising a translucent substance allowing an inscription or picture to be made visible by means of a light behind. The lines themselves express Scott's hopes for a new era in the Buccleuch family fortunes following on from the premature deaths of his friends and patrons, Charles William Henry Scott, the 4th Duke (1772–1819), and his wife the Duchess, Harriet Katherine Townshend (1773–1814). The allusion to the lore of shepherds in the final two lines would have been well matched to the occasion, in view of the Duke's large ownership of sheep farms in the surrounding countryside.

120.   Epistle to John Gibson Lockhart

Textual Note
This verse epistle of 1824 was first printed in J. G. Lockhart's *Life* of Scott (1837–38), 5.370–71, presumably as a result of Lockhart, its original addressee at his Edinburgh home in Northumberland Street, having maintained possession of the letter. Lockhart also includes Scott's postscript following his verses: 'P.S.—*Hoc jocose* [this jokingly]—but I am nevertheless in literal earnest. You incur my serious displeasure if you move one inch in this contemptible rumpus. So adieu till to-morrow' (371). No manuscript of the original letter has been discovered, and the text provided in the Grierson edition of the *Letters* (8.418–20) is from Lockhart's *Life* (evidently the second edition—see also below). Lockhart's preamble in the *Life* states that 'on the … 12th of November [1824], being the Poet's last day at Abbotsford for the long vacation, he indited the following rhymes—which savour of his recent overhauling of Swift and [Thomas] Sheridan's doggrel epistles' (370). According to Corson, however, Scott actually returned to Edinburgh on 15 November, so that the 'to-morrow' of his postscript indicates that it was written on Sunday, 14 November (*N&I*, 241, note to 8.418 *n.* 1). With the 10-volume second edition of the *Life* (1839) the verses acquired a handful of small changes (7.279–281), probably originating from the printer rather than any direct intervention by Lockhart: most noticeably the transposition of 'look' and 'rather' (to read 'might rather look') at line 27, and the replacement of a comma with an exclamation mark and dash after 'peace' in line 37 ('peace!—on').

These changes are carried over into subsequent editions of Lockhart's *Life*, as well as posthumous collections of Scott's poetry starting with the one-volume *Poetical Works* (Edinburgh, 1841), 704, where the now self-standing verses are also given a title (as 'To J. G. Lockhart, Esq. On the Composition of Maida's Epitaph'). The text there also adopts two sizeable footnotes originally found in Lockhart, the first concerning the origin and meaning of 'speates and raxes', the second identifying 'Fatsman' (see also Explanatory Notes below). In J. Logie Robertson's *The Poetical Works of Sir Walter Scott* (London, 1904), 751–52, the title is extended further to 'Epistle to his Son-in Law, John Gibson Lockhart, on the Composition of Maida's Epitaph', though the Lockhart notes are no longer evident, being replaced by four very short ones.

The present text follows the first edition of Lockhart's *Life*, 5.370–71, as the printed version probably closest to Scott's original verse epistle. The notes in Lockhart are excluded, as not originating from Scott, while the title has been supplied editorially.

Historical Note

This verse epistle relates to circumstances following on from the production of a Latin inscription to serve as an epitaph on an effigy of Scott's dog Maida placed by the porch at the main entrance to Abbotsford. A large male deerhound, named after the battle in the toe of Italy against the French in 1806, in which British infantry forces prevailed, Maida had been gifted to Scott by Alexander Ranaldson Macdonell of Glengarry (1773–1828) in 1816. He soon established himself as a familiar in the household at Abbotsford, featuring in a number of paintings associated with Scott, including David Wilkie's rustic representation of the 'Abbotsford Family' in 1817. The effigy was placed in position in February 1824, several months before Maida's death in October that year and the inscription cut on the pedestal 21–23 October (*N&I*, 241, note to 8.412 *n*. 1). Scott quoted the inscription in letters to his sons Walter and Charles on 26 October, that to Charles also supplying an English version:

> Old Maida died quietly on his straw last week ... He is buried below his monument on which the following epitaph is engraved: though it is great audacity to send Teviotdale Latin to Brazen nose:
>
> > Maidæ marmorea dormis sub imagine Maida
> > Ad januam domini sit tibi terra levis.
>
> Thus Englishd by an eminent hand
>
> > Beneath the sculptured form which late you wore
> > Sleep soundly Maida at the masters door. (*Letters*, 8.412)

Scott's mention of Brasenose College, which Charles (1805–41) had just entered as a student, points to an awareness on Scott's part of the differences between his own education in Latin, at the Edinburgh High School and College and as a Scottish Advocate, and the Classical Latin taught at Oxford University—a distinction which also tended to apply in the case of the Oxford-educated J. G. Lockhart, who had previously written scathingly about the limited teaching of Latin in Scotland in his *Peter's Letters to His Kinsfolk* (1819). Lockhart's present account describes Scott broaching the subject of an epitaph 'over his glass of toddy and cigar' at the Lockharts' summer home Chiefswood on the Abbotsford estate:

> He said it must be in Latin, because *Maida* seemed made on purpose to close a Latin hexameter—and begged, as I was fresher off the irons than himself, that I would try to help him. The unfortunate couplet ... was what suggested itself at the moment—and though his own English version of it, extemporized next minute, was so much better, on his way home he gave directions to have it engraved ... (*Life*, 5.367–68).

The next ingredient in the story occurs with a report on 27 October in the *Edinburgh Weekly Journal* by James Ballantyne (1772–1833), Scott's printer and the paper's proprietor and editor:

> Sir Walter Scott's fine old stag-hound, Maida ... died a few days since. Some months ago an effigy of the noble animal was placed at the door of the principal entrance to Abbotsford; and he has been buried below it, with the following epitaph cut on the effigy:–
>
> > Maidæ marmorea jaces sub imagine, Maida,
> > Ad januam Domini. Sit tibi terra levis!

For uncertain reasons, though perhaps reflecting Ballantyne's preference for the literal, in the first line *jaces* ('you lie') here is substituted for *dormis* ('you sleep'), in the process altering the scansion of the line. This same report appeared widely in other papers, featuring in the *Caledonian Mercury* on the following day, and reaching the *Morning Post* in London on 6 November. According to Lockhart several newspapers in Edinburgh and London picked up the 'false quantities' in Scott's lines, pre-empting a simple rectification by Scott on the sculpture itself. The alleged errors were made plain enough in a letter to the editor by Lionel Thomas Berguer published in the *Morning Post* of 8 November: 'There are two gross blunders in the prosody of Sir Walter Scott's Epitaph upon his Dog Maida, as it appears in your columns ... The first syllable in *"jăces"*, which is *short*, being made *long*; and the first in *"jānuam"*, which is *long*, being made *short*.' Berguer goes on to exonerate Scott himself, laying blame on the reportage, and offers as an alternative a (wrong) version of the couplet as it originally stood, before venturing to improve even on that. At this point, Scott intervened to bring the matter to a halt, writing from Abbotsford on 12 November a letter to the Editor under his own name, published in the *Morning Post* five days later: 'The two lines were written in mere whim, and without the least intention of their being made public. In the first line, the word *jaces* is a mistake of the transcriber (whoever took that trouble), the phrase is *dormis*, which I believe is good prosody. The error in the second line, *ad januam*, certainly exists, and I bow to the castigation' (see also *Letters*, 8.417–18). In other areas Scott is likely to have been less temperate, with Ballantyne probably receiving at least one reprimand, while an abject apology from Berguer of 18 November indicates that he had received a hurtful personal letter: 'I can make no reparation ... I shall never *forgive myself*' (NLS, MS 868, f. 113v). Scott's verse epistle clearly follows on from this situation, though adopting a more satirical and familiar tone: one which, as Lockhart's account (see Textual Note) suggests, bears similarities to Jonathan Swift's poetical interchanges with his friend and associate Thomas Sheridan (1687–1738), of which Scott no doubt would have been reminded when revising his *Works* of Swift for a second edition earlier in the year.

Explanatory Notes
272.2 Fat worship referring (somewhat unflatteringly) to James Ballantyne (see also Historical Note). Compare the cognomen 'Fatsman' at line 43.
272.2 *jaces ... dormis* Latin 'you lie' [in the recumbent sense], 'you sleep'. In the report of Scott's Latin epitaph in the *Edinburgh Weekly Journal*, 27 October 1824, *jaces* had replaced the original *dormis* without authorisation (see also Historical Note).
272.3 Southrons southerners, Englishmen. Not individually identified, though Lockhart claims that mistakes noted in the epitaph as given in the *Edinburgh Weekly Journal* had been observed 'in the newspapers both in Edinburgh and in London' (*Life*, 5.368).
272.3 *januam* Latin door (accusative).
272.4 twitch to both ears referring to accusations of a false quantity (faulty pronunciation or metrical use of a vowel in verse) in two cases in Scott's epitaph as reported in the newspapers. The image of the braying ass as applied to pedants and false critics is a common feature of early 18th-century satire.
272.4 Priscian's cranium Priscianus Caesariensis (fl. AD 500), commonly known as Priscian, Latin grammarian. His *Institutiones Grammaticae* (*Institutes of Grammar*) became the standard Latin grammar in the Middle Ages. Compare Jonathan Swift, 'The Pardon', 'another Blow / Would break the head of Priscian' (lines 5–6): in *Works of Swift*, ed. Scott, 2nd edn, 19 vols (1824), 15.101. Priscian's concern over 'false quantities' (see previous note) in verse is alluded to in similar terms in Alexander Pope's *Dunciad* (1728), Bk 3:

'Some free from rhyme or reason, rule or check, / Break *Priscian*'s head and *Pegasus*'s neck' (lines 155–56).

272.5   Lionel Berguer   Lionel Thomas Berguer (b. 1789), English poet, pamphleteer, and cleric; author of the letter in the *Morning Post* of 8 November 1824 commenting on 'two gross blunders' in the epitaph, while not too convincingly exonerating Scott in the process (see also Historical Note). Berguer had previously dedicated a long poem ('Stanzas, Occasioned by a Visit to Edinburgh in 1815') to Scott in his *Trifles in Verse, including some experiments in Latin rhyme* (Edinburgh, 1817: *ALC*), and appears to have been rather an unctuous presence in shadowing him.

272.8   rowt in the papers   referring to Scott's riposte to Berguer (see previous note) in a letter of 12 November to the Editor of the *Morning Post* and published there on 17 November; *rowt* is used here in the sense of an outcry or uproar.

272.10   gudeson   son-in-law, i.e. J. G. Lockhart.

272.11–12   James .... banter in Blackwood   intimating that James Ballanytne had informed him of Lockhart's intention to make capital about the incident in *Blackwood's Edinburgh Magazine*.

272.12   dog-Latin   the creation of a phrase or jargon in imitation of Latin, often by 'translating' English words into Latin by conjugating or declining them as if they were Latin words; also used to describe a poor-quality attempt at writing genuine Latin. While the Latin in the inscription is in fact both proper and grammatical, an extra applicability of the term in view of its subject will be self-evident.

272.19   bacon be saved   proverbial (to escape personal injury): *ODEP*, 700.

272.22   resetter   a harbourer of criminals; receiver of stolen or fraudulently acquired goods (*Scots law*).

272.23   don't care a boddle   mind not a bit. A *boddle* is a copper coin of small value.

272.24   noddle   back of the head.

272.25   as Benlomon's   as that of Ben Lomond, distinctive peak (974 m) in the Scottish Highlands, situated on the E shore of Loch Lomond. For the spelling compare Joanna Baillie: 'The clouds seen in my youthful days floating across Benlomon': see *Collected Letters*, Vol. 1, ed. Judith Bailey Slagle (Madison, 1999), 13.

272.28   scribe of Valerius   J. G. Lockhart was the anonymous author of the novel *Valerius; a Roman Story*, 3 vols (Edinburgh, 1821).

272.31   stet pro ratione voluntas   *Latin* let my will stand as the voucher for the deed. Compare Juvenal, *Satires*, 6.222: 'Sit pro ratione voluntas', where *sit* (let it be) differs from the slightly more affirmative *stet* (let it stand). The use of 'stet' also reflects the common instruction to printers to negate previous corrections, allowing the original text on a proof to remain unchanged.

272.31   tractile   capable of being drawn out to a thread; ductile.

272.32   dactyl   metrical foot consisting of a long syllable followed by two short ones (or, in modern verse, an accented syllable by two unaccented).

273.34   town for the winter-course   the winter legal term in Edinburgh normally ran from 12 November to 24 December. In 1824 Scott returned from Abbotsford on Monday, 15 November.

273.36   pye-house daughter's   Sophia (1799–1837), Scott's elder daughter, had married J. G. Lockhart in 1820, and had settled with him at the couple's Edinburgh home at 25 Northumberland Street by April 1822. Scott's humorous characterisation of Sophia as the keeper of a pie shop matches her depiction as a milkmaid in David Wilkie's portrait of the 'Abbotsford Family' (1817). There is also possibly here a pun on the word 'pious', alluding to childhood errors in spelling by Sophia; and perhaps too, with the classically-educated Lockhart in mind, an echo of 'pious Aeneas', a phrase repeated some 20 times in Virgil's *Aeneid*.

273.36　prog　provisions; a meal.

273.39　spondees　a *spondee* is a metrical foot consisting of two long syllables.

273.40　Dominie Grundys　a *dominie* in Scots is a schoolmaster and/or clergyman; from the Latin for 'sir', vocative of *dominus*, a master. The surname Grundy is used proverbially of an imaginary person (most usually Mrs Grundy) representing the tyranny of conventional propriety. Mrs Grundy herself apparently derives from a character in Thomas Morton's play *Speed the Plough* (1798).

273.41　dry thrapples　thirsty throats.

273.42　Speates and raxes　as partly explained by Lockhart in a note to this passage in the *Life* (5.371n), this relates to an incident from 1474 in Scott's edition of *Memorie of the Somervilles*, 2 vols (Edinburgh, 1815), 1.240–43, in which the wife of the then Lord Somerville misinterprets a written request from him to provide '*Speates and Raxes*' for the entertainment of the King as a call for '*Speares and Jacks*', that is instruments of war. Scott in the *Memorie* annotates 'Speates and Raxes' as 'Spits and Ranges; the latter being the appendage to the kitchen grate, on which the spit turns' (1.241n).

273.42　ere five　according to Henry Cockburn, in Edinburgh the 'prevailing dinner hour was about three o'clock', this eventually reaching 'five, which however was thought positively revolutionary', and finally slipping to six or later: see *Memorials of His Time* (Edinburgh, 1856), 33–34.

273.43　Fatsman　according to Lockhart, 'one of Mr James Ballantyne's many *aliases*' (*Life*, 5. 371n). See also note to 272.2.

273.43　haver　talk, gossip.

273.44　Dame Peveril　character (Lady Peveril) in Scott's novel *Peveril of the Peak* (1822), and presumably here referring to Scott's wife, Lady Scott. It also echoes an occasion near the end of the novel: 'And now, Dame Peveril, to dinner, to dinner!' (*Peveril of the Peak*, ed. Alison Lumsden, EEWN 14 (Edinburgh, 2007), 484).

273.45　Oury and Anne　*Oury* is a variant of Ourisk or Whisk, a Highland terrier bitch belonging to Lady Scott. This dog is mentioned alongside Maida in R. P. Gillies's recollections of Scott's recovery from illness in 1819: 'he was able once more to ride out with no other companionship but that of the pony, Maida … and Ourisk': *Memoirs of a Literary Veteran*, 3 vols (London, 1851), 2.254. The *ourisk* or *urisk* in the Highlands of Scotland is a supernatural being supposed to haunt lonely places such as mountain streams and waterfalls. Compare Scott's footnote to *The Lady of the Lake* (1810), Canto 3, stanza 26: 'The *Urisk*, or Highland satyr' (133n). Anne refers to Scott's younger daughter (1803–33).

273.46　Janua　Latin door (nominative).

121.　Come ower the Tweed Adam

Textual Note

The only known surviving record of this song is found in a typed transcript with manuscript annotations in NLS, MS 1753, ff. 81–82, as part of a volume consisting mainly of materials rejected for inclusion in Grierson's edition of the *Letters*. (A microfilm held at NLS, Mf. MSS 63, containing images from the collection of Miss Helen Bayley, the source of the original manuscript, on inspection proves not to include this item, merely a record of the transcript in MS 1753.) The transcript itself incorporates five deletions by Scott, which are numbered in ink and noted as such at the foot, this indicating that the original manuscript was written in a spontaneous fashion. In line 14, for example, Scott had originally written 'tall' after 'guests' before deleting this in favour of 'too'. An ink note on the typescript also comments that 'quanie' might read 'queenie' (line 25), while the same hand adds square brackets round 'us all' at the end of the final line, suggesting that these two words might have been added editorially in the typescript. The song remained unpublished until appearing as item 7 in W. M. Parker's 'Sir Walter Scott: Thirteen New Poems?', *Poetry Review*, 40: 4 (August–September 1949), 263–75 (pp. 270–71). Parker's version adds routine punctuation, while omitting the refrain 'Come ower the Tweed Adam' in the first and second stanzas, as well as the instruction 'Dacapo' at the end of the first. It also retains the final 'us all'.

The present text follows the typescript in NLS, MS 1753, ff. 81–82, removing the deletions noted there, accepting 'queenie' (line 25) as a likely spelling in the manuscript, and retaining 'us all' as the appropriate ending of the whole. Full stops have been added at the end of stanzas where absent. The following emendations have also been made:

273.4   all. (Editorial) / all
273.5   welcome (Editorial) / wellcome
273.6   We'll (Editorial) / W ell
273.7   broth, (Editorial) / broth
273.9   ower (Editorial) / oer
273.music instruction   *Da capo* (Editorial) / Dacapo
274.13   hall. (Editorial) / hall
274.20   dram, (Editorial) / dram
274.21   song, (Editorial) / song
274.22   call. (Editorial) / call

Historical Note
This item was evidently written some time during the residence of Scott's close friend Sir Adam Ferguson (1771–1855) at Gattonside House, on the north bank of the river Tweed, facing Melrose on the other side, and some 5 km (3 miles) downstream from Abbotsford. Previously Ferguson with his sisters had occupied the house at Huntlyburn on the Abbotsford estate, granted to them by Scott after the death of their father, the philosopher and historian Adam Ferguson (1723–1816). Sir Adam had then moved to Gattonside after his marriage to Margaret Stewart in April 1821, the occupancy apparently lasting between 1821 and 1825 (see *Letters*, 6.425, 9.147). Evidence within the poem, however, makes it possible to narrow down these parameters to a more specific moment in early February 1825. On 3 February the marriage had finally taken place in Edinburgh between Scott's elder son Walter and Jane Jobson, after a degree of resistance from the bride's widowed mother, Mrs William Jobson (1775–1863), some of it apparently eased by Sir Adam and Lady Ferguson (the latter being a sister of Mrs Jobson). The newly-wedded couple then honeymooned at Abbotsford by themselves, before being joined by Scott on 10 February, prior to them leaving for Ireland where Walter was stationed. The intervening period by Scott's own account was one of great festivity, and natu-

rally involved his close friends from across the river. As he wrote to Maria Edgeworth on 14 February:

> They were married on 3rd February, and came here to reside quietly for a little. Since I joined them on the 10th we have seen the Scotts of Harden and the Fergusons, and my little landlady [i.e. Jane] did the honours of her chateau with very pretty embarrassment. … We join them in Edinburgh to-morrow, and in four or five days afterwards [they] set out for London, and then for green Erin. (*Letters*, 9.2)

Reference to 'Mrs. Jeanie' (line 24) in particular seems to refer to the newly-married Jane, Scott in a number of contemporary letters applying this cognomen to her (see also note to 274.24, below). Granted that this indeed represents the occasion of the present song, then it reflects an especially buoyant time in Scott's life, as domestic plans involving both friends and relations appeared to have arrived at fruition.

The designated air, alternatively called 'Over the Water to Charlie', relates to a popular Jacobite song, expressing loyalty to the exiled Charles Edward Stuart (1720–88), grandson of James VII and II, and leader of the Jacobite Rising in 1745–46. A version had recently appeared in James Hogg's *Jacobite Relics of Scotland*, 2 vols (Edinburgh, 1819–21), 2.76–77, 290; and another is given in Robert Chambers, *Scottish Songs*, 2 vols (Edinburgh, 1829), 2.448–49. Scott not uncharacteristically appropriates an erstwhile political song for a contemporary domestic purpose.

Explanatory Notes
273.2 Sir Adam Scott had been instrumental in acquiring the post of Deputy Keeper of the Scottish Regalia for Adam Ferguson (see above) in 1818, then a knighthood, the latter being conferred by George IV during the royal visit to Edinburgh in August 1822.
273.7 boullie *French* gruel, porridge.
273.music instruction *Da capo Italian* repeat from the beginning (literally from the head).
274.10 your dear lady Margaret Stewart Ferguson (d. 1857), wife of Sir Adam. Described by Scott as 'a good humourd purpose-like body *of no particular age*' (*Letters*, 6.425) when they were married on 16 April 1821, she became a familiar and welcome guest at Abbotsford.
274.16 In especiall in particular, especially.
274.16 Miss Arnot not identified.
274.24 Mrs. Jeanie very possibly referring to Jane Jobson (d. 1877), afterwards Lady Scott, who married Scott's son Walter on 3 February 1825 (see also Historical Note). Scott refers to her several times as Jeanie Jobson in correspondence at this period, sometimes transferring the name to quotations from popular songs and ballads (see *Letters*, 8.487, 497; 9.91). 'Mrs Jeanie' is also used to describe Scott's Jeanie Deans in *The Heart of Mid-Lothian*: see *The Heart of Mid-Lothian*, ed. David Hewitt and Alison Lumsden, EEWN 6 (Edinburgh, 2004), 368.18, 39.
274.25 queenie used in Scots to refer to a female, lass, or girl, especially one in early womanhood.

122. The Bonnets of Bonnie Dundee

Textual Note
The first clear reference to these verses occurs in a Journal entry for 22 December 1825, where Scott writes: 'The air of "Bonnie Dundee" running in

my head to-day I [wrote] a few verses to it before dinner, taking the key-note from the story of Claverse leaving the Scottish Convention of Estates in 1688–9. I wonder if they are good' (*Journal*, 45). Subsequently Scott moved quickly to promote the song and test out its suitability for musical rendition amongst members of his own family and close associates. On 26 December, in writing J. G. Lockhart, he enclosed for his daughter Sophia's use 'a Jacobite song seven verses of which she may get up if she likes' (*Letters*, 9.350). On 27 December he recorded how 'Sir Adam Fergusson came over and tried to marry my verses to the tune of "Bonnie Dundee"', adding that 'They seem well adapted to each other' (*Journal*, 49). And on 29 December he wrote to his daughter-in-law, Jane Jobson, enclosing another copy of the verses and advising on sources for the tune to be adopted. The song was not to be made public, though Jane might judiciously introduce it to influential friends creating in the process an air of mystery about its origin (*Letters*, 9.355–56). After a short delay, Scott then wrote to Anna Jane Maclean Clephane on 11 February 1826, this time inscribing the song (consisting of 11 verses plus the chorus) within the letter, part of which, including the verses, survives in an autograph album held by the National Trust at Belton House, Lincolnshire (47.D.3, p. 64; letter printed without the verses in *Letters*, 9.423–25). In keeping with the earlier letters, Scott encourages singing of the song, advising her to send it to her sister Lady Compton '[i]f you think it will stand the sea' (9.425).

After this, the trail tends to go cold until the first appearance of the song in print, under the title 'The Bonnets of Bonnie Dundee', in *The Christmas Box* (London, 1828), 27–33 (including editorial matter), a keepsake annual for juveniles, edited by Thomas Crofton Croker (1798–1854), first published in London on 19 November 1827. No specific evidence of how the verses arrived at this destination has been discovered, but Scott had been communicating for some time with Croker, mainly concerning the latter's *Fairy Legends and Traditions of the South of Ireland*, and was the dedicatee of its second series (1828). In this version the song consists of ten verses with the chorus supplied in full after the first and final stanzas. No direct indication of a tune is given, and the text is supplemented by a headnote outlining the general historical backdrop along with twenty explanatory footnotes, all supplied by the editor. Scott's name does not appear above the verses, but his authorship is acknowledged in the Preface to the anthology, which draws attention to the contemporaneous publication of the first series of Scott's own juvenile history, *Tales of a Grandfather* (1828). Scott's authorship is also implied in a note on the verso of the volume's half-title: 'The Publisher begs to inform the Composers of Music and Music-sellers, that Mr. James Power, of the Strand, Music-seller, is the only person authorised by him to publish *The Bonnets of Bonnie Dundee* by Sir Walter Scott.' No such song-sheet has been discovered, though the song ('published by special permission of the Proprietor') subsequently featured in George Thomson's *The Melodies of Scotland*, 5 vols [folio edn] (Edinburgh, 1831), 2.item 100, set to 'The Campbells are Coming' and 'With new Symphonies and Accompaniments, composed in 1829'. The letterpress text here likewise involves the same ten stanzas with the chorus repeated twice, though conflated to appear as six octets, and with a handful of small verbal variants compared with the '1827' *Christmas Box* text.

A more substantial body of variants is found when Scott lastly introduced the verses as an inset song in his play *The Doom of Devorgoil* (Edinburgh, 1830), 113–15. Headed here simply 'Song', and with the Air given as 'The Bonnets of Bonny Dundee', this was reproduced as part of *The Doom* in the 11-volume octavo *Poetical Works* (Edinburgh, 1830), 11.143–45, as well as providing the copy-text of the version in the posthumous Lockhart set of 1833–34 (12.194–

97), where again the song appears only as part of the play. Most noticeable in this later '1830' version is the presence of an additional ninth stanza (making 11 in all), reading:

> There's brass on the target of barken'd bull-hide,
> There's steel in the scabbard that dangles beside;
> The brass shall be burnish'd, the steel shall flash free,
> At a toss of the bonnet of Bonny Dundee.

Some thirty more local verbal variants compared with the '1827' version include: 'shall fall' not 'go down' (line 2); 'Whigs ... cramm'd' not 'saints ... pang'd' (19); 'speak twa words or three' not 'three vollies let flee' (31); and 'in the midst of your glee' not 'tho' triumphant ye be' (46). Judged purely on a simple comparison, one might posit a relatively straightforward two-phase textual development, but the true record (already complicated by the Thomson version) is more diverse than this, as is evident in the surviving manuscript record. In all five autograph MS versions have been discovered, as follows:

i) *Dundee Central Library, MS 1833.* Consisting of a four-page booklet, leaf size approx. 26 x 20.5 cm, and with the watermark 'A COWAN / 1823[?]', this appears to be an early working copy, with multiple alterations by Scott utilising both rectos and versos. All eleven stanzas however are in place, with Scott at one point deleting the 'additional' ninth stanza, then reinstating it as 'Verse omitted' on a facing page. Interestingly a further series of alterations, in pencil and by another hand, have the effect of revising the wording to match that as found in the '1827' *Christmas Box* version. This MS was owned earlier by Miss K. H. Gordon, a grand-daughter of George Huntly Gordon (1796–1868), who himself had worked as Scott's amanuensis and cataloguer at Abbotsford, and a slip of paper attached to the MS includes what appears to be an attempted variorum involving the '1830' version in Gordon's hand. This is partly explained by an accompanying letter from J. G. Lockhart to Gordon advising him to send 'your copy of the original MS.' and list of variants to the publisher Robert Cadell for possible use in the twelfth volume of the 1833–34 *Poetical Works*, though adding that the song had 'been deliberately placed in the Drama of Devorgoil' by 'the Poet's arrangement'.

ii) *Princeton University Library, Manuscripts Division, Robert H. Taylor Collection of English and American Literature (RTCo1).* Unlike the preceding item, this represents a fair copy, and bears an 1824 watermark. Apart from its inclusion of the 'additional' ninth stanza, the text almost exactly matches that in the '1827' *Christmas Box* printed version, suggesting that it may well have been prepared by Scott for that purpose, either as the copy-text or as a record of what he had sent. This MS had been at Abbotsford since Scott's death until it was taken by Major-General Walter Maxwell-Scott in August 1946 for auction in New York.

iii) *Belton House, 47.D.3, p. 64.* As suggested above, the February 1826 date of the containing letter to Miss Clephane places this 11-stanza version fairly early in the chronological sequence, and almost certainly before the Princeton fair copy. On the other hand it already shows signs of representing a kind of textual hybrid, with a number of components already pointing more in the direction of the '1830' rather than '1827' printed states, with Scott for example opting for 'Whigs' rather than 'saints' at line 19 and 'Lowlands' rather than 'Southland' at line 40. The presence of the 'additional' ninth stanza within the main sequence of verses indicates too that it had become an integral part of the poem by this stage.

iv) *Morgan Library, Scott 09, MA 435.2*. The first of two autograph manu-
scripts bound together in a dark-green leather volume, and evidently acquired
by the library in 1907. This one is accompanied by an undated letter, bearing
an 1825 watermark, in which Scott informs an unknown addressee that he is
sending 'the promised verses [of which] only two or three need to be sung'.
The verses themselves are on three leaves in the bound volume, each measur-
ing approx. 23.0 x 19.1 cm, and there is the watermark of 'J WHATMAN /
TURKEY MILL / 1825' on the second leaf. In this case the text consists of
just ten numbered verses, the 'additional' ninth stanza being omitted, but in
other respects is markedly closer to the '1830' printed state, and includes both
the readings 'speak two words or three' and 'in the midst of your glee' at lines
31 and 46 respectively. At the same time it contains a small number of variants
apparently unique to itself, such as 'cheek' (as opposed to 'face' and 'look') in
line 21, indicating that Scott was still engaged in the creative process as he wrote
out versions for different purposes.

v) *Morgan Library, Scott 09, MA 435.3*. Consisting of eight larger leaves,
each measuring approx. 26.9 x 20.5 cm, this version includes a transcription
(also in Scott's hand) of the passage from Sir John Dalrymple's *Memoirs of Great
Britain and Ireland* (see also Historical Note) which professedly provided the
narrative basis for the song, and which eventually was to appear as a long foot-
note in the posthumous 1833–34 collected edition. Other marks on the MS indi-
cate too that it was destined for one of the late collected sets, and it might seem
safe to assume this represents Scott's final version. At other points, however, the
text not only displays the '1827' reading (as in 'high [rather than 'proud'] Castle
rock' at line 29), but also occasionally offers a distinct reading of its own (as with
'squadron' instead of 'horsemen' at line 50).

For such reasons it is difficult to produce any clear graph of linear progression.
Rather Scott appears to have been engaged throughout in introducing new
terms while intermittently exchanging others, a procedure in keeping with the
tradition of the oral song, and in this case (especially in the earlier stages) further
influenced by a concern to provide the best combination for singing.

The present text follows that in *The Christmas Box* (London, 1828), 29–33,
as representing the first printed version of the song, and one almost certainly
authorised by Scott. It however does not incorporate the 'additional' ninth
stanza, notwithstanding its appearance in the Princeton MS (see ii above), partly
on the grounds that this exclusion might have carried Scott's approval, and
partly because the same verse can be found omitted elsewhere. (It will neverthe-
less be included as part of the *Doom of Devorgoil* in a later volume of EEWSP.) Also
excluded are the headnote and explanatory footnotes provided in the *Christmas
Box* by Thomas Crofton Croker as its editor. The following emendations have
been made, as probably reflecting Scott's own preferences:

275.11   douce (Princeton MS) / douse
275.12   Town (Princeton MS) / town
275.29   Castle Rock (Princeton MS) / castle rock
275.36   Grace (Princeton MS) / grace

Historical Note
According to Scott's earliest communications about his new song, the trigger for its
narrative line came from a passage in Sir John Dalrymple's *Memoirs of Great Britain
and Ireland*, 3 vols (London, 1790; *ALC*) concerning John Graham, 1st Viscount
of Dundee, the Royalist general who had previously featured as the ambiguously

heroic Claverhouse in his novel *The Tale of Old Mortality* (1816), drawing fierce accusations from Presbyterian critics of bias on Scott's part. By Dalrymple's account, as the Scottish Convention of Estates in Edinburgh moved unerringly in March 1689 towards accepting William III as the new King, and under the threat of rumoured assassination, 'Dundee left the house in a rage, mounted his horse, and with a troop of 50 horsemen, who had deserted to him from his regiment in England, galloped through the city' (2.305). As Scott explained to his daughter-in-law Jane: 'You know among my foibles I am a most incorrigible Jacobite and the other day I lighted on the passage in Baron Dalrymples memoirs of great Britain … in which there is a very spirited description of the viscount of Dundee leaving Edinr. to go north to raise the Highlands' (*Letters*, 9.355). Scott also acknowledged having drawn on a traditional Scottish song, 'Bonny Dundee', which in previous versions had linked the seduction of a young girl with the town of Dundee. In particular his chorus matches closely that found in a coarse and parodic version, 'Jockey's Escape from Dundee; and the Parsons Daughter whom he had Mow'd', from Thomas Durfey's *Wit and Mirth: or, Pills to Purge Melancholy*, 6 vols (1719–20), 5.17–19: *ALC*. (The same chorus is quoted by Scott in *Rob Roy* (1818), at a point where MacGregor is anxious to get out of the Tolbooth of Glasgow: *Rob Roy*, ed. David Hewitt, EEWN 5 (Edinburgh, 2008), 189.6–9.) Noticeably gentler adaptations, focusing more on the feelings of the girl, were subsequently produced by Robert Burns (see Kinsley, no. 157) and James Hogg, the latter employing the fuller title of 'The Bonnets o' Bonny Dundee' when first publishing his piece in the *Scots Magazine* for July 1804 (66.534). In all these instances, however, it is the town of Dundee rather than the historical personage that is concerned. A previous shift on Scott's part in the latter direction is found in a letter to Lord Montagu of 13 November 1819, in relation to the Radical disturbances of that year:

> The accounts from the west sometimes make me wish our little Duke [of Buccleuch] five or six years older and able to get on horseback: it seems approaching to the old song
>
>> Come fill up your cup come fill up your can
>> Come saddle the horses and call up our men
>> Come open the gates and let us go free
>> And we'll shew them the bonnets of bonny Dundee. (*Letters*, 6.15)

It is not unlikely that near the close of 1825, faced with the prospect of financial ruin, but at a moment when escape seemed temporarily possible, Scott sought a similar kind of release in identifying with Viscount Dundee's exhilarating (if ultimately futile) act of defiance in the face of seemingly impossible odds.

The tune of 'Bonny Dundee' is at least as old as the seventeenth century, a simple version called 'Adew Dundie' appearing in the Skene Mandora collection, NLS, Adv. MS 5.2.15, 151–53, around 1630 (for a fuller account, including the setting to Burns's song, see 'Music Note' to 'Bonny Dundee', in James Hogg, *The Forest Minstrel*, ed. P. D. Garside and Richard D. Jackson (Edinburgh, 2006), 229–31). In writing to Jane Jobson, in helping her recognise the tune, Scott points to three instances where it had been used, these including a song ('The Charge is Prepared') from John Gay's *Beggar's Opera* (1728): see *Letters*, 9.355–56; also 350. At times, however, Scott appears to show some unease about matching the tune to his own verses, a factor perhaps partly underlying his not infrequent local changes to the wording.

Explanatory Notes
274.1 Lords of Convention referring to members of the Convention of Estates (Scottish Parliament), which on 11 April 1689 adopted the Claim of

Right, laying down the constitutional and legal principles by which it wished William III and Mary to govern, and stating among other things that the royal prerogative could not override the law.

274.1   Clavers   John Graham of Claverhouse (pronounced 'Clavers') (1648?–89), created Viscount Dundee in 1688. See also Historical Note.

275.7   West-port   one of the old city gates of Edinburgh (demolished in 1786), at the W end of the Grassmarket, and leading in the direction of Glasgow and the more fordable parts of the Forth.

275.10   rung backwards   bells were rung in reverse order, starting with the lowest pitch, as a signal of alarm at a fire or other danger.

275.11   Provost   principal magistrate of a Scottish burgh; equivalent to a mayor in England and other countries.

275.11   douce   respectable, sensible, sober.

275.12   The Town   Edinburgh. In some other versions the sobriquet 'Gude Town' is used.

275.14   the Bow   the West Bow, a precipitous street leading down to the Grassmarket from the Lawnmarket (upper High Street) in Edinburgh. It is said to have been the dwelling place of many Covenanting Presbyterians, hence Scott's here mainly ironical 'sanctified' (see also note to 275.19).

275.15   carline   old woman, hag.

275.15   flyting   scolding.

275.15   pow   head.

275.16   plants of grace   compare Isaac Watts, *The Psalms of David* (London, 1719: see *ALC*), Psalm 92, Second Part, line 9: 'The Plants of Grace shall ever live' (238).

275.16   couthy and slee   friendly and sly; secretly sympathetic.

275.19   saints   alluding to the representation of religious victims of Royalist oppression as saints in Covenanting hagiography. See also Psalm 37.9, 11, and 22, where those 'that wait upon the Lord', the meek, and 'such as be blessed' by God (collectively 'the saints') 'shall inherit the earth'.

275.19   Grass-market   the open space to the S of Edinburgh Castle, where many Covenanters were executed after 1660.

275.19   pang'd   packed tight, crammed.

275.20   the West   the West of Scotland, a stronghold of Presbyterian Whig support and opposition.

275.20   set tryste   made an arrangement (a *tryste* referring to an agreed assignation or rendezvous).

275.24   cowls of Kilmarnock   woollen, conical skull-caps worn as nightgear or by indoor workers such as weavers: named after the town in the W of Scotland 34 km (21 miles) SW of Glasgow where they were manufactured. The hat suggests lower-class, Presbyterian sympathies.

275.25   lang-hafted gullies   long-handled knives. A *gully* in Scots often refers to a knife blunted with use, sometimes associated with animal butchery.

275.26   close-heads   the upper ends of narrow alleyways.

275.26   causeway   the paved part of the street.

275.29   Castle Rock   volcanic plug in the middle of Edinburgh upon which Edinburgh Castle sits, 130 m above sea level, with rocky cliffs to the S, W and N, rearing up to 80 m from the surrounding landscape. Scott probably imagines Dundee approaching from the E up Castle Hill.

275.30   gay Gordon   George Gordon (*c.* 1649–1716), 1st Duke of Gordon, Governor of Edinburgh Castle from 1686 to 1689. For a while he held out the Castle against the Convention of Estates in the name of the exiled James VII and II (1633–1701), though finally capitulating on 14 July 1689. The epithet *gey* or *gay*, as traditionally used in relation to the Highland Gordon clan (and now more familiarly associated with a dance), conveys an idea of showiness and brilliance.

275.31 Mons Meg name of a large cannon gifted to James II of Scotland in 1454, used in sieges in the 16th century, and otherwise located in Edinburgh Castle until 1754, when it was relocated in the Tower of London. Scott campaigned for its return, which was eventually effected in 1829.

275.31 marrows associates, accomplices; fellow-cannon.

275.35 Wherever ... spirit of Montrose compare Sir John Dalrymple, *Memoirs of Great Britain and Ireland* (London, 1790), where the querist is another person: 'Being asked by one of his friends, who stopt him, Where he was going? He waved his hat, and is reported to have answered, "Wherever the spirit of Montrose shall direct me."' (2.305). Montrose refers to James Graham (1612–50), 1st Marquess of Montrose, who after supporting the National Covenant changed sides and in 1644–45 fought a brilliant but savage military campaign in favour of King Charles I, ending in his defeat at the battle of Philiphaugh and leading to his eventual execution at Edinburgh in 1650. Montrose's fate might be said to have foreshadowed Dundee's own death later in 1689 at the battle of Killiecrankie, at an otherwise highpoint in a fierce but brief royalist insurgency supported by Highland troops.

276.39 Pentland the Pentland Hills, on the SW boundary of modern Edinburgh, stretching further SW for about 32 km (20 miles).

276.39 Forth the Firth of Forth, the large estuary separating the Lothians from Fife on its N shore.

276.40 Southland in this context, southern Scotland. Represented as 'Lowlands' in some other versions.

276.41 dunnie-wassels from the *Gaelic* 'duin' uasal', denoting a gentleman.

276.42 *Hoigh!* a loud whoop or cry of exhilaration, as uttered by the male dancers during a Highland reel.

276.51 Ravelston Craigs on the E slopes of Corstorphine Hill, 5 km (3 miles) NW of central Edinburgh.

276.51 Clermiston lee Clermiston is a district of modern Edinburgh slightly to the W of Corstorphine Hill (see previous note).

123. When Noble Duke

Textual Note
The manuscript of this uncompleted poem is now held in Fordham University Library, Bronx, New York (Modern Manuscripts Collection), having been given to that University by Major-General Walter Maxwell-Scott in August 1946 from papers held at Abbotsford. Consisting of a single torn half sheet, measuring approx. 14 x 21 cm, it bears the watermark of '[C]OWAN' without a visible date. As the following transcript shows, there are fairly extensive deletions, indicative of a working draft, and the final line suggests an uncompleted couplet:

> <When last>
> <Th> When Noble Duke in joy we met
> <Where th> The shout of thousands ownd a debt
> A debt so weighty and so large
> <As ne'er the Nation can discharge>
> As never Britain can discharge
> To One whose triumphs did not cease

> Till She had Triumph Europe peace
> \<And> ↑While↓ some folks thought the thrift[i]est way
> Was rather \<it> to disown than pay
> But not so Sunderlands stout tars
> Wellcomed the Ender of our wars
> \<Not so grey Durhams Patriarch Prince
> Wellcomed our Heroe short time since>
> The Patriarch Prince of Durham grey

This poem has not previously appeared in print. The present edited version regularises Scott's spelling, lowers some initial letters in words, and supplies the apostrophe in 'Sunderland's' (line 9). A title is provided from the first line. Four punctuation marks are also added to help guide sense, as listed below:

276.6   triumph, Europe peace. (Editorial) / Triumph Europe peace
276.8   pay, (Editorial) / pay
276.10   wars. (Editorial) / wars

Historical Note
This fragment refers to events held in celebration of the Duke of Wellington's visit to County Durham early in October 1827, at which Scott was also an honoured guest. According to Scott's *Journal* entry for 3 October, the Duke was greeted on arrival at Durham by 'bells and cannon and drums trumpets and banners besides a fine troop of yeomanry' (358). That evening a formal dinner was held at the palace of the Bishop of Durham, followed by a visit the following day to Sunderland where 'the Duke was brilliantly received by an immense population chiefly of Seamen' (360). (For subsequent festivities at Sunderland that evening, see no. 126, 'Verses to Sir Cuthbert Sharp'.) During the proceedings Scott found an opportunity to talk briefly with the Duke on a private footing, mainly on topics relating to Napoleon. It is not unlikely that Scott composed these lines when staying at nearby Ravensworth Castle as a guest of the Liddell family.

Explanatory Notes
276.1   Noble Duke   Arthur Wellesley (1769–1852), field marshal and commander at the battle of Waterloo, was created Duke of Wellington in 1814. He was to become Prime Minister in January 1828.
276.7–8   some folks … pay   by the end of the Napoleonic wars in 1815 Britain's national debt had risen to an inflated amount, repayable only by retrenchment in government expenditure or by increased taxes. The manufacturing interest in particular was opposed to levies upon the increasing production of British industry. Scott may also have been thinking of those, mainly from the Whig party, who had earlier argued for peace on the grounds that the Continental blockade was ruining Britain's commercial interests. A personal dimension possibly exists too in view of Scott's determination to pay off his own debts after his insolvency in 1826. A similar reference is found in no. 126, 'Verses to Sir Cuthbert Sharp', lines 10–12.
276.9   Sunderland's stout tars   the port of Sunderland had been a major exporter of coal since the 17th century, with major improvements to its harbour and piers from the later 18th century. The 'tars' (sailors) mentioned here were presumably mainly merchant seamen.
276.11   Patriarch Prince   Dr William Van Mildert (1765–1836), recently installed as Bishop of Durham in 1826. According to Scott's letter to his son

Walter of 9 October 1827: 'The old prelate contrived to sustain admirably the character of a Count Palatine with that of a Bishop' (*Letters*, 10.287).
276.11   Durham grey   Compare *Harold the Dauntless* (1817): 'Grey towers of Durham!' (Canto 3, stanza 1).

124.   Translation from Grillparzer

Textual Note
These verses were contributed by Scott early in 1828 to an album, bound in red leather, belonging to Charlotte, the wife of the composer and keyboard virtuoso Ignaz Moscheles (1794–1870), which is now BL, Zweig MS 215. Scott's verses are on page 16, written directly into the album itself rather than on a separate paper subsequently pasted in. The size of the album page is approx. 21 x 27.8 cm with no watermark visible. Scott's verses are on the verso of a leaf, the recto of which bears the poem by Franz Seraphicus Grillparzer (1791–1872), presumably in his own hand and end-dated from Vienna on 24 October 1826, of which Scott's lines are a translation. In her biography of her husband Charlotte Moscheles is unclear as to when precisely Scott's translation was written, although it was probably during the couple's Edinburgh stay in January 1828 since she records that Scott returned the album only a few hours after he was sent it: see *Life of Moscheles, with Selections from his Diaries and Correspondence*, trans. A. D. Coleridge, 2 vols (London, 1873), 1.206. Scott's lines were never published in his lifetime, although included subsequently in Charlotte Moscheles' biography of her husband, first published in German in 1872, the English version of which appeared the following year (*Life of Moscheles*, 1.207).
The present text is taken directly from the autograph album, BL, Zweig MS 215, p. 16, with an appropriate title being supplied editorially. In addition to the following listed emendations routine apostrophes have been introduced as required, as have full stops at the ends of stanzas.

277.2   Painting, Music, (Editorial) / Painting Music
277.7   tower (Editorial) / Tower
277.8   O'er (Editorial) / Oer
277.13   freest (Editorial) / Freest
277.15   Music, (Editorial) / Music

Historical Note
Ignaz Moscheles, the virtuoso pianist and composer, and his wife visited Edinburgh in January 1828 to give a series of concerts, where the couple met Scott. Moscheles had been born in Prague in 1794 to a well-to-do German Jewish merchant family, and he married Charlotte Emden, the daughter of a Jewish banker, in the Frankfurt synagogue shortly before pursuing his career in London between 1825 and 1846. Scott records in his Journal that the couple came to breakfast with him on Monday, 21 January, and mentions this visit again in the entry of 23 January which records in more detail his favourable impression both of Moscheles's playing and of his wife's beauty and charm: 'he an excellent performer on the pianoforte, she a beautiful young creature "and one that adores me" as Sir Toby says, that is in my poetical capacity' (*Journal*, 417–18). He also attended Moscheles's final concert on Saturday, 26 January, at which he 'was amused, the more so that I had Mrs. M. herself to flirt a little with. To have so much beauty as she really possesses and to be accomplishd and well-read, she is an unaffected and pleasant person' (*Journal*, 419).

At the first of his concerts Moscheles (according to a review of 'Mr Moscheles' Concert' in the *Caledonian Mercury* of 10 January) played a piece presumably prepared especially for the occasion entitled 'Anticipations of Scotland', which included the Scottish air of 'Kelvin Grove' with variations. Scott's liking for Moscheles's playing was no doubt enhanced by his adoption of Scottish airs in his Edinburgh performances, and in particular the tune to which Scott had written his own 'Pibroch of Donald Dhu' (see no. 92). In the course of a conversation about Highland music during the couple's breakfast-time visit to Scott on 21 January (see 'Mr Moscheles', *Caledonian Mercury*, 26 January 1828) Scott quoted this poem and asked one of the company if he would sing the tune for Moscheles. On the company moving into the drawing-room, Moscheles sat down at the piano and gave a spirited improvisation upon it. This was subsequently included in Moscheles's *Fantaisie sur des Airs des Bardes Écossais* (opus 80, 1828), a work dedicated to Scott and published in English with the title *Sir Walter Scott's Favourite Strains of the Scottish Bards*. Scott graciously accepted the dedication in his letter of 18 October 1828 (*Letters*, 11.18). At some point he also sent a copy of *Tales of a Grandfather* inscribed 'To Adolphus and Emily Moscheles, from the Grandfather' to the couple's two infant children (*Life of Moscheles*, 1.204) as a sign of continuing friendship.

Above his verses in the album Scott had modestly written, 'I am afraid the verses of Mr. Grillparzer and Mad^e Moschelles valuable album are only disgraced by the following small attempt at translation Walter Scott'. Scott's contribution was perhaps triggered by his discovery of a blank page in the album following the Grillparzer lines complimenting musicians such as Moscheles. Franz Seraphicus Grillparzer (1791–1872) was known in Scotland chiefly for his dramas, notably *Die Ahnfrau* (1816). An unpublished translation by R. P. Gillies (1789–1858) was the subject of an enthusiastic account in 'Horae Germanicae. No. II', in *Blackwood's Edinburgh Magazine*, 6 (December 1819), 247–56. Grillparzer's poem praises music as being uniquely able in an anxious and difficult time to communicate a freedom that petty officials will not allow to pass in words, and painting does not enter into the comparison at all although it is implicit in the expression 'Schwesterkünste drei' (three sister arts). Scott's version of Grillparzer's poem in Mrs Moscheles's album, removed from the Austrian context of extreme and illiberal censorship, expresses similar ideas while inevitably appearing more generalised.

Explanatory Notes
277.1 **Nine** the nine Muses, goddesses associated with particular arts in classical Greece: Calliope (epic poetry); Clio (history); Euterpe (flute-playing); Melpomene (tragedy); Terpsichore (dancing); Erato (the lyre); Polyhymnia (sacred song); Urania (astronomy); and Thalia (comedy).
277.1 **loveliest three** poetry, painting and music do not correspond precisely to any of the nine muses of the ancient world: the reference to them as the three sister arts is more recent.

125. Song from the German

Textual Note
Scott appears to have sent these lines in a letter to Charlotte, wife of the virtuoso keyboard player and composer Ignaz Moscheles (1794–1870), shortly after attending his final Edinburgh concert on Saturday, 26 January 1828, but it seems likely that he had written a similar translation many years earlier.

According to Moscheles's later recollections: 'Between the parts he asked my wife if she knew Bürger's poem "Der Dichter liebt den guten Wein," and, on her answering in the affirmative, he told her how he delighted in this poem, which he had translated into English, adding, "Would you like to have it? I shall send it you"': see Charlotte Moscheles, *Life of Moscheles, with Selections from his Diaries and Correspondence*, trans. A. D. Coleridge, 2 vols (London, 1873), 1.205. Moscheles adds that Scott sent it to her with a note on the following day.

The mistaken attribution of the original poem to Bürger (see Historical Note), several of whose poems Scott had translated in the 1790s, suggests that he had translated the poem very early in his poetic career. The German original, accompanied by an anonymous English translation, had been published in *The Athenaeum, A Magazine of Literary and Miscellaneous Information*, 1 (March 1807), 277–78. Scott was an established poet by this date and a most desirable contributor, although one who was unlikely to have contributed directly to a two-shilling magazine edited for its brief three-year run by John Aikin (1747–1822), who moved in English radical and dissenting circles. (This English translation was reprinted subsequently in *Poetical Register*, 7 (1808–09), 354.) A slightly different version of the translation was then published more than a decade afterwards in *The Tickler* for 1 September 1819, 159. Scott was perhaps even more unlikely to have contributed directly to this poorly-produced sixpenny miscellany produced in London from December 1818 up until 1824. There are significant verbal differences between the translation as given in *The Athenaeum* and in *The Tickler*: for instance, lines 4–5 of the former read 'For him her sparkling juice refine, / And fairest clusters swell' whereas in the latter they read 'For him her flexile tendrils twine, / And bid her clusters swell'. The translation in *The Tickler*, however, names Walter Scott as the author, adding 'One of his earliest Effusions', and the two printings do appear to be distinct versions of the same translation.

No uncertainty exists as to the provenance or authenticity of the translation given in Scott's letter to Mrs Moscheles. Scott's letter, with the poem in his own hand, survives in Cornell University Library, MS 4600, Box 51, and is end-dated 'Edin^r Saturday 2^d Feb^y' by Scott, a week in fact after Moscheles's final concert. It was sent to Mrs Moscheles at the couple's lodging in Frederick Street, but arrived after their departure for London and had to be forwarded to them there, possibly by Scott's son Walter on a visit to London, since in his letter to Moscheles of 21 February 1828 (Fales Library, New York University, MSS 001, Box 153, Folder 8) Scott mentions that his son left Edinburgh 'a few days ago' and carried with him 'a card for Mrs Moscheles containing some lines I promised her'.

Notwithstanding resemblances between the earlier periodical translation and the text of Scott's later manuscript, there are also substantial differences. In the first stanza, for instance, the rhyming second and fifth lines in *The Tickler* read 'And if the bard sings well' then 'And bid her clusters swell', while in Scott's manuscript they read 'And if his verse be good' then 'To cheer him with her blood', a final line incidentally which is closer to the original German 'Und opfert ihm ihr Blut' (And offers him her blood). One possible explanation is that Scott first translated the German poem early in his career and then, in attempting to call to mind his translation in order to fulfil his promise to Charlotte Moscheles, effectively recreated it. This translation of 1828 was apparently never printed in Scott's lifetime (nor in the Lockhart 1833–34 posthumous edition), the accompanying letter being included without the poem itself in Charlotte Moscheles's *Life of Moscheles*, 1.205.

The present text is taken from Scott's manuscript in Cornell University Library, MS 4600, Box 51, as a probable late version with a secure provenance, that of the earlier versions presently being doubtful. In addition to the following listed emendations routine apostrophes have been introduced as required, as have full stops at the ends of stanzas.

277.sub-title   liebt den guten Wein (Editorial) / liebe den guten wein
278.7   traitor's (Editorial) / traiters
278.10   yields (Editorial) / yeilds
278.12   mine: (Editorial) / mine

Historical Note
In January 1828 the virtuoso pianist and composer, Ignaz Moscheles and his wife visited Edinburgh where Moscheles gave several public concerts and became acquainted with Scott (for details see Historical Note to no. 124, 'Translation from Grillparzer'). Moscheles recalled that during his final concert on 26 January, after Scott had offered to send Charlotte Moscheles his translation, she had 'begged him to recite the song in the original; this, to my wife's great delight, he willingly assented to, while all around listened eagerly' (*Life of Moscheles*, 1.205). Scott alludes to this circumstance in his letter: 'As you are determined to have me murder the pretty song twice first by repeating it in bad german & then by turning it into little better English I send the promised version' (Cornell University Library, MS 4600, Box 51).
This German-language original was, in fact, the work of the Danish poet Jens Immanuel Baggesen (1764–1826), who composed both in Danish and in German and had travelled widely in Germany, supporting peaceful co-existence and cultural exchange between the two countries despite an atmosphere of chauvinistic nationalism in his native Denmark. It was first published, as 'Lied. (Als ich auf den Alpen eine Traube fand.)' (Song. When I found a bunch of grapes in the Alps), in the *Musenalmanach für das Jahr 1797*, ed. Johann Heinrich Voss (Hamburg, [1796]), 49. The mistaken attribution of the poem to Gottfried Augustus Bürger (1747–94) may, of course, be due to Moscheles's imperfect recollection of Scott's conversation with his wife, but if reported accurately was probably a simple slip of memory on Scott's part as he thought back to the translations of German Romantic poetry that had been a major preoccupation at the start of his poetic career.

Explanatory Notes
277.sub-title   **Der Dichter ... Wein &c.**   the first line of the poem in the original German, meaning 'The poet loves good wine'.
278.13   **gaudy stars and ribbands**   a star of some form constitutes part of the insignia of an order of knighthood. A *ribband* or ribbon is the badge of an order of knighthood, or by transference a sign of high distinction in anything.

126.   Verses to Sir Cuthbert Sharp

Textual Note
The original manuscript for this poem survives in the form of an unpublished letter from Scott to Sir Cuthbert Sharp (1781–1849), the Durham antiquary, now held in the Pforzheimer Collection, New York Public Library (Scott Misc MS 1300). Consisting of two conjugate leaves each measuring approx. 22.8 x 18.4 cm, and with the watermark 'A COWAN & SON / 1827', the letter

comprises the verses at its head followed by a short note by Scott end-dated 13 March [1828]. This evidently formed the basis of the broadside version, of which a final copy plus two proofs (with MS additions by Sharp) can be found in the Bodleian Library (13 THETA 114: nos 5, 10, 14). Measuring approx. 22 x 14 cm and unwatermarked, with the verso left blank, this was privately commissioned by Sharp in a letter of 15 March (no. 6) to the Newcastle-upon-Tyne printer John Sykes in a run of just 56 copies. The same volume of papers in the Bodleian Library also contains a transcript by Sharp of the verses from Scott's letter (no. 4), presumably prepared as a copy-text for the printer, and with later interventions, some possibly by Sykes in response. Here Scott's 'you' has been subsequently altered to 'thee' at lines 1, 9, and 17; and in line 1 'gallant' has also been replaced by 'worthy', both overriding Scott's original 'knightly'. Uncertainty about the meaning of the penultimate word in line 18 resulted in a space initially being left, the lacuna subsequently being filled not too convincingly with the word 'bridle [diddles]'. Compared with the autograph letter, the transcript supplies some additional question and exclamation marks, to which the printed version adds a modicum of more conventional punctuation. The text of the broadside's header can found (apparently in Sharp's hand) at the foot of a note from Sykes (no. 11) responding to some of the issues posed by Scott's text and among other things approving of the spelling of 'Liddles' (line 20).

The text of the poem as found in the letter to Sharp was later published in J. G. Lockhart's *Life of Scott* (7.76–77), along with a cut-down version of its accompanying note. In this case 'twiddle diddles' is interpreted even more fancifully as 'dumpty-diddles'. 'In which' (line 15), common to both manuscript and broadside, also becomes 'In what'; and 'Liddles' at line 20 is altered to the more conventional '*Liddells*'. This poem is not found in any of the collected sets of Scott's verse up to and including the Lockhart posthumous 1833–34 edition.

The present text follows that of the 1828 broadside, as the first printed version complete with punctuation, and preserves the header found there as providing a useful context. 'Verses to Sir Cuthbert Sharp' is added editorially as a convenient main title. The following emendations have also been made:

278.1   you (MS) / thee
278.1   knightly (MS) / worthy
278.9   you (MS) / thee
279.17   you (MS) / thee
279.18   twiddle (MS) / bridle
279.21   you (MS) / thee

Historical Note
These verses describe features of a grand dinner held in honour of the Duke of Wellington at Sunderland in County Durham on 4 October 1827. An immediate prompt underlying their composition came in the form of letters subsequently sent to Scott by Sir Cuthbert Sharp, the Vice President at the dinner, who was offering advice on a planned further visit by Scott to Northumberland and Durham in the following Spring. In particular, at the start of a letter of 24 November 1827, Sharp had written: 'I'm sure you have not forgotten us—but if you have, the enclosed sketch will recall us to your remembrance' (NLS, MS 3905, f. 170r). The 'enclosed sketch', later referred to in the same letter as a 'tract', most probably refers to the small pamphlet titled *The Duke of Wellington's Visit to Sunderland, 1827*, printed in Durham by Francis Humble, which gives an account of the dinner (as attended by 204 guests), the main officials present,

and the various responses to toasts. Occupying the Chair was the 3rd Marquess of Londonderry (1778–1854), a veteran of the Peninsular War, now engaged in developing coalfields and port facilities in lands he had acquired in County Durham. Other dignitaries included Earl Bathhurst, Viscount Castlereagh, and Lord Ravensworth (see also note to 279.20 below). Bathurst in particular in his speech drew attention to the extraordinary conjunction of 'the greatest Captain of the Age' in Wellington and 'the Poet and Historian' Scott (17). Scott's own health was proposed by the Chairman in the following terms:

> As a plain and ordinary soldier ... I desire to offer my tribute to the merits of Sir Walter Scott—(*loud applause*)—to whom the army are greatly indebted for the gratification and instruction they derived from his works. During the war, Waverly [*sic*] was ever to be found in the camp and in the field, as well as the other works of the same author, and the fatigues and anxieties of the campaign were often forgotten in the perusal of these interesting volumes—(*Applause.*) The health of Sir Walter Scott was drunk with 3 times 3, and loud applause. (21–22)

Sir Cuthbert Sharp's response to a toast in his favour focuses on the town of Sunderland, then in a state of rapid industrial development as a manufacturing centre and exporter of coal.

No mention is made of problems such as slum dwellings and outbreaks of typhoid fever then affecting industrial communities, nor of the political unrest which was shortly to break out in Reform agitation. For his part Scott undoubtedly would have approved of such demonstrations of loyalty, and used his own speech to celebrate the end of Anglo-Scottish rivalries: 'How much more gratifying it is to find the kindred forces of England and Scotland, joined with those of Ireland, uniting against the common foe—those forces which, when the Hero of Waterloo gave the word "advance", proceeded jointly against the troops of France, and scattered them to the storm. (*Loud applause*).' (22–23) Other evidence, however, indicates that the noise of the dinner and bustle of a following ball, as well as the sense of being on display, were not entirely to his taste, coming after another such event held at the Bishop of Durham's on the previous day. As he wrote to his son Walter on 9 October 1827: 'Next day we went to Sunderland where there was a most suffocating croud. The Duke was received in triumph and I as a jackal of the Show had my share of attention and such a shaking of hands as made me wish the regulation had been announced that "Gentlemen & Ladies were requested not to touch the animals."' (*Letters*, 10.287–88). An even greater sense of suffocation is conveyed by a *Journal* entry for 4 October:

> Our party went to-day to Sunderland where the Duke was brilliantly received by an immense population chiefly of Seamen. The difficulty of getting into the rooms was dreadful for we chanced to march in the rear of an immense Gibraltar gun etc. all composed of glass which is here manufactured in great quantity. The disturbance created by this thing, which by the way I never saw afterwards, occasiond an ebbing and flowing of the crowd which nearly took me off my legs. I have seen the day I would have minded it little. The entertainment was handsome; about two hundred dined and appeard most hearty in the cause which had convend them ... After the dinnerparty broke up there was a ball, numerously attended, where there was a prodigious anxiety discoverd for shaking of hands. The Duke had enough of it and I came in for my share for though as Jackall to the lion I got some part in whatever was going. We got home about half past two in the morning sufficiently tired. The Duke went to Seaham, a house of Lord Londonderry. After all, this Sunderland trip might have been spared. (360)

In this light, Scott's eventual recollection of the event with this poem in such lively terms exhibits a certain degree of graciousness on his part, and there is no suggestion that he was anticipating its publication.

Explanatory Notes
278.1 knightly fere *fere* in the sense of friend, companion. The
combination 'trewe fere' occurs several times in Scott's edition of *Sir Tristrem*
(Edinburgh, 1804), and is glossed there 'trusty companion' ('Glossary', viii);
'noble fere' and 'worthy fere' are also common in Elizabethan literature.
278.6 canny Sunderland presumably referring to the town rather than
an individual person, with *canny* conveying something of the peculiar Geordie
sense of 'good, or fine'. Lockhart in his version in the *Life* places 'canny
Sunderland' in quotation marks. 'Canny awd Sunderland' also features as the
first song in a chapbook collection *The Sunderland Songster* (*c.* 1840), and may
well have had an earlier history in chapbook form.
278.11 Disown the debt for topical reference to the national debt
accumulated during the Napoleonic wars, as well as a possible personal
dimension in view of Scott's determination to pay off his own debts after
insolvency in 1826, see no. 123, 'When Noble Duke', note to 276.7–8.
279.16 my Surtees in a ball room Robert Surtees of Mainsforth
(1779–1834), fellow-antiquary of Scott and Sharp, and one of Scott's oldest
acquaintances in the region. According to a later report he avoided the main
part of the celebrations, not being able to 'endure great "bungalow" dinners',
but managed to meet Scott in the ante-room to the ball-room, where the two
'sat down in a corner and had a long *tête-à-tête*': George Taylor, *Memoir of
Robert Surtees, Esq.*, ed. James Raine, Publications of the Surtees Society
(Durham, 1852), 226. Surtees is not found in the list of those present in *The
Duke of Wellington's Visit to Sunderland* (1827), 31–33.
279.18 twiddle diddles compare John Burgoyne's comedy, *The Heiress*
(1786), where after the stage instruction 'Takes the harp and plays a few bars of
a lively air', Alscrip says: 'Oh! the sweet little twiddle-diddles' (Act 3, Scene 1).
279.20 the Liddles an important local family. Members at the dinner
included Thomas Henry Liddell, 1st Baron Ravensworth (1775–1855); and his
elder son, Henry Thomas Liddell (1797–1878), Tory MP for Northumberland
1826–30. Scott was a guest of the family, and spent the day at Ravensworth
Castle after the Sunderland celebrations (see *Journal* entry for 5 October 1827).

127. The Death of Keeldar

Textual Note
'The Death of Keeldar' was contributed by Scott to, and first published in,
the 1829 volume of *The Gem, A Literary Annual*, ed. Thomas Hood (London,
[1828]), 13–17, where it accompanied an engraving of a watercolour sketch of
that name by Abraham Cooper (1787–1868). Scott's poem was composed some
months after receiving the original painting from the artist on 7 February 1828
(*Journal*, 424). In his letter to Cooper of 21 September that year Scott mentions
sending his verses two or three days previously to Thomas Hood (1799–1845)
as editor of *The Gem*, while also assuring Cooper 'the autograph is for you if
you care about such things' (*Letters*, 10.504). Scott's manuscript in BL, Egerton
MS 2075, ff. 5–6, was thus almost certainly both copy for the annual and a pres-
entation manuscript. It consists of two leaves of unwatermarked paper now
measuring approx. 22.3 x 18.3 cm, though possibly trimmed to fit the existing
mount. Scott's text, written on both sides of the paper, is not fully punctuated
and contains a few revisions and corrections: for instance, he revises the original
'sylvan fancy' in line 23 to 'wildering fancy'. *The Gem* was published in London
on 8 October 1828, but despite the short interval between the sending of the

manuscript and publication Scott was sent a proof, which has not apparently survived but which he duly returned to Hood with a letter of 26 September 1828, requesting 'that my corrections are attended to' (Beinecke, GEN MSS 266, Box 1, Folder 18). 'The Death of Keeldar' is fully punctuated in *The Gem*, and Scott's spelling is regularised so that, for instance, Cooper's name is correctly and consistently spelled in both poem and headnote. Other changes, however, suggest authorial revision more than the work of a printer, such as the substitution of 'Alnwick's Earl' in line 11 for the manuscript's 'the stout Earl' and of 'moan or quiver' in line 44 for the manuscript's 'moan or groan'.

   'The Death of Keeldar' was not included in the 8vo or 18mo editions of Scott's *Poetical Works* of 1830, nor in Lockhart's posthumous collected edition of 1833–34. The present text follows that of the 1829 volume of *The Gem, A Literary Annual*, ed. Thomas Hood (London, [1828]), 13–17, and is accompanied by the engraving there of Cooper's picture. No emendations have been made.

Historical Note
Abraham Cooper's paintings were largely of animals such as horses and dogs, although from around 1815 he also depicted battle-scenes. Scott had professed himself an admirer in his letter to Cooper of 7 September 1826 (*Letters*, 10.98–99), and was plainly delighted to receive the water-colour sketch of 'The Death of Keeldar' which, according to Corson, hung in the breakfast parlour at Abbotsford until at least 1840, although its present whereabouts is apparently unknown (*N&I*, 285, note to 10.380 *n*. 2). During 1828 relations between author and artist were strengthened when each sought the assistance of the other, Cooper wanting Scott to write lines for an engraving of 'The Death of Keeldar' for *The Gem* and Scott wishing to enrol Cooper among the illustrators of his projected Magnum Opus edition of the Waverley Novels. This helps to account for Scott's readiness to contribute to a literary annual on the present occasion. Certainly Robert Cadell saw Scott's poem as a lever in negotiating with the artist, reminding Scott of his intention to write verses for Cooper's picture in his letter of 29 July 1828 from London, which also alludes to Cooper's promised illustrations, both for scenes involving horses, to *The Antiquary* and *The Tale of Old Mortality* (NLS, MS 3907, ff. 38–39). In total Cooper provided seven designs for the Magnum Opus edition. See also *Introductions and Notes from the Magnum Opus*, ed. J. H. Alexander with P. D. Garside and Claire Lamont, EEWN 25a (Edinburgh, 2012), 101, 136, 174, 215 and EEWN 25b (Edinburgh, 2012), 108, 135, 163.

   There are many stories of a hunter mistakenly killing his faithful dog. In the Welsh legend of Gelert, for instance, the faithful animal comes to meet his master Llywelyn ab Iorwerth, Prince of Gwynedd (*c.* 1173–1240), with blood around his mouth, and when the prince sees the cradle of his infant son overturned he kills Gelert, only to notice subsequently the corpse of the wolf from whom Gelert had in fact defended the baby. Beddgelert (meaning the grave of Gelert) is a village near the confluence of the rivers Glaslyn and Colwyn in Snowdonia. The scene depicted by Cooper seems to be generic rather than specific, and certainly the remorseful hunter's clothing appears better suited to a medieval courtier than to a Border Reiver. The name Keeldar, however, was perhaps familiar to Cooper through Leyden's poem 'The Cout of Keeldar' in Scott's *Minstrelsy* (2.389–406), which is another story of an unfortunate hunting expedition. Scott interpreted the scene as a precursor (what Hollywood would now term a prequel) of the traditional 'Ballad of Parcy Reed', a manuscript version of which in another hand is tipped into the back of the copy of Robert

Roxby's *The Lay of the Reedwater Minstrel* (Newcastle, 1809) in the Abbotsford Library. Subsequently Scott sent a copy of this ballad to Cooper with his letter of 2 December 1830 (*Letters*, 11.426–27 [letter only]; BL, Egerton MS 2075, ff. 18–20 [ballad]), having previously admitted in his letter to Cooper of 1 February 1830 that 'Percy Reed was a real person and actually slain by a clan calld Crossar so I intrusted him to the imaginary death of Keeldar' (*Letters*, 11.293). Scott's headnote to 'The Death of Keeldar' thus elides the difference between the genuine tradition of Reed's death and the invented tradition of his shooting his dog, while erroneously suggesting that Cooper had in mind in producing his picture the tradition subsequently invented by Scott himself.

Explanatory Notes
279.headnote   Percival Rede, of Trochend Troughend is a settlement in Elsdon parish, Northumberland about 12 km (7½ miles) NE of Bellingham. As Scott wrote in his letter to Cooper of 2 December 1830, in which he sent his copy of 'The Ballad of Parcy Reed': 'Troughend is the ancient inheritance of the family of Reed who have evidently derived their name from the river and are therefore probably an ancient race. The hamlet is opposite to the much more famous village of Otterbourn on the south side of Reed, and it is said ... that the Reeds have dwelt there for nine hundred years' (*Letters*, 11.426). The Reeds were one of the Border Reiver families, who lived by blackmail and cattle-rustling in the 15th and 16th centuries: Percival Reed himself is believed to have lived in the 1580s and 1590s.
279.headnote   clan called Crossar the Crossars (also often spelled Crozier, or Croser) were a family of Border Reivers associated with the Armstrongs, Nixons, and Elliots, who launched their forays across the Border from Liddesdale in Scotland. The chief branch of the family was based at Riccarton, about 21 km (13 miles) SE of Hawick in Roxburghshire. In the 'Ballad of Parcy Reed' the Crosers of Liddesdale began a feud against the Reeds when Percival Reed, Keeper of Redesdale, arrested Whinton Croser for raiding. The Halls, who were old friends of Percy Reed, betrayed him and conspired with the Crosers to trap him while he was out hunting. When the Crosers ambushed Percy Reed, the Halls watched as he was murdered. His ghost was afterwards supposed to have haunted Redesdale. With his letter to Cooper of 2 December 1830 Scott sent a copy of the 'Ballad of Parcy Reed' (*Letters*, 11. 426–27 [letter only]; BL, Egerton MS 2075, ff. 18–20 [ballad]). Scott mentions in his letter that he had taken down the story 'from the recitation of a shepherd belonging to these wilds', but he also refers to Robert Roxby's account in *The Lay of the Reedwater Minstrel* (Newcastle, 1809). Scott had previously alluded to this story in a note to Canto 1, stanza 20 of *Rokeby* (1813), 'Notes to Canto First', xx–xxi.
279.3   couples a brace or leash for hounds.
279.5   palfrey a saddle-horse for ordinary riding, as opposed to a war-horse.
281.11   Alnwick's Earl Henry Percy, 1st Earl of Northumberland (1341–1408), whose chief stronghold was Alnwick Castle. His eldest son, Sir Henry Percy, known as Hotspur (1364–1403), was the Percy who actually led the ill-fated expedition into Scotland.
281.12   Cheviot's rueful day the well-known 'Ballad of Chevy Chase' relates the consequences of an ill-omened hunting expedition in the Cheviot Hills led by Hotspur, the eldest son of the English Earl of Northumberland in 1388. The Scottish Earl of Douglas interpreted this as an invasion of Scotland and a bloody battle resulted at Otterburn, on the opposite bank of the Rede

from Troughend, in which Hotspur was captured by the Scots. There are both English and Scottish versions of the ballad, the former being published in Thomas Percy, *Reliques of Ancient English Poetry*, 3 vols (London, 1765; see *ALC*), 1.1–17, and the latter as 'Battle of Otterbourne' in *Minstrelsy*, I. 27–47. The Cheviots are a range of hills extending along the English Border with Scotland.

281.14   Tarras   the horse is named presumably from Tarras Water, a fast-flowing stream in Eskdale, S Dumfriesshire.

281.37   faithless yew   bows for archery were commonly made of yew-wood.

281.40   grey-goose wing   an arrow was traditionally fletched with four feathers, evenly spaced at the back and set at a slight angle to give stability to its flight and create spin.

283.75   fearful odds in deadly feud   according to the copy of the 'Ballad of Parcy Reed' Scott sent to Cooper (BL, Egerton MS 2075, ff. 18–20) Percy Reed had to fight five of the Crosers.

283.79   treacherous ambush   in the 'Ballad of Parcy Reed' the three Halls who accompanied Reed on his hunting expedition steal his gunpowder, pour water in his gun, and fix his sword in his sheath while he is asleep, in preparation for the arrival of the Crosers.

283.84   Oblivion's river   Lethe, the river of oblivion or forgetfulness, flowed through Hades, or the underworld, according to classical mythology.

128.   To General David Stewart of Garth

Textual Note

Scott's poem was appended to a letter to General David Stewart of Garth of 18 October 1828 (Basel University Library, Autog. Geigy-Hagenbach 2605), the letter-paper consisting of a sheet folded in two with Scott's letter occupying both sides of the first of the two resulting leaves and the poem in numbered couplets on the recto of the second, its verso being left blank. The lines were clearly intended as a private *jeu d'esprit*, since Scott added in a postscript below them, 'Pray dont let the papers get this offhand nonsense'. They were accordingly not published in any of the lifetime collected editions of Scott's poetry nor in the Lockhart 1833–34 posthumous edition. An undated manuscript copy in the hand of Scott's daughter, Sophia, on unwatermarked paper measuring approx. 18.1 x 11.3 cm, survives in NLS, MS 921, f. 1. The verses remained unpublished until the end of the nineteenth century, when they featured in 'An Interesting Letter and Verses of Sir Walter Scott', *Life and Work*, 17 (January 1895), 4–5, the article, including the poem, being reprinted from there in *The Scotsman* of 26 December 1894. W. M. Parker afterwards included the verses as item 13 in 'Sir Walter Scott: Thirteen New Poems?', *Poetry Review*, 40: 4 (August–September 1949), 263–75 (p. 275), this providing an imperfect version, which was corrected by James C. Corson in a letter to the editor in *Poetry Review*, 41: 1 (January–February 1950), 49.

The present text follows Scott's manuscript letter to David Stewart of Garth of 18 October 1828 (Basel University Library, Autogr. Geigy-Hagenbach 2605), a title being editorially supplied from the name of the recipient. In addition to the following listed emendations, ampersands have been routinely expanded to 'and', verb forms ending with 'd' to 'ed', routine apostrophes have been introduced as required, and full stops have been placed at the end of the individual couplets.

284.4   blame, (Editorial) / blame
284.6   yet, (Editorial) / yet
284.10   friend (Editorial) / freind

Historical Note
Scott's old friend David Stewart of Garth (1772–1829) wrote to him at Abbotsford on 6 October 1828 regretting that he would not see Scott again before leaving the country to take up his new appointment as Governor of the island of St Lucia in the Caribbean and requesting that, as several ladies among his friends were anxious to have Scott's autograph, Scott would therefore 'favour me with a few lines, and scribble your signature as often as the paper will hold' (NLS, MS 3907, ff. 144–45). Scott's reply of 18 October, to which the verses are appended, congratulates Stewart on his new post and says that he would have come to say farewell to him in Edinburgh had he known details of his departure earlier (*Letters*, 12.459–60 [letter only]). While the terms of Stewart's request raise the possibility that Scott might have expected the individual verses of his poem to have been separated from one another for distribution among Stewart's autograph-hunting female friends, they do seem to build towards a climax in the final couplet and in the event the letter was not cut up.

Stewart was an army officer from a well-known Perthshire Jacobite family and an outspoken critic of the Highland Clearances, which he viewed as an abnegation of the obligations of a Highland landlord and chieftain towards his tenants, an opinion permeating his *Sketches of the Character, Manners, and Present State of the Highlanders of Scotland* (1822). Founder in 1820 of the Celtic Society of Edinburgh, he had assisted Scott with arrangements for the visit of George IV to Edinburgh in 1822. Scott praised him in a letter to Lockhart of 14 July 1828 as 'a highlander of the old stamp' (*Letters*, 10.468). The melancholy tone of the third and the seventh couplets perhaps reflects that the separation was likely to be a final one, since the climate of St Lucia was notoriously unhealthy and Scott himself was suffering some of the infirmities of old age.

Explanatory Notes
284.3   Waverley   Scott's first novel, *Waverley*, published anonymously in 1814, portrays the Highland clans at the time of the Jacobite Rising of 1745: Scott's authorship had been publicly acknowledged as recently as February 1827. Scott's letter with his verses refers to Stewart's sending him, at the request of his friend Menzies of Pitfoddells, a manuscript by Menzies's Jacobite uncle, James Maxwell of Kirkconnell (1708–62), who was an eyewitness of many of the events of the events of 1744–46 concerning the Rising: see *Waverley*, ed. P. D. Garside, EEWN 1 (Edinburgh, 2007), 520 n9. This gift probably helped to bring the topic to the forefront of Scott's mind.
284.7   Trees did he plant   Scott's notebook for setting out his grounds at Abbotsford, 'Sylva Abbotsfordienses', has been transcribed by Gerrard Carruthers and Alison Lumsden, at http://www.advocates.org.uk/media/1606/sylvafinalrevisedtranscript-web-version-010512.pdf. The topic is also pursued at length in his article 'On Planting Waste Lands', *Quarterly Review*, 36 (October 1827), 558–600.
284.8   Darnick   a village immediately to the W of Melrose, in the vicinity of Scott's country estate of Abbotsford.
284.11   Highland Chiefs he had a vote   alluding to Scott's dealings with the chiefs of various Highland clans in preparation for the visit of George IV to Edinburgh in 1822. Stewart of Garth had served on Scott's committee to arrange the details, with particular responsibility to organise, muster and drill

bodies of Highlanders for performing in various public spectacles: see John Prebble, *The King's Jaunt* (London, 1988), 87.

284.13   greyhounds good   Scott kept greyhounds for hare-coursing for many years.

284.15   reck   take heed of, take thought for.

129.   Farewell Address for Mrs Siddons

Textual Note

Scott's lines were written for the actress Harriet Siddons (1783–1844) to speak at the Theatre Royal on 29 March 1830, at the conclusion of her final performance before her retirement from the Edinburgh stage, and they appear to have been composed not long before that event. Of the two surviving manuscripts in Scott's hand, the first appears to be a rough draft (NLS, MS 23049). This consists of a single leaf of paper measuring approx. 25.2 x 19.4 cm bearing part of a plumed shield device watermark. Scott has docketed it sideways after folding 'Mrs Siddons parting Address'. It includes a seven-line deleted passage in which Scott variously attempts to secure the sympathies of the Edinburgh theatre-goers for William Henry Murray (1790–1852), who was to continue running the Theatre Royal after his sister's retirement. The second manuscript in Scott's hand was clearly his fair copy since it forms part of his letter of 17 March 1830 sent from Abbotsford to Mrs Siddons in Edinburgh, directed to her Windsor Street address and duly postmarked. Scott, still recovering from his recent apoplectic seizure on 15 February, comments that the lines may 'smell of the apoplexy' and makes Mrs Siddons welcome to 'put them in the fire' rather than use them and to 'take your scissors at your discretion'. However, he also promises, 'I will attend to any criticism on the inclosed if there is time for it but I see by your announce that your time is but brief' (NLS, MS 9609, ff. 50–51).

There is apparently no surviving correspondence between Scott and Mrs Siddons between 17 and 29 March, nor any indication that the two met in person during that time. Scott remained at Abbotsford, apart from a brief visit to the Duke and Duchess of Buccleuch at Bowhill, while Mrs Siddons was almost certainly fixed in Edinburgh by a series of performances of her favourite theatrical roles from 20 March onwards that were intended to precede her farewell performance: see 'The Theatre—Mrs H. Siddons' in *The Scotsman* of 20 March 1830. In view of Scott's ill-health and the time-constraints involved it seems virtually certain that any changes for performance were made by Siddons herself or her theatrical advisors.

A version of the address was published in reports of Mrs Siddons's final performance in various contemporary papers, but this differs substantially from the text in Scott's letter of 17 March and probably represents the poem as altered at the theatre for performance. It appeared in papers such as *The Scotsman* (31 March) and *Edinburgh Literary Journal* (3 April), and subsequently in English papers also, such as the *Morning Post* (3 April) and *John Bull* (5 April). The text varies somewhat from paper to paper, but of the 42 lines of Scott's fair-copy manuscript only 26 survive in the version printed in *The Scotsman*, which is closest to Scott's manuscript. *The Scotsman* provides a text mixing Scott's material with new verse-lines, presumably interpolated by the theatre management: the first 16 lines agree with those in Scott's manuscript (with minor variations of wording), but are then succeeded by 16 new lines replacing lines 17–32 of Scott's poem, after which this text follows Scott's poem to its conclusion before adding a second new passage of eight closing lines. The nature of the new mate-

rial supports the idea that the changes were made at the theatre, for the replace-
ment passage of 16 lines substitutes for the pathetic allusion in Scott's poem to
the actress's widowhood an expression of how in future she will look back fondly
from her retirement in England to the years she has spent in Scotland, and the
additional closing passage restores the focus of the conclusion from Murray as
Siddons's successor to the moment of her speaking her Edinburgh farewell. Mrs
Siddons and her advisers probably did not consider Scott's poem ideally suited
to the occasion of her retirement from the Edinburgh stage, but were reluctant
to lose the prestige and publicity that would result from her speaking an original
address written for the occasion by Sir Walter Scott, who had in his accompany-
ing letter authorised her, after all, to 'take your scissors at your discretion'.

It is hardly surprising that Scott's retirement address for Mrs Siddons was
not included in the octavo *Poetical Works* of 1830, for less than a month elapsed
between the theatrical occasion and the London publication of this edition. Nor
was it included in the Lockhart 1833–34 posthumous edition.

The present text of the address follows that of Scott's letter to Mrs Siddons
of 17 March 1830 in NLS, MS 9609, ff. 50–51. There it is headed 'Epilogue'
to indicate that it was intended to be spoken at the end of the evening, but the
poem is not an epilogue to the play performed (*The Provoked Husband*), and in
the present text the title 'Farewell Address for Mrs Siddons' has been adopted
editorially. In addition to the following listed emendations, ampersands have
been routinely expanded to 'and', verb forms ending with 'd' to 'ed', routine
apostrophes have been introduced as required, as have full stops at the end of
verse paragraphs.

285.2	remains, (Editorial) / remains
285.10	Fare (Editorial) / fare
285.14	public life, (Editorial) / publick life
285.15	To hopes, to doubts, (Editorial) / To hopes to doubts
285.16	scenic (Editorial) / scenick
285.18	bloom, (Editorial) / bloom
285.20	eyes. (Editorial) / eyes
285.22	debt. (Editorial) / debt
285.26	gratitude? (Editorial) / gratitude.
285.27	soothers (Editorial) / Soothers
285.28	Despise (Editorial) / Depise
285.32	close: (Editorial) / close
285.34	ear? (Editorial) / ear
286.35	far, (Editorial) / far
286.35	patrons, (Editorial) / patrons
286.36	behind! (Editorial) / behind
286.38	origin, (Editorial) / origin
286.38	name. (Editorial) / name

Historical Note

After the death in April 1815 of Henry Siddons (1774–1815), the manager and
holder of the patent of Edinburgh's Theatre Royal, his widow continued with
the theatre, her brother, William Henry Murray, acting as manager on her
behalf. By the time the patent expired in 1830 Mrs Siddons had paid up the pur-
chase money and so became the owner of the theatre, but since her health had
been poor recently she decided to retire at this point, leaving the Theatre Royal
under her brother's management. Scott's letter to Mrs Siddons of 17 March
1830 indicates that she had communicated her plans to him and appealed to him

to write a theatrical address for her final Edinburgh performance: it seems pos-
sible that she intended to move to London, since in his letter Scott invited her
to visit Abbotsford on her way south afterwards.

Scott himself was far from well (see Textual Note above), but did his best
to oblige. He had previously written a farewell address for Harriet Siddons to
mark the end of her engagement in Dublin in 1821, which was never used (see
no. 111, 'For Mrs Siddons's Farewell to Dublin'), and clearly he reworked
the initial sentiments of this for her farewell address to the Edinburgh stage
in 1830, while naturally reflecting also on the history of their association. This
perhaps is what prompted his allusion to Mrs Siddons's anxious widowhood in
1815, although fifteen years later she was a secure and prosperous woman and
may well have considered these lines somewhat inappropriate to her current
situation.

Newspaper comment on the address generally noted Scott's authorship and
added a word of praise, although the *Edinburgh Literary Journal* of 3 April 1830
in its notice of 'The Drama' considered it 'fully as poor as such compositions
usually are', terming its reflections on the word farewell 'commonplace' and the
appeal to the public for continued support for her brother's management of the
theatre 'a puff collateral' that was 'in very bad taste' (207).

Explanatory Notes
285.24   Misery's hours of deprivation   Henry Siddons had died on 12
April 1815, leaving his affairs in an embarrassed condition. Murray stated
at the time that 'the management will begin in November next with a debt
of £3100', Siddons's private property having all been swallowed up by the
expenses of the theatre: see James C. Dibdin, *The Annals of the Edinburgh
Stage* (Edinburgh, 1888), 270.
285.29   warrant high is given   both Old and New Testaments urge care
and compassion for widows, and Job counts among the good deeds of his
prosperous days that he 'caused the widow's heart to sing for joy' (Job 29.13).
286.38   Scottish origin, a Scottish name   William Henry Murray's
grandfather was the Jacobite agent John Murray of Broughton (1714/15?–77),
who had been secretary to Charles Edward Stuart (1720–88) and was widely
regarded as a traitor for having betrayed his associates to the Hanoverian
authorities. His name was therefore a somewhat dubious recommendation to
an Edinburgh audience.

130.   Ettricke's Forest and Fountains

Textual Note
This poem, a tribute to the young bride of the Duke of Buccleuch, was almost
certainly written for her album during Scott's visit to Bowhill on 24 March
1830. Although end-dated 'Bowhill 24 february / 1830', it seems likely that
Scott, still suffering from the after-effects of a serious stroke on 15 February
(*Life*, 7.203–04), inadvertently wrote the previous month at the end of his
manuscript. Scott's manuscript is now in the Beinecke Library, Osborn MSS,
File 13273, and consists of a single leaf of unwatermarked paper measuring
approx. 23.7 x 17.4 cm. This is probably a leaf taken from an album, since
Scott's poem on the recto is followed by a poem in another hand on the verso
entitled 'Paraphrase of a passage in Corinne'. There are a few corrections, which
suggest that Scott may have been drafting directly into the album: 'were' in the
second line, for instance, has been inserted above the line, while in line 8 the

original 'set' has been deleted in favour of 'have set'. Scott also seems to have had trouble with the penultimate line, first of all writing 'Yet may whose' and then substituting 'But that' above the line.

The poem has never apparently been published. The present text follows that of Scott's manuscript in the Beinecke Library, Osborn MSS, File 13273. A title, taken from the wording of the first line, has been supplied editorially. In addition to the following listed emendations, verb forms ending with 'd' have been expanded to 'ed' and full stops inserted at the end of stanzas.

286.10	verse, gentle Lady, (Editorial) / verse gentle Lady
286.13	youth, (Editorial) / youth
286.17	affliction (Editorial) / afliction
286.20	worth. (Editorial) / worth,
287.end-date	March (Editorial) / february

Historical Note
Scott's two-day visit to the Buccleuch mansion of Bowhill near Selkirk in March 1830 must have seemed a happy omen that his longstanding ties with the Buccleuch family were to be continued into another generation in his old age. Walter, 5th Duke of Buccleuch (1806–84) had written to Scott on 28 July 1829 announcing his imminent marriage to Lady Charlotte Thynne (1811–95), the youngest daughter of the Marquess of Bath, and Scott replied on 31 July:

> I hope you will in an hour of influence bespeak a portion of her regard for the old man who held you in his arms at your christening and had the honour to be early protected by your excellent grandfather and to spend so much of his life (when it was in its better days) in the intimacy of your lamented parents (*Letters*, 11.221)

In his postscript Scott expressed his wish that the young couple should spend time at Bowhill as the place 'where your father and mother enjoyd some of their happiest days' and which he hoped might 'revive again in all its old honours' (222). He seems to have had to wait until the following spring before meeting the new Duchess, but he and his daughter Anne then dined and stayed overnight at Dalkeith Palace on 3 March 1830 (Johnson, 2.1125). Towards the end of the same month, on 22 March, the young couple paid a two-day visit to Abbotsford and Scott and Anne afterwards accompanied them to Bowhill for a further two days (*Letters*, 11.321).

Explanatory Notes
286.2 flowrets were weeded away recalling 'The flowers of the forest are a' wede away', a line from a popular song written to the traditional tune of 'The Flowers of the Forest', a lament for the men of Ettrick Forest killed at the Battle of Flodden in 1513 which is sometimes performed at funeral or memorial services in Scotland. One of the most popular sets of words to this traditional tune was written by Jean Elliot (1727–1805), as included by Scott in *Minstrelsy*, 1.274–78. In his headnote there Scott states that the line alluded to in the present poem is ancient.
286.3 Day Spring daybreak, particularly in the metaphorical sense of a new dawn, as in Luke 1.78, 'the dayspring from on high hath visited us'.
286.8 those that have set an allusion to the death of the Duke's parents, Charles, 4th Duke of Buccleuch (1772–1819) and his wife Harriet (1773–1814).
286.16 desire to be pleased and to please Scott described the new Duchess in a letter to his son Charles of 1 April 1830 as 'extremely amiable

and shews an anxious wish to please and to be pleased which seldom fails to be gratified' (*Letters*, 11.321).

286.18 true to the North   the Duchess was English by birth, but by her marriage Scott counts her a Scot.

286.20 object of spirit and worth   the young Duke of Buccleuch. Scott had written of him to Lady Louisa Stuart on 21 February 1825 'The little Buccleuch turns out a goodly youth with fine points of sense and generosity about him' (*Letters*, 9.13).

131.   Inscription for the Monument

Textual Note
The original manuscript for this epitaph survives in the National Records of Scotland [NRS], GD157/2012/26/1, accompanied by two separate letters to Mrs Harriet Scott of Harden (1773–1853) concerning the early death of her son George. Headed 'Inscription', it is written on black-bordered mourning paper, measuring approx. 22.4 x 18.2 cm, and with the watermark 'J GREEN & SON / 1828'. The text contains two alterations made by Scott in the course of composition, with 'flattering' replacing a repetitive 'opening' at line 7, and 'murmuring' being substituted for 'sorrowing' in the penultimate line. There is only minimum punctuation, a deficiency which in a short undated note beneath the poem Scott offers to supply through his printer James Ballantyne:

> You will readily believe Madam that in a case in which I am sincerely and affectionately interested the inclosed are the best verses that have occurd to me. They do not please me but I have not been able to substitute any thing better Should you think of having them used I will cause them to be *set up* as it is calld & pointed by my printer & sent [*sic*] you one or two copies I dont understand punctuation perfectly

Another manuscript version, now held in NLS, MS 894, f. 59, is in the hand of Mrs Scott of Harden, and was enclosed by her in lieu of returning Scott's own holograph verses in a letter of November 1830: 'I send you a copy of them which I hope will equally do for you to send to the Printer & if you have some Printed copies struck off I shall be very glad to have some for all those nearest & dearest to our departed angel & for a few friends who really knew him' (NLS, MS 3915, f. 118r). This transcript successfully replicates Scott's final wording, apart from the representation in the penultimate line of 'murmuring' as 'mourning', presumably as a result of misreading. In his reply to this letter, Scott promises that when the lines are 'thrown off I will send you all that are of them except a copy for myself' (NRS, GD157/2012/27). No printed copies of the verses in this form have been discovered.

The inscription first appeared publicly, under its present title, in the Lockhart posthumous collected edition of 1833–34 (11.376), along with the following footnote: 'This young gentleman, a son of the Author's friend and relation, Hugh Scott of Harden, Esq., became Rector of Kentisbeare, in Devonshire, in 1828, and died there the 9th June, 1830. This epitaph appears on his tomb in the chancel there.' No mention is made here of a source for the text, though most probably it would have been one of the original privately printed copies, possibly as made available to Lockhart by Mrs Scott of Harden, and from which the punctuation in the Lockhart edition is then likely to have at least partly derived. In its wording the text matches that found in Mrs Scott's transcript of Scott's manuscript, apart from 'mourning' in line 9, which has been transferred to 'sorrowing' (a word rejected earlier by Scott) apparently in an effort to improve scansion.

The present text is based on that in the 1833–34 Lockhart edition, 11.376, representing the first known surviving printing, and whose fuller descriptive title is adopted. The following emendation, restoring Scott's final choice in his manuscript, has also been made:

287.9   murmuring (NRS MS) / sorrowing

Historical Note

The Rev. George William Scott (1804–30) was the fourth son of Hugh and Harriet Scott of Harden, the present heads of a branch of the Scott clan with which Scott claimed kinship; and, at Mertoun House near St Boswells, close neighbours with whom he had personally enjoyed friendship over several decades. Scott first heard the news of the death through a letter of 11 June 1830 from George's brother Henry reporting 'your old favourite George has been carried off by a severe typhous fever' (NLS, MS 3913, f. 178r). Scott's personal sadness is reflected in a *Journal* entry of 15 June: 'Poor George Scott Harden is dead of the typhous fever. Poor dear boy! I am sorry for him and yet more for his parents' (597). According to another *Journal* entry of 25 October 1827, the seriousness of purpose which had led to George's early incumbency as an Anglican rector at Kentisbeare, some 25 km (16 miles) NE of Exeter, coexisted with a more adventurous nature: 'We arrived at Mertoun yesterday and heard with some surprize that George had gone up in an Air balloon and ascended two miles and a half above this sublunary earth. ... Honest George, I certainly did not suspect him of being so flighty' (368).

The request that Scott compose an inscription was first made by Harriet Scott in a letter of 19 September 1830: 'I enclose to you what we intend to have engraved on a Tablet in the Church at Kentisbeare ... It would be a great satisfaction to us if you would write a few lines, to be engraved below the enclosed inscription, merely expressive of your own kind feeling as a friend and a relation' (NLS, MS 3914, f. 49). In a reply of 26 September Scott graciously accepted the task as one close to his heart: 'I cannot be at all sure that I shall be in the least successful on the subject you mention but I will attempt that subject with deep feeling on my own part and a sympathy with your sorrows and will send you the scroll in the course of a few days' (NRS, GD157/2012/25). Scott, however, makes no mention of a request also made by Mrs Scott in her letter that 'your name may be also engraved below your lines' (NLS, MS 3914, f. 49v). In the actual marble monument on the south chancel wall in Kentisbeare church, Scott's inscription is placed on a scroll hanging over a stone coffin, as revealed by a naked cherub figure. In a letter to Lockhart of 6 October 1832, in which she mentions [John Edward] Carew (*c*. 1782–1868) as the sculptor, Mrs Scott seems convinced that this represents Scott's 'Last Poetical Lines' (NLS, MS 1554, f. 60v), though such is not the case.

Explanatory Notes

287.9   murmuring thought   in the Bible *murmuring* often denotes a faithless questioning of God's purpose (see, for example, Psalm 106.25).

132.   Fantastic Maid

Textual Note

The manuscript containing this verse is presently found in a brown envelope at Abbotsford, inscribed 'Sir Walter Scott / 7 Autograph Poems': the remainder of a larger collection, some of whose contents were dispersed by Major-General Walter Maxwell-Scott in 1946. Consisting of a single leaf, approx. 22.5 x 18.5 cm, without a visible watermark, it contains 17 lines on the recto, and a further three overleaf. 'No. XIII' has also been written apparently in another hand down the side of the verso. The text is extremely hard to decipher, and a typewritten transcript in the same envelope (also copied at NLS, MS 3581, f. 123) leaves a number of gaps. The three lines on the verso seem particularly fragmentary and resistant to interpretation, and it is by no means clear whether these represent a continuation of the recto text or independent jottings:

> Since this old last[?] was new
> A hundred herad[?] years or more
> And made a circle round the glebe

However, the preceding text has more the air of a sustained flow of composition, and arguably becomes clearer in the form of two distinct octets if the twelfth line there ('Which <sad> bad my fancy') is seen as partly representing a false start:

> Fanticke Maid whos step from dewy morn
> Till Evenings sober shad<of> I oft have traced
> And evry shadowy change obscurely scene
> Grow fresher wilder in thy by the slipper traced
> And can it be and must I say farewell
> Because adancine time hath markd with gray
> The hair<t> which once was tinged with youthful brown
> <Gave> While pale Decmber fogs the bloom of May
> It will not Aid the fairy tinge is gone
> That painted oer each scene with fancies new
> Far oer my aged head the glance is flown
> Which <sad> bad my fancy
> Reality assume Romance's tone
> Oft have I thought amid thy wandering train
> O things that ownd their beings to our selves
> Entangled in the mesh we wove ourselves
> that thou<gh> and eye were lik the nettn brd

The presence of several characteristics of Scott's late hand—including homophones as well as a more general kind of scriptorial stuttering—also makes it possible to conjecture more confidently here his original intentions.

The present text, based on the Abbotsford manuscript, through such means attempts to reconstitute two stanzas of what was probably embarked on as a somewhat larger piece, and which arguably shows signs of already losing momentum in its last full lines. The title is provided editorially from the first line. In addition to a number of conjectural verbal emendations, which can be traced through comparison with the above transcript, the following punctuation has been provided to facilitate reading:

288.4   fresher, (Editorial) / fresher
288.4   traced. (Editorial) / traced
288.8   May? (Editorial) / May
288.9   aid, (Editorial) / Aid
288.12   tone. (Editorial) / tone
288.16   bird. (Editorial) / brd

Historical Note
No information about the possible circumstances underlying these verses has been discovered. The preoccupation with age and loss, combined with bursts of vivid recollection, places them close to some of his very last poems, such as 'Verses Written at the Request of the Countess Wolkonsky' (no. 134). Thematically there is also a similarity to his 'Farewell to the Muse' (no. 103), written in 1818 but at a time of grave illness and expressing uncertainty about the continuation of his poetical powers. While such might lead one to interpret the Maid of the present fragment as Scott's Muse, it is tempting as well to associate the long-standing relationship figured there with Scott's wife, Charlotte, and more particularly with his grief at her death in May 1826, as so poignantly recorded in the *Journal*: 'that yellow masque with pinchd features which seems to mock life rather than emulate it, can it be the face that was once so full of lively expression?' (145). If this is the case, then such an unusually private dimension might help explain both the apparent non-completion of the piece and its remaining at Abbotsford so long.

Explanatory Notes
288.12   Reality assume Romance's tone   reversing the situation as enunciated in John Logan's 'On the Death of a Young Lady' ('The wild romance of life is done; / The real history is begun'), printed in *English Minstrelsy*, ed. Scott, 2 vols (Edinburgh, 1810), 1.184–88. Compare *Waverley*, ed. P. D. Garside, EEWN 1 (Edinburgh, 2007), 606, note to 301.29–30.
288.16   netted bird   compare Psalm 124.7: 'Our soul is escaped as a bird out of the snare of the fowlers'.

133.   Lines Written in Dora Wordsworth's Album

Textual Note
This poem was written by Scott into an album kept by Dora (1804–47), William Wordsworth's daughter, during a visit paid by the pair to Abbotsford in early autumn 1831, immediately before Scott headed south to begin his excursion to Malta and Naples in an effort to restore his failing health. Now preserved by the Wordsworth Trust at Grasmere (DCMS 122), and containing verse and drawings by various contemporaries between 1830 and 1850, the album consists of 88 unnumbered leaves measuring approx. 12.5 x 11.5 cm and is bound in green tooled morocco leather. Scott's poem, end-dated 'Abbotsford/22 September 1831', is found on the recto of leaf 20, with a transcription and brief note in another hand concerning the underlying circumstances of the composition on the facing verso. The original text contains two small areas of deletion, indicating that Scott was at least partly in the process of composition as he wrote. It also lacks a concluding word after 'idle' in line 8, and the final line includes the misspelling 'Gorious'. On the following leaf (21r) there is a transcript of Wordsworth's sonnet 'On Sir Walter Scott's quitting Abbotsford for Naples', dated 1831, possibly as dictated by Wordsworth to Dora and with his end-signature.
     Another apparent holograph version of the poem, pasted into an album of autographs located at Belton House (National Trust, 47.D.3, p. 63), has been identified as a facsimile. The first known printings are found in *A Selection from the Works of Sir Walter Scott, Bart.*, ed. Mortimer Collins (London, 1866), 255–56, and Charles Wordsworth's *Annals of My Early Life* (London, 1891), 114, both of which add punctuation and normalise spelling. A photograph and

transcription of the verses appear in *Dora Wordsworth: Her Book*, ed. F. V. Morley (London, 1924), 78–79.

The present text is based on the original manuscript, from Dora Wordsworth's album, at the Wordsworth Trust, Grasmere, DCMS 122.item 19. Full stops are added at the end of each stanza, and Scott's initial capital letters have been retained. The title is supplied editorially. The following emendations have also been made:

288.5   hint, (Editorial) / hint
288.7   turns, (Editorial) / turns
288.8   idle dream (Editorial) / idle
289.10   deafened (Editorial) / deafend
289.12   seem doomed (Editorial) / seemd doom
289.16   thou Glorious (Editorial) / though Gorious

Historical Note
The Wordsworths' visit to Abbotsford, which took place between 19 and 22 September 1831, proved to be the last in a series of exchanges which had commenced with the arrival of William and his sister Dorothy Wordsworth at Lasswade in 1803, followed by Scott's visit with his wife to Dove Cottage at Grasmere in 1805 (for the latter see Historical Note to no. 55, 'Hellvellyn'). On Tuesday, 20 September 1831 Scott had accompanied his guests to Newark Castle in Yarrow, an event memorialised in Wordsworth's poem 'Yarrow Revisited'. According to Wordsworth's later notes to that poem, as dictated to his friend Isabella Fenwick in 1843, it was early on the morning of their departure on 22 September that Scott's own poetical intervention took place:

> At noon on Thursday we left Abbotsford & in the morng. of that day Sir W. & I had a serious conversation tête-à-tête when he spoke with gratitude of the happy life which upon the whole he had led. He had written in my daughter's Album, before he came into the breakfast room that morning, a few Stanzas addressed to her & while putting the book into her hand, in his own Study standing by his desk, he said to her in my presence, 'I should not have done any thing of this kind but for your Father's sake; they are probably the last verses I shall ever write'. (*The Fenwick Notes of William Wordsworth*, ed. Jared Curtis (London, 1993), 51)

The occasion is also recorded by Scott in his Journal, in a retrospective passage written after his arrival in London: 'Wordsworth and his daughter, a fine girl, were with us on the last day. I tried to write in her Diary and made an ill favourd botch' (*Journal*, 661). Wordsworth in his longer account similarly comments on Scott's current difficulties in expression as evidenced in the verses: 'They shew how much his mind was impaired not by the strain of thought but by the execution, some of the lines being imperfect, & one Stanza wanting corresponding rhymes. One letter, the initial S, had been omitted in the spelling of his own name' (*Fenwick Notes*, 51). In fact, in the manuscript a long-tailed 's' before Scott's surname is clearly apparent, though there is some possibility that this might have been added by another hand later. This Wordsworthian testimony nevertheless helped propagate a notion of the deleterious effects of Scott's illness in this supposedly last effort, as found most notably in Matthew Arnold's 1855 poem 'Haworth Churchyard': 'chief glory of all, / Scott had bestowed there his last / Breathings of song, with a pen / Tottering, a death-stricken hand'.

While the manuscript bears several marks of Scott's stuttering hand at this time, the poem itself has a tightly organised structure, and is responsive both to the immediate situation and Scott's longer term friendship with Wordsworth. Its first stanza evidently refers to the earlier imaginative relationship between the two, and Scott's present reduced creative capacities. The second addresses Dora, then in her mid-twenties and as yet unmarried, offering a somewhat sombre warning about life's uncertainties. The final two stanzas concern the current political situation, where Scott and Wordsworth shared similarly pessimistic views about the movement for Reform. In March 1831, Scott had been hissed by a crowd in Jedburgh as he attempted a valedictory political speech warning about the inherent dangers to social stability. Since then the Whig reformers had gained a parliamentary majority, and on 21 September 1831 (just one day prior to Scott's writing of the poem) a Second Reform Bill was approved in the House of Commons.

Explanatory Notes

288.1 gifted eye as used elsewhere by Scott in referring to the visionary capacities of the Seer: compare no. 33, 'Glenfinlas' ('No more is given to gifted eye!': line 124), and no. 84, 'The Dance of Death' ('But the seer's gifted eye was dim': line 145). In this case Scott is apparently referring to Wordsworth's imaginative qualities when the poets first met.

288.6 vain is worldly esteem echoing the title and theme of Samuel Johnson's poem *The Vanity of Human Wishes* (1749), a favourite poem of Scott's. Scansion is arguably improved if allowance is made for Scott's 'Berwickshire *burr*' (see *Letters*, 7.63), which would have led to a pronunciation more like 'waraldly esteem'.

289.10 palsied hand between February 1830 and April 1831 Scott had suffered three strokes. Writing to William Rowan Harrison on 27 October 1831, Wordsworth reports how 'I found him a great deal changed within the last three or four years, in consequence of some Shocks of the apoplectic kind; but his friends say that he is very much better': Juliet Barker, *Wordsworth: A Life in Letters* (London, 2003), 214. Dora in a letter to her friend Maria Jane Dewsbury noted a 'melancholy' in Scott's disposition, though adding that she had heard 'he was much better both in health & spirits' since arriving in London: *Letters of Dora Wordsworth*, ed. Howard P. Vincent (Chicago, 1944), 91.

134. Verses Written at the Request of the Countess Wolkonsky

Textual Note

According to Edgar Johnson, this item was composed in Naples early in 1832 at the request of 'A Russian lady, possibly the Countess Wolkonsky': 'She pleaded for a piece of verse from him; Scott found it hard to resist a pretty woman's coaxing and promised that he would try. A little later he did begin some irregular stanzas, but the only copy preserved among his papers breaks off after twenty-two lines' (Johnson, 2.1233). These verses (as then quoted by Johnson) consequently postdate Scott's contribution to Dora Wordsworth's Album (see no. 133), written shortly before leaving Abbotsford for his Mediterranean trip, and traditionally considered to represent his last poetical attempt. Johnson, however, is wrong in suggesting that there is only one manuscript; in fact, there is evidence of at least three surviving autograph versions, each representing a distinct phase in development. These (in probable order of development) are as follows:

i) *NLS, MS 877, ff. 203–04.* This consists of two conjugate leaves, measuring approx. 24.8 x 20 cm, with the watermark 'J WHATMAN / 1830'. Headed in Scott's hand 'Lines writ / To the Countess of Wollenluss[?] / at / her request', the text consists of some 30 lines, containing multiple alterations, and with Scott striking out with two downward strokes five lines of an attempted conclusion followed by his end-signature (also deleted). These are followed by a few patchy additional lines, which can be found more fully worked up elsewhere, encouraging the view that this represents the earliest remaining draft. The presence of this MS as part of the Abbotsford Collection in the NLS suggests that it was among papers returning along with Scott to Abbotsford.

ii) *NLS, MS 2208, f. 41.* Consisting of a single leaf, approx. 24.8 x 19 cm, with the watermark 'J WHATMAN', and apparently on similar paper to the above. Headed 'verses / Written/ by [*sic*] / The Countess of Wollenluss[?] / Reques [*sic*] a Russian Lady' in Scott's hand, this contains the text used by Edgar Johnson (see above). According to James B. Kerr, 'On supposed Unpublished Verses by Sir Walter Scott', in *History of the Berwickshire Naturalists' Club*, 9: 1 (1879), 171–75, it originally formed part of a small collection of Scott-related documents possessed by John Nicholson (1802–40), Scott's valet, which had come to Kerr via Nicholson's niece in 1878. Nicholson had arrived in Naples as Scott's servant along with Walter junior and Anne Scott in December 1831: see William Gell, *Reminiscences of Sir Walter Scott's Residence in Italy, 1832*, ed. James C. Corson (London, 1957), xv. The text here is relatively clean, and notably ends with a solitary 'And' on its final line, to which Johnson editorially adds a long dash. Johnson's transcription also misreads a number of individual words, as well as conflating the final two of three distinct stanzas. This MS was once owned by the Society of Antiquaries of Scotland, before coming into the custody of the NLS.

iii) *The Times, Friday, 19 August 1932, 13–14.* In an article headed 'The Last Verses of Walter Scott', Philippa (wife of Major-General Frank Russell), daughter of Henry James Baillie (1803–85), recounts how her father had rooms in the Palazzo Caramanico, in Naples, at the same time that Scott was lodged there, and how on 'the evening of April 14' the 'Countess Wallendoff [*sic*], a Russian lady' had been 'persistent in begging Scott to write some lines for her album'. Scott had duly supplied the lines, only to be informed by his daughter Anne that the Countess had departed from Naples that same morning, with Baillie as a result being left with them prior to Scott embarking on his homeward journey. The article then gives a transcript of the verses, comprising 27 lines, this being accompanied by a photograph of the manuscript, with the title 'Verses written to the Countess of Wollenluss[?] / a Russian Lady', but showing only the first sixteen lines. In this version, according to the transcript text, Scott can be seen providing a kind of resolution with a new concluding stanza:

> The genial breath of waking day
>   Wakes the chill limbs and torpid hand;
> And the Poor Bard attempts to show
>   What sparks remain in Life's decay.
> Fashion, fair Dame, at thy command
>   A sample [of] my earlier hand.

Mrs Russell goes on to say how Lockhart had tried to procure the verses for his biography, but that her father had then been travelling in the East. Baillie's earlier proximity to Scott in Naples is supported by an anecdote in Gell's *Reminiscences*, ed. Corson, 6, 43n18. He also features as part of the circle surrounding Scott and as a suitable match for Anne Scott in *Life in the South: The Naples Journal of Marianne Talbot 1829–32*, ed. Michael Heafford (Cambridge, 2012), 153n, 169, 170. In advancing elements first found in item ii), and in providing a conclusion where that had broken off, there are indications that this represents the last in the sequence. However, the part of the MS reproduced in the newspaper article shows a number of alterations, untypical of a presentation copy, and it seems slightly odd that Scott should title the piece as to 'a Russian Lady' if formally directed to her. Comparison between the transcript in the article and that part of the MS reproduced in the photograph reveals a number of misreadings in the former, in turn casting doubt on the reliability of the remaining transcript, which as a whole imposes its own system of punctuation. The present whereabouts of this MS has not been discovered.

Seen together, the MS record presents a number of difficulties. The first item (for reasons suggested) is the most obvious draft, albeit offering valuable information about the poem's genesis. The faltering end of item ii) might also seem to indicate an uncompleted draft, though it could also be claimed that the poem as found there has a kind of inner integrity, offering a particularly poignant expression of Scott's crippling inability to fulfil moments of creative desire. The third item, while in a sense providing the obligatory ending, still fails to achieve this with any air of finality, and it is not impossible that one further version was prepared for and even received by its addressee. Another difficulty in the case of item iii) is the uneven surviving textual record, as detailed above.

In response, the present edition provides a text based on NLS, MS 2208, f. 41 (see item ii above), where the manuscript evidence is complete, and the verses arguably at their most cohesive. The title, incorporating main elements of Scott's own while correcting the spelling of the addressee's name, is supplied editorially. Verb forms ending with a shortening 'd' have been normalised as 'ed', one ampersand expanded, apostrophes supplied as conventionally required, and full stops added at the end of the first two stanzas. In addition the following emendations have been made:

289.6	Grow feeble mid (MS item (iii): see above) / Decay in the
289.7	Until (Editorial) / Untill
289.9	Text— (Editorial) / Text
289.10	briars, (Editorial) / briars
289.11	Wolkonsky (Editorial) / Wollenluss[?]
289.12	thorn? (Editorial) / thorn
289.14	new (Editorial) / now[?]
	MS may also possibly read 'new'.
290.18	April wears (Editorial) / april wear
290.21	blood (Editorial) / bloon[?]

Historical Note
The intended addressee of these verses can be identified with some certainty as Princess Zinaida Aleksandrovna Volkonskaya [Зинаида Александровна Волконская] (1789–1862), also represented in English as Princess Zenaide Wolkonsky, who had married Prince Nikita Wolkonsky (1781–1844), an aide-de-camp to Czar Alexander I, in 1810. She had settled in Rome in 1829, where her singing, acting, and conversational skills led to her becoming a popular hostess: see Raymond Lamont-Brown, '"Countess Wollenluss" and Scott's "Last Verses"', *Scott Newsletter*, no. 27 (Summer 1995), 6–12; and Maria Fairweather, *The Pilgrim Princess. A Life of Zinaida Volkonsky* (London, 1999), xv–xix and passim. Her presence in Naples at a ball given by the Austrian Minister early in December 1831 was noted by Marianne Talbot, shortly before Scott settled in lodgings there later that month having arrived from Malta: see *Life in the South*, ed. Heafford, 145–47. If Scott indeed wrote the poem in Naples, then composition must have taken place before he departed for Rome on 16 April 1832. Scott's

apparent uncertainty over the spelling of his addressee's name, which may have resulted from his only having heard it pronounced rather than written, certainly seems to suggest an early or fleeting rather than full acquaintance. On the other hand, an incident in Gell's *Reminiscences of Sir Walter Scott's Residence in Italy* (repeated in Lockhart), which may refer to the requested verses, is firmly placed in Rome, from where Scott eventually departed for home on 11 May 1832:

> At Rome ... [a] lady requested him to do something which was very disagreeable to him. He was asked whether he had consented. He replied, 'Yes'. He was then questioned why he had agreed to do what was so inconvenient to him. 'Why', said he, 'I thought it was goodnatured to do it, so as I am now good for nothing else, I thought it as well to be goodnatured, as she seemed anxious about it.' (28; compare *Life*, 7.367–68)

According to an additional note supplied by a correspondent in James B. Kerr's article (cited in the Textual Note), the grounds at Villa Wolkonsky (later used as the residence of the British ambassador) contained an upright stone in Scott's memory, with an inscription in French (174). Whatever their precise origin, Scott's verses poignantly reflect his situation while in Italy, lionised as a Scottish and international celebrity, eager to participate in a culturally vibrant setting, but debilitated as a result of a succession of strokes which made even the physical act of writing challenging.

Explanatory Notes
289.9   so says the Text   compare Matthew 7.16: 'Do men gather grapes of thorns, or figs of thistles?'
289.15   shades upon the Dial   probably alluding to the sun-dial, in 2 Kings 20.10–11 and Isaiah 38.8, where the dying Hezekiah is spared by God in response to the prophet Isaiah's prayers. God agrees to give him a sign of recovery and the prophet asks whether he would prefer the shadow on the sun dial to be moved forward ten degrees or backward ten degrees, with Hezekiah choosing backwards on the grounds that it is relatively easy to move the shadow forwards but virtually impossible to move time back. Compare Scott's letter to J. G. Lockhart from Naples end-dated 1 March 1832: 'I could not expect the shadow to go backward on the Dial and if I get no better I must be contented with getting no worse' (NLS, MS 1752, f. 537).

APPENDIX:
SUPPOSITIOUS AND DOUBTFUL WORKS

Several poems previously attributed to or otherwise associated with Scott have been excluded from the present volume, because research has enabled the editors to demonstrate that they are the work of another author or were published before Scott's time. These poems are listed in Part A of this Appendix.

A further group of poems previously attributed to Scott has been excluded from the present volume, because research has not provided the present editors with sufficient evidence to decide in favour of Scott's authorship and thus attribution to him remains doubtful. These poems are listed in Part B of this Appendix.

Poems are given in alphabetical order by title supplemented by first words in brackets (or by first words alone where no title is given). In each case the source or reference(s) which apparently gave rise to the attribution to Scott is listed, followed by information concerning an alternative attribution (where discovered) and/or other reasons for not accepting Scott's authorship. The abbreviations used for the Combined Editorial Notes of the present volume are also employed here.

PART A.   POEMS OTHERWISE IDENTIFIED

A: 1
Addition to 'Auld Robin Gray' [Nae langer she wept, her tears were a' spent]. 4 lines (single stanza).

> Printed as by Scott in George Thomson, *The Select Melodies of Scotland*, 5 vols (Edinburgh, 1822–23), 3.item 33, as 'Added by the Author of Waverley', probably following its use as a motto to Vol. 2, Ch. 14 of *The Pirate*, published in December 1821, and described there as from a '*Continuation of Auld Robin Gray*' (see ed. Mark Weinstein and Alison Lumsden, EEWN 12, 245). Also implicitly attributed to Scott in T&B, no. 180A.
> Scott himself printed these lines as the second stanza of Lady Anne Barnard's own continuation in his Bannatyne Club printing of *Auld Robin Gray: A Ballad* (Edinburgh, 1825), 11. In his letter to her of 14 July 1823 he says that he had heard seven or eight verses of the continuation many

years previously from his relation Christian Rutherford, who herself had
no doubt of Lady Anne's authorship (*Letters*, 8.39).

Rejected as work of Lady Anne Barnard (formerly Lindsay).

A: 2

Bridal Song [And did you not hear of a mirth befel]. 28 lines
(7 x 4-line stanzas).

Joseph Strutt, *Queenhoo-Hall, A Romance*, 4 vols (Edinburgh and
London, 1808), 4.76–77. Scott completed this work for publication in
1808: see Notes to no. 64, 'Hunting Song'. Reprinted in Appendix 2,
'General Preface' (1829) to The Magnum Opus edn of the *Waverley
Novels* (*Introductions and Notes from the Magnus Opus: Waverley to A
Legend of Montrose*, ed. J. H. Alexander with P. D. Garside and Claire
Lamont, EEWN 25a, 45–46).
Attributed to Scott: Ruff, no. 77, T&B, no. 32Aa; also EEWN 25a, 410,
note to 45.13–46.12 (as 'probably Scott's own composition').
Actually from 'The Famous Historie of Fryer Bacon' (*c*. 1555): reprinted
in *A Collection of Early Prose Romances*, ed. William J. Thoms, 3 vols
(London, 1828), 1.51 (*ALC*).

Rejected due to provenance earlier than Scott's writing career.

A: 3

[For her love in sleep I slake]. 9 lines (single stanza).

Included as an extract among the poems Scott sent to 'Jessie' in NAL,
MS 470, Vol. 1, f. 73; and reprinted from there in *New Love-Poems by Sir
Walter Scott*, ed. Davidson Cook (Oxford, 1932), 23.
Old spelling text (as 'V. A Love Song') in Joseph Ritson, *Ancient Songs,
from the Time of King Henry the Third, to the Revolution* (London, 1790),
26–29. Ritson includes this in 'Class I. Comprehending the Reigns of
Henry IIII. Edward I. Edward II. Edward III. and Richard II.', and as
originating in Harley MS 2253. Scott's modernised version comprises
lines 80-83, 1–3, with repeated refrain and slightly different layout.

Rejected due to provenance earlier than Scott's writing career.

A: 4

King Gathol's Chair [Dead were this spirit, by my fay]. 86 lines
(6 verse paragraphs).

Printed in *Fraser's Magazine*, 4 (October 1831), 376–77, as 'by Sir Walter
Scott'.
Confirmed as Scott's in T&B, no. 251A. Part of a typical Fraserian spoof,
with Oliver Yorke, the supposed editor of the magazine, appealing to
a range of contemporary poets for a poem to commemorate the recent
coronation of William IV and supposedly receiving in return a letter and
poem from each in characteristic style: see 'Coronation Coronal', *Fraser's
Magazine*, 4 (October 1831), 375–86. The poem purportedly by Scott
includes passages such as 'Oh for a cataract of verse! / The wondrous
history to rehearse / Of England's regal chair' (377).

Rejected as a parody of Scott.

A: 5
Lines on Lady Cochrane [I knew thee Lady by that glorious eye]. 36 lines (6 x 6-line stanzas).

Manuscript in another hand in NRS, GD233/43/14/9/2, with initials of 'W. S.' at the foot of the poem, and with an accompanying envelope on which is written in pencil, 'W Scott / Lines on Lady Cochrane / In 1825—'. The heading to this transcript reads 'From the Morning Post of Wednesday / 19 October 1825', but the MS itself must be of a later date since the paper bears a watermark 'J WHATMAN / 1842'.

The named source in the *Morning Post* of 19 October 1825 has the initials 'H. G. B.' at the end, probably signifying Henry Glassford Bell (1803–74).

Rejected as the work of H. G. B., the commonly-used signature of Henry Glassford Bell.

A: 6
Lines on the Death of Lord Byron [He's gone,—the glorious spirit's fled]. 48 lines (6 x 8-line stanzas).

Attribution to Scott in two manuscripts, neither of them authorial: NRS, GD157/2013 and Nottingham University Library, MY 1760/1. NRS transcription is headed 'Lines on the Death of Ld Biron [*sic*] by Sir W. S.'. Nottingham transcription (on paper having an 1824 watermark) is followed by a 'Parody on Sir W Scotts "Lines on the Death of Byron"' (My 1760/2).

Published as the final item in a poetry collection by John Malcolm (*c*. 1795–1835), *The Buccaneer, and Other Poems* (Edinburgh, 1824), 200–02, and often reprinted as Malcolm's work.

Rejected as the work of John Malcolm.

A: 7
[Sir Hilary fought at Agincourt]. 14 lines (2 x 7-line stanzas).

Printed as by Scott in W. M. Parker, 'Sir Walter Scott: Thirteen New Poems', *Poetry Review*, 40: 4 (August–September 1949), 263–75 (p. 271). Parker introduces it as a charade quoted as 'said to be "by my father"' in a letter from Scott's son, Walter, of 3 January 1839, to his younger brother Charles.

Appeared as by 'Vyvyan Joyeuse' in *Knight's Quarterly Magazine*, 2 (January–April 1824), 469. This was a pseudonym of Winthrop Mackworth Praed (1802–39), and the verses were subsequently included in *The Poems of Winthrop Mackworth Praed*, 2 vols (London, 1864), 2.[387].

Rejected as the work of Winthrop Mackworth Praed.

A: 8
Song on an Inconstant Mistress [Some time I loved as you might see]. 45 lines (9 x 4-line stanzas with refrain).

Included among the poems Scott sent to 'Jessie' in NAL, MS 470, Vol. 1, ff. 74–75; and reprinted from there in *New Love-Poems by Sir Walter Scott*, ed. Davidson Cook (Oxford, 1932), 24–25.

Old spelling text (as 'VI. A Song on an Inconstant Mistress') in Joseph
Ritson, *Ancient Songs, from the Time of King Henry the Third, to the
Revolution* (London, 1790), 72–74. Ritson includes this in 'Class II.
Comprehending the Reigns of Henry IV. Henry V. and Henry VI.', and
as 'From MSS More. Ff. I. 6'.

Rejected due to provenance earlier than Scott's writing career.

A: 9

[Thus bold, thus great, and all in the extreme]. 14 lines (couplets).

Printed from an unspecified MS in Scott's hand in W. M. Parker, 'Sir
Walter Scott: Thirteen New Poems', *Poetry Review*, 40: 4 (August–
September 1949), 263–75 (pp. 274–75).

Matches lines 66–79 of 'A Panegyrick on the Author of *Absolom and
Achitophel*' (1699), by the political writer William Pittis (1673/74–1724).

Rejected as the work of William Pittis.

A: 10

Tod, The [Eh quo the Tod it's a braw light night]. 20 lines
(5 x 4-line stanzas).

Manuscript among the papers of William Scott, 6th Laird of Raeburn
(1773–1855). Not in Scott's hand, but with 'Eh quo' the Tod / Sir
Walter Scott' written on the verso of the leaf (NLS, MS 2890, f. 221).

Printed as Scott's own version in W. M. Parker, 'Sir Walter Scott:
Thirteen New Poems', *Poetry Review*, 40: 4 (August–September 1949),
263–75 (pp. 264–65).

Scott in a letter to Lady Ann Barnard, 14 July 1823 (*Letters*, 8.38), cites
the opening two lines as from one of the songs of 'Soph Johnstone', that
is Sophia Johnston (1716–1810), daughter of Robert Johnston of Hilton,
Berwickshire.

**Rejected as primarily by Sophia Johnston, though the final
stanza (referring to 'Raeburn's Yetts') may have been specially
adapted by Scott.**

A: 11

[When the nightingale sings the woods waxen green]. 4 lines
(single stanza).

Included as an extract among the poems Scott sent to 'Jessie' in NAL,
MS 470, Vol. 1, f. 73; and reprinted from there in *New Love-Poems by Sir
Walter Scott*, ed. Davidson Cook (Oxford, 1932), 23.

Old spelling text (as 'VI. A Song on his Mistress') in Joseph Ritson,
Ancient Songs, From the Time of King Henry the Third, to the Revolution
(London, 1790), 30 (lines 1–4). Ritson includes this in 'Class I.
Comprehending the Reigns of Henry IIII. Edward I. Edward II. Edward
III. and Richard II.', and as originating in Harley MS 2253.

Rejected due to provenance earlier than Scott's writing career.

PART B. POEMS OF DUBIOUS ATTRIBUTION

B: 1

Additional Lines to Burns's 'Scots Wha Hae' [By Bannockburn proud Edward lay]. 8 lines (single stanza).

> Published by H. Bartle G. Frere in 'Walter Scott and Burns', *Macmillan's Magazine*, 26 (June 1872), 168, giving a son of Robert Shortreed (1762–1829) as the source. Frere relates that Scott wrote it down 'on the fly-leaf of [a] volume of Burns'. Another version in two 4-line stanzas was published in a letter by Oliver Hilson, 'Sir Walter Scott and Bannockburn' in *The Scotsman* of 12 January 1927, on the authority of Mary H. Shortreed, a grand-daughter of Robert Shortreed, this being followed by further accounts from memory in letters to the paper on 15 January.

Excluded, as the lines and their attribution to Scott rest upon hearsay.

B: 2

[All hail the shouting trumpet]. 40 lines (5 x 8-line stanzas).

> Unsigned and end-dated 'Edinburgh, April 1802' in the *Monthly Magazine*, 13 (July 1802), 559.
>
> Speculative attribution ('Scott might well have known the author of this martial poem, or perhaps have been himself responsible') in T&B, no. 114A, noting its Edinburgh provenance and appearance in the same issue as a prose account of the Battle of Sempach, itself stated as having possibly influenced Scott's choice of a subject for his own 'The Battle of Sempach' (no. 68). No evidence of alternative authorship, but the poem's praise of the temporary cessation of hostilities between Britain and France in the Napoleonic Wars brought about by the Treaty of Amiens of 27 March 1802 renders Scott's involvement improbable.

Excluded, due to insufficient evidence of Scott's authorship and inherent lack of probability of subject-matter.

B: 3

Bonnie Laddie, Highland Laddie [Where have ye been a' day]. 64 lines (16 x 4-line stanzas).

> Manuscript in Scott's hand, Morgan Library, MA 451.3, the paper of which is watermarked 'T STAINS / 1815'. As the catalogue entry notes 'Bonnie Laddie Highland Laddie' is a Jacobite song with many versions, this strongly resembling the longer version in Robert Chambers, *The Scottish Songs*, 2 vols (Edinburgh, 1829), 2.503–06. Of these 64 lines, for instance, only 8 are not in the version printed by Chambers, which, however, contains 32 lines not in this manuscript. It seems probable that the manuscript is Scott's transcription of a traditional Jacobite song, possibly (given the date of the paper) intended as a contribution towards James Hogg's materials for his *Jacobite Relics* (1819, 1821), since Hogg gratefully acknowledged Scott's assistance with the project.

Excluded, as almost certainly a traditional Jacobite song only recorded by Scott.

B: 4

Canadian Boat Song [Listen to me, as when ye heard our father]. 30 lines (5 x 6-line stanzas).

   Printed in *Blackwood's Edinburgh Magazine*, 26 (September 1829), 400, as part of 'Noctes Ambrosianae No. XLVI'.

   Scott is one among many candidates for authorship. Linda Dowler in 'The Authorship of the "Canadian Boat Song": A Bibliographical Note' in the online journal *Canadian Poetry*, 6 (Spring/Summer 1980) reviews the evidence for eight authorial candidates and decides that Scott is perhaps the least likely.

Excluded, due to insufficient evidence of Scott's authorship.

B: 5

[Don't talk to me, I tell ye it's a shame]. 89 lines plus stage-directions.

   Printed in 'Theatre', *Caledonian Mercury*, 6 November 1828, and 'imputed to a great well known author'.

   While the address is clearly the production of someone intimately acquainted with the workings of the Edinburgh Theatre Royal and its management, contemporary newspaper attribution to Scott is guarded and hesitant. Although subsequently included in *The Farewell and Occasional Addresses Delivered by W. H. Murray, Esq., in the Theatres Royal and Adelphi, Edinburgh* (Edinburgh, 1851), 41–43, the 'Advertisement' there makes it clear that the collection was put together from newspaper reports without reference to Murray himself. Also printed in James C. Dibdin, *The Annals of the Edinburgh Stage* (Edinburgh, 1888), as 'from the pen of Sir Walter Scott' (323), though the text (493–94) likewise seems to have been taken from contemporary newspapers. It could as well have been the work of Murray himself or another member of his theatrical troupe as that of Scott.

Excluded, due to insufficient evidence of Scott's authorship.

B: 6

[Droop not fair lily on thy stem]. 28 lines (7 x 4-line stanzas).

   Manuscript in the Holland House papers (BL, Add. MS 51,968, f. 51), enclosed in a letter from Gertrude Russell to Caroline Fox of 18 January 1812 (f. 50), not in Scott's hand but in that of the letter-writer. Caroline Fox (1767–1845) was the daughter of Stephen Fox, 2nd Baron Holland (1745–74), while Gertrude Russell's letter is addressed from Woburn Abbey, probably indicating that she was a connection of the Bedford family (a former Gertrude Russell had been the Duchess of the 4th Duke of Bedford and great-aunt to Caroline Fox). The letter claims that the enclosure, sent in fulfilment of an earlier promise, is of 'Walter Scott's Verses, which were sent to the Duchess with Campbell's Poems'. The 'Duchess' in this connection was most probably Georgiana, Duchess of Bedford (1781–1853), daughter of Alexander Gordon, 4th Duke of Gordon (1743–1827), who had married John Russell, 6th Duke of Bedford (1766–1839) in 1803. Scott was certainly acquainted with the

Duke of Gordon as well as the Bedfords (see *Letters*, 1.381–82), but politically opposed to the aristocratic Whigs of Holland House. The verses are signed as from 'A Minstrel of Ettricke Foreste', but this could indicate a number of contemporary Selkirkshire poets, and some of the expressions employed (the 'lark's warbling Throat', 'the languid lingering Hour') seem too conventional for Scott.

Excluded, as the lines and their attribution to Scott rest upon hearsay.

B: 7

Farrier's Garland, The [The devil would be shod]. 30 lines (5 x 6-line stanzas).

> Manuscript in Sophia Scott's hand, NLS, MS 876, ff. 30–31, the paper of which is watermarked 'D & A COWAN / 1817'. Also with a note by Sophia stating 'This was written for Papa'. Also published in *Letters from and to Charles Kirkpatrick Sharpe*, ed. A. Allardyce, 2 vols (Edinburgh, 1888), 2.202–03, with a note of 29 May 1819 by Sharpe: 'Composed by W. Scott, on a print in a book I sent him' (203). Printed in turn as part of a letter from Scott in *Letters*, 5.390–91.
>
> Playing on the legend of St Dunstan accounting for why a horse-shoe nailed up by a door is lucky, the verses seem too cumbersome by Scott's standard, and may have a chapbook origin, though one reference there is modern ('Wellington boot' in line 5).

Excluded, due to insufficient evidence of Scott's authorship.

B: 8

Head and Tail [Of old, as Menenius Agrippa could tell ye]. 56 lines (14 x 4-line stanzas).

> Manuscript (not in Scott's hand) in NLS, MS 856, ff. 74–75, where it appears in the context of a volume of Shortreed papers, mostly transcripts of letters from Scott to Robert Shortreed by his son Andrew. A note on the top right-hand corner states, 'I have reason to believe this poem was published somewhere—but where I cannot discover—not certainly in the Collected edition of the Works. But this is not a solitary omission, as I can testify'.
>
> Attributed to Scott by W. M. Parker, firstly in 'Additions to Scott's Poems', *TLS*, 13 December 1941, 636; and subsequently in 'Sir Walter Scott: Thirteen New Poems', *Poetry Review*, 40: 4 (August–September 1949), 263–75 (pp. 271–73).
>
> An elaborate satirical allegory, presumably political, in an Augustan manner.

Excluded, due to insufficient evidence of Scott's authorship.

B: 9

Muckle Stain, The, or the Bleeding Stone of Kilburn Priory [For the blessed rood of Sir Gervase the good]. 92 lines (23 x 4-line stanzas).

A rare printed copy of *The Bleeding Stone of Kilburn* survives in the
Abbotsford Library, with a London 1817 imprint reading 'Printed
for William Atkinson Esq. Grove End, St John's Wood; by B. M.
M'Millan, Bow-Street, Covent-Garden', and with the words 'for
William Atkinson Esq. Grove End, St John's Wood' crossed out in ink.
The architect William Atkinson (1774/5–1839), who worked on Scott's
home at Abbotsford, built his own villa of Grove End House in London,
the legend described in the piece apparently relating to ornaments
originating from Kilburn Priory, and in particular to a red-stained stone
sent from Whitby, as incorporated into the garden at Grove End. The
poem was republished in September 1820 in *The Cornucopia; or Literary
and Dramatic Bouquet* (1: 1, 2–4) as a legendary ballad 'divested merely of
its ancient orthography', and with no mention of Scott. Scott, however,
is named as its author by H. G. Atkinson, the son of the architect, who
published the poem in the *Athenaeum* of 17 September 1881 (368–69),
with a prefatory letter stating that Scott had been prompted to write
it having visited Atkinson's garden, 'as a kind of friendly offering for
services rendered' at Abbotsford, and that a 'copy' had been found by his
sister among their father's papers. It was subsequently published several
times with Scott's name.
H. G. Atkinson's account seems improbable. Scott did not visit London
between 1815 and 1821, and William Atkinson does not appear to have
visited Abbotsford in 1817, while no direct correspondence between the
two seems to have survived before 1818, negotiations being conducted
primarily through Scott's close friend, the actor-manager Daniel Terry.
The poem itself also offers little support for Scott's authorship, and
might have been written by anyone with some familiarity with the
traditional ballad, while the rhymes do not suggest a Scottish phonology.
Moreover, the 'copy' referred to by H. G. Atkinson is not described as
a holograph manuscript and was more probably in another hand or a
printed copy similar to that at Abbotsford. As a whole the verses seem
more likely to be the work of William Atkinson himself—as the one with
an emotional and financial investment in the Grove End garden—or an
unnamed third person.
Excluded, due to insufficient evidence of Scott's authorship.

B: 10
[Now will I of that fell dragoun]. 8 lines (single stanza).
Inscribed by Scott on the verso of the Contents leaf of the first volume
of the Abbotsford copy of Joseph Ritson, *Ancient Engleish Metrical
Romances*, 3 vols (London, [1802]), subscribed 'Stevens' at foot.
Attributed to Scott in *ALC* entry, as 'a satirical verse by him on Ritson's
dispute with Percy'. Although not apparently recorded as the work of
the literary editor George Steevens (1736–1800), he and Ritson had
quarrelled in 1783 after Ritson's remarks on Steevens' contributions to
Samuel Johnson's Shakespeare, in *Remarks, Critical and Illustrative, on
the Text and Notes of the Last Edition of Shakespeare* (1783).
**Excluded, as more likely (given Scott's own ascription) to be
the work of George Steevens.**

B: 11
Vision of the Coronation, A [The steady foxhound, staunch and true]. 157 lines (4 numbered paragraphs).

> Printed in the *Court Journal*, 10 September 1831, 620.
>
> Attributed to Scott in T&B, no. 250A, on the grounds of its being initialled 'W. S.', with the editorial footnote: 'The illustrious author of the foregoing must also have had, in his dreams, a vision of the *Times*, which is the only paper, so far as we have seen, which has stated that the Princess Victoria was present at the Ceremony [the coronation of William IV].' Reprinted as 'By Sir Walter Scott' in *Museum of Foreign Literature, Science, and Art*, new series 12 (November 1831), 594–95.

Excluded, due to insufficient evidence of Scott's authorship.

INDEX OF TITLES

In the following alphabetical index of titles, locations are given by item number. Titles beginning with 'On', 'To', 'Lines' or 'Verses' or where the poem may be most easily remembered from its association with a particular person, place, or event have been cross-referenced by key words wherever this has been deemed helpful to the reader. Where poems are commonly known by another title or name, this title is also cross-referenced to the title used in the present volume. A final section indexes titles given in the Appendix of Suppositious and Doubtful Works.

APPENDIX

Where no title is given in the source, or commonly ascribed to an item, the first line of the item is given within square brackets.

INDEX OF FIRST LINES

In the following alphabetical index of first lines, locations are given by item number. The line given is the first line of the poem itself and not that of Scott's headnote, preliminary dating or motto. End-of-line punctuation is not included. A final section indexes first lines of items listed in the Appendix of Suppositious and Doubtful Works.

APPENDIX